Isaac Bashevis Singer

THREE COMPLETE NOVELS

Isaac Bashevis Singer

THREE COMPLETE NOVELS

THE SLAVE

ENEMIES, A LOVE STORY

SHOSHA

AVENEL BOOKS

New York

Translated from the Yiddish
by the author and Cecil Hemley.
The author wishes to thank
Miss Elizabeth Pollet for her
assistance in the preparation
of this book.

This 1982 edition is published by Avenel Books
distributed by Crown Publishers, Inc. by arrangement with
Farrar, Straus & Giroux, Inc.

Manufactured in the United States of America

Library of Congress Cataloging in Publication Data
Singer, Isaac Bashevis, 1904–
    Isaac Bashevis Singer, three complete novels.

    Contents: The slave—Enemies, a love story—
Shosha.
    1. Singer, Isaac Bashevis, 1904–   —Translations,
English.   I. Title.
PJ5129.S49A2   1982   839′.0933   82-11346

ISBN: 0-517-385805

h g f e d c b a

Contents

The Slave

■

PART ONE

Wanda

CHAPTER ONE

1

A single bird call began the day. Each day the same bird, the same call. It was as if the bird signaled the approach of dawn to its brood. Jacob opened his eyes. The four cows lay on their mats of straw and dung. In the middle of the barn were a few blackened stones and charred branches, the fireplace over which Jacob cooked the rye and buckwheat cakes he ate with milk. Jacob's bed was made of straw and hay and at night he covered himself with a coarse linen sheet which he used during the day to gather grass and herbs for the cattle. It was summer, but the nights were cold in the mountains. Jacob would rise more than once in the middle of the night and warm his hands and feet on the animals' bodies.

It was still dark in the barn, but the red of dawn shone through a crack in the door. Jacob sat up and finished his final allotment of sleep. He had dreamed he was in the study house at Josefov, lecturing the young men on the Talmud.

He stretched out his hand blindly, reaching for the pitcher of water. Three times he washed his hands, the left hand first and then the right, alternating, according to the law. He had murmured even before washing, "I thank Thee," a prayer not mentioning God's name and therefore utterable before cleaning oneself. A cow stood up and turned its horned head, looking over its shoulder as if curious to see how a man starts his day. The creature's large eyes, almost all pupil, reflected the purple of the dawn.

"Good morning, Kwiatula," Jacob said. "You had a good sleep, didn't you?"

He had become accustomed to speak to the cows, to himself even, so as not to forget Yiddish. He threw open the barn door and saw the mountains stretching into the distance. Some of the peaks, their slopes overgrown with forests, seemed close at hand, giants with green beards. Mist rising from the woods like tenuous curls made Jacob think of Samson. The ascending sun, a heavenly lamp, cast a fiery sheen over everything. Here and there, smoke drifted upward from a summit as if the mountains were burning within. A hawk, wings outstretched, glided tranquilly with a strange slowness beyond all earthly anxieties. It appeared to Jacob that the bird had been flying without interruption since creation.

3

The more distant mountains were bluish, and there were others, the most distant of all, that were scarcely visible—unsubstantial. It was always dusk in that most remote region. Caps of clouds sat on the heads of those unearthly titans, inhabitants at the world's end where no man walked and no cow grazed. Wanda, Jan Bzik's daughter, said that that was where Baba Yaga lived, a witch who flew about in a huge mortar, driving her vehicle with a pestle. Baba Yaga's broom was larger than the tallest fir tree, and it was she who swept away the light of the world.

Jacob stood gazing at the hills, a tall, straight man, blue-eyed, with long brown hair and a brown beard. He wore linen trousers which did not reach to his ankles and a torn, patched coat. On his head was a sheepskin cap, but his feet were bare. Though he was out of doors so much, he remained as pale as a city dweller. His skin did not tan and Wanda said that he resembled the men in the holy pictures that hung in the chapel in the valley. The other peasant women agreed with Wanda. The Gazdas, as the mountaineers were called, had wanted to marry him to one of their daughters, build him a hut, and make him a member of the village, but Jacob had refused to forsake the Jewish faith, and Jan Bzik, his owner, kept him all summer and until late fall in the barn high on the mountain where the cattle could not find food and one had to feed them with grass pulled from among the rocks. The village was at a high elevation and lacked sufficient pastures.

Before he milked the cows, Jacob said his introductory prayer. Reaching the sentence, "Thou hast not made me a slave," he paused. Could these words be spoken by him? He was Jan Bzik's slave. True, according to Polish law, not even the gentry had the right to force a Jew into servitude. But who in this remote village obeyed the law of the land? And of what value was the code of the gentiles even prior to Chmielnicki's massacre? Jacob of Josefov took the privations Providence had sent him without rancor. In other regions the Cossacks had beheaded, hanged, garroted, and impaled many honest Jews. Chaste women had been raped and disemboweled. He, Jacob, had not been destined for martyrdom. He had fled from the murderers and Polish robbers had dragged him off to somewhere in the mountains and had sold him as a slave to Jan Bzik. He had lived here for four years now and did not know whether his wife and children were still alive. He was without prayer shawl and phylacteries, fringed garment or holy book. Circumcision was the only sign on his body that he was a Jew. But heaven be thanked, he knew his prayers by heart, a few chapters of the Mishnah, some pages of the Gemara, a host of Psalms, as well as passages from various parts of the Bible. He would wake in the middle of the night with lines from the Gemara that he himself had not been aware he knew running through his head. His memory played hide and seek with him. If he had had pen and paper, he would have written down what came to him, but where were such things to be found here?

He turned his face to the east, looked straight ahead, and recited the holy words. The crags glowed in the sunlight, and close by a cowherd yodeled, his voice lingering on each note, resonant with yearning as if he too were being held in captivity and longed to thrust himself into freedom. It was hard to believe that such melodies came from men who ate dogs, cats, field mice, and indulged in every sort of abomination. The peasants here had not even risen to the level of the Christians. They still followed the customs of the ancient pagans.

There had been a time when Jacob had planned to run away, but nothing had come of his schemes. He did not know the mountains; the forests were filled with predatory animals. Snow fell even in summer. The peasants kept guard over him and did not permit him to go beyond the bridge in the village. There was an agreement among them that anyone who saw him on the other side of the stream should immediately kill him. Among the peasants there were those who wanted to kill him anyway. Jacob might be a wizard or a braider of elflocks. But Zagayek, the count's bailiff, had ordered that the stranger be permitted to live. Jacob not only gathered more grass than any other cowherd, but his cattle were very sleek, gave abundant milk, and bore healthy calves. As long as the village did not suffer from famine, epidemic, or fire, the Jew was to be left in peace.

It was time for the cows to be milked and so Jacob hurried through his prayers. Returning to the barn he mixed with the grass in the trough the chopped straw and turnips he had prepared the day before. On a shelf in the barn were the milking pail and some large earthen pots; the churn stood in a corner. Every day late in the afternoon Wanda came up, bringing Jacob his food and bearing two large pitchers in which to carry the milk back to the village.

Jacob milked the cows and hummed a tune from Josefov. The sun climbed beyond the mountains and the coils of fog dissolved. He had been here so long now and had become so acquainted with the plants that he could detect the odor of each flower and each variety of grass, and he breathed in deeply as the smells of vegetation were wafted into the barn through the open door. Every sunrise in the mountains was like a miracle; one clearly discerned God's hand among the flaming clouds. God had punished His people and had hidden His face from them, but He continued to superintend the world. As a sign of the covenant which He had made after the Flood, He had hung the rainbow in the sky to show that day and night, summer and winter, sowing and reaping would not cease.

2

All day Jacob climbed on the mountain. After gathering a sheetful of grass, he carried it to the barn, and then returned once more to the woods. The other cowherds, when he had first come, had attacked and beaten him, but now he had learned how to strike back, and these days carried an oaken stick. He scampered over the rocks with the agility of a monkey, mindful of which herbs and grasses were good for the cattle and which harmful. All those things which are required of a cowherd he could do: light a fire by rubbing wood against wood, milk the cows, deliver a calf. For himself, he picked mushrooms, wild strawberries, blueberries, whatever the earth produced, and each afternoon Wanda brought him a slice of coarse black bread from the village, and sometimes, also, a radish, carrot, or onion, or maybe an apple or pear from the orchard. In the beginning Jan Bzik had jokingly sought to force a piece of sausage into his mouth, but Jacob had refused stubbornly to partake of forbidden food. He did not gather herbs on the Sabbath, but gave the animals feed he had prepared during the week. The mountaineers no longer molested him.

But this was not true of the girls who slept in the barn and tended the sheep. Night and day they bothered him. Attracted by his tall figure, they sought him out and talked and laughed and behaved little better than beasts. In his presence they relieved themselves, and they were perpetually pulling up their skirts to show him insect bites on their hips and thighs. "Lay me," a girl would shamelessly demand, but Jacob acted as if he were deaf and blind. It was not only because fornication was a mortal sin. These women were unclean, and had vermin in their clothes and elflocks in their hair; often their skins were covered with rashes and boils, they ate field rodents and the rotting carcasses of fowls. Some of them could scarcely speak Polish, grunted like animals, made signs with their hands, screamed and laughed madly. The village abounded in cripples, boys and girls with goiters, distended heads and disfiguring birth marks; there were also mutes, epileptics, freaks who had been born with six fingers on their hands or six toes on their feet. In summer, the parents of these deformed children kept them on the mountains with the cattle, and they ran wild. There, men and women copulated in public; the women became pregnant, but, climbing as they did all day on the rocks, bearing heavy packs, they often miscarried. The district had no midwife and mothers in labor were forced to cut the umbilical cord themselves. If the child died, they buried it in a ditch without Christian rites or else threw it into the mountain stream. Often, the women bled to death. If someone descended to the valley to fetch Dziobak, the priest, to confess the dying and administer Extreme Unction, nothing came of it. Dziobak had a game leg and besides he was always drunk.

In comparison with these savages, Wanda, Jan Bzik's widowed daughter, seemed city-bred. She dressed in a skirt, blouse and apron, and wore a kerchief on her head; moreover, her speech could be understood. A bolt of lightning had killed her husband Stach and from then on she had been courted by all the bachelors and widowers of the village; she was constantly saying no. Wanda was twenty-five and taller than most of the other women. She had blond hair, blue eyes, a fair skin, and well-modeled features. She braided her hair and twisted it around her head like a wreath of wheat. When she smiled, her cheeks dimpled and her teeth were so strong she could crush the toughest of pits. Her nose was straight and she had a narrow chin. She was a skillful seamstress and could knit, cook, and tell stories which made one's hair stand on end. In the village she had been nicknamed "The Lady." As Jacob knew very well, according to the law he must avoid her, but if it had not been for Wanda he would have forgotten that he had a tongue in his head. Besides she assisted him in fulfilling his obligations as a Jew. Thus, when in winter, on the Sabbath, her father commanded him to light the oven, she got up before Jacob and lit the kindling herself and added the firewood. Unbeknown to her parents, she brought him barley kasha, honey, fruit from the orchard, cucumbers from the garden. Once when Jacob had sprained his ankle and his foot had swollen, Wanda had snapped the bone back into the socket and applied lotions. Another time, a snake had bitten him in the arm, and she had put the wound to her mouth and sucked out the venom. This had not been the only time Wanda had saved his life.

Yet Jacob knew that all this had been contrived by Satan; throughout the day he missed her and could not overcome his longing. The instant he awoke he would start to count the hours before she would come to him. Often he would walk to the sundial that he had made from a stone to see how much the shadow had moved. If a heavy downpour or cloudburst prevented her coming, he would walk about morosely. This did not stop him from praying to God to preserve him from sinful thoughts, but again and again the thoughts returned. How could he keep his heart pure when he had no phylacteries to put on and no fringed garment to wear? Lacking as he did a calendar, he could not even observe the holy days properly. Like the Ancients he reckoned the beginning of the month by the appearance of the new moon, and at the end of his fourth year, he rectified his computations by adding an extra month. But, despite all these efforts, he was aware hat he had probably made some error in his calculations.

As he figured it, this long and warm day was the fourth of the month of Tammuz. He gathered great quantities of grass and leaves; he prayed, studied several chapters of the Mishnah, said those few pages of the Gemara which he repeated daily. Finally he recited one of the Psalms and chanted a prayer in Yiddish that he himself had composed. He begged the Almighty to redeem him from captivity and allow him to live the life of a Jew once more. This day, he ate a slice of bread left from the day before and cooked a pot of groats over the fireplace in the barn. Having said the benediction, he felt tired, and walked outside and lay down under a tree. He had found it necessary to keep a dog to protect the cattle from wild animals. At first he had disliked the black creature with its pointed muzzle and sharp teeth, repelled by its barking and obsequious licking which had reminded him of what the Talmud said on the subject and how the holy Isaac Luria, along with other cabalists, compared canines to the satanic hosts. But at length Jacob had grown accustomed to his dog, and had even named him, calling him Balaam. No sooner had Jacob lain under the tree, than Balaam sat down near him, stretched out his paws, and kept watch.

Jacob's eyes closed, and the sun, red and summery, shone through his lids. Above him the tree was filled with birds, twittering, singing, trilling. He was neither awake nor asleep, having retreated into the weariness of his body. So be it. This was the way God had willed it.

Ceaselessly he had prayed for death; he had even contemplated self-destruction. But now that mood had passed, and he had become inured to living among strangers, distant from his home, doing hard labor. As he drowsed, he heard pine cones falling and the coo of a cuckoo in the distance. He opened his eyes. The web of branches and pine needles strained the sunlight like a sieve, and the reflected light became a rainbow-colored mesh. A last drop of dew flamed, glistened, exploded into thin molten fibers. There was not a cloud to sully the perfect blue of the sky. It was difficult to believe in God's mercy when murderers buried children alive. But God's wisdom was evident everywhere.

Jacob fell asleep and Wanda walked into his dreams.

3

The sun had moved westward; the day was nearing its end. High overhead an eagle glided, large and slow, like a celestial sailboat. The sky was still clear but a milk-white fog was forming in the woods. Twisting itself into small ovals, the mist thrust out tongues, and sought to evolve into some coherent shape. Its inchoateness made Jacob think of that primeval substance which, according to the philosophers, gave birth to all things.

When he stood at the barn, Jacob could see for miles around. The mountains remained as deserted as in the days of the Creation. One above the other, the forests rose like steps, first the leaf-bearing trees, and then the pines and firs. Beyond the woods were the open ledges, and the pale snow, like gray linen unfolding, was slowly moving down from the summits ready to enshroud the world in winter. Jacob recited the prayer of Minchah and walked to the hill from which one could see the path to the village. Yes, Wanda was on her way up. He recognized her by her figure, her kerchief, her manner of walking. She looked no larger than a finger, like one of those imps or sprites about whom she told so many stories, fairies who lived in the crevasses of rocks, in the hollows of tree trunks, under the eaves of toadstools and who came out at dusk to play, dressed in small green coats and wearing blue caps and red boots. He could not remove his eyes from her, charmed by her walk, by the way she paused to rest, by her disappearance among the trees, then by the sight of her, emerging from the woods higher up the slope. Now and again, the metal pitcher in her hand gleamed like a diamond. He saw that she was carrying the basket in which she brought him food.

As she approached nearer and nearer, she grew larger and larger, and Jacob ran toward her, ostensibly to be of assistance, although the pitchers she was carrying were still empty. She caught sight of him and stopped. He was moving toward her like a bridegroom seeing his bride. When he reached her, shyness and affection, both equally intense, mingled within him. Jewish law, he knew, forbade him to look at her, yet he saw everything: her eyes which were sometimes blue, sometimes green, her full lips, her long, slim neck, her womanly bosom. Like any other peasant she worked in the fields, but her hands remained feminine. He felt awkward standing beside her. His hair was unkempt, his pants too short and as ragged as a beggar's. Being descended on his mother's side from Jews who had had constant dealings with the nobility and had rented their fields, he had been taught Polish as a child, and now in his captivity he had learned to speak the language like a gentile. At times, he even forgot the Yiddish name for some object.

"Good evening, Wanda."

"Good evening, Jacob."

"I watched you coming up the mountain."

"Did you?"

The blood rushed to her face.

"You looked no larger than a pea."

"Things look that way from a distance."

"They do," Jacob said. "The stars are as large as the whole world, but they are so far off, they appear to be little dots."

Wanda became silent. He often used strange words which she did not understand. He had told her his story, and she knew that he was descended from Jews who lived in a far-off place, that he had studied books, and that he had had a wife and children whom the Cossacks had slaughtered. But what were Jews? What was written in their books? Who were the Cossacks? All of these things were beyond her comprehension. Nor did she understand his statement that the stars were as large as the earth. If they were really that large, how could so many cluster above the village? But Wanda had long since decided that Jacob was a profound thinker. Who knew, perhaps he was a wizard as was whispered by the women in the valley? But whatever he was, she loved him. Evening for her was the festive part of the day.

He took the pitchers from her and they finished the ascent together. Another man would have taken her by the arm or placed a hand upon her shoulder, but Jacob walked beside her with the timidity of a boy, exuding a sunny warmth and trailing the odors of grass and barn. Yet Wanda had already proposed marriage, or, if he was unwilling to commit himself to that, cohabitation without the priest's blessing. He had pretended not to hear her suggestion and only later had he remarked that fornication was forbidden. God looked down from heaven and rewarded and punished each man according to his deeds.

As if she were unaware of that! But in the village love was a random matter. The priest had fathered a half dozen bastards. Such a proposal as she had made to Jacob would have been refused by no other man. Were not all the villagers pursuing her, including Stephan, the bailiff's son? Not a week passed without some boy's mother or sister approaching her to arrange a match. She was forever receiving and returning gifts. Wanda found Jacob's attitude perplexing and she walked with bowed head thinking about this puzzle which she was unable to solve. She had fallen in love with the slave at first sight, and though over the years they had been much together, he had stayed remote. Many times she had come to the conclusion that from this dough would come no bread, and that she was wasting her youth on him. But the strength of the attraction he exerted upon her did not abate, and she could scarcely endure waiting for evening. She had become the subject of gossip in the village. The women laughed at her and passed sly comments. It was said that the slave had bewitched her; whatever it was, she was unable to free herself.

Thoughtfully she bent down, plucked a flower, and tearing away its petals began, "He loves me; he loves me not." The last petal assured her that the answer was "yes." But if so, how long would he go on tormenting her?

Now the sun sank rapidly, dropped behind the mountains. Accompanied by the croaking and screaming of birds, the day ended. Smoke rose from the bushes and the cowherds yodeled. The women were already preparing the evening meal, perhaps roasting some animal which had fallen into a trap.

4

In addition to bread and vegetables, Wanda, without the knowledge of her mother and sister, had brought Jacob a rare gift, an egg laid by the white hen, and while she milked the cows, he prepared supper. He placed a few dry branches on the stones, lit a fire, and boiled the egg. He had left the barn door open although it was already dark, and the flames from the pine branches mottled Wanda's face with fiery spots and were reflected in her eyes. He sat on a log remembering the meal eaten before the fast of the ninth day of the month of Ob. An egg was consumed then as a sign of mourning: a rolling egg symbolized the changeability of man's fate. He washed his hands, let them dry, said grace, and dipped his bread into the salt. There was no table in the barn and so he used a pail turned upside down. He gained his sustenance from vegetables and fruit; meat he never tasted. As he ate, he glanced at Wanda out of the corner of his eyes, Wanda who was as devoted to him as a wife, and who every day prepared him something special. "In the mercy of the nations is sin," he said to himself, quoting a commentary on a passage from the Bible and trying to strangle the love he felt for her. Had all this been done by her for the sake of God? No, it was desire for him that had prompted her. Her love depended upon outward show, and should he become a cripple, God forbid, or lose his manhood, her love would cease. And yet such was the power of the flesh that man looked only at the surface and did not probe into such matters too deeply. He heard the sound of the milk falling into the pail and he paused in his eating to listen. Grasshoppers were singing and there was a buzzing and humming of bees, gnats, flies, multitude upon multitude of creatures each with its own voice. The stars in the heavens had kindled their fires. A sickle of a moon was aloft in the sky.

"Is the egg all right?" Wanda asked.

"Good and fresh."

"Could anything be fresher? I saw the hen lay it. The moment it fell to the straw, I thought, this is for Jacob. The shell was still warm."

"You're a good woman, Wanda."

"I can be bad as well. It depends on whom I'm with. I was bad to Stach, peace be with him."

"Why was that?"

"I don't know. He demanded, he never asked. If he wanted me in the night, he woke me from the middle of sleep. In the daytime, he would push me down in an open field."

Her words aroused both passion and disgust in Jacob.

"That was not right."

"What does a peasant know of right or wrong? He just takes what he wants. I was sick once and my forehead was as hot as an oven but he came to me and I had to give myself."

"The Torah says that a man must not force his wife," Jacob said. "She must be wooed by him until she is willing."

"Where is the Torah? In Josefov?"

"The Torah is everywhere."

"How can it be everywhere?"

"The Torah tells how a man should conduct himself."

Wanda was silent.

"That's for the city. Here the men are wild bulls. Swear to me that you'll never reveal what I tell you."

"Whom would I tell?"

"My own brother threw himself on me. I was only eleven years old. He'd come back from the tavern. Mother was asleep but my screams woke her. She picked up the pail of slops and poured it over him."

Jacob paused a moment before speaking again.

"Things like that don't happen among the Jews."

"That's what you say. They killed our God."

"How can a man kill a God?"

"Don't ask me. I'm only telling you what the priest says. Really, are you a Jew?"

"Yes, a Jew."

"It's hard for me to believe. Become one of us and we'll get married. I'll be a good wife and we'll have our hut in the valley. Zagayek will give us our share of land. We'll work our time for the count, and what's left over we'll have for ourselves. There's nothing we won't have—cows, pigs, chickens, geese, ducks. You know how to read and write and when Zagayek dies you'll take his place."

It was some time before Jacob answered.

"No, I cannot. I am a Jew. For all I know, my wife is alive."

"You've said many times that everyone was killed. But even if she still lives, what's the difference? She's there and you're here."

"God is everywhere."

"And it will hurt God if you are a free man instead of a slave? You walk around barefoot, half naked. Summers you spend in the barn, winters you freeze in the granary. Sooner or later they'll kill you."

"Who will kill me?"

"Oh, they'll kill you all right."

"And so then I'll be with the other holy spirits."

"I pity you, Jacob. I pity you."

Both fell into a long silence and in the barn there was quiet except when a cow now and again stamped its hoof. The last embers in the fireplace died, and when Jacob had finished eating he walked out into the open air to say the benediction in a place unpolluted by dung. Evening had fallen but in the west the last shreds of the sunset lingered. Usually, the women who brought food to the cowherds did not loiter on the mountain since at night the way home was considered dangerous. But Wanda would often stay late despite her mother's scolding and the women's persistent gossip. She was as strong as a man and she knew the proper incantations to drive off the evil spirits. She had finished milking the cows and, in the darkness of the barn, she poured milk from the pail into the pitchers. She scrubbed the churn with straw and cleaned globs of mud off the hips of the cows. All this she did swiftly and with great skill. Her tasks accomplished, she went outside, and the dog ran from Jacob to her, wagged its tail and jumped on her with its front paws. She bent down and he licked her face.

"Balaam, enough," she ordered. "He's more affectionate than you," she said to Jacob.

"An animal has no obligations."

"But they too have souls."

She delayed going home, sat down near the barn, and Jacob sat also. They always spent some time together and always on exactly the same rocks. If the moon was not out, she saw him by the light of the stars, but it was as bright this evening as at the full moon. Gazing at her in silence, Jacob was seized by love and desire, and restrained himself with difficulty. The blood in his veins seethed like water about to boil, and hot and cold fire zigzagged down his spine. "Remember this world is only a corridor," he warned himself. "The true palace lies beyond. Don't let yourself be barred from it for the sake of a moment's pleasure."

5

"What's new with your family?" Jacob inquired.

Wanda awoke from her reverie.

"What could be new? Father works, chops down trees in the woods and drags them home. He's so weak the logs almost knock him down. He wants to rebuild our hut, or God knows what. At his age! He's so tired at evening he can't swallow his food, and drops on the bed as though his legs had been cut off. He won't live much longer."

Jacob's brow furrowed.

"That's no way to talk."

"It's the truth."

"No one knows the decrees of Heaven."

"Maybe not, but when your strength gives out, you die. I can tell who's going to go—not only the old and sick, but the young and healthy too. I take one look and it comes to me. Sometimes I'm afraid to say anything because I don't want to be thought a witch. But all the same, I know. There's no change with Mother, she spins a little, cooks a little, plays at being sick. We only see Antek on Sundays, and sometimes not even then. Marisha is pregnant, will be in labor soon. Basha is lazy. Mother calls her the lazy cat. But a dance or a party revives her. Wojciech gets crazier and crazier."

"What about the grain? Is the crop good?"

"When has it ever been good?" Wanda answered. "In the valley you get rich, black earth, but here it's all stony. You could drive a cart of oxen between the stalks. We still have some rye from last year, but most of the peasants eat their knuckles. What little good earth we have belongs to the count and anyway Zagayek steals everything."

"Doesn't the count ever come here?"

"Just about never. He lives in another country and doesn't even know he owns this village. About six years ago, a bunch of them descended upon us in the middle of summer—like now, before harvest. They got the idea they wanted to go hunting and tramped back and forth in the fields with their horses and dogs. Their servants snatched calves, chickens, goats, even a peasant's rabbit. Zagayek crawled after them kissing everyone's behind. Oh, he's high and mighty enough with the people around here, but as soon as he meets someone from the city he becomes a boot licker. When they went away, there was nothing but a wasteland left. The peasants starved that winter; the children turned yellow and died."

"Couldn't someone have spoken to them?"

"The nobles? They were always drunk. The peasants kissed their feet and all the thanks they got were a few strokes with a riding crop. The girls got raped; they arrived home with bloody shifts and an ache in their hearts. Nine months later they gave birth to bastards."

"We do not have such murderers among the Jews."

"No? What do the Jewish aristocrats do?"

"The Jews have no gentry."

"Who owns the land?"

"The Jews have no land. When they had a country of their own, they worked the earth themselves and possessed vineyards and olive groves. But here in Poland, they live by trade and handicraft."

"Why is that? We have it bad, but if you work hard and have a good wife, you at least own something. Stach was strong but lazy. He should have been Basha's husband, not mine. He kept putting off everything; he'd cut the hay and let it lie around until the rain soaked it. All he wanted to do was sit in the inn and talk. The truth was his time was up. On our wedding night I dreamed he was dead and his face black as a pot. I didn't tell anyone but I was sure he wouldn't last long. The day it happened, the weather wasn't bad. All of a sudden lightning struck and came straight through our window. It rolled along like a fiery apple, looking for Stach. He wasn't in the hut, but it went into the granary and found him. When I reached him his face was charred like soot."

"Don't you ever see anything good in your dreams?"

"Yes, I've told you. I foresaw that you would come to us. But I wasn't dreaming, I was wide awake. Mother was frying rye cakes and father had slaughtered a chicken that was starving because it had a growth in its beak. I poured some soup on the cakes and I looked into the bowl which was filled with great circles of fat. A mist rose and I saw you there as plain as I see you now."

"Where did you get such powers?" Jacob asked after a pause.

"I don't know, Jacob. But I've known all along that we were fated for each other. My heart knocked like a hammer when father brought you home from the fair. You weren't wearing a shirt and I gave you one of Stach's. Wacek and I were about to be betrothed, but when I saw you his image was erased from my heart. Marila has been laughing ever since. He fell into her hands like ripe fruit. I saw him at a wedding a short time ago and he was drunk. He started to cry and talk to me the way he used to. Marila was beside herself. But I don't want him, Jacob."

"Wanda, you must get such ideas out of your head."

"Why, Jacob, why?"

"I've already told you why."

"I never understand you, Jacob."

"Your faith is not my faith."

"Haven't I said that I'm willing to change my faith?"

"One can't belong to my faith unless one believes in God and his Torah. Just because one wants a man is not enough."

"I believe in what you believe."

"Where would we live? If a Christian becomes a Jew here, he's burned at the stake."

"There must be some place."

"Perhaps among the Turks."

"All right, let's escape."

"I don't know the mountains."

"I know them."

"The country of the Turks is very distant. We'd be arrested on the road."

The two once more fell into silence. Wanda's face was completely wreathed in shadows. From somewhere in the distance came a cowherd's yodel, muted and languorous as if the singer was expressing Wanda and Jacob's dilemma and bewailing the harshness of fate. A breeze had begun to blow and the rustle of branches mingled with the sound of the mountain stream as it coursed among the rocks.

"Come to me," Wanda said and her words were half command and half entreaty. "I must have you."

"No. I cannot. It is forbidden."

CHAPTER TWO

2

For Wanda the way down the mountain was more difficult than the way up. She was burdened now by the two pitchers filled with milk, and a heavy heart. But, terrified, she almost ran down the slopes. The path took her through towering grass, underbrush, forests; strange murmurs and rustles came from the thickets. Hostile imps and derisive spirits were abroad, she knew. They might play nasty pranks on her. A rock might be put in the path; the imps might swing from the pitchers and make them heavier; they might weave elflocks in her hair or dirty the milk with devil's dung. Demons abounded in the village and surrounding mountains. Each house had its familiar spirit dwelling behind the stove. Werewolves and trolls swarmed the roads, each monster with its own peculiar type of cunning. An owl hooted. Frogs croaked with human voices. Kobalt, the devil who spoke with his belly, was wandering somewhere in the neighborhood; Wanda heard his heavy breathing which sounded like a death rattle. And yet fear could not dull the pain of love. Her rejection by the Jewish slave intensified her desire. She was ready to leave the village, her parents, her family, and follow Jacob naked and empty-handed. She had told herself many times that she was a fool to be angry. Who was this man? If she wished she could get one of the village boys to kill him, and no tears would be shed. But what was the use of murder when you loved the victim? The ache in her throat choked her. Her face stung as if it had been slapped. Men had always chased after her—her own brother, the urchin who tended the geese. Jacob's spirit was stronger.

"A sorcerer!" Wanda said to herself. "He's bewitched me."

But where was the charm hidden? Slipped into a knot in her dress? Tied to a fringe of her shawl? It might be hidden in a lock of her hair. She searched everywhere, found nothing. Ought she to consult old Maciocha, the village witch? But the woman was insane, babbled out all her secrets. No, Maciocha could not be trusted. Wanda became so occupied with her thoughts she didn't know how she managed the descent. But suddenly she was at the bottom of the mountain approaching her father's hut. It was little more than a hovel with crumbling beams overgrown with moss and birds' nests hanging from the thatch. The building had two windows, one covered with a cow's bladder and the other open to permit the smoke from the fire to escape. In summer Jan Bzik permitted no illumination but on winter evenings a wick burned in a shard or kindling was lit. Wanda entered, and though it was dark inside, she saw as clearly as if it had been day.

Her father lay on the bed. He was barefoot and in torn clothes. He seldom undressed. She couldn't tell whether he was asleep or just resting. Her mother and her sister Basha were busy braiding a rope of straw. The bed that Jan Bzik lay on was the only one in the hut; the whole family slept in it, Wanda included. Years before when her brother Antek had still been unmarried Jan Bzik would have intercourse with his wife before going to sleep and the children would have something to amuse them. But Antek no longer lived at home and the couple had become too old for such games. Everyone expected Jan Bzik to die shortly. Antek who was anxious to take over the house appeared every few days to ask shamelessly, "Well, is the old man still alive?"

"Yes, still alive," his mother would answer. She also wanted to be rid of this nuisance. He wasn't worth the bread he ate. He had become weak, morose, irritable. All day he belched. Like a beaver, he kept gathering wood, but the thin, crooked logs he brought home were only good for the fire.

They scarcely spoke to each other in that hut. The old woman had a grudge against Wanda for not remarrying. Basha's husband Wojciech had gone home to live with his own parents; he had become despondent after the marriage. Basha had already borne three children, one by her husband, and two bastards; all of them had died. Jan Bzik and his wife had also buried two sons, boys who had been as strong as oaks. The family had become embogged in bitterness and sadness; silent antagonism simmered and bubbled in that household like kasha on a stove.

Wanda didn't say a word to any of them. She poured the milk from the pitchers into some jars. Half of what the cows gave belonged to Zagayek the bailiff; he owned a dairy in the village where cheese was made. The Bziks would use their half the following day for cooking and drinking with bread. The family lived well compared to those around them. In a shed behind the house were two sacks, one of rye and one of barley, and also a handmill in which to grind the grain. Bzik's fields, unlike most, had been partially cleared of stones over the years and the rocks used to build a fence. But food isn't everything. Jan Bzik continued to mourn his dead sons. He couldn't tolerate Antek or his daughter-in-law Marisha. Basha he disliked because of her indiscretions. Wanda was the only one he loved and she had been a widow for years and had brought him no joy. Antek, Basha, and the old woman had become allies. They kept their secrets from Wanda as though she were a stranger. But Wanda managed the household. Her father even consulted her on how to sow and reap. She had a man's brain. If she said something, you could rely on it.

Stach's death had brought her humiliation. She had been forced to return to her parents and again sleep with them and Basha in one bed. Now she would often spend the night in the hayloft or granary, although these places were crawling with rats and mice. She decided to sleep in the granary that night. The hut stank. Her family conducted themselves like animals. It hadn't occurred to any of them that the stream that flowed before their house could be used for bathing. It was the same one that passed near Jacob's barn.

Wanda picked up her pillow; it was stuffed with straw and hay. She walked toward the door.

"Sleeping in the granary?" her mother asked.

"Yes, in the granary."

"You'll be back tomorrow with your nose bitten off."

"Better to have your nose bitten than your soul."

Often Wanda herself was amazed by the words that issued from her lips. At times they had the pithiness and wit of a bishop's talk. Basha and her mother gaped. Jan Bzik stirred and murmured something. He liked to boast that Wanda resembled him and had inherited his brain. But what was intelligence worth if you didn't have luck?

2

The peasants went to bed early. Why sit around in the dark? Anyway they had to get up again at four. But there were always a few who hung around the tavern until it was late. The tavern was presumably the property of the count; it was in fact owned by Zagayek. He supplied its liquor from his still. That evening Antek was among the customers. One of Zagayek's bastard daughters waited on tables. The peasants nibbled pork sausage and drank. All sorts of strange and curious occurrences were discussed. The previous harvest a malevolent spirit named the Polonidca had appeared in the fields, carrying a sickle and dressed in white. The Polonidca had wandered around asking difficult riddles and demanding answers of all she met. For example: What four brothers chase but never catch each other? Answer: The four wheels of a wagon. What is dressed in white but black to the sight and wherever it goes speaks right? Answer: A letter. What eats like a horse, drinks like a horse, but sees with its tail as well as with its eyes? Answer: A blind horse. If the peasant didn't know the right answer the Polonidca tried to cut off his head with her sickle. She would pursue the man as far as the chapel. He would become ill and lie sick for many days.

The Dizwosina was another savage spirit. This terrifying succubus had stringy hair and came from Bohemia on the other side of the mountains. Recently she had entered the hut of old Maciek and had tickled his heels until he had died from laughter. She had taken three of the village boys as her lovers and had forced them to lie in the fields and do her will. One boy had become so emaciated he had died of the phthisis. It was also the custom of the Dizwosina to lie in wait for girls and win their confidence by braiding their hair, putting garlands around their necks, and dancing with them in a circle. But then after amusing herself with the maidens, she would spatter and cover them with filth.

Skrzots also had been seen this year in the granaries. This was a bird that dragged its wings and tail on the ground. As was well known, it came from an egg which had been hatched in a human armpit. But who in the village would do such mischief? It clearly couldn't be the men; only women would have the time and patience for things like that. In the winter the Skrzot got cold in the granary and would knock at the door of a hut and seek to be let in. Then the Skrzot brought good luck. But in all other respects it was harmful and consumed vast amounts of grain. If its excrement fell on the human eye, blindness followed. The opinion of those in the tavern was that a search party should be organized to find out what women were carrying eggs under their arms. But by far the strangest thing that had happened recently concerned a young virgin. The girl swore she had been attacked by a vampire. The monster had fastened its teeth to her breasts and had drunk until dawn. In the morning the girl had been found in a swoon, the teethmarks on her skin clearly visible.

And yet concerned though they were with vampires and succubuses, they spoke even more about Jacob who lived on the mountain and who tended Jan Bzik's cattle. It was a sin, they said, to maintain an infidel in a Christian village. Who knew where this man came from or what his intentions were? He said that he was a Jew, but if that was so he had murdered Jesus Christ. Why, then, should he be given asylum? Antek said that as soon as his father "croaked," he would take care of Jacob. But the listeners replied that they couldn't wait that long.

"You've seen how your sister crawls to him every day," one peasant remarked to Antek. "It'll end up with her giving birth to a monster."

Antek deliberated before he replied.

"She claims he doesn't touch her."

"Eh, woman's talk!"

"Her belly's flat."

"Flat today, swollen tomorrow," another peasant interjected. "Did you hear about the beggar that came to Lippica? This one was a fine talker and the women followed him around. Three months after he left, five monsters were born. They had nails, teeth, and spurs. Four were strangled but one woman out of pity tried secretly to nurse hers. It bit off her nipple."

"What did she do then?"

"She screamed and her brother picked up a flail and killed it."

"Bah, such things happen," an old peasant said, licking the pork fat off his mustache.

The tavern was half in ruins. Its roof was broken; mushrooms grew on its walls. Two tables and four benches were in the room which was lit by a wick burning in a shard; the single flame smoked and sputtered. The peasants cast heavy shadows on the wall. There was no floor. One of the men got up to relieve himself and stood at a heap of garbage in the corner. Zagayek's daughter laughed with her toothless gums.

"Too lazy to go outside, little father?"

Heavy steps could be heard, and a groaning and snorting. Dziobak, the priest, entered. He was a short, broad-shouldered man; he looked as if he had been sawed in half and glued and nailed together again. His eyes were green as gooseberries, his eyebrows dense as brushes. He had a thick nose with pimples and a receding chin.

Dziobak's robe was covered with stains. He was bent and hunched up, supported himself by two heavy canes. Priests are clean shaven, but coarse, stiff hairs like the bristles of a pig sprouted on his chin. For years the charge had been made that he neglected his duties. Rain leaked into the chapel. Half of the Virgin's head had been smashed. On Sundays when it was time to say Mass Dziobak often lay in a drunken stupor. But his one defender was Zagayek, who ignored all the denunciations. As for the majority of the peasants, they continued to worship the ancient idols that had been the gods of Poland before the truth had been revealed.

"Well, good householders, I see you're all busy with the bottle," Dziobak's hollow voice came from his chest as if from a barrel. "Yes, one needs a drink to burn out the devil."

"Well, it's a drink," Antek said, "but it doesn't burn."

"Does she mix it with water?" Dziobak asked, pointing at the barmaid. "Are you swindling the householders?"

"There's not a drop of water there, little Father. They run from water like the devil from incense."

"Well said."

"Why don't you sit down, Father?"

"Yes, my small feet do ache. It's a hard job for them to carry the weight of me."

Grandiose language was still available to him; he had studied in a seminary in Crakow, but everything else he had learned he had forgotten. He opened his froglike mouth, exposing his one long black tooth which resembled a cleat.

"Won't you have a drink, Father?" the barmaid asked.

"A drink," Dziobak repeated after her.

She brought him a wooden mug filled with vodka. Dziobak eyed it suspiciously and with visible distaste. He grimaced as if he had a pain in his stomach.

"Well, good people, to your health." He quickly gulped down the liquid. His face became more distorted; disappointment gleamed in his green eyes. It was as if he had been served vinegar.

"We're talking about the Jew Jan Bzik keeps on the mountain, Father." Dziobak became incensed.

"What's there to talk about? Climb up and dispose of him in God's name. I warned you, did I not, little brothers? I said he would bring only misfortune."

"Zagayek has forbidden it."

"I count Zagayek as my friend and defender. We can be sure that he does not want the village to fall into the hands of Lucifer."

Dziobak peeked at the wooden mug out of the corner of his eyes.

"Just another drop."

3

Jacob awoke in the middle of the night. His body was hot and tense; his heart was pounding. He had been dreaming of Wanda. Passion overwhelmed him and an idea leaped into his brain. He must run down to the valley and find her. He knew she sometimes slept in the granary. "I'm damned already," he told himself. But even as he said it he was aware it was Satan speaking within him.

He must calm himself. He walked to the stream. The brook had its source in glacial snows and its waters were ice cold even in summer. But it was necessary for Jacob to perform his ablutions. What else remained for him but the doing of such acts? He took off his pants and waded into the stream. The moon had already set, but the night was thick with stars. Rumor had it that a water devil made its home in these waters and sang so beautifully in the evening that boys and girls were lured to their destruction. But Jacob knew that a Jew had no right to be afraid of witchcraft or astrology. And if he were dragged down into the current, he would be better off.

"Let it be His will that my death redeem all my sins," he murmured, choosing those words which in ancient times had been spoken by those put to death by the Sanhedrin. The stream was shallow and filled with rocks, but at one spot the water reached to his chest. Jacob walked carefully. He slipped, almost fell. He was afraid that Balaam would begin barking, but the dog continued to sleep in his kennel. He reached the spot that was deepest and immersed himself. How strange. The coldness did not extinguish his lust. A passage from the Song of Songs came to his mind: Many waters cannot quench love, neither can the floods drown it. "What a comparison," he admonished himself. The love referred to in Scriptures was the love of God for his Chosen People. Each word was filled with mystery upon mystery. Jacob continued to immerse himself until he became calmer.

He came out of the water. Before, desire had made him tremble but now he shivered from the cold. He walked to the barn and threw his sheet over him. He murmured a prayer: "Lord, of the universe, remove me from this world, before I stumble and arouse Thy wrath. I am sick of being a wanderer among idolaters and murderers. Return me to that source from whence I came."

He had now become a man at war with himself. One half of him prayed to God to save him from temptation, and the other sought some way to surrender to the flesh. Wanda was not married, she was a widow, the recalcitrant part of him argued. True, she did not undergo ablution after her periods, but the stream was here, available to her for this ritual. Were there any other interdictions? Only the one that forbade the marrying of a gentile. But this interdiction did not apply here. These were unusual circumstances. Had not Moses married a woman from Ethiopia? Did not King Solomon take as his wife Pharaoh's daughter? Of course, these women had become Jewesses. But so could Wanda. The Talmudic law stating that a man who cohabits with a gentile could be put to death by anyone in the community was only valid if there had first been a warning and the adultery was seen by witnesses.

In Jacob's case the normal order of things had been reversed. It was God who spoke in the simplest language while evil overflowed with learned quotations. How long did one live in this world? How long was one young? Was it worth while to destroy this existence and the one that would follow for a few moments of pleasure? "It's all because I don't study the Torah," Jacob said to himself. He started to mumble verses from the Psalms, and then an idea came to him. Hereafter to occupy his time he would enumerate the two hundred and forty-eight commandments and the three hundred and sixty-five prohibitions to be found in the Torah. Although he didn't know them by heart, his years of exile had taught him what a miser the human memory is. It didn't like to give, but if one remained stubborn and did not cease asking, it would pay out even more than what was demanded. Never left in peace, it would at last return all that had been deposited within it.

To be fruitful and multiply was the first of all the commandments. ("Perhaps have a child by Wanda," the legalist within Jacob interjected.) What was the second commandment? Circumcision. And the third? Jacob could not think of another commandment in the entire book of Genesis. So he began to reflect upon Exodus. What was the first commandment in that book? Very likely the

eating of the Passover offering and of the unleavened bread. Yes, but what was
the use of remembering these things when tomorrow he might forget them? He
must find a way to write everything down. Suddenly he realized that he could
do what Moses had done. If Moses had been able to chisel the Ten Commandments
into stone, why couldn't he? Chiseling wasn't even necessary; he could scratch
with an awl or a nail pried from one of the rafters. He recollected having seen
a bent hook somewhere in the barn. Now Jacob found it impossible to return to
sleep. A man must be clever in battling the Evil One. He must anticipate all of
the Devil's stratagems. Jacob sat waiting for the light of the morning star. The
barn was quiet. The cows slept. He heard the sound of the stream. The entire
earth seemed to be holding its breath awaiting the new day. Now he had forgotten
his lust. Once more he remembered that while he was sitting here in Jan Bzik's
barn God continued to direct the world. Rivers flowed; waves billowed on the
ocean. Each of the stars continued on its prescribed way. The grain in the fields
would ripen soon and the harvest would begin. But who had ripened the grain?
How could a stalk of wheat rise from a kernel? How could tree, leaf, branch,
fruit emerge from a pit? How could man appear from a drop of semen in a
woman's womb? These were all miracles, wonders of wonders. Yes, there were
many questions one might ask of God. But who was man to comprehend the
acts of divinity?

Jacob was now too impatient to wait for sunrise. "I thank Thee," he said,
rising, and then he washed his hands. As he did so a purple beam appeared in
the crack beneath the door. He walked outside. The sun had just risen from
behind the mountains. The bird which always announced the coming of day
chirped shrilly. This was one creature that did not oversleep.

It had become light enough to reach for the hook. Its place was on the shelf
where the milk pots were stored. But it had disappeared. Well, that was Satan's
work, Jacob thought. He did not wish Jacob to engrave the six hundred and
thirteen laws. Jacob took down the earthen pots, one by one, and put them back
on the shelf. He rummaged on the ground, searching among the straw. He
remained hopeful. The important thing was not to give up. Good things never
came easily.

At last he found it. It had slipped into a crack on the shelf. He didn't
understand how he could have missed it. Yes, everything, it seemed, was ordained.
Years before someone had left the hook there so that Jacob could engrave God's
edicts.

He left the barn to find a suitable stone. He did not have to search far.
Behind the barn a large rock protruded from the earth. There it stood as ready
as the ram which Father Abraham had sacrificed as a burnt offering instead of
Isaac. The stone had been waiting ever since Creation.

What he wrote would be visible to no one; it would be hidden behind the
barn. Balaam began to wag his tail and jump as if his canine soul comprehended
what his master was preparing to do.

4

Harvest time was approaching and Jan Bzik brought Jacob down from the mountain.
How painful it was for the slave to leave his solitude! He had already scratched

forty-three commandments and sixty-nine interdictions into the rock. What wonders issued from his mind. He tortured memory and things he had long forgotten appeared. His was a never ending struggle with Purah, the lord of oblivion. In this battle force and persuasion were both necessary; patience was also required, but concentration was most important of all. Jacob sat midway between the barn and rock, concealing himself with weeds and the branches of a midget pine. He mined within himself as men dig for treasure in the earth. It was slow work; he scratched sentences, fragments of sentences, single words into the stone. The Torah had not disappeared. It lay hidden in the nooks and crannies of his brain.

But now he was forced to interrupt his task.

It had been a dry summer, and though there was never much of a harvest in the village, this year's crop was particularly meager. The stalks of grain grew further apart than usual and their kernels were small and brittle. As always, the peasants prayed to both the image of the Virgin and the old lime trees which commanded the rain spirits.

These were not the only rites. Pine branches, lurers of rain, were set among the furrows. The village's wooden rooster, a relic of ancient times, was wrapped in green wheat stalks and decked with saplings. Dancing around the lime trees with the decorated image, the villagers doused it with water. In addition to such public ceremonies, each peasant had his own unique rituals which had been handed down from father to son. Relatives of men who had hanged themselves visited the suicides' graves and begged the unsanctified bones not to cause drought. But rain was not the only problem. As everyone knew, a wicked Baba hid in the stalks and an evil Dziad in the tips. As soon as one furrow was reaped the Baba and Dziad fled and concealed themselves in another. Even when the whole crop had been bound in sheaves, no one could be sure that the danger was over as tiny Babas and minuscule Dziads sought final refuge in the unhusked kernels, and had to be thrashed out with flails. Until the last small Baba had been crushed, the crop was not safe.

This year all the customs had been scrupulously followed, but somehow had been of no avail. There was a grumbling among the peasants when they learned that Jan Bzik had brought Jacob down from the mountain. The poorness of the harvest was perhaps his work. A complaint was made to the bailiff Zagayek, but his answer was, "Let him do his job first. It's never too late to kill him."

So from early morning until sunset Jacob stood in the fields, and Wanda did not leave him. It was she who taught him how to reap, showed him how the scythe should be sharpened, brought him the food he was permitted to eat: bread, onions, fruit. The law did not allow him to drink milk now since he had not been present at the milkings. But fortunately the chickens were laying well and Wanda secretly gave him an egg each day, which he drank raw. He could also take sour milk and butter since the law stated that the milk of unclean animals does not turn. His sin was heinous enough merely eating the bread of the gentile; his soul could not tolerate further sullying.

The work was difficult, and his fellow harvesters never stopped ridiculing him. Here was a man who wouldn't drink soup or milk and never touched pork. This fellow fasted while he worked.

"You'll wither away," he was warned. "The next thing you know you'll be stretched out flat."

"God gives me strength," Jacob answered.

"What God? Yours must live in the city."

"God is everywhere, in both city and country."

"You don't cut straight. You'll ruin the straw."

The women and girls giggled and whispered.

"Do you see, Wanda, how your man sweats?"

"He's the strongest in the village."

Hearing that remark, Jacob cautioned her.

"The man who can control his passions is the most powerful."

"What's that fool saying?"

The women winked at each other and laughed, exchanged lewd gestures. One girl ran over to Jacob and pulled up her skirts. This made the peasants whinny with laughter.

"That's a fine show for you, Jew."

As he reaped, Jacob kept up a constant recitation, repeating to himself Psalms and passages of the Mishnah and Gemara. He had been there when the oxen plowed the fields and the seed was sowed. Now he was harvesting the grain. Weeds grew among the stalks and corn flowers on the sides of the furrows. As the scythes moved, field mice ran from their blades, but other creatures remained in the harvested fields: grasshoppers, lady bugs, beetles, flyers and crawlers, every variety of insect, and each with its own particular structure. Surely some Hand had created all this. Some Eye was watching over it. From the mountains came grasshoppers and birds that spoke with human voices, and the peasants killed them with their shovels. Their efforts were to no avail, since the more they killed, the more gathered. Jacob was reminded of the plague of locusts that God had visited upon the Egyptians. He himself killed nothing. It was one thing to slaughter an animal according to the law and in such a way as to redeem its soul, another to step on and crush tiny creatures that sought no more than man did—merely to eat and multiply. At dusk when the fields were alive with toads, Jacob walked carefully, so as not to tread on their exposed bodies.

Now and again when the ribald songs of the harvesters resounded in the fields, Jacob would take up a chant of his own, the Sabbath service, or the liturgies of Rosh Hashana and Yom Kippur, or sing the Akdamoth, a Pentecost song. Wanda joined in, for she had picked up the tunes from Jacob, singing Jewish chants and recitatives with a voice that had been accustomed to ballads of a different kind. Jacob's soul throbbed with music. He kept up a constant debate with the Almighty. "How long will the unholy multitudes rule the world and the scandal and darkness of Egypt hold dominion? Reveal Thy Light, Father in Heaven. Let there be an end to pain and idolatry and the shedding of blood. Scourge us no longer with plagues and famines. Do not allow the weak to go down to defeat and the wicked to triumph. . . . Yes, Free Will was necessary, and Your face had to be hidden, but there has been enough of concealment. We are already up to our necks in water." So absorbed did he become in his chant that he did not notice that all the others had become silent. His voice sang alone and everyone was listening. The peasants clapped hands, laughed, and mimicked him. Jacob stood with bent head, ashamed.

"Pray, Jew, pray. Not even your God can make this a good harvest."

"Do you think he's cursing us?"

"What language is that you're speaking, Jew?"

"The Holy Language."

"What Holy Language?"

"The language of the Bible."
"The Bible? What's the Bible?"
"God's Law."
"What's God's Law?"
"That one neither kill nor steal nor covet a man's wife."
"Dziobak says things like that in the chapel."
"It all comes from the Bible."
The peasants became silent. One of them handed Jacob a turnip.
"Eat, stranger. You won't get strong from fasting."

5

The crop had been poor, but nevertheless the peasants celebrated. Girls appeared in the fields with wreaths on their heads and the older women assembled also. The time had come for Zagayek to superintend the selection of the maiden who would reap the last Baba. The choice was made by drawing lots and the girl chosen cut the last sheaf of grain, thereby becoming a Baba herself. Once selected, she was wrapped in stalks tied round her body by flax, and paraded from hut to hut in a wooden-wheeled cart drawn by four boys. The whole village accompanied the procession, laughing and singing and clapping hands. It was said that in ancient times when the people had still been idol worshipers the Baba was thrown into the stream and drowned, but now the village was Christian.

The night following this ceremony, the peasants danced and drank. The Baba performed with the boy who was chosen to be rooster. The rooster crowed, chased chickens, did all kinds of antics. He had a pair of wings on his shoulders, a cockscomb on his head and on his heels wooden spurs. Last year's rooster was also there, and the two fought, pushing out their chests, charging each other, tearing each other's feathers. It was so funny the girls couldn't stop laughing. This year's rooster always won, and then danced with the Baba who was now disguised as a witch, her face smeared with soot, and with the broom in her hand on which she rode to the Black Mass. The Baba seated herself in a barrel hoop and lifted her skirts, preparing to make a journey. The peasants forgot their troubles. The children refused to go to bed, sipped vodka, laughed and giggled.

Since it was no longer permissible to drown the real Baba, the boys made an effigy from straw. So skillfully did they model face, breasts, hips and feet, that the scarecrow, with two coals in the head for eyes, seemed alive. Just as the sun rose, the Baba was led to the stream. The women scolded the scapegoat, demanding that she take with her the evil eye and all their misfortunes and illnesses. The men and children spat on her, and then she was thrown into the stream. Everyone watched the straw Baba move downstream, bobbing up and down in the current. As the peasants knew, the river flowed into the Vistula and the Vistula emptied into the sea where bad spirits were awaiting the Baba. Though she wasn't alive, the over-compassionate girls wept for her. Was there such a great difference between flesh and straw? The ceremony over, vodka was passed around, and Jacob was given a drink. Wanda whispered into his ear, "I wish I were the Baba. I would swim with you to the end of the world."

The next day, the threshing began. From sunrise to sunset there was the sound of flails rising and falling. Occasionally a muffled cry or sob rose from the stalks. One of the small Babas was dying. The evenings were still warm enough for the threshers to stay out of doors, and so after supper they gathered branches and lit a fire. Chestnuts were roasted, riddles asked, stories told of werewolves, hobgoblins, demons. The most spine-tingling tale concerned the black field where only black grain sprouted and where a black reaper reaped with a long black scythe. The girls screamed and clutched each other, huddled closer to the boys. The autumn days were brilliant, but the nights were dark. Stars fell; frogs croaked, spoke with human voices from the bogs. Bats appeared and the girls scurried, covering their heads and screaming. If one of these nocturnal creatures entangled itself in a girl's hair, it meant that she would not live out the year.

Someone asked Jacob to sing and he performed a lullaby he had learned from his mother. The song pleased the peasants. He was asked for a story. He told them several tales from the Gemara and Midrash. The one they liked best was about a man who had heard of a harlot living in a distant country whose fee was four hundred gulden. When the man went to the harlot, he found she had prepared six silver beds with silver ladders and one golden bed with a golden ladder. The harlot had sat before him naked, but the fringes of his ritual garment had suddenly risen and struck him angrily in the face. At the end of the story the man converted the harlot to the Jewish faith and the beds she had prepared for him were finally used on their wedding night. The story was not easy to translate into Polish, but Jacob managed to make the peasants understand. They became fascinated by the fringes. What kind of fringes were they? Jacob explained. The glow from the fire lit up Wanda's face. She pulled his arm to her lips, kissed and then bit it. He sought to free himself but she hung to him tenaciously. Her breasts rubbed against his shoulder and the heat she gave off was like an oven's.

The story had been told for her, he knew. In the form of a parable he had promised that if she did not force him to cohabit with her now, later he would take her as a wife. But could he make such a promise? His wife might be alive. How could Wanda become a Jew? In Poland a Christian who became a Jewish convert was put to death; moreover, Jewish law forebade the conversion of gentiles for reasons other than faith.

"Well, every day I sink deeper into the abyss," Jacob thought.

Then on the last day of the threshing, a circus arrived in town. It was the first time Jacob had seen anyone from another district. The troupe included two men beside the owner, and they had a monkey, and a parrot who not only talked but told fortunes by selecting cards with his beak. The village was in an uproar. The performance was given in an open field near Zagayek's house and all of the men showed up with their wives and children. Jacob was permitted to go also. The bear whirled around on his hind legs, the monkey smoked a pipe and did somersaults. One of the men was an acrobat and did stunts like walking on his hands and lying bare-backed on a board of nails. The other was a musician and played a fiddle, a trumpet, and a drum with bells. The peasants screamed with joy and Wanda jumped up and down like a little girl. But Jacob disapproved of such entertainment, which he considered only one step away from witchcraft. More than a desire for amusement had brought him there. Circus men wandered from town to town, and perhaps this troupe had stopped at Josefov. They might have news of Jacob's family. So when the performance was done and the monkey and bear had been chained to a tree, Jacob followed the performers into their tent. The proprietor looked at Jacob in astonishment when he heard his question: had the circus stopped at Josefov.

"What business is it of yours where I've been?"

"I come from Josefov. I am a Jew and a teacher. I am a survivor of the massacre."

"How do you happen to be here?"

Jacob told the proprietor and the man snapped his whip.

"If the Jews knew where you were would they ransom you?"

"Yes, to free a captive is considered a holy act."

"Would they pay me if I told them you were alive?"

"Yes, they would."

"Give me your name. And I must have a way to convince them that I am telling the truth."

Jacob confided to the circus owner the names of his wife and children as well as that of his father-in-law who had been one of the community elders. Although the man could not write, he made a knot in a piece of string and told Jacob that he had not as yet been to Josefov, but he might well stop there. If any Jews were left in the town he would tell them that Jacob was alive and where he could be found.

CHAPTER THREE

1

After the harvest, Jacob returned to the barn on the mountain. He knew that he would not be there long. Soon the cold weather would set in and the cattle would have no food. Already the days had become shorter and when he gathered grass in the morning, he found the fields covered with frost. Haze hung over the autumn hills and it was increasingly difficult to distinguish between fog rising from the earth and the smoke of camp fires. The birds screamed and croaked more shrilly these days, and the winds blowing down from the summits carried the taste of snow. Though Jacob gathered as much fodder as he could, it was never enough for the cows. The hungry beasts bellowed, stamped on the earth, even pounded with their hoofs while they were being milked. Once more Jacob proceeded with his task of engraving the six hundred and thirteen laws of the Torah onto a stone, but he had little spare time during the day and at night it was too dark to work.

On the seventh day of the month of Elul—according to Jacob's calculations— dusk came quickly. The sun fell behind a massive cloud which covered the entire west. But was it really that date? For all he knew his reckonings might be erroneous and when the ram's horn was blown all over the world and the Rosh

Hashana litanies sung, he would be out as usual gathering fodder. He sat in the barn and thought about his life. For as long as he could remember he had been considered lucky. His father had been a wealthy contractor who bought up the gentry's timber, supervised the felling of the trees and floated the logs down the Bug River to the Vistula and from thence to Danzig. Whenever his father had gone off on such trips, he had returned bearing gifts for Jacob and his sisters. Elka Sisel, Jacob's mother, was a rabbi's daughter and came from Prussia where she had been brought up in comfortable circumstances. Susschen, as she was called, spoke German and wrote Hebrew and conducted herself differently from the other women. She had rugs on the floor of her house and brass latches on the door. Coffee, a rarity even among the rich, was served daily in her home. An expert cook, seamstress, knitter, she taught her daughters how to do needlepoint and instructed them in Bible reading. The girls married young. Jacob himself was only twelve when he became engaged to Zelda Leah, who was two years younger, and the daughter of the town's elder. He had always been a good student. At eight he had read a complete page of the Gemara unassisted; at his engagement party he delivered a speech. He wrote in a fine, bold hand, had a good singing voice, and was a gifted draughtsman and wood carver. On a canvas on the east wall of the synagogue he painted the twelve constellations in red, green, blue and purple circling Jehovah's name, and in the corners put four animals: a deer, a lion, a leopard, and an eagle. At Pentecost he decorated the windows of the town's most important citizens and for the feast of Succoth adorned the tabernacle with lanterns and streamers.

Tall and healthy, when he made a fist, six boys could not force it open. His father had taught him to swim side and breast stroke. Zelda Leah, on the other hand, was thin and small—prematurely old, his sisters maintained. But of what possible interest was this ten-year-old child to Jacob? He was more interested in his father-in-law's library of rare books. Jacob received four hundred gulden as dowry, room and board at his in-laws for life.

The wedding was noisy and boisterous. Josefov was only a small town but after his marriage Jacob immersed himself so deeply in study that he forgot the outside world. True, his wife, he discovered, had odd habits. If her mother scolded her, she petulantly kicked off her shoes and stockings and overturned the soup bowl. She was a married woman and had not as yet menstruated. When her period finally came, she bled like a slaughtered calf. Every time Jacob approached her, she howled in pain. She was a perpetual sufferer from heartburn, headaches, and back aches. She screwed up her face, wept, complained. But Jacob was given to understand that only daughters were always like that. Her mother was constantly tugging her from him, but Zelda Leah bore him three children, Jacob scarcely knew how. Her recriminations and sarcasms sounded like the babblings of fools or school children; she belonged to that class of spoiled daughters whose whims can never be satisfied. Her mother, she said, was envious of her good looks. Her father had forgotten her; Jacob didn't love her. It never seemed to occur to her that she should try being lovable. Her eyes grew prematurely old from too much crying and her nose turned red. She didn't even take care of the children. That too became her mother's responsibility.

When the rabbi died, Jacob's father-in-law wanted him to take over the office, but Zaddock, the late rabbi's son, had a considerable following. True, Jacob's backer was the town's elder, a rich and influential man, but the people of Josefov had decided that this one time they were not going to let him have his way. Despite himself, Jacob found that he was involved in a quarrel. He didn't want to become rabbi, was actually in favor of Zaddock, and because of this his father-in-law became his enemy. If he refused to become rabbi, let him at least lecture to the boys in the study house. Jacob would have liked to stay in the library, studying the Gemara and its commentaries, meditating on philosophy and cabala, subjects he preferred even to the Talmud. From childhood on he had been searching for the meaning of existence and trying to comprehend the ways of God. He was acquainted with the thought of Plato, Aristotle, and the Epicureans through the quotations he had found in *A Guide for the Perplexed,* the *Chuzary, The Beliefs and Ideas,* and similar works. He knew the cabalistic systems of Rabbi Moshe of Cordova and the holy Isaac Luria. He was well aware that Judaism was based upon faith and not knowledge and yet he sought to understand wherever it was possible. Why had God created the world? Why had He found it necessary to have pain, sin, evil? Even though each of the great sages had given his answer, the questions remained unsolved. An all-powerful Creator did not need to be sustained by the agony of small children and the sacrifice of His people to bands of assassins. The atrocities of the Cossacks had been talked about for years before the attack on Josefov. Hearts had long been frozen with fear, then one day death had struck.

Jacob had just turned twenty-five when the Cossacks had advanced on Josefov. He was now past twenty-nine, so he had lived a seventh of his life in this remote mountain village, deprived of family and community, separated from books, like one of those souls who wander naked in Tophet. And here it was the end of summer; the short days, the cold nights had come. He could reach out his hand and actually touch the darkness of Egypt, the void from which God's face was absent. Dejection is only one small step from denial. Satan became arrogant and spoke to Jacob insolently: "There is no God. There is no world beyond this one." He bid Jacob become a pagan among the pagans; he commanded him to marry Wanda or at the very least to lie with her.

2

The cowherds also had their autumn celebration. They had sought by threats and promises to make Jacob join them ever since he had first appeared upon the mountain with Jan Bzik's herd. But, one way or another, he had always put them off. He was forbidden to eat their food or listen to their licentious songs and brutal jokes. For the most part, they were a crippled, half-mad crew with scabs and elflocks on their heads and rashes on their bodies. Shame was unknown to them, as if they had been conceived before the eating of the forbidden fruit. Jacob often reflected that as yet this rabble had not developed the capacity to choose freely. They seemed to him survivors of those worlds, which, according to the Midrash, God had created and destroyed before fashioning this one. Jacob, when he saw them approaching, had acquired the habit of turning his head, or looking through them as if they didn't exist. If they foraged for grass on the lower slopes, he moved up toward the summit. He avoided them like filth. They were crawling all about him on the mountain, yet he went days and weeks without meeting any. Nor was it only disgust that kept him apart from this vermin; they were dangerous and, like wolves, would attack for no reason. Sickness, suffering, the sight of blood amused them.

That year they had made up their minds to seize him by force, and one evening after Wanda had left they surrounded the barn, deploying themselves like soldiers stealthily preparing to storm a fortress. One moment there was a stillness in which only the song of the grasshoppers was heard, and the next, the silence had been broken by howling and shrieking as both men and girls charged from all sides. The attackers were equipped with sticks, stones, and ropes. Jacob thought hey had come to kill him, and like his Biblical namesake prepared to fight, or, if possible, to ransom himself through entreaties and a "gift" (the shirt off his back). He picked up a heavy club and swung it, knowing that his adversaries were so debilitated by illness he might be able to drive them off. Soon an emissary stepped forward, a cowherd who was more fluent than the others, and who assured Jacob no harm was intended. They had merely come to invite him to drink and dance with them. The man dribbled, stammered, mispronounced words. His companions were already drunk and laughed and screamed wildly. They held their stomachs and rolled about on the ground. He would not be let off this time, Jacob knew.

"All right," he finally said, "I'll go with you, but I'll eat nothing."   ·

"Jew, Jew. Come. Come. Seize him. Seize him."

A dozen hands grasped Jacob and started to tug him. He descended the hill on which the barn was located, half running, half sliding. An awful stench rose from that mob; the odors of sweat and urine mingled with the stink of something for which there is no name, as if these bodies were putrefying while still alive. Jacob was forced to hold his nose and the girls laughed until they wept. The men hee-hawed and whinnied, supported themselves on each other's shoulders, and barked like dogs. Some collapsed on the path, but their companions did not pause to assist them, but stepped over the recumbent bodies. Jacob was perplexed. How could the sons of Adam created in God's image fall to such depths? These men and women also had fathers and mothers and hearts and brains. They too possessed eyes that could see God's wonders.

Jacob was led to a clearing where the grass was already trampled and soiled with vomit. A keg of vodka three-quarters empty stood near an almost extinguished fire. Drunken musicians were performing on drums, pipes, on a ram's horn very like that blown on Rosh Hashana, on a lute strung with the guts of some animal. But those who were being entertained were too intoxicated to do more than wallow on the ground; grunting like pigs, licking the earth, babbling to rocks. Many lay stretched out like carcasses. There was a full moon in the sky, and one girl flung her arms around a tree trunk and cried bitterly. A cowherd walked over, threw branches on the fire, and nearly fell into the flames. Almost immediately a woolly looking shepherd attempted to put out the blaze by urinating on it. The girls howled, screamed, cat-called. Jacob felt himself choking. He had heard these cries many times before, but each time he was terrified by them.

"Well, now I have seen it," he said to himself. "These are those abominations which prompted God to demand the slaying of entire peoples."

As a boy, this had been one of his quarrels with the Lord. What sin had been committed by the small children of the nations Moses had been told to annihilate? But now that Jacob observed this rabble he understood that some forms of corruption can only be cleansed by fire. Thousands of years of idolatry survived in these savages. Baal, Astoreth, and Moloch stared from their bloodshot and dilated eyes. He was offered a cup of vodka by one of the merrymakers but the liquid seared his lips and throat; his stomach burned as though he had been forced to drink molten lead like those culprits the Sanhedrin had condemned to death at the stake in ancient times. Jacob shuddered. Had he been poisoned? Was this the end?

His face became contorted and he doubled up.

The cowherd who had given him the drink let out a yell, "Bring him more. Make the Jew drink. Fill up his cup."

"Give him pork," someone else shouted.

A pock-marked fellow with a face like a turnip grater tried to push a piece of sausage into Jacob's mouth. Jacob gave the man a shove. The cowherd fell and lay as still as a log.

"Hey, he's killed him."

Jacob approached the fallen man with trembling knees. Had this also been destined? Thank God, the man was alive. He lay there, foam bubbling from his lips, the sausage still clutched between his fingers, screaming abuse. His comrades laughed, threatened, cursed.

"God murderer. Jew. Scabhead. Leper."

A few feet away a cowherd jumped on a girl but was too drunk to do anything. Yet the two wrestled and squirmed like a dog and a bitch. The surrounding company laughed, spat, dribbled from their noses, and goaded the lovers on. A monstrous square-headed girl with a goiter on her neck and tangled matted hair sat on a tree stump sobbing out a name over and over again. She was wringing her hands, which were as long as a monkey's and as broad as a man's, their nails rotted away. Her feet were covered with boils and as flat as a goose's. Some of the cowherds sought to comfort her and gave her a cup of vodka. Her crooked mouth opened, exposing a single tooth, but she only wailed louder.

"Father! Father! Father!"

So she also cried out, Jacob thought, to a father in heaven. Compassion for this creature who had fallen from the womb deformed and misshapen, a mooncalf, swept over Jacob. Who could tell what frightened her mother at the moment of conception, or what sinful soul had been incarcerated in the girl's body? Hers was not an ordinary cry but the wail of a spirit who has gazed into the abyss and seen a torment from which there is no escape. Through some miracle this animal comprehended its own bestiality and mourned its lot.

Jacob wanted to go and comfort her, but he saw in her half-shut eyes a fury undiminished by suffering. Such a woman might spring at him like a beast of prey. He sat down and chanted the third chapter of Psalms: "Lord, how are they increased that trouble me! Many are they that rise against me. Many there be which say of my soul, there is no help for him in God. Selah."

3

It stormed in the middle of the night. A flash of lightning lit up the interior of the barn, and the cows, dung heaps, earthen pots became visible for an instant.

Thunder rumbled. After washing his hands, Jacob recited "The One Who Does the Work of Creation" and "His Power and Strength Fill the World." A gust of wind blew open the barn door. The downpour beat on the roof like hail. The rain lashed Jacob as he closed and latched the door. This was the beginning of bad weather, he feared, and not merely one of those torrential cloudbursts that occur in summer. So it was; for a few hours later, though the rain ceased, the sky remained overcast. An icy wind blew from the mountains. At dawn the storm started all over again. Though the sun had risen, the morning was as gray as twilight. There would be no foraging for grass and other vegetation on the slopes today. Jacob would have to feed his herd with the fodder he had prepared for the Sabbath. He built a small fire to make things more cheerful and sat by it praying; he rose, faced to the east, and recited the eighteen benedictions. A cow turned its head and gazed at him with a blank humility, yet the expression of the black muzzle, wet with saliva and bristling with a few sparse hairs, made Jacob think that the creature nursed some grievance. It often seemed to him that the cattle complained, "You are a man and we are only cows. What justice is there to that?" He placated them by stroking their necks, slapping their sides, and feeding them tidbits. "Father," he often prayed, "Thou knowest why Thou hast created them. They are the work of Thy hand. At the end of days, they too must have salvation."

That morning his breakfast consisted of bread and milk and an apple brought the day before. If the rain continued, Wanda would not come. He would have to sustain himself on sour milk, a dish which he could no longer stomach. He chewed each bite of the apple slowly to savor the full flavor. In his father-in-law's house he had not known that one could have such an appetite and that bread with bran could be so delicious. As he swallowed each mouthful, he seemed to feel the marrow in his bones increase. The wind had died down, the door of the barn was now open, and from time to time he glanced up at the sky. Perhaps the weather would clear: wasn't it too early for the autumn rains? No longer was there a vista of distant places—nothing was visible but the flat crest of the hill surrounding the barn. Sky, mountains, valleys, forests, had dissolved and disappeared. Fog drifted across the ground. Mist rose from the pines as though the wet trees were burning. Here in his exile Jacob at last understood what was meant when the cabala spoke of God's hidden face and the shrinking of His light. Yesterday everything had been bright; now it was gray. Distances had shrunk; the skies had collapsed like the canvas of a tent; the tangible had lost substance. If so much could vanish for the physical eye, how much more could elude the spiritual. Every man comprehended according to his merit. Infinite worlds, angels, seraphim, mansions and sacred chariots surrounded man, but he did not see them because he was small and sinful and immersed in the vanities of the body.

As always when it rained, a variety of creatures sought shelter in the barn: butterflies, grasshoppers, gnats, beetles. One insect had two pairs of wings. A white butterfly with black markings resembling script alighted on a stone near the fire and appeared to be warming or drying itself. Jacob placed a crumb of bread near it, but it remained motionless. He touched it, but it didn't stir, and he realized it was dead. Sorrow overcame him. Here was one that would never flutter again. He would have liked to eulogize this handsome creature which had lived a day, or even less, and had never tasted sin. Its wings were smoother than silk and covered with an ethereal dust. It rested on the stone like a shrouded corpse.

Of necessity, Jacob had to war with flies and vermin which bit both him and the cows. He had no alternative but to kill. As he walked about, he could not avoid treading on worms and toads, and when he gathered grass he often encountered venomous snakes which would hiss and strike at him and which he crushed with a club or stone. But each time something like that happened he judged himself a murderer. He silently blamed the Creator for forcing one creature to annihilate another. Of all the questions he asked about the universe, he found this the most difficult.

There was nothing for him to do that day and so he stretched out on the straw and covered himself with his sheet. No, Wanda would not come. He was ashamed that he longed so much for this gentile woman, but the harder he tried to rid himself of desire, the stronger it became. His yearning stayed with him praying and studying, sleeping and waking. He knew the bitter truth: compared to his passion for Wanda, his mourning for his wife and children and his love for God were weak. If the desires of the flesh came from Satan, then he was in the Devil's net. "Well, I have lost both worlds," he muttered, and through half-shut eyes he maintained his watch. The petals of a flower stirred among the wet bushes. Field mice, weasels, moles, skunks, and hedgehogs were hiding in the thickets. All of these small creatures waited with impatience for the sun to shine. The birds, like clusters of fruit, weighed down the trees and the instant the rain let up, whistling, chirruping, croaking began.

From somewhere far off came a muted yodel. A cowherd was singing in the foul dampness, and his distant voice pleaded and demanded, lamented the injustice visited on all living things: Jews, gentiles, animals, even the flies and gnats crawling on the hips of the cattle.

4

Though the rain ceased before evening, it was clear that this was only a short respite. Thunderheads lay low in the west, red and sulphurous, charged with lightning, and the air was heavy with mist that might at any moment turn to rain. Crows dived and cawed. There was no hope that Wanda would come in such weather, and yet when Jacob ascended his lookout hill, he saw her climbing toward him, carrying her two pitchers and the food basket. Tears came to his eyes. Someone remembered him and cared. He prayed that the storm would hold off until she reached him, and apparently his plea was answered; a moment after she entered the barn the deluge came, pouring down from the heavens as if from barrels. Neither Jacob nor Wanda spoke much to each other that afternoon. She sat down and immediately began to milk the cows. She was strangely shy and embarrassed and so was Jacob. Now and again a flash of lightning illuminated the twilight of the barn and he saw her bathed in such a heavenly glow that it seemed to him the woman he had known before had only been a sign or a husk. Had she not been created in God's image? Did not her form reflect that emanation through which the Eternal reflected His beauty? Had not Esau come from the seed of Abraham and Isaac? Jacob knew only too well where these meditations were leading, but he could not push them from him. He ate, said the benediction, recited the evening prayer, but still they did not leave him. The weather did not clear; Wanda would be unable to return home. At this late hour, moreover, the road back had already become dangerous.

"I'll sleep here in the barn," Wanda said, "unless you drive me out."

"I drive you out? You are the mistress."

They sat conversing quietly with the ease that intimacy brings. Wanda spoke of Zagayek and his paralytic wife, of their son Stephan who continued to pursue Wanda, of Zagayek's daughter Zosia whom everyone knew consorted with her father. But the bailiff had a dozen mistresses besides his daughter and so many bastards he could not remember their names. He did not conduct himself like a retainer but like a lord or king. He exacted from the peasant brides "the right of the first night," a law that was no longer in force. The peasants he treated as slaves, although they had their own fields and were only required to work for the count two days a week. He whipped them with wet rods, illegally forced them to do his business, levied private taxes upon vodka, performed operations on the sick against their will, tearing out teeth with pliers, amputating fingers with a cleaver, opening up breasts with a kitchen knife. Often he acted as midwife and demanded a handsome payment for his services.

"There's nothing he doesn't want," Wanda said. "He would swallow the village whole if he could."

Wanda's bed was not difficult to prepare. Jacob spread out some straw and she lay down on it, covering herself with her shawl. He slept in one corner of the barn and she in another. In the silence the cows could be heard chewing their cud. She went outside to relieve herself and returned drenched from the rain. "So modesty exists even among these people," Jacob reflected. They both lay there without saying a word. "I must be sure not to snore," Jacob warned himself. He feared that he would be unable to sleep, but weariness overcame him. His jaw sagged and darkness flooded his mind. Every night he dropped onto his bed like a log. Thank God there was something stronger than his lust.

<hr />

5

He awoke trembling, opened his eyes, and discovered Wanda lying next to him on the straw. The air in the barn was cool but he felt the burning heat of her body. She caught hold of him, pressed herself against him, and touched his cheek with her lips. Though he was conscious, he submitted in silence, amazed not only at what was happening but at the fierceness of his own desire. When he sought to push her from him, she clung to him with uncanny strength. He attempted to speak to her, but she stopped his lips with her mouth. He remembered the story of Ruth and Boaz and knew that his lust was more powerful than he. "I am forfeiting the world to come," he said to himself. He heard Wanda's hoarse voice imploring him; she was panting like an animal.

He lay numb, unable now to deny either her or himself, as if he had lost his freedom of will. Suddenly a passage from the Gemara entered his mind: should a man be overcome by the Evil One, let him dress himself in dark clothing, and cover himself in black, and indulge his heart's desire. This precept appeared to have been lurking in his memory for the specific purpose of breaking down his last defense. His legs became heavy and taut, and he was dragged down by a weight he could not withstand. "Wanda," he said, and his voice was trembling, "you must first go and bathe in the stream."

"I have already washed and I have combed my hair."

"No, you must immerse yourself in the water."

"Now?"

"God's law requires it."

She lay there in silence, perplexed by this strange demand, and then finally said, "I will do this also."

She rose, and still holding tight to him, opened the barn door. The rain had stopped but the night was mired in darkness and wet. There was not a trace of the sky and the only evidence of the stream was the sound of water churning and bubbling as it rushed downward. Wanda clutched Jacob's hand as they groped blindly and with the abandon of those who no longer fear for their bodies. They stumbled over stones and shrubs, were splashed by the moisture dripping from trees. They were seeking the one spot in that shallow, rock-cluttered torrent where the stream was deep enough for a man to immerse himself. When they reached it, she refused to enter the water without him, and he, forgetting to slip out of his linen trousers, followed her in. The shock of the cold water touching him took away his breath; he almost lost his footing, so swollen was the stream because of the rains. They clung to each other as if undergoing martyrdom. Thus, at the time of the massacres Jews had plunged into fire and water. At last, his feet on a firm bottom, Jacob said to Wanda, "Immerse yourself."

She let go his hand and submerged in the water. He reached about, unable to find her. She reappeared, and his eyes, now accustomed to the darkness, made out the dim contours of her face.

"Hurry," he said.

"I have done this for you."

He took her hand and together they ran back to the barn. The cold, he realized, had not extinguished the fire in his veins. Both of them burned with the heat of newly lit kindling. He dried Wanda's naked body with his sheet, breathing heavily, his teeth chattering. Wanda's eyes shone through the darkness. He heard her say to him again, "I have done this for you."

"No, not for me," he answered, "for God," and the blasphemy of his words frightened him.

Nothing could restrain him now. He lifted her in his arms and carried her to the straw.

CHAPTER FOUR

1

The sun rose and red could be seen through the chinks in the door. A purple beam of light fell across Wanda's face. They had been asleep, but awakened by lust they again sought each other. He had never known such passion as hers. She spoke words he had never heard before, called him in her peasant dialect her buck, her lion, her wolf, her bull, and even stranger epithets. He possessed her but it did not quench his desire. She blazed with an ecstasy—was it from heaven or hell? "More, more," she cried in a loud voice, "master, husband." He found himself possessed of powers that did not seem to be his—was it miracle or witchcraft? For the first time in his life he recognized the mysteries of the body. How was such desire possible? "For Love is as strong as Death," the Song of Songs said, and at last he understood. As the sun rose, he sought to tear himself from her. She clung to his neck and again thirstily kissed him. "My husband," she said, "I want to die for you."

"Why die? You are still young."

"Take me away from here to your Jews. I want to be your wife and bear you a son."

"You must believe in God to become a daughter of Israel."

"I believe in Him. I believe."

She was screaming so loudly that he covered her mouth with his hand so the cowherds outside would not hear. He was no longer ashamed before God, but he feared the ridicule of men. Even the cows turned their heads and stared. He pulled himself from her and was baffled to discover morning brought no repentance. The opposite rather! He was astonished now that he had endured his desire. The pitcher had overturned and he could not wash his hands. He didn't even say "I thank Thee," fearing to utter holy words after what had happened. His clothes were damp, but he put them on anyway, and Wanda also tidied herself. He walked out into the cool, clear Elul morning, leaving her with the cows. Dew covered the grass and each droplet gleamed. Birds were singing, and in the distance a cow lowed, the sound echoing like the blast from a ram's horn. "Yes, I have forfeited the world beyond," Jacob muttered, and immediately Satan whispered into his ear, "Shouldn't you also give up being a Jew?" Jacob glanced at the rock on which he had already scratched a third of the commandments and interdictions and it seemed to him like a battered ruin, all that was left to him from a war that had been lost. "Well, but I am still a Jew," he said, quoting the Talmud in an attempt to rally his spirits. He washed his hands in the stream and said, "I thank Thee," and then he began the introductory prayer. When he came to the words, "Lead us not into temptation," he paused. Not even the sainted Joseph had been as tempted as he. The Midrash said that when Joseph had been about to sin, his father's image had been revealed to him. So Heaven had interceded in his behalf.

As he mumbled his prayers, he searched in himself for some extenuation of what he had done. According to the strict letter of the law, this woman was neither unclean nor married. Even the Ancients had had concubines. She could still be a pious Jewish matron. "Something done selfishly may end up as a godly act." But, nevertheless, as he prayed he contrasted, despite himself, Wanda and Zelda, peace be with her. His wife had also been a woman, but frigid and cold, forever distracted. She had been a constant stream of complaints: headaches, toothaches, cramps in the stomach, and always fearful of breaking the law. How could he have known that such passion and love as Wanda's existed? He again heard Wanda's voice, the words she had whispered to him, her groans, the swift intake of her breath, and he again felt the touch of her tongue and the sharpness of her teeth. She had left marks on his body. She was willing to flee with him across the mountains in the middle of the night. She spoke to him exactly as Ruth had spoken: "Where thou goest, I go. Thy people are my people. Thy God is my God." Her body exuded the warmth of the sun, the breezes of summer, the fragrance of wood, field, flower, leaf, just as milk gave off the odor of the grass the cattle fed on. He yawned while he prayed. He recited the Shema and stretched his arms. He had scarcely closed his eyes the night before and lacked the strength to go hunting for grass. Bending his head low, Jacob was aware of his own weariness. During the few brief moments of sleep, he had dreamed, and although he did not remember his dream clearly, its aftertaste lingered. It seemed to him that he had been descending steps into a ritual bath or cave and had wandered across hills, ditches, and graves. He had met someone whose beard was composed of the roots of a plant. Who could it have been? His father? Had the man spoken to him? Wanda thrust her head out of the barn and gave him a wifely smile.

"Why are you standing there?"

He pointed to his lips to signify that she must not interrupt his prayer.

Her eyes shone with affection; she winked and nodded. Jacob closed his eyelids. Did he repent? He did not feel so much contrition as annoyance that he had been placed in a situation which made his sin possible. He stared into himself as though he were looking down the shaft of a deep well. What he saw there frightened him. Like a snake, passion lay curled at the bottom.

2

Rosh Hashana, Yom Kippur, and Succoth, according to Jacob's calendar, were past. The day which he thought to be Simchath Torah, Jan Bzik appeared on the mountain accompanied by Antek, Wanda, and Basha. The smell of snow was in the air; the time had come to drive the cattle down the valley. Both bringing them up and taking them down were difficult tasks. Cows are not mountain goats and do not climb slopes nimbly. The beasts had to be held by short, thick ropes, and restrained at every step. A cow might dig its hoofs into the ground and then one man would be forced to drag the creature while another whipped it. Others might stampede and break backs or legs bolting from the herd. But on this occasion all went well. An hour or so after the cattle had entered Jan Bzik's barn, snow fell. The mountains were no longer accessible, and were enveloped by columns of mist. The village, turned white, looked unfamiliar. Food was not plentiful in the homes of the peasants, but there was no lack of wood; smoke rose from the chimneys. The frames of the windows had been weather-proofed with lime and sealed with straw. The peasant girls had also made out of straw long-nosed monsters with horns on their heads whose task was to tease and annoy Winter.

This year, as every year, Jacob was asked to move into the hut with the family, but he preferred to take up his old abode in the granary. He made himself a straw bed and Wanda sewed him a pillow stuffed with hay; he had a horse blanket for a cover. The granary had no windows but light seeped through the cracks in the wall. Now Jacob longed for the mountains. It was better up there than down here. How strange and remote his peak seemed to him, a giant with a white beard, coiffured in clouds and with curls of mist. Jacob's heart cried out. The Jews were celebrating Simchath Torah, were reciting "Unto Thee it was shown," and circling the lectern. The Bridegroom of the Torah, who would finish the reading of the Pentateuch, was being called up from the congregation, to be followed by the Bridegroom of Genesis who would start once more the Mosaic Books, beginning with the Creation. Even boys were being summoned to the lectern, while those too young to participate were parading with flags decorated with candles and apples. Girls also were coming to the study house to kiss the holy scrolls and to wish for long life and happiness. There was dancing and drinking; people were going from house to house, partaking of wine and mead, strudel, tarts, cabbage with raisins and cream of tartar. This year, if Jacob was correct, Simchath Torah had fallen on a Friday, and the women were preparing the Sabbath pudding, dressed in their velvet capes and satin dresses.

But now all of this seemed dreamlike to him. He had been torn from his home not four but forty years ago! Indeed, were there Jews remaining in Josefov? Had Chmielnicki left a saving remnant? And if so, could the survivors rejoice in the Torah as they once had, now that all of them were mourners? Jacob stood in front of the granary and watched the snow falling. Some of the flakes dropped straight to earth and others swirled and eddied as if seeking to return to the heavenly storehouses. The rotting thatch of the roofs was covered with white, and the clutter of broken wheels, logs, poles, and piles of shavings was decorated with fleece and the dust of diamonds. The roosters were crowing with wintery voices.

Jacob reentered the granary and sat down. Some lines from the Simchath Torah liturgy which he had not thought of for four years came to his mind:

> *Gather you angels*
> *And converse with each other.*
> *Who was he? What was his name,*
> *The man who ascended the heights*
> *And brought down the strength of confidence?*
>
> *Moses ascended the heights*
> *And brought down the strength of confidence.*

Jacob started to sing these words to the traditional Simchath Torah melody. Even the cantor had usually been a trifle tipsy by the time he reached this song. Every year it had been the same, the rabbi finding it necessary to admonish those of priestly descent not to bless the congregation while under the influence of wine. Jacob's father-in-law had himself brewed beer and vodka using grain raised in the fields he leased from the town's overlord. At this time of year, a keg with a straw in it had always stood near the water barrel of his house, and nearby had hung a side of smoked mutton. Whoever visited the house sipped vodka from the straw and took a nibble of the smoked meat.

Jacob sat there in the dark, alone with his thoughts. Slowly the door was pushed open, and Wanda entered, carrying two pieces of oak bark, and some rags and string.

"I've made you a pair of shoes," she said.

He was ashamed of how dirty his feet were, but she lifted them to her lap, and while taking their measure, caressed them with her warm fingers. She took a long time making certain the shoes fit. When she was satisfied, she insisted that Jacob get up and walk about to see if they were comfortable, just as Michael the shoemaker had him do in Josefov.

"They fit, don't they?"

"Yes, they do."

"Why are you so sad, then, Jacob? Now that you are near me, I can take care of you. I don't have to climb the mountain to see you."

"Yes."

"Doesn't that please you? I was looking forward so much to this day."

3

The day began as though it were already ending. The sun flickered like a candle about to go out. Zagayek and his men were in the woods hunting bear, and the bailiff's son Stephan strode about the village in high boots, dressed in a rawhide jacket embroidered with red, a marten cap with ear flaps on his head, and a riding whip in his right hand. Stephan was called Zagayek the Second by the peasants. His career with girls had started early and by now he had his own crop of bastards. He was a short, broad-shouldered man, with a square head, a nose as flat as a bulldog's, and a chin which dimpled in the middle. He had the reputation of being a fine horseman and kept himself busy training his father's dogs and setting traps for birds and animals.

Stephan took over in the village whenever his father went hunting. On such days he went from hut to hut, throwing open doors and sticking in his head and sniffing. The peasants always had something which by law belonged to the landlord. That morning he entered the tavern and ordered vodka. His half-sister, one of Zagayek's bastards, waited on him, but their relationship did not prevent him from hiking her skirts. Then, after having his drink, Stephan proceeded to Jan Bzik's. Bzik had once been a man of importance in the village, one of those whom Zagayek had taken under his protection, but now the old man was worn out and sick. The day he had brought the cattle down from the mountain he had had a seizure and he now lay on top of the oven as his strength ebbed. He talked, spat, muttered to himself. Bzik was a small, lean man; his hair, long and matted, surrounded a single bald spot. He had deep sunken cheeks, a face as red as raw meat, and bulging, bloodshot eyes underlined by two puffy bags, a few scraggly hairs drooping from his chin. That winter he had been so sick they had measured him for a coffin. But then his condition had improved. He lay, his face turned toward the room, one eye glued shut, the other only half open. Ill though he was, this did not prevent him from running the household and overseeing each detail. "It's no good," he would grumble often. "Butter fingers!"

"If you don't like the way we're doing things, climb down from the oven and do them yourself," his wife would answer. She was a small, dark, half-bald woman, with a wart-covered face, and the slanty eyes of a Tartar. The couple did not live in peace; she kept insisting that her husband was finished and that it was time to cart him off to the graveyard.

Basha resembled her mother. Stocky and dark, she had inherited the high cheekbones and almond eyes of the older woman. She was known for her indolence. At he moment she sat at the edge of the bed studying her toes and every now and again searching for lice between her breasts. Wanda was at the oven, removing a loaf of bread with a shovel. As she bustled about the kitchen, she repeated to herself the lesson Jacob had taught her: The Almighty had created the world. Abraham had been the first to recognize God. Jacob was the father of the Jews. She had never before received any instruction and Jacob's words had fallen on her brain like a shower on a parched field. She had even memorized the names of the Twelve Tribes and knew how Joseph's brothers had sold him into Egypt. When Stephan entered, he stood at the open door listening to her mutterings.

"What's that you're saying?" he asked. "Some sort of an incantation?"

"Close the door, Pan," she directed over her shoulder. "You're letting in the cold."

"You're hot enough to keep from freezing."

Stephan walked into the room.

"Where's the Jew?"

"In the granary."

"Won't he come into the house?"

"He doesn't want to."

"They say he lays you."

Basha opened her wide, gap-toothed mouth in laughter; she licked her lips with delight, hearing her proud sister insulted. The old woman left off spinning, and Bzik wriggled his feet.

"Dirty mouths will say anything."

"I understand you're carrying his bastard."

"Pan, that's a lie," the old woman interrupted. "She just got over her period."

"How do you know? Did you investigate?"

"There was blood on the snow in front of the house," the old woman testified.

Stephan struck his boot tops with his whip.

"The householders want to get rid of him," he said after a slight hesitation.

"Who does he hurt?"

"He's a sorcerer, and that's the least of it. How is it your cows give more milk than anyone else's?"

"Jacob feeds them better."

"All sorts of things are said about him. He'll be done away with. Father will haul him into court."

"For what reason?"

"Don't grasp at straws, Wanda. He'll be taken care of, and you'll give birth to a demon."

Wanda could no longer restrain herself. Not everything the wicked desire comes true, she told Stephan. There was a God in heaven who avenged those who suffered injustice. Stephan pursed his lips as if about to whistle.

"Where did you hear that? From the Jew?"

"Dziobak says so also."

"It was the Jew, the Jew, who told you," Stephan said. "If his God is such a great defender, how come he's a slave? Well, answer that!"

Wanda could think of nothing to say. There was a lump in her throat and her eyes were burning; she could scarcely keep back the tears. She wanted to run quickly to Jacob and ask him this difficult question. With fingers that had become inured to heat, she picked up a fresh loaf of bread and sprinkled it with water. Anger had made her face, flushed already from the warmth of the oven, even redder. Stephan stood surveying her legs and buttocks like a connoisseur. He winked at the old woman and Basha. The latter responded flirtatiously, smiled obsequiously at him with her gap teeth. At length he walked out whistling, slamming the door behind him. Wanda stood at the window and watched him stride off in the direction of the mountain. He was a man filled with iniquity like Esau or Pharaoh. Ever since she could remember he had spoken of little else but killing and torturing. It was Stephan who assisted his father in the slaughtering and scalding of the pigs. It was he who did the actual whipping when Zagayek ordered a peasant punished. Even the trail left by Stephan's boots in the snow seemed evil to Wanda. "Father in Heaven," she began to pray, "how long will You remain silent? Send down plagues as you did against Pharaoh. Drown him in the sea."

"He wants you, Wanda. He wants you," she heard her mother saying.

"Well, he'll just keep on wanting."

"Wanda, he's Zagayek's son. He may set fire to the hut. What would we do then? Sleep in the fields?"

"God will not permit it."

Basha started to guffaw.

"What are you laughing about, Basha?"

Basha didn't answer. Wanda knew that her mother and sister were on Stephan's side. They wanted to see her humiliated. There was a crooked wrinkle on the old woman's forehead and her toothless mouth was fixed in a smile which seemed to say, "Why quarrel over such nonsense? Stephan's powerful. There's no alternative."

The old man lying on the stove mumbled something.

"Did you say something, Father?"

"What did he want?"

The old woman laughed nastily.

"What does a tomcat usually want?"

"Father's forgotten about that kind of thing," Basha said scornfully.

"You did right, Wanda. Don't let him put a bastard into your belly." Bzik spoke haltingly and with the dirge-like tone of the mortally sick uttering a last testament. "The moment you're with child, that skunk will forget you. He has enough bastards already." The old man's singsong voice was mournful, other-worldly. Wanda remembered the Ten Commandments Jacob had taught her; one must honor one's father and mother.

"Do you want something, Father?"

Jan Bzik did not answer.

"Are you hungry or thirsty?"

He had to pass water, he said in a voice which was half cry, half yawn.

"Well, crawl outside," his wife ordered. "This isn't a stable."

"I'm cold."

"Here, Father." Wanda gave him a pan.

The old man sought to raise himself from the oven but the low ceiling interfered. He attempted to pass water and Basha giggled when he couldn't. His wife shook her head contemptuously. His member had shrunk to the size of a child's. A single drop of water fell into the pan.

"He's worthless," the old woman said.

"Mother, he's your husband and our father," Wanda replied sharply. "We must honor him."

Basha began to guffaw again. Wanda felt a cry rising in her throat. Jacob said that God was just, that He rewarded the good and punished the wicked, but Stephan, idler, whoremaster, assassin, flourished like the oak, while her father, whose whole life had been dedicated to work and who had done injustice to no one, crumbled into ruins. What sort of justice was this? She gazed toward the window. The answer could come only from Jacob in the granary.

4

Jacob in the old days would have considered himself ridiculed if anyone had ever suggested to him that a time would come when he would discuss such matters as the freedom of the will, the meaning of existence, and the problem of evil with a peasant woman. But one never knows where events are leading. Wanda asked questions and Jacob answered them to the best of his ability. He lay close to her in the granary, the same blanket covering them both, a sinner who ignored the restrictions of the Talmud, seeking to explain in a strange tongue those things he had studied in the holy books. He told her that God is eternal, that His Powers and Nature have existed without beginning, but that, nevertheless, all that was possible for Him had not as yet been accomplished before Creation. For example, how could He have been Father until His children were born? How could He have shown pity until there was someone to pity? How could He have been redeemer and helper until there were creatures to redeem? God had the power to create not only this world but a host of others. However, Creation would have been impossible if He, Himself, had completely filled the void. So that the world might appear, it had been necessary for Him to dim his effulgence. Had He not done this, whatever He created would have been consumed and blinded by His brilliance. Darkness and the void had been required, and these were synonymous with pain and evil.

What was the purpose of Creation? Free Will! Man must choose for himself between good and evil. This was the reason God had sent forth man's soul from the Throne of Glory. A father may carry his child, but he wishes the infant to learn to walk by itself. God was our Father, we His children, and He loved us. He blessed us with His mercy, and if now and again He let us slip and fall, it was to accustom us to walking alone. He continued to watch over us, and when we were in peril of falling into ditches and pits, He raised us aloft in His holy arms.

Outside, frost glowed everywhere, but it wasn't too cold in the granary. Wanda snuggled close to Jacob, her body tight against his, her mouth leaning toward his. He spoke and she continued to question. At first it seemed to him that he was both a fool and a betrayer of Israel. How could a peasant's brain comprehend such profundities? But the more Wanda questioned, the more obvious it became to him that she grasped his meaning. She even posed problems he could not solve. If the animals did not possess Free Will, why was it necessary for them to suffer? And if the Jews alone were God's children, why were gentiles created? She clasped him so tightly he could hear her heart beating; her hands dug into his ribs. She lusted for knowledge almost as fiercely as she did for the flesh.

"Where is the soul?" she inquired. "In the eye?"

"Yes, in the eyes, but in the brain also. The soul gives life to the entire body."

"Where does the soul go when a man dies?"

"Back to heaven."

"Does a calf have a soul?"

"No, it has a spirit."

"What happens to the spirit when the calf is slaughtered?"

"It sometimes enters the body of the eater."

"Does a pig have a spirit too?"

"Yes. No. I guess so. It has to have something."

"Why can't a Jew eat pork?"

"God's Law forbids it. It is His Will."

"When I become a Jew, will I also be God's daughter?"

"Yes, if you let Him enter your heart."

"I will, Jacob."

"You must become one of us not because of love for me but because you believe in God."

"I believe, Jacob. Honestly I do. But you must teach me. Without you I am blind."

A plan was forming in Wanda's mind; they would run away together; she knew the mountains. True, a Christian could not become a Jew, but she would disguise herself as a Jewess. She would shave her head and not mix meat with milk; Jacob would teach her to speak Yiddish. She insisted that he begin immediately. She said a word in Polish and he repeated it in Yiddish. *Chleb* meant bread; *wol* was an ox; *stol*, a table, and *lawka*, a bench. Some words were the same in both languages. Wanda asked him if the two tongues were really identical.

"The Jews spoke the sacred tongue when they lived in the Land of Israel," Jacob replied. "The tongue they speak today is a mixture of many languages."

"Why aren't the Jews still in their own country?"

"Because they transgressed."

"What did they do?"

"They bowed down to idols and stole from the poor."

"Don't they do that any more?"

"They don't worship idols."

"What about the poor?"

Jacob considered this question carefully before answering it.

"The poor are not treated justly."

"Who is ever just to the poor? The peasants work hard all year round and yet go naked. Zagayek wouldn't think of soiling his hands, but he takes everything, the best grain, the finest cattle."

"Every man will have to make an accounting."

"When, Jacob? Where?"

"Not in this world."

"Jacob, I must go. It's almost sunrise."

She clung to his neck, pressed deeply into his mouth, kissing him one final time. Her face became hot once again, but finally she tore herself from him. As she threw open the granary door, she murmured something and smiled shyly. There was no moon but the reflection of the snow fell across her face. Jacob recalled the story of Lilith, she who seeks out men at night and corrupts them. He and Wanda had now lived together for weeks, and yet each time he thought of his transgression he shivered anew. How had it happened? He had resisted temptation for years, then suddenly had fallen. He had changed since he had cohabited with Wanda. At times he didn't recognize himself; it seemed to him his soul had deserted him and he was sustained like an animal by something else. He prayed but without concentration. He still recited Psalms and portions of the Mishnah but his heart did not hear what his lips uttered. Whatever was within him had frozen. He no longer hummed and sang the old melodies, and was ashamed to think about his wife and children and all the other martyrs whom the Cossacks had slaughtered. What connection did he have with such saints? They were holy and he, unclean. They had sacrificed themselves for the Sacred Name while he had made a covenant with Satan. Jacob could no longer control his thoughts. Every kind of absurdity and non sequitur crammed his brain. He imagined himself eating cake, roast chicken, marzipan; drinking wine, mead, beer; hunting among the rocks and finding diamonds, gold coins, becoming a rich man, and riding around in coaches. His lust for Wanda reached such intensity that the moment she left the granary he began to miss her.

As with the soul, so with the body! He grew lazy and wanted only to lie on the straw. He suffered more from the cold that year than any other. When he chopped wood, the ax stuck and he couldn't pull it free. When he shoveled the snow from the yard, he tired quickly and had to rest. How strange it was! Even the cows he had reared sensed his predicament and turned nasty. Several times they tried to kick and gore him when he was milking them. The dog barked at him as if he were a stranger.

His dreams changed also. His father and mother no longer appeared in them. The moment he fell asleep he was with Wanda. Together they roamed through forests, crawled through caves, fell into pits, ravines, abysses, sank into swamps filled with putrefaction and filth. Rats and beasts with shaggy tails, large udders, and pouches chased him; they shrieked with strange voices, dribbled, spat, and vomited upon him. He awoke from these nightmares in a cold sweat but still burning with passion. A voice within him called out constantly for Wanda. He even found it difficult to stay away from her on those days when the Mosaic law declared her unclean.

5

The moon shone in a cloudless sky. That night, it was nearly as bright as day. Jacob, standing at the door of the granary, looked up at mile upon mile of mountains. Crags rising from the forests resembled shrouded corpses, beasts standing erect on their hind legs, monsters from another world. The silence in the village was so intense Jacob's ears rang as though a multitude of grasshoppers were singing under the snow. Although it had stopped snowing, occasional flakes drifted slowly to earth. A crow started from sleep and cawed once. In the granary and surrounding sheds, field mice and weasels scratched in their winter burrows as if expecting the sudden advent of spring. Even Jacob awaited a miracle. Perhaps summer would come more quickly than usual this year. There was nothing beyond God's power. The Almighty, if he wished, could remove the sun's cover as he had in the time of Abraham. But for whom would the Lord perform such a miracle? For Jacob the profligate, Jacob the sinner? He looked about him at the trees in the yard, snow hanging from their branches like white pears, petals of ice dropping from the twigs. He listened intently. Why didn't she come? The hut was dark, it seemed like a mushroom protruding from the drifts. Yet Jacob thought that he heard footsteps and voices. The door of the hut opened and Wanda appeared, but not as usual barefooted and enveloped in a shawl. She had on shoes and a sheepskin coat and she carried a cane. "Father is dead," she said, walking over to Jacob.

His mind froze.

"When? How?"

"He went to sleep like always, groaned, and that was the end of it. He died as silently as a chicken."

"Where are you going?"

"To fetch Antek."

They stood there in silence, and then Wanda said, "Hard times have begun for us. Antek's no friend of yours. He wants to kill you."

"What can I do?"

"Be careful."

She turned away from him; Jacob stood and watched her move into the distance, diminishing in size until she appeared no larger than an icicle. There had been no tears, but he knew she was grieving. She had loved her father—at times she had even used that word "father" addressing Jacob—now she had lost him. Whatever soul a peasant possessed had deserted the old man's body. But where was it now? Still in the hut? Or had it already begun its ascent? Had its departure been like smoke through the chimney? The custom of the village required Jacob to visit the family and say a few words of comfort. But he was doubtful whether he ought to go. Without Wanda the hut was a nest of snakes.

He was not even certain Jewish law permitted him to make this condolence call, but at length he decided to. He opened the door of the hut. The old woman and Basha stood in the middle of the room; a wick was burning in a shard. On the bed lay the body, its appearance altered by death, the face yellow as clay, the ears chalk white, only a hole where once the mouth had been. How difficult to imagine that only a few minutes before, this corpse had been alive. Yet in the wrinkled eyelids and sockets a hint of the live Jan Bzik remained, a smile, the look of a man who has encountered something both comic and propitious. The old woman sobbed hoarsely.

"He's gone, finished."

"May God comfort you."

"There wasn't a thing wrong with him at dinner. He ate a whole bowl of barley dumplings." Her remarks were only half directed at Jacob.

He stood there while the neighbors gathered. The women arrived in shawls and battered shoes, the men in sheepskins and boots made of rags. One woman wrung her hands, forced tears from her eyes, crossed herself. The widow kept repeating the identical sentence. "He had barley dumplings for supper and ate every morsel." With these words she was accusing death and giving evidence of what an exemplary wife she had been. All the faces were immersed in shadow, filled with the mystery of the night. Soon the air became fetid. Someone went to fetch Dziobak; the coffin maker arrived to take Jan Bzik's measure. Jacob slipped out of the hut. He was an alien among these people, but not as much a stranger now since Jan Bzik could almost be regarded as his father-in-law. The thought of this frightened him. "Well, aren't we all descended from Terah and Laban?" he said to himself. He was cold and his teeth were chattering. Jan Bzik had been good and just, had never ridiculed him, nor called him by a nickname. Jacob had become accustomed to him. There had been a secret understanding between the two men as if Bzik had somehow sensed that some day his cherished Wanda would belong to Jacob. "Well, it's a mystery," Jacob said to himself, "the profoundest mystery. All men are made in God's image. Perhaps Jan Bzik will sit with the other God-fearing gentiles in paradise."

Again he yearned for Wanda. What was keeping her? Well, from now on there would be an end of peace. The dog barked; more and more peasants were entering the hut. Zagayek arrived, a small rotund man dressed in a coat of fox pelts, felt boots, and a fur cap similar to those Jews wore on the Sabbath. Zagayek's mustaches flared underneath his thick nose like the whiskers of a tomcat. Dawn broke and the stars faded. The sky paled and turned rose. The sun blossomed behind the mountains and reddish specks of light glistened on the snow. The shrill voices of winter birds were heard, chattering. Jacob entered the barn and found that Kwiatula, the youngest of the cows who only a short time before had been a heifer, was about to give birth. She stood with bloated stomach, saliva dripping from her black muzzle. Her moist eyes looked straight at Jacob as though imploring his help.

He started to prepare the feed. It was also necessary to milk the animals. He mixed chopped straw, bran, and turnips together. "Well, we are all slaves," Jacob murmured to the cattle, "God's slaves." Suddenly the door opened and Wanda came in. Her cheeks were moist and red. Wanda, taking hold of Jacob, cried out as had his mother, peace be with her, before she rolled the large candle preparing for Yom Kippur Eve. "Now I have no one but you," she said.

CHAPTER FIVE

1

The scarcity of food in the village was rarely discussed, and Christmas was celebrated with great pomp despite the dearth. Though many of the peasants had already slaughtered their hogs and suckling pigs, there was sufficient meat for the holiday meal, nor was there a lack of vodka. Children went from hut to hut singing carols. The older boys collected gifts, leading around one of their company dressed as a wolf. Since the roof of the chapel leaked, the creche showing the birth in the manger had been set up in Zagayek's granary; there, too, was put on the pageant showing the arrival of the kings and wise men come to adore God's newborn son. Staffs, flaxen beards, the gilded star, everything required for the play was on hand, having been used year after year. But the sheep were real and the sound of their bleating cheered up the dejected spirits of the peasants.

The winter had been a hard one. Sickness and pestilence! The number of small and large graves had increased in the cemetery, and gales had toppled most of the new wooden crosses. But now the time to be merry was here, Zagayek distributed toys to the children and he gave white flour to the women so that the wafers could be baked. Wanda now knew from Jacob that the Jews believed in a God who had neither son nor division into persons. Yet she had to participate in the holiday and go with the others Christmas Eve to Midnight Mass. She even took part in the pageant, stood near Stephan with a halo around her head looking like one of the saints. Stephan wore a mask, a white beard, and a miter. His breath stank of liquor, and he surreptitiously pinched Wanda and whispered obscene words into her ears.

Time after time Wanda had begged Jacob to enter the hut and take part with the others in the feasting. Even Jacob's enemy Antek sought to make peace during the holidays. Inside the hut stood a Christmas tree hung with ribbons and wreaths. The old woman had made pretzels, baked pork, stuffed cabbage, and a variety of other dishes. An extra man was needed to even out the number of guests, but Jacob remained stubborn. None of the food was kosher; all of this was idolatry, and it was well known that it was better to die than participate in such ceremonies. He stayed in the granary and ate dry bread as usual. It hurt Wanda to see him separate himself from the others and hide. The girls ridiculed him and her as well since he was her lover. Her mother openly spoke of the need to rid themselves of that accursed Jew who had brought bad luck and disgrace to the family. Now Wanda was more careful about seeking him out at night, knowing that the boys were planning to play all sorts of tricks on him. They considered dragging him out of the barn and forcing him to eat pork. Someone suggested that he be thrown into the stream as a sacrifice to the river spirit or be castrated. Wanda had brought him a knife so he might defend himself. She began to drink vodka to dispel the bitterness in her heart.

On the third day after Christmas, the village celebrated the sacred day of Turon that honored the ancient god of horses and courage, wind and power. Dziobak demanded the abolition of this pagan holiday, pointing out that with

Jesus' birth all the idols had been deprived of their power, and in addition that no one in the large cities ever remembered such days. But the village paid no attention to him and there was dancing at Zagayek's house and in the huts. The musicians fiddled, banged cymbals, beat drums, played "The Little Shoemaker," "The Shepherd," "The Dove," "Good Night," and the "Dirge of a Dying Man," the last of which brought tears to the eyes of the women. The boys and girls danced a mazurka, a polka, a cracowiak, a goralsky. Everyone forgot his troubles. Sleighs crowded with young people raced across the snow, the bells on the reins and harnesses of the horses jingling. Here and there a sled yoked to a dog passed. Wanda had promised Jacob not to participate in these pagan revels, but with each passing hour she grew more restive. She had to dance and drink with the peasants. As long as she stayed in the village, it was impossible not to be one of them. The very fact that she planned to run away with him and accept his faith made the avoidance of suspicion more necessary. She hurried into the granary, her face flushed, and her eyes shining. Hurriedly she threw Jacob a few kisses, put her face on his chest, and started to sob. "Don't be angry with me," she said. "I've already become a stranger in my own home."

———————

2

This was the first of the month of Nissan according to Jacob's calendar, two weeks before Passover. Not once in his captivity had he eaten bread during that holiday, subsisting those eight days on milk, cheese, and vegetables. The cold had set in again and a heavy snow had fallen. Antek had gone to buy another cow in a nearby village, and had taken Wanda along to get her opinion. She had been forced to agree to the trip, fearing to quarrel with her brother as long as Jacob was there. Jacob spent the morning milking the cows and chopping wood for the fire, which was the work he liked best. His ax rose and fell and the chips flew. The heavier pieces he split by hammering wedges into them. Little by little the pile grew until there was a sizable quantity. He went into the granary to rest, lay down, closed his eyes and dreamed of Wanda, but this dream did not have the village as its setting. Suddenly he felt himself being poked and he opened his eyes. The granary door was ajar and Basha stood near him. "Get up," she said. "You're wanted at Zagayek's."

"How do you know?"

"He's sent one of his men."

Jacob rose, realizing only too well what had happened. Zagayek had learned of his plan to escape and this was the end. Only recently Stephan had prophesied to Wanda that the Jew would be disposed of. "Well, my time has come," Jacob thought. All through the years he had been expecting this outcome. His knees trembled, and crossing the threshold, he bent over, picked up a handful of snow, and rubbed the palms of his hands with it so that he might pray. "Let it be Thy Will that my death redeem all my sins," he mumbled. For one instant he thought of making a break for it, but then saw how useless it would be. He was barefoot and without a sheepskin. "No, I won't run," he decided. "I have sinned and earned my punishment." Zagayek's man was waiting outside; he was unarmed. "Let's go," he said to Jacob. "The gentlemen are waiting."

"What gentlemen?"

"How the devil do I know?"

"So they are going to try me," Jacob said to himself. The barking of the dog brought the old woman out of the hut; she stood there, broad and squat, yellow-faced, neither joy nor pity in her slanty eyes. Basha stood next to her mother, another one of those who, cow-like, accept docilely. The dog became silent and his tail drooped. Jacob was relieved that Wanda was not there; by the time she returned it might be all over. He thought of reciting, "Hear, O Israel," but decided he should do that when the noose was fixed about his neck. His stomach felt heavy; he was cold. He hiccupped, belched, started to recite the third chapter of Psalms, but paused when he came to the verse, "For Thou, O Lord, art a shield to me, my glory, and the lifter of my head." It was too late for such hopes. When he nodded at the old woman and Basha, they remained as unresponsive as stuffed images. The one thing that astonished Jacob was that not only was his attendant unarmed but he made no attempt to manacle him. "Well, there is an end to everything," Jacob thought, walking with bowed head and measured steps. For years he had been curious about what lay on the other side of flesh and blood. He was only anxious to get the death agony over with, and was prepared to sanctify God's name if he were asked to deny or blaspheme Him.

Women came from their hovels to stare blankly. Barking dogs ran after him; others peacefully wagged their tails. A duck waddled across his path. "Well, you'll outlive me," Jacob comforted the creature. He bid the world and the village goodbye. "Do not let anxiety make her ill," he prayed, thinking of Wanda. She had not been destined to reach the truth and he sorrowed for her. He raised his eyes and saw that the sky was once more blue and vernal. The only cloud resembled a single horned beast with a long neck. The mountains looked down on him from the distance, those hills to which he had planned to flee from slavery. "It has been ordained that I be with them," he said, thinking of his father and mother and his wife and children.

The man led him to Zagayek's house and there in front of the building stood a covered wagon hitched to a team of horses. Jacob didn't think that either the wagon or the team were from the neighborhood. The horses were covered with blankets and their harnesses were decorated with brass; a lantern hung from the rear axle of the vehicle. Jacob walked up a meticulously scrubbed staircase to the second floor. He had almost forgotten staircases existed, but here, it seemed, was a piece of the city in the center of this hamlet. As he walked down the hall, he smelled cabbage cooking; the midday meal was being prepared. He passed doors which had the kind of brass latches his parents' house had had. Straw mats lay before them. A door was thrown open and what he saw was strange and dream-like. Three men sat at a table, Jews with beards, sidelocks, and skull caps. The coat of one was unbuttoned and a fringed garment peeped through. Jacob recognized another but in his confusion forgot where he had met him. Jacob stood with his mouth open, and the Jews gaped back. At last one of them addressed him in Yiddish, "Are you Jacob from Zamosc?"

Everything went dark before Jacob's eyes.

"Yes, I am," he answered, speaking with a Polish accent.

"Reb Abraham of Josefov's son-in-law?"

"Yes."

"Don't you recognize me?"

Jacob stared. The face was familiar but he couldn't place it. "So this is not the day of my death," he thought. He still was unable to grasp what was happening, but he was ashamed that he was barefoot and dressed in peasant clothes. Inside of him all was still and frozen and he became as tongue-tied and shy as a boy. "Perhaps I am already on the other side," he thought. He wanted to say something, but couldn't utter a word. For the moment Yiddish eluded him. Another door opened and in walked Zagayek, short and stocky, red-nosed, his pointed mustaches resembling two mouse tails. He had on a braided green coat and low boots. The riding crop he carried had a rabbit's foot for a handle. Though it was early in the day, he had already drunk enough to make him walk unsteadily. His eyes were bloodshot and watery. "Well, is this your Jew?" he shouted.

The man who had just addressed Jacob spoke hesitantly. "Yes, this is he."

"All right, then, take him and go. Where's your money?"

One of the Jews, a small, pampered-looking man with a broad fanlike beard and dark eyes set widely apart, silently pulled a purse from his coat and commenced to count out gold pieces. Zagayek tested each of the coins by placing them between his thumb and index finger and trying to bend them. Only now did Jacob realize what had happened. These Jews had come for him; he was being ransomed. The man with the familiar face was from Josefov, one of the town elders. Suddenly Jacob felt terribly awkward as though the nearly five years he had lived in the mountains had taken effect this very instant and changed him into an uncouth peasant. He didn't know where to hide his calloused hands and dirty feet. He was ashamed of his torn jacket, and his unruly hair, resting upon his shoulders. A desire to bow peasant-like to the Jews and grasp their hands and kiss them seized him. The man who had counted out the gold pieces lifted his eyes.

"Blessed be Thou who revivest the dead."

3

The speed with which things now happened to Jacob was eerie. Zagayek extended his hand and wished him a pleasant trip. A moment later, the Jews escorted him outside and told him to get into the covered wagon. A number of peasants had gathered at Zagayek's house, but none of Jan Bzik's family was in the group. Before Jacob could say anything, the gentile driver—Jacob had not noticed him before—snapped his whip and the wagon careened downhill. Jacob thought of Wanda, but he didn't mention her. What was there to say? Could he ask that his peasant mistress be taken along? She was not in the village and so he couldn't even say goodbye to her. With the same suddenness that he had been enslaved he had now been ransomed. In the wagon the men spoke to him all at once and confused him so he scarcely knew what they were saying. Their speech sounded almost like a foreign tongue. A quilt was thrown over his shoulders and a skull cap placed on his head. He sat among them feeling naked. Slowly he grew accustomed to their words, gesticulations, odor, and asked how they had known his whereabouts. "A circus proprietor informed us," they said.

He became silent again.

"What happened to my family?" he asked.

"Your sister Miriam is alive."

"No one else?"

They didn't reply.

"Should I rend my clothes?" he inquired, intending the question not merely for them but for himself also. "I have forgotten the law."

"Yes, for your father and mother. But not for your children. More than thirty days have passed."

"Yes, that is now a distant event," Jacob said, employing the technical term.

Although he had known all along that his loved ones were dead, he sat there grieving. Miriam was the only one of the family who had survived. He feared to ask for details, kept looking straight ahead; the men spoke, for the most part, to each other. They discussed the clothes he must have: a shirt, a fringed garment, trousers, shoes. One of them remarked that his hair must be cut, and another untied a leather sack and rummaged in it. The third offered him cake, vodka, jam. Jacob refused to eat: he must remain in mourning for at least one day. Now he recollected the name of the man from Josefov: Reb Moishe Zakolkower, one of the town's seven most prominent citizens. The last time Jacob had seen him, he had been a young man sprouting his first growth of beard.

"It's exactly like Joseph and his brethren," one of the men remarked.

"Now we have lived to see this, we must say a benediction," another interjected, and he started to intone, "Oh, Thou who hast sustained me and made me live to reach this time."

"And I must say 'Thou hast done mercy,' " Jacob mumbled as if to prove that he too was a Jew and that no error had been made in ransoming him. But even as he said this, he was conscious of having erred. The correct thing was to praise God without further ado, but his voice sounded so coarse to him, he was embarrassed to speak before such fine people. His companions were small in stature but his head touched the roof of the wagon. He felt penned in, and so unfamiliar was the smell of the vehicle, it was difficult for him to keep from sneezing. These men should be thanked, but he didn't know the correct words for the occasion. Each time he tried to say something, Yiddish and Polish mingled in his head. Like an ignoramus about to talk to learned men he knew in advance that he would make a fool of himself. But he did ask finally, "Who is left in Josefov?"

The men appeared to have been waiting for this question and all started talking at once. The Cossacks had nearly leveled the town, had killed, slaughtered, burned, hanged, but there had been some survivors, widows and old men mostly, and a few children who had hidden in attics and cellars or taken refuge in peasant hamlets. The men mentioned some names Jacob knew, but others, since Josefov had acquired new inhabitants, that he had never heard before. The wagon continued to roll downhill, sunlight seeping through the covering, and the conversation remained elegiac. Every sentence ended with the word "killed." Now and then Jacob heard "died in the plague." Yes, the Angel of Death had been busy. The massacres and burnings had been followed by sickness, and people had died like flies. Jacob found it difficult to comprehend so much calamity. But as always, there was a saving remnant. The speakers appeared weighed down by an enormous burden and Jacob bowed his head. It was as if he had slept seventy years, like the legendary Choney, and awakened in another age. Josefov was no longer Josefov. Everything was gone: the synagogue, the study house, the ritual bath, the poor house. The murderers had even torn up the tombstones. Not a single chapter of the Holy Scroll, not a page from the books in the study house remained intact. The town was inhabited by fools, cripples, and madmen. "Why did this happen to us?" one of the men asked. "Josefov was a home of Torah."

"It was God's will," a second answered.

"But why? What sins did the small children commit? They were buried alive."

"The hill behind the synagogue shook for three days. They tore out Hanan Berish's tongue, cut off Beila Itche's breasts."

"What harm did we do them?"

No one answered these questions and they raised their eyes and stared at Jacob as if expecting him to reply. But he sat in silence. The explanation he had given Wanda that free will could not exist without evil nor mercy without sorrow now sounded too pat, indeed almost blasphemous. Did the Creator require the assistance of Cossacks to reveal His nature? Was this a sufficient cause to bury infants alive? He remembered his own children, little Isaac, Breina, the baby; he imagined them thrown into a ditch of lime and buried alive. He heard their stifled screams. Even if these souls rose to the most splendid mansion and were given the finest rewards, would that cancel out the agony and horror? Jacob wondered how it had been possible for him to forget them for an instant. Through forgetfulness, he had also been guilty of murder.

"Yes, I am a murderer," he said to himself, "I am no better than they."

CHAPTER SIX

1

Passover was at an end. Pentecost came and went. At first each day was so crammed with incident it seemed like a year to Jacob. Not an hour passed, scarcely a minute, without his coming upon something new or something he had half forgotten. Was it so trivial a matter to return to Jewish books, clothes, holidays, after years of slavery among the pagans? Alone in the mountain barn or in the Bziks' granary, he had felt that no trace of this world remained. Chmielnicki and his Cossacks had wiped out everything. At other times he had been half convinced that there never had been a Josefov and that all his memories were illusions. Suddenly he found himself dressed again as a Jew, praying in synagogues, putting on phylacteries, wearing a fringed garment, and eating strictly kosher food. His trip down the road from Cracow to Josefov had been one long continual holiday. Rabbis and elders had greeted and feasted him in every town. Women had brought their children to be blessed and had asked him to touch coins and speak incantations over pieces of amber. The martyrs were beyond help, and so everyone's goodness was lavished on this man who had been ransomed from captivity.

His sister Miriam and her daughter Binele awaited him in Josefov. Besides these two only a few distant relations were left to him. Josefov was so changed it was unrecognizable: grass was growing where houses had once been, buildings now stood where goats had pastured. There were graves in the middle of the synagogue yard. The rabbi, his assistant, and most of the elders came from other towns. Jacob was given a room and the authorities scratched together a yeshiva class so that he could support himself teaching. His sister Miriam had once been well-to-do, but now she was toothless and in rags. Meeting Jacob, she ran to him with a wail and never stopped sobbing and crying until she returned to Zamosc. He feared she was out of her mind. She screamed, pressed against him, bobbed up and down, all the time wringing her hands, pinching her cheeks, and enumerating all the tortures the family had undergone. She made Jacob think of those mourners and hand clappers who in the old days, according to the Talmud, had been hired for funerals. Her voice became so shrill at times that Jacob covered his ears.

"Alas, poor Dinah, they ripped open her stomach and put a dog in. You could hear it barking."

"They impaled Moishe Bunim, and he didn't stop groaning all night."

"Twenty Cossacks raped your sister Leah and then they cut her to pieces."

Jacob was not under the misapprehension that one had a right to forget how the dead had been tortured. What was said in the Bible of Amalek was true of all Israel's enemies. Yet, he did beg Miriam not to heap so many horrors on him at once. There was a limit to what the human mind could accept. It was beyond the power of any man to contemplate all these atrocities and mourn them adequately. A new Tischab'ov and a new seventeenth day of Tammuz had to be proclaimed. The year was not long enough to pray for and lament each of these saints singly. Jacob would have liked to run off and hide in some ruined building where he could remain in silence. But there was no such place in Josefov, which was all hustle and bustle. Houses were being built, buildings roofed; on every side men were mixing lime and carrying bricks. There were new stores in the market place and once again the peasants flocked to town on market day to deal with the Jews. Jacob, returning, was immediately involved in religious activities. It was the time when the matzoth were baked and he helped prepare them for the town's most pious citizens, drawing the water and assisting in the rolling. On the first night of Passover he entertained some widows at his seder, and it seemed strange to him now to speak of the miracles that had transpired in Egypt when in his day a new Pharaoh had brought to pass what the old Pharaoh had been unable to accomplish. There was not a prayer, law, passage in the Talmud that did not seem altered to him. The questions that he asked about Providence became increasingly sharp and searching and he found he had lost the power to stop asking them.

But, as he realized with astonishment, what was so new for him was stale for everyone else. The yeshiva boys laughed and played practical jokes on each other. Alert young men wove chains of casuistry. Merchants were busy making money, and the women gossiped in the same old way. As for the Almighty, He maintained his usual silence. Jacob saw that he must follow God's example, seal his lips, and forget the fool within, with his fruitless questions.

So the days flew by: Passover, Pentecost! Jacob's body had returned home but his spirit remained restless. No, if anything, his condition was worse, for now he had nothing to hope for. To prevent himself from thinking, he kept busy all day: teaching, studying, praying, reciting Psalms. Other towns had contributed a number of worn out, dog-eared books to Josefov and Jacob mended the pages and filled in the missing letters and words. The new study house needed a beadle, and he took that job also. His day began at dawn and did not end until he was ready to collapse from exhaustion. If his thought could dwell only on complaints against Heaven or on memories of lechery in a barn on a mountain, then it was unclean. Let those whose minds were pure indulge in meditation.

Those pious women who took care of Jacob sought to repay him for his years of exile, but an undeclared war developed between them and their charge. They prepared him a bed of down and he stretched out on the hard floor and lay there all night. They cooked him soups and broths, and he wanted dry bread and water from the well. When visitors came to speak to him about his years of absence, he answered curtly. How else could he behave? The windows of the study house overlooked the hill where his wife and children lay buried. He could see cows grazing there in the newly grown pasture. His parents, relations, friends, had been tortured. As a boy he had pitied the watchman in the cemetery at Zamosc whose life had been passed near the cleansing house, but now the whole of Poland had become one vast cemetery. The people around him accommodated themselves to this, but he found it impossible to come to terms with. The best he could do was to stop thinking and desiring. He was determined to question no longer. How could one conceivably justify the torments of another?

One day seated alone in the study house, Jacob said to God, "I have no doubt that you are the Almighty and that whatever you do is for the best, but it is impossible for me to obey the commandment, Thou Shalt Love Thy God. No, I cannot, Father, not in this life."

2

How revolting to lust for some peasant woman and not adore the Creator. Out of contrition, one should bury oneself alive. But what then could be done with the gross body and its desires? How silence the criminal within? Jacob lay on the floor moving neither hand nor foot. The window was open and the night billowed in. He traced the path of the constellation in the ascendant and saw the stars drift from roof to roof, noting how these lights, whiter than the sun, twinkled and shimmered. The same God, who had given the Cossacks strength to chop off heads and rip open stomachs, directed this heavenly multitude. The midnight moon floated in mother-of-pearl and its face, said by the children to be Joshua's, stared straight at Jacob.

Josefov by day was a confusion of sounds: chopping, sawing; carts arriving from the villages with grain, vegetables, fire wood, lumber; horses neighing, cows bellowing; children chanting the alphabet, the Pentateuch, the commentaries of Rashi, the Gemara. The same peasants who had helped Chmielnicki's butchers strip the Jewish homes now turned logs into lumber, split shingles, laid floors, built ovens, painted buildings. A Jew had opened a tavern where the peasants came to swill beer and vodka. The gentry, having blotted out the memory of the massacres, again leased their fields, woods, and mills to Jewish contractors. One had to do business with murderers and shake their hands in order to close a deal. It was rumored that Jews, too, had fattened on the catastrophe, dealing in stolen goods and digging up caches hidden by refugees. Deserted wives were another subject of gossip. These women wandered through town searching for their husbands or for witnesses to testify they were dead. Many Jews had not been strong enough to resist conversion and the Polish government had decreed that those unwillingly baptized might reassume their own faith.

But the greatest sensation of all was caused by the Cossack wives, Jewish women forced into marriage, who now fled the steppes and returned. One of them, Tirza Temma, who had arrived in Josefov shortly before Jacob, had forgotten how to speak Yiddish. Her first husband was still alive, having escaped to the forest where he had lived on roots at the time of the massacre. He had not recognized Tirza Temma and had denied it was she. She had exhibited her evidence in the bath house, a honey-colored speck on one of her breasts and a second birthmark on her back. But her petition that her husband be forced to divorce his second wife had been denied. Tirza Temma, informed by the court that it was she who would be divorced, had berated the community in Cossack, and still persistently sought to break into her old home and take over the household. Another woman had been possessed by a dybbuk. One girl barked like a dog. A bride whose groom had been murdered on their wedding day suffered from melancholia and spent her nights in the cemetery dressed in her bridal gown and veil. Only now, years after the calamity, did Jacob realize how deep were the wounds. Moreover, new wars and insurrections were feared. The Cossacks on the steppes were again preparing an invasion of Poland, and Muscovites, Prussians, and Swedes stood poised with sharpened swords. The Polish nobility did nothing but drink, fornicate, whip peasants, and quarrel among themselves over the distribution of honors, privileges, and titles.

Only at night was there silence—the song of grasshoppers and the croak of frogs. Warm breezes wafted the smell of flowers, weeds, ripening grain from the fields, and Jacob recognized each faint aroma. He heard birds and animals stirring among the thickets. Lately he had taken a solemn oath, to root Wanda from his heart and never think of her again. She was a daughter of Esau who had lured him into adultery, a woman whose desire to accept his faith came from impure motives. In addition she was there, he here. What good was this brooding? Nothing but sins and imps born of evil thoughts arose from it. He marshaled the images of the cripples he had seen on the road and here in Josefov, men without noses, ears, tongues—each time he lusted for her, he thought of them. He should be more concerned with the misery of these unfortunates than with dreams of luxury in the lap of their torturer's sister. He determined to punish himself: every time he thought of Wanda he would fast until sunset. He drew up lists of torments: pebbles in his shoes, a stone beneath his pillow, bolting his food without chewing it, going without sleep. The debt he owed for allowing Satan to ensnare him had to be paid off once and for all. But Belial was as persistent as a rat. Who was the rat? Jacob, himself? Some force beyond him?

But there was, as he well knew, a Spirit of Good and a Spirit of Evil. In his case the latter was more firmly seated in his brain and had much more to say. The instant Jacob dozed off, Evil took over, sketched lascivious pictures, brought Wanda's voice to the sleeper's ears, revealed her naked body to him, defiled and polluted Jacob. Sometimes he heard her voice even when he was awake. "Jacob, Jacob," she called. The sound came from without, not within him: he saw her working in the fields, grinding the grain, bearing food to the cowherd who this year slept in the barn with the cattle. She had taken up residence within him and he could not drive her forth. She nestled close to him beneath the prayer shawl when he prayed. She studied with him as he sat poring over the Torah. "Why did you show me how to be a Jew if you meant to leave me among the idolaters?" she complained. "Why did you pull me to you only to thrust me away?" He looked into her eyes, heard her sob, walked with her among the cattle in the fields. Once more they bathed together in the mountain stream and he bore her in his arms to the straw. Balaam barked; the mountain birds sang. He heard her panting, "More, more." She whispered, bit his ear, and kissed it.

The matchmakers were busy trying to marry off Jacob, and one of the men who had ransomed him was among those who had found a prospect. Jacob at first said "no" to all these suggestions. He had no intention of remarrying, would remain celibate. But the contention was that he should not travel so dangerous a road. Why endure temptation daily? Moreover, he should obey the precept: "Be fruitful and multiply." A widow from Hrubyeshoyv was among the possibilities and she was to come to Josefov shortly to meet him. She had a drygoods store in the Hrubyeshoyv market and a house that the Cossacks had neglected to burn. The widow was a few years older than he and had a grown daughter, but this was no great handicap. The Jew does not tempt Evil by denying the body but harnesses it in the service of God. Jacob knew that he could never love this woman from Hrubyeshoyv, but possibly he might be able to find forgetfulness with her.

He was exhausted by the struggle within him, sleepless at night, weary during the day. He found he lacked the patience to teach and had lost his taste for Torah and prayer. He sat in the study house longing for the open air, dreaming of gathering grass again, scaling crags, chopping wood. The Jews had ransomed him but he remained a slave. Passion held him like a dog on a leash. The hounds of Egypt bayed but he could not drive them off.

One day when he was seated in the study house explaining the procedures involving the horns of rams sacrificed as burnt offerings, a small boy entered and said, "My father would like to see you, Reb Jacob." Jacob shivered as he always did now when he saw a child.

"Who is your father?"

"Moishe Zakolkower."

"Do you know what he wants with me?"

"The widow from Hrubyeshoyv is here."

The class burst out laughing and Jacob, becoming confused, blushed. "Recite the Gemara while I am gone," he directed. But even before he left the building, he heard his pupils pounding on the table and arguing querulously. Active boys, accustomed to playing wolf and goat, hide and go seek, tag, they were forever joking among themselves and laughing boisterously. One of the principal objects of their humor was gloomy Jacob seated before them lost in somber thoughts, and, now that he was being led away to meet a woman, they had something more to ridicule. Jacob walked beside the boy, having decided not to go home to change to his Saturday gabardines. The child, who had not even been alive at the time of the massacres, prattled about a bird that had flown through his bedroom window. They came to Moishe Zakolkower's newly erected house, even more comfortable than the one the Cossacks had burned, and Jacob, entering, found himself in a hall, smelled food, cutlets, and onions frying. The door of the kitchen was open and he could see Moishe's second wife (his first had been killed) standing near the oven. Another woman was kneading dough and a girl was grinding pepper in a mortar. For a moment he caught a whiff of the past and then Moishe, the man who had counted out the gold pieces for Zagayek, opened the living room door and bade Jacob enter. In the room, Jacob noted the newness of everything, walls, floors, tables, chairs, newly bound books from Lublin in the bookcases. The evil ones destroyed, the Jews created. Once more Jewish books were being printed and authors were traveling here and there to sign up subscribers. Jacob felt a stab in his heart every time he saw the past visibly resurrected. No doubt the living must go on living, but this very affirmation betrayed the dead. A song he had heard a wedding jester sing came to his mind: "What is life but a dance across graves?" Yes, his coming to meet a prospective bride was a scandal. Only a few feet from here his wife and children lay buried. Yet better a wife than this perpetual brooding about a gentile woman.

Moishe and he were deep in a discussion of yeshiva and community matters when the woman of the household entered, bringing cookies and a dish of cherries—the hospitality of the wealthy. Blushing, she apologized for not being properly dressed, and nodded as if to say, "I know what you think, but you can't do a thing about it. This isn't a man's world." Finally the widow from Hrubyeshoyv arrived, a small dumpy woman, decked out in a silk dress and satin cape, wearing a matron's bonnet decorated with colored ribbons and pearls. Her round face had so many wrinkles that it looked as if it had been pieced together, and her eyes were black and soft, resembling those pulps found in cherry brandy. From her neck hung a gold chain with a dangling pendant, her fingers gleamed with rings. The odor of honey and cinnamon trailed into the room with her, and she looked Jacob over shrewdly.

"My, what a giant of a man! May the evil eye not fall on you."

"We are as God created us."

"True, but better big than a midget."

She spoke with a lilt and a sob, and kept wiping her nose with a batiste handkerchief. The wagon that had brought her to Josefov had lost a wheel, she said, and they had had to stop for repairs at a blacksmith's. Then she sighed and began to fan herself, meanwhile talking about her drygoods store and how hard it was to get the goods that the customers wanted. She refused the refreshments that Moishe's wife offered her, and then broke down and drained a glass of blueberry wine while she swallowed three cookies. Some crumbs fell on the folds of her cape and she picked them up and ate them. True, her business was large, thank God, but the girls she had working for her, on the other hand, couldn't be trusted. "A stranger's hand is useful only for poking a fire," she said, quoting the proverb and looking at Jacob slyly from the corners of her eyes. "One needs a man in the house, otherwise everything goes."

She liked him, Jacob saw, and was ready to sit down and write the preliminary agreement. But he hesitated. This woman was too old and syrupy, too cunning. He didn't want to spend his life overseeing clerks and bargaining with customers. Such a person needed a husband who was wrapped up, body and soul, in money. She was going to add a new wing to the house, she said, and also enlarge the store. The more she spoke, the more disconsolate Jacob became. I have ceased being a part of this world, he said to himself, the match would be good for neither of us. "I am not a business man by nature," he said aloud.

"Who's born a business man?" she asked, picking up a cluster of cherries with her flabby fingers.

She began to examine Jacob on his years of captivity—a subject usually avoided since the Jews regarded time spent among the pagans as wasted and better not discussed—but such a wealthy woman did not have to conform to convention. Jacob told her of Jan Bzik, of the barn on the mountain in which he had spent his summers, of the granary where he had slept in the winter. "How did you get food when you were on the mountain?" she asked.

"It was brought from the valley."

"Who brought it? The peasant?"

"No, his daughter."

"Unmarried?"

"A widow."

"Did you collect grass on the Sabbath?"

"I never broke the Sabbath. Nor did I eat unkosher food." He was ashamed to hear himself boasting of his piety.

The woman thought over what he had said carefully, and then remarked as she reached out her hand to take another cookie, "What choice did you have? Oh, what those murderers did to us!"

3

It was noon; the boys went for their midday meals, some to their families and others to the houses where they boarded. Alone in the study house, Jacob prepared a lecture. He was pleased to be once more deep in the study of books, yet he found earning his living by teaching distasteful. Most of his students were bored and the clever ones spent their time in hair-splitting or in complicating the obvious. His years away from Torah had changed his views. Now conscious of much he had not realized, he saw that one law in the Torah generated a dozen in the Mishnah, and five dozen in the Gemara; in the later commentaries laws were as numerous as the sands of the desert. Each generation added its own strictures, and during his years of exile the Shulcran Oruch had been further interpreted and additional forbiddances added. A wry thought occurred to him: if this continued, nothing would be kosher. What would the Jews live on then? Hot coals? And why had these interdictions and commandments not preserved the Jews from Cossack atrocities? What more did God require of his martyred people?

Moreover, as Jacob looked about him, he saw that the community observed the laws and customs involving the Almighty, but broke the code regulating man's treatment of man with impunity. His return before Passover had brought him to town when a quarrel was in progress. Flour for matzoths was scarce and the rabbi, finding no proscription in the Mosaic Law, in the Talmud, or even in Maimonides, had authorized the eating of peas and beans during the holidays. This ruling had incensed certain members of the congregation, some because they wanted to show how pious they were, others because they were angry at the rabbi; and they had broken the windows in the rabbi's house and driven nails into his bench at the east wall. One of the zealots had approached Jacob and sounded him out about becoming rabbi. Yes, men and women who would rather have died than break the smallest of these ritualistic laws, slandered and gossiped openly, and treated the poor with contempt. Scholars lorded it over the ignorant; the elders divided privileges and preferments among themselves and their relatives and exploited the people generally. Money lenders gouged their clients—using loopholes in the law against usury; merchandise was kept off the market until it became scarce. Some went so far as to give false weight and measure. But when Jacob entered the study house he met them all: the angry, the haughty, the obsequious, the crooked. They prayed and schemed, erected tall towers of legalisms while they broke God's commandments. The catastrophe had impoverished the community, but the town still had more than its share of hatred and envy. Moishe Zakolkower told Jacob that there were those who were anxious to prevent his match with the widow of Hrubyeshoyv. An anonymous letter had been received denouncing Jacob.

Yet Jacob's thoughts worried him, since he knew his concern with such things was of evil origin. Satan tried to prove that corruption being general, sin could be taken lightly. The Spirit of Good replied: "Why concern yourself with what others do? Look to yourself." But Jacob had no peace. Everywhere he heard people asserting things that their eyes denied. Piety was the cloak for envy and avarice. The Jews had learned nothing from their ordeal; rather suffering had pushed them lower.

Chanting as he studied, he found it difficult now to keep the lilt of the cowherds' songs out of his voice. Moments came when he longed for the barn. His love for the Jews had been wholehearted when he was distant from them. He had forgotten the shifty eyes and barbed tongues of the petty—their tricks, stratagems and quarrels. True, he had suffered from the primitiveness and savagery of the cowherds, but what could be expected from such a rabble?

The marriage contract was almost completed, the date of the wedding set for the Friday after Tischab'ov. The widow, though well along in her thirties, could still bear children and was anxious to have a son. Already flatterers considered Jacob a rich man and showered him with compliments. Yet he lay awake worrying, still uncertain about this marriage. The widow needed a business man, a good mixer; he was withdrawn, a recluse. The years of slavery had estranged him from life; he looked healthy, but was shattered within. He kept rummaging in the cabala and leafing through books of philosophy. Sometimes he was overwhelmed by the desire to flee, but he didn't know where. He doubted everything, with, as the saying goes, the kind of doubt which "the heart does not share with the lips." He had not tasted meat in all the years of slavery and the idea of feeding on God's creatures now repelled him. Meat and fish were both eaten customarily on the Sabbath, but the food stuck in his throat. Jews treated animals as Cossacks treated Jews. The words "head," "neck," "liver," "gizzards," made him shudder. Meat in his mouth gave him the fantasy he was devouring his own children. On several occasions he had gone outside and vomited after the Sabbath dinner.

He was alone in the study house, not studying, but merely leafing through volume after volume. Possibly Maimonides had the answer. Or the *Chuzary*. Might it be contained in *The Duty of the Heart* or *The Vineyard?* He read a few words, turned the page, opened another book in the middle, turned pages again. Putting his hands to his face, he closed his eyes. He longed for both Wanda and the grave. The instant his desire for her left him, he wished to die. "Father in Heaven," his lips said as if possessed of a will of their own, "take me."

Footsteps approached; a charity worker entered, bringing him a bowl of soup. Jacob studied her. Lame though she was, with a wart on her nose and hair on her chin, this woman was a saint. Kindness, gentleness, candor dwelt in her eyes. She had lost her husband and children but exhibited no bitterness, envied no one, nursed no grievances, uttered no slander. She washed Jacob's linen, cooked for him, waited on him like a maid, and would not allow him even to thank her. Her answer to his praise was, "for what other reason were we created?"

She placed the bowl on the table and brought bread, salt, a knife, as well as a pitcher of water for him to wash his hands; and then stood humbly at the door waiting for him to finish. What was the source of her kindness? Jacob wondered. Only the wise behaved as she. Even if she were the sole representative of virtue in Josefov, she would still be a witness to God's mercy, and this was the woman he should marry. Would she consider marriage, he asked, if a proper husband were found for her? Her eyes clouded. "God willing, in the next world with my Baruch David."

4

Wanda came to Jacob one night as he lay sleeping. He saw her in the flesh, her body surrounded by light, her cheeks tear-stained, and knew she was pregnant. The smell of fields and haystacks entered with her. "Why did you leave me?" she asked wanly. "What will happen to your child? It will be brought up among pagans." Startled, Jacob awoke; the image lingered an instant at the boundary of sleep and waking. When it at last dissolved, the darkness retained an afterglow as if a lamp had just been extinguished. Hearing Wanda's voice re-echo in his ears, Jacob trembled. He could almost feel the warmth of her body. Straining his ears, he waited for her to reveal herself again. He dozed off. She reappeared, wearing a calico apron, carrying a kerchief with a fringed border, and approaching him, threw her arms about him and kissed him. Because of the child she bore, he had to bend to her and he tasted her lips and the salt of her tears. "It's yours," she said, "your flesh and blood."

Once more he awoke, and did not close his eyes again that night. He had seen her, she was carrying his child. Jacob began to recite Psalms. The eastern sky became scarlet; he rose and washed his hands. All was clear to him now. The law obliged him to rescue Wanda and his child from the idolaters. He had money, for as sole heir of his father-in-law he had received fifty gulden for the property in the market place where the old house had stood. He threw his belongings into a burlap sack and walked to the study house. Reb Moishe, always one of the first ten to enter God's house, had his Gemara already open, and was busily studying. His dark eyes grew large seeing Jacob approach with a sack slung over his shoulder.

"What are you up to?"

"I'm off to Lublin."

"But the date of the wedding's been set."

"I can't go through with it."

"What'll happen to your class?"

"You'll find another teacher."

"Why? And so suddenly?"

Wanting neither to lie nor tell the truth, Jacob said nothing. He counted out twenty gulden from a small bag. "Here's part of the money the town spent ransoming me." Astonished, Reb Moishe tugged at his beard. "Repaying the community," he mumbled. "We can expect the Messiah any day."

"It should be of some assistance."

"What do I tell the widow of Hrubyeshoyv?"

"Say we weren't meant for each other."

"Are you coming back?"

"I don't know."

"What's your plan—to become a recluse?"

Without waiting for the arrival of a quorum, Jacob turned his head and began the morning prayer. He had learned the day before that a wagon would leave for Lublin in the morning, and quickly finishing his devotions, he set out to find Leibush the carter. If he passed someone carrying a filled container, he had decided that would be an omen that there would be room on the wagon, and that Heaven approved of the trip. Lo and behold, there was Calman the water carrier lugging two pails of water. "Well, we can always squeeze in one more," Leibush said.

The morning was warm; the village quiet. It was late in the month of Sivan. Shutters opened. Sleepy-eyed women poked out their bonneted heads. Men converged on the study house carrying bags containing their prayer shawls and phylacteries. Cows were being led to pasture. A great golden sun was aloft in the east, but dew continued to fall on the grass and the young trees planted after the destruction. Birds sang and pecked at the oats fallen from the horses' feedbags. On such a morning it was difficult to believe this a world in which children were slain and buried alive, and that the earth still drank of blood as in the days of Cain. "You sit with me on the box," Leibush said to Jacob. The other passengers were mostly women off to buy goods in the Lublin stores.

One woman had forgotten something. Another had to run home to nurse her baby. A man arrived with a package to be delivered to the Lublin inn. So the wagon did not start immediately as scheduled. Two men, storekeepers, who were seated among the women whiled away the time swapping spicy stories and innuendoes with the giggling matrons. Jacob heard his name mentioned and then the name of the widow of Hrubyeshoyv. Unintentionally, he had humiliated her.

No matter what one does one stumbles into sin, he thought. He had been reading books of ethics, filled with the best advice on how to avoid the pitfalls of evil, but Satan always outwitted one. He participated in all business transactions and marriages; no human enterprise proceeded without him: touch something and you hurt someone. Have a little success, and, no matter how decent you were, you provoked envy. But why was he on his way to Lublin? He told himself he didn't know. He wanted advice from the city's wisest rabbis and would do as they recommended. Yet all the time he was aware he was traveling to Wanda, like one of the Israelite rabble that had wanted to turn and march back to Egypt and slavery for a kettle of meat. But did he dare let his child grow up among the pagans? He had not thought that the gentile woman would become pregnant. Generally he had withdrawn and spilled his seed like Onan.

Well, it makes no difference whether I go or stay, Jacob remarked to himself. I'm lost either way. The wagon had begun to move without his noticing it, and was now passing fields where the peasants were weeding and transplanting. How beautiful the countryside was and how contrary to his despair. Doubt, dissension, discord dwelt within him, but the fields exuded harmony, tranquillity, fruitfulness. The sky was blue, the weather warm with the mercy of summer, the air fragrant as honey, each flower exhaling its own perfume. A hidden hand had shaped and modeled each stalk, blade of grass, leaf, worm, fly. Each hovering butterfly's wings exhibited a unique design; every bird sang with its own call. Breathing deeply, Jacob realized how much he had missed the country. Grainfields, trees, every single growing thing refreshed his eyes. If only I could live in perpetual summer and do harm to no one, he murmured, as the wagon entered a pine wood which seemed less a forest than some heavenly mansion. The trees were as tall and straight as pillars and the sky leaned on their green tops. Brooches, rings, gold coins were embossed on the bark of their trunks. The earth, carpeted with moss and other vegetation, gave off an intoxicating odor. A shallow stream coursed through the woodland, and perched on rocks in the water were birds Jacob had never seen in the mountains. All of these creatures knew what was expected of them. None sought to rebel against its Creator. Man alone acted viciously. Jacob heard the women behind him slandering the whole of Josefov. Raising his eyes, he gazed through the screen of branches and needles where jewels glittered. The light which filtered through shone with all the colors of the rainbow. Cuckoos sang, woodpeckers drummed. Gnats circled quickly, dark, eddying specks. Jacob closed his eyes as though begrudging himself the sight of so much splendor. A roseate light seeped through his lids. Gold mingled with blue, green with purple, and, out of this whirlpool of color, Wanda's image formed.

5

Great crowds filled the community house in Lublin. The Council of the Four Countries was not in session, but the Council of Poland was. Deserted wives petitioning for the right to remarry, "Cossack brides" returned from the steppes and Russian Orthodoxy, widows whose brothers-in-law had refused to perform the Levirate ceremony or had insisted on being payed exorbitantly to do so, moved through the rooms. Mingled with them were husbands whose wives had run off or gone mad and who needed the consent of a hundred rabbis to remarry, fathers looking for prospective sons-in-law, authors asking religious authorities for endorsements, contractors seeking partners to invest in the lumber business, and individuals who merely wanted witnesses for wills. Both social and commercial activity went on in the Lublin community house. Merchants passed around samples; jewelers and goldsmiths displayed their wares; authors hawked their books and met with printers and paper jobbers; usurers discussed loans with builders and contractors; managers of estates brought objects their gentile patrons wanted to pawn or sell—a carved ivory hand ornamented with rubies, a lady's gold comb and hairpins, a silver pistol with a mother-of-pearl handle studded with diamonds.

Despite the upheaval, Poland's commerce remained in the hands of the Jews. They even dealt in church decorations, although this trade was forbidden them by law. Jewish traders traveled to Prussia, Bohemia, Austria, and Italy, importing into the country silk, velvet, wine, coffee, spices, jewelry, weapons, and exporting salt, oil, flax, butter, eggs, rye, wheat, barley, honey, hides. Neither the aristocracy nor the peasantry had any real knowledge of business. The Polish guilds continued to protect themselves through every form of privilege, but nevertheless their products were more expensive than those of the Jews and often inferior in workmanship. Nearly every manor harbored Jewish craftsmen, and, although the king had forbidden Jews to be apothecaries, the people had confidence in no others. Jewish doctors were sent for, sometimes from abroad. The priests, particularly the Jesuits, harangued against infidel medicine from their pulpits, published pamphlets on the subject, petitioned the Sejm and the governors to disqualify Jews from medical practice, but no sooner did one of the clergy fall ill, than he called in a Jew to attend him.

Jacob had come to Lublin to get advice from the local rabbi or from the members of the Council, but he loitered in the city doing nothing. The Sabbath came and went. The more he reflected on the question perplexing him, the clearer it became that no one could advise him. He was familiar with the law. Would he find a man anywhere who could determine the authenticity of a vision or who could weigh in the scales which was the greater transgression, the abandonment of one's issue to the idolaters or the conversion of a woman lacking a true vocation? Once more Jacob remembered the saying, "Something done selfishly may end up as a godly act," and argued accordingly. Cakes, candies, and almonds were given a child starting cheder to encourage him to love the Torah. Didn't one speak of a convert as new-born? Who could know all the motives of those who had become Jews in the past? No saint was entirely selfless. Jacob decided to take the sin upon himself and instruct Wanda in the tenets of his faith. Now that the Polish government permitted converted Jews to return to their religion, Wanda could pass as one of them. No one would bother to investigate. She would shave her head, put on a matron's bonnet, and he would teach her every single law.

In Lublin, Jacob was known as that man from Josefov who spent so many years a slave. Speaking thus, they set him apart. The scholars addressed him as if he were a simpleton who had forgotten all he learned. When they mentioned a Hebrew word or quoted the Talmud, they translated it into Yiddish for his benefit. In his presence they whispered among themselves and smiled patronizingly as city people do when they converse with bumpkins. The elders were interested in how he had conducted himself in slavery: had he kept the Sabbath and the dietary laws? How odd that he had not attempted to escape but had waited to be ransomed. Jacob became convinced they knew something dreadful they dared not say to his face. Could they have been told about Wanda? Zagayek might have passed a comment to the group who had come to ransom him. If so, his secret was traveling from mouth to mouth.

From the first he had noted the difference between himself and the others, and the longer he stayed in Lublin, the sharper the contrast seemed. He was tall, blond, blue-eyed; they, for the most part, were short, dark-eyed, black-bearded. They liked esoteric scholarly jokes, used snuff, smoked tobacco, knew the names of all the rich contractors, were acquainted with who had married whom, and what Jew was the favorite of which nobleman. All this was foreign to Jacob. I have turned into a peasant, he said, rebuking himself. But he recalled that it had not been so different before the calamity. The rabbis, elders, and rich men in the old days had also been of one party and he of another. They had eyed him suspiciously as if they suspected he had gentile blood. But how could this have been? Descended from an eminent family, his grandfathers, and their fathers also, had all been Polish rabbis.

Stranger than this, however, was the attitude of the Jews who, having just survived their greatest calamity, behaved as if they no longer remembered. They groaned and sighed, but without feeling. The rabbis and elders were again quarreling over money and power. The problem of the deserted wives and "the Cossack brides" was for them an opportunity to display their casuistic brilliance in long, time-consuming discussions little connected with the spirit of the law. The unhappy petitioners waited weeks and months for verdicts that could have been handed down in a few days. The Council of the Four Countries had taken upon itself the task of collecting the Crown taxes in addition to those which went for its own support, and everywhere complaints were heard that the burden of the tax was inequitably distributed and the rate excessive. Occasionally an accuser pointed a finger at these eminent men, threatening to complain to the administration, to stand up in the synagogue and denounce them before the reading of the Torah, or to wait for them outside and give them a good beating. The man was immediately made a member of the elite, offered a few crumbs, and sent out to sing the praises of the very individuals he had been defaming. Jacob even heard of emissaries who misappropriated money they collected or took too high a percentage for themselves. The catastrophes over, the stomachs of many of the rabbis and elders had increased in size; their necks wrinkled with fat. All this flesh was dressed in velvet, silk, and sables. They were so heavy they wheezed; their eyes shone greedily. They spoke an only half comprehensible language of innuendoes, winks, and whispered asides. Outside the community house, angry men proclaimed these rulers robbers and thieves and warned prophetically of the plagues and afflictions their sins would produce.

Yes, it was clear to Jacob that these, the grabbers, were worthless, but there were also the givers, and more of these than the others. Thank God, not all Jews were community elders. Men still prayed, studied, and recited Psalms in God's house. Many of them still bore the wounds they had received from the Cossacks. Jacob saw cripple after cripple, men deprived of ears, fingers, noses, teeth, eyes, and all sang: "We will sanctify"; "Bless ye." They listened to the sermons, sat down to pore over the Mishnah. Anniversary candles were lit and men continued to mourn.

Wandering through the narrow alleys, Jacob saw how great the poverty was. Many lived in what were only dark burrows; tradesmen worked in shops that looked like kennels. A stench rose from the gutters; ragged women, often on the point of giving birth, foraged for wood shavings and dung to be used for heat. Half naked children with scabby heads and rashes walked around barefoot. Many of the urchins had rickety legs, sores on their eyes, puffed bellies, distended heads. There was some kind of epidemic in progress and hearses with corpses in them passed constantly, each followed by lamenting women. A beadle rattled his alms box and cried out, "Charity will preserve you from death." The insane were everywhere, wild in the streets, another remembrance of the Cossacks.

It shamed Jacob that he thought so much of Wanda. People were starving before his eyes. A groschen here could save a life. He was continually changing silver to smaller coins and distributing his money. But what he gave was little when confronted with this vast need. Bands of beggars pursued him, clutched at his coat, blessing and cursing him. They hissed, spat at him, threw lice in his direction, and he was barely able to escape. Where was God? How could he look down on such want and keep silent? Unless, Heaven forbid, there was no God.

CHAPTER SEVEN

1

Jacob traveled from Lublin to Cracow by wagon. Changing to peasant dress, he proceeded on foot from Cracow to the mountains. The sack slung over his shoulder contained bread, cheese, a prayer book and shawl, phylacteries, a volume of the Mishnah, and presents for Wanda: a matron's bonnet, a dress, a pair of shoes. He had made his plans in advance; he would avoid the high road and take meadow and forest trails. The sun had gone down before he left Cracow, and all night he walked, aware of the dangers around him. Wild beasts and robbers lived in the hills; he remembered Wanda's stories of vampire owls disguised as cats and of witches' mares galloping through darkness on their evil errands.

The roads were dangerous at night, as Jacob knew. The King's Daughter, filthiest of witches, confused travelers and shoved them into bogs. The demonic Lillies made their homes in caves and the hollows of tree trunks. Ygereth, Machlath, and Shibta enticed men off the highways until they defiled themselves with nocturnal emissions. Shabriry and Briry polluted the waters of springs and rivers. Zachulphi, Jejknufi, Michiaru, survivors of the generation that had built the Tower of Babel, confounded men's speech and drove them mad or into the mountains of darkness. But Jacob's longing for Wanda made him willing to take any risk. Even though the journey must result in sin, he sang Psalms and begged God to keep him safe. His investigations of the cabala since his return had uncovered the doctrine that all lust was of divine origin, even Zimri's lust for Kozbi, the daughter of Zur. Coupling was the universal act underlying everything; Torah, prayer, the Commandments, God's holy names themselves were mysterious unions of the male and female principles. Jacob thrashed this way and that, constantly seeking exoneration: a soul would be saved from idolatry; his seed would not be mingled with that of Esau. Such virtuous acts must tip the scales in his favor.

The summer night passed, but Jacob could not have told how. The sun rose and he discovered himself in a forest with a stream close by. Washing his hands, he recited the Shema, and said the morning prayer in his shawl and phylacteries. He breakfasted on bread, dried cheese, and water, and then, having said grace, rested his head on the sack and fell asleep. The analogy between him and his Biblical namesake had already occurred to him. Jacob had left Beersheba and journeyed to Haran for love of Rachel and had toiled seven years to win her. Had she not been the daughter of a pagan? Awaking with such thoughts in his mind, he resumed his own journey, heading upstream past mushrooms and blackberry brambles in bud, noting which plants were edible. Uncertain of the road, he kept his eye out for the blazes the Gazdas notched into trees. Cows bellowed close at hand; he could see camp fires. As long as the path climbed, it was taking him to Wanda.

Late in the afternoon, when the sun was moving westward, a strange figure appeared as if risen from the earth. White-haired, bearded, the man wore a brown robe and felt boots. A rosary and crucifix hung from his neck. He stopped before Jacob, leaning on a crooked staff. "Where are you bound for, my son?" he asked.

Jacob told him the name of the village.

"There is the way," the old man said, and he showed him the path.

Before leaving, he blessed Jacob. If it had not been for the cross he wore, the old man might have been mistaken for the prophet Elijah. But, perhaps, Jacob thought, he was an emissary of Esau, sent by those powers who wished Jews and gentiles to mate. Jacob was now nearing the village, and he lengthened his stride. He felt anxious: Wanda might have remarried or fallen ill. God forbid, she might be dead. She might be in love with someone else. The sun went down; though it was midsummer, it became cold. Columns of mist rose from the mountains. In the distance, a huge bird, an eagle perhaps, hung suspended in mid air, wings motionless as though kept aloft by cabala. The moon rose and one by one, like candles being lit, stars appeared. Suddenly there was a noise, a kind of roaring. An animal or the wind? Jacob wondered. Though he was prepared to fight, he recognized that Providence would be justified in allowing some predatory creature to destroy him. How had he deserved better?

Stopping, he looked about him. He was as solitary here as the original Adam, with no sign anywhere of man and his works. The birds silent, only the song of the grasshoppers and the bubbling of a stream were heard. Glacial breezes blew from the mountains. Jacob breathed in deeply, savoring the familiar odors. Strange how he had missed not only Wanda but this. The stale air of Josefov had been unbearable, windows tightly shut, nothing but books all day. Tired though he was from his exertion, the journey had invigorated him. The body required use as well as the soul. It was good for men to haul, drag, chop, run, perspire, to hunger and thirst and become weary. Raising his eyes, he saw more stars appearing, large and brilliant here in the mountains. The workings of the heavens were visible to him, each orbiting light going its prescribed way and fulfilling its function. Notions he had had as a boy returned to him. Suppose he had wings and flew in one direction forever, would he come to the end of space? But how could space end? What extended beyond? Or was the material world infinite? But if it was, infinity stretched both to the east and west, and how could there be twice infinity? And what of time? How could even God have had no beginning? How could anything be eternal? Where had everything come from? These questions were impertinent, he knew, impermissible, pushing the inquirer toward heresy and madness.

He continued to walk. How strange and feeble was man. Surrounded on every side by eternity, in the midst of powers, angels, seraphim, cherubim, arcane worlds, and divine mysteries, all he could lust for was flesh and blood. Yet man's smallness was no less a wonder than God's greatness.

Pausing, he took some dry cheese from his sack and refreshed himself. Would he find Wanda today or have to wait until tomorrow? He feared the peasants and their dogs. He began to mumble prayers—a slave returning to bondage, a Jew again putting on Egypt's yoke.

2

Jacob entered the village at midnight, stealing through fields and pastures at the back of the huts. The moon had set, but it was light enough for him to recognize each house and granary. The mountain where he had spent five summers was visible also and he constantly lifted his eyes to it. Those years seemed dreamlike now, a vanished miracle, an interlude achieved by sorcery. Thank God, the dogs slept. His feet no longer felt heavy and his steps were faunlike; his body was buoyant from lack of food. He broke into a run, down the hill leading to Jan Bzik's hut, his single desire to find Wanda. Was she in the house? In the granary? Could she have gone to Antek's? He thought of his life and was amazed at what had happened to him. He had been taken captive; his family had been wiped out. Now, disguised as a peasant, he was hurrying to find his beloved. This was the sort of ballad his sisters had told or sung when his father was absent, not daring to when the pious man was at home, knowing that he regarded the female voice as lascivious.

Jacob stopped and held his breath. There it was, Jan Bzik's hut. He was trembling. He could make out every detail: the thatched roof, the windows, the granary, even the stump on which he had chopped wood. The kennel in the center of the yard appeared to be empty. Tiptoeing toward the granary, he smelled an odor he only now remembered. Was Wanda there? Could he be sure she would not cry out and wake everyone? He recollected the code she had used during those months when he had feared an attack by Antek or Stephan—three knocks, two loud and one soft. He rapped out the signal. There was no answer. Now for the first time he realized how dangerous this undertaking was. If he were discovered, he might be killed as a thief. And what if he did find Wanda, where could they go? This adventure was putting him in constant jeopardy. The Christians burned gentiles who became Jews. Nor would the Jews accept the convert. It was still not too late to turn back, he knew. He tingled with anxiety. Where had passion led him? Quietly he pushed open the granary door, meanwhile defending himself—I am no longer responsible for my acts. He heard breathing. Wanda was there. Hands ready to stifle her scream, he approached. Now he saw her in the darkness: she lay on the straw, her breasts exposed, half-naked. The story of Ruth and Boaz floated through his brain. He was awake, yet dreaming. He put down his sack.

"Wanda."

Her breathing stopped.

"Wanda, don't scream. It's me, Jacob." He broke off, unable to say more. She sighed. "Who is it?"

"Jacob. Don't scream."

Thank God she did not, but sat up like someone delirious from fever.

"Who are you?" she said uncomprehendingly.

"Jacob. I've come for you. Don't scream."

At that very instant she did. Her scream made Jacob shudder and he was certain those in the hut must have heard. He fell to the straw, and, struggling with her in the darkness, he clamped his hand over her mouth. She freed herself, got to her feet, and he clutched her again, glancing at the open door, expecting to see peasants running toward the granary.

"Be still," he said, his breath coming in gasps. "They'll kill me. I've come for you, Wanda. I couldn't get you out of my mind."

Scarcely knowing what he was doing, he pulled her closer. They dared not stay there, the granary was a trap. He was breathing hard and sweating; his heart was pounding. "We must leave here while it's still dark," he whispered.

No longer struggling, trembling now, she pressed herself to him, her teeth chattering as though it were winter. "Is it really you?" he heard her say:

"Yes, I. Hurry, we must go."

"Jacob. Jacob."

The scream must have gone unnoticed as no one was coming. But perhaps the peasants lay in wait outside. Now, for the first time, it occurred to him that this was not the Wanda of his vision. There was no indication that she bore his child. A dream had deceived him. Her arms about his neck, she whimpered like a sick animal, "Jacob, Jacob." He could not doubt that she had been longing for him. But every minute counted now. Over and over again he cautioned her that she must dress quickly and come with him. He grasped her by the wrists, shook her, begged her not to delay—they were in great peril. She pulled him to her again, pressing her face against his. In his anxiety he couldn't make out what she was saying. "We must leave," he warned her.

"One minute."

Turning, she ran from the granary. He saw her enter the hut and wondered if she would tell the old woman. He lifted his sack and walked out into the open air, prepared to run for the fields if there was trouble. It was difficult for him to believe that the woman he had awakened was Wanda. She looked smaller and thinner than she had been, more like a girl than a woman. Outside it was dark and still—that moment before dawn when night borders on day. Sky, earth, and mountains waited in an expectant hush. Though he remained terrified and shocked at what he had done, there was also a silence in Jacob. His mind seemed frozen. He no longer cared what the outcome of this adventure would be. His fate was decided. He had passed beyond freedom, was both himself and another. The still point within him watched as though his actions were those of a stranger.

He waited, but Wanda did not come. Had she decided not to leave with him? The sun must have risen already on the other side of the mountains. He stood enveloped in the chill darkness of dawn. Suddenly Wanda ran from the hut, now wearing shoes and with a kerchief on her head. A sack was slung over her shoulder. "Did you wake them?" he asked.

"No, they sleep like the dead."

3

Wanda chose another route to leave the village than the one he had had in mind. Like an elusive shadow she ran before him scarcely visible in the darkness. His legs shook from too much walking and too little sleep. He stumbled over rocks, slid into ditches. He wanted to call to her not to get too far ahead, but dared not raise his voice. How could she run so quickly bearing a sack? He felt drowsy; he kept dreaming. Something rose from the darkness. He drew back startled and instantly the image dissolved. An alien voice spoke inside him. Things were happening, but he didn't know what. Wanda had dressed and packed without waking her mother and sister—how? An absurd idea, patently false, came to him: could she have strangled them?

That instant a fragment of day fell on the mountains and made them shine. The east reddened and the sun lifted itself behind the peaks. Jacob caught up with Wanda and saw that they were in a meadow at the edge of the forest. He noticed that she had on the fringed kerchief and the calico apron she had worn in his dream. Yes, she had altered, was shrunken and emaciated. Though her face was tinted purple by the sun, nevertheless her complexion was as pale as that of a consumptive. Her eyes had grown large and protruded from their sockets. It was even more difficult now to understand how she could have run so swiftly.

"Let's stop for a moment," he said.

"Not here—in the forest," she answered in a whisper.

But they did not stop immediately upon entering the woods. Among the trees Wanda's figure became more elusive than ever, and Jacob feared he would lose sight of her. The grade became steeper. He slipped on the pine needles. Wanda climbed like a bear, or a doe. He had returned to a changed woman. How could she have altered so quickly?

The forest grew lighter as if a lamp had been lit. Golden light fell over everything. Birds whistled and sang. Dew fell. Wanda stopped at the narrow opening of a cave. She threw her sack into the aperture and crept in head first, her feet kicking outside for a second. Jacob pushed his sack in and followed her through the opening. He recalled the commentary in the Talmud on the passage in the Bible, "And the pit was empty, there was no water in it." The Talmud added, "There was no water in it, but there were snakes and lizards." Well, whatever happens, happens, Jacob said to himself. It was as if he had entered the mouth of an abyss. He slipped and Wanda gripped him by the shoulders. The dampness choked him. He stumbled into her, and they fell over the sacks. Finally the cave became larger and he was able to sit up. When he spoke, his muffled voice sounded far off and unfamiliar to him.

"How did you know about this cave?" he asked.

"I knew. I knew."

"What's wrong with you? Are you sick?"

Wanda did not speak immediately.

"If you'd waited a little longer, you would have found me dead."

"What's wrong?"

Wanda paused again.

"Why did you go away? Where did they take you? I was told you'd never come back."

"You knew that the Jews had ransomed me?"

"All they said was that some devils had seized you."

"What do you mean? They paid Zagayek fifty gulden. They arrived in a wagon."

"When I was out of the village. But I knew I wouldn't find you when I got back. I didn't need the women to tell me."

"How did you know?"

"I know everything, everything. I was walking with Antek and the sun became black as night. The horse Wojciech was riding began to laugh at me."

"The horse?"

"Yes, and then I knew that my enemies would revenge themselves on me."

Jacob considered what she had told him.

"I was lying in the granary, when your sister came to call me."

"That! I know. As soon as I came into the village, they all laughed at my bad luck. How did the Jews know where you were?"

"I spoke to that circus proprietor and he carried the message."

"Where to? Palestine?"

"No, to Josefov."

"You didn't even say goodbye to me. It was as if the earth had swallowed you up, as if there had never been a Jacob. Stephan came to me but I spat in his face. He got back at me by killing the dog. Mother and Basha said I was either possessed or crazy. The peasants wanted to tie me to a tree trunk but I ran away to the mountains and I stayed there until they brought up the herd. For four weeks I didn't taste a thing but snow and cold water from the stream."

"It wasn't my fault, Wanda. The Jews came and took me. What could I have told them? The wagon was waiting. When Zagayek sent for me I thought I was going to be hanged."

"You should have waited. You shouldn't have left me like that. If I'd had a child by you I would have had some comfort. But all I was left with was the stone behind the barn and what you had scratched on it. I beat my head against it."

"But I did come."

"I knew you would. You called to me but I didn't have the strength to wait. I went to the coffin maker and had myself measured. I had the priest confess me and I chose a grave next to father's."

"But you told me you no longer believed in Dziobak."

"What? He sent for me and I came. I fell on my knees and kissed his feet. All I wanted was to lie near Father."

"You'll live, but as a daughter of Israel."

"Where will you take me? I'm sick. I can't be a wife to you now. The witch told me what to do—it was she who brought you here and no one else."

"Wanda, what are you telling me? One cannot use witchcraft."

"You didn't come of your own free will, Jacob. I made a clay image of you and I wrapped it in my hair. I bought an egg laid by a black hen and buried it at the crossroads with a piece of glass from a broken mirror. I looked into it and I saw your eyes. . . ."

"When?"

"After midnight."

"One mustn't do such things. That's sorcery. It's not allowed."

"You wouldn't have come by yourself."

Suddenly clutching him, she let out a wail that made Jacob shudder. Crying, she kissed his face, licked his hand. A howl tore itself from her throat.

"Jacob, don't leave me again, Jacob."

PART TWO

■

Sarah

CHAPTER EIGHT

1

Once more the Cossacks attacked Poland, once more they slaughtered Jews in Lublin and the surrounding areas. Polish soldiers dispatched many of the survivors. Then the Muscovites invaded from the east and the Swedes from the north. It was a time of upheaval and yet the Jews had to conduct business, supervise the tilling of leased fields, borrow money, pay taxes, even marry off daughters. A house built today would be burned tomorrow. Today a girl was engaged, a few days later raped. One day a man was rich, the next poor. Banquets were held one day, the next funerals for martyrs. The Jews were constantly on the march, from Lemberg and back to Lemberg, from Lublin and back to Lublin. A city that was secure one day was under siege the next. A wealthy man would wake to find he must carry a beggar's sack. Entire communities of Jews turned Christian and though some later reassumed their own faith, others remained in darkness. Poland teemed with deserted wives, raped women, brides run away from their gentile husbands, men who had been ransomed or who had escaped from prison. God's wrath poured down on his people. But the moment the Jews caught their breath, they returned to Judaism. What else could they do? Accept the religion of the murderer?

A handful of Jews, survivors of burned-out and pillaged towns, gathered in Pilitz, a village on the other side of the Vistula, having gained the consent of the overlord to settle there. The Swedish war had ruined Adam Pilitzky, but not even the Swedes could steal earth, sky, and water. Again the peasants plowed and sowed. Again the earth, soaked with the blood of the innocent and the guilty, brought forth wheat and rye, buckwheat and barley, fruit and vegetables. The retreating Swedish army had set fire to Pilitzky's castle, but a rain storm had extinguished the blaze. A revolt of the peasantry had followed the withdrawal of the Swedes and one of Pilitzky's marshals had been stabbed. Arming his retainers, Pilitzky attacked the rebels, hanging some, and flogging others to death. He ordered the heads of the executed to be placed on poles and publicly exhibited as a warning to the serfs. Birds pecked at the flesh until only naked skulls remained.

Pilitzky had no time for his manor and was a poor manager; his Polish bailiffs were drunkards, drones, and thieves. True, the Jews also swindled if they got the chance, but the owner could brandish a whip over them. A Jew could be flogged like a peasant, imprisoned in a sty, even beheaded. Moreover the Jew was thrifty, saved money, and put it out for usury. One could always go bankrupt and make a settlement with him.

Though Adam Pilitzky was already fifty-four, he looked much younger. He was tall, dark, had brown hair untouched by gray, black eyes and a small goatee. He had spent his youth in France and Italy and had returned with what he termed new ideas. For a time he flirted with Protestantism, but that mood passed and he soon became a zealous Catholic and an enemy of the Reformation. The neighboring landowners found him strange, spoke of him as an "odd bird." He continually predicted the collapse of Poland. All of the prominent leaders were rascals, thieves, scum. He himself had taken no part in the Cossack and Swedish wars but accused his countrymen of cowardice. He swore by all that was holy that everyone in Poland could be bought, from the smallest clerk in a town hall to the king. Phrases from the diatribes of the priest Skarga were perpetually on his lips, though he drank heavily and was considered a libertine. The *jus primae noctis* (obsolete elsewhere) was in force in his estates. It was said that his daughter had drowned herself after having been possessed by him. His son had gone mad and had died of jaundice. The rumor was that his wife Theresa was his procuress and had taken the coachman as her lover. Another report was that she copulated with a stallion. Both wife and husband had recently become religious enthusiasts. When the monastery at Czestochow was besieged and Kordecki put up his heroic resistance, they had worked themselves into a religious frenzy.

Pilitzky's castle was crowded with his and his wife's relatives, who, though they belonged to the aristocracy, did the work of maids and lackeys. Once when Lady Pilitzky found a hole in the tablecloth she emptied a glass of wine over a female cousin. She required that the tablecloths, towels, shirts, underwear, silver, and porcelain be counted weekly. When Adam Pilitzky became angry, he took a rod and beat the old maids. The great fortune he and his wife had inherited between them had been dissipated. The neighborhood joke was that all that remained of Theresa Pilitzky's jewelry was a single gold hairpin. At every opportunity Adam Pilitzky warned that Poland would have no peace until all Protestants, Cossacks, and Jews were killed—particularly the Jews who had secretly bribed the traitor Radziszewski and conspired with the Swedes. Pilitzky had given his word to the priests that when Poland was rid of its enemies, no Jew would lay foot on his property. But, as usual, he did the opposite of what he said. First he permitted a Jewish contractor to settle. This Jew began to complain that he needed a quorum. Soon the Jews were granted the right to build a synagogue. Someone died and a cemetery was necessary. Finally the Jews of Pilitz imported a rabbi and a ritual slaughterer. So now Pilitz had become a community. Adam Pilitzky cursed and spat, but the Jews had done much to get him back on his feet. It was they who saw to it that the peasants plowed, harvested, mowed hay. They paid cash to Pilitzky for grain and cattle, repaired the pond in which he stocked fish, built a dairy. They even brought beehives for honey into the estate. Pilitzky no longer had to go looking for a tailor, a shoemaker, a furrier, a bell maker. Jewish craftsmen repaired his castle, patched the roof, rebuilt the ovens. Jews could do anything; rebind books, mend parquet floors, put glass in windows, frame pictures. When someone was ill, a Jewish doctor bled him or applied leeches and had a stock of medicines ready. A Jewish goldsmith made a bracelet for Lady Pilitzky and took a note instead of cash. Even the Jesuits, despite their slander and pamphlets, dealt with the Jews and used their handicraft.

At first Pilitzky had kept count of the number of Jews who settled on his property. But before long, he lost track. He didn't know their language and could scarcely tell one Jew from another. He warned constantly, "Unless the Poles change radically, there'll be another Chmielnicki. Anyway, everything's collapsing."

2

One day a man and woman trudged into Pilitz, sacks on their shoulders, bundles in their hands. The Jews emerged from stores and workshops to welcome the newcomers. The man, tall, broad-shouldered, blue-eyed, had a brown beard. Wearing a kerchief, seemingly younger than her husband, the woman looked almost gentile. The man was called Jacob. Asked where he was from, he mentioned the name of a distant city. The women soon learned that the young wife was a mute, and at first were amazed that so handsome a man should have made such a marriage. But, then, was it so astonishing? Marriages were made in heaven. Jacob gave his wife's name as Sarah, and she was immediately nicknamed, "Dumb Sarah."

The Jews inquired if Jacob was a scholar because they were looking for a teacher. "I know a chapter or two of the Pentateuch," Jacob said hesitantly.

"That's all that's needed."

It was springtime, the period between Passover and Pentecost. So now Pilitz had a school. Jacob and his mute wife were given a room and promised a house of their own if Jacob proved a good teacher. Pilitzsky owned many forests and lumber was cheap in the town. The new teacher was supplied with a table, a dunce's stool, and a cat-o'-nine-tails; he whittled a pointer and printed the letters of the alphabet on paper. Most of the children were in the early grades and the class assembled under a tree. Jacob sat with his charges in the shade, teaching them the alphabet, how to read syllables and words, instructing each child according to his age and knowledge. Because of the great amount of construction in progress, logs and lumber were piled all around, and the children built swings out of the boards and made little houses from chips and shavings. The town had no woman teacher and some of the parents sent daughters as well as sons to the cheder to learn their prayers and master a little writing. The girls made mud pies and sang and danced in a circle. The smaller boys and girls played house. The husband went to the synagogue to pray, his wife fixed supper for him and served it on a broken plate. The bread was a sliver of bark, the soup sand, the meat a pine cone. Jacob misplaced his cat-o'-nine-tails. He never whipped the children or scolded them, but lovingly pinched their cheeks and kissed their foreheads. These children had been born after the catastrophe.

The community liked Jacob immediately and pitied him for having a mute wife. True, Dumb Sarah behaved as a Jewess should, went to the ritual bath, soaked the meat and salted it, on Friday prepared the Sabbath pudding, burned a piece of chalah dough, blessed the candles; on the Sabbath, she stood in the woman's section of the synagogue and moved her lips as though praying. But sometimes she behaved in a way unbecoming a teacher's wife, took off her shoes and walked barefooted, laughed unrestrainedly, exhibiting a mouthful of unblemished peasant-like teeth. Dumb Sarah labored wih the skill of a country woman, chopped wood, tended a vegetable garden she had planted behind the house, washed clothes in the river. When her own washing was done, she helped other women who had small children. She was remarkably strong and worked for everyone—and for nothing. Once she undressed in front of the women and swam in the river naked. Certain that she would drown at the spot where the waters swirled dangerously, the matrons, none of whom knew how to swim, broke into screams. But Dumb Sarah fearlessly crossed the whirlpool. Her audience was astounded. Dumb all right! Just like an animal.

This incident was soon followed by another which gave the people of Pilitz more to gossip about. The construction of Jacob's house was begun; and not only did Jacob assist in the work but Sarah also, although she was already pregnant and had stopped going to the ritual bath. Jacob went to the forest and felled trees, trimmed them with his ax and dragged them to the village. Sarah hauled logs and lumber as though she were a man. The house didn't cost the community a groschen. Nor was Jacob as unlearned as everyone had believed. One Saturday the reader lost his voice and Jacob read from the scroll; several times he was observed opening a Gemara in the study house. When he prayed he stood in a corner, swaying piously, and occasionally sighing. He said little about his past and the community concluded that he must have lost his family in the massacres. If they sought to engage him in conversation, he walked away, saying, "What happened happened. One must start over again."

The men respected him and the women liked him. When the matrons sat on their benches in front of their houses Sabbath afternoons, they agreed among themselves that Dumb Sarah had more luck than brains. No one denied that she was young, good-looking, and healthy, but what did a man want with a dumbbell? A husband liked to talk to his wife and hear her opinions. What a calamity, God forbid, if the child should take after its mother. Such things happened. One woman known as a wit remarked: "Well, some men would regard a silent wife as a blessing. No tongue, no torment."

"Oh, that's just talk."

"Well, it's better than having a blind one."

"Have you noticed," a young woman asked, "that as soon as it's dark she closes the shutters?"

"What does that prove?"

"That she loves him."

"Who wouldn't?"

On the Sabbath, Dumb Sarah discarded her kerchief, put on a bonnet, pointed shoes, an embroidered apron, and a dress with flowers that she had brought from far off. Going to synagogue, she held a prayer book in one hand and a handkerchief in the other. [This was allowed since the town of Pilitz had been enclosed in a wire which removed the Sabbath ban against carrying things.] When the women tried to communicate with her by hand signs, she smiled and shook her head, apparently unable to understand. The women poked fun at her, yet agreed she had a kind heart. She visited the sick and massaged their bodies with turpentine and alcohol. She prepared stewed apples and prunes as a treat for her husband's pupils on the Sabbath afternoon. Her stomach swelled, became pointed, and the women calculated she would give birth around Succoth or early in the month of Cheshvan.

Since the mute are also deaf, the women did not watch their words in her presence. Once, while Sarah sat with her prayer book open, a woman remarked, "She reads as well as the sacrificial rooster."

"Perhaps she's been taught."

"How can you teach the dumb?"

"Maybe she became dumb with fright."

"She doesn't look frightened."

"Perhaps the murderers cut out her tongue."

The women asked to see her tongue. At first, Sarah didn't seem to understand, then she began to laugh and her cheeks dimpled. She stuck out a pink tongue, as pointed as a dog's.

3

Wanda, not Jacob, had thought of playing the mute, realizing Yiddish would take her too long to learn; the few words she knew she spoke like a gentile. Her idea of passing herself off as a "Cossack bride" who could now only speak the language of the steppes was discarded because she didn't know that tongue either. She was not an adroit liar and would have been unmasked immediately. Jacob and she underwent many hardships and dangers before she decided on the role of a mute. They went to distant Pilitz because Jacob was too famous in Lublin and the surrounding areas as the slave who had returned. At night when Sarah, as all Jewish converts were called, closed the shutters, Jacob spoke with her and instructed her in their religion. He had already taught her the prayers and how to write Yiddish and now they studied the Pentateuch, the Books of Samuel and Kings, the Code of the Jewish Law; he told her stories from the Gemara and Midrash. Her diligence was amazing, her memory good; many of the questions she asked were the same the commentators had raised. Teaching her, he dared not lift his voice. Not only did he dread the gentiles and their laws, but also the Jews who would expel him from the village if they learned his wife was a convert. Sarah's presence in Pilitz imperiled the town. If the Polish authorities learned that a Christian girl had been seduced into Judaism, there would be reprisals. God knows what accusations would be made. The priests only wanted a pretext. And if the Jews got wind of it, the elders would immediately investigate the circumstances of the conversion and would guess correctly that Sarah had left her own religion because of Jacob—women being little interested in speculative matters; and Jacob would be excommunicated.

There was so much concern with the lineage and matrimonial connections of scholars that Jacob had not divulged that he was learned. The few scholarly books he had brought he kept hidden. He built his house with thick walls and constructed an alcove, windowless and hidden from the world by a clump of trees, where he and his beloved wife could study in secret. True, they had lived together illicitly, but since then they had fulfilled the law of Moses and Israel by standing under the canopy. Sarah now fervently believed in God and the Torah and obeyed all the laws. Now and then she erred, doing things upside down according to her peasant understanding, or speaking in a manner that was inappropriate. But Jacob corrected her kindly and made her understand the reason for each law and custom. Teaching others, Jacob realized, one also instructed oneself; correcting Sarah's behavior, answering her questions, eradicating her errors, many problems about which he would not have otherwise thought were clarified for him. Often her questions demanded answers which were not to be found in this world. She asked: "If murder is a crime, why did God permit the Israelites to wage war and even kill old people and small children?" If the nations distant from the Jews, such as her own people, were ignorant of the Torah, how could they be blamed for being idol worshipers? If Father Abraham was a saint, why did he drive Hagar and her son Ishmael into the desert with a gourd of water? The question that recurred more often than any other was why did the good suffer and the evil prosper. Jacob told her repeatedly he couldn't solve all the world's riddles, but Sarah kept on insisting, "You know everything."

He had warned her many times about the unclean days, reminding her that when she was menstruating she could not sit on the same bench with him, take any object from his hand, nor even eat at the same table unless there was a screen between her plate and his. He was not allowed to sit on her bed, nor she on his; not even the headboards of their beds ought to touch at this time. But these were some of the things that Sarah either forgot or ignored, for she kept on insisting she must be near him. She was capable of running over and kissing him in the middle of her period. Jacob rebuked her and told her such acts were forbidden by the Torah, but she took these restrictions lightly, and this caused Jacob sorrow. She was very scrupulous about less important things. She immersed all the dishes in the ritual bath, and kept on inquiring about milk and meat. At times she forgot she was a mute and broke into song. Jacob trembled. Not only was there the danger of her being heard, but a pious daughter of Israel should not provoke lust with the lascivious sound of her voice. Nor had she let the bath attendant shave her head like the other women's, though Jacob had asked her to. Sarah cut her own hair with shears; occasionally ringlets pushed out from under her kerchief.

Though Jacob had built them a house, Sarah complained nightly that she wished to leave Pilitz. She could not remain silent forever, and she feared what would happen to her child. The young must be taught to speak, and given love. She kept asking whether her Yiddish had improved; Jacob assured her she was doing well but it wasn't so. She mispronounced the words, twisted the constructions, and whatever she uttered came out upside down. Often her mistakes made Jacob laugh. Even a few words dropping from her tongue and there was no mistaking she had been born a gentile. Now that she was pregnant Jacob was more frightened than ever. A woman in labor cannot control her screams. Unless she could endure the birth pangs in silence, Sarah would give herself away.

Yes, the day Jacob had left Josefov for the village where he had been a slave for five years, he had picked up a burden which became heavier with the passage of time. His years of enforced slavery had been succeeded by a slavery that would last as long as he lived. "Well, Gehenna is for people and not for dogs," he had once heard a water carrier say. Yet he had saved a soul from idolatry, even though he had stumbled into transgression. At night when Sarah and he lay in their beds which were arranged so as to form a right angle (the room wasn't long enough to have one at the foot of the other), the couple whispered to each other for hours without tiring. Jacob informed Sarah about the moral life, spicing his text with little parables. She spoke of how much she loved him. They often recalled the summers he had lived in the barn when she had brought food to him. Now those days were far off and as shadowy as a dream. Sarah found it difficult to believe that the village still existed and that Basha and Antek and possibly her mother still lived there. According to the law, Jacob said, she no longer was a member of her family. A convert was like a newborn child and had a fresh soul. Sarah was like Mother Eve who had been formed from Adam's rib; her husband was her only relative. "But," Sarah argued, "my father is still my father," and she began to cry about Jan Bzik who had had so hard a life and now lay buried among idolaters. "You will have to bring him into Paradise," she told Jacob. "I won't go without him."

4

The peasants, now busy in the fields preparing for harvest, rarely brought produce to town. Jewish peddlers traveled to the country with packs on their backs to buy chickens, millet and corn. Sarah, needing supplies, picked up a sack and set out, though Jacob had insisted this was no errand for a pregnant woman, much less the wife of a teacher. But Sarah longed for the fields and pastures. The moment Pilitz was behind her, she kicked off her shoes and slung them over her shoulder. The townswomen smirked, seeing her go, asked each other, "Now how will the dumbbell bargain?"

Sarah's presumed deafness left the women free to slander and ridicule her in her presence. She was referred to as a dumb animal, a golem, a simpleton, a cabbage head. Jacob was pitied for having brought home such a goose. The guess was she had a rich father who had given a substantial dowry to marry her off. Still, Jacob was a fool to have led such a nanny goat under the canopy. Sarah had to keep smiling though she could scarcely retain her tears. The peasants were openly scornful. Running their fingers across their throats, they would point toward the road, pretending the Cossacks were coming. Pan Pilitzky, they said, was infesting Poland with Jewish lice, and they prophesied wars, plagues, and famines, Heaven's revenge for permitting the God murderers to settle there. Sarah found it difficult to remain silent.

When she was alone with Jacob at night she cried and repeated what the Jews said. "You must not repeat such things," Jacob scolded her. "That's calumny. It's as great a sin as eating pork."

"So they're allowed to abuse us but I can say nothing?"

"No, they're not behaving properly either."

"Well, they all do it, even Breina, and she's the wife of an elder."

"Those who do such things will be punished in Heaven. The sacred books warn that all those who gossip, ridicule, or speak evil of others, will burn in the fires of Gehenna."

"All of them?"

"There's no lack of room in Gehenna."

"The rabbi's wife laughed too."

"There are no favorites in Heaven. When Moses sinned, he was punished."

Sarah became thoughtful.

"No, speaking evil can't be one thousandth the sin of eating pork, or no one would do it."

"Come, I'll show you what it says in the Torah."

Jacob, opening the Pentateuch, translated the text and told her how each of the sins had been interpreted by the Gemara. Several times he walked to the door to assure himself no one was listening or looking through the keyhole. "Why do the Jews obey some laws and break others?" Sarah whispered.

Jacob shook his head.

"That's the way it's always been. The prophets denounced it. The temple was destroyed for that reason. It's easier not to eat pig than to curb your tongue. Come and I will read you a chapter from Isaiah."

Jacob turned to Isaiah and translated the first chapter. Sarah listened in amazement. The prophet said the same things as Jacob: God had had enough of the blood of bullocks and the fat of lambs; people were not to come into his presence with bloody hands. The elders of Israel were compared by the prophet to the lords of Sodom God had destroyed. Late though it was, the wick in the shard continued to burn and moths circled the flame. The shadow of Jacob's head wavered on the ceiling. A cricket chirped from behind the oven. Love and fear mingled in Sarah. She dreaded the angry God who dwelled in Heaven and overheard every word and thought; she feared the peasants desirous of murdering Jews again and burying children alive; she was anxious about the Jews who were provoking the Almighty by obeying only one part of the Torah. Sarah promised not to repeat the evil gossip she heard, though as it was she had not told him everything. It was said in town that one of the storekeepers gave false measure. There was a rumor that a man had stolen from his partner at the time of the massacres. Sarah had been told that the Jews were the chosen people and she wanted to ask how they could be so favored when they committed such crimes. But that Jacob was righteous was evident to her. If God loved him as much as she did, he would live forever.

In her prayers she told God that she had no one but Jacob. She could never love another. She had joined a community but felt like a stranger. Though she had fled the peasants, she had not become one of the Jews of Pilitz. Jacob was husband, father, and brother to her. The moment the candle was extinguished she called him to her bed. "You, gentile," Jacob said jokingly: "Don't you know that a daughter of Israel mustn't be immodest or she'll be divorced without a settlement?"

"What can a daughter of Israel do?"

"Bear children and serve God."

"I intend to bear you a dozen."

He would not lie with her immediately, but first told her stories of upright men and women. She asked what went on in Paradise and what would occur when the Messiah came. Would Jacob still be her husband? Would they speak Hebrew? Would he take her with him to the rebuilt temple? When the Messiah came, Jacob said, each day would be as long as a year, the sun would be seven times as bright, and the Saints would feed on leviathan and the wild ox and drink the wine prepared for the days of redemption.

"How many wives will each man have?" Sarah asked.

"I'll have only you."

"I'll be old by then."

"We'll be young forever."

"What kind of a dress will I wear?"

Lying with Jacob was for her a foretaste of Paradise. She often wished that the night would last forever and she could continue to listen to his words and receive his caresses. That hour in the darkness was her reward for what she had endured during the day. When she fell asleep, her dreams took her to her native village; she entered the hut where she had lived; she stood on the mountain. Strange events involving Antek, Basha, and her mother occurred. Her father, once more alive, spoke wisely to her, and though she forgot his words as soon as she awoke, their resonance rang in her ears. Sometimes she dreamed Jacob had left her, and cried in her sleep. Jacob always awakened her.

"Oh, Jacob, you're still here. Thank God." His face would become hot and wet from her tears.

5

A coach drawn by a team of four horses, with two coachmen in front and two footmen in the rear, rode into the market place at noon. One of the coachmen blew his horn. The Jews of Pilitz became alarmed. Pilitzky rarely came to town in such pomp, and never in summer before the harvest. He was carrying a sword; he looked drunk. Leaping from the coach, he drew his sword from its scabbard and screamed, "Where is Gershon? I'm going to cut off his head. I'm going to tear him to pieces and pour acid into his wounds—him and his family as well. I'm going to throw the whole batch of them to the dogs."

Some of the Jews scurried off. Others rushed to Pilitzky and threw themselves at his feet. The women began to wail. The children in Jacob's class heard the tumult and came running to have a look at the lord, at the coach, at the horses with their heads held high in their fine harnesses. One of Gershon's sycophants hastened to him and warned him that Pilitzky was drunk and looking for him. Gershon was the most powerful man in Pilitz, since he leased the fields of the manor and managed them as if they were his own. He was known in town as a shady dealer. He'd built himself a large house and had acquired three sons-in-law, all from wealthy families, who had become respectively the town's rabbi, ritual slaughterer and public contractor. The last supplied the flour at Passover and had built the synagogue. Gershon had retained the wardenship of the burial society and charged exorbitant prices for graves, although Pilitzky had donated the land for the cemetery. Gershon also collected the taxes, usurping the function of the town's seven elders as set forth by the Council of the Four Countries. Taxation in Pilitz worked on the principle that the friends and flatterers of Gershon paid little or nothing; all ohers tottered under the weight of his levies. Gershon was ignorant but had granted himself the title "Our Teacher" and did not allow the cantor to intone the eighteen benedictions until he, Gershon, had said them over to himself. When he got the whim to take a steam bath in the middle of the week, the bath attendant was forced to heat the water at the community's expense.

Those whom Gershon had trampled threatened to denounce him to Pilitzky and to the Council in Lublin, but Gershon feared no man. He had friends who sat on the Council and he held Pilitzky's note for a thousand gulden. He was an intimate of other landowners, Pilitzky's enemies. Gershon, it seemed, had forgotten that the Jews were in exile. Yes, Pilitzky was looking for him and Gershon was advised to take cover in an attic or cellar until the wrath of the lord of Pilitz subsided. But Gershon was not one to have himself thought a coward, and he put on his silk overcoat, his sable hat, wrapped a sash around his waist, and walked out to meet Adam Pilitzky. Though Gershon dressed like a rabbi, he had the florid complexion of a butcher. His nose was flat, his lips thick; his belly stuck out as though he were pregnant. One of his eyes was higher and set in a larger socket than the other. He had heavy, bushy eyebrows. Not only was he aggressive but stubborn. When he rose to make a speech, every third word was a barbarism; he babbled until everyone fell asleep, and the opposition never had a chance to voice its opinion.

Now, walking slowly, Gershon approached his overlord. He did not come alone but accompanied by his entourage: the butchers, the horse dealers, and the men of the burial society whom he banqueted twice a year and who got all the sinecures in town. Before Gershon could open his mouth, Pilitzky screamed: "Where's the red bull?"

Gershon considered the question for a moment and then replied. "I sold him to the butcher, my lord."

"You dirty Jew. You sold my bull."

"Sir, while I lease the manor land, I'm in control."

"So you're in control. Seize him, boys. We'll hang him here." All the Jews shouted in terror—even Gershon's enemies joined in. Gershon tried to speak and retreated a few steps, but the coachmen and footmen caught hold of him. Pilitzky cried out, "Get the rope."

Some of the Jews fell to their knees, prostrated themselves, bowed—as on Yom Kippur when the cantor repeats the ritual service of the ancient temple in Jerusalem. Women screamed. Gershon struggled with his captors. The sash was torn from his waist. Pilitzky shouted, "A pole. Bring me a pole."

"We can hang him from the lamp post, my lord."

Jacob, hearing the clamor which was not unlike that when the Cossacks had attacked Josefov, came running. Gershon's wife was clasping one of Pilitzky's knees, refusing to let go. Pilitzky was trying to shake himself free of her and had his sword raised as if about to sever her head. The women were pushing and milling and wailing insanely. One dug her nails into her cheeks, another clutched her breasts, a third scratched at her husband to do something. Gershon was a crass man. The Jews of Pilitz disliked him but they could not stand by and see him hanged summarily. Gershon's daughters-in-law fell into each other's arms. The rabbi also prostrated himself at Pilitzky's feet; his skull cap having come off, his long side locks dragged in the dirt. It was almost as if the massacres had again begun. Gershon's followers, instead of disarming Pilitzky's servants which they might have done easily, just stood gaping with legs spread wide, amazed it seemed at their own impotence. But when had a Jew ever defied a Polish noble? Then out of the study house walked the beadle bearing the holy scroll as if it would quiet Pilitzky's wrath. There were shouts bidding the old man advance closer; others among the crowd motioned him back, protesting the sacrilege. He stood swaying indecisively on his rickety legs as though about to fall. Seeing him totter, a great cry of lamentation rose from the people. Jacob stood transfixed, knowing he must say nothing, yet equally certain he could not remain silent. Stepping forward, he ran quickly to Pilitzky and took off his hat.

"Mighty lord, a man is not killed for selling a bull."

The market place became quiet. Everyone knew that Gershon had declared war on Jacob because Jacob had taken the place of the reader. Gershon didn't like scholars, would never have tolerated Jacob's appointment if he had known that this was a man who could understand both text and footnotes. Now Jacob came to his assistance. Astonished, Pilitzky stared at the Jew in front of him.

"Who are you?"

"I am the teacher."

"What's your name?"

"Jacob."

"Oh! Are you that Jacob who cheated Esau out of his birthright?" An inhuman laugh burst from Pilitzky's throat.

Hearing the lord of Pilitz laugh, everyone joined in—the Jews, Pilitzky's men; Pilitzky doubled up with mirth. Was it merely a joke, a nobleman's prank such as the Polish landowners often played on their Jewish tenants? These games always terrified the Jews since such fun sometimes turned serious. But the men still held onto Gershon—who was the only one not laughing. His yellow eyes had lost none of their arrogance; his thick, mustached lip was drawn back into a snarl, revealing sparse, yellow teeth. Gershon looked like an animal at bay about to die in a struggle with a stronger adversary. Pilitzky howled with laughter, clapped his hands, clutched at his knees, and gasped. Those who had prostrated themselves rose and, relieved, bellowed with a mad exuberance. Even the rabbi laughed. The women collapsed into each other's arms, their knees buckling, their laughter turning to tears.

"Mommalas, Poppalas, tsitselas," Pilitzky mimicked and started braying again. The whole community joined in, every face with its own particular expression and grimace. The sight of one old matron, who had lost her bonnet and whose unevenly clipped scalp resembled a newly sheared ewe, started the women off once more, but this time their laughter was genuine.

Then all laughter ceased. Pilitzky gave a final burst and scowled again.

"Who are you? What are you doing here?" he asked Jacob. "Answer me, Jew."

"I am the teacher, my lord."

"What do you teach? How to steal the host? How to poison wells? How to use Christian blood to make matzoth?"

"God forbid, my lord. Such acts are prohibited by Jewish law."

"Prohibited, are they? We know. We know. Your cursed Talmud teaches you how to fool the Christian mob. You've been driven from every country, but King Casimir opened our gates wide to you. And how do you repay us? You've established a new Palestine here. You ridicule and curse us in Hebrew. You spit on our relics. You blaspheme our God ten times a day. Chmielnicki taught you a lesson, but you need a stronger one. You love all Poland's enemies—Swedes, Muscovites, Prussians. Who gave you permission to come here?" Pilitzky screamed at Jacob, shaking his fist. "This is my earth, not yours. My ancestors shed blood for it. I don't need you to teach Jewish vermin how to defile my country. We have enough parasites already. We're more dead than alive."

Pilitzky ceased his invective and foamed at the mouth. Once more, eyeing each other in dread, the Jews bent, ready to fall to the ground and beg for mercy. The elders signaled among themselves. Picking up his skull cap, the rabbi placed it, still dirty, on his head. The woman whose bonnet had fallen off clapped it back on, askew, its beaded front to the side. Pilitzky's men tugged at Gershon again, as though trying to shake him out of his clothes. The beadle still swayed back and forth with the scroll. Evidently the story was not to end happily. Men and women began to detach themselves from the crowd and to slip away, some going to close their shops, others running into their houses and locking the doors. "Don't run away, Jews," Pilitzky shouted. "There's no escape. I'll strangle you wherever you are. When I finish with you, you'll mourn the day your wretched mothers squeezed you from their leprous wombs."

"Magnanimous lord, we are not running away. Mighty benefactor, we await your pleasure."

"I have asked you something," Pilitzky shouted, turning to Jacob. "Answer me."

Jacob didn't remember the question. Pilitzky reached out as if to grab the teacher by his collar. But Jacob was too tall for him.

"Forgive me, my lord," Jacob bowed his head. "I have forgotten the question."

Pilitzky, having forgotten himself, looked confused. He had noticed that this Jew, unlike the others, spoke good Polish. His anger left him and he felt something akin to shame at having made such a display before these paupers, the survivors of Chmielnicki's blood bath. He had always considered himself a compassionate man. Tears came to his eyes. Prayers to Jesus and the apostles passed through his head. From boyhood on, he had expected to die young; a fortune teller had predicted an early end. Now he looked for some excuse to terminate this saturnalia. His turbulent spirit stood midway between contrition and anger. Should he ask forgiveness of the Jews, that wilful people God had chosen? There was a bitter taste in his mouth and his nose tickled. I wouldn't behave this way if my life weren't chaos. That cursed woman has ruined me. Suddenly he had an impulse to toss coins to the crowd. That would show them that he was no Haman. But when he reached into his pocket he remembered he didn't have a groschen, and he was overwhelmed with self-pity. That's what these Jews have done to me, he thought, bled me dry. Seeing the old beadle, swaying unsteadily with the holy scroll on his shoulder, he yelled, "Why did you bring out the scroll? How can that help you? It would be better if you followed what is written there instead of using it to mask your crimes. Carry it back to the synagogue, you old rascal."

From every side shouts came, "Carry back the scroll. Carry back the scroll." The lord of Pilitz had relented, the Jews sensed. The beadle gave a final sway and bore the scroll into the study house. But the men still held Gershon pinioned. Pilitzky's mood might change again. He surveyed the crowd, a bitter look in his eyes as if searching for another victim. Dumb Sarah walked into the square carrying an apronful of herbs. Having gone into the fields, she had not heard the noise of Pilitzky's arrival and knew nothing of what had happened. She saw the coach and horses, Pilitzky's men, Pilitzky himself, and Jacob, hat in hand, standing humbly before the lord of Pilitz. Sarah raised her arms, wailed, and the herbs fell from her apron. What she had dreaded had come to pass. Her nightmares had been true omens. Breaking through the crowd, she pushed her way to Jacob, and screaming wildly threw herself at Pilitzky's feet. Pilitzky turned pale and retreated. She followed him, crawling like a worm and clutching at his legs. "Have pity, Pan," she lamented in Polish. "Mercy, gentle lord. He's all I've got. I carry his child in my womb. Kill me instead. My head for his. Let him go free, Pan. Let him go free."

"Who is this woman? Get up."

"Forgive him, my lord. Forgive him. He's committed no crime. He's honest, my lord. A holy man."

Jacob bent to raise her and then paused, terrified. Only then did he realize that Sarah had given herself away: she had spoken. In the confusion, no one appeared to have understood what had happened. Then men spread their hands and raised their eyebrows; women clutched their heads; Pilitzky's servants momentarily let go of Gershon. Even the horses, until then standing silently, lost in equine meditations remote from the struggles of men, turned their heads. Gershon looked baffled and outraged. Like many overbearing men, he resented having things happen he could neither control nor comprehend. A woman slapped both of her cheeks screaming, "Oh, I've seen everything."

"What is this? Who is she?" Pilitzky asked.

"My lord, she's a mute."

"What? A mute?"

"Gracious lord, she's as dumb as a fish. Deaf and dumb."

"Yes, gracious lord, dumb, dumb, a mute." Cries came from all directions.

"Hey, rabbi, is that a fact? Is this woman a mute?" Pilitzky said, turning to the rabbi.

"Yes, my lord, she's the wife of the teacher. She's deaf and dumb. This is a miracle."

"Children, I'm going to faint"—and a woman fell to the ground.

"Help. Water! Water!"

"Oh, my God"—and another woman fainted.

Jacob, bending, pulled Sarah to her feet. Her limp body lay against his shoulder, supported by his arm; she trembled, gasping, sobbing. Pilitzky rested his hand on the hilt of his sword. "What is this, Jew? Some kind of farce?"

"No farce, my lord. She's deaf and dumb. Deaf as the wall and dumb as a fish."

"My lord, we all know she's mute," witnesses from the crowd attested.

"Are you prepared to swear to that?"

"My lord, we've invented nothing."

"Hey, you, Jew, is your wife really dumb?"

"Yes, my lord."

"Always been that way?"

"As long as we've been married."

Jacob did not consider this a lie since Sarah had assumed her role before stepping under the canopy. All around him the townswomen were screaming that it was indeed so, swearing by their husbands and their children that this was Dumb Sarah who everyone knew was unable to talk. Pilitzky's men stood gaping while their master considered this strange occurrence.

"I don't believe you, Jews, not a word of it. This is just another one of your tricks. You want to fool me and make me look ridiculous. Remember Jews, if this is a lie, you'll be flayed alive, I'll herd you into your synagogue and set it on fire. We'll roast you slowly, as sure as my name is Adam Pilitzky."

"Gracious lord, we are telling the truth."

6

Pilitzky realized the Jews were telling the truth. Their open mouths and bewildered looks told him this was a miracle. Adam Pilitzky had been waiting for a miracle ever since the start of the wars and invasions. One was needed to save Poland. Prior Chodecki's resistance at Czestochow and Stephan Czanecki's campaign against the Swedes, which had rallied the Polish armies and revived the cause of Catholicism, had seemed to be that miracle. Now from every side came reports of new wonders. An image of the Virgin had wept real tears which the people gathered in a silver chalice. On church steeples stone crosses flamed in the dark of night. Dead armies, dressed in the uniforms of a hundred years ago, marched against the enemies of Poland and drove them from fortified positions. Ghost riders were seen galloping on phantom horses. Legendary heroes, dressed in helmets and breastplates, brandished swords and spears as they led charges. Monks and nuns, long since residents of Paradise, put on bodies again and roamed the countryside comforting the people and urging them to pray.

Here a church bell rang by itself, and there an ancient coach was seen driving down a road into a wall and disappearing as if swallowed up. Birds spoke with human voices and a dog led a battalion out of ambush. In one village it had rained blood, in another fishes and toads. In one instance wine had been lacking for the mass and God's mother had opened her lips and wine had flowed out. An almost blind crone had watched a flaming ship flying the Polish ensign sail across the sky. These signs and portents had invigorated the nation's spirit and renewed its belief in heaven.

Nevertheless, Adam Pilitzky had seen no miracles himself and resented this. The devil subverted and denied the wonders of God in a thousand ways; hidden in every heart was some doubt. Often when Pilitzky lay awake thinking of what was going on in the country, Lucifer came and whispered in his ear: "Don't they all speak of miracles? The Greek Orthodox, the Protestants, even the infidel Turks? How does it come about that God sometimes rides with the Protestants bringing them victories? Why doesn't he visit them with the plagues of Pharaoh or rain down stones as he will on Gog and Magog?" Pilitzky listened to Lucifer; at heart, he may have believed man merely an animal who returns to dust, and hence condoned his wife's licentiousness.

The revolt of his serfs and the cruelties with which he had suppressed the rebellion had further mortified Pilitzky's spirit. He knew that widows and orphans sorrowed because of him. At night he had visions of bodies hanging from the gibbets, their feet blue, their eyes glassy, their tongues extended. He suffered from cramps and headaches; his skin itched. There were days when he prayed for death or planned suicide. Not even wine and vodka could calm him now. Nor were the pleasures of the body as intense as they had been. He was always on the lookout for new sensations to stave off impotency. Because of the perverseness of that witch Theresa, now only her infidelities aroused his lust. He made her describe her affairs in detail. When she had exhausted the catalog of her debauchery, he forced her to invent adventures. Husband and wife had driven each other into an insane labyrinth of vice. He procured for her and she procured for him. She watched him corrupt peasant girls and he eavesdropped on her and her lovers. He had warned her many times that he would stab her, she teased about poisoning his food. But both were pious, lit candles, went to confession, and contributed money for the building of churches and religious monuments. Often Adam Pilitzky opened the door of their private chapel and found Theresa, her cheeks wet with tears, a crucifix pressed to her bosom, kneeling before the altar deep in contemplation. Theresa spoke of entering a nunnery; Pilitzky toyed with the idea of becoming a monk.

Pilitzky could never have described the torments he had endured during the last few years. Only God, aware of all the temptations and pitfalls besetting man, and compassionately viewing His creatures' follies and weaknesses, knew how much Pilitzky had suffered through shame and guilt. What the lord of Pilitz wanted was a sign that some supernal eye looked down and took notice, some proof that more than blind chance governed the world. Now heaven, it seemed, had decided to put an end to his doubts.

Pilitzky looked at Sarah and Jacob, the wife clinging to the husband. No, this was no fraud. He could see the Jews glancing at each other and staring at the couple incredulously. There was a lump in Pilitzky's throat; he found it difficult to keep from crying. Then, remembering that the mute had spoken of Jacob as a holy man, he said in a firm voice, "Forgive me, Jacob. I did not mean to insult you. If you are truly a holy man as the mute has attested, I respect you even though you are a Jew."

"Gracious lord, there is nothing holy about me. I am an ordinary individual, a Jew like all the others; perhaps even less than they."

"What? Saints are all modest. Hey, there, men, let that crook Gershon go. I'll settle with him some other time. You are no longer my tenant, Gershon," Pilitzky said. "Don't step on my land again or let me see your face. If I find you trespassing, I'll unleash the dogs."

"Your excellency owes me money," Gershon said. His voice did not waver; his manner showed he did not fear the bluster of overlords. "I have leased the manor lands. I have a contract and your note."

"Huh? Jew, you have nothing. You can wipe yourself with those papers."

"My lord, this is not just. A man's word is sacred. There is a court in Poland."

"Drag me into court, will you, Jew? You're crazy, Jew. You'd be already swinging and the birds would be eating the flesh of your head, as the Bible says, if what just happened had not. You thief, you swindler. I've heard that you filch from the Jews, even. I intend to investigate and see you're punished. As for the court: I fear no one. I am the court and the law. I rule supreme on my manor. Poland is not France where the king tyrannizes over the nobles. Here we have more power than the king. We make and break our kings. Keep that in mind and you'll also keep your head on your shoulders."

"I have paid for the contract."

"What you paid, you got back a long time ago. I'll have no further dealings with you. Move—before I break every bone in your body."

There was a murmuring among the Jews. Gershon's friends and family whispered to him to leave the market place immediately. His wife and daughter tugged at his sleeves, begging him to come home. But Gershon shook his head; his nose wrinkled and his heavy under lip sagged. Powerless though a Jew was against a nobleman, Gershon did not intend to stand by and see himself ruined. He had friends who were richer and more eminent than Pilitzky. He knew that the lord of Pilitz had broken every law of church and state. Moreover, he was involved in law suits that threatened to ruin him. The nobility still preserved their code and demanded that notes and contracts be honored, even those made with the contemptible Jews. Gershon took a step forward.

"I am still the tenant until the expiration of my lease."

"All you are is a dead dog."

Adam Pilitzky turned violently, drew his sword, and ran at Gershon. The Jews wailed and screamed.

CHAPTER NINE

1

Jacob saw that he had lost control of himself. Satan fiddled and he danced. "Transgression draws transgression in its train," the Book of Aboth said, and this was surely true in his case. His lust for a forbidden woman had involved him in deception. An entire Jewish community—no, not merely one, a host of them—had been deluded into believing his wife was a mute. Now, grieving women sought out Sarah who was already in her eighth month and begged her to lay her hands on them and bless them. Nor would the elders of Pilitz hear of Jacob not accepting Pilitzky's offer. Gershon had lost the contract; Pilitzky warned that if Jacob refused to become his administrator, he would import one from another town. He even threatened to expel the Jews from Pilitz. A deputation of the elders, led by the rabbi, came to plead with Jacob. Gershon let it be tacitly understood that he was not opposed to this arrangement; Jacob should administer the estate for the time being. Gershon's appraisal was that the teacher, unable to distinguish rye from wheat, would mismanage Pilitzky's interests and this would lead the nobleman to conclude that Gershon was indispensable.

As is usual in the affairs of men, the relationships were complex, and all were based on deception. Woe to the house founded on falsehood. But what could Jacob do? If he told the truth, Sarah and he would be burned at the stake. Sacred though the truth was, the law did not permit one to sacrifice oneself for it.

Lying awake at night, Jacob addressed God: "I know that I have forfeited the world to come, but nevertheless you are still God and I remain your creation. Castigate me, Father, I will submit to your punishment willingly."

The punishment might arrive any day. Sarah would shortly go into labor, and might scream and talk. The truth would sooner or later make itself known. Jacob waited for the rod to strike and worked; there was more than enough for him to do. God had blessed the fields with plenty; the Polish and Swedish armies had not trampled the newly sown crops that year. Jacob woke early and retired late; the lord of Pilitz expected a profit. Gershon also anticipated getting a covert share. However, Jacob, unlike Gershon, received no contract and was only Pilitzky's manager, supervising the peasants and dealing with the grain merchants. He took as wages merely what he needed to subsist.

It was strange to be in the fields surrounded by vegetation again. Sarah and Jacob lived in the house Gershon had built for himself near the castle. Jacob's own house as well as the school he had begun to build remained unfinished. The town was looking for a new teacher—meanwhile someone tutored the children a few hours a day—and the current joke was that since Jacob was managing Pilitz, Gershon should take over the cheder.

Jacob had always been aware that everything in this world is transitory. What was man? Today alive, tomorrow in his grave. The Talmud spoke of the world as a wedding; the poet in the liturgy compared man to a drifting cloud, to a wilting flower, to a fading dream. Yes, everything passed. But never before had Jacob felt the transience of things so keenly. One week a field of grain stood ripening; the next the field was bare. The days were now bright and clear, but rain and snow would soon follow. Jacob had become important in Pilitz; the lord of the manor was now accessible to him. When he passed peasants, they tipped their caps and addressed him as "Pan." The Jews considered him the husband of a holy woman. Jacob knew the end of all this would be disgrace and a walk to the gallows. But meanwhile he saw to it that the grain was harvested, threshed, and stored. He superintended the autumn plowing and the sowing of the winter crop. What he had learned in those years of slavery had become useful. Now when Sarah and he retired at night, they discussed not only the Torah but also the affairs of the manor. Even though Jacob did not keep the account books, little by little he uncovered evidence of Gershon's bad practices. True, Pilitzky in turn stole from the peasantry and he who robs a thief is guilty of no crime; nevertheless Gershon had broken the Eighth Commandment, made enemies for Israel, and committed sacrilege. Well, but everyone has his temptations.

Jacob had risen in the world, but he knew his ascent was of that kind of which it is written, "Pride goeth before a fall." The peasants did not seek to trick him, as they had Gershon, but followed his instructions and even offered him advice. The inhabitants of the castle, Pilitzky's dependents as well as his servants, respected Jacob. The dogs, whose ferocity had made Gershon tremble, for some mysterious reason took to Jacob immediately, wagging their tails when he approached the gate. Everyone in the castle was kind to him, and Lady Pilitzky sent a maid to help the pregnant and mute Sarah. Pilitzky, himself, went out of his way to talk to Jacob and admired the manager's fluent Polish. Gershon had been another sort, an ignoramus unable to answer any of his patron's questions about Jews and their religion. Jacob replied quoting the holy books. Accustomed to discussing difficult questions lucidly, he invented parables the gentile mind could accept. Pilitzky brought up the same problems that had disturbed Wanda.

One day when Pilitzky sat with Jacob in the library showing him a Bible concordance in Latin which had Hebrew marginalia, Lady Pilitzky entered. Jacob rose from his chair and bowed deeply. Theresa Pilitzky was a small, plump woman with a round face, short neck, and a high bosom. Her blond hair, twisted in a coronet, reminded Jacob of a Rosh Hashana chalah. She had on a pleated, black silk dress, decorated with ribbons, and around her neck lay a gold cross set with jewels. She had a small nose, full lips, bright dark eyes and a smooh forehead. Jacob had been told that she behaved like a whore, but she walked with sprightly steps and seemed almost girlish, despite her stoutness. She smiled upon seeing the men and her cheeks dimpled. Pilitzky winked at her, "This is Jacob."

"Of course, I've seen you many times from my window."

Lady Pilitzky offered her hand to Jacob who hesitated an instant and then, bowing again, carried her fingers to his lips. One more sin, Jacob thought, kissing her hand, and blushing to the roots of his hair. Pilitzky laughed.

"Well, now that that's done let's have a glass of wine together."

"Forgive me, my lord, but my religion forbids it."

Pilitzky's body tensed.

"Oh, so you're forbidden. It's all right to fleece the Christians, but you mustn't drink wine with them. And who forbids it? The Talmud, naturally, which teaches you how to cheat the Christians."

"The Talmud makes no mention of Christians, only idolators."

"The Talmud considers Christians idolators. Your people gave the world the Bible, but then you denied God's only begotten son, thereby turning from the Father. Today Chmielnicki punishes you; tomorrow another *hetman* will continue your castigation. The Jews will never have peace until they recognize the truth and . . ."

Lady Pilitzky frowned. "Adam, these discussions have no value."

"No, I will not keep back the truth. That Jew Gershon was a crook and a jackass besides. He didn't know a thing, not even his own Bible. Jacob appears to be not only honest but well-educated. That's why I want to ask him a few questions."

"Not now, Adam. He's busy seeing to the fields."

"Where are the fields running? Sit down, Jew. I'm not going to hurt you. Sit here. Very good! Neither Lady Pilitzky nor I believe in forcing our Faith on anyone. We don't have an inquisition here as they do in Spain. Poland is a free country, too free for its own good. That's why it's collapsing. But that's not your fault. Let me ask you this. You've been waiting for the Messiah for a thousand years—what am I talking about?—for more than fifteen hundred, and he doesn't appear. The reason is clear. He has come already and revealed God's truth. But you are a stubborn people. You keep yourself apart. You regard our meat as unclean, our wine as an abomination. You are not permitted to marry our daughters. You believe you are God's chosen people. Well, what has he chosen you for? To live in dark ghettos and wear yellow patches. I've been out of the country and seen how Jews live abroad. They're all rich and all they think about is profit. Everywhere they're treated like spiders. Why don't you take a good look at yourself and throw away the Talmud? Perhaps the Christians are right after all. Have any of you visited heaven?''

"Really these religious arguments are stupid," Theresa Pilitzky protested.

"What's so stupid about them? People have to discuss things. I'm not speaking to him in anger, but as an equal. If he can convince me that the Jews are right, I'll become a Jew." Pilitzky laughed.

"I can convince no one, my lord," Jacob began to stammer. "I inherited my faith from my parents and I follow it to the best of my ability."

"The idolators had fathers and mothers too. And they were taught that a stone is God. But you Jews demanded the destruction of their temples and the annihilation of their children. The Old Testament says so. Doesn't that prove that one doesn't necessarily follow the parents' faith?"

"The Christians also regard the Bible as sacred."

"Naturally. But one must be logical. Everyone but your people and the infidel Turks have accepted Christianity. You Jews consider yourself cleverer than anyone in Europe or the world. All right, God loves you. What kind of love?—your wives are raped and your children buried alive.''

Jacob swallowed hard. "Those were the acts of the Christians."

"What? The Cossacks are no more Christians than I am Zoroastrian. Only the Catholics are Christian. The Russian Orthodox are as idolatrous as their allies the Turks. Protestants are even worse. But this is all irrelevant, Jew."

"None of us knows the ways of Providence, my lord. The Catholics also suffer. They wage war against each other . . ." Jacob broke off in the middle of his sentence.

For a moment Adam Pilitzky meditated in silence on Jacob's words.

"Of course we suffer. As the Bible says, man was born to suffer. But we suffer for a reason. Our souls are purified through what we endure and rise to heaven. But the real torment begins for the unbeliever after death."

Theresa Pilitzky shook her head. "Really, Adam, where's this getting you? The truth cannot be proved. It can only be found here." Theresa Pilitzky pointed to her heart.

"Yes, that is true, my lady," Jacob said softly.

"Well, I suppose it is. But of what use is this stiff-necked clinging to your faith? In your misguided way, you are attentive to God, and your synagogues are always filled. Once when I was in Lublin, I walked past your prayer houses. Such ecstatic singing! A song rose as if from a thousand voices. But a few years later ten thousand Jews were slaughtered. I talked to someone who saw the Cossacks enter Lublin. The Jews crushed each other in their panic. More died from being trampled on than were killed by the invaders. While this went on, was the sky any less blue? Did the sun stop shining? Where was the God you praise and beseech, whose dear children you claim to be? How do you deal with these facts, Jew? How can you sleep at night remembering?"

"When you're tired enough, your eyes close by themselves."

"I see you avoid answering me . . .''

"He's right, Adam, he's right. What's there to say? Can we explain our misfortunes any better than he can his? Even searching for an answer is blasphemous. You know that very well."

Pilitzky drew his eyeballs downward and stared cross-eyed at Lady Pilitzky.

"I know nothing, Theresa. Sometimes I think that the Epicureans and Cynics were right. Have you ever heard of Democritus, Jew?"

"No, my lord."

"Democritus was a philosopher who said that chance ruled everything. The Church has proscribed his writings, but I read him. He believed in neither idols nor God. The world, he said, was the result of blind powers."

"Don't repeat those heresies," Theresa Pilitzky said, interrupting.

"Perhaps he was right."

"Really, Adam."

"Very well, I'll go and lie down. Your eyes close by themselves," he said, echoing Jacob. "Isn't there something you have to say to Jacob, Theresa?"

"Yes, there is."

"Goodbye, then, and don't be afraid of us. Is your wife really a mute?"

"Yes, my lord."

"That means that miracles also happen among the Jews, doesn't it?"

"Yes, my lord."

"Well, I'll go and take a nap."

2

As he left the room, Pilitzky glanced back over his shoulder. Jacob bowed. Lady Pilitzky slowly moved her fan of peacock feathers.

"Sit down. So! Where do such discussions ever lead? One has to trust that God knows how to manage the world. When the Swedes took the manor, they flogged me in my own castle. I thought it was the end. But the Almighty wanted me to continue living."

Jacob paled. "They flogged you, my lady?"

Lady Pilitzky smiled.

"My dear Jacob, the rod is not particular about rank. Dukes, ladies, your royal highnesses even, are all the same to it. It strikes. The officers found it more amusing just because I was an aristocrat."

"Why did they do this, my lady?"

"Because I said no to the general. My husband was in hiding and I had no one to protect me. If my suitor had been young and handsome, or at least healthy" (Lady Pilitzky's tone changed) "I might have been tempted. 'All's fair in love and war,' as they say. But not with that ugly ape. One look and I said, 'Sir, death is preferable.' "

"I had thought such behavior was limited to Muscovites and Cossacks."

Lady Pilitzky smiled. "Ah, the Swedes are angels? No, Jacob, all men are alike. Frankly, I don't blame them. Women have only one use for them. A child must nurse and doesn't care if the breast belongs to a peasant or a princess. Men are like children."

Demureness and coquetry met in Lady Pilitzky's smile. She looked Jacob straight in the eye and fluttered her lids slightly. Jacob's neck became hot.

"A man has his wife."

"What? To begin with, in wartime, wives don't count. Secondly, one gets tired of a woman. My tailor makes me an expensive dress; so after I wear it three times I'm bored with it and give it to one of my husband's cousins. Men feel the same way. A woman's no longer attractive to a man when he can have her as much as he pleases—and he's off after another. But why should I tell you this? You're a man—tall and with blue eyes . . ."

The blood rushed to Jacob's face. "The Jews do not behave so."

Lady Pilitzky petulantly shook her fan. "Jew or Tartar, a man is a man. Why, your men were allowed a host of wives. The great kings and prophets had harems."

"Now that's forbidden."

"Who forbade it?"

"Rabbi Gershom, the Light of the Diaspora. He issued the edict."

"The Christians forbid it too. But what does human nature care about edicts? I don't condemn a man for wanting. If he gets a woman to say 'yes' I don't condemn her either. My view is that everything comes from God—including lust. And not everyone's a saint, and not every saint was always saintly. Anyway, how does it hurt God? Some take the position that a secret sin where there is no sacrilege injures no one. My husband spent a few years in Italy. There the ladies have both a husband and lover. The lover is called an 'amico.' When a lady goes to the theater, she is escorted by both her gentlemen. Don't forget this happens in the shadow of the Vatican. The amico is often a cardinal or some other Church dignitary. The Pope knows of it, and, if it were such a crime would he tolerate it?"

There was a pause in the conversation. Finally, Jacob said, "Nothing like that occurs among the Jews. A man may not even glance at another woman."

"Just the same they do glance. I know a man's a hypocrite if he claims to be only interested in his wife. Let me ask you something."

"Yes, my lady."

"Where are you from? How does it happen you settled here? Don't think it odd that I pry; I have my reasons. It seems strange that you married a mute. Most Jews aren't as good-looking as you, or as well-bred, and you speak good Polish. You could have had the prettiest girl."

Jacob shook his head. "This is my second marriage."

"What happened to your first wife?"

"The Cossacks killed her and our children."

"In what town?"

"I am from Zamosc."

"Well, that is sad. What do they have against the women and children? And where does your present wife come from?"

"From near Zamosc."

"Why did you marry her? There must have been other women."

"Only a few. Most of the women were killed."

"You must have liked her. It can't be denied that she's good-looking."

"Yes, I did."

Lady Pilitzky rested her fan on her bosom.

"I'll be frank with you, Jacob. Your enemies among the Jews—don't think you don't have any—are spreading the story that your wife is not as mute as she pretends. When my husband first heard this, he was out of his mind with rage, and he wanted to put your Sarah to the test. But I dissuaded him. His idea was to shoot off a pistol behind her and see what happened. I told him you don't play such tricks on a pregnant woman. Adam Pilitzky listens to me. He does whatever I tell him to. In this one respect he's an unusually good husband. You understand yourself that the Jews of Pilitz will suffer if there was no miracle. The clergy in this part of the country, particularly the Jesuits, have their own interests to look out for. All that I want you to know is that you have a close friend in me. Don't be shy and secretive. We are all only flesh and blood underneath our clothes. I want to protect you, Jacob, and I am afraid that you may need protection.''

Jacob raised his head slowly.

"Who is spreading these rumors?''

"People have mouths. Gershon is sly and even conspires against my husband. He will come to a bad end, but before that happens he will make trouble.''

3

Fear such as he had felt when Zagayek sent for him, arose in Jacob. But now Sarah's life was in danger, also. The Jesuits had interests to protect. Pistols were to be fired near Sarah! I am in a trap, thought Jacob. I must flee. But the child must be born first. With winter approaching, where could he run? What course should he follow—tell Lady Pilitzky the truth? Deny the rumor? He sat silent and helpless, ashamed of his cowardice. Lady Pilitzky surveyed him expertly out of the corner of her eyes, a polished smile on her lips.

"Don't be afraid, Jacob. You remember the saying, 'A great wind but a small rain.' Nothing bad will happen.''

"I trust not. Thank you, my lady. I can't thank you enough.''

"You can thank me later. Have you seen the castle?''

"No, only this room.''

"Come, I will show it to you. The invaders did a great deal of damage, but they left something. At times I agree with my husband—everything's collapsing. The peasants report having seen a huge comet in the sky with a tail stretching from one horizon to the other. It's as it was at the end of the first millennium, or during the Black Plague.''

"When did they see the comet? I've seen nothing.''

"Nor have I. But my husband has. It's a sign that we can expect some cataclysm: war, pestilence or flood. The Turks are sharpening their scimitars. Suddenly the Muscovites are a power. The Prussians, of course, are always ready for pillage. 'Eat, drink, and be merry. For tomorrow we die.' ''

"A life lived in constant fear loses its flavor.''

"What? Some have the opposite attitude. I've been through one war after another. But I know how to keep calm when others shiver. I laugh when most people cry. 'Draw the curtains,' I order my maid, and say to myself, 'Theresa, you have only one more hour to live.' Do you ever drink in bed?''

"Only when I'm sick . . .''

"No, when you're well. My husband's room is across the hall from mine and so I can isolate myself completely. I prop myself up with a pillow and order the maid to bring me wine. I like mead especially, although it's supposed to be a peasant's drink. They call it 'the nectar of the Slavs' in other countries. But I'm happy when I'm just this side of being drunk. When my mind's a trifle foggy, I don't worry; I lose all sense of obligation. I only do those things that please me.''

"Yes, my lady."

"Follow me."

As Lady Pilitzky led Jacob through the halls and chambers, he did not know what to admire first: the furniture, the rugs, the tapestries or the paintings. Everywhere were trophies of the hunt: stags' and boars' heads staring down from the walls; stuffed pheasants, peacocks, partridges, grouse, looking as if they were alive. In the armory were displayed swords, spears, helmets, and breastplates. Lady Pilitzky pointed out the portraits of the lords of Pilitz and their families. Pictures of the kings of Poland were also on the walls: the Casimirs, the Wladislaws, the Jagelos, King Stephan Batory, along with famous statesmen from the ancient families of Czartoryski, and Zamoyski. Whichever way he turned, Jacob's eyes fell on crosses, swords, nude statuary, paintings of battles, tournaments, and the chase. The very air of the castle smelled of violence, idolatry, and concupiscence. Lady Pilitzky threw open the door of a room in the center of which was a large canopied bed. Jacob caught sight of himself in a mirror, but his image, standing as it were in deep water, was barely recognizable. He saw himself hatless, blushing, his hair and beard disheveled, resembling, it seemed, one of the savages portrayed in the other room. "It isn't the best taste to show the bedrooms," Lady Pilitzky said, "but you Jews don't go in too much for courtly forms. My father had a manor Jew whom we were all fond of. He was very vivacious and would dress up like a bear when we had a ball. You know, he could dance exactly like a bear! But he wouldn't drink and though he took part in the fun, he stayed sober. My father always said only a Jew could do that."

"He had to do it."

"Do you know, not only could he speak in rhymes but in a mixture of Polish, Yiddish, and the patois of the peasants? The Jews considered him a scholar. He married his daughter to the son of a rabbi and the fellow lived at his expense and just sat swaying over prayer books."

"What happened?"

"You mean to the old fellow? He was killed by brigands."

Strange, but Jacob had known she was going to say that. His skin prickled. When Lady Pilitzky spoke, he had the impression she understood that what she told him had made him sad.

"Well, he had had a full life. But what difference does it make how long one lives? One thing is certain; we all die. Sometimes I find it impossible to believe that the world will go on after I'm gone, that the sun will shine, the trees blossom—but I won't be there. No, it's unimaginable. But then, one often hears old people speak of things that happened before one was born. Well, while one's here one longs for happiness, particularly at night. I lie by myself with the darkness surrounding me. Jacob, have you ever seen a werewolf?''

"No, my lady."

"Nor have I. But there are such creatures. There are nights when I want to crawl out into the dark on my hands and knees and howl."

"Why, my lady?"

"Oh, for no reason. I may decide to visit you one of these nights, Jacob, and then be on your guard because I'm dangerous."

Suddenly Lady Pilitzky took hold of Jacob's wrists and said, "I am not so old yet. Kiss me."

"My lady, I am not allowed to. My religion forbids it. I must humbly beg your pardon, your excellency."

"Don't apologize. I'm a fool and you're a Jew. You have borscht, not blood in your veins."

"My lady, I fear God."

"Well, go to him."

4

It was a warm, summerlike evening in the month of Elul. The crops had been harvested and the fields lay bare. A tepid mist rose from the empty furrows. Jacob as he walked heard the croak of frogs; he kept his eyes fixed on the heavens where a half moon shone, attended by a brilliant blue-green star twinkling with a strange light. Jacob could almost see this small point as the vast orb it really was. Here on earth he was as good as destroyed by the dangers hemming him in on every side. But it was a comfort to realize that God and his angels and seraphim dwelt in their heavenly mansions. Jacob, not wanting to lay himself open to investigation and persecution, had to be careful about opening a book in Pilitz; he did not want to be known as a scholar and certainly not as a cabalist. But here on the manor, he could study whatever he wanted in his free moments. He had brought with him the *Book of Creation, Angel Raziel,* and the *Zohar* to use as charms against devils and to put under Sarah's pillow when she was in labor. These were the books he kept returning to now. A man like himself could not expect to understand what was written in such volumes, but the very words had a sacred look about them. Merely gazing at a page edified him. Even if you were a sinner, it was a privilege to exist surrounded by so many spheres, chariots, powers, and potentates. Jacob remembered from his readings in *The Tree of Life* that evil, synonymous with absolute emptiness, only arose because God had contracted and hidden his face. Repentance could change sins to pieties, justice to mercy. A transgression might at times even lead to good. So, he, Jacob, had sinned when he had lusted for Wanda, but now Wanda had become Sarah, the daughter of Abraham, and in giving birth to a child was about to summon a Jewish soul from the Throne of Glory. It had been right for him to rebuff Lady Pilitzky but would his virtue help him avoid the traps lying all around him?

He was walking on an embankment between fields and insects and other small creatures scurried from beneath his advancing tread. They had received their share of wisdom, but the Creator had left their bodies unprotected. Whoever had feet trod on them; they killed and fed on each other. Yet Jacob found no sadness anywhere but within himself. The summer night throbbed with joy; from all sides came music. Warm winds bore the smells of grain, fruit, and pine trees to him. Itself a cabalistic book, the night was crowded with sacred names and symbols—mystery upon mystery. In the distance where sky and earth merged, lightning flashed, but no thunder followed. The stars looked like letters of the alphabet, vowel points, notes of music. Sparks flickered above the bare furrows. The world was a parchment scrawled with words and song. Every now and then Jacob heard a murmur in his ear as if some unseen being was whispering to him. He was surrounded by powers, some good, some evil, some cruel, some merciful, but each with its own nature and its own task to perform. At times he heard laughter, at other times sighs. He tripped but his foot was guided to the ground. The struggle was going on without as well as within him. He trembled thinking of Lady Pilitzky's wrath but thanked God continually that he had not involved himself with her. He longed for Sarah who might already be in labor, and wished he were home. The maid was in the house, and in an emergency the servants' midwife could be sent for, but Jacob wanted a daughter of Israel to bring the baby into the world. He would not stay on in the manor during the High Holidays. The moment he had finished his most important work he would move back to Pilitz. That is if he were still alive.

"Don't be frightened," Jacob said to himself to keep up his courage, and suddenly a few lines of commentary entered his mind. They concerned the Biblical passage in which the patriarch Jacob blesses his son Jehudah, saying, "Jehudah thee shall thy brethren praise." His teacher at cheder had given the following gloss: Jehudah had been hiding in a corner from his father afraid that he would be reminded of his transgression with Tamar. But Jacob had said reassuringly, "Don't be afraid and don't tremble. Thy brethren will praise you because King David will descend from your loins."

So many years had passed since he had been a school boy, but his teacher's voice still rang in his ears. The old man had died a martyr; Jacob could see his wrinkled face and his gesticulating hands. He remembered the cheder boys also, each with his particular facial expression and mannerism. Where were Moishe'le, Kople, Chaim Berl? Probably dead; and inhabitants now of higher worlds, where thousands upon thousands of mysteries had already been revealed to them. As Jacob walked, his shadow paced with him, a double shadow, composed of a light shell and a dark kernel. He had come to a swamp and, fearful of sinking into the slime, retraced his steps and made a long detour. Nets of moonlight fell in front of him; he heard the hissing and rapid retreat of frightened snakes. Sorcery lay all around him. The castle appeared and disappeared, one moment in front of him, the next to the rear, and he realized that he was lost. He noticed a light in one of the castle windows and thought he caught a glimpse of Lady Pilitzky.

When, at length, he reached home, he found Sarah preparing supper on a tripod, and looking almost girlish despite her pregnancy. Thank God she was all right. The pine branches over which she was cooking blazed and smoked and Jacob smelled the odors of resin and fresh milk. Before he had a chance to speak, Sarah pointed to the rear. On a log outside the house sat three women and a man who had heard of Sarah's miracle and come to be blessed.

Jacob covered his face with his hands. His lies had made him a party to this abominable fraud. These people had left home, wasted their money, exhausted themselves to seek out Sarah. He walked outside and saw a broad-shouldered man with a ragged beard, heavy eyebrows, and a pimply nose. The man's tattered coat was unbuttoned revealing his hairy chest and long fringed garment. A beggar's sack stood close by on the ground. The man rose upon seeing Jacob.

The three women were all small and wore kerchiefs and aprons. One of them had a bundle in her lap, the second a basket; the third nibbled on a piece of turnip. They also rose when Jacob appeared.

"Good evening, visitors. Bless you."

"Good evening, rabbi," the man answered in a deep, gruff voice.

"I am not a rabbi," Jacob said, "only a humble Jew."

"God has granted you a saint for a wife," one of the women answered, "so you must be a saint also."

<hr />

5

The guests were invited to remain for the night and Sarah prepared supper for them. When the meal was over she blessed the travelers, placing her hands on the women's heads and mouthing a silent prayer over the man. Then, knowing that this was a wasted evening, she wearily retired to her bed in the alcove. There would be no studying of the Torah that night; the guests had to be hospitably treated. Though the women had had beds made up for them in the adjoining bedroom, and the man his in the shed, none of the travelers felt like retiring and they walked out into the warm evening. Jacob followed, anticipating that this would be one of those nights when he would not close his eyes. The incident with Lady Pilitzky had made his position untenable. He expected to be arrested at any moment.

As always the talk turned to the catastrophe. In a rasping voice, the man, Zeinvel Bear, told how he had fled Chmielnicki's Cossacks.

"Yes, I ran. No, my body ran. I was scared. I meant to stay with my family, but my feet said 'no.' Look, I'm a wanderer now. Well, in the old days I just stayed put. All I did was pound cleats into shoes. So how did I, a shoemaker, know where to go? I'd heard of two hamlets, Lipcy and Maidan. In Lipcy there was this fellow who would walk through fire for me. Only a peasant, but a builder and wood carver too. The count humored him, let him dress like one of the gentry. I made his boots. Such boots aren't made any more. The king's aren't as good. But Maidan had a bad reputation. The peasants there were sorcerers and brigands, and secret allies of the murderers. So, there I stood at the crossroads, wanting to get to Lipcy, but not knowing whether it was right or left. Suddenly I saw a dog. Where had it come from? Out of the earth. It wagged its tail, and pointed its nose straight at me. It couldn't talk, but it was saying, 'Follow me.' It started off down one of the roads and kept turning its head. It was making sure that I was following. Where did it lead me? Right into Lipcy. When I saw the town I went to pat the dog and give it a piece of bread. But it vanished before my eyes. I knew then that it wasn't a dog at all but a messenger sent from heaven."

"Did the gentile really hide you?"

"I lived in the granary for weeks and he brought me everything I needed."

"What became of your family?"

"None of them are left."

The woman with the basket nodded her head.

"Heaven wanted you to be saved, so you were. But why was I kept alive? My husband and my little swallows were killed in front of me. Woe to a mother who must endure that. I begged them to do away with me first but they wanted to torture me. Two Cossacks held me while the others did their dirty work. They discussed the plans that they had for me. One of them had a rabbit and they were going to sew it into my stomach. Suddenly there was a scream and they ran like crazy. I still don't know who screamed. It was such an awful yell I get cold shivers even now when I think of it."

"They must have thought it was some soldiers."

"What soldiers?"

The woman, still holding on to her turnip, took a bite and spat it out. "Trine, tell them about the Cossacks," she said to the woman with the bundle.

Trine didn't answer.

"What's wrong? Are you angry?"

"What's there to tell?"

"She was the wife of a Cossack for three years."

"Be quiet. Why talk? It was worse than when the temple was destroyed. I look old, but I'm not as old as all that. I'll be thirty-six on the fast day, the seventeenth of Tammuz. My husband was a scholar and known all over Poland. When the rabbis were stumped by a question, they came to him. He would pick up a book and open it: there was the answer. They wanted to make him assistant rabbi, but he would have no part of it. 'When the town buys you bread, soon you wish you were dead.' He sat and studied and I took care of our drygoods store. When a fair opened, I went there with our stock, and God did not forsake me. My only grief was that I had no children. Ten years after our marriage, my mother-in-law (may it not be held against her) said that my husband should divorce me because I was barren. We married young. I was eleven and he twelve. He was bar-mitzvahed in my father's house. My mother-in-law had the law on her side, but my husband answered, 'Trine is mine.' He liked to talk in rhyme. He would have been a good wedding jester. Well, the murderers came. We all ran to hide, but he put on his prayer shawl and walked out to meet them. They made him dig his own grave. As he dug, he prayed. I sat in the cellar for days and I didn't have the strength to rise. I fainted from hunger. The others went out at night to hunt for food. I was already in the other world and I saw my mother. There was music and I didn't walk but floated like a bird. My mother flew beside me. We came to two mountains with a pass between. The pass was as red as sunset and smelled of the spices of Paradise. My mother skimmed through, but when I tried to follow someone drove me back."

"An angel?" the shoemaker asked.

"I don't know."

"What happened then?"

"I cried, 'Mother, why are you leaving me?' I couldn't make out her answer. It was just a faint echo in my ear. I opened my eyes and someone was dragging me. It was dark out. I was being pulled from the cellar by a Cossack. I begged him to kill me, but those who want to die live. He tied me to his horse. His name was Vassil."

"Is that the one you married?"

"Married-shmarried."

"Where did he take you?"

"Who knows? Some place on the steppes. We rode day and night. Maybe a week, maybe a month. I didn't even know when it was Sabbath."

"So?"

"Please let me alone."

"He kept her for three years," the woman with the basket said.

"I'll bet you had children by him, huh?" Zeinvel Bear asked.

His question remained unanswered.

No one spoke for a while, and everyone looked up at the moon. Then Zeinvel Bear asked, "What about the steppes? Is it like here?"

"It's beautiful, beautiful. They have strange birds there that talk like people. The grass is very tall and you have to watch out for snakes. The horses are small but faster than our big ones. The Cossacks ride bareback and laugh at anyone who uses a saddle. The women ride too. All the men wear a single earring, and they carry riding crops. When they get angry, they hit with their whips, first from the right, then from the left. They'll beat their own mothers. When a boy comes of age, he and his father wrestle in front of the village. They call it *stanitza*. If the son throws the father, they're jubilant, even the mother. We milk cows but they milk mares. I saw a lot of Tartars where I was. The Tartars shave off their hair and leave only a pigtail. They gamble with hard-boiled eggs on holidays. We do everything inside the house, but they wash and cook outside. They make a fire in a hole, and if they don't have wood, they burn cow dung. They don't have a king. If they have to decide something, all the men get together and talk it over. Every Cossack has his own sword and saber. If a man suspects his wife's unfaithful, he just kills her and no one says anything. Everyone sings there, even the women. At dusk they sit around in a circle and an old man starts the chant and the others join in. They also know how to dance and play musical instruments.

"When I got there, I was more dead than alive. My Cossack had ridden with me all day and half of the night. We didn't eat much, mostly only mushrooms and berries and whatever else he could find in the forest. When he went to look for food, he'd tie his horse to a tree and me to the horse. One time it started to rain and thunder and I tried to get free. But when they tie you up, you stay tied. The horse got frightened too and started to stamp his hoofs and neigh. He came back carrying a wild boar. I refused to put the meat in my mouth. He'd roasted it but it was still half raw. They all eat meat that's hard as a rock and filled with blood. I started to vomit, but he pushed the filthy stuff into my mouth. When a Cossack stops beating his wife, it means he doesn't love her any more. He doesn't beat her in private, but outside in front of everyone, and while he's doing it, he talks to the neighbors. All the men have beards just like the Jews.

"Where was I? Oh, yes, he takes me to the *stanitza* and I can't speak a word of their language. I already had hair on my head, but not as much as the Cossack women. Everyone came to watch him untie me from the horse. An old woman, dressed in pants and as ugly as a witch, began to mumble and spit. It was his mother. She ran at him and began to hit him with her fists and he drove her away with his whip. Then a young woman—it was his wife—came rushing up, screaming and cursing. I stood there like a clay image, ragged, half-naked, barefoot, as emaciated as the dead. I didn't know what to do but they all kept pointing at me as if asking, 'What do you need such a carcass for?' They looked me over as if I were a freak. He had already defiled me but I started to make my confession. What does a woman remember? 'Hear, O Israel.' 'I put my spirit into thy hands.' And a few benedictions. I spoke to God in Yiddish, knowing He understands all languages. 'Father in heaven, take me to you. Death is better than such a life.' But when one wants to go, one doesn't. They brought me into the house and put me to tending geese. They tried the Cossack for bringing home a foreign woman. The young men wanted to behead him, but the old men sided with him.

"What? No, I have no children. That's all I would have needed. He had children by the other one, and they loved me more than their own mother. She'd fly into rages when he wasn't around and beat me until I bled. But then she'd get sorry and bring me a bowl of soup. At first I wouldn't eat unkosher food but finally I had to. I threw up more than I swallowed. They know nothing about Jews. They live like savages. Do you know how they take a bath? They go outside and the husband pours a bucket over his wife and then she pours one over him. All the while the neighbors chat. When they kill a pig, it's a great event. Instead of cutting off its head, they all stab it with spears—men, women, and children. The old crones run up with a pot and catch the blood.

"They got to like me. Even the old bitch. I learned some Cossack, and they picked up some Yiddish. The old woman was always fighting with her daughter-in-law and she began to make up to me. I understood about one word in ten, but she kept on raving and chattering until I had water on the ear. You know they hardly fed her. She slept on a pile of straw and was half eaten by vermin. She didn't have a tooth in her head. Her son didn't know she existed. I gave her whatever I could. When she was dying, she left me her bracelets. I hid them carefully. The daughter-in-law would have devoured me if she had known.

"I thought about only one thing, running away. But where can you run to on the steppes? There are wild animals everywhere. It's so hot in summer that the earth burns your feet. In the winter the snow is piled as high as your head. I didn't have clothes or money. But even if you have money there's not much to do with it. One thing I did not forget: I was a daughter of Israel. When I opened my eyes in the morning, I said, 'I thank Thee.' He'd ask me, 'What's that you're mumbling?' and I'd answer, 'None of your business.' If I'd known their language I could have converted them. They said to me openly, 'We want to become Jews.' If I'd been a man something would have come of that. But what use is a woman? I myself can't tell up from down. They know a little about the Christian holidays, but it's all topsy-turvy. Their priest has a wife. If his wife dies, he has to take another right away. Until he does, they won't listen to him bleating. During Lent they don't eat milk, butter, cheese, or eggs. Only cabbage and vodka. They have everything there but salt and wine which are as expensive as gold. The country's fine except for the flies and locusts which descend like the plagues of Egypt. And they give you elflocks. . . ."

"How did you manage to get away?"

"What's the difference? I'm here. My mother came to me in a dream and told me to leave. When a Tartar passed through, I gave him the old woman's bracelets. He sold me what he had on him—a *bashmet* and a pair of their shoes— they're called *tshuviakis*. I started off trusting in God and good angels to lead me. A small flame ran before me and showed me the road. If I'm lying, may I not see another Yom Kippur. Animals chased me. A huge bird swooped down and tried to carry me off. I screamed and it flew away. But, dear friends, if I told you everything, we would be here for three days and nights. I got help. Yes, help was sent to me. But to whom or what was I running? I didn't even find a grave. I am all by myself in God's world, shamed and despised. When I remember all I went through, I spit on myself.''

"So why have you come to be blessed?'' Zeinvel Bear asked.

"I keep wandering. So as not to stay in one place. Perhaps there is some comfort for me somewhere in the world. When that blessed woman put her hands on me, a stone dropped from my heart.''

Zeinvel Bear pointed with his finger, "See, a falling star!''

6

The door of Lady Pilitzky's bedroom opened. The moon shone through the curtains. Lady Pilitzky opened her eyes. "Is that you, Adam?'' she asked in a soft, intimate voice.

"Yes, Theresa. Did I wake you?''

"No, I was just napping.''

"I can't sleep. What should I do about that Jew? About all the Jews? I let in a few and suddenly there's a city. Savitzky is boiling. He's already consigned me to hell. Our dear neighbors are also conspiring. Each of them has his own little Jew, but when it comes to me, they're all pious Christians. This business with that mute is a farce. Even the Jews are laughing at me. It's just another of those damned Jewish tricks.''

"Why are you standing? Sit down or come into bed.''

"All right, I'll sit. I'm hot. Why has it turned so warm in the middle of the night? Maybe the world's coming to an end or something of the sort. I don't want those Jews around any longer. Gershon's a crook, and that Jacob's a trickster. Why should a woman pretend to be dumb? I just don't understand it.''

"Perhaps she's not pretending. She may really be a mute.''

"You said yourself that he admitted she wasn't.''

"I said nothing of the kind. All I said was that he remained silent and didn't protest. Who knows what goes on among these people? They're a special tribe. It's best to ignore them.''

"How can I ignore them? They have a finger in everything.''

"Your Catholic administrators aren't any better.''

"What is any good? The whole of Poland's collapsing. Mark my word, we'll be completely eradicated. What the Jewish lice don't eat, the Prussians or Muscovites will. You won't find our nobility crying. No, they consider every Polish defeat their personal victory. Things like this only happen in Poland. Every other country's anxious to prosper; we strangle ourselves.''

"I don't know, Adam. I don't know anything any more!''

"Why did you start with that Jew? It was like spitting in my face.''

Theresa hesitated.

"But that's what you enjoy.''

"Not when it's a Jew. You shouldn't have done it. I used to sleep at night. Now I don't. I wake every few minutes. I'm beginning to think I'm possessed. Theresa, I want to bring this matter to an end.''

"What matter? What kind of an end?"

"I'll take some men and we'll march down to Pilitz and cut off a few Jewish heads. The rest of them will just pack up and run."

"Adam, you're mad. Whose heads? We have enemies all around us. Do something like that and you'll find yourself standing trial."

"Because of some Jews?"

"You know your enemies are just looking for something. All right, they hate the Jews, but if they find it useful, they'll take their side."

"I must do something."

"Do nothing, Adam. Go to sleep. Lie perfectly still with your eyes closed, and sleep will come. We must bide our time. Adam, dear, we must wait. What else is there to life? You wait and the days pass, and death comes and everything is over."

"I can't just lie waiting for death. Those spinster cousins are too much for me. They walk around glaring at me as if I were their worst enemy; and they're always whispering. This castle is filled with whisperers. You'd think I was keeping them imprisoned. If they're so unhappy, let them go elsewhere. I can't support all my distant relatives. It's not my fault that my uncles and aunts produced only spinsters."

"I've been saying just that for years."

"Yes, it was you who poisoned me against them. That's the tragedy. But now that your venom's worked, suddenly you're their protector and good angel."

"I knew it. Sooner or later everything ends up being my fault."

"Well, it's so. You're the cause of all my troubles. I've quarreled with everyone on account of you. You've isolated me. But I want to be finished with all this." Pilitzky's voice rose to a scream.

"Why must you shout? You'll wake everyone. You know that they eavesdrop."

"Here no one needs to eavesdrop. They all know everything. I can see it in their faces and hear it in their laughs. Theresa, this time you've gone too far."

"I? No, it was you who pushed me, Adam. If I were at the point of death, I would say it over again. You did it. When I testify before God, I will not change my story. No one but you was responsible. I came to you as an innocent girl and you—"

"I know, I know. That story's already grown a beard. You were pure as snow, as innocent as a white rose, and so on. What do you want me to do? Return your hymen?"

"No, all I want from you is a little peace."

"I can't go on living like this. What makes you think Jacob won't talk? I don't want those dirty Jews pointing their fingers at me."

"He won't say anything. He'll keep still. He has his own troubles. His wife's a puzzle—I don't know the answer, but there is one. He's as frightened as he is large and awkward. Maybe he ran away from jail. God knows what. Sooner or later the truth will out."

"Yes, and my shame also."

"You wanted it that way, Adam. For years you urged me to indulge you in your fantasies. God alone knows how I struggled against you and what I endured."

"Don't mention God."

"Who else? I have no one but Him. You drove our children to their deaths. It was as if you killed them with your own hands. Me you made—I dare not say the word; it would disgrace the souls of our parents in heaven. What you have done can not be undone."

Both husband and wife lapsed into silence and then Pilitzky said, "I ordered Antonia to kill the hog tomorrow afternoon."

"No, Adam, I am no longer interested. I don't want it to happen. Let the beast live."

"I have already told Antonia."

"I was not serious when I said it. I don't want to watch. It doesn't help anyway. Holy Mother, what has become of me? God in heaven strike me dead this instant. I want no tomorrow."

Theresa moaned, half in pain and half in disgust. Her body contorted on the bed as if she had been seized by a spasm.

"Take me, death."

CHAPTER TEN

1

The Jews of Pilitz were preparing for the High Holidays. The beadle blew his horn daily to scare off Satan, the Seducer, who led men into sin and then testified against them in heaven. Sarah, having moved back to Pilitz from the manor, in addition to holiday preparations, made ready for childbirth. Jacob had placed *The Book of Creation* and a knife under her pillow to discourage those she-devils who hover around women in labor and injure the newborn—Lilith, for example, or Shibta who broke the necks of children being delivered. Jacob had also acquired a talisman from a scribe which had the power to keep off Ygereth, the queen of the demons, Machlath, her attendant, as well as the Lillies who resembled humans but had bat wings, ate fire, and lived in shadows of the moon and tree trunks. As for Sarah, she secretly practiced the magic native to her village. Though now a daughter of Israel, who had learned the prayers said on the High Holidays, still she wore on her throat a piece of a meteorite; and she took the shell of a newly hatched chick, mixed it with dry horse manure and frogs' ashes and drank the concoction in milk. Another charm required her to sit naked on a pot in which mustard seed was burning, allowing the smoke to enter her. The prediction of the women of Pilitz was that she would give birth to a boy since her stomach was not round but pointed upward. Jacob had already bought a gold embroidered skull cap from a traveling pedlar as well as a bracelet that protected from the evil eye.

On Rosh Hashana it was Jacob who arose to begin the prayer, an honor which Gershon had bitterly opposed. On the previous Sabbath he had delayed the reading of the Torah while he railed against the community for allowing a stranger to stand at the lectern as its representative, but the elders had outvoted him. Jacob stood in his prayer shawl and robe singing "the King" and Sarah could not keep back her tears. She could remember him when he had been a barefooted slave who slept in her father's barn. Now he looked like a venerable sage. She, too, had changed, wore a gold colored dress, earrings which Jacob had ordered from a goldsmith and on which money was still owed, and a string of imitation pearls. She held a prayer book in her hands and its brass covers reflected her image—the image of a lady. Her lips moved in silent prayer. Jacob had been so scrupulous in his teaching that she knew more than most of the women around her. How strange it all was: her love for Jacob at first sight, his leaving her and returning to get her, their years of wandering together. Those had been years of constant danger and her life had almost been forfeited many times. God alone knew how many miracles had been required to rescue Jacob and her.

Next to her in the women's gallery stood Beile Pesche, Gershon's wife, dressed in silk and velvet and with a string of real pearls around her neck. But Sarah didn't envy her her finery, felt herself to be superior. Beile Pesche was old, couldn't read, had to listen to a woman reader, and was married to an ignoramus who was not allowed to represent the community at prayer. But Sarah was young, could read and understand a little Hebrew, and was married to a scholar. If the town only knew what a scholar Jacob really was! More than that, Jacob was Pilitzky's administrator, and was received at the castle. Those years that separated Sarah from her peasant past stretched behind her like an eternity. What had occurred before must have happened to someone else. It was as if she had read about it in a story. She had once been Wanda, the wife of Stach, a drunken peasant. Whenever that thought came to her, she shivered, but often she went days without remembering it. She had become a Jewess. What Jacob had said was true: she had been born with a Jewish soul and he had merely brought her back to her point of origin.

Jacob's voice rang loud and clear as he sang and intoned. Her eyes misted. What had she done to deserve these blessings? She bore his child in her womb. Why had she been chosen from all the other Polish women? Her only special merit had been the suffering which had set her apart from childhood; sorrow and longing had always been part of her. She had had strange thoughts even before she could talk. Often she had cried for no reason. Asleep or awake she had odd dreams whose meanings she had not understood until now. She had always been afraid to talk to Jacob about them, fearing he would think her mad. When her grandfather had died—her father's father—she had seen the dead man standing among the mourners, and he had walked with the peasants as his body was carried for burial. She had wanted to scream out to him, but he had raised a finger and put it to his nose as a sign for her to be silent. Only when the cortege had reached the graveyard had the image dissolved slowly like a pocket of mist when the sun starts shining.

The next night her grandfather had come and left flowers on her bed.

She had had other visions as well, had foreseen Jacob's arrival and for this reason had refused other men. The truth was that since childhood she had been expecting and longing for him.

Around her now, the women motioned and made signs to her, assuming that she heard neither her husband intoning the prayers nor the ram's horn being blown. When they spoke to each other, they did so disregarding her presence. Only Beile Pesche loudly warned that she was no mute at all but a fraud. So great was this woman's hatred that when Sarah nodded a silent Good New Year to her after the prayers, Beile Pesche turned her back. At home the holiday dinner Sarah had prepared was waiting, the head of a fish, carrots, all the customary dishes that are eaten on Rosh Hashana. Jacob said the benediction over the wine and passed the goblet to her so that she might drink, and cut her a slice of chalah with honey. As she ate, she imagined she saw God in the pale, blue sky, seated on a fiery throne with the book of life and death open before Him, while angels trembled and fluttered their wings and the hand of each man inscribed his fate for the year. A secret fear gnawed at her. Perhaps her death had already been decreed. If so, at least Jacob and the baby must be allowed to live.

When the meal was over, Jacob went to the study house to recite Psalms. Sarah lay down on the bed. She could feel the child moving in her womb. It would soon be Yom Kippur when those who have lost their parents say the memorial prayer. But whom should she pray for? Jan Bzik, her father? She had asked Jacob, who had concluded after some hesitation that she should omit that part of the prayer where the names of the dead are mentioned. For she, Sarah, had not been orphaned through the death of Jan Bzik. Her real father was the patriarch Abraham.

2

In the middle of the night Jacob felt himself being shaken. He opened his eyes. Sarah stood by his bed.

"Jacob, it's begun."

"What, the spasms?"

"Yes."

Though he was still exhausted and longed for sleep, he rose quickly, yawning. Then he remembered and was afraid. In the half light Sarah's bloated body seemed a barrel taut with suffering.

"I'll go for the midwife."

"Wait. Perhaps there's still time."

She spoke in a whisper. No matter what happened, she continued to insist, she would not utter a word, not even in labor. But who could be certain how flesh and blood would behave at such a time? Jacob was surrounded by danger. He went and opened the shutters. The half moon that shines during the ten days of repentance had set, but stars glittered. Should he bring her something to eat, he wondered. That summer she had made gooseberry, currant, and blackberry jam, and some cherry wine. He glanced at the water barrel, saw it was half empty, and decided to go to the well for more water. He would not have left a woman about to go into labor alone if there had not been charms and inscriptions on the wall to protect her. But even so he kept the door open and he directed her to recite the incantation a scribe had written out for her:

> *The mountain is high; the sky is my skin.*
> *The earth is my shoe; the sky is my dress.*
> *Save me, Lord God.*

Let no sword cut me,
No horn gore me,
No tooth bite me,
No waters flow over me.

Under the black sea lies a white stone.
In the throat of the hawk a hard bone is stuck.
YUHAH will guard me!
SHADDAI will save me!
TAFTIFIAH will be a wall for me.

During the period between Rosh Hashana and Yom Kippur the townspeople attended night prayers at the study house. Jacob had not gone this year because Sarah was approaching labor. But he had seen Gershon walking with the others. Only a few days before this wilful man who dictated to everyone had been threatening violence if Jacob was allowed to become reader; he had even implied he would denounce Jacob to the nobles. Everyone knew how Gershon had acquired his wealth; during the massacres monies and other valuables had been entrusted to him for safekeeping by someone he knew. The man had perished and when his heirs had asked for their father's fortune, Gershon had denied ever receiving it, perjuring himself. Yet now he went with his wife, his daughters, and his sons-in-law to night prayers. Did he believe he could fool the Almighty? Despite the thirty-odd years he had lived in the world, Jacob was continually astonished at how many Jews obeyed only one half of the Torah. The very same people, who strictly observed the minor rituals and customs which were not even rooted in the Talmud, broke without thinking twice the most sacred laws, even the Ten Commandments. They wanted to be kind to God and not to man; but what did God need of man and his favors? What does a father want from his children but that they should not do injustice to each other? Jacob, leaning over the well, sighed. This was the cry of the prophets. Perhaps it was the reason the Messiah did not come. He pulled up a pail of water and hurried back to Sarah. She stood at the threshold bent double with pain.

"Get the midwife."

Leaving the pail of water standing, Jacob ran for the midwife, but when he knocked at her shutters, nobody answered. Jacob hurried to the study house and entered the woman's section, although it was not the correct thing to do. But childbirth is dangerous. He looked around and saw she wasn't there.

"My wife's in labor," he said aloud. "Where's the midwife?"

Several of the women scowled and slapped their prayer books, angry at the interruption. Others whispered words of advice and informed him that the midwife was delivering another child. One woman, however, closed her prayer book and rose.

"Life is more important than anything," she said. "I'll go to your wife."

Still in search of the midwife, Jacob found himself traveling down a street filled with bumps and holes and small hillocks. The house of the woman in labor had been described to him and he knew it was one of those he was passing but couldn't decide which, not hearing any screams. The only sound disturbing the silence was the chant rising from the study house. "Adonai! Adonai! Gracious and Merciful God." How strange the prayer sounded echoing in the dark with that peculiar intonation characteristic of night prayers. Despite all their catastrophes, the Jews still spoke of God as merciful and gracious. Jacob stared vacantly about him, uncertain whether to continue his search or hurry home. Sweat ran from his face, wetting his shirt. "Father in Heaven, preserve her," he said aloud, looking up at the sky crowded with stars. When his first wife, peace be with her, had given birth, he had been scarcely more than a boy. What went on among women had been a mystery to him, protected as he had been by his mother, sisters, aunts, and cousins. He had been reading when the women had come in to tell him that he was a father and wish him mazeltov. It had been that way with the second and third child also. But now all of this was so distant it seemed to have taken place in another life. Raising his voice, he called out the name of the midwife, and his cry echoed as though he were in a forest. Then, turning, he ran back home to find a fire already burning in the oven and a pot of water boiling. The woman who had come from the study house had also laid out linen and towels and had lit a wick in a shard of oil. Her sleeves were rolled up and her face wore the expression of one who is an expert in female matters. If she hadn't been there, Jacob would have asked Sarah how she felt. Sarah lay silent on the bed, her face contorted.

"Did you get the midwife?" the woman asked.

"No, I couldn't find her."

"Well, don't get upset. Nothing's happening yet. It doesn't go that easily." And she thrust another piece of wood into the oven.

Behind the anguish in Sarah's eyes was the trace of a smile which seemed to say, "Don't worry so." Jacob looked at her with both love and astonishment. This was Wanda, Jan Bzik's daughter, who every afternoon had brought food to him on the mountain. On her head was the kerchief worn by daughters of Israel, and around her throat a talisman. The walls of the room were hung with charms and verses from the Psalms, and under the pillow lay *The Book of Creation*. He had wrenched this woman from generations of gentiles, robbed her of mother, sister, sister-in-law, all her family. He had even deprived her of her speech. And what had he given in return? Only himself. He had wed her to dangers from which only a miracle could rescue her. For the first time he realized the ordeal to which she had been subjected, and came close to her and stroked her head. Responding like a peasant, she caught his hands in hers and kissed them. If the other woman had seen, the people of Pilitz would have had more to gossip about and ridicule.

3

Can a mute cry? Can she scream in pain? Sarah wept and screamed but said nothing. From the first, signs had indicated a difficult labor. The afternoon following the night of her first spasms she still had not given birth. Her body was wet with perspiration and her eyes protruded. The midwife hurried in and out; there was an assistant, an old crone who delivered the peasants' babies and who had left her turnip patch to run to the bedside; she also bustled about, her unwashed hands black with loam. Neighbors entered, having heard it was a difficult labor, and offered contradictory advice and suggestions. Some of the women stayed outside talking to Jacob, others approached the bed to signal to the mute. Various magical attempts were made to ease the delivery. A young nursing mother squeezed milk from her nipples and gave it to Sarah to drink. A piece of matzoth left over from Passover was placed between the suffering woman's teeth and she was directed to hold it there. A pious matron, noted for her acts of charity, placed her hand on Sarah's stomach and recited a spell. The man who had read the Torah on Rosh Hashana was sent for and he intoned the following passage, resting one hand on the mezuzah: "The captive exile hasteneth that he may be loosed and that he should not die in the pit." He also repeated the verse beginning, "And the Lord visited Sarah," three times, continuing to the words, "at the set time of which God had spoken to him." It was known that Beile Pesche had a bowl inscribed with sacred letters which if placed on the navel of a woman in labor pulled the child out—sometimes the woman's intestines as well if it were left on the body too long. But when Beile Pesche was asked to lend it, she said it had been broken.

When darkness fell and Sarah continued to scream, the women started to bicker. Should she be given the milk of a bitch mixed with honey? Or pigeon droppings in wine? A tip of the lemon used at Succoth was offered and a coin blessed by the pious Rabbi Michael of Zlotchev. Nothing worked. There was only one hope left—the most powerful of all remedies. A long string was brought and attached to Sarah's wrist, its other end carried to the study house and tied to the door of the Ark. Sarah tugged with her wrist as commanded, but instead of the door opening as it should have, the string snapped. This was a bad omen. The midwife said: "I'm afraid there'll be no bread from this oven."

"We must at least try to save the child."

The women spoke loudly, believing there was no need to watch their words.

"What would the widower do with a newborn baby?"

"Oh, he'll find a woman to help."

"Imagine, God already decreed this misfortune on Rosh Hashana," the pious woman remarked.

"No, you're wrong, the fates don't become final until Yom Kippur."

The words Sarah had been trying to hold back tore themselves from her throat:

"Don't bury me yet, I'm not dead." She spoke in Yiddish.

The women drew back.

"Oh, my God, she's speaking."

"It's a second miracle."

"Miracle nothing. She's not a mute."

"Gershon was right."

One of the women called out that her head was spinning and fainted.

Jacob, who had run to the beadle's to fetch more Passover matzoth since the piece in use had fallen from Sarah's lips and was spattered with blood, was not present. Everyone in the room began to yell at once and there was such a tumult it was heard on the street. From all sides people came running to Jacob's, among them the burial society women who supposed Sarah had died and were ready to lay the corpse on the floor and light the candles. Soon there was such a crush in the room that the bed on which Sarah lay was almost broken. Terrified, she started to shout in her native Polish:

"What do you want from me? Get out of here. You play at being good, but you're all rotten. You want to bury me and marry off Jacob to one of your own, but I'm still living. I'm alive and my baby's alive too. You're rejoicing too quickly, neighbors. If God had wanted me to die, He wouldn't have made me go through what I have."

Sarah's Polish was not that of a Jewess but that of a gentile and the women turned pale.

"That's a dybbuk speaking."

"There's a dybbuk in Sarah," a voice called out into the night.

Many strange events had occurred recently, but the Jews of Pilitz had never heard of a dybbuk entering a woman in labor, and of all things during the days of repentance. Now everyone came, screaming and running. Mothers warned their daughters not to go see the dybbuk unless they wore two aprons, one in the front and one in the rear. Even school children tried to shove into the room where Sarah lay uncovered, but the women turned them back at the door. The stool on which the wick stood was jostled and the light went out; the oil was spilled when someone attempted to light it from the oven. Those on the inside sought to get out and those on the outside tried to squeeze in. People blocked the door and quarrels started. Madness, it seemed, had become universal in Pilitz. Bonnets and kerchiefs fell to the floor, dresses were torn; a string of beads was ripped from a woman's neck. Rising above all this came Sarah's periodic screams. The darkness in the room frightened her and she spoke in a mixture of Polish and Yiddish.

"Why is the room so dark? I'm still living. I'm not in the grave. Where's Jacob? Jacob. Has he run off? Has he forgotten his Wanda?"

"Who's Wanda?" someone asked.

"Let me have light. I'm dying," the woman in labor moaned.

A piece of kindling was found and lit and fiery shadows danced on the walls. In the semi-darkness all the faces seemed distorted. The midwife who had been out of the room pushed her way through the crowd.

"What's come over you? Who's Wanda? Push down hard. Push, daughter."

"He's too big, too big. He takes after Jacob," Sarah cried in Polish. "He's tearing out my insides."

"Who are you? How did you enter Sarah?" a woman inquired of the dybbuk.

Realizing what she had done, Sarah did not reply. The spasms subsided momentarily and she lay exhausted, her hair damp, her body bathed in sweat, her lips and nose swollen. Her legs felt as heavy as logs, her fingers as if they had been stretched. She knew what a dybbuk was, having heard the women speak about them frequently.

"Who are you? How did you enter Sarah?" the women demanded again.

"I entered and here I am," Sarah said. "What do you care? Get out of here. All of you. I don't need you. You're my enemies."

She was speaking in Polish.

"Who is Wanda?"

"She is who she is. Get out of here. Out of here. Let me die in peace. Grant me this. Have pity on me."

The spasms returned and she let out a terrifying wail.

4

Jacob had been told that a dybbuk had entered Sarah and his arrival started the crowd milling again. Somehow he managed to squeeze his way through.

"What's going on here?" he asked, annoyed and fearful.

"There's a dybbuk inside of her," a woman answered. "It talks Polish. It calls itself Wanda."

Jacob shrugged. "Where's the midwife?"

Sarah's mouth twisted into an expression of mockery.

"No midwife can help me," she said in Polish. "Your son is too large for my hips. Both of us are on our way there," and she pointed toward the cemetery.

Jacob stood, knowing all was lost, speechless with sorrow and shame.

"Save her," he begged those around him. "Please save her."

"No one can save me, Jacob," Sarah said. "The witch predicted I wouldn't live long. Now I see she was right. Forgive me, Jacob."

"Who are you? Where do you come from?" a woman asked.

"Bring the rabbi," another woman cried. "Let him exorcise the dybbuk."

"It's too late for that," Sarah said. "What's he going to drive out? When you bury me, I won't be here any more and you won't have to trouble yourself gossiping about me. Don't think I didn't hear your nasty talk." Sarah's tone changed. "I heard every word. But I had to play the fool. Now I'm dying, I want you to know the truth. You call yourself Jews but you don't obey the Torah. You pray and bow your heads but you speak evil of everyone and begrudge each other a crust of bread. Gershon, the man who rules you, is a swindler. He robbed a Jew whom the Cossacks killed and because of that his son-in-law's a rabbi and—"

Jacob turned white. "What are you talking about, Sarah?"

"Be quiet, Jacob. My sorrow speaks, not I. I can no longer be silent. I kept still for two years, but now that I'm dying, I must talk. I'll burst if I don't. Thank you, Jacob, for everything. You are the cause of my death but I don't hold it against you. How is it your fault? You're a man. You'll find another woman. They're already talking of matches. The town won't let you remain single long. Pray for me, Jacob, because I have forsaken the God of my parents. And I don't know if your God will allow me into heaven. If you ever meet my sister Basha or my brother Antek, tell them how their sister died."

"What is she saying? What is she saying?" voices asked from all sides.

"It's a dybbuk, a dybbuk."

"Yes, a dybbuk. What are you going to do about it? I'll be in my grave along with my child before you can harm me."

Sarah suddenly started to howl. The spasms had begun again. Jacob was pushed from the room and rebuked for being there. He found himself among the men, women, and girls who had not been able to get in. Questions came at him from all sides but he did not answer.

"Why don't they bring the rabbi?"

"They went to get him."

"First they must remove the child and then the dybbuk," one man said.

"Why didn't Gershon's wife lend her bowl?"

"Because she's so noble."

"What's the sex of this dybbuk, male or female?"

"Female."

"I never heard of one female entering another."

There was silence and everyone listened to Sarah's groans. Men bowed their heads; women covered their faces as if ashamed of Eve's curse. The midwife stuck her head out the door.

"Run and bring the bowl. She's sinking fast."

Jacob lunged. "Let me in."

"No, not now."

The rabbi had entered the street, accompanied by his father-in-law, Gershon, and his brother-in-law, the ritual slaughterer. The latter was carrying a utensil, which was at first thought to be Beile Pesche's bowl, but turned out to be a pan filled with burning coals. A ram's horn was stuck in the rabbi's pocket. At Gershon's command the crowd parted and the dignitaries walked through. Trailing behind, carrying a white robe and a prayer shawl, was Joel, the beadle and town grave digger. Gershon, as befitted his position, began to talk loudly.

"Women, make way for the rabbi. We are going to exorcise the dybbuk."

"No men can come in now," a woman called from inside.

"We can't just stand here and wait."

"It's not a dybbuk," Jacob said. "There's no dybbuk."

"What is it then?" Gershon asked, even though Jacob and he were not on speaking terms.

"Leave her in peace."

"Men, in that room is a demon residing in the body of a woman. Dare we permit her to defile this whole community?" Gershon said, haranguing the crowd. Then, pointing at Jacob, he continued, "He came to us a mere teacher but now he's become a big man. He has a wife with a devil inside her. Because of such people plagues are sent down."

"First the child must be removed," a woman said sagely.

"Perhaps there isn't any child in her womb," another woman suggested. "It may be the dybbuk."

"I have seen the child's head."

"Demons have heads too."

"Demons have hair."

"No."

"If she dies with the child in her womb, the whole community will be imperiled," the rabbi warned.

"Shouldn't we blow the ram's horn out here?" the beadle asked.

"No, first we must implore the dybbuk to leave her," the rabbi announced.

Again there was silence. Roosters began to crow, answering each other. These fowl would be sacrificed on the day before Yom Kippur; there was something both solemn and awesome in their recitative as if they already knew what lay in store for them. The dogs, hanging around the butcher shops, started barking. A warm breeze blew from the fields and swamps; the night had turned hot and humid. Jacob covered his face with his hands.

"Father in heaven, save her."

5

I will say nothing, Jacob decided. Now that she is speaking I must be still. He stood, lips tightly sealed, determined to endure his tribulations to the end, knowing that now he could not escape unharmed. Sarah mortally ill, probably delirious, had divulged their closely guarded secret. Prayer alone was left to him but his lips refused to open even to prayer. Sarah's fate had been decided by heaven which had determined also that he and probably the child too must die with her. I must recite my confession, he thought, and he murmured inwardly: We have trespassed, we have been faithless, we have robbed, we have spoken basely. . . . He heard people talking to him but the words made no sense. Sarah wept continually, and then finally became silent. But she could not have died, because again they were speaking about driving out the dybbuk. The men were arguing unsuccessfully with the women who were now in charge, about entering the room. A compromise was reached: the men would stand in the doorway. Admonishing the dybbuk, the rabbi pleaded with it to desert the woman's body, but no voice issued from Sarah. At the rabbi's command, the beadle blew the ram's horn; first a long blast, then three staccato ones, then nine swift grace notes in succession. A few minutes later, Pilitzky's carriages drove up to the house accompanied by retainers bearing torches. The entourage resembled an invading army or demons parading in Gehenna. Pilitzky dismounted, inquiring:

"What's going on here, Jews? Has the devil taken over?"

"My lord," someone answered, "a dybbuk has entered Jacob's wife. It's been screaming from her throat."

"I don't hear any screams. Where is she?"

"She's in labor. It was screaming before. Here's Jacob."

Pilitzky glanced at Jacob.

"What's going on with your wife? Is she talking again?"

"I know nothing, my lord. I have ceased knowing anything."

"Well, it's clear enough to me. She's as dumb as I'm blind. I want to speak to her."

"My lord, no men are allowed," the women called from inside.

"Nevertheless, I'm going in."

"Cover her. Cover her."

Pilitzky entered and addressed Sarah, but she did not answer. The women listened in silence. The younger matrons had already gone home to nurse their babies, and many of the older women had hastened off to the study house. The rabbi had left too. Gershon lounged against a tree ouside, appearing asleep on his feet. He had removed his hat on Pilitzky's arrival and had been about to run and kiss his master's hand, but he lord of Pilitz had turned his back on him. This was Jacob's second sleepless night, and he stood numb from fatigue but with his eyes still open. He had wrestled with God as had the Patriarch Jacob, but his defeat had brought more than a dislocated thigh. He, Jacob, the son of Eliezer, had been utterly destroyed by heaven. No longer did he fear anything, not even Gehenna. He deserved no better, having cohabited with the daughter of Jan Bzik and then illicitly converted her. What did he expect? In these days justice ruled untempered by mercy. Jacob heard Sarah groaning.

"Gracious lord, let me die in peace."

"So you are not dumb. You never have been. This was a little comedy that you and your husband played."

"It's the dybbuk, my lord, the dybbuk," someone interrupted.

"Silence. You don't have to tell me. I know what a dybbuk is," Pilitzky said, raising his voice. "When the devil enters a woman, he speaks with his own voice. She uses *her* own. That's the same voice I heard when she thought I meant to harm her husband. Isn't that true? What's your name? Sarah?"

"Let me die, worthy lord, let me die."

"You'll die, you'll die. And when your soul leaves your body, I won't stop it. But for the moment you're living. Tell me, why did you pretend to be mute?"

"I can tell you nothing."

"If you won't, your husband will. We'll pour hot oil on his head, then he'll talk."

"My lord, what do you wish from me? Have you no pity for the dying?"

"Tell the truth before you die. Don't go to the grave still lying."

"The truth is that I loved him and still love him. I regret nothing, my lord. No, nothing."

"Who are you? You speak like a mountaineer, not like a Jewess."

"I am a daughter of Israel, my lord. Jacob's God is my God. Where is the rabbi? I want to make my confession. Where is Jacob? Jacob, where are you?"

Jacob pushed his way through the crowd.

"Here is my husband. Why don't you eat something? Women, give him something to eat. Don't be so pale, Jacob, and frightened. I'll sit with the angels and look down on you. I'll see that no harm befalls you. I'll sing with the choiring angels and pray to God for you."

Sarah intoned all this in Polish and the women stood open-mouthed. Neither Sarah's way of speaking nor her manner was that of a daughter of Israel. Suddenly they remembered she didn't look Jewish, that she had a snub nose, high cheekbones, teeth which were strangely white, strong, and sharp, unlike those found among the Jews. Pilitzky asked:

"Where are you from? The mountains?"

"I have nobody, my lord, neither father, nor mother, nor sister, nor brother. I have erased them from my mind. My father was a good man, and I'll meet him if he's in heaven. Remember, all of you, don't hurt Jacob. You can find him a wife when I'm dead, but don't torture him with your talk. I'll defend him. I'll kneel before God's throne and pray for his safety."

"You were born a Christian, weren't you?"

"I was born when Jacob found me."

"Well, everything's clear."

"What's clear, my lord? It's clear that I'm dying and will take my child with me to the grave. And I had hoped that God would grant me a son, and that I would still have a few good years with my husband . . ."

Suddenly Sarah started to sing in a half yodel, half sob. The song was one Jacob had often heard on the mountain, the ballad of an orphaned girl who fell into the hands of a forest spirit and was carried to a Smok's cave. The Smok made her his concubine and, forced to endure his demonic love, she longed for the mountains, the Gazdas, and her lover at home. Now it seemed as if Sarah no longer knew where she was. She lay, her cheeks swollen, her eyes half shut, her head uncovered, and chanted in a hoarse voice. Pilitzky crossed himself. The women wrung their hands. Suddenly Sarah was silent, her thoughts turned inward. Then, again, she started chanting; Jacob's eyes clouded and he viewed everything as if through water. He remembered a passage from the Book of Aboth: "Whosoever profanes the Name of Heaven in secret will suffer the penalty of it in public." He wanted to go and comfort Sarah, wipe the sweat from her brow, but his feet were like wood. Pilitzky took him by the arm and led him outside.

"Look, you'd better leave town," he said conspiratorially. "The priests will burn you. And they'll be right to do it."

"How can I run away at such a time?"

"She'll be dead shortly. I pity you, Jew. That's why I'm warning you."

Pilitzky stepped into his carriage and drove off.

CHAPTER ELEVEN

1

The baby, a boy, born the next day, arrived crying too loudly for a newborn child. Sarah remained in a stupor and the women took care of the infant; a young mother with an abundance of milk nursed him. It was the day before Yom Kippur and the townspeople were busy with the sacrificial fowl and preparations for the holiday. Yet Gershon demanded a meeting of the community elders. What was said in this secret conclave was never told; but the rabbi forbade the cheder boys to read the Shema at Sarah's bedside, and prohibited attendance at the ceremony requesting peace for the male child customarily held on the Sabbath after the birth. The rabbi went further and instructed his brother-in-law, the ritual slaughterer who also performed the circumcisions, that for the time being the child should not be circumcised. Pilitz was in an uproar. The uninstructed misunderstood the rabbi's decision and maintained that it was Gershon who had instigated his son-in-law to humiliate Jacob. But those who knew the Talmud explained the verdict. According to the law, the child is born into its mother's faith. It was clear Sarah was a gentile—even the name substantiated that she was a convert. But what rabbinical court would have upheld the conversion of a gentile when the punishment for such an act was death? How could the community accept her when acceptance meant a criminal indictment? God forbid. Misfortunes and evils could only attend such an act. In the study house, Gershon demanded that Jacob be excommunicated, publicly exhibited in an ox cart and driven out of Pilitz. What a heinous crime, Gershon shouted. Jacob from mere lust had passed off a gentile as a daughter of Israel. Now even those who had sided with Jacob agreed with Gershon. And since Gershon remained out of favor with Pilitzky another envoy was sent to explain the position taken by the Jews.

The next day Sarah still lay helpless. The women refused to visit her knowing that according to Polish law she too had committed a capital crime. Only one old woman came a few times to inquire after her and leave some chicken broth which Sarah couldn't swallow. Yom Kippur would begin at sundown and although eating before the fast day was considered an act of piety, Jacob had no food in the house nor could he have tolerated eating. He sat at the bedside and recited Psalms. The woman who was acting as wet nurse had taken the child to her own home and Jacob could not go to visit his son since he had no one to leave with Sarah. Nor was it certain that the family would have permitted him to enter their house, for though he had not as yet been officially excommunicated he soon would be. The townspeople, he noticed, no longer passed by his house. His acts, in a perverse way, were an offense to the government, the community and to God. He was ashamed to say the verses of the Psalms. How could his lips utter such holy words? How could his prayer be acceptable? Now he was receiving his retribution in all its harshness. Any day he might be burned at the stake.

As he sat with the sick woman, holding the Book of Psalms in his hands, he made a spiritual accounting. His family had been killed; for five years he had been Jan Bzik's slave, sleeping with the cattle in the barn or with the mice in the granary. True, he had lusted for Jan Bzik's daughter and had wanted her as his wife. But had not the author of the Psalms, King David, lusted for Bathsheba? And if the Bible was to be accepted as the literal truth, then David had committed a far worse sin than he had. God had forgiven David. Why not Jacob, who had never sent a man out to be killed in battle?

But Jacob knew that these thoughts themselves were forbidden. The Talmud explained that King David had not been a sinner, that Uriah the Hittite had left a divorce for Bathsheba before he marched out to battle. The Gemara and the Midrash also defended the people of the Bible. But, just the same, those great ancient figures had lusted carnally, and had married outside of their nation. Moses had taken an Ethiopian as a wife, and Miriam had become leprous when she slandered him. Jehudah who had given his name to the Jews had had intercourse with a woman he thought was a harlot. King Solomon, himself, the greatest sage, had married the daughter of Pharaoh, and yet the Song of Songs and the Proverbs were holy. And what of the Jews now? Did they all strictly obey the commands of the Torah? His years of wandering with Sarah had made him aware of many wrongs he had ignored before. Legalisms and rituals proliferated without diminishing the narrow-mindedness of the people; the leaders ruled tyrannically; hatred, envy, and competition never ceased. Before Yom Kippur the Jews made peace with one another, but the night after quarrels broke out all over again. Perhaps that was why God sent men like Chmielnicki, why the exile lasted so long and the Messiah did not come.

Jacob dipped a finger in water to moisten Sarah's lips, bent over her, touched her forehead, and whispered to her. She lay as if already in the beyond, sunk in contemplation, receiving, it seemed to Jacob, the answers to those unanswerable questions that the living ask. Her chin trembled; the veins of her temples throbbed. It was as if she were arguing with the higher powers. Is that how it is? the smile that occasionally came to her lips seemed to say. How could I, Jan Bzik's daughter, ever have known that? I wouldn't have guessed it in a million years.

She is good, he thought, really a saint, a thousand times better than any of the others. Have they been to heaven and learned what God likes? Worry and fear, the isolation in which he found himself, had made him rebellious. He was even ready to struggle with God himself. Of course, God was the only God, awesome and all powerful, but it was only fair that his justice be universal. He should not be a tyrant like Gershon, fawning on the strong and spitting at the weak. Was it Sarah's fault who her parents were? Had she had the freedom to choose her mother's womb? If such as she must burn in Gehenna, then there was even inequity in heaven.

Dusk was beginning to fall, and the Jews were going in slippers or in their stockinged feet to pray. They wore white robes, prayer shawls, and on their heads gold-embroidered miters. The women were adorned with capes, fancy headgear, dresses with trains. Candles burned in the windows. A wailing rose from the houses. Everyone in Pilitz had lost someone in the massacres, and now Jacob's anger turned to pity. A tortured people. A people whom God had chosen for affliction, raining down on them all the tortures in the Book of Punishment.

The door opened and the old woman entered bearing half a chicken, a chalah, and a piece of fish for Jacob to eat before the fast started. No one else would come near him but at her age she had nothing to lose. Her face was yellow as wax, dry as a fig, and the wrinkles on her forehead were like the script on an ancient parchment. For a few moments she stood at the sick woman's bedside, her eyes still young, looking up at Jacob with a motherly understanding. Her hairy chin shook as she made an effort to speak. Finally she said:

"Let your prayer for a good year be answered. Everything can still be all right. God is good."

The old woman raised her voice in a wail.

2

Late that night, Sarah opened her eyes. Her lips moved and Jacob heard her half-choked voice coming to him as if from a distance. He had the feeling that her voice and body were no longer connected. He bent over her, and she muttered in Polish.

"Jacob, is it Yom Kippur yet?"

"Yes, Sarah, Yom Kippur eve."'

"Why aren't you in the synagogue?"

"I'll go there again as soon as you are well."

Sarah closed her eyes and meditated on this. Jacob thought she had fallen asleep. When she opened her eyes again, she said:

"I will be dead soon."

"No, you will get better and live many more years."

"Jacob, my feet are dead already."

He tried to feed her some broth, but her teeth locked, and the soup dribbled out. He remained leaning over her, clasping her hands. He had prayed so much in the last days and weeks, but now he had given up and even the wish for prayer had evaporated. Heaven had not listened to his supplications. The gates of mercy had been closed to him. He looked at Sarah, realizing that he was her murderer. If he had not touched her, if she had remained in her village, she would still be healthy and vital. Every sin, no matter how small, ends in murder, Jacob said to himself. He felt a love such as he had never known before, but equally a helplessness. There was a midnight silence in the room. Two candles standing in a box of sand flickered and cast shadows. The kerchief had fallen from Sarah's head and her scalp, covered with short hair like a boy's, was the color of straw and fire. He didn't know what to do. Should he go and get someone? Disturb people on the holiday? No one could help anyway. He sat on a stool by the bed, unable even to think now. Within him there was a great emptiness. Crush me, Father in heaven, crush me! In the Psalmist's words, "And my sorrow is continually before me." Now his only desire was to die with her. He had forgotten the child. He wanted to descend into Sheol from which none return.

Suddenly Sarah opened her eyes and spoke, her voice firm and clear as if she were again well.

"Jacob—see Father."

Jacob looked around.

"What did you say?"

"Don't you see him? There he is." Sarah stared at the door.

"Good evening, Father," she said. "You've come for your Wanda. You haven't forgotten. I'll come with you soon, Father. But wait, wait another few minutes. How well you look, Father, all in light."

Jacob turned to the door and saw nothing. Sarah was silent. Her eyes began to shrink in their sockets, the pupils contracting into opaqueness. Jacob spoke to her but she did not answer, nor give any sign that she heard. Then she said:

"See Grandmother too. How beautiful you look. I was your favorite granddaughter. You've come for me too. Oh, how I loved you. You and Father. Now we'll always be together."

"Sarah," Jacob cried. "You'll get better. You are the mother of a child. You have a son."

"Yes."

"You must live—for him and for me."

"No, Jacob."

He continued to call to her but she did not answer. Her eyes stayed shut. She lay absorbed in meditations that could not be interrupted. Something was happening within her. Jacob could see that the journey to where she was going was not easy. She seemed to be engaged in a dispute with some power external to her, arguing with it, struggling. Whatever power was forcing her from life also would not accept her in death. An accusation was being made and her glazed eyes seemed to be imploring: No more. No more. I'm tired. Leave me in peace. Jacob sought to have her make her confession, wanted her to die with the words, Hear O Israel, on her lips, but it was too late for that. How strange that these gentile spirits had found their way here on all nights Yom Kippur eve. But who knew the secrets of heaven and earth? Again and again, Jacob turned to look at the door. Perhaps he too would see the ghost of Jan Bzik.

His head slumped forward and he fell into the sweet forgetfulness of sleep.

He awoke, glanced at Sarah, and knew that she was dead. Her jaw had sagged, one of her eyes was open, one closed. The face was no longer recognizable. Now the struggle had ended, her chapped lips seemed to say, I've passed through everything. All is well now. The face was peaceful and acquiescent; this was no longer the sick, the tormented, the martyred Sarah who had estranged herself from both Jews and gentiles, and lost her home and her language. The corpse, at last beyond the reach of finite good and evil, forgave. Sarah's body was here, but her spirit had already climbed to heights unreachable for flesh. Jacob's sight became as if visionary, and he saw her entering a heavenly mansion. He did not cry but his cheeks became damp. His love for her had begun with lust; now nine years later he watched over the body of a saint. But the burial society, Jacob knew, would refuse to inter her in a Jewish cemetery. Moreover, the gentiles threatened him direly. Nothing that was related to this earth was of any importance to him now. In the presence of this peace, all anxiety left him. He bent down and kissed her forehead.

"Holy soul."

The door opened and a few men and women from the burial society entered. A tall man in a fur hat and white robe cried out:

"What are you doing? That's forbidden."

"He's out of his head," another said.

A woman put a feather to Sarah's nostrils. The feather did not move.

3

Gershon breached custom once more and called a meeting of the elders and the burial society immediately Yom Kippur ended. After the debate had gone on for an hour, Jacob was sent for. He was sitting watch over the corpse, but the beadle now took his place. Offered cake and wine by the rabbi's wife, Jacob refused.

"A second Yom Kippur has begun for me," he said.

"You should eat. One fast day is sufficient," the rabbi answered.

At the insistence of those present, Jacob took a spoonful of rice and a cup of water. The meeting wanted information from Jacob, nothing less than the complete truth.

"What you have done bears on the welfare of the whole community," the rabbi pointed out. "We imperil the town if we break the law. You know well enough what we have suffered. So tell us the truth. If you have sinned, don't be ashamed. This is the night after Yom Kippur and all Jews have been purified."

The speech was unnecessary since Jacob had already decided to tell the truth. As soon as he started to talk everyone became quiet. He told them who he was, who his father and grandfather had been, how Polish robbers had captured him and sold him to Jan Bzik, and how he had lain illicitly with Bzik's daughter, how the Jews of Josefov had ransomed him, how, longing for Wanda, he had later returned to the village, and how, since she could not speak Yiddish correctly, she had pretended to be mute. So quiet was it in the study house that the buzzing of a fly could have been heard. Every once in a while a listener sighed. This was not the first strange story those assembled had listened to. Ever since the massacres all sorts of peculiar things had been heard of: Jews turned Christian or Mohammedan; daughters of Israel married to Cossacks, sold into harems; women who remarried only to find their husbands returning. Stories to tell for generations to come! Yet, that a young scholar from a fine family should fall in love with a peasant girl, convert her in defiance of both the Jewish and gentile law—this was something new. Gershon's yellow eyes bulged, his mustache quivered like a tomcat's, and he clenched his fist on the table. The others glanced at one another and shook their heads. The moment Jacob stopped talking, Gershon said:

"You have betrayed Israel. You're a monster!"

"Men, this is no time to preach morality," a white-bearded elder interrupted.

"You know the law," the rabbi said hesitantly to Jacob. "Your son is not a Jew. The mother was not converted with the consent of the community."

"She went to the ritual bath. She observed the laws."

"That is immaterial. She was not accepted. Moreover, the laws of this country apply to us, too."

"These are unusual times. Is it the child's fault?"

"He was born and conceived in sin."

"Must he remain uncircumcised?"

"Take your bastard and go elsewhere," Gershon shouted. "We're not going to pay with our heads for your lechery."

"What about the body?" the white-bearded elder asked.

"Interment in the cemetery is out of the question."

They were still arguing when Jacob rose and left. He walked slowly through the streets with bowed head. Now he knew what he was: a branch torn from its trunk. Excommunication was certain. He wanted to see the child but decided it was more important to watch over the corpse. While he had been sitting night and day at the sick bed, he had been meditating. What happened was no accident. Everything was preordained. True, the will was free, but heaven also made its ordinances. He had been driven, he knew, by powers stronger than himself. How else could he have found his way back from Josefov to the mountain village? It had been his feet that had led him. And Sarah had hinted, even before she became pregnant, that she would die giving birth. The night before, her words had returned to him, and he knew she must have been granted some prophetic power. But whom could he tell such things? Who would believe him?

But now he at least understood his religion: its essence was the relation between man and his fellows. Man's obligations toward God were easy to perform. Didn't Gershon have two kitchens, one for milk, and one for meat? Men like Gershon cheated, but they ate matzoth prepared according to the strictest requirements. They slandered their fellow men, but demanded meat doubly kosher. They envied, fought, hated their fellow Jews, yet still put on a second pair of phylacteries. Rather than troubling himself to induce a Jew to eat pork or kindle a fire on the Sabbath, Satan did easier and more important work, advocating those sins deeply rooted in human nature.

But what could he, Jacob, do? Become a prophet and castigate the people? He who had himself broken the Torah?

He arrived home and relieved the beadle, sat down to watch over the body. The corpse lay on the floor now, covered by his overcoat, the feet towards the door. Behind the head, the stumps of yesterday's candles still burned. The previous night, it had seemed to him several times that the corpse had moved, and he had uncovered Sarah's face, and tried to wake her, suspecting catalepsy. But hour by hour, she had grown stiffer. The body was altering, and one could see that she was moving further and further from this earth. Jacob raised the eyelids, but the pupils were blank. Even the expression of acquiescence had vanished. Clearly, she was no longer there. Unable to gaze at her longer, Jacob covered her again. He took out the Psalter from his bookcase and began to recite the Psalm: "Deliver me out of the mire, and let me not sink. . . . Reproach hath broken my heart; and I am full of heaviness. . . . Make haste, O God, to deliver me; make haste to help me, O Lord."

4

The clatter of horses' hoofs sounded in the night. Jacob knew what that meant. The door slammed open and a dragoon with a plumed helmet and twisted mustache thrust his head in. He saw the corpse lying on the floor and was silent for a moment. Then he spoke:

"If you're Jacob, come with me."

"Who will watch over the body?"

"Let's go, I have my orders."

Jacob bent and for the last time uncovered Sarah's face, which seemed to be smiling. He had closed the mouth but the jaws opened again; the teeth no longer seemed to fit the gums; the tongue was lumpy and blackish. He wanted to say goodbye but he didn't know how. I should take some clothes or a shirt, he thought, but he didn't move. Again he covered the body and said:

"All right, I'm ready."

The moment he was in the street he thought of his prayer shawl and phylacteries and asked the soldier to let him return for them. But the soldier blocked his way. The moon, not yet full, had crossed the sky to the horizon. Everywhere, shutters were closed. Even the grasshoppers and frogs were silent. A mounted dragoon held the first one's horse by the reins. Jacob had the feeling that he had lived through this before or seen it in a dream. He thought of calling out to the people not to leave Sarah's body unattended, but was held back by a youthful embarrassment. He was trembling, not from fear but from the cold. He recalled that the night before a mouse had approached the body and he had had to chase it away. But what difference did it make whether the corpse was eaten by mice or worms? The first dragoon dragged out a long chain, tied one end to Jacob's wrist, and attached the other to his saddle. The second dragoon dismounted to help, the two handling the prisoner like butchers trussing an ox to be led to slaughter. They spoke, but only to each other. Only now did Jacob remember the child. Well, the boy would have neither father nor mother. He had been born under a dark star. Jacob wanted to ask the soldiers to take him to the house where the baby was but realized that his request would be refused. He fixed his eyes on the chinks in the shutter where could be seen the glimmer of the candles burning at the head of the corpse. Does she know what's happening to me? he asked himself. Or is her soul so distant it is no longer connected with this world? The dragoons rode slowly, Jacob following. He realized they were taking him to another town. Pilitz was left behind, and they moved past fields that had already been harvested. He was marching to his death, yet Jacob breathed in deeply, filling his lungs with the cool night air. For days now he had done nothing but sit with the sick woman and then with her corpse. Inactivity and stale air had enervated him. He was no longer accustomed to not using his body. His feet wanted movement, his hands demanded work. Now he walked between the horses, fearful they might step on his feet or crush his ribs, although surely such a death was more honorable than being hanged. He wanted to recite chapters from the Psalms, but the chatter of the soldiers distracted him. The taller of the dragoons, the one who had arrested Jacob, said:

"All right, Czeslaw, how many men do you think Kasia's had already?"

"More than you have hairs on your head."

"She only has one bastard."

"You can have her for half a grivnik."

"Still, she has a way with her."

"It's all false. She smiles at you with one eye and at your worst enemy with the other. She'll kiss you all over, but the moment you go she curses you and your mother. Then she's off to the priest to confess how she accidentally stepped on a cross of straw."

"That's a fact. Now all she talks about is getting married."

"Why not? Once she's your wife, she'll tell you to go whistle. You'll rot in camp and she'll do what she wants. You'll come home and she'll have a belly ache. With strangers she'll dance; with you she'll groan. Every year she'll present you with another bastard."

"Well, I've got to marry someone."

"Why?"

"Should I take my horse for a wife?"

"Your horse would be more faithful than Kasia."

Jacob wondered how a man who had just looked on death could speak so. Didn't these men ever contemplate their own fate? They lead me to the gallows and never bother to ask why. As if guessing his thoughts the soldiers became silent. The horses' pace slackened. Jacob, cooled by a breeze, felt a calm such as he had never known before, and raised his eyes to the sky. So, the heavens were still there, created by the same God who had formed both the rider and the horse. He had made the chain strong. Suddenly it occurred to Jacob that sometimes chains could be broken. Nowhere was it written that a man must consent to his own destruction. Instantly his mood changed. He was angry. Powers slumbering within him awoke. He now knew what to do. He wanted to laugh. The moon had set, he noticed. Edging over toward Czeslaw, the smaller of the two dragoons, he struck his horse with an elbow. The animal broke into a gallop, veered off into the underbrush. The tall dragoon shouted, reached for his sword. Jacob yanked the chain and the tall dragoon's saddle came apart. The horse stumbled and nearly fell. Regaining its balance, this mare also bolted. Jacob ran into the fields with a speed and lightness that astounded him. There was no place to hide, but the dragoons would not risk injuring the legs of their mounts pursuing him across the stubble. Soon all was silent and he was surrounded by darkness.

I must reach a forest before sunrise, he warned himself, amazed at what had happened. But which way should he run? He had outwitted the powerful, broken the chain of slavery, but despite his escape, he felt no elation. He kept on going blindly and for how long he did not know. Time had become dreamlike. The chain dragged; he felt its weight on his hand. Bending down, he groped on the ground, not realizing at first what he was looking for. He found a stone and used it to pry the chain from his wrist. Where would he hide it? There was no ditch or stream around; like a dog with a bone, he dug a hole with his fingers and buried the chain. Only half awake, he knew he was in the fields, but at the same time he seemed to be in Josefov. He was surprised to discover that Gershon and the widow of Hrubyeshoyv were married. How could this be? Gershon's wife hadn't died. Had the edict of Rabbi Gershom the Light of the Diaspora come to an end? Shaking his head to clear it, Jacob got up and stumbled on across the stubble. Sky and earth fused in the darkness. He heard someone sighing, and knew that it was neither man nor beast but one of those who hover in the night; something wet and warm, like spittle, fell on Jacob's forehead. Under his feet, the earth seemed to sway. He walked dragging his legs as if they were no longer a part of his body. He saw a red pool shining like blood on the ground before him. Billowing smoke mingled with sparks rose in front of him as if from a burning village. He fell face down on the ground, overcome by sleep.

He awoke and it was day. Coils of mist hovered over the naked fields. A crow flew low and croaked. At the edge of the horizon to his left a forest stretched like a sash of blue, and emerging from it like the head of a newborn child, small and bloody red, came the sun.

5

Jacob lay in the forest and slept. But even in his sleep he clutched a heavy stick. The day was warm and the sunlight filtered through the pines. His was the deep sleep of those who have ceased to hope. Each time he woke, he wondered, Where am I running? Why did I escape?—and then exhaustion overwhelmed him again. He dreamed he was in the barn on the mountain and Wanda brought him food. He stood on the rock and watched her climbing from the valley dressed like a queen in jewels and purple robes, a crown on her head, golden milk pails in her hands. When, he asked himself, did Wanda become a Polish queen? Where was her retinue? Why did she need gold milk pails? It must be a dream. He awoke. The forest echoed with the songs of birds. His stomach ached with hunger. He dozed again. Today is her funeral, he said to himself, waking. They will give her a donkey's burial, outside the fence. His grief was too great to permit him to stay awake. Sleep like an opiate drugged him.

He was with her again, but now she was both Wanda and Sarah; Sarah-Wanda, he called her, amazed at the coupling of these names. How strange: Josefov and the mountain hamlet had also merged. Wanda was his wife, and he sat in his father-in-law's library and she brought him the Sabbath fruit. The massacres and the years of slavery had become the dream. But as he told Sarah-Wanda this, her eyes filled with tears and her face paled.

"No, Jacob, it happened."

He heard her speak and knew she was dead.

"What must I do now?"

"Fear not, Jacob my slave."

"Where shall I go?"

"Go with the child."

"Where?"

"To the other side of the Vistula."

"I want to be with you."

"Not yet."

"Where are you?"

She did not answer. Her smile awoke him and for a few moments her image lingered, white and shining, framed between the tree trunks. He reached out his hands and she disappeared. Again he slept and when he awoke the setting sun shone red in the thickets, while above the crowns of the pines, the sky flamed. Jacob remembered that he had not put on phylacteries since he had fled but this was his first day of mourning and so praying in prayer shawl and phylacteries was forbidden him. He moved into the brush searching for food: the blueberries had withered, but not the blackberries, and he gorged himself. Yet he remained hungry. Evening had fallen but the forest murmurs did not cease. Eerie laughter came from the branches, night birds calling. Another nocturnal bird repeated the same shrill warning over and over again like a prophet. The moon rose and dew fell as if through a heavenly sieve. The moss gave off warm, spicy odors. Jacob's head ached. He stumbled through a tangle of underbrush and trees, knowing he couldn't stay where he was. Here he would starve or fall prey to wolves. But there was no path out. He caught sight of a figure among the trees, ran calling to it, and saw it evaporate. Voices were chattering all around him and he wondered if he were already in the hands of the demons. To protect himself, he recited, "Hear O Israel," and then forced himself to envisage each letter of the word, Jehovah. His foot plunged into mud as he skirted a swamp; pine cones struck him as if thrown by hidden hands. He slid on beds of fallen pine needles. He walked toward the moon. The forest was savage yet he knew that even here Providence tended each fern and grub. He listened and heard the many voices around him, each unique, and, uniting all, the inimitable voice of the forest. Overcome by fatigue, he sat down on a couch of moss near a tree trunk. He felt the approach of death and once more cried out to Wanda.

His strength ebbed from him and the earth he rested on became suddenly near and dear. The grave is a bed, he thought, a most comfortable bed. If men knew this, they would not be so fearful.

6

Sand dunes stretched out and down like steps and at the bottom Jacob saw the Vistula quiet, deep, half silver, half a greenish black. Walking and dreaming, he had come to the edge of he forest. The landscape was as empty as on the first day of Creation. Jacob walked and the moon walked with him. The pleated sand, here and there as white as chalk, brought to his mind the deserts he had read of in the Pentateuch. The sight of the river made him hasten—he had not tasted water since the day before. The closer he came to it, the wider the river became. At the shore, bending down to drink from his cupped hands, he recalled the story of Gideon in the Book of Judges. He sat down to rest in the cool breeze and saw shadowy nets trembling on the surface of the water as if cast by some unseen fisherman. Stars dropped from the sky into the waves and hovering glowworms flared. Jacob again wanted to sleep but some power warned him not to, and, overcoming his weariness, he rose, climbed a pile of rocks and looked about him. Far off to the right, he saw something which could be a barge, a raft, a mill. He walked along the shore toward it.

Nearing the object, he discovered that it was a ferryboat, moored by thick ropes to piles; not far from the boat were a hut and a dog house. As he approached the landing, a barking dog ran toward him and a moment later a man came out of the hut. He was as black as a gipsy, barefoot, half naked, with long, curly hair, and wore trousers turned up to the knee. Scolding the dog in a rasping voice, he walked up to Jacob and said:

"The ferry doesn't run at night."

"Where does it go?"

"Where? To the other side."

"Is there a town there?"

"A stone's throw away."

"What's its name?"

The stranger informed Jacob. After a moment's silence, he asked:

"You a Jew?"

"Yes, a Jew."

"How come you're not carrying bundles?"

"I don't have any."

"If you're a beggar, where's your sack?"

"This stick is all I own."

"So that's it. Some have too much, others too little. In my lifetime, I've seen everything. What happened? Were you robbed?"

"Robbers don't worry me," Jacob said, amazed at his own statement.

"You're right. What have we got to lose? More than your trousers they can't take. But I do keep a spear, and you've seen the dog. Around here, they'd even run off with the ferryboat if they could. And how far would they get? Once we were crossing and his peasant woman's goose jumped into the Vistula. Two men had to keep her from going in after it. We got the goose back later. I said to her, 'Can you swim?' 'No,' she said, 'not a stroke.' 'How come you tried to jump overboard, then?' You know what she said: 'Well, it's my goose, isn't it?' Where are you from?"

"Josefov."

"Never heard of it. It must be far away."

"It is."

"Well, people come and people go. The kings don't even sit still. Everyone's come this way; the Swedes, the Muscovites, Chmielnicki. Whoever has a sword wants to live by it. But someone's got to do the work or we'd all chew rags. I'm a nobody, but I have two eyes in my head. Time's one thing I have enough of. I do plenty of thinking. You must be hungry."

"I don't have any money."

"You're entitled to a piece of bread. Even jailbirds get bread and water."

The ferryman walked into the hut and returned with a slab of bread and an apple.

"Here, eat."

"Do you have a pitcher in which I can wash my hands?"

"Yes. What do you want to do that for?"

Jacob washed his hands with the water that the ferryman brought him and wiped them on his coat. After saying grace, he bit into the bread.

"I owe you thanks, but first I must thank God."

"You don't owe me a thing, or God either. I have bread so I give it to you. If I didn't have any, I'd go begging. God owns everything but the rich receive it all."

"God is the author of all riches."

"If there is a God. Have you seen Him? I had one passenger, an aristocrat, who said there wasn't."

"What kind of an aristocrat?"

"Crazy! But he talked sense. What does anyone know? In India they worship snakes. The Jews put little black boxes on their heads, and shawls. I know. A lot of them used to use this ferry. But along gallops Chmielnicki; there were so many corpses floating in the Vistula the river stank. That's what their God did for them."

"The evildoers will be punished."

"Where? There was a brute of a count in Parchev who flogged I don't know how many hundreds of peasants to death but he lived to be ninety-eight. His serfs set his castle on fire, and down came the rain and saved it. He died peacefully sipping a glass of wine. I say: the worms get everyone, good and bad."

"Yet, you give me bread."

"So! Don't take it as an insult but I feed hungry animals, too."

7

The ferryman, whose name was Waclaw, took Jacob into his hut and gave him a pillow stuffed with straw. There was only one bench to sleep on so Jacob lay on the floor. The ferryman talked:

"One thing I've learned in my life: don't get attached to anything. You own a cow or a horse and you're its slave. Marry and you're the slave of your wife, her bastards, and her mother. Look at Pilitzky, all his life scared he'll be robbed, while he's being bled dry. When he married that whore, she only had to look twice at a man and he was sending around his seconds. The worst bitch this side of the Vistula. A hunk of filth. She's had a stallion as her lover, and of course the coachman. Did you know her husband finds her lovers? If that isn't being a slave, what is? When I hear such things, I say to myself, Waclaw, not you. You'll be nobody's slave. I'm not a peasant. I have noble blood. True, I don't know who my father was, but what's the difference? My mother came from a fine house. They wanted to apprentice me to a shoemaker and marry me off to his daughter. A dowry and all the trimmings went with her. So did a mother, grandmother, and sisters. The dust didn't settle under my feet. Here at the ferry I'm as free as a bird. I think what I please. Twice a day the passengers come and I do my job. No one bothers me the rest of the time. I don't even go to church. What does the priest want? To put another rope around my neck.''

"No, man cannot be entirely free," Jacob said, after some consideration.

"Why not?"

"Somebody must plow and sow and reap. Children must be raised.''

"Well, not by me. Let the others do it.''

"A woman bore you and brought you up.''

"I didn't ask for it. She wanted to have a man, so she did.''

"But if there is a child, it must be fed, clothed, and taught, or it will grow up a wild animal.''

"Let them grow as they please.''

Waclaw began to snore. Yes, it is true, Jacob meditated, only half asleep himself, man goes in harness, every desire is a strand of the rope that yokes him. Jacob fell asleep, awoke, dozed off again, woke with a start. What should he do? Leave and desert the child? But where would he go? What would he do? Marry again? He had already stepped under the canopy twice, and now his two wives and three children were in the other world. He would be more at home there than here. A cold wind was blowing from the Vistula and he tried to warm himself with the heat from his own body. His brain stayed awake and he could hear himself snoring. He mustn't stay here long; people would soon be coming to the crossing, and the dragoons might be on his trail. But perhaps it was better to be caught and hanged.

Jacob fell into a deep sleep, and when he opened his eyes the sun was shining. Waclaw stood over him.

"You got yourself a little sleep, eh?''

"I was exhausted.''

"Go on sleeping. There's nothing better. If someone who doesn't belong here shows up, I'll let you know.''

"Why do you do all this?''

"Your head must be worth a couple of grivniks . . .'' And Waclaw winked.

As Waclaw left, closing the door behind him, Jacob heard the sound of approaching wagons and realized there must be a road across the dunes. Soon wagons began to pass, shaking the hut, and through chinks in the walls came smells of horse dung, tar, and sausage. He heard many people talking, though it was still early and the ferry wouldn't leave for hours. There was no water in the hut to wash with before praying. So Jacob recited, 'I thank,'' a prayer one could say without ablutions. Blessed spirit, he murmured, where are you now? Your body must have been buried like carrion. He thought of the child, his and Sarah's, the grandson of Rabbi Eliezer of Zamosc and of Jan Bzik. He could not desert it. Did not the first Jacob rear the grandchildren of Terah and Laban? His own son must grow up instructed in the Torah. For God, whose purpose requires both life and death, there was no such thing as good birth. In God's mills even chaff becomes flour.

Rising, he walked to the front wall and peered through the cracks. It looked like market day outside—everywhere peasants, carts, oxen, pigs, calves. On the ferryboat near a sack stood a strange little man in a prayer shawl and phylacteries, his face turned away from Jacob toward the east. His white gabardine and embroidered prayer shawl were unlike any seen in Poland, and he was wearing sandals and white stockings. He bowed so low praying that the phylactery on his head almost touched the deck; he seemed to be reciting the eighteen benedictions. When he turned, Jacob saw the stranger's white beard that extended to his waist, and knew that this man had been sent to him. Degraded as he was, heaven no longer trusted in his wisdom to choose freely, but was leading him step by step along the road that he must follow. Jacob could no longer remain in the hut, but had to go and present himself to the stranger.

8

The man finished his prayers, replaced his phylacteries in their cases and put on an *abaya*, the kind of coat worn by messengers from the Holy Land and by Jews from Egypt, Yemen, Persia. Jacob approached the man and greeted him with a Sholom, expecting to receive a reply in Aramaic or Hebrew, but when the stranger spoke, it was in Yiddish.

"A Jew, eh? This place is crawling with gentiles. But I say my prayers wherever I am."

"You must be an emissary from the Holy Land."

"Yes, an emissary. The need in the land of Israel is great. We had a drought this year and on top of that a plague of locusts. When the Arab's in trouble, what's left for the Jews? Starvation is everywhere. And thirst. Water is bought by the cupful. Well, but the Jews all over the world are merciful. Stretch out a hand to them and they give."

"When do you go back?"

"I'm on my way now, though I still must visit a few communities. Then I board ship at Constance."

"How do the Jews maintain themselves in the Holy Land?"

The emissary paused to think this over.

"Which ones? It depends. The majority are paupers and what you don't give, they don't have. But there are a few rich men. All of us were struck dumb when we heard what was going on here in Poland. The news came about Chmielnicki—may his name be blotted out—and we had a second Tischab'ov. We ran to the sacred graves and the Wailing Wall and prayed. But we were no help. The massacres must have been already decreed. How do we know what's going on in heaven? Since the destruction of the temple, the rigor of the law has prevailed. But there are signs, many signs, that the End of Days is near."

"What signs?"

"It would take too long to tell you. The Book of Daniel makes it clear to those who understand that the Redemption will come in the year 5426. Don't think we do nothing. The cabalists are busy and have uncovered all kinds of portents. Of course, everything is in God's hands but much can be done through the power of the holy names. Pure and sacred men dressed in white sit and pore over these mysteries. Are you a man of the Torah?"

"I have studied."

"Have you ever looked into the *Zohar?*"

"Occasionally."

"Well, the sacred names govern everything. As the Gemara says, there is an angel for each blade of grass. And if that is so, the Redemption will only come through the holy combinations. Our cabalists fast, study all night, and at dawn visit the graves of saints. The older generation is gone; we have been deprived of our pious Rabbi Isaac Luria as well as Rabbis Chaim Vital and Shlomo Alkabetz. But the tabernacle of peace in Sefad still exists and Yephtah is the Samuel of this generation. But can a man live without bread? Even Rabbi Chanina, the son of Dusso, had to have his share of St. John's bread each week. Jews all over the world must do their part. What is your name?"

"Jacob."

"Give me a little something, Reb Jacob."

And the emissary pulled out a wooden alms box. Jacob blushed.

"You won't believe me but I don't have even half a groschen."

The alms box quickly disappeared.

"How can you travel without money?"

"I am a mourner, I should be sitting shivah."

"So why aren't you?"

"I'm escaping from the gentiles."

"Then, it's you who should be receiving. Does it matter where a Jew suffers? We all have the same Father. Why are you running away?"

Jacob didn't know whether to laugh or cry. Again his story must be told. The secrets he had kept for years were now being divulged to everyone. So seemingly chance occurrences led to a predetermined end. He said to the emissary:

"Come into the hut. My story is long. I must not be seen."

"But what about the ferryman?"

"He is letting me use it."

Before seating himself on the bench, the emissary ascertained that there was no cloth there woven of both wool and linen. He was so short his legs didn't reach the floor and Jacob placed a log for his feet. Then, leaning against the wall, Jacob told everything, denied nothing, from the day the Cosacks took him captive until the night he escaped from the dragoons. The emissary nodded, grimaced, chewed his beard, rubbed his forehead, and occasionally pulled at one of his sidelocks. The deeper Jacob got into his story the more pained the emissary became. He spread his hands, raised his eyebrows, tugged at his beard. His eyes expressed sadness, compassion, astonishment. From time to time, he sighed deeply. When Jacob finished, the emissary covered his face with his hands, which were small and bony, and his lips, hidden behind his beard, murmured and shook as if he were reciting a prayer or an incantation. After a while he lowered his hands. His face seemed altered, grayer, more drawn, with deeper pockets under the eyes.

"The community is right. Your wife was a gentile and so is your son. The child follows its mother. This is the law. But behind the law, there is mercy. Without mercy, there would be no law."

"Yes, yes."

"How could you have thought of doing such a thing? Well, it's done now."

"I am ready for my punishment."

"What? It's all because of the massacres and the destruction. Don't ask me what I've seen here. Nevertheless you are a learned man."

"It was not within my power to act differently."

"It seems it was not. Free will exists, but so does foreknowledge. 'All is foreseen but the choice is given.' Each soul must accomplish its task, or it would not have been sent here. The sons of Keturah were also the sons of Abraham."

"What shall I do now?"

"You must save yourself and you must save your child. First of all, he must be circumcised. When he grows up, he may have to be converted—I don't remember the law exactly but meanwhile let him be brought up as a Jew. It is written somewhere that before the Messiah will come, all the pious gentiles will have been converted."

"I don't remember the passage."

"It's somewhere in the Talmud or Midrash—what's the difference? I'll give you two guldens and when you have money, God willing, you'll give it back. Not to me personally, but to another emissary. Does it matter? The money goes to the Holy Land. The fact that you found me here is odd: I was to have preached a sermon and I would have collected a nice sum of money. But suddenly I was seized by a desire to travel. That's the way Heaven manages things."

For a while both men were silent. Then the emissary said:

"If she has already been buried, you are obliged to pray today. Take my prayer shawl and phylacteries. I'll wait and then we'll have breakfast."

CHAPTER TWELVE

1

The emissary tried to persuade Jacob that it would be dangerous to return to Pilitz immediately. A man's life is too important, he said, and anyway the infant was too small and weak to be moved. Besides, the day after tomorrow was Succoth, and a holiday is a holiday. He suggested that Jacob go to the city with him and stay here until after Simchath Torah. But Jacob was unyielding. He longed to see the child, and he wanted to visit Sarah's grave. Money was hidden in his room; perhaps no one had as yet stolen it; he could not suddenly start begging. In his years of slavery and wandering, Jacob had grown used to overcoming obstacles. Distances no longer frightened him, nor dark forests, beasts, robbers; even his terror of devils and hobgoblins had vanished. The strength he had gathered had to be used. His escape from the dragoons meant that the king was not as powerful as he had imagined. What would happen to the might of the wicked if the just were not so craven? Stories he had heard of how the Jews had behaved during the massacres shamed him. Nobody had dared lift a hand against the butchers while they slaughtered entire communities. Though for generations Jewish blacksmiths had forged swords, it had never occurred to the Jews to meet their attackers with weapons. The Jews of Josefov, when Jacob had spoken of this, had shrugged their shoulders. The sword is for Esau, not for Jacob. Nevertheless, must a man agree to his own destruction? Wanda had often asked Jacob: Why did the Jews permit it? The ancient Jews of the Bible stories had been heroic. Jacob never really knew how to answer her.

Breakfasting with the emissary on bread, cheese, and plums, Jacob hesitated, then took the two guldens, promising to return them as soon as he could. The emissary who had to stay a few more weeks in Poland told Jacob his route. Passengers, as well as horses, cows, oxen and sheep were still coming aboard the ferry. Amid the hubbub of the peasants, the neighing, bellowing, baying of the animals, the emissary advised Jacob on his future conduct. The Messiah was coming, so why stay in Poland? It was a great act of piety to settle in the Holy Land. When the Redeemer came, the Jews in the land of Israel would be the first to greet him. Moreover, a Jew could breathe more freely in the country of the Turks, where the Torah was respected. Many rich Jews lived in Istanbul, Smyrna, Damascus, and Cairo. Of course there were sometimes hostile edicts and people were falsely accused, but such catastrophes as those that happened in Poland—never. Further, since he, Jacob, had broken the ecclesiastical laws of the Christians, and the Jews too had good reason to censure his conduct, why not bring his child to the Holy Land and settle in a place where scholars were supported? He could always learn a trade or go into business if he wished. God willing by next summer the child would not be too frail to make the journey. The emissary's words were laden with half-spoken promises. He hinted that the Messiah already existed, and that where he was and when he would reveal himself was known to the most esoteric of the cabalists. He said to Jacob:

"My lips are sealed. A word to the wise is sufficient."

The emissary was about to say more, but suddenly the ferry began to move and Jacob jumped ashore. The emissary called out:

"Comfort and aid are coming. We'll live to see it—in our own lifetimes."

2

At dusk Jacob started for Pilitz and reached it by late evening. All the shutters were closed. Pilitz slept. A three-quarter moon shone in the sky. The Succoth booths, covered with green branches, had already been set up, though a few were yet unfinished. Walking abreast of his shadow, Jacob carried an oak stick and in his breast pocket a knife Waclaw had lent him. Jacob now heeded the advice of the Book of Aboth: "If one comes upon thee, to kill thee, rise first and kill him." Passing the market place quickly, he came to the house in which Sarah had died. There was no light, a sign that the corpse had already been removed. Standing momentarily at the door, overcome by terror, he sensed the presence of the corpse, not the body, nor even the soul, but something shapeless and horrible. He pushed in the door. The moonlit room resembled a ruin, the bare floor littered with straw and rags; the body must have been cleansed on the spot. Everything had been removed, all the clothing and linen, even the pots from the oven. There was something uncanny, hostile in the fetid air. The room had a wintry dankness though it was still late summer. What's wrong with me?

Why should I fear her? Jacob said to himself in reproach. Wasn't she more a part of me than my own body? But he left the door open; his heart pounded, and he breathed heavily. He searched through the straw mattress but realized immediately that the money he had hidden there was gone. Thieves! And Yom Kippur had hardly passed. The men of the burial society might even have stolen it. Despite his anxiety, Jacob was overcome with anger. They had devastated his house. The robbed had become robbers. It was a world of grabbers; whoever could, stole, and now they were going to sit in the tabernacle and invite the Holy Guests to join them. Jacob's few books were missing too. "Naked came I out of my mother's womb, and naked shall I return thither."

After kissing the mezuzah, Jacob left. Be a witness, he said. He strode toward the cemetery. Even at a distance, the new grave was visible, a fresh mound of earth far removed from the others. When he reached the mound, Jacob saw a marker, and on it the words: "Here lies Sarah, the daughter of the Patriach Abraham." Jacob's eyes grew moist. Here lay Wanda, Sarah, the woman he loved. Although he tried to recite Kaddish , he choked on the words. Darkness enveloped him. Had the moon been extinguished? Throwing himself to the earth, he pressed his face against the grave: I am here, Sarah.

He listened as if expecting her voice to issue from the grave. A goulish idea came to him: exhume her body, or at least to thrust his hand into the earth and touch her. He wanted to kiss her once more. It's forbidden, it's crazy, a sacrilege, he warned himself. Even though it was a sin, he prayed for his own death: I have wandered too long in this world. Everyone I love is there. Lying prostrate, waiting for death, he had forgotten the child. For a while his strength seemed to ebb. His legs became numb and wooden, his brain like stone. He slept as though dead, then awoke. His prayer had not been answered. Rising, he began to mumble Kaddish. The marker had fallen to one side; he straightened it.

Brushing the earth from his face, Jacob stepped back a few paces. He looked for a large rock, wanting like the Patriarch Jacob to lay a stone on the grave of his beloved wife, but there were none. Jacob returned to Pilitz. Passing the study house where a single candle burned, he opened the door. An old man sat at a stand, looking into a book. Jacob recognized Reb Tobias, of whose eight children only one daughter, the wife of Naphtali the leather merchant, remained. In the glimmering light Reb Tobias' face with its matted and dirty beard seemed dark as earth. His gabardine was bloated like the garment of a pregnant woman; since he was ruptured, every few weeks his intestines had to be pushed back in place by a woman, the only person in Pilitz who knew how, and the fact that he had to allow a woman to touch his private parts caused him more grief than the physical pain. Now at midnight he sat studying the Torah. He's not a thief, God forbid, Jacob defended him, but a victim of other people's sins. The thieves are a minority.

Jacob stood watching but the old man did not stir. Deaf and half-blind, he held the book so close his eyelids almost touched the letters and at the same time hummed with a kind of moaning singsong. Because of such men as this, God had preserved the Jews. Suddenly, as Jacob stood there, he knew exactly what he must become: an ascetic who eats no meat, drinks no wine, does not sleep in a bed. He must atone for his sins. In winter he would immerse himself in cold baths, in summer lie on thorns and thistles; the sun would burn him, the flies and mosquitoes bite him. For the rest of his life and until his last breath, he must repent and ask forgiveness of God and of Sarah's sacred soul. Perhaps then he would not have to linger too long in this most imperfect of worlds.

But what if in that other world Zelda Leah claimed him? She was there with her children. But would she want him after what he had done following her death? They had never belonged together spiritually, had never truly mated; most likely she had ascended to realms of purity that he, a man of earthly passions, could never enter. And as for the children, their holy souls were undoubtedly at the very Throne of Glory.

3

Jacob knew where the young woman lived to whom he had given his child, but in the night, with all the shutters closed, her house was indistinguishable from the others. It seemed to Jacob that during even his brief absence changes had occurred in Pilitz. Lurking outside, he listened for a baby's cry. But he could not remain here forever, so, after hesitating, he decided to try one house. He raised the latch to knock, the door opened, and by the light of the moon he saw two beds and two cradles. A man grunted, a woman woke, and a child began to cry. The man asked harshly:

"Who's there, huh?"

"I'm sorry. It's me, Jacob, the baby's father."

In the uneasy silence even the child stopped crying.

"Woe is me," the woman groaned.

"Did they let you out of prison?" the man asked.

"I escaped. I've come for my baby."

Once more there was silence. Then the woman said:

"Woe is me! Where will you take an infant like this one in the middle of the night? He's too small to be moved. The least wind and, God forbid . . .''

"I have no choice. The soldiers s45after me."

"Make a light. Make a light," the woman told her husband. "They'll arrest us. I've heard the count wants the baby. Woe, Woe. What messes people get into."

"I won't give up the child without the consent of the community," the husband said firmly. "They gave it to me, let them take it back. I don't have to suffer for other people's bastards."

"I'll pay you for your trouble."

"It's not a question of money."

The woman, after covering herself with a shawl, stood at the oven and blew into the embers. Then she lit a wick and set it in a shard of oil. Its dim light illumined the unplastered walls, the smoke-stained ceiling, the two benches— one for dairy dishes, one for meat—on which stood pots, bowls, and in a wooden trough covered with rags a loaf of dough. Diapers, swaddling clothes, and straw whisks littered the room. Garbage floated in a pan of slops. A chamber pot stood next to one bed. In one cradle lay the child who had been crying. In the other, beneath a dirty quilt lay Jacob's son: tiny, red, bald, with a large head and pale eyelids. The baby's face looked old and grief-worn. A smile reminiscent of death touched its tiny lips and unformed forehead. Jacob stared. Only now did he realize that he had a son. The woman stood on the other side of the cradle.

"Where will you take such a little baby?"

"It's murder," her husband said, from his bed where he was propped up. His fringed garment was stained; pillow feathers stuck to his skull cap, and his beard and sidelocks were stippled with wisps of down. In his black eyes there was the look of a man trapped by domesticity. Jacob knew they were right, but he realized that if he did not take the baby now he would never see it again. Recalling the dream and Sarah's words, he girded himself stubbornly.

"I'll take care of him. The night is warm."

"It's not so warm. At dawn it gets cold."

"I don't want Pilitzky to get my son."

No one spoke; this was an unanswerable argument. Jacob took out a gulden.

"This is for what you have done. I'd pay more, but they stole everything, even the dishes."

"I know. I know everything. The burial society really outdid itself. They thought that you, God forbid, would never return."

"They all grabbed except us," the husband said. "They stripped the house."

"They took my money out of the straw mattress. And right after Yom Kippur!"

"Don't fast and don't steal, my mother, peace be with her, always said," the woman commented. "She'll intercede for us in Paradise. Other people's property is sacred, she always maintained."

"That's the reason we live as we do," her husband said.

"Where will you take the baby? Well, I'd better not ask."

The woman began to move about the room. She found a basket, padded it with rags and diapers, laid the baby inside and covered it with a quilt. The infant whimpered once. The woman looked at Jacob:

"He has to be nursed every few hours."

"I'll get somebody."

"When? How? Oh Mother."

And the woman began to cry.

Suddenly she said:

"Wait. I'll draw some milk from my breast. Where's the bottle?"

Her husband left his bed. Below the torn shirt, his legs were thin, crooked, hairy. He found the bottle for his wife. The noise in the room had waked the animals. The cat stretched, chickens clucked, worms crawled, a mouse poked its head out of a hole in the floor. The woman turned to the wall and squeezed milk from her breast. After a while she gave Jacob the bottle, its neck stoppered with a bit of cloth, and showed him how to pour single drops into the baby's mouth so that it would not choke. Jacob knew he was risking the child's life as well as his own; carrying the infant, he would be unable to defend himself if attacked. But he could not leave his own child, and Sarah's, among strangers and enemies. If he was destined to live, he would live. Jacob thanked the couple repeatedly, speaking of a debt which only the Almighty could pay. Then he walked out into the night, moving in the direction of the forest, the Vistula, and the ferry. He lifted his gaze to the stars: "Father, what do you want?"

A passage from Psalms came to his lips: "O spare me, that I may recover strength, before I go hence, and be no more."

4

The moon had set and it was dark in the forest. Slowly Jacob felt his way along a path, pausing occasionally to listen to the child's breathing or to ascertain by a kiss whether it was warm enough. He had endured many tribulations in his life, but never a more anxious night than this one. Praying so hard his lips swelled, he put himself completely into the hands of Providence, knowing he was acting improperly in relying on miracles. But thrusting his burden on God was now his only recourse. He had nothing left but his faith.

Jacob's footsteps aroused the sleeping forest. Twigs snapped under his feet; birds rose from the thickets; animals scurried for cover. He kept one hand raised over the basket to ward off branches. Every conceivable disaster occurred to him. Bears and wild boars inhabited the forest. Several times he thought he heard a wolf howling and reached for the stick thrust through his belt. Let there be day, let the sun rise, he commanded imploringly, realizing that his ambiguous words meant also: Let the Redemption come, and there be an end to this dark exile. It was safer to keep quiet, but instead he recited aloud passages of the Psalms, the Prophets, the Book of Prayer, and cried out to God: I have reached the end of the road. The waters are swirling around me. I lack the strength to endure these afflictions. Suddenly he had a desire to sing and he chanted a Yom Kippur melody which turned midway into one of the mountain songs. Each note reminded him of Sarah. As he sang, he wept.

All at once, a strange light flooded the forest, and for a second Jacob thought Heaven had heard him. All the birds began to scream and sing at once: the trunks of the pine trees seemed aflame. Far off in a clearing between the trees he saw a conflagration. A moment later, he realized it was the sun. Jacob gazed at the child, sat down, and offered it the cloth moistened with milk. At first it seemed to rebel at not receiving the breast, but finally it started to suck. For the first time in weeks, Jacob was joyful. No, not everything was lost; he still had his son. Let him, Jacob, reach the Vistula, he would cross it on the ferry and find somebody to nurse his son!

At that instant, the name he must give the boy came to Jacob: Benjamin. Like the first Benjamin, this child was a Ben-oni, a child born of sorrow.

Before long he sighted the dunes that bordered the Vistula and knew he had not gone astray. Coming out of the forest, he looked around for the ferry, and walked in the direction where he was sure the crossing lay. The Vistula flowed, red mingling with black; a large bird skimming the surface dipped so low at times that its wings ruffled the waters. The river's calmness, purity, and radiance refuted the darkness of the night. Set against this luminosity even death seemed only a bad dream. Neither the sky, nor the river, nor the dunes were dead. Everything was alive, the earth, the sun, each stone. Not death, but suffering was the real enigma. What place did it have in God's Creation? Jacob stopped again to look at the baby. Did it already suffer? Yes, there were signs of suffering.

But such sorrow did not come from anything it had yet endured. Its wide brow seemed furrowed in thought, and its lips moved as if it were saying something. He is only partly here, Jacob thought, no, not yet here; he is still meditating on his past before birth.

Jacob remembered the words his namesake had spoken on his deathbed: "And as for me, when I came from Padan, Rachel died by me in the land of Canaan in the way, when yet there was a little way to come into Ephrath; and I buried her there. . . ."

His name was Jacob also; he too had lost a beloved wife, the daughter of an idolater, among strangers; Sarah too was buried by the way and had left him a son. Like the Biblical Jacob, he was crossing the river, bearing only a staff, pursued by another Esau. Everything remained the same: the ancient love, the ancient grief. Perhaps four thousand years would again pass; somewhere, at another river, another Jacob would walk mourning another Rachel. Or who knew, perhaps it was always the same Jacob and the same Rachel. Well, but the Redemption has to come. All of this can't last forever.

Jacob lifted his gaze: Lead, God, lead. It is thy world.

PART THREE

The Return

CHAPTER THIRTEEN

1

Almost twenty years had passed and Pilitz, grown into a city belonged now to the son of one of Pilitzky's creditors, who had taken possession after a protracted lawsuit. Both the lord of Pilitz and his wife Theresa were dead, he having finally carried out his threat to hang himself. The widow had immediately begun an affair with an impoverished young noble and had been so infatuated that she gave him the last of what she had. One day he disappeared. Theresa became melancholic, locked herself in an attic room in the castle, grew sick and emaciated, and never reappeared. All of her cousins and relatives deserted her. When the new owner moved to dispossess the widow, the bailiff found her dead surrounded by her cats. The peasants commented that although Theresa had been dead for days, her cats, ravenous from lack of food, had not touched the body—evidence that animals are grateful to their benefactors.

The castle had been rebuilt, but the young noble was seldom there, spending most of his time in Warsaw or abroad. The bailiff stole, and Gershon's youngest son-in-law, as dishonest as Gershon himself, now leased the manor fields. The peasants starved; most of the Jews were also poor; yet the city grew. Gentile craftsmen now competed with the Jewish artisans, and the priests sent delegates to the king to revoke the ancient Jewish privileges. But when one trade was taken from a Jew, he found another. Jews sapped the trees for turpentine, sent lumber down the Vistula to Danzig, brewed vodka and beer, made mead from honey, wove cloth, tanned hides, and even traded in minerals. And although the Muscovites sharpened their swords and the Cossacks attacked at every opportunity, nevertheless between invasions they bought Polish goods. Jewish merchants extended credit, conducted business with Russians, Prussians, Bohemians, even with the distant Italians. There were Jewish banks in Danzig, Leipzig, Cracow, Warsaw, Prague, Padua, Venice. The Jewish banker did not waste money on luxuries, kept his capital in a bag tucked into his fringed garment, and sat in the study house praying. But when he gave someone a letter of credit, the recipient could present it in Paris or in Amsterdam and get money.

At the time of Sabbatai Zevi, the false Messiah who later put on the fez and became a Mohammedan, Pilitz was torn by dissension. The community excommunicated his followers, but they retaliated by publicly cursing the rabbi and the town elders. Men not only damned but even attacked each other physically. Some of the members of the sect ripped the roofs from their houses, packed their belongings in barrels and trunks, and prepared to fly to the land of Israel. Some indulged in cabala, tried to tap wine from walls, to create pigeons by the arcane powers of the Book of Creation. Others ceased to follow the Torah, believing the law would be annulled with the coming of the Messiah. Still others ferreted out hints in the Bible that to be utterly evil was the way to redemption, and they indulged in every variety of abomination. There was a teacher in Pilitz whose imagination was so strong that while praying in prayer shawl and phylacteries he could fancy himself copulating and have an ejaculation. The cursed sect considered this so great an achievement that they made him their leader.

After a while, most of the Jews recognized their error, realized Satan had seduced them, and lost faith in the false Messiah. But some still conspired and kept up their pernicious idolatry. They met at fairs in distant cities and made themselves known to each other through various signs. They wrote the initials S-Z on the books, tools and other merchandise sold in their stores, and they exhibited talismans invented by Sabbatai Zevi. They were united not merely by the illusion that Sabbatai Zevi would return and rebuild Jerusalem, but by commerce. They bought and sold from each other, formed combines, worked for each other's profit, and intrigued against their enemies. When one was accused of swindling, the others testified to his honesty and threw the blame on someone else. They soon became wealthy and powerful. At their meetings, they ridiculed the righteous—pointing out how easy it was to deceive them.

The city grew and so did the cemetery, until the graves spread to the spot where Sarah lay. Her grave became an issue. Some of the elders said her bones should be exhumed and buried elsewhere, since according to the law she was not Jewish and it was a sacrilege to let her remain among the corpses of the pious. The opposition maintained that digging up her bones was not only wrong but might have evil consequences. Besides, the marker had rotted away, the mound flattened, and no one was sure where the body lay. The wisest thing was to leave well enough alone. And the cemetery kept on growing. As usual in new cities where there is no book of chronicles and no old men to hand down the traditional stories, Sarah was soon forgotten and even Jacob was seldom remembered. Many of their contemporaries had died; new citizens had moved in; and Pilitz now had a stone synagogue, a study house, a poorhouse, an inn—even a community outhouse for those who were ashamed to use the gutter. In a little hut across from the cemetery lived the gravedigger, Reb Eber.

One day in the month of Ob, a tall, white-bearded man, in a white gabardine and white hat, sandals on his bare feet, a bag on his shoulder, appeared at the cemetery. In his right hand he held a stick. He did not look like a Polish Jew. His waist was circled with a broad sash like those worn by emissaries from the Holy Land. Moving among the graves, he poked, searched, bent down to read the headstones. Observing him from a window, Eber wondered what he was doing in the cemetery. Was he looking for someone? The settlement was not old; there were no saints' graves here. Eber went to find out.

"Who are you looking for? I'm in charge here."

"So? There used to be a convert's grave here. Sarah, the daughter of the

Patriarch Abraham. They buried her at a distance, but I see the cemetery has grown.''

"A convert, here? Has she a stone?"

"No, a marker."

"When did she die?"

"Some twenty years ago."

"I've only been here six. What was she to you?"

"My wife."

"Who are you? What's your name?"

"Jacob. I lived here once, a little after the massacres."

"Was conversion allowed in Poland?"

"She had a Jewish soul."

"I don't know. The place is overgrown with weeds. They added a piece of ground years ago. The whole city fasted."

2

Jacob continued to search, poking with his stick, and sniffing at the ground; then he stretched out on the wild grass, whispering to the earth. The sun was setting when Jacob walked through the city, looked around, stopped, gaped. It was a different Pilitz with different people. Seeing the study house, he entered. A single anniversary candle flickered in the menorah, and above the tables were shelves of books. Jacob took one out, looked inside, kissed it, and put it back. Then he took out another and seated himself. He had come from the Land of Israel to disinter Sarah's bones and take them back. Their son, Benjamin Eliezer, was now a lecturer in a yeshiva in Jerusalem. Jacob had never told him of his mother's origins. There are truths which must remain hidden. Why divide his spirit? Benjamin Eliezer had grown up a prodigy and at thirteen had already dipped into the cabala. This was in the time of Sabbatai Zevi and both father and son were misled by the false Messiah. The emissary Jacob had met on the ferryboat had been one of his legates and in old age had put on the fez.

Jacob had been through so much in those twenty years. The voyage to Jerusalem had taken many weeks and the vessel he had been traveling on had been attacked by pirates. He had seen half of his fellow passengers murdered before his eyes. The baby had suffered from dysentery and would have died if Sarah had not come to Jacob in a dream and given him a remedy. He too had become critically ill. Scarcely had he recovered when a Turk accused him of stealing and the captain had wanted to hang Jacob. A storm had come up and the ship lay on its side for three days. When Jacob arrived at Jerusalem, he found the city suffering a famine. Moreover, there was scarcely any water to drink. Every few years the city was swept by pestilence. Jacob was present when Sabbatai Zevi had been driven out of Jerusalem; he knew Nathan of Gaza and Samuel Primu. During the days of his error, he had worn the talismans of the accursed sect and had eaten on Tischab'ov and the seventeenth day of Tammuz. He had almost put on the fez like all the others. God alone knew how many miracles had happened to him. All that he had seen and endured could not have

been told in seven days and seven nights. It is impossible to convey the torment
he had undergone when he realized that he was sinking into the lowest abyss!
Even his present trip to Poland had been beset by many pitfalls, proving again
that no moment is without its misfortune. Every day he experienced another
miracle. But that Benjamin should have become an instructor in a yeshiva at
twenty and the son-in-law of a rabbi was an unalloyed gift from Heaven. Heaven
had decreed that Jacob should not perish a heretic. It had been willed that Sarah
and he were to leave issue.

But the disappearance of Sarah's grave was a blow to Jacob, and it seemed
that the trip had been made in vain. Jacob wanted to bury Sarah's bones on the
Mount of Olives and to prepare a grave for himself close by. He hoped that
since he had not been able to be with her alive, at least his body should rest
near her in death.

Well, but everything God did was for the good. The older Jacob grew, the
clearer this truth became to him. An eye was watching, a hand guiding, each
sin had its significance. Not even Sabbatai Zevi had come in vain. False birth
pains sometimes precede the true. Jacob, journeying through the Turkish countries
from the Holy Land to Poland, had come to know things he had not understood
before. Each generation had its lost tribes. Some portion always longs to return
to Egypt. There are always frightened spies, Samsons, Abimelechs, Jethros,
Ruths. The leaves drop from the tree, but the branches remain; the trunk still
has its roots. Israel's lost children live in every land. Each community has within
it those who stay apart. Men blossom and wither like plants. Heaven writes the
story and only there is the truth known. In the end each man is responsible only
for himself.

When Jacob had still been close to the sect of Sabbatai Zevi, they had tried
to persuade him to marry. Women of wealth and fine family were available. He
had never been free of carnal desires, but a power stronger than passion had
said no. Later too, when he had repented, the rabbi and the cabalists had argued
that according to the law and the cabala, he should find a new mate. But even
when his lips said yes, an inner voice shouted no. It often seemed to him that
Sarah was still with him. She spoke to him, he answered. She accompanied him
to the ruins and the holy graves, warned him against all kinds of dangers, and
advised him how to bring up Benjamin. If he put a pot on the stove and forgot
it, she called him when the food was about to burn. . . .

How could he tell such things? He would be considered insane or possessed
by devils, but every heart has secrets it dares not tell.

Jacob nodded over the book open before him. How wonderful there were
study houses and books everywhere! Jacob had never forgotten the years on the
mountain when he had to dig Torah from his memory. His love for books had
grown continually. Sometimes when they tried to marry him off he wanted to
answer, the Torah is my wife. No day passed without his going over a few
chapters of the Bible, and he had read the Midrash many times. His love for
the Torah had not ceased even when he belonged to the Sabbatai Zevi sect. A
chapter of the Psalms was like manna which tasted exactly as each man wished
it to. Jacob refreshed himself with the moral truths of Proverbs; he satisfied his
hunger with sections of the Mishna. Everything he studied he explained to Sarah
in Yiddish, sometimes in Polish, as if she were sitting beside him. On the voyage
he had drawn her attention to the waves, the islands, the flying fish, the con-

stellations. Look, Sarah, God's wonders! It was perilous for a Jew to walk alone on the roads in the Holy Land, but he had wandered with her among the Arabs, through deserts where caravans of camels passed. Sarah watched that no evil befell him. Arabs with wild eyes and knives at their waists gave him figs, dates, St. John's bread, and provided him with shelter for the night. Many times he came upon venomous snakes—which turned away from him. "Thou shalt tread upon the lion: the adder and the dragon shalt thou trample under feet."

But why had he been sent on this long journey if he could not find Sarah's bones and bring them to the Holy Land? His son had tried to dissuade him from the trip. The cabalists had pleaded with him, saying that every Jew was needed in the Holy Land. The pangs accompanying the birth of the Messiah were almost over, and signs indicated that the battle of Gog and Magog was imminent. Satan was drawing up a list of heavy accusations. The Lord of Edom girt his loins for the bitter struggle. Soon would come that battle when the evil hosts would attempt to overturn the scale of mercy. Then would Asmodeus, Lilith, each demon, every hobgoblin, bark, hiss, spit, foam; led by the primeval snake, packs of dogs, adders, hawks, and hyenas would march to Batsrah where the final conflict would take place. Not a single pious Jew, prayer, benediction, or act of piety, could be spared with the Redemption hanging in the balance. Jacob was needed here, not in some distant country. Sarah, too, argued against his going: Why bring my bones when soon the underground caverns will be filled with skeletons rolling to the Land of Israel? But for the first time in twenty years, Jacob demurred. An irresistible power within him forced him to make the trip.

Jacob's losses had been great, but he still had the holy books to cling to. Resigned long since to the loss of both the joys of this world and of heaven, he served God without hope, prepared each moment for the fires of Gehenna.

3

The men who came to the study house for the evening prayer greeted the stranger and asked where he came from.

"From the Land of Israel," he answered. "But once I lived here in Pilitz."

"What is your name?"

"Jacob. In those days I was known as Jacob the teacher, or as Jacob, Dumb Sarah's husband."

There was an outcry. Though most of the men present had not known Jacob, a few of the older inhabitants remembered him well. The man whose wife had nursed Jacob's baby clutched his head, and ran to tell his wife the news. She came into the study house among the men and began to cry and scream as if she were praying for someone who had fallen ill.

"Dear man, a day hasn't passed without my thinking of you. How's the baby?"

"He lectures in a yeshiva in Jerusalem and is the father of three children."

"That I should have lived to see this! There is a God."

Once more she began to wail.

The cantor had difficulty keeping the people silent until after the Minchah prayer, and immediately upon the completion of the eighteen benedictions the tumult resumed. Though few had known Jacob and his mute wife, many had heard of them. Even in the villages ouside of Pilitz, the story was told of how Jacob had escaped from the dragoons and come in the middle of the night to claim his son. This story had been particularly popular when the Messianists were dominant in Pilitz. That sect had believed in physical action, had contended that Israel should either seize Esau's sword or intermarry with his seed and that of Ishmael until all the descendants of Abraham had become one nation. They cited Jacob and Sarah as precursors of the Redemption. The new lord of Pilitz had even regarded the sect of Sabbatai Zevi with favor. At that time the mound over Sarah's grave was still visible, the marker still there, and women and girls had gone to the grave and recited prayers.

But when it was heard that Sabbatai Zevi had accepted the Koran, the warden of the burial society in Pilitz ordered his men to level the ground over Sarah's grave. Not long after, the new plot of ground was added to the cemetery and soon no one remembered where Sarah lay. Now, hearing that Jacob had returned from the Land of Israel, the secret followers of Sabbatai Zevi approached him, bid him welcome, and one of them invited him to stay at his house. But, refusing to be anyone's guest, Jacob replied he would sleep in the poorhouse. At the mention of Sabbatai Zevi's name, Jacob spat and cried out loudly, "Let his name and memory be blotted out."

Many questions were put to Jacob about what had happened to him. He spoke of the land of Israel, of the Jews living there, of the yeshivas, the holy graves, the ruins. He explained how the true cabalists were attempting to bring about the End of Days. He described the Wailing Wall, the Double Cave, Rachel's grave, and exhibited a few Turkish coins. A young man asked him if on his sea voyage he had seen any of those creatures, half man, half fish, who sing so sweetly that a man must stop up his ears or he will expire wih delight. Jacob said that he himself had not seen any. Long after the evening prayer was over, the men continued to talk and converse. Why had Jacob come? someone asked. When he replied that it was to disinter Sarah's bones and transport them to the Holy Land, there was a long silence. Then the warden of the burial society remarked:

"Might as well look for a needle in a haystack."

"It seems that it was not fated," Jacob said.

The people began to turn their backs on him. Everyone had heard of the bones of saints of important people being carried to the Land of Israel—but that a man should return after twenty years to hunt for the bones of some female who had been given a donkey's burial? That was peculiar. Some murmured that the guest must be out of his mind; others suspected him of belonging to the excommunicated sect; still others concluded that he was a liar and had not come from the Land of Israel. The followers of Sabbatai Zevi walked over to him, but everything they said, he disputed. Finally all the older men left, and without Jacob. Soon the woman who had nursed Jacob's child entered, bringing kasha and beef broth for him, but he told her he never ate flesh: neither meat nor fish nor anything else from a living creature, not even cheese or eggs. The woman asked:

"What do you live on? Burning coals?"

"Bread and olives."

"We have no olives."

"Also I take radish, onion, or garlic with my bread."

"How do you keep your strength that way?"

"God gives strength."

"Well, eat the bread."

Jacob washed his hands at the water barrel and sat down to eat the dry bread. A few boys whose turn it was to study at this time of the night began to ridicule the stranger.

"Why are you so scared of flesh?"

"We are flesh ourselves."

"What do you take on the Sabbath?"

"The same as on weekdays."

"You're not allowed to torment yourself on the Sabbath."

"Nor must one torment others."

"What do you put into the Sabbath pudding?"

"Olive oil."

"If everybody lived as you do, what would the ritual slaughterer live on?"

"One can survive without slaughter."

One boy tried to convince Jacob that he was breaking the law, while the others pinched themselves, giggled, whispered. He knew they were ridiculing him, but Jacob answered seriously, clearly. Jacob, who had his own ways of thinking and acting, who interpreted the Torah in his own manner, was accustomed to suspicion and mockery. Even as a child he had been a misfit. Despite his brief association with the followers of Sabbatai Zevi (and even there he had been on the outer fringe), he had always remained aloof. Even his own son, Benjamin Eliezer, had at times reproached him for his strange conduct. In the Holy Land, the community had wanted to support him out of funds given to aid scholars, but he had refused to accept charity, and had done all kinds of hard labor, such as digging ditches, cleaning outhouses, carrying heavy loads usually transported by donkeys. He was offered steady work, but refused to stay long in one place. One day he would go to Safad, another to Shechem; sometimes he journeyed to Jaffa, other times he wandered through the desert on the way to the Dead Sea. When he was sleepy, he would lie down in the sand, placing a stone under his head. There was even a rumor that Jacob was not a born Jew but a convert. Years passed, yet some of those who knew him never discovered that he was a learned man and considered him an ignoramus.

He had always been the same Jacob, in Zamosc, in Josefov, in the hamlet on the mountain, in Pilitz, in Jerusalem. His thoughts seemed clear to him, but others found them confused. At times, Jacob accused himself of stubbornness and disobedience since the Torah itself said that one should accept the majority and follow the leaders of each generation. But even so, Jacob could not be other than he was. Besides he could not forget the years he had spent in Jan Bzik's barn on the mountain, surrounded by animals and savage shepherds. The years with Sarah had left their mark upon him. He had great patience with the weak but he resisted the strong. For long periods he could remain silent, but when he spoke it was always the truth. He had made long journeys to repay half a piastre. He dared defy armed Arabs or Turks. He took the most difficult tasks upon himself, carried the paralyzed, cleansed the lice-infected sick. Men avoided him, but pious women considered him a saint, one of the thirty-six righteous men who are the pillars of the world.

Now Jacob sat in the study house, reproaching himself for having come. Of the money he had saved for the trip, there was not enough left for the return journey. He had placed himself in a situation where he would have to ask others for help, and, God forbid, he might become sick in Poland, or on the ship where those who die are buried at sea. I am mad, he said to himself. My mother, peace be with her, when she called me a rattlebrain, was right. As soon as he had finished the passages he had set himself, he walked to the poorhouse. The boys had told him he could sleep in the study house, but this he considered sacrilege. His rule was to prefer the difficult to the easy. Sometimes Jacob was amazed at the burdens he required his body and his soul to carry.

———————

4

Opening the door of the poorhouse, Jacob entered. In the darkness, he heard sighing and groaning, snoring, and the uneasy coughing of those he had disturbed. A man's voice asked:

"Who's there?"

"A guest. A stranger."

"In the middle of the night?"

"It's not midnight yet."

"The candle is out already."

"I will do without it."

"Can you see in the dark?"

"I'll lie down on the floor."

"There's a bundle of straw somewhere. Wait, I'll get it for you."

"Don't bother."

"Once I'm awakened, I can't close my eyes all night."

Jacob stood there while his eyes grew accustomed to the darkness and his nose to the stench. Even though it was summer, all the windows were tightly shut. The moon wasn't shining, but the sky outside was filled with stars. Jacob could discern the sleeping forms of men and women. He was familiar with all of this, the smells, the moaning; it was the same everywhere, in the Holy Land, in the countries of the Arabs and the Turks, in Poland. In whatever town Jacob found himself, he always went to the poorhouse to help the old and the sick, to wash them, rub them with turpentine, bring them fresh straw. Now, bringing a pile of straw and spreading it on the floor, someone was helping him. Jacob had read Shema before coming, so that the holy words need not be defiled by this unclean place; now he only needed to say the last prayer before sleep. He lay down, carefully stretching out his legs to avoid touching anyone. A woman complained:

"All night they drag themselves around, and now they come and wake up sick people. May their legs drop off!"

"Don't curse, woman, don't curse. You'll have time enough to sleep."

"In the grave maybe."

"Who are you? Where are you from?" the man who had brought Jacob the straw asked. He lay on a bench nearby.

"I came from the Holy Land."

"You aren't that Reb Jacob who was in the study house today?" the man said, astonished.

"Yes,I am."

"Didn't anyone offer you a bed? You lived here once. I remember when you first came. You were the teacher. My own son learned the alphabet from you. We were talking about you earlier."

"It couldn't be the same Jacob," a woman said.

"Yes, the same."

"No wonder they call Pilitz Sodom," the man said. "But even in Sodom there was a Lot, and he took in strangers."

"What's your name?" Jacob asked the man.

"Mine? Leibush Mayer."

"Reb Leibush Mayer, one should look for the good in people, not the bad. How do you know no one invited me? The truth is, several men did. But it's not my habit to be anyone's guest. What's the matter with the poorhouse?"

"My enemies should rot in poorhouses," said the woman who had cursed Jacob.

"He knows what he's doing," Leibush Mayer defended Jacob. "How many of you here come from Pilitz? The devil knows where you're from. You land in Pilitz and eat up the town. But I came the very first day. There were only three houses here, then. It was right after the massacres. Gershon, may his soul burn in hell, had already grabbed Pilitzky's fields. In those days we didn't even have a quorum. I came with Menasha, my little boy. I'd lost my wife and the other two children. Menasha's gone too, now. I was a carpenter, and there was plenty of work to do. We had one tutor—he left before you came," he said, turning to Jacob. "Another teacher was supposed to come from the other side of the Vistula. Then you showed up. I remember it as if it were yesterday. What do these beggars know about that. You taught my Menasha and he learned a lot. In a few months he could read. Well, and so you took over the fields from Gershon. What didn't happen, then! We've talked about you; we've talked. Just last week I told these paupers here your whole story. Then you show up! But why did you come back from the Holy Land?"

Jacob was silent for a moment.

"To visit my wife's grave."

"Did you find it? The burial society people blotted it out. Don't think, Reb Jacob, there weren't people on your side." The man's tone changed. "I remember that meeting at the rabbi's the night after Yom Kippur. I went. True, I was only a carpenter, but I was invited. Wasn't I a householder? Didn't I know the small letters? I stood at the door and listened. I wanted to cry out, 'Don't be so harsh. He's punished enough.' But Gershon, his bones should turn in his grave, shook his fist at me. And who gave the verdict? The rabbi, Gershon's son-in-law. We know who was the real rabbi. It was Gershon too who denounced you to the priests. I'll testify to that before God Himself. Gershon almost turned to steam when he heard you'd taken the baby. He almost ruined the man for letting you have it. Did the child live?"

"He has three children of his own now."

"Where is he?"

"In Jerusalem."

"How did you get there with such a small baby?"

"It's a long story."

"They wanted me to be a member of the burial society, but I wasn't going to lick Gershon's boots. They didn't even cleanse your wife's body properly, just threw her into a ditch in her clothes. I was there. I saw it. The beadle was about to recite Kaddish, but Gershon said no. They stole everything you had. The corpse was still lying on the floor, and they were stripping the room. They even took the broom. And they turned the place upside down looking for money."

"I forgave them a long time ago."

"All right, you forgave. But has God? In Heaven everything's written down—from the biggest sin to the smallest. Gershon took to his bed before the year was out. His belly was always big but it swelled up and he looked like a barrel. There wasn't a feather bed large enough to cover him and the town rang with his hiccups. Your wife, Sarah, may she dwell in Paradise, was not at peace in her grave. Maybe I shouldn't tell you, but she came to women in dreams and complained: I am naked and without shrouds. She was also seen walking in the room where she died. Even in summer that room stayed icy. Everyone knew why she walked. The house was finally bought by a gentile."

"It's gone now," Jacob said.

"It burned down. Suddenly one night it blazed up like straw. The women swore they saw her image in the flames."

"Whose?"

"Your wife's."

5

Jacob awoke before dawn. Something heavy lay on his heart; his stomach was swollen; his limbs were weak. Am I getting sick? What's happening to me? he asked himself. His tongue was coated; his head lolled. Never before had he been so ill. He found he didn't have the strength to sit up. He lay amazed, watching the sun through he window, a red ball rising in the east. Dawn was like dusk; the birds twittered feebly. Were the window panes so dusty? Were his eyes misted? Somehow he raised himself and looked around. Men and women lay all about him on straw pallets amid garbage and rags: the old, the sick, the paralyzed, some with distorted faces. They muttered, snored, grunted, whined through their noses. Jacob sank back again closing his eyes.

He was not asleep, yet he saw Sarah standing near him dressed in luminous drapes and surrounded by light. The joy of the sunrise emanated from her. Smiling at him like a mother, like a wife, with a love greater than he had ever known, she said:

"Mazeltov, Jacob. We have been separated long enough."

Jacob opened his eyes. He knew the truth: his time had come. Well, is this what I came for, to die? Here, and not in the Holy Land? This seemed to him a harsh decree: his son and grandchildren were there; Benjamin Eliezer would not know of his death, would not know he should say Kaddish. But Jacob warned himself not to question the Lord of the Universe. If this was Heaven's decree so be it. "All that God does is for the good." Jacob glanced at his sack in which he carried his prayer shawl, his phylacteries, and a few books, a Pentateuch, a volume of the Mishnah, a prayer book. How can I recite holy words in this filthy place? he asked himself. He wanted to pray, but his lips would not move. Finally, he began to murmur a chapter of the Psalms, omitting to pronounce the names of God. "None of them can by any means redeem his brother, nor give to God a ransom for him. . . . That he should still live for ever, and not see corruption."

Jacob dozed off, woke, fell asleep, and woke once more. Even as he closed his eyes, his dreams rushed in on him. Phantoms walked, ran, screamed, behaved in indescribable ways. And when he opened his eyes, they remained for a time etched against the glare of the daylight, speaking a tongue that Jacob understood without hearing. He lay there seeming to sleep. A man with a gray disheveled beard and a wrinkled earthy face put his feet down from his bench and nudged Jacob.

"Reb Jacob, it's morning."

Jacob stirred.

"You don't want to be late with your Shema."

"I have no water to wash my hands."

"Wash your hands in the barrel. They don't bring you pitchers around here."

"I'm afraid I'm not well," Jacob said.

"What? You do look a little yellow."

The man stretched out his hand, touched Jacob's forehead, and frowned.

"I'll go for the healer."

"No, don't trouble."

"Caring for the sick is a sacred obligation."

The man put on his gabardine and his shoes and left. Soon the women and the children began to wake; they yawned, coughed, sneezed. One old crone sat up cursing. Everyone deloused himself. Despite his stuffed nose, Jacob was aware of the stench. Worms crawled on the floor and walls. Rabbis had many times denounced the lodging of men and women in the same room in the poorhouse but the practice persisted, the justification being that Satan had no power over the sick and the old. Modesty did not exist here. One woman bared breasts which hung down like empty sacks. Jacob averted his eyes. His wish had always been to die in the shadow of the holy ruins, near the graves of saints, surrounded by cabalists and ascetics, and to be buried on the Mount of Olives. He had imagined himself bringing Sarah's bones to the Mount and had intended to raise one stone for both of them. He had always pictured his son Benjamin Eliezer standing at his grave reciting Kaddish. Yet it was fortunate that he had had the foresight to carry with him a small bag of earth from the Holy Land. He lay silent while half-naked children crawled over him. A woman rebuked him.

"As if it wasn't crowded enough. The devil had to drag in another."

It was some time before Jacob realized that she was referring to him and he wanted to apologize but he lacked both the words and the strength with which to talk. Jacob listened to what was going on within him. How had it all happened so quickly? He had gone to sleep a strong man and had awakened moribund. His stomach had stopped digesting, his intestines were frozen; his teeth felt loose in his gums. Usually in the morning he had to urinate, but today there was no need even for that. He watched from under his eyelids the women and children eating, and the sight seemed foreign to him. But finally he summoned up enough strength to rise. He washed his hands at the barrel, and walked outside on unsteady legs to cleanse himself of urine before prayers. Standing at the wall, he forced out single drops. The heat was already oppressive. The sun blazed. Next to the poorhouse, in garbage and excrement, grew grass and wildflowers— white blooms, yellow blooms, feathery seed puffs, hairlike green fringes. Butterflies fluttered, and blue-gold flies buzzed on a heap of goat turds as if holding a meeting. A dog limped down the street sniffing the ground. For a moment the wind brought the clean scent of the fields, but then shifting bore only the smell of the outhouses. Feathers whirled in the air as in slaughter houses. Roosters crowed; chickens clucked; geese honked. On a patch of grass and weeds a crow picked at the guts from a chicken. Jacob stood openmouthed. This was the world he must soon leave. He returned to the poorhouse and tried to lift his sack. He could not stay there; the room, as the woman had pointed out, was too crowded. It was one thing to go among the poor to aid them, and another to infringe on the space that they needed. Only yesterday the sack had felt light; now he could barely raise it. At last, having pulled it over his shoulder, he said to everyone:

"Goodbye. Forgive me."

"The poor man is sick. Don't let him leave," screamed the same woman who had reproached him for being there.

"Where will you go, Reb Jacob?" voices called to him.

"To the study house."

"Oh, it's terrible. He can hardly walk," another woman screamed.

"Get him some water."

"Thank you. There's no need. Don't be offended."

Jacob kissed the mezuzah and walked to the study house, which was just across the street, taking small steps and stopping frequently to rest. He heard the voices of the men praying and the boys studying. Lingering in the antechamber, Jacob quickly thought over his life and tried to make an accounting, but his brain was as sluggish as his guts were. Nothing but exhaustion remained. Nevertheless, he marshaled his strength, and before saying the words which are customarily spoken before entering a holy place, he dipped his fingers into the copper font. He remembered having read in a book of ethics that even the man who dies in bed is a martyr. The very act of dying is a sacrificial offering.

6

Jacob became faint during his prayers and fell sprawling in his prayer shawl and phylacteries. There was consternation in the study house. He was lifted to his feet and a man who had no children took him home and gave him a room; the man's wife assisted Jacob.

Chanina the healer was sent for, and all kinds of remedies were applied— bleeding, leeches, herbs—but to no avail. Jacob grew weaker from hour to hour. His voice became so low one could barely hear him. The next morning he asked for his prayer shawl and phylacteries but lacked the strength to put on the shawl or bind the thongs to his arms. The men of Pilitz came to visit him and the rabbi came also. Jacob asked the rabbi to recite the confession. "And for the sin," Jacob said, as it is said on Yom Kippur; with hands that now lacked the strength to close he fruitlessly attempted to beat his breast. He remembered that he had been strong all his life; now he was as weak as he had once been powerful. He couldn't even turn on his other side. Merely to open his mouth and swallow a spoonful of warm water was too difficult.

Jacob wanted only to doze. He lay there with his eyelids closed, absorbed in an activity unknown to the healthy. He did not think but something in him approached the higher truths. From nowhere, images came to him: his father, peace be with him, his mother, peace be with her, his sisters, Zelda Leah, the children, Sarah. Even Jan Bzik visited him, no longer a peasant, but a saint from Paradise. They were debating something among themselves but without hostility, and Jacob too was being consulted. Both sides were in their own way right, and even though Jacob was not sure what the question was or what it meant, he was amazed. If only men could apprehend these things while they were still strong, he said to himself, they would serve the Lord differently. No one would lack confidence. No one would become sad. But how could these truths be conveyed to the vigorous? No, it was impossible. Already there was an impenetrable wall between Jacob and those who came to visit him. They wished him a speedy recovery, murmured the customary words of comfort and hope, gave him all kinds of advice, but though he heard them their words seemed empty, unrelated to anything he cared for. He did not want to recover; he no longer needed his body, and his devotion to it had passed.

Already, several times, he, Jacob had found himself outside his body looking down on it as if it were discarded clothing. The body lay, wrapped in linen, huddled in bed, sick, yellow, crumpled. You have already served your time— Jacob said to it—you are torn and stained with sins and must be cleansed. In one night the healthy Jacob had torn free from the moribund; he had traveled over fields, mountains, seas to the house of Benjamin Eliezer in Jerusalem. He had entered the room where his son sat studying by the light of an oil lamp, had spoken to him, given him a sign, but Benjamin Eliezer, engrossed in his book, had not responded. Before long some power had whisked Jacob back to Pilitz and he had again become imprisoned in his body and its suffering.

Jacob's death agony had begun. He breathed hoarsely, his chest heaved, single words of Yiddish and Polish bubbled from his throat. Those present thought he was dead, but when a member of the burial society laid a feather to his nostrils, it still moved. His body in its own way resisted the sentence of death. It tried to hold on, to function again, to digest, eliminate, belch, sweat, but its efforts were like the twitching of a slaughtered animal. The heart fluttered like a half-torn wing; the blood moved sluggishly; the eyes did not see the burning candle. The flame of life was guttering, and those on the other side, who waited for Jacob like relatives waiting on the shore for the ship to anchor, called to him and stretched out their hands. Jacob saw Sarah near Zelda Leah, and even though his thoughts were no longer earthly, he wondered. Well, but up there things happened differently. . . .

Jacob's body died, but he was already so busy greeting those who had come to meet him that he did not look back. His dark cabin with its rags and refuse was left behind on the ship. The voyagers would clean it out, those who must still continue to journey on the stormy seas. He, Jacob, had arrived.

The men of the burial society lifted the corpse, opened the window, and recited the justification of God's decree. They placed Jacob with his feet toward the door and set two candles at his head. Pious men gathered to recite the Psalms. The news that Jacob had died spread swiftly through the district. Even though he had lived in obscurity for twenty years in the land of Israel, how he had conducted himself was not unknown, and he was thought of as a righteous man. The original cemetery plot was long since fully occupied, so Jacob was given ground in the new part. The body was cleansed and taken to the study house where the rabbi spoke the eulogy. The whole town attended Jacob's funeral. When the gravedigger broke ground for Jacob's grave, his spade struck bones. He began to dig more carefully, and soon a body was seen that had not yet completely decomposed, perhaps because the earth there was so sandy and dry. From the skeleton and from pieces of clothing, the burial society women saw that it was a female. Strands of blond hair still entwined the skull, and it soon became clear that this was the grave of Sarah, who had been buried unshrouded in her own dress. The community had buried Sarah outside but the dead had gathered to take her in. The cemetery itself had ordained it; Sarah was a Jewish daughter and a sanctified corpse.

Pilitz was in an uproar. Women cried; the pious fasted. Many came, even young girls and children, for a look at the body that had lain twenty years in the earth and was still recognizable. The cemetery was as crowded as in the month of Elul when everyone visits the graves. All saw the hand of Providence in this event. It was like one of the ancient miracles, a sign that there is an Eye which sees and a scale wherein even the acts of the stranger are weighed. The elders called a meeting and decided to bury Jacob near Sarah.

Thus judgment was rendered. Jacob, enveloped in a prayer shawl, with shards on his eyes, and a stem of myrtle between his fingers, was buried near Sarah. And the community undertook to erect a common tombstone as recompense to Sarah for the injustice done her by Gershon and his men. After the thirty days of mourning, the engraver began to chisel their stone. At the crest were two doves facing each other, their beaks joined in a kiss. But only the outlines were formed in keeping with the Mosaic interdiction against images. Deeply incised were the names of the deceased: Jacob the son of Eliezer; Sarah the daughter of the Patriarch Abraham. Jacob was honored with the words, "Our teacher, the saint"; and inscribed near Sarah's name was the line from Proverbs, "Who can find a virtuous woman?"

The epitaph was completed by a passage from the Bible encircling their names: "Lovely and pleasant in their lives and in their death they were not divided."

Enemies, A Love Story

AUTHOR'S NOTE

Although I did not have the privilege of going through the Hitler holocaust, I have lived for years in New York with refugees from this ordeal. I therefore hasten to say that this novel is by no means the story of the typical refugee, his life, and struggle. Like most of my fictional works, this book presents an exceptional case with unique heroes and a unique combination of events. The characters are not only Nazi victims but victims of their own personalities and fates. If they fit into the general picture, it is because the exception is rooted in the rule. As a matter of fact, in literature the exception *is* the rule.

The novel was first published in *The Jewish Daily Forward* in 1966 under the title ''Sonim, di Geshichte fun a Liebe.'' It was translated by Aliza Shevrin an Elizabeth Shub and edited by the latter, Rachel MacKenzie, and Robert Giroux. Gratitude to all of them.

I.B.S.

PART ONE

████████

CHAPTER ONE

1

Herman Broder turned over and opened one eye. In his dreamy state, he wondered whether he was in America, in Tzivkev, or in a German camp. He even imagined himself hiding in the hayloft in Lipsk. Occasionally all these places fused in his mind. He knew he was in Brooklyn, but he heard Nazis shouting. They were jabbing with their bayonets, trying to flush him out, while he pressed deeper and deeper into the hay. The blade of a bayonet touched his head.

Full awakening required an act of volition. "Enough!" he told himself, and sat up. It was mid-morning. Yadwiga had been dressed for some time. In the mirror on the wall opposite the bed he caught sight of himself—face drawn, his few remaining hairs, once red, now yellowish and streaked with gray. Blue eyes, piercing yet mild, beneath disheveled eyebrows, nose narrow, cheeks sunken, the lips thin.

Herman always woke up shabby and rumpled, looking as if he had spent the night wrestling. This morning there was even a black-and-blue mark on his high forehead. He touched the bruise. "What is this?" he asked himself. Could it have been caused by the bayonet in his dream? The thought made him smile. He had probably bumped against the edge of the closet door on the way to the bathroom during the night.

"Yadwiga!" he called in a sleepy voice.

Yadwiga appeared in the doorway. She was a Polish woman with rosy cheeks, pug nose, light-colored eyes; her hair was light as flax, combed back in a bun and held in place by a single pin. She had high cheekbones and a full lower lip. In one hand she held a dust mop and in the other a small watering can. She wore a dress with red and green squares in a design uncommon in this country, and on her feet were run-over house slippers.

Yadwiga had spent a year with Herman in the German camp after the war and had been living in America for three years, but she had retained the freshness and shyness of a Polish village girl. She used no cosmetics. She had learned only a few English words. It even seemed to Herman that she carried with her the odors of Lipsk; in bed she smelled of camomile. From the kitchen now came the aroma of beets cooking, of new potatoes, of dill, and something else summery and earthy that he couldn't name but that evoked a memory of Lipsk.

She looked at him with good-natured reproach, shaking her head. "It's late," she said. "I've done the laundry and the shopping. I've had my breakfast, but I'm ready to eat again."

Yadwiga spoke a peasant Polish. Herman talked to her in Polish or sometimes in Yiddish, which she did not understand; he would throw in a few Biblical quotations in the holy tongue or even phrases from the Talmud, as the mood struck him. She always listened.

"Shikseh, what time is it?" he said.

"Almost ten o'clock."

"Well, I'll get dressed."

"Would you like some tea?"

"No, it's not necessary."

"Don't walk around barefoot. I'll get your slippers. I polished them."

"You've polished them again? Who polishes slippers?"

"They were all dried up."

Herman shrugged. "What did you polish them with? Tar? You're still a peasant from Lipsk."

Yadwiga went to the clothes closet and brought his bathrobe and slippers.

Though she was his wife and the neighbors called her Mrs. Broder, she behaved toward Herman as if they were still in Tzivkev and she still a servant in the house of his father, Reb Shmuel Leib Broder. Herman's entire family had been wiped out in the holocaust. Herman was alive because Yadwiga had hidden him in a hayloft in her native village of Lipsk. Her own mother had been unaware of his hiding place. After the liberation in 1945, Herman learned from an eyewitness that his wife, Tamara, had been shot after their children had been taken from her to be killed. Herman left with Yadwiga for Germany and the camp for displaced persons and later, when he obtained an American visa, had married her in a civil ceremony. Yadwiga had been ready to adopt the Jewish faith, but it seemed senseless to burden her with a religion that he himself no longer observed.

The slow, hazardous trip to Germany, the voyage on the military ship to Halifax, the bus trip to New York had so bewildered Yadwiga that to this day she was afraid of traveling alone on the subway. She never went farther than a few blocks from the house in which she lived. She really did not need to go anywhere. Mermaid Avenue provided her with everything she needed—bread, fruit, greens, kosher meat (Herman did not eat pork), an occasional pair of shoes or a dress.

On the days Herman stayed home, he and Yadwiga would stroll together on the Boardwalk. Though he told her repeatedly that she needn't cling to him— he was not about to run away from her—Yadwiga always held him firmly by the arm. Her ears were deafened by the noise and clamor; everything vibrated and shook before her eyes. Her neighbors urged her to go with them to the beach, but since the crossing to America Yadwiga had a dread of the ocean. A mere glance at the leaping waves and her stomach began to churn.

Occasionally Herman took Yadwiga to a cafeteria in Brighton Beach, but she could not accustom herself to the trains hurtling by on the El with their deafening roar, or the screeching automobiles racing this way and that, or to the hordes of people in the streets. Herman had bought her a locket to wear, containing a slip of paper with her name and address written on it in case she got lost, but it was no comfort to Yadwiga; she didn't trust anything in writing.

The change in Yadwiga's life seemed like an act of Providence. For three years Herman had depended on her utterly. She had brought food and water to him in the loft and carried out his waste. Whenever Marianna, her sister, needed to go to the hayloft, Yadwiga would climb up the ladder and warn Herman to burrow himself deeper into the space he had hollowed out in the depths of the hay. During the summer, when the fresh-cut hay was being stored away, Yadwiga hid him in the potato cellar. She put her mother and sister in constant jeopardy; if the Nazis discovered that a Jew was hiding out in the barn, they would have shot all three women and perhaps burned down the village as well.

Now Yadwiga lived on an upper floor of an apartment house in Brooklyn. She had two princely rooms, a foyer, a bathroom, a kitchen with a refrigerator, a gas oven, electricity, and even a telephone on which Herman called her when he was away on his book-selling trips. Herman's business might be in distant places, but his voice brought him close to her. When he was in the mood, he would sing her favorite song to her over the telephone:

> *"Oh, if we were to have a boy.*
> *Praise the Lord on high!*
> *In what would we cradle our joy?*
> *Praise the Lord on High!*
> *In the street below*
> *There's a tub in the snow.*
> *In that would our little son lie*
> *As we sang him a sweet lullaby.*
>
> *Oh, if we were to have a boy.*
> *Praise the Lord of the poor!*
> *In what would we swaddle our joy?*
> *Praise the Lord of the poor!*
> *In your apron full*
> *And my muffler of wool.*
> *In these would we wrap him secure*
> *Against the cold, he'd be safe and sure."*

The song remained a song: Herman took care not to make Yadwiga pregnant. In a world in which one's children could be dragged away from their mother and shot, one had no right to have more children. For Yadwiga, the apartment he gave her made up for not having children. It was like an enchanted palace in the stories that old village wives used to tell while spinning flax or stripping feathers for down. You pushed a button on the wall and lights went on. Hot and cold water flowed from faucets. You turned a knob and a flame appeared on which you could cook. There was a tub for daily baths that kept you clean and free of lice and fleas. And the radio! Herman would set the dial on a station that broadcast in Polish in the morning and evening, and Polish songs, mazurkas, polkas, on Sunday a sermon by a priest, and news from Poland, which had fallen to the Bolsheviks, filled the room.

Yadwiga could neither read nor write, but Herman would write letters for her to her mother and sister. When a reply came, written by the village teacher, Herman would read it to her. Sometimes Marianna enclosed a kernel of grain in the envelope, a little stalk with a leaf from an apple tree, or a small flower—reminders of Lipsk in faraway America.

Yes, in this distant country Herman was Yadwiga's husband, brother, father, God. She had loved him even when she was a servant in his father's house. Living with him in foreign lands, she realized how right she had been about his worth and intelligence. He knew his way in the world—he rode on trains and buses; he read books and newspapers; he earned money. If she needed anything for the house, all she had to do was tell him and he would bring it himself or an Express man would deliver it. Yadwiga would sign her name with three little circles as he had taught her to do.

Once on May 17, her name day, Herman had brought her two parakeets, as they were called here. The yellow one was a male and the blue one a female. Yadwiga named them Woytus and Marianna, after her beloved father and sister. Yadwiga had never got along with her mother. After Yadwiga's father died, her mother had taken a second husband, who beat his stepchildren. Because of him, Yadwiga had to leave home and work as a servant for Jews.

If only Herman stayed home more often, or at least slept at home every night, Yadwiga would have considered her good fortune complete. But he traveled about selling books for a living. When he was away, Yadwiga kept the door chained for fear of thieves, and also to keep the neighbors out. The old women who lived in the apartment house talked to her in a mixture of Russian, English, and Yiddish. They pried into her life, asking where she came from and what her husband did. Herman warned her to tell them as little as possible. He taught her to say in English, "Excuse me, I have no time."

2

Herman shaved while the bathtub filled with water. His beard grew fast. Overnight his face became as prickly as a grater. He stood before the mirror of the medicine cabinet—a man of slight build, somewhat taller than average, his narrow chest covered with tufts of hair resembling the clumps of stuffing that stick out of old sofas and armchairs. He ate as much as he wanted, but he remained lean. The outline of his ribs could be seen, and there were deep hollows between his neck and shoulders. His Adam's apple moved up and down as if of its own accord. His whole appearance expressed weariness. Standing there, he began spinning a fantasy. The Nazis had come back into power and occupied New York. Herman was hiding out in this bathroom. Yadwiga had had the door walled up and painted so that it looked like the rest of the wall.

"Where would I sit? Here on the toilet seat. I could sleep in the bathtub. No, too short." Herman examined the tile floor to see if there was enough room for him to stretch out. But even if he were to lie down diagonally, he would have to draw his knees up. Well, at least he would have light and air here. The bathroom had a window opening on a small courtyard.

Herman began to calculate how much food Yadwiga would need to bring him each day for him to survive: two or three potatoes, a slice of bread, a piece of cheese, a spoonful of vegetable oil, from time to time a vitamin pill. It would cost her no more than one dollar a week—at the most, one dollar and a half. Herman would have some books here, and writing paper. Compared to the hayloft in Lipsk, this would be luxurious. He would keep a loaded revolver at hand, or perhaps a machine gun. When the Nazis discovered his hiding place and came to arrest him, he would welcome them with a volley of bullets and leave one bullet for himself.

The tub almost overflowed; the bathroom was filled with steam. Quickly Herman turned off the faucets. These daydreams had taken on the character of obsessions.

As soon as he was in the tub, Yadwiga opened the door. "Here's some soap."

"I still have a piece left."

"Perfumed soap. Smell. Three for a dime."

Yadwiga smelled the cake of soap herself and handed it to him. Her hands were still as rough as a peasant's. In Lipsk, she had done the work of a man. She had sown, mowed, threshed, planted potatoes, even sawed and chopped wood. Her neighbors in Brooklyn gave her all kinds of lotions to soften her hands, but they remained as calloused as a laborer's. Her calves were muscular, hard as stone. All the other parts of her body were feminine and smooth. Her breasts were full and white; her hips were round. She looked younger than her thirty-three years.

From sunup until she went to sleep, Yadwiga never rested for a moment. She always found work to do. The apartment was not far from the ocean, but a good deal of dust blew in through the open windows, and all day Yadwiga washed, scoured, polished, and scraped. Herman remembered how his mother had praised her for her industriousness.

"Come, I'll soap you," Yadwiga said.

Actually, he felt like being alone. He hadn't finished figuring out the details of how to hide himself from the Nazis here in Brooklyn. For instance, the window would have to be camouflaged so the Germans wouldn't see it. But how?

Yadwiga started to soap his back, his arms, his loins. He had frustrated her longing to bear children and so had taken the place of child for her. She fondled him, played with him. Every time he went away from home, she feared that he would not return—he would lose his way in the turmoil and vastness of America. His every homecoming seemed a miracle. She knew that today he was to go to Philadelphia, where he would stay overnight, but at least he would eat breakfast with her.

The aroma of coffee and of bread baking drifted in from the kitchen. Yadwiga had taught herself how to make poppyseed rolls like the ones in Tzivkev. She prepared all kinds of delicacies for him and cooked his favorite dishes: dumplings, matzo balls with borscht, millet with milk, groats with gravy.

She had a freshly ironed shirt, underwear, and socks ready for him every day. She wanted to do so much for him, but he needed so little. He was more often on the road than at home. She had a burning desire to talk to him. "What time does the train leave?" she asked.

"What? Two o'clock."

"Yesterday you said three o'clock."

"A few minutes past two."

"Where is this city?"

"You mean Philadelphia? In America. Where should it be?"

"Is it far away?"

"In Lipsk it would be far, but here it's just a few hours away by train."

"How do you know who wants to buy books?"

Herman was thoughtful. "I don't know. I try to find buyers."

"Why don't you sell books here? There are so many people here."

"You mean Coney Island? Here they come to eat popcorn, not to read books."

"What kinds of books are they?"

"Oh, different kinds: how to build bridges, how to lose weight, how to run the government. And books of songs, stories, plays, the life of Hitler—"

Yadwiga's face became serious. "They write books about such swine?"

"They write about all kinds of swine."

"Well." And Yadwiga went into the kitchen. After a while Herman followed her.

Yadwiga had opened the little door of the birdcage and the parakeets were flying about the room. The yellow parakeet, Woytus, perched himself on Herman's shoulders. He liked to pick at Herman's earlobe and nibble crumbs from his lips or the tip of his tongue. Yadwiga was amazed at how much younger, fresher, and happier Herman appeared after he had bathed and shaved.

She served him warm rolls, black bread, an omelet, and coffee with cream. She tried to feed him well, but he didn't eat properly. He bit off a piece of the roll and put it aside. He only tasted the omelet. His stomach had surely shrunk during the war, but Yadwiga recalled that he had always eaten sparingly. His mother would quarrel with him about it every time he came home from Warsaw, where he was studying at the university.

Yadwiga shook her head in concern. He swallowed without chewing. Even though there was plenty of time before two o'clock, he kept looking at his watch. He sat on the edge of his chair as if he were about to jump up at any moment. His eyes seemed to be staring off beyond the wall.

Abruptly he shook off his mood and said, "Tonight I'll be eating supper in Philadelphia."

"Who will you eat with? Alone?"

He started talking to Yadwiga in Yiddish. "Alone. That's what you think! I'll be eating with the Queen of Sheba. I'm as much a book salesman as you're the Pope's wife! That faker of a rabbi I work for—still, if it weren't for him, we'd be starving. And that female in the Bronx is a sphinx altogether. What with the three of you, it's an absolute miracle I haven't gone out of my mind. Pif-pof!"

"Talk so I can understand you!"

"Why do you want to understand? 'For in much wisdom is much grief,' Ecclesiastes said. The truth will be known—not here, but in the hereafter, providing anything is left of our miserable souls. If not, we'll have to make do without the truth—"

"More coffee?"

"Yes, more coffee."

"What's in the newspaper?"

"Oh, they've made a truce, but it won't last. They'll start fighting again soon—those buffaloes. They never have their fill of it."

"Where is this?"

"In Korea, China—you name it."

"The radio said that Hitler is still alive."

"If one Hitler is dead, there are a million ready to take his place."

Yadwiga was silent a moment. She leaned on her broom. Then she said, "The neighbor with the white hair who lives on the ground floor told me I could earn twenty-five dollars a week in a factory."

"You want to go to work?"

"It gets lonesome sitting in the house by myself. But the factories are so far away. If they were nearer, then I'd work."

"Nothing is near in New York. You have to ride on the subways or you're stuck where you are."

"I don't know English."

"You could take a course. I can enroll you in one if you like."

"The old woman said they don't accept anyone who doesn't know the alphabet."

"I'll teach it to you."

"When? You're never at home."

Herman knew she was right. And at her age it was difficult to learn. When she had to sign anything with her three little circles, she reddened and perspired. It was hard for her to pronounce even the simplest English word.

Generally, Herman understood her peasant Polish, but sometimes at night, when she was overcome with passion, she would chatter a village gibberish that he couldn't follow—words and expressions he had never heard before. Could it be the speech of ancient peasant tribes, perhaps from pagan times? Herman had long been aware that the mind contains more than is gathered in one lifetime. The genes seem to remember other epochs. Even Woytus and Marianna seemed to have a language inherited from generations of parakeets. They obviously carried on conversations, and the way they would take flight together in the same direction, within a fraction of a second, indicated that they knew one another's thoughts.

As for Herman, he was a riddle to himself. The entanglements he involved himself in were mad. He was a fraud, a transgressor—a hypocrite, too. The sermons he wrote for Rabbi Lampert were a disgrace and a mockery.

He got up and went to the window. A few blocks away, the ocean heaved. From the Boardwalk and Surf Avenue came the noises of a Coney Island summer morning. Yet, on the little street between Mermaid and Neptune Avenues, everything was quiet. A light breeze was blowing; a few trees grew there. Birds twittered in the branches. The incoming tide brought with it a smell of fish, and something undefinable, a stench of putrefaction. When Herman put his head out of the window, he could see old shipwrecks that had been abandoned in the bay. Armored creatures had attached themselves to the slimy hulls—half alive, half sunk in primeval sleep.

Herman heard Yadwiga saying reproachfully, "The coffee is getting cold. Come back to the table!"

3

Herman left the apartment and ran down the stairs. If he didn't disappear quickly, Yadwiga might call him back. Every time he went away, she said goodbye as if the Nazis were ruling America and his life was in danger. She laid her hot cheek against his, begged him to be careful of cars, not to forget his meals, to remember to phone her. She clung to him with the devotion of a dog. Herman often teased her, called her silly, but he could never forget the sacrifice she had made for him. She was as direct and truthful as he was devious and enmeshed in lies. Still, he couldn't stay with her day and night.

The house in which Herman lived with Yadwiga was an old building. Many elderly refugee couples who needed fresh air for their health had settled there. They prayed in the little synagogue nearby and read the Yiddish papers. On hot days they brought benches and folding chairs out on the street and sat around chatting about the old country, their American children and grandchildren, about the Wall Street crash in 1929, about the cures worked by steam baths, vitamins, and mineral waters at Saratoga Springs.

Herman occasionally had the desire to strike up an acquaintance with these Jews and their wives, but the complications of his life made it necessary to avoid them. Now he hurried down the shaky steps and turned quickly to the right into the street before any of them could stop him. He was late with his work for Rabbi Lampert.

Herman's office was in a building on Twenty-third Street near Fourth Avenue. He could get to the subway at Stillwell Avenue by walking down Mermaid, Neptune, or Surf Avenues, or by the Boardwalk. Each of these routes had its attractions, but today he chose Mermaid Avenue. This street had an Eastern European flavor. Last year's posters announcing cantors and rabbis and the prices of synagogue pews for the High Holy Days still hung on the walls. From the restaurants and cafeterias came the smells of chicken soup, kasha, chopped liver. The bakeries sold bagels and egg cookies, strudel and onion rolls. In front of a shop, women were groping in barrels for dill pickles.

Even if he never had had a large appetite, the hunger of the Nazi years had left Herman with a sense of excitement at the sight of food. Sunlight fell on crates and bushel baskets of oranges, bananas, cherries, strawberries, and tomatoes. Jews were allowed to live freely here! On the main avenue and on the side streets, Hebrew schools displayed their signs. There was even a Yiddish school. As Herman walked along, his eye sought hiding places in case the Nazis were to come to New York. Could a bunker be dug somewhere nearby? Could he hide himself in the steeple of the Catholic church? He had never been a partisan, but now he often thought of positions from which it would be possible to shoot.

On Stillwell Avenue, Herman turned right, and the hot wind struck him with the sweet smell of popcorn. Barkers urged people into amusement parks and side shows. There were carousels, shooting galleries, mediums who would conjure the spirits of the dead for fifty cents. At the subway entrance, a puffy-eyed Italian was banging a long knife against an iron bar, calling out a single word again and again, in a voice that carried over all the tumult. He was selling cotton candy and soft ice cream that melted as soon as it was put into a cone. On the other side of the Boardwalk, the ocean sparkled beyond a swarm of bodies. The richness of color, the abundance, the freedom—cheap and shoddy as everything was—surprised Herman each time he saw it.

He went into the subway. Passengers, mostly young people, streamed out of every train. In Europe Herman had never seen such wild faces as these. But here the young seemed dominated by lust for enjoyment rather than for mischief. The boys ran, screeching, shoving one another like rams. Many of them had dark eyes, low foreheads, and curly hair. There were Italians, Greeks, Puerto Ricans. The small girls with their broad hips and high breasts carried lunch bags, blankets to spread out on the sand, suntan lotion, and umbrellas to protect them from the sun. They laughed and chewed gum.

Herman went up the stairs to the El, and a train soon arrived. When the doors opened, he felt a blast of heat. The ventilators hummed. Bare lightbulbs dazzled the eye; newspapers and peanut shells were strewn over the red cement floor. Some passengers were having their shoes shined by half-naked black boys, who knelt at their feet like ancient idol-worshippers.

A Yiddish newspaper that someone had left behind was lying on a seat and Herman picked it up and read the headlines. Stalin had declared in an interview that Communism and ·capitalism could co-exist. In China there were battles between the Red and Chiang Kai-shek's armies. On the inside pages of the paper, refugees described the terrors of Majdanek, Treblinka, Auschwitz. An escaped witness gave an account of a slave-labor camp in north Russia, where rabbis, socialists, liberals, priests, Zionists, and Trotskyites were digging for gold, dying of hunger and beriberi. Herman thought he had become inured to such horrors. Yet each new outrage shocked him. This article ended with the promise that some day there would be established a system based on equality and justice that would cure the sickness of the world.

"So? They are still intent on curing?" Herman dropped the paper to the floor. Phrases like a "better world" and a "brighter tomorrow" seemed to him a blasphemy on the ashes of the tormented. Whenever he heard the cliché that those sacrificed had not died in vain, his anger rose. "But what can I do? I contribute my share of evil."

Herman opened his briefcase, took out a manuscript, and read it, making notes. His livelihood was as bizarre as everything else that had happened to him. He had become a ghost writer for a rabbi. He, too, promised a "better world" in the Garden of Eden.

As Herman read, he grimaced. The rabbi was selling God as Terah sold idols. Herman could find only one justification for himself: most of the people who listened to the rabbi's sermons or read his essays were not completely honest either. Modern Judaism had one aim: to ape the Gentile.

The doors of the train opened and shut; Herman looked up each time. No doubt there were Nazis roaming about New York. The Allies had proclaimed amnesty for three-quarters of a million "small Nazis." The promises to bring the murderers to trial were lies from the very beginning. Who would sentence whom? Their justice was deceit. Lacking the courage to commit suicide, Herman had to shut his eyes, stop up his ears, close his mind, live like a worm.

Herman was to have changed from the express to the local train at Union

Square and then get off at Twenty-third Street, but when he looked out, he saw that the train had already reached the Thirty-fourth Street station. He took the stairs to the opposite platform, where he boarded a train going downtown. But again he missed his station and rode too far—to Canal Street.

These mistakes in the subway, his habit of putting things away and not remembering where, straying into wrong streets, losing manuscripts, books, and notebooks hung over Herman like a curse. He was always searching through his pockets for something he had lost. His fountain pen or his sunglasses would be missing; his wallet would vanish; his own phone number would slip from his mind. He would buy an umbrella and leave it somewhere within the day. He would put on a pair of rubbers and lose them in a matter of hours. Sometimes he imagined that imps and goblins were playing tricks on him. Finally he got to his office, located in one of the buildings owned by the rabbi.

4

Rabbi Milton Lampert had no congregation. He published articles in Hebrew journals in Israel and contributed to Anglo-Jewish periodicals in America and England. He had book contracts with several publishing houses. He was in demand for lectures at community centers, and even at universities. The rabbi had neither the time nor the patience to study or write. He had amassed a fortune from real estate. He owned half a dozen convalescent homes, had built apartment houses in Borough Park and Williamsburg, was a partner in a company that contracted for building projects worth millions of dollars. He had an elderly secretary, a Mrs. Regal, whom he continued to employ although she neglected her work. He had been separated from his wife, but they were again living together.

The rabbi referred to what Herman did for him as "research." Actually, Herman ghosted the rabbi's books, his articles, his speeches. He wrote them in Hebrew or in Yiddish, someone translated them into English, and a third person edited them.

Herman had been working for Rabbi Lampert for several years. The rabbi was many things at once: thick-skinned, goodhearted, sentimental, sly, brutal, naïve. He could recall obscure commentaries from the Prepared Table, but make errors in quoting a verse from the Pentateuch. He played the stock market, gambled, and raised money for all sorts of charitable causes. He was over six feet tall, had a potbelly, and weighed two hundred and sixty pounds. He played the role of a Don Juan, but it soon became apparent to Herman that the rabbi had no luck with women. He was still searching for his true love and often made himself ridiculous in this seemingly hopeless quest. It had gone so far that once he was punched in the nose by a husband in an Atlantic City hotel. His expenses were often greater than his income—at least that's what he reported on his tax return. He went to bed at two and woke up at seven in the morning. He ate two-pound steaks, smoked Havana cigars, drank champagne. His blood pressure was dangerously high and his doctor kept warning him about a heart attack. At sixty-four, his energy had not flagged and he was known as "the dynamic rabbi."

He had served as an army chaplain during the war and boasted to Herman that he had reached the rank of colonel.

No sooner had Herman crossed the threshold of his office than the telephone rang. He answered it and from the other end of the line the rabbi immediately began shouting at him in his strong bass voice. "Where the heck have you been? You were supposed to check in the first thing this morning! Where is my speech for Atlantic City? You forget that I still have to go over it, in addition to everything else I have to do. And what do you mean by moving into a house that doesn't have a telephone? When a person works for me, I have to be able to reach him, not have him stuck in a hole like a mouse! Ach, you're still a greenhorn! This is New York, not Tzivkev! America is a free country; you don't have to hide here. Unless you're making money illegally or the devil knows what! I'm telling you today for the last time—get a telephone where you live or our business is goodbye. Wait, I'm coming over. I have to talk to you about something. Stay where you are!" Rabbi Lampert hung up.

Herman started writing quickly in small letters. When he first met the rabbi, he had been afraid to admit that he was married to a Polish peasant. He had said he was a widower and had rented the spare room of a poor friend from the old country—a tailor who didn't have a phone. Herman's telephone in Brooklyn was listed under the name of Yadwiga Pracz.

Rabbi Lampert had often asked if he might visit Herman at the tailor's. It gave the rabbi special pleasure to drive his Cadillac down the streets of a poor neighborhood. He also enjoyed the impression made by his great bulk and smart clothes. And he loved doing favors—finding jobs for the needy, writing letters recommending admission to philanthropic institutions. Herman thus far had been able to talk the rabbi out of visiting him. He had explained that the tailor was too shy for company, and that as a result of his life in the camps he was somewhat unbalanced and might not even let the rabbi into the house. Herman had also dampened the rabbi's interest by casually mentioning that the tailor's wife was lame and that the couple had no children. The rabbi preferred families with daughters.

The rabbi told Herman over and over again that he should move. He went so far as to suggest a match for him. He offered him an apartment in one of his own houses. Herman explained that the old tailor had saved his life in Tzivkev and needed the few dollars of rent money that Herman paid him. One lie led to another. The rabbi made speeches and wrote articles opposing mixed marriages. More than once, Herman himself had to expound on this theme in his writings for the rabbi, warning against mingling with the "enemies of Israel."

How could his actions ever be explained to make sense? He had sinned against Judaism, American law, morality. He was deceiving not only the rabbi but Masha. But he was unable to behave differently. Yadwiga's sheer goodness bored him; when he talked to her, it was as if he were alone. Masha was so complicated, stubborn, and neurotic that he couldn't tell her the truth either. He had convinced her that Yadwiga was frigid and he had made a solemn vow that as soon as Masha divorced her husband, Leon Tortshiner, he would free himself from Yadwiga.

Herman heard heavy footsteps and the rabbi opened the door. He could barely get through the doorway: tall, broad—an enormous man with a red face, thick lips, a hooked nose, and bulging black eyes. He wore a light-colored suit, yellow shoes, and a gold-stitched tie with a pearl stickpin. In his mouth was a long cigar. His gray-streaked black hair stuck out from beneath his Panama hat. Ruby cuff-links glittered at his wrists and a diamond signet ring shone on his left hand.

He took the cigar from his mouth, flicked the ashes on the floor, and shouted, "*Now* you're starting to write. It should have been ready days ago! I can't wait like this till the last minute. What have you got scribbled there? It looks too long already. A conference of rabbis isn't a meeting of the elders of Tzivkev! This is America, not Poland. Well, and how about the essay on Bal Shem? It should have gone off. There's a deadline! If you can't manage it, please tell me and I'll find someone else—or I'll talk into a dictaphone and let Mrs. Regal type it."

"Everything will be ready today."

"Hand me the pages you've done and, once and for all, give me your address. Where do you live—in hell? In Asmodeus' castle? I'm beginning to think that you have a wife somewhere and are hiding her from me."

Herman's mouth felt dry. "I wish I had a wife."

"If you wanted one, you'd have one. I picked out a fine woman for you, but you won't even meet her. What are you afraid of? No one is going to drag you to the wedding canopy by force. Now what's your address?"

"Really, it isn't necessary."

"I insist that you give it to me. I have my address book right here. Well?"

Herman gave him an address in the Bronx.

"What is your landsman's name?"

"Joe Pracz."

"Protsch. An unusual name. How do you spell it? I'll have them put in a phone and tell them to send the bill to this office."

"You can't install one without his consent."

"Why should he care?"

"The ringing frightens him. It reminds him of the camp."

"There are other refugees and they have telephones. Have it put in your room. It will be better for him, too. If he's a sick person, he should be able to call a doctor or get help. Lunatics! Crazy people! This is why we have a war every few years; this is why Hitlers rise up. I insist that you spend six hours a day in the office—that's what we agreed. I'm paying rent and taking it off for tax purposes. If an office is always locked, then it's not an office. I have enough trouble without you."

Rabbi Lampert paused, then he said, "I wanted us to be friends, but there's something about you that makes it difficult. I could help you a great deal, but you shut yourself up like an oyster. What secrets are you hiding behind those proverbial seven locks?"

Herman didn't reply at once. "Anyone who's gone through all that I have is no longer a part of this world," he said finally.

"Clichés, empty words. You're as much a part of this world as the rest of us. You may have been a step away from death a thousand times, but so long as you're alive and eat and walk and, pardon me, go to the toilet, then you're flesh and blood like everyone else. I know hundreds of concentration-camp survivors, some of them were practically on the way to the ovens—they're right here in America, they drive cars, they do business. Either you're in the other world or you're in this world. You can't stand with one foot on the ground and the other in the sky. You're playing a role, that's all. But why? You should be open with me of all people."

"I am."

"What's troubling you? Are you sick?"

"No. Not really."

"Maybe you're impotent? That's all nerves. It's not organic."

"I'm not impotent."

"What is it then? Well, I won't force my friendship on you. But I'm calling today and having them put in a telephone."

"Please wait a while."

"Why? A telephone isn't a Nazi; it doesn't eat people. If you have a neurosis, go see a doctor. Maybe you need an analyst. Don't let it scare you. It doesn't mean you're crazy. The best people go to them. Even I went to an analyst for a time. I have a friend, a Dr. Berchovsky from Warsaw. If I send you to him, he won't overcharge you."

"Honestly, Rabbi, there's nothing wrong with me."

"All right, nothing. My wife also insists there's nothing wrong with her, but she's a sick woman just the same. She turns on the stove and goes shopping. She lets the water run in the tub and leaves a washcloth in it that stops up the drain. I sit at my desk, and suddenly I see a puddle on the carpet. I ask her why she does these things, and she becomes hysterical and begins to curse me. That's why there are psychiatrists—to help us before we get so sick that we have to be put away."

"Yes, yes."

"Well, wasted words. Let's see what you've written."

CHAPTER TWO

1

Whenever Herman pretended to be on the road selling books, he spent the nights with Masha in the Bronx. He had a room in her apartment. Masha had survived years in the ghetto and concentration camps. She worked as a cashier in a cafeteria on Tremont Avenue.

Masha's father, Meyer Bloch, had been the son of a rich man, Reb Mendl Bloch, who owned property in Warsaw and had had the honor of sitting at the table of the Alexandrover rabbi. Meyer spoke German, became a Hebrew writer of some reputation, and was a patron of the arts. He escaped from Warsaw before the Nazis occupied the country, only to die later of malnutrition and dysentery in Kazakhstan. Masha had attended the Beth Yaakov schools at the insistence of her Orthodox mother, and later had studied at a Hebrew-Polish high school in Warsaw. During the war, her mother, Shifrah Puah, was sent to one ghetto, Masha to another. They didn't see each other again until they met in Lublin after the liberation in 1945.

Even though Herman had himself managed to survive the Hitler catastrophe, he could never figure out how these two women had been able to rescue themselves. He had spent almost three years hiding in a hayloft. It was a gap in his life which could never be filled. The summer the Nazis invaded Poland, he was visiting his parents in Tzivkev, while his wife, Tamara, had gone with both children to her family in Nalenczew, a spa where her father owned a villa. Herman had hidden himself first in Tzivkev, then at Yadwiga's in Lipsk, and so avoided the forced labor of both ghetto and concentration camp. He had heard the shouts of the Nazis and the sound of their guns, but had been spared looking into their faces. Weeks had passed without his seeing the light of day. His eyes had grown accustomed to darkness; his hands and feet had become numb with disuse. He had been bitten by insects, field mice, rats. He had developed a high fever and Yadwiga had cured him with herbs she picked in the fields and with vodka she stole from her mother. In his thoughts, Herman had often likened himself to the Talmudic sage, Choni Hamagol, who according to legend slept for seventy years and when he awoke found the world so strange that he prayed for death.

Herman had met Masha and Shifrah Puah in Germany. Masha was married to a Dr. Leon Tortshiner, a scientist who was said to have discovered, or to have helped discover, some new vitamin. But in Germany he spent entire days and half the nights playing cards with a band of smugglers. He spoke a flowery Polish and dropped the names of professors and universities with which he claimed to have been associated. He managed financially on what the "Joint" gave him and on the meager income Masha earned mending and altering clothes.

Masha, Shifrah Puah, and Leon Tortshiner had preceded Herman to America. When Herman arrived in New York, he ran into Masha again. He worked first as a teacher in a Talmud torah and then as proofreader in a small printing shop, where he met the rabbi. By that time Masha had been separated from her husband, who as it turned out neither had made any discoveries nor had any right to the title of Doctor. He was now the lover of a wealthy elderly woman, the widow of a real-estate man. Herman and Masha had fallen in love when they were still in Germany. Masha swore that a gypsy fortuneteller had foretold her meeting with Herman. The gypsy had described him down to the smallest detail and had warned her of the pain and troubles their love would bring. While predicting Masha's future, the gypsy had fallen into a trance and fainted.

Herman and Tamara, his first wife, had both grown up in well-to-do homes. Tamara's father, Reb Shachnah Luria, had been a lumber dealer, and partner with a brother-in-law in a glass business. He had two daughters—Tamara and Sheva. Sheva had died in a concentration camp.

Herman was an only child. His father Reb Shmuel Leib Broder, a follower of the Rabbi of Hushatin, was a wealthy man who owned several houses in Tzivkev. He hired a rabbi to instruct his son in Jewishness and a Polish tutor to teach him secular subjects. Reb Shmuel Leib hoped his only son would become a modern rabbi. Herman's mother, who had attended a German gymnasium in Lemberg, wanted her son to become a doctor. At nineteen, Herman went to Warsaw, passed his matriculation exams, and enrolled in the school of philosophy at the university. He had shown a leaning toward philosophy even as a youngster.

He had read all the philosophic books he could find in the Tzivkev library. In Warsaw, against the wishes of his parents, he had married Tamara, a student of biology at the Wszchnica, who was active in leftist movements. Almost from the very beginning they did not get along. A disciple of Schopenhauer, Herman had determined never to marry and bring new generations into the world. He had told Tamara of his resolve, but she became pregnant, refused to have an abortion, and enlisted her family to force him into marriage. A boy was born. For a time she was an ardent Communist and even planned to go to live in Soviet Russia with her child. Later she dropped Communism and became a member of the Poalay Zion Party. Neither Tamara's parents nor Herman's were in a position to continue supporting the young couple and they earned their living by tutoring. Three years after their marriage, Tamara gave birth to a girl— according to Otto Weininger (at the time considered by Herman to be the most consistent philosopher), a creature with "no sense of logic, no memory, amoral, nothing but a vessel of sex."

During the war and in the years after, Herman had time enough to regret his behavior to his family. But basically he remained the same: without belief in himself or in the human race; a fatalistic hedonist who lived in presuicidal gloom. Religions lied. Philosophy was bankrupt from the beginning. The idle promises of progress were no more than a spit in the face of the martyrs of all generations. If time is just a form of perception, or a category of reason, the past is as present as today: Cain continues to murder Abel. Nebuchadnezzar is still slaughtering the sons of Zedekiah and putting out Zedekiah's eyes. The pogrom in Kesheniev never ceases. Jews are forever being burned in Auschwitz. Those without courage to make an end to their existence have only one other way out: to deaden their consciousness, choke their memory, extinguish the last vestige of hope.

2

When Herman left the rabbi's office, he took the subway to the Bronx. People were hurrying and shoving in the heat of the summer day. On the Bronx express train, all the seats were taken. Herman gripped a strap. Above his head a fan whirred, but the air it stirred was not cool. He hadn't bought an afternoon paper, so he read the advertisements—for stockings, chocolate, canned soups, "dignified" burials. The train sped into a narrow tunnel. Even the bright lights of the car did not keep out the stony darkness. At each station new clusters of passengers pushed their way in. The smell of perfume and perspiration mingled in the air. Makeup melted on the women's faces; their mascara streaked and caked.

Gradually the crowd thinned; the train now rode above-ground, on the El. Through factory windows Herman could see white and black women moving briskly around machines. In a hall with a low metal ceiling, half-naked youths were playing pool. A girl in a bathing suit lay on a folding cot on a flat roof, taking a sunbath in the setting sun. A bird flew through the pale-blue sky. Even though the buildings didn't seem old, an air of age and decay hovered over the city. A dusty mist, golden and fiery, hovered above everything, as if the earth had entered the tail of a comet.

The El stopped, and Herman bolted out through the door. He ran down the iron steps and walked on into a park. Trees and grass grew there, just as they would in the middle of a field; birds hopped about and chirped in the branches. In the evening, the park benches would be full, but now only a few elderly people occupied them. One old man was reading a Yiddish newspaper through a pair of blue spectacles and a magnifying glass. Another had rolled his trouser leg up to the knee and was warming his rheumatic leg. An old woman was knitting a jacket from coarse gray wool.

Herman turned left onto the street where Masha lived with Shifrah Puah. It had only a few houses, separated by empty lots overgrown with weeds. There was an old warehouse, with bricked-up windows and a gate that was always shut. In one dilapidated house, a carpenter was making furniture that he sold "unfinished." A "For Sale" sign hung on an empty house whose windows had been knocked out. It seemed to Herman that the street couldn't make up its mind whether to remain part of the neighborhood or to give up and disappear.

Shifrah Puah and Masha lived on the third floor of a house with a broken porch and a vacant ground floor, the windows of which were covered with boards and tin. A shaky stoop led to the entrance.

Herman climbed up two flights and stopped—not because he was tired, but because he needed time to complete a fantasy. What would happen if the earth were to split into two parts, exactly between the Bronx and Brooklyn? He would have to remain here. The half with Yadwiga would be drawn into a different constellation by another star. What would happen then? If Nietszche's theory about the eternal return was true, perhaps this had already occurred a quadrillion years ago. God does everything that he is capable of doing, Spinoza wrote somewhere.

Herman knocked on the kitchen door and Masha opened it immediately. She wasn't tall, but her slenderness and the way she held her head gave the impression that she was. Her hair was dark with a reddish cast. Herman liked to say that it was fire and pitch. Her complexion was dazzlingly white, her eyes light blue with flecks of green, her nose thin, her chin pointed. She had high cheekbones and hollow cheeks. A cigarette dangled between her full lips. Her face reflected the strength of those who have survived peril. Masha now weighed one hundred and ten pounds, but at the time of the liberation she had weighed seventy-two.

"Where's your mother?" Herman asked.

"In her room. She'll be out soon. Sit down."

"Here, I've brought you a present." Herman handed her a package.

"A present? You mustn't bring me presents all the time. What is it?"

"It's a box for holding stamps."

"Stamps? That will come in handy. Are there stamps already in it? There are. I have about a hundred letters to write, but weeks pass and I can't seem to pick up a pen. The excuse I give myself is that there are no stamps in the house. Now I won't have any excuse left. Thanks, dear, thanks. You shouldn't have spent the money. Well, let's eat. I've cooked something you like—stewed meat and groats."

"You promised me not to cook meat any more."

"I promised myself, too, but without meat there's nothing to cook. God himself eats meat—human flesh. There are no vegetarians—none. If you had seen what I have seen, you would know that God approves of slaughter."

"You don't have to do everything God wants."

"You do, you do."

The door from the other room opened and Shifrah Puah came in—taller than Masha, a brunette with dark eyes, black hair streaked with gray, which she wore pulled back in a bun, a sharp nose, and eyebrows that grew together. She had a mole on her upper lip; hairs grew on her chin. There was a scar on her left cheek, made by a Nazi bayonet in the first weeks of the Hitler invasion.

It was easy to see that she had once been an attractive woman. Meyer Bloch had fallen in love with her, had written Hebrew songs to her. But the camps and illness had ruined her. Shifrah Puah always wore black. She still mourned for her husband, her parents, sisters, and brothers—all exterminated in the ghettos and camps. Now she squinted like someone who suddenly comes out of the dark into the light. She raised her small, long-fingered hands, as if to smooth her hair, and said, "Oh, Herman! I hardly recognized you. I've got into the habit of sitting down and falling off to sleep. At night I lie wide awake till morning, thinking. During the day my eyes yearn for sleep. Did I sleep long?"

"Who knows? I didn't even know you were asleep," Masha said. "She walks around the house as quiet as a mouse. There are real mice here, and I can't tell the difference any more. She walks around all night and doesn't even bother to turn on the light. One of these days, you'll fall in the dark and break a leg. Mark my words."

"You're beginning again. I don't really sleep, but a curtain seems to fall over my face and my mind turns blank. It shouldn't happen to you. What do I smell? Is something burning?"

"Nothing's burning, Mama, nothing's burning. My mother has a peculiar habit—everything she does herself she blames on me. She burns everything she cooks, and as soon as I make something, she smells it burning. If she pours herself a glass of milk, she lets it run over, and she warns me to be careful. It must be a Hitler sickness. In our camp, there was a woman who informed on others—she accused them of the very things she had done herself. It was pathological and funny, too. There are no crazy people; the mad only pretend to be crazy."

"Everyone's sane—only your mother is crazy," Shifrah Puah grumbled.

"I didn't mean that, Mama. Don't put words in my mouth. Sit down, Herman, sit down. He brought me a little box to keep stamps in. Now I'll have to write letters. I should have cleaned your room today, Herman, but I got involved in a thousand other things. I've told you: be a boarder like all other boarders—if you don't demand that your room be kept neat and clean, you'll live in dirt. The Nazis forced me to do things for so long that I can't do anything of my own free will any more. If I want to do something, I have to imagine that a German is standing over me with a gun. Here in America, I've come to realize that slavery isn't such a tragedy after all—for getting things done, there's nothing better than a whip."

"Listen to her carrying on. Ask her what she's talking about," Shifrah Puah complained. "She has to say something contrary, that's all. She inherited it from her father's family—he should rest in the Garden of Eden. They all loved to argue. My father—may he rest in peace—your grandfather, once said, 'Their Talmudic arguments are brilliant, but somehow they end up proving that one is allowed to eat bread on Passover.' "

"How did bread on Passover get into this? Do me a favor, Mama, and sit down. I can't bear to see you standing up. She's so shaky I imagine she's going to fall any minute. And she does fall. A day doesn't pass without her falling.''

"What will you think up about me next? I was lying in the hospital in Lublin and was at death's door. I was at peace at last. Suddenly she appears and calls me back from the other world. What did you need me for if you keep making up lies about me? It's good to die, it's a pleasure. Whoever has tasted death has no more use for life. I thought she was dead too. Suddenly I find out she's alive and has come looking for me. One day she finds me, and the next day she's already talking back to me and pricking me with a thousand needles. If I should tell it all, anyone listening would think I was out of my mind.''

"You are, Mama, you are. I would need a barrel of ink to describe the condition she was in when I brought her out of Poland. But one thing I can say with a clear conscience: no one has ever tormented me the way she does.''

"What have I done to you, daughter, to make you talk like this? You were healthy even then—may no evil eye befall you—and I was dead. I told her openly, 'I don't want to live any more. I've had enough.' But she pulled me back to life with a fury. You can destroy a person with anger, but you can bring him back to life with it too. Why did you need me? It suited her fancy to have a mother, that's all. And that husband of hers, Leon, didn't appeal to me from the beginning. I took one look at him and I said, 'Daughter, he's a charlatan.' Everything is written on a person's forehead, they say, if you know how to read. My daughter can read the most difficult books, but when it comes to people, she doesn't know her hands from her feet. Now she's been left sitting here, a deserted wife, a grass widow forever.''

"If I want to get married, I won't wait for a divorce.''

"What! We're still Jews, not Gentiles. What's happening to the stew? How long does a stew have to sit on the fire? The meat will dissolve. Just let me look at it. Oh, my God! There's not a drop of water in the pot. Oh, you can't depend on her! I smelled it burning. They made a cripple out of me, those fiends, but I still have my sense of smell. Where are your eyes? You've read too many ridiculous books, God pity me!''

3

Masha smoked while she ate. She alternated between a bite of food and a puff on her cigarette. She tasted a bit of each dish and pushed the plate away, but she kept passing food to Herman, urging him to eat. "Imagine you're in the hayloft in Lipsk and your peasant has served you a piece of pork. How do we know what tomorrow will bring? It can happen again. Slaughtering Jews is part of nature. Jews must be slaughtered—that's what God wants.''

"Daughter, you're breaking my heart.''

"It's the truth. Papa always said that everything comes from God. You say it, too, Mama. But if God could allow the Jews of Europe to be killed, what reason is there to think He would prevent the extermination of Jews of America? God doesn't care. That's how God is. Right, Herman?''

"Who knows?''

"You have the same answer for everything: 'Who knows?' Someone must know! If God is almighty and omnipotent, He ought to be able to stand up for His beloved people. If He sits in heaven and stays silent, that means it must bother Him as much as last year's frost."

"Daughter, are you going to leave Herman in peace or aren't you? First you burn the meat, then you pester him with questions while he's trying to eat."

"It doesn't matter," Herman said. "I wish I knew the answer. It could be that suffering is an attribute of God. If one agrees that everything is God, then we are God too, and if I beat you, it means that God has been beaten."

"Why should God beat Himself? Eat up. Don't leave anything on your plate. Is that your philosophy? If the Jew is God and the Nazi is God, then there's nothing to talk about. Mama baked a kuchen. I'll bring you a piece."

"Daughter, first he has to eat the compote."

"What's the difference what he eats first? It all gets mixed up in the stomach anyway. You're a dictator, Mama, that's what you are. All right, bring him the compote."

"I beg you, don't quarrel on my account. What I eat first is of no importance. If you two can't live together peacefully, how can there ever be peace? The last two people on earth will kill each other."

"Do you doubt it?" Masha asked. "I don't. They'll stand opposite one another with atomic bombs and starve to death, because neither will give the other a chance to eat. If one were to take time out to eat, the other would throw the bomb. Papa always took me with him to the movies. She hates movies"— Masha nodded toward her mother—"but Papa was crazy about them. He used to say that when he was at the movies, he forgot all his troubles. I'm not interested in them now, but then I loved them too. I used to sit with him and he would let me hold his cane. When Papa left Warsaw, that day when all the men went away across the Praga bridge, he pointed to his cane and said, 'As long as I have this, I'm not lost.' Why am I bringing this up? Oh, yes! In one movie, they showed two deer—bucks—fighting over a female. They locked antlers and thrashed about till one of them fell dead. The survivor was half dead himself. The whole time, the female stood by chewing grass as if she wasn't involved at all. I was a child—in the second year of high school. I thought then, if God can instill such violence in innocent beasts, there is no hope. I often thought of that film in the camps. It made me hate God."

"Daughter, you shouldn't talk that way."

"I do many things I shouldn't do. Bring the compote!"

"How can we understand God?" Sifrah Puah went to the stove.

"Really, you shouldn't argue with her so much," Herman said quietly. "What can you accomplish by it? If my mother were alive now, I wouldn't talk back to her."

"You're teaching me how to act? I have to live with her—not you. Five days out of the week, you stay with your peasant, and when you finally come here, you start preaching. She infuriates me with her piety and narrow-mindedness. If God is so right, why does she raise such a fuss because the soup isn't ready as fast as she wants it to be? If you want my opinion, she's more devoted to material things than any atheist. First, she urged me to marry Leon Tortshiner because he used to bring her little cakes. Later, she started to find fault with him—God knows why. What difference was it to me who I married? After all

I'd been through, how could it matter? But tell me, how is your little peasant? Did you tell her you were going on a book-selling trip again?''

"What else?''

"Where are you today?''

"In Philadelphia.''

"What happens if she finds out about us?''

"She'll never find out.''

"There's always the possibility.''

"You may be sure she will never separate us.''

"I'm not so sure. If you can spend so much time with an illiterate goose, then you certainly don't have a need for anything better. And what sense is there in doing the dirty work for a swindler of a rabbi? At least become a rabbi and swindle in your own name.''

"I can't do that.''

"You're still hiding in your hayloft. That's the truth!''

"Yes, it's the truth. There are soldiers who can drop a bomb on a city and kill a thousand people, but they can't bring themselves to slaughter a hen. As long as I don't see the reader I deceive and he doesn't see me, I can stand it. Besides, what I write for the rabbi doesn't do any harm. On the contrary.''

"Does that mean you're not a fraud?''

"I am and let's stop talking about it!''

Shifrah Puah returned. "Here's the compote. Wait, let it cool. What's she saying about me, my daughter? What is she saying? You would think I was her worst enemy, the way she talks.''

"Mama, you know the proverb: 'God protect me from my friends, I'll protect myself from my enemies.' ''

"I saw how you protected yourself from them. Oh well, since I'm still alive after they butchered my family and my people, you are right. You alone, Masha, are responsible. I would have been at rest now if it hadn't been for you.''

4

After supper, Herman went to his room. It was a tiny room with a single window overlooking a small yard. Below there was grass growing and a crooked tree. The bed was rumpled. Books, manuscripts, and scraps of paper covered with Herman's doodles lay scattered about.

Just as Masha always had to hold a cigarette between her fingers, so Herman had to hold a pen or a pencil. He wrote and made notes even in the hayloft in Lipsk, whenever there was enough light coming through the cracks in the roof. He practiced an ornate calligraphy, elaborating the letters with flourishes. He drew pictures of outlandish creatures with protruding ears, long beaks, and round eyes, and surrounded them with trumpets, horns, and adders. He even wrote in his dreams—on yellowish paper in Rashi script, a combination of a story book, cabalistic revelations, and scientific discoveries. He sometimes woke up with a cramp in his wrist from too much writing.

Herman's room was under the roof, and during the summer it was always hot, except early in the morning before the sun rose. Heavy soot sifted in through the open window. Although Masha changed the sheets and pillow cases frequently, the bedding always looked grimy. There were holes in the floor, and at night mice could be heard scratching underneath. Several times Masha set a trap, but the sound of the trapped creatures in agony was too much for Herman. He would get up in the middle of the night and free them.

As soon as he came into his room, Herman stretched out on the bed. His body was racked by pain. He suffered from rheumatism and sciatica; sometimes he thought he was walking around with a spinal tumor. He had neither the patience to go to doctors nor confidence in them. The years of Hitlerism had left him with a fatigue he never quite got rid of except when he made love to Masha. After eating, his stomach ached. Every little draft clogged his nose. Often his throat was sore, and he grew hoarse. Something in his ear pained him—an abscess, a growth? The one thing his organism escaped was fever.

It was evening, but the sky was still light. A single star shone brightly, blue and green, near and far, with a glow and substantiality that baffled him. A straight line led from its height in the universe directly to Herman's eye. This heavenly body (if it was a body) twinkled with cosmic joy; it laughed at the physical and spiritual smallness of a being that possessed only a talent for suffering.

The door opened and Masha came in. In the twilight her face was a mosaic of shadows. Her eyes seemed to generate their own light. She had a cigarette between her lips. Herman repeatedly warned her that one day she would start a fire with her cigarettes. "Sooner or later I will burn," she always replied. Now she stood at the door, inhaling. The glow of the cigarette made her face seem fiery and fantastic for a moment. Then she removed a book and magazine from a chair and sat down. She said, "God in heaven, it's hot as hell here."

Despite the heat, Masha would not undress as long as her mother was awake. For appearance's sake, she had put bedding on the sofa in the living room.

Meyer Bloch, Masha's father, had considered himself an unbeliever, but Shifrah Puah remained devout and maintained a strictly kosher kitchen. She even wore a wig on the High Holy Days when she went to pray. On the Sabbath, she insisted that Meyer Bloch perform the sanctification ceremony and sing the Sabbath hymns, although after the meal he would lock himself in his study and write poetry in Hebrew.

The ghetto, the concentration camps, the displaced-person camps, had unsettled the traditions of both mother and daughter. In the German camp where Shifrah Puah had lived with Masha after the war, couples copulated openly. When Masha married Leon Tortshiner, Shifrah Puah slept in one room with her daughter and son-in-law, separated only by a screen.

Shifrah Puah would say that the soul, like the body, could take so many blows and no more; then it stopped feeling pain. In America, her piety intensified. She prayed three times a day and often went around with a cloth covering her hair, imposing restrictions upon herself that she hadn't observed even in Warsaw. She continued to live in spirit with those who had been gassed and tortured. She was always lighting paraffin-filled glasses—memorial candles for friends and relatives. In the Yiddish newspapers she read nothing but the accounts of those who had survived the ghettos and concentration camps. She saved money from her food budget to buy books about Majdanek, Treblinka, Auschwitz.

Other refugees used to say that with time one forgets, but neither Shifrah Puah nor Masha would ever forget. On the contrary, the further removed they were from the holocaust, the closer it seemed to become. Masha would attack her mother for grieving so much for the dead victims, but when her mother was silent, Masha would take over. When she talked of German atrocities, she would run to the mezuzah on the door and spit on it.

Shifrah Puah would pinch her own cheeks. "Spit, daughter, blaspheme! We've had one catastrophe here, and we'll have another one there!" And she would point to the sky.

Masha's separation from Leon Tortshiner and the affair she was carrying on with Herman Broder, the husband of a Gentile woman, were to Shifrah Puah a continuation of the horrors that had begun in 1939; it seemed they would never cease. But, nevertheless, Shifrah Puah felt close to Herman and called him "my child." She was impressed by his knowledge of Judaism.

Every day in her prayers, she implored the Almighty to make Leon Tortshiner agree to divorce Masha, and Herman separate from his Gentile wife, and let her, Shifrah Puah, live to have the joy of leading her daughter to the wedding canopy. But it appeared that such rewards were not to be hers. Shifrah Puah blamed herself: she had rebelled against her parents, she treated Meyer badly, she had paid too little attention to Masha when she was growing up, when it would have been possible to instill the fear of God in her. And the greatest sin she had committed was to have remained alive when so many innocent men and women had been martyred.

Shifrah Puah was in the kitchen, washing the dishes and mumbling to herself. She seemed to be arguing with an unseen person. She turned off the light and turned it on again. She recited the prayer to be said before retiring, took a sleeping pill, filled the hot-water bottle. Shifrah Puah suffered from heart, liver, kidney, and lung ailments. Every few months she would fall into a coma and the doctors would give her up, but each time she gradually recovered. Masha listened to every move her mother made, always on the alert should help be needed. Mother and daughter loved one another, yet held innumerable grudges against each other. Their grievances dated back to the time when Meyer Bloch was still alive. He had carried on an allegedly platonic love affair with a Hebrew poetess, a teacher of Masha's. Masha would say jestingly that the love affair had started with a discussion about some rule in Hebrew grammar and had never gone any further. But Shifrah Puah had not forgiven Meyer even this small unfaithfulness.

Shifrah Puah's room was dark now, and still Masha sat on the chair in Herman's room, smoking one cigarette after another. Herman knew that she was preparing some unusual story for their love play. Masha compared herself to Scheherazade. The kissing, the fondling, the passionate love-making was always accompanied by stories from the ghettos, the camps, her own wandering through the ruins of Poland. Through them all, men pursued her: in bunkers, in the forest, in the hospital where she had worked as a nurse.

Masha had collected scores of adventures. Sometimes it seemed she must be making them up, but Herman knew she was not a liar. Her most complicated experiences had come after the liberation. The moral of all her tales was that if it had been God's purpose to improve His chosen people by Hitler's persecution,

He had failed. The religious Jews had been practically wiped out. The worldly Jews who managed to escape had, with few exceptions, learned nothing from all the terror. Masha boasted and confessed at the same time. Herman would warn her not to smoke in bed, but she would kiss him and blow smoke rings at him. Sparks from her cigarettes would land on the sheet. She would chew gum, munch chocolates, drink Coca-Cola. She would bring Herman food from the kitchen. Their love-making was not merely a matter of a man and a woman having intercourse, but a ritual that often lasted till daybreak. It reminded Herman of the ancients, who would relate the miracle of the exodus from Egypt until the morning star rose.

Many of the heroes and heroines that peopled Masha's dramas had been killed, had died in epidemics, or were trapped in Soviet Russia. Others had settled in Canada, Israel, in New York. Once Masha had gone into a bakery to buy a cake and the baker had turned out to be a former Capo. Refugees recognized her in the cafeteria on Tremont Avenue, where she was a cashier. Some had become rich in America—had opened factories, hotels, supermarkets. The widowers had taken new wives, the widows new husbands. Women who had lost their children and were still young had other children in new marriages. Men who had been smugglers in Nazi Germany and dealt in black-market goods had married German girls, sometimes the daughters and sisters of Nazis. No one had repented his sins—neither the aggressor nor the victim. Take Leon Tortshiner, for example.

Masha never tired of talking about Leon Tortshiner and his trickery. He was everything at once: a pathological liar, a drunkard, a braggart, a sex maniac, a gambler who would wager the shirt on his back. He invited his mistress to the wedding banquet that Masha and her mother had paid for with their last pfennigs. He dyed his hair; he assumed the title of Doctor, to which he had no right; he had been accused of plagiarism. He belonged at one and the same time to the Zionist Revisionist Party and to the Communist Party. The New York judge who had granted Masha a legal separation had allotted her fifteen dollars a week alimony, but Leon Tortshiner had yet to pay one cent. On the contrary, he used every device to get money out of her. He still telephoned her, wrote her letters, and begged her to return to him.

More than once, Herman had made Masha promise not to stay up late. They both needed to get up in the morning to go to work. But Masha seemed hardly to require sleep. She could doze off and wake up refreshed a few minutes later. Her dreams plagued her. She would shout in her sleep; talk German, Russian, Polish. The dead revealed themselves to her. She would use a flashlight and show Herman the scars the dead had left on her arms, her breasts, her thighs. Her father appeared to her in a dream and read her verses he had written in the other world. A stanza had remained in her mind and she had recited it to Herman.

Even though Masha had had love affairs of her own in the past, she could never forgive Herman his former relationships with women—not even with those who had died. Had he ever loved Tamara, the mother of his children? Had her body been more attractive to him than Masha's? In what way? Well, and what about that student of romance languages, the girl with the long braids? And Yadwiga? Was she really as cold as he said she was? And what would happen if Yadwiga were suddenly to die—if she were to commit suicide? If Masha were to die—how long would he remember her? How long would he wait before finding someone else? If he would just once be honest with her!

"How long would *you* wait?" Herman asked.

"I would never have anyone again."

"Is that the truth?"

"Yes, you devil, it's the holy truth." And she kissed him long and passionately. It became so still in the room that the scratching of a mouse could be heard under the flooring.

Masha possessed the suppleness of an acrobat. She aroused in him desires and powers he didn't know he had. In some mystical way she could temporarily stop the bleeding during her period. Even though neither Masha nor Herman was perverse, they talked endlessly to each other of unusual sexual behavior and perversions. Would she enjoy torturing a Nazi murderer? Would she make love to women if there were no men left on earth? Could Herman turn homosexual? Would he copulate with an animal if all humans had perished? It was only since his affair with Masha that Herman had begun to understand why union, the joining of male and female, was so important in the Cabala.

At moments when Herman fantasized about a new metaphysic, or even a new religion, he based everything on the attraction of the sexes. In the beginning was lust. The godly, as well as the human, principle is desire. Gravity, light, magnetism, thought may be aspects of the same universal longing. Suffering, emptiness, darkness are nothing more than interruptions of a cosmic orgasm that grows forever in intensity . . .

———————————

5

Today Masha had morning hours at the cafeteria. Herman had slept late; it was a quarter to eleven when he awoke. The sun was shining, and the sound of birds and the rumble of a delivery truck came through the open window. In the other room, Shifrah Puah was reading the Yiddish newspaper, occasionally heaving a deep sigh over the troubles of the Jews and human cruelty in general. Herman went into the bathroom, shaved, and bathed. His clothing was in the Coney Island apartment, but he kept some shirts, handkerchiefs, and underwear here in the Bronx. Shifrah Puah had washed and ironed a fresh shirt for him. She behaved toward him like a mother-in-law. Even before he was dressed, she had started to make his omelet; she had bought strawberries especially for him. Herman felt catered to and at the same time embarrassed when he ate breakfast with Shifrah Puah. She insisted that he wash his hands from a pitcher, according to the Orthodox ritual. Now that Masha wasn't at home, she gave him his hat to wear when he recited the prayer over the hand-washing and later for the benediction. She sat opposite him at the table, nodding and muttering. Herman knew what she was thinking: in the camps one hadn't allowed oneself to so much as imagine a feast like this. There a person would have risked his life for a piece of bread, a potato. Shifrah Puah picked up a slice of bread as if she were touching a sacred object. She bit into it carefully. Guilt stared out of her dark eyes. Could she permit herself to enjoy God's bounty when so many God-fearing Jews had died of starvation? Shifrah Puah often maintained that she had been permitted to survive only because of her sins. The blessed souls, the pious Jews, God had taken to Himself.

"Eat up everything, Herman. It's forbidden to leave anything."

"Thanks. The omelet is excellent."

"How can it be bad? Fresh eggs, fresh butter. America—long may it prosper—is full of good things. Let's hope we don't lose it through sinfulness. Wait, I'll bring the coffee."

In the kitchen, while she poured out the coffee, Shifrah Puah broke a glass. Breaking dishes was one of her failings. Masha often scolded her because of this and Shifrah Puah was ashamed of her weakness. Her vision wasn't what it should be. In the past, she assured Herman, she had never broken a thing, but she had come out of the camps a bundle of nerves. Only God in heaven knew how much she suffered, how tortured she was by nightmares. How can one stay alive remembering all she remembered? That very moment, as she stood at the stove, she had seen in her mind's eye a young Jewish girl stripped naked and balancing on a log over a pit of excrement. All around her stood groups of Germans, Ukrainians, Lithuanians, taking bets on how long she would be able to stand there. They shouted insults at her and at the Jews; half drunk, they watched until this eighteen-year-old beauty, this daughter of rabbis and esteemed Jews, slipped and fell into offal.

Shifrah Puah recalled a hundred such incidents to Herman. It was this memory that had caused her to drop the glass. Herman went to help her pick up the pieces, but she wouldn't let him. He might—God forbid—cut his fingers. She swept up the slivers of glass with a brush and dustpan and then carried in his coffee. He often had the feeling that whatever she touched became holy. He drank his coffee and ate a piece of cake she had baked especially for him (the doctor had put her on a strict diet). He was sunk in thoughts so old and familiar that they were no longer expressible in words.

Herman didn't have to go to his office. Masha was through at noon and he went to the cafeteria to meet her. She was to get her first vacation this summer—one week. She was anxious to go somewhere with him, but where? Herman walked down Tremont Avenue toward the cafeteria. He passed shops selling fancy goods, ladies' wear, stationery. Salesmen and saleswomen sat and waited for customers just as in Tzivkev. Chain stores had driven many of the small businesses into bankruptcy. Here and there a for-rent sign hung on the door. There was always someone ready to try his luck again.

Herman entered the cafeteria through the revolving door and saw Masha. There she stood, the daughter of Meyer Bloch and Shifrah Puah, accepting checks, counting money, selling chewing gum and cigarettes. She caught sight of him and smiled. According to the cafeteria clock, Masha had twenty minutes more to work, so Herman sat down at a table. He preferred a table next to the wall or, if possible, in a corner between two walls, so that no one could come up behind him. Despite the big meal he had just eaten, he bought a cup of coffee and some rice pudding at the counter. It seemed impossible for him to put on weight. It was as if a fire in him consumed everything. From a distance, he watched Masha. Although the sun shone in through the windows, the electric lights were on. At neighboring tables men were openly reading Yiddish newspapers.

They didn't need to hide from anyone. It always seemed like a miracle to Herman. "How long can this last?" he would ask himself.

One of the customers was reading a Communist paper. He probably felt dissatisfied with America, hoped for a revolution, for the masses to swarm into the street, to break the store windows Herman had just passed, and drag the salespeople off to prison or to slave-labor camps.

Herman sat quietly, preoccupied with the complexities of his situation. He had remained in the Bronx for three days. He had telephoned Yadwiga and told her that he had had to go on from Philadelphia to Baltimore, and had promised to be back this evening. But he wasn't sure that Masha would let him go; they had talked of going to a film together. She used every device to keep him with her, and made things as difficult as she could. Her hatred of Yadwiga approached the irrational. If Herman had a stain on his clothing or a button was missing from his coat, Masha would accuse Yadwiga of being indifferent to him, of living with him only because he was supporting her. Masha was the best argument Herman knew for Schopenhauer's thesis that intelligence is nothing more than a servant of blind will.

Masha finished her work at the cash register, gave the money and the checks to the cashier who was relieving her, and came over to Herman's table with her lunch on a tray. She had slept very little the night before and had awakened early, but she didn't look tired. The usual cigarette hung between her lips, and she had already had quite a few cups of coffee. She loved spicy food—sauerkraut, dill pickles, mustard; she added salt and pepper to everything she ate, drank her coffee black without sugar. She took a sip of coffee and drew deeply on her cigarette. She left three-fourths of the meal uneaten.

"Well, how is my mother?" she asked.

"Everything's all right."

"All right? I have to take her to the doctor tomorrow."

"When is your vacation?"

"I'm not sure yet. Come, let's get out of here! You promised to take me to the zoo."

Both Masha and Herman could walk for miles. Masha stopped often at store windows. She belittled American luxuries, but she had a keen interest in bargains. Businesses that were closing down might be selling goods at great reductions—sometimes less than half price. For pennies Masha would buy remnants of fabric from which she made clothes for herself and her mother. She also sewed bedspreads, curtains, even slip covers for the furniture. But who came to visit her? And where did she go? She had alienated her refugee friends—first, to avoid Leon Tortshiner, who was in their circle, and second, because of her life with Herman. There was always the danger that he might meet someone who knew him from Coney Island.

They stopped at the Botanical Gardens to look at the flowers, palms, cactuses, the innumerable plants grown in the synthetic climate of hothouses. The thought occurred to Herman that Jewry was a hothouse growth—it was kept thriving in an alien environment nourished by the belief in a Messiah, the hope of justice to come, the promises of the Bible—the Book that had hypnotized them forever.

After a while Herman and Masha continued on to the Bronx Zoo. Its reputation had reached them even in Warsaw. Two polar bears dozed in the shadow of an overhanging ledge by a pool of water, undoubtedly dreaming of snow and icebergs. Each animal and bird conveyed something in its own wordless language, a story handed down from prehistoric times, both revealing and concealing the patterns of continuous creation. The lion slept, and from time to time lazily opened his golden eyes, which expressed the despondency of those who are allowed neither to live nor to die, and with his mighty tail swept away the flies. The wolf paced to and fro, circling his own madness. The tiger sniffed at the flooring, seeking a spot on which to lie down. Two camels stood immobile and proud, a pair of Oriental princes. Herman often compared the zoo to a concentration camp. The air here was full of longing—for deserts, hills, valleys, dens, families. Like the Jews, the animals had been dragged here from all parts of the world, condemned to isolation and boredom. Some of them cried out their woes; others remained mute. Parrots demanded their rights with raucous screeching. A bird with a banana-shaped beak turned its head from right to left as if looking for the culprit who had played this trick on him. Chance? Darwinism? No, there was a plan—or at least a game played by conscious powers. Herman was reminded of Masha's words about the Nazis in heaven. Wasn't it possible that a Hitler presided on high and inflicted suffering on imprisoned souls? He had equipped them with flesh, blood, teeth, claws, horns, anger. They had either to commit evil or to perish.

Masha threw her cigarette away. "What are you thinking about—which came first, the chicken or the egg? Come, buy me some ice cream."

CHAPTER THREE

1

Herman spent two days with Yadwiga. Since he planned to go away with Masha for her week's vacation he was careful to tell Yadwiga beforehand about a trip he would have to take to faraway Chicago. To make it up to her in advance, he took her on a one-day outing. Right after breakfast, they walked to the Boardwalk and he bought rides on a carousel. Yadwiga almost screamed when Herman sat her on a lion—he mounted a tiger. With one hand she held on to the lion's mane and with the other she held an ice-cream cone. Next they rode on the Wonder Wheel and the little car in which they sat hurtled back and forth. Yadwiga fell over Herman and laughed with fright and glee. After a lunch of knishes, stuffed derma, and coffee, they strolled over to Sheepshead Bay, where they took a boat to Breezy Point. Yadwiga was afraid she might become seasick, but the water stayed calm; the waves, a mixture of green and gold, barely moved. The breeze had tousled Yadwiga's hair and she tied it back with a kerchief. Music was playing at the pier where the boat stopped, and Yadwiga drank lemonade. In the evening, after a fish dinner, Herman took her to a musical film full of dancing, singing, beautiful women, and magnificent palaces. He translated for her so that she would know what was happening. Yadwiga snuggled up close to him, held his hand, and from time to time raised it to her lips. "I'm so happy . . . so lucky," she whispered. "God himself has sent you to me!"

That night, after a few hours of sleep, Yadwiga awakened, filled with desire. She begged him, as she had so many times before, to give her a child, to arrange for her conversion to Judaism. He promised her everything she asked.

In the morning, Masha telephoned Herman to say that her vacation had been postponed for a few days, because the cashier who was to substitute for her was ill. Herman told Yadwiga that the Chicago trip, on which he had hoped to sell a lot of books, had to be put off and instead he was going to Trenton, close by. He made a brief stop at the rabbi's office on Twenty-third Street, then he took the subway to Masha's house. He should have been content, but he was tormented by the foreboding of some catastrophe. What would it be—would he be taken sick? Would some misfortune befall Masha or Yadwiga, God forbid? Would he be arrested or deported for failing to pay taxes? True, he probably didn't earn enough, but still he should have filled out the form; it was possible he owed the federal government or the state a few dollars. Herman was aware that some of his fellow countrymen from Tzivkev knew he was in America and made efforts to get in touch with him, but he preferred to keep his distance. Every human contact was a potential danger to him. He even knew he had distant relatives somewhere in America but he neither asked nor wanted to know where they were.

That evening Herman spent with Masha. They quarreled, made up, quarreled again. As always, their conversation abounded with promises they both knew would never be kept, with fantasies of pleasures not to be achieved, with questions asked as a spur to their mutual excitement. Masha wondered if she would have allowed him to sleep with her sister, if she had had one. Would she enjoy sharing Herman and his brother, if he had had a brother? What would she do if her father were still alive and had developed an incestuous passion for her? Would Herman still find her desirable if she decided to go back to Leon Tortshiner, or marry some rich man for his money? If her mother were dead, would Masha move in with Herman and Yadwiga? Would she leave him if he became impotent? Often their conversations culminated in talk of death. They both believed they would die young. Masha urged Herman again and again to acquire a cemetery plot for the two of them so that they could be buried together. In her passion, Masha assured Herman that she would visit him in his grave and they would make love. How could it be otherwise?

Masha had to leave for the cafeteria early in the morning, and Herman remained in bed. As usual, he was behind in his work for Rabbi Lampert, and he resolved to finish the manuscript that had been promised. He had given the rabbi a false address at which to have a telephone installed, but it seemed the rabbi had forgotten all about it. Thank God, he was too preoccupied with his own business to remember. The rabbi made notes, but he never consulted them. None of the old philosophers and thinkers could have foreseen an epoch such as this one: the helter-skelter epoch. Work in haste, eat in haste, speak in haste, even die in haste. Perhaps rushing was one of God's attributes. Judging by the swiftness of electromagnetic flow and the momentum with which the galaxies move outward from the center of the universe, one might conclude that God is impatient. He prods the angel Metatron; Metatron pushes the angel Sandalphon, the seraphim, cherubim, Ophanim, Erelim. Molecules, atoms, and electrons move with mad speed. Time itself is pressed for time in which to carry out the tasks it has taken upon itself in endless space, in infinite dimensions.

Herman fell asleep again. His dreams too were hurried, running into one another, wiping out the law of identity, negating the categories of reason. He dreamed that while he was having intercourse with Masha, the upper part of her body had become separated from the lower part and was standing before a mirror chiding him and pointing out that he was copulating with only half a woman. Herman opened his eyes. It was fifteen minutes past ten. Shifrah Puah was saying her morning prayers in the other room—slowly, syllable by syllable. He dressed and went into the kitchen, where, as always, she had breakfast ready for him. A Yiddish newspaper lay on the table.

Herman leafed through it while he drank his coffee. Suddenly he saw his own name. It was in the "Personals" section: "Mr. Herman Broder of Tzivkev, please contact Reb Abraham Nissen Yaroslaver." There was an address on East Broadway, as well as a telephone number. Herman sat rigid. It was pure chance that he had seen it. Generally he contented himself with skimming the headlines on the front page. He knew who Reb Abraham Nissen Yaroslaver was—an uncle of his dead wife, Tamara, a learned man, an Alexandrover Hasid. When Herman first arrived in America, he had visited him and promised that he would come again. Even though his niece was no longer alive, Reb Abraham Nissen wanted to help Herman, but Herman avoided him because he didn't want him to know that he was married to a Gentile woman. And here was Reb Abraham Nissen looking for him in the newspaper!

"What can this mean?" Herman asked himself. He was frightened of this man who was involved with the Tzivkev Landsleit. I'll pretend I didn't see it, he decided. But he sat a long time, staring at the notice. The telephone rang and Shifrah Puah answered it. She said, "Herman, it's for you. Masha."

Masha called to say that she had to work an extra hour and would meet Herman at four. While they talked, Shifrah Puah picked up the paper. She saw his name and turned her head toward him in surprise, pointing to the paper with her finger. As soon as Herman hung up, Shifrah Puah said, "They're looking for you in the newspaper. Here."

"Yes, I saw it."

"Call up. They give a phone number. Who is it?"

"Who knows? Probably someone from the old country."

"Call them up. If they put it in the paper, it must be important."

"Not for me."

Shifrah Puah raised her eyebrows. Herman remained at the table. After a while he tore out the notice. He showed her that there was nothing on the back of it but another advertisement and that no text would be missing that she might want to read. Then he said, "They want to drag me into the Landsmanscaft, but I neither have the time for it nor the patience."

"Maybe some relative has turned up."

"There is no one left."

"Nowadays if someone is looked for, it's no small matter."

Herman had determined earlier to go back to his room and put in a few hours' work. Instead, he said goodbye to Shifrah Puah and went out. With slow steps he walked toward Tremont Avenue. He thought he would go to the park, sit on a bench, and go over the manuscript, but his legs carried him to a phone booth. He felt depressed, and he realized that the premonition that had nagged him for the past few days must have to do with this advertisement. There was such a thing as telepathy, clairvoyance—whatever it might be called.

He turned into Tremont Avenue and went into a drugstore. He dialed the number given in the newspaper. "I'm getting myself into a mess," he thought. He could hear the telephone ringing, but there was no answer.

"Well, it's better this way," he decided. "I won't call again."

At that moment Reb Abraham Nissen's voice asked, "Who is it? Hello?" The voice sounded old, cracked, and familiar, even though Herman had only spoken to the man once, and then not on the telephone.

Herman cleared his throat. "This is Herman," he said. "Herman Broder."

There was a silence, as if Reb Abraham Nissen had been caught by surprise. After a moment he seemed to collect himself; his voice became louder and clearer. "Herman? You saw the notice in the newspaper? I have news for you, but don't be frightened. It isn't—God forbid— bad news. On the contrary. Don't get nervous."

"What is it?"

"I have information about Tamar Rachel—Tamara. She's alive."

Herman didn't answer. Apparently somewhere in his mind he had allowed for the possibility that this might happen, because he was not as shocked as he might have been. "And the children?" he asked.

"The children are gone."

Herman said nothing for a long time. The quirks of his own fate had been so extraordinary that nothing could surprise him any more. He heard himself saying, "How can this be? A witness saw her being shot—what was his name? I can't think of it."

"Yes, it's true, she was shot, but she remained alive. She escaped to a friendly Gentile's house. Later she made her way to Russia."

"Where is she now?"

"Here in my house."

Again the silence between the two men was long. Then Herman asked, "When did she arrive?"

"She's been here since Friday. She just knocked at the door and came in. We've been looking all over New York for you. Just a minute, I'll call her to the phone."

"No, I'll come right over."

"What? Well—"

"I'll come right over," Herman repeated. He tried to hang up the receiver, but it fell from his hand and dangled at the end of the cord. He thought he heard Reb Abraham Nissen's voice still coming from it. He opened the door of the booth. He stared at a counter opposite him where a woman was sitting on a stool sipping a drink through a straw while a man served her some cookies. She was flirting with the man and all the wrinkles in her rouged face smiled imploringly, with the humility of those who can no longer demand but only beg. Herman replaced the receiver, left the booth, and walked to the door.

Masha often accused him of being a "mechanical man" and at this moment he agreed with her. His feelings were dammed up and his mind was calculating coldly. He was to meet Masha at four o'clock. He had promised Yadwiga he would be home in the evening. He still had the rabbi's manuscript to finish. As he stood in the doorway of the drugstore, customers going in and out bumped into him. He was reminded of Spinoza's definition of wonder: "When the mind is without motion because the imagination of this particular thing has no connection with the rest . . ."

Herman started to walk, but he could not remember in which direction the cafeteria was located. He stopped in front of a mailbox.

"Tamara, alive!" He said the words out loud. This hysterical woman, who had tormented him and whom he had been about to divorce when the war broke out, had risen from the dead. He wanted to laugh. His metaphysical joker had played him a fatal trick.

Herman knew that every minute was precious, but he was unable to move. He leaned against the mailbox. A woman dropped a letter into it and eyed him suspiciously. Run away? Where to? With whom? Masha couldn't leave her mother. He had no money. Yesterday he had changed a ten-dollar bill and until the rabbi gave him a check he was left with four dollars and some change. And what would he say to Masha? Her mother would certainly tell her about the notice.

He concentrated on his watch. The small hand pointed to the eleven and the big one to the three, but their meaning didn't register. He became absorbed in the watch face as if some mental exertion were required to read the time.

"If only I were wearing my good suit!" For the first time Herman felt the common ambition of the refugee: to show that he had achieved a degree of success in America. At the same time, something in him mocked this trite desire.

2

Herman walked to the El and climbed the steps. Except for its impact on him, Tamara's return had changed nothing. The passengers read their newspapers and chewed gum as always. The train's fans made the same rumbling noise. Herman picked up a discarded newspaper from the floor and tried to read it. It was a horse-racing sheet. He turned the page, read a joke, and smiled. Along with the subjectivity of appearances, there is a mystic objectivity.

Herman pulled his hat brim down to keep the light from shining through his eyelids. "Bigamy? Yes, bigamy." In a sense, he could be accused of polygamy. During the years he believed Tamara dead, he had tried to remember her good qualities. She had loved him. She was essentially a spiritual person. He had often spoken to her soul, begged her forgiveness. At the same time, he knew that her death had spared him misery. Even the years wasted in the hayloft in Lipsk had sometimes seemed a respite when set against the trouble Tamara had caused him during their years together.

Herman no longer remembered exactly why he had quarreled so bitterly with her, why he had left her and neglected their children. The conflict between husband and wife had become an endless haggle in which one party was never able to convince the other. Tamara talked incessantly of the redemption of humanity, the plight of the Jews, the role of woman in society. She praised books which Herman considered little better than pulp, was enthusiastic about plays that revolted him, sang the current song hits with gusto, and attended the lectures of all the party demagogues. When she was a Communist, she wore a leather jacket á la Cheka; when she became a Zionist, she wore a Star of David around her neck. She was constantly celebrating, protesting, signing petitions, and raising funds for all kinds of party purposes. In the late thirties, when the Nazi leaders visited Poland and nationalist students beat up Jews and forced Jewish students to stand during the lectures at the university, Tamara, like many others, had turned to religion. She began to light candles on Friday night and to keep a kosher household. She seemed to Herman to be the incarnation of the masses, always following some leader, hypnotized by slogans, never really having an opinion of her own.

In his irritation he had overlooked her devotion to him and the children, the fact that she was always there to help him and others. Even when he had moved out of the house and lived in a furnished room, she would come and clean it for him and bring him food. She nursed him when he was sick, mended his clothes, and washed his linen. She even typed his dissertation, although in her opinion it was anti-humanistic, anti-feminist, and depressing in outlook.

"Could she possibly have calmed down?" Herman asked himself. "Let's see, how old would she be?" He couldn't figure out her age exactly, but she was older than he. Herman tried to bring events into some order, to piece together what must have happened. The children had been taken from her. She had been shot; with the bullet lodged in her body, she had found refuge in a Gentile home. Her wound had healed; she had been smuggled into Russia. It must have happened before 1941. Well, and where had she been all those years? Why hadn't he heard from her since 1945? True, Herman hadn't searched for her. He had never looked through the lists that were published in the Yiddish newspapers for those seeking lost relatives. Had anyone ever been in such a predicament? Herman asked himself. No. Trillions, quadrillions of years would have to pass before this combination of circumstances repeated itself. Again Herman felt like laughing. Some heavenly intelligence was conducting experiments on him, similar to those the German doctors had carried out on the Jews.

The train stopped and Herman jumped up—Fourteenth Street! He climbed the stairs to the street, turned east, and walked to the bus stop to wait for an east-bound bus. The morning had been cool, but it was becoming hotter by the minute. Herman's shirt clung to his back. Some article of clothing was making him uncomfortable, but he was unable to identify it. Was it his collar, the elastic waistband of his underwear, perhaps his shoes? He passed a mirror and saw his reflection: lean and wasted, a bit stooped, wearing a battered hat and rumpled trousers. His tie was twisted. Herman had shaved just a few hours ago, but his beard already made a shadow on his face. "I can't go there looking like this!" he said to himself in alarm. He slowed his pace. He looked into the store windows. Perhaps he could pick up a cheap shirt. Maybe there was a place nearby where he could get his suit pressed. At least he could get his shoes shined. He stopped at a shoeshine stand and a young black boy started to smear shoe polish on his shoes with his fingers, tickling Herman's toes through the leather. The warm air, filled with dust, gasoline fumes, odors of asphalt and sweat, was nauseating. "How long can the lungs endure it?" he wondered. "How long can such a suicidal civilization last? They'll all suffocate—first they'll go mad, then choke."

The black boy started to say something about Herman's shoes, but Herman didn't understand his English. Only the first syllable of each word reached his ears. The boy was half naked. His square-shaped head was sweating.

"How's business?" Herman asked, trying to make conversation, and he answered, "Pretty good."

3

Herman sat on the bus that went from Union Square to East Broadway and looked out the window. The neighborhood had changed since his arrival in America. Now many Puerto Ricans lived there. Whole blocks of buildings had been torn down. Nevertheless, one still occasionally saw a sign in Yiddish and, here and there, a synagogue, a yeshiva, a home for the aged. Somewhere in the area was the headquarters of the Tzivkev Landsleit Society that Herman was so anxious to avoid. The bus passed kosher restaurants, a Yiddish film-theater, a ritual bath, a hall that could be rented for weddings or bar mitzvahs, and a Jewish funeral parlor. Herman saw young boys with earlocks longer than any he had seen in Warsaw, their heads covered by broad-brimmed velvet hats. It was in this section and on the other side of the bridge in Williamsburg that the Hungarian Hasidim, followers of the rabbis of Sącz, Belz, and Bobow, had settled, continuing the old feuds. Some of the extremist Hasidim even refused to recognize the land of Israel.

On East Broadway, where Herman got off the bus, he glimpsed through a basement window a group of white-bearded men studying the Talmud. Their eyes under heavy brows expressed scholarly sharpness. The wrinkles on their high foreheads reminded Herman of the ruled lines of parchment scrolls used by scribes to guide their letters. The faces of the old men reflected a stubborn grief as ancient as the books they studied. For an instant Herman toyed with the idea of joining them. How long would it be before he too was a graybeard?

Herman recalled what he had learned from a landsman about the circumstances of Reb Abraham Nissen Yaroslaver's coming to America a few weeks before Hitler's invasion of Poland. In Lublin he had owned a small establishment that published rare religious books. He had traveled to Oxford to copy an old manuscript that had been discovered there. In 1939 he had come to New York to enlist prenumerants for printing this manuscript, and was prevented from returning by the Nazi invasion. He lost his wife, but in New York had married the widow of a rabbi. He had given up his plan to publish the Oxford manuscript and instead had begun work on an anthology of the writings of the rabbis who had perished at the hands of the Nazis. His present wife, Sheva Haddas, helped him. Both of them had taken it upon themselves to observe mourning one day a week— Monday—for the martyrs in Europe. On that day, they fasted, sat in their stocking feet on low stools, and observed all the rules of shiva.

Herman approached the house on East Broadway and glanced up at the windows of Reb Abraham Nissen's ground-floor apartment. They were hung with half curtains, like those used in the old country. He climbed the short flight of stairs and rang the doorbell. There was no response at first. He thought he heard whispering behind the door, as if those inside were debating whether or not to let him in. The door opened slowly and an old woman, obviously Sheva Haddas, stood on the threshold. She was short, thin, had wrinkled cheeks and a sunken mouth, and wore a pair of spectacles on her hooked nose. In her high-collar dress and bonnet, she looked exactly like the pious women in Poland. There was no trace of America in her appearance, or any indication of hurry or excitement; from her manner, it would seem that such a reunion between husband and wife was an everyday occurrence.

Herman greeted her and she nodded. They walked down a long foyer without speaking. Reb Abraham Nissen stood in the living room—short, stocky, stooped, with a pale face, a full yellow-and-gray beard, and disheveled sidelocks. He had a high forehead, a flattened skullcap sat on his head. The brown eyes under the gray-yellow eyebrows expressed both confidence and sorrow. A broad, fringed garment could be seen beneath his unbuttoned robe. Even the house smell seemed to belong to the past—fried onions, garlic, chicory, wax. Reb Abraham Nissen looked at Herman and his gaze seemed to say, "Words are superfluous." He glanced at a door that led to another room.

"Call her in," he ordered his wife. Calmly, the old woman left the room. Reb Abraham Nissen said, "A miracle from heaven!"

It seemed to take a long time. Again, Herman imagined he heard a whispered argument. The door opened and Sheva Haddas led Tamara into the room as if she were leading a bride to the canopy.

Herman took everything in at once. Tamara had aged a little, but she appeared surprisingly young. She was wearing American clothes and had obviously visited a beauty parlor. Her hair was jet black and had the artificial sheen of fresh dye, her cheeks were rouged, her eyebrows plucked, her fingernails red. She made Herman think of a stale loaf of bread put into a hot oven to be freshened up. Her hazel eyes seemed to look at him sideways. Until this moment, Herman would have sworn that he remembered Tamara's features perfectly. But now he noticed something that he had entirely forgotten: a crease at the corner of her mouth that had always been there and that gave her an expression combining vexation, suspicion, and irony. He stared at her: the same nose, the same cheek-bones, the same set of the mouth, the same chin, lips, ears. He heard himself saying, "I hope you recognize me."

"Yes, I recognize you," she answered, and it was Tamara's voice, although it was somewhat changed—perhaps because of its guarded tone.

Reb Abraham Nissen motioned to his wife and they both left the room. Herman and Tamara remained silent a long time.

"Why is she wearing pink?" Herman thought. His embarrassment had subsided and he experienced a feeling of irritation that the woman who had seen their children taken away to be killed allowed herself to be dressed in this fashion. Now he was glad that he hadn't changed into his good clothes. He again became the Herman he used to be—the man who didn't get along with his wife, the husband who had turned away from her. "I didn't know you were alive," he said. And he was ashamed of his own words.

"That's something you *never* knew," Tamara retorted sharply in her old way.

"Well, sit down—here on the sofa."

Tamara sat. She was wearing nylon stockings. She pulled down her dress, which had risen above her knees. In silence, Herman stood across the room from her. It occurred to him that the spirits of the newly dead encountered one another in this way, speaking the words of the living, not yet knowing the language of the dead. "How did you come here—by boat?" he asked.

"No, by plane."

"From Germany?"

"No, from Stockholm."

"Where were you all this time? In Russia?"

Tamara seemed to be mulling over his question. Then she said, "Yes, in Russia."

"I didn't know you were alive until this morning. An eyewitness came to me and told me that he had seen you being shot."

"Who was he? Nobody came out alive. Unless he was a Nazi."

"He was a Jew."

"It can't be. They shot two bullets into me. One is in my body to this day," Tamara said, indicating her left hip.

"Can't it be removed?"

"Perhaps here in America."

"It's as if you've risen from the dead."

"Yes."

"Where did it happen? In Nalenczew?"

"In a field on the outskirts. I managed to get away at night, though my wounds were bleeding. It was raining, or else the Nazis would have seen me."

"Who was the Gentile?"

"Pawel Czechonski. My father had done business with him. I went to him, thinking, 'What could possibly happen now? At the worst, he'll report me.'"

"He saved your life?"

"I stayed there four months. They couldn't trust a doctor. He was my doctor. He and his wife."

"Have you heard from them since?"

"They're no longer alive."

They were both silent. Then Tamara asked, "How is it that my uncle didn't know your address? We had to put an advertisement in the paper."

"I don't have my own apartment. I live with someone else."

"You could have left him your address."

"What for? I don't see anyone."

"Why don't you?"

He wanted to reply, but the words wouldn't come. He pulled a chair from the table and sat down on the edge of it. He knew that he should ask her about the children, but he was unable to do so. Even when he heard people talking about children who were alive and healthy, he felt something akin to panic. Every time Yadwiga or Masha expressed the wish to have a child by him, he would change the subject. Somewhere among his papers there were photographs of little Yocheved and David, but he never dared to look at them. Herman had not behaved toward them as a father should. At one time he had even denied their existence and played the role of a bachelor. And here was Tamara—the witness of his crime. He was afraid that she would begin to cry, but she retained her composure.

"When did you find out that I was alive?" he asked.

"When? After the war. By an extraordinary coincidence. An acquaintance of mine—actually, a close friend—was wrapping a package in a Yiddish newspaper from Munich and happened to see your name in it.''

"Where were you then? Still in Russia?''

Tamara didn't answer, and he didn't repeat his question. From his own experience with Masha and other survivors of the German camps, he knew that the whole truth would never be learned from those who had survived the concentration camps or the wandering through Russia—not because they lied but because it was impossible for them to tell it all.

"Where do you live?'' Tamara asked. "What do you do?'' In the bus Herman had imagined that Tamara would ask these questions. Nevertheless, he sat in stunned silence.

"I didn't know you were alive and—''

Tamara smiled wryly. "Who is the lucky woman who has taken my place?''

"She isn't Jewish. She's the daughter of the Pole in whose house I hid.''

Tamara considered his reply. "A peasant?''

"Yes.''

"Was that how you repaid her?''

"You might say it was that.''

Tamara looked at him but didn't answer. She had the absent expression of someone who is saying one thing and thinking another.

"What kind of work do you do?'' she repeated.

"I work for a rabbi—an American rabbi.''

"What do you do for the rabbi? Answer questions on ritual law?''

"I write books for him.''

"And what does he do? Dance with shiksehs?''

"That's not as far from the truth as you might think. I see you've already learned a great deal in this country.''

"There was an American woman in our camp. She had come to Russia looking for social justice and was immediately packed off to a camp, the camp I was in. She died there of diarrhea and starvation. I have the address of her sister somewhere. She held my hand before she died and made me promise to locate her relatives and tell them the truth.''

"Her family is also Communist?''

"It would seem so.''

"They won't believe you. They're all hypnotized.''

"There were mass deportations to the camps. They took men, starved them, and made them do work that would destroy even the strongest within a year. I witnessed it myself. If I hadn't seen it, I wouldn't believe it either.''

"What happened to you?''

Tamara bit her lower lip. She shook her head as if to indicate the futility of relating what was beyond belief. This was not the garrulous Tamara he had known but a different person. The odd thought occurred to him that perhaps this wasn't Tamara but her sister. Then suddenly she began to speak.

"What happened to me can never be fully told. The truth is, I don't really know myself. So much happened that I sometimes imagine nothing happened. I have completely forgotten many things, even about our life together. I remember lying on a wooden plank in Kazakhstan, trying to recall why, during the summer of 1939, I took the children on a visit to my father, but I simply couldn't find any sense or reason for what I had done.

"We sawed logs in the forest—twelve and fourteen hours a day. At night it was so cold I couldn't sleep at all. It stank so, I couldn't breathe. Many of the people suffered from beriberi. One minute a person would be talking to you, making plans, and suddenly he would be silent. You spoke to him and he didn't answer. You moved closer and saw that he was dead.

"So I lay there and asked myself, 'Why didn't I go with Herman to Tzivkev?' But I couldn't recall a thing. This, they tell me, is a psychological illness. I suffer from it. Sometimes I remember everything and sometimes nothing. The Bolsheviks taught us to be atheists, but I still believe everything is predestined. It was fated that I had to stand by and watch those monsters rip out my father's beard and a piece of his cheek as well. Anyone who did not see my father at that moment doesn't know what it means to be a Jew. I never knew it myself or I would have followed in his footsteps.

"My mother fell at their feet and they trampled on her with their boots and spat at her. They would have raped me, but I was having my period and you know how I bleed. Oh, later it stopped, it stopped all right. Where does one get blood if one doesn't have bread? You ask what happened to me? A speck of dust blown by the wind across land and desert can't tell where it's been. Who was the Gentile who hid you?"

"It was our servant. You knew her—Yadwiga."

"You married *her*?" Tamara looked as if she were about to laugh.

"Yes."

"Forgive me, but wasn't she simple-minded? Your mother used to make fun of her. She didn't even know how to put on a pair of shoes. I remember your mother telling me how she tried to put the left shoe on the right foot. If she was given money to buy something, she would lose it."

"She saved my life."

"Yes, I suppose one's life is worth more than anything else. Where did you marry her—in Poland?"

"In Germany."

"Was there no other way to repay her? Well, I'd better not ask."

"There isn't anything to ask. That's the way it is."

Tamara stared at her leg. She raised her dress a bit and scratched her knee, then quickly pulled her skirt down over it. "Where do you live? Here in New York?"

"In Brooklyn. It's part of New York."

"I know. I was given an address there. I have a book full of addresses. I would need a whole year just to go around telling relatives how this one died, how that one died. I've already been to Brooklyn. My aunt explained the way, and I went alone by subway. I came to a house and no one there knew a word of Yiddish. I tried to speak in Russian, Polish, German, but they knew only English. I tried sign language to indicate to them that their aunt had died. The children simply laughed at me. The mother looked like a fine woman, but without a trace of Jewishness in her. People know a little, a drop in the ocean, about what the Nazis did. But the world knows nothing about what Stalin did and is still doing. Not even those who live in Russia know the whole story. What did you say your job was—a writer for a rabbi?"

Herman nodded. "Yes, in a way. I am also a book salesman." He found himself lying out of habit.

"You do that in addition? What kind of books do you sell? Yiddish books?"

"Yiddish, English, Hebrew. I am a so-called traveling salesman."

"Where do you travel?"

"Different cities."

"And what does your wife do when you go away?"

"What do other wives do when their husbands travel? Here in America, selling is an important profession."

"Do you have any children by her?"

"Children? No!"

"It wouldn't shock me if you did have. I met young Jews who married former Nazis, and when it comes to talking about what some girls did to save their skins, I'd better be quiet. People became totally depraved. In a bed next to mine, a brother and sister were carrying on. They couldn't even wait till it grew dark. So what can surprise me any more? Where did she hide you?"

"I told you, in a hayloft."

"And her parents didn't know?"

"She has a mother and a sister. No father. They didn't know."

"Of course they knew. Peasants are crafty. They figured out that after the war you would marry her and take her to America. I assume you crawled into bed with her even when you were with me."

"I didn't crawl into her bed. You're talking nonsense. How could they know that I would get a visa to America? As a matter of fact, I had intended to go to Palestine."

"They knew, they knew. Yadwiga may be an idiot, but her mother talked it over with other peasants and they helped her figure it out. Everyone wants to come to America. The whole world is dying to come to America. If the quotas were opened, America would become so jammed there wouldn't be room for as much as another pin. Don't think I'm angry at you. In the first place, I'm not angry at anyone any more. In the second place, you didn't know I was alive. You deceived me while we lived together. You ran away from the children. You didn't even write me a letter during those last few weeks, knowing that the war was about to break out at any moment. I know of fathers who risked their lives crossing frontiers in order to be with their children. Men who had managed to escape to Russia turned themselves over to the Nazis out of longing for their families. But you remained in Tzivkev and crept into a hayloft with your lover. How can I even pretend to have any claims on such a person? Well, why don't you have any children by her?"

"I don't and that's that."

"Why look at me like that? *You* married her. Since my father's grandchildren weren't good enough for you and you were as ashamed of them as if they were scabs on your scalp, why shouldn't you have other children by Yadwiga? Her father was certainly a finer man than mine."

"Well, for a moment I thought you had changed, but I see you're still the same."

"No, not the same. You are looking at a different woman. Tamara who left her murdered children and fled to Skiba—that's the name of the village—is another Tamara. I am dead, and when his wife is dead, the husband may do as he pleases. It's true, this body of mine is still dragging itself about. It has even dragged itself to New York. They put nylon stockings on me, dyed my hair, and polished my fingernails, God help me, but Gentiles have always prettied up their corpses, and Jews nowadays are Gentiles. So I bear no grudges against anyone, nor am I dependent on anyone. I wouldn't have been surprised to hear that you married a Nazi, one of those who danced on corpses and ground her heels into the eyes of Jewish daughters. How can you possibly know what happened? I just hope you're not playing the same tricks on your new wife that you played on me."

Footsteps and voices could be heard from behind the door that led to the foyer and the kitchen. Reb Abraham Nissen Yaroslaver came in, followed by Sheva Haddas. Both husband and wife shuffled rather than walked. Reb Abraham Nissen addressed Herman.

"You probably don't have an apartment as yet. You may stay with us till you find one. Hospitality is an act of charity, and besides, you are relatives. As the Holy Book says, 'And thou shalt not hide thyself from thine own flesh.'"

Tamara interrupted. "Uncle, he has another wife." Sheva Haddas clasped her hands. Reb Abraham Nissen looked baffled.

"Well, that's another story—"

"There was an eyewitness who testified that he saw how they were—" Herman stopped himself. He had neglected to warn Tamara not to tell them that his wife was a Gentile. He looked toward Tamara and shook his head. He had a childish impulse to leave the room before being disgraced. He moved toward the door, hardly aware of what he was doing.

"Don't run away. I won't force you into anything," Tamara said.

"Truly it's something one only reads about in the newspaper," Sheva Haddas said.

"You haven't, God forbid, committed any sin," Abraham Nissen said. "Had you known she was alive, it would have meant you were living illegally with a woman. But in this case, Rabbi Gershom's interdiction does not apply to you. One thing is definite: you'll have to divorce your present wife. Why didn't you tell us?"

"I didn't want to trouble you."

Herman signaled to Tamara, this time with his finger on his lips. Reb Abraham Nissen grasped his beard. Sheva Haddas's eyes expressed a motherly grief. Her head, covered by its bonnet, nodded submission to the ancient prerogative of masculine infidelity, the passion for new embraces that even the most righteous man could not resist. It has always been this way and so it will remain, she seemed to be thinking.

"These are issues a man and wife must discuss alone," she said. "Meanwhile, I'll make something to eat." She turned toward the door.

"I've just eaten, thank you," Herman said quickly.

"His wife is a good cook. She has undoubtedly prepared some greasy soup for his supper." Tamara grimaced with derision in the way Orthodox Jews sometimes do when they mention pork.

"A glass of tea with a cookie?" Sheva Haddas asked.

"No, nothing, really."

"Perhaps you should go into the other room and talk it over," Reb Abraham Nissen said. "As they say, 'These are matters between him and her alone.' If I can help you, I will certainly do so." In a changed tone, the old man continued,

"This is a time of moral chaos. The guilty ones are the wicked murderers. Do not take the blame on yourself. There was no choice."

"Uncle, there is no lack of wicked people among the Jews. Who do you think dragged us away to that meadow? Jewish police. Before dawn they broke down all the doors, searched in cellars and attics. If they found people hiding, they beat them with rubber clubs. They corraled us with ropes as if we were cattle going to slaughter. I said a word to one of them and he kicked me so hard I'll never forget it. They didn't know, the fools, that they wouldn't be spared either."

"As it is said, 'Ignorance is the root of all evil.' "

"The GPU in Russia were no better than the Nazis."

"Well, the prophet Isaiah said, 'And man is bowed down and man is humbled.' When people stop believing in the Creator, anarchy prevails."

"It's the human species," Herman said, as if to himself.

"The Torah says, 'For the imagination of man's heart is evil from his youth.' But that's why there is a Torah. Yes, go in there and talk it over together."

Reb Abraham Nissen opened the door to a bedroom. There were two beds in it, covered with European spreads and placed lengthwise, head to head, as in the old country. Tamara shrugged her shoulders and went in first; Herman followed. It reminded him of the bridal chambers into which, years ago, brides and grooms were escorted on their wedding night.

New York hurried along outside, but here behind the half curtains a part of Nalenczew or Tzivkev survived. Everything re-created a picture of bygone years: the faded yellow of the walls, the high ceiling, the floorboards, even the style of the chest of drawers and the upholstery of the armchair. An experienced stage director couldn't have selected a more suitable setting, Herman thought. He smelled the odor of snuff. He sat down in the armchair and Tamara seated herself on the edge of the bed.

Herman said, "You needn't tell me, but—if you assumed I was dead, then you must surely have—with others—"

He couldn't go on. His shirt was wet again.

Tamara examined him, slyly.

"You want to know? Everything at once?"

"You don't have to tell me. But I've been honest with you and deserve—"

"Did you have any choice? You had to tell me the truth. According to the law, I'm your wife, which means that you have two wives. They're strict about such things in America. No matter what I did, I want you to know one thing: love is no sport for me."

"I didn't say it was a sport."

"You made a caricature of our marriage. I came to you an innocent girl and—"

"Stop it!"

"The fact is that no matter how much we suffered, never knowing whether we would live another day or even another hour, we needed love. We craved it more than when things were normal. People lay in bunkers or in attics, hungry and lousy, but they kissed and held hands. I would never have guessed that people could be so passionate in such circumstances. To you I was less than nothing, but men devoured me with their eyes. God help me! My children had been murdered and men wanted me to carry on affairs with them. They offered me a loaf of bread, a bit of fat, or some privilege at work. Don't imagine these were small matters. A crust of bread was a dream. A few potatoes were a fortune. There was business going on in the camps all the time, deals being made a few steps away from the gas chamber. The total merchandise could fit into a shoe, but that's how desperate people were to save their lives. Handsome men, younger than I, husbands of attractive wives, ran after me and promised me the moon.

"It didn't occur to me that you might be alive, but even if you were, I owed you no loyalty. On the contrary, I wanted to forget you. But wanting is one thing and being able to do it is something else again. I have to love a man or sex is disgusting to me. I used to envy those women for whom love was a game. What then is it, after all, if not a game? But there is something in me, the accursed blood of my God-fearing grandmothers, that stopped me.

"I told myself that I was a damned fool, but when a man touched me I had to pull away. They thought I was crazy and they were right too. They called me hypocrite. People became rough. One highly esteemed man tried to rape me. In the middle of all this, my camp mates in Jambul set about arranging a match for me. They all said the same thing: 'You are young and must get married.' But you are the one who got married, not I. One thing I know, the merciful God in whom we believed does not exist."

"Then there was no one?"

"You sound disappointed. No, I had no one and will never have anyone again, I want to stand pure before the souls of my children."

"I thought you said God does not exist."

"If God was able to watch all this horror and remain silent, then He's no God. I talked to devout Jews, even rabbis. There was a young man in our camp—he had been a rabbi in Old Dzikow. He was so pious—there aren't any left like him. He had to work in the forest, though he didn't have the strength for it. Those Reds knew well enough that his work was worthless, but torturing a rabbi was considered a good deed. On Saturdays, he wouldn't take his portion of bread, because of the law against carrying anything on the Sabbath. His mother, the old rabbi's wife, was a holy person. Only God in heaven knows how she comforted others and how she gave away the last of what she owned to help. She became blind as a result of the conditions in the camp. But she knew all the prayers by heart and recited them up to her last moment.

"Once I asked the son, 'How can God allow such tragedies?' He tried to give me all kinds of excuses. 'We don't know God's ways,' and all the rest of it. I didn't argue with him, but I felt bitter. I told him about our children and he turned pale as chalk and looked ashamed—as if he himself had been responsible. Finally, he said, 'I beg of you, don't speak any more.'"

"Yes, yes."

"You don't even ask about the children."

Herman waited a minute. "What is there to ask?"

"No, don't ask. I knew that there were great people among adults, but that children—small children—can become great, I would never have believed. They grew up overnight. I tried to give them some of my rations, but they refused to eat any of my share. They went to their deaths like saints. Souls exist; it's God who doesn't. Don't try to contradict me. That's my conviction. I want you to know that our little David and Yocheved come to me. Not in my dreams, but when I am awake. Naturally, you think I'm crazy, but that doesn't bother me in the least.''

"What do they say to you?"

"Oh, different things. Where they are they are children again. What do you want to do? Divorce me?"

"No."

"Then what shall I do? Move in with your wife?"

"First of all, you must get yourself an apartment."

"Yes. I can't stay here."

CHAPTER FOUR

1

"Well, the impossible is possible," Herman said to himself. "It's really happened."

He walked along Fourteenth Street, muttering. He had left Tamara at her uncle's house and was on his way to Masha, having phoned her from a cafeteria on East Broadway to tell her that a distant relative of his from Tzivkev had turned up. Sardonically he had given the relative a name—Feivl Lemberger—and had described him as a Talmudic scholar, a man in his sixties. "Are you sure it isn't Eva Kracover, a former girl friend of yours in her thirties?" Masha had asked.

"If you like, I'll introduce you to him," Herman had replied.

Now Herman stopped at a drugstore to phone Yadwiga. All the phone booths were occupied and he had to wait. What was so bewildering was not so much the event itself, but the fact that in all his fantasies and imaginings the possibility that Tamara was alive had not occurred to him. Perhaps his children too would rise up from the dead? The scroll of life would roll back and all that had been would be once again. As long as the Powers were playing with him, they undoubtedly had something more in store. Had they not created a Hitler and a Stalin? One could rely on their ingenuity.

After ten minutes all five telephone booths were still occupied. One man gesticulated as he talked, as if the party at the other end of the line could see him. A second moved his lips in an uninterrupted monologue. A third talked and smoked while lining up the change he needed to prolong the conversation. A girl laughed and kept looking at the red fingernails of her left hand, as if the dialogue with her telephone partner concerned those nails, their shape and color. Each of the talkers was apparently involved in a situation that demanded explanations, apologies, subterfuge. Their faces expressed deceit, curiosity, worry.

At last a booth became vacant and Herman entered, breathing the odor and warmth of another man. He dialed the number and Yadwiga answered at once, as if she had been standing by the phone, waiting.

"Yadzia darling, it's me."

"Oh, yes!"

"How are you?"

"Where are you calling from?"

"From Baltimore."

Yadwiga paused a second. "Where is that? Well, it makes no difference."

"A few hundred miles from New York. Can you hear me clearly?"

"Yes. Very well."

"I'm trying to sell books."

"Are they buying?"

"It's hard work, but they're buying. They're the ones who pay our rent. How did the day go for you?"

"Oh, I did the laundry—things get so grimy here," Yadwiga said, unaware that she always said the same things. "The laundries here tear the clothes to shreds."

"How are the birds?"

"They're chattering. They're together all day and they kiss each other."

"Lucky creatures. I'll spend the night here in Baltimore. Tomorrow I'm going to Washington, which is even farther away, but I'll speak to you on the phone. The telephone doesn't care about distances. Electricity carries the voice a hundred and eighty thousand miles a second," Herman said, not knowing why he was giving her this information. Perhaps he wanted to impress upon her how far away he was, so that she would not expect him to return home soon. He could hear the chirping of the birds. "Has anyone been to see you? I mean, one of the neighbors?" he asked.

"No. But the doorbell rang. I opened the door with the chain on and a man was standing there with a machine that sucked up dust. He wanted to show me how it worked, but I said that I couldn't let anyone in without you."

"You did the right thing. He was probably a vacuum-cleaner salesman, but he might also have been a thief or a murderer."

"I didn't let him in."

"What will you do tonight?"

"Oh, I'll wash dishes. Then your shirts need ironing."

"They can do without it."

"When will you call?"

"Tomorrow."

"Where will you eat supper?"

"Philadelphia, I mean Baltimore, is full of restaurants."

"Don't eat any meat. You'll ruin your stomach."

"Everything is ruined anyhow."

"Go to bed early."

"Yes. I love you."

"When will you come home?"

"Not before the day after tomorrow."

"Come soon, it's lonesome without you."

"I miss you too. I'll bring you a gift."

And Herman hung up the receiver.

"A gentle soul," Herman said to himself. "How is it that such goodness survives in this corrupt world? That is a mystery—unless one believes in the transmigration of souls." Herman remembered Masha's insinuation that Yadwiga too might have a lover. "It's not true," he thought, becoming angry. "She is truth itself.'' Nevertheless, he let himself imagine a Pole standing close to Yadwiga while she spoke to Herman on the phone. The Pole was playing the very same tricks that were so familiar to Herman. ''Well, one can be certain of only one thing—death.''

Herman thought of Rabbi Lampert. If he didn't deliver the promised chapter that day, the rabbi might fire him once and for all. It was rent time again, in the Bronx and in Brooklyn. ''I'll run away! It's simply too much. It will be the end of me.''

When he reached a station, he went down the steps to the subway. Such heat and humidity! Young blacks ran quickly, shouting in tones as much African as New York. Women whose dresses were wet under the armpits jostled each other with their packages and purses, their eyes glinting in fury. Herman put his hand into his trousers pocket for a handkerchief, but it was wet. On the platform, a dense crowd was waiting, bodies pushed against one another. The train rode into the station with a shrill whistling, as if it would fly right past the platform, the cars already packed. The crowd on the platform lurched toward the opening doors before the passengers inside could make their way out. An irresistible force shoved Herman into the car. Hips, breasts, elbows pressed against him. Here, at least, the illusion of free will had vanished. Here man was tossed about like a pebble or like a meteor in space.

Herman stood trapped in the congestion and envied the tall men, the six-footers, who could catch a breath of cool air from the ventilators. It hadn't been this hot even during the summer in the hayloft. Jews must have been packed together like this in the freight cars that carried them to the gas chambers.

Herman shut his eyes. What should he do now? Where should he begin? Tamara almost certainly had come without money. She would receive some support from the Joint Distribution Committee if she concealed the fact that she had a husband. But she had already said that she had no intention of deceiving the American philanthropists. And now he was a bigamist and had a lover as well. If he were discovered, he could be arrested and deported to Poland.

''I must see a lawyer. I must go to a lawyer right away!'' But how could he explain such a situation? American lawyers had simple solutions for everything: ''Which one do you love? Divorce the other one. End the affair. Find a job. Go to a psychoanalyst.'' Herman imagined the judge sentencing him, pointing at him with his index finger: ''You have abused American hospitality.''

''I want to have all three, that's the shameful truth,'' he admitted to himself. Tamara's become prettier, calmer, more interesting. She's suffered an even worse hell than Masha. Divorcing her would mean driving her to other men. As for love, these professionals used the word as if it were capable of clear definition—when no one had yet discovered its true meaning.

2

Masha was at home when Herman arrived. She was apparently in a good mood. She removed the cigarette from her lips and kissed him full on the mouth. From the kitchen he heard the hissing sounds of cooking. He smelled frying meat, garlic, borscht, new potatoes. He heard Shifrah Puah's voice.

Coming to this house always roused his appetite. Mother and daughter were endlessly cooking, baking, handling pots, pans, salting boards, noodle boards. It reminded him of his parents' home in Tzivkev. On the Sabbath, Shifrah Puah and Masha prepared cholent and kugl. Perhaps because he lived with a Gentile, Masha made sure that her Sabbath candles were lighted, the sanctification goblet polished, the table set according to law and custom. Shifrah Puah would often consult Herman on questions of dietary law: she had accidentally washed a dairy spoon together with a meat fork; tallow from a candle had dripped onto a tray; the chicken had no gall. To this last question Herman remembered replying, "Taste the liver and see if it's bitter."

"Yes, it's bitter."

"If it's bitter, it's kosher."

Herman was eating potatoes and schav when Masha asked him about the relative who had gotten in touch with him. He almost choked on the mouthful of food he was eating. He could not remember the name he had given her on the phone. Nevertheless, he began to speak, accustomed as he was to such improvisation.

"Yes, I didn't even know this relative of mine was alive."

"A man or a woman?"

"I told you—a man."

"You say many things. Who is he? Where's he from?"

The name he had invented came back to him—Feivl Lemberger.

"How is he related to you?"

"On my mother's side."

"How?"

"The son of my mother's brother."

"Your mother's maiden name was Lemberger? Seems to me you once mentioned some other name."

"You're mistaken."

"You said on the phone he was a man in his sixties. How can you have such an old cousin?"

"My mother was the youngest. My uncle was twenty years older than she."

"What was your uncle's name?"

"Tuvye."

"Tuvye? How old was your mother when she died?"

"Fifty-one."

"The whole thing sounds fishy. It's an old girl friend. She missed you so badly, she put a notice in the newspaper. Why did you tear it out? You were afraid I'd see the name and phone number. Well, I bought another paper. I'm going to call up right now and find out the truth. This time you've hung yourself with your own belt," Masha said. Hatred and satisfaction were written on her face.

Herman pushed his plate away.

"Why don't you call right now and end this ridiculous cross examination!" he said. "Go ahead, dial the number! I'm bored with your ugly accusations!"

Masha's expression changed. "I'll call when I feel like it. Don't let the potatoes get cold."

"If you haven't any faith in me at all, then our whole relationship is senseless."

"It's senseless all right. Eat the potatoes anyway. If he's your mother's nephew, why did you refer to him as a distant relative?"

"All relatives are distant to me."

"You have your shikseh and you have me, but some bitch from Europe shows up and you leave me to run off and meet her. A whore like that probably has syphilis too."

Shifrah Puah came to the table. "Why don't you let him eat?"

"Mama, don't interfere!" Masha said threateningly.

"I'm not interfering. Are my words worth nothing to you? When a person is eating, don't bother him with complaints. I know of a case where someone, God protect us, choked to death—"

"You have a story for everything! He's a liar, a faker. He's even too stupid to know how to get away with it," Masha said, half to her mother, half to Herman.

Herman picked up a small potato with his spoon; it was round, new, moist with butter, sprinkled with parsley. He was about to put it in his mouth, but stopped himself. He had found his wife but lost his mistress. Was this the joke destiny had in store for him?

Even though he had carefully rehearsed the details of what he would tell Masha about his relative, his memory refused to function. He cut the tender little potato in half with the edge of his spoon. "Should I tell her the truth?" he asked himself. But no answer came. How strange that despite his distress Herman felt calm. It was the resignation of a criminal caught red-handed who accepted the inevitable punishment.

"Why don't you phone?" he said.

"Eat. I'll bring the dumpling."

He ate the potatoes and each mouthful filled him with energy. He had had no lunch, and he felt drained by the day's events. He thought of himself as a prisoner eating his last meal before execution. Masha would know the truth soon. Rabbi Lampert would surely fire him. He had only two dollars in his pocket. He couldn't apply for government aid—his double life might be exposed. What kind of work could he find? He was even incapable of getting a job as a dishwasher.

Masha served him a pudding and an apple compote with tea. Herman had planned to work on the rabbi's manuscript after supper, but his stomach felt heavy. When he thanked mother and daughter for the meal, Shifrah Puah said, "Why thank us? Thank Him above." She brought Herman a bowl of water in which to wash his fingers and a skullcap so that he might say the benediction. Herman mumbled the first verse of the blessing and retired to his room. Masha filled the sink with water to wash the dishes. It was still light outside, and it seemed to Herman that he heard·birds singing in the back-yard tree, but these were not the voices of the sparrows that usually twittered among the branches. Herman played with the thought that they were the spirits of birds of another age, from before the time of Columbus, or even from a prehistoric era, that awakened and sang toward evening. In his room, at night, he had often found beetles so huge and strange that he could not believe they were a product of either this climate or the present time.

The day seemed longer to Herman than any summer day he could recall. He remembered David Hume's words that there was no logical proof the sun would rise the following morning. In that case, neither was there a guarantee that the sun would set this day.

It was hot. He often wondered why the room didn't set itself on fire from the high temperature. On particularly turgid evenings, he imagined flames bursting forth from the ceiling, the walls, the bedding, the books and manuscripts. He stretched out on the bed, alternately dozing and brooding. Tamara had asked for his address and telephone number, but instead he had told her he would call her the following evening. What was it they all wanted? To forget for a while their loneliness and the inevitability of death. Poor and worthless as he was, some people still depended on him. But it was Masha who made it all meaningful. If she were to leave him, then Tamara and Yadwiga would become no more than burdens.

He fell asleep, and when he awoke, it was evening. In the other room, he could hear Masha talking on the telephone. Was she talking to Reb Abraham Nissen Yaroslaver? Or to Tamara? Herman strained to hear. No, she was talking to the other cashier at the cafeteria. After a few minutes, she came into his room. She spoke into the semi-darkness.

"Are you asleep?"

"I've just wakened."

"You lie down and fall right asleep. You must have a clear conscience."

"I haven't murdered anyone."

"One can murder without a knife." Then, in a changed voice, she said, "Herman, I can take my vacation now."

"Starting when?"

"We can leave Sunday morning."

Herman was silent for a moment. "All I have is two dollars and a few pennies."

"Aren't you supposed to get a check from the rabbi?"

"I'm not so sure now."

"You want to stay with your peasant—or perhaps someone else. All year you've promised to take me to the country, but at the last minute you change your mind. I shouldn't say it, but compared to you Leon Tortshiner was an honest man. He lied too, but he bragged harmlessly and thought up silly fantasies. Did you put that notice in the paper yourself? I wouldn't be surprised. All I need to do is dial the number. I'll soon know your tricks."

"Call and find out. For a few cents, you'll know the truth."

"Who did you go to see?"

"My dead wife, Tamara, has risen from the grave. She's polished her nails and come to New York."

"Yes, of course. What happened between you and the rabbi?"

"I'm behind in my work."

"You did it deliberately so that you wouldn't be able to go away with me. I don't need you. Sunday morning I'm going to pack a suitcase and go wherever my eyes lead me. If I don't get out of this city for a few days, I'll lose my mind. I've never been so tired, not even in the camp."

"Why don't you lie down?"

"Thanks for the suggestion; it won't help. I lie there and remember all the savagery, all the humiliations. If I do fall asleep, then I'm back with them immediately. They're dragging me, beating me, chasing me. They come running from all sides, like hounds after a hare. Has anyone ever died from nightmares? Wait, I must get a cigarette."

Masha left the room. Herman got up and looked out the window. The sky shone pale and dull. The tree below stood motionless. The air smelled of marshes and the tropics. The earth was turning from west to east as it had done from time immemorial. The sun was racing off somewhere with its planets in tow. The Milky Way turned on its axis. In the midst of these cosmic adventures, Herman stood with his handful of reality, with his ridiculous little troubles. It would take only a length of rope, a drop of poison, and they would vanish together with him. "Why doesn't she phone? What is she waiting for?" Herman asked himself. "Maybe she's afraid of the truth."

Masha came back with a cigarette between her lips. "If you want to come with me, I'll pay for you."

"Do you have the money?"

"I'll borrow it from the union."

"You know I don't deserve it."

"No, but if you need a thief, you rescue him from the gallows."

3

Herman planned to spend Friday, Saturday, and Sunday in Brooklyn with Yadwiga. Monday he intended to go to the country with Masha.

He had finished the chapter and delivered it to the rabbi, promising solemnly not to be late with his work again. It was his good luck that Rabbi Lampert was always so busy that he never had time to carry out his threats. The rabbi took the manuscript and paid Herman at once. The two telephones on the rabbi's desk kept ringing. He was flying to Detroit that day to give a lecture. When Herman took leave of him, the rabbi shook his head. He seemed to be saying: "Don't think that you're fooling me, greenhorn. I know more than you think." He didn't give Herman his whole hand to shake, only two fingers.

When Herman reached the door, Mrs. Regal, the secretary, called out, "What about your phone?"

"I gave the rabbi the address." And he shut the door behind him.

Each time Herman received a check from Rabbi Lampert, it seemed like a miracle to him. He cashed it as quickly as he could in a bank where the rabbi was known. He himself would have nothing to do with checks. He carried his cash with him in the rear pocket of his trousers even though he was afraid of being robbed. It was Friday, and according to the wall clock of the bank, it was fifteen minutes past eleven. The rabbi had an office on West Fifty-seventh Street, where the bank was also located.

Herman headed in the direction of Broadway. Should he call Tamara? Judging by the way Masha had talked to him from the cafeteria, there could be no doubt that she had already telephoned Reb Abraham Nissen Yaroslaver. She must by now know that Tamara was actually alive. "This time I'll come out of it with every bone broken." Herman realized he was repeating an expression his father had often used.

Herman went into a store to phone and dialed Reb Abraham Nissen Yaroslaver's number. After a few seconds he heard Sheva Haddas's voice.

"Who is this?"

"It's Herman Broder, Tamara's husband." He spoke the words hesitatingly.

"I'll call her."

He couldn't tell how long he waited—a minute, two, five. The fact that Tamara didn't come at once could only mean that Masha had called. At last he heard Tamara's voice—it sounded different from yesterday. Speaking too loudly, she said, "Herman, is that you?"

"Yes, it's me. I still don't believe that what has happened has really happened."

"Well, it really has. I'm looking out of the window and I see a street in New York, full of Jews, God bless them. I can even hear the sounds of fish being chopped."

"You're in a Jewish neighborhood."

"There were Jews in Stockholm, too, good Jews, but here it's a little like Nalenczew."

"Yes, a trace of it has survived. Has anyone phoned you?"

Tamara didn't reply at once. Then she said, "Who should have phoned? I don't know anyone in New York. There are—what are they called?—Landsleit. My uncle was supposed to check on some of them, but—"

"You haven't asked about renting a room yet, have you?"

"Who shall I ask? Monday, I'm going to the organization. Perhaps they will advise me. You promised to phone yesterday evening."

"My promises aren't worth a penny."

"It really is strange. In Russia, things were pretty bad, but at least people were together; whether we were in the camp or in the forest, we were always a group of prisoners. In Stockholm we stayed together too. Here, for the first time, I'm alone. I look out of the window and I feel I don't belong here. Can you come over? My uncle is out and my aunt is going shopping. We could talk."

"All right. I'll come."

"Come. After all, we were once related," Tamara said, and she hung up.

A cab came along just as Herman stepped out into the street. He barely earned enough money for a crust of bread, but he had to hurry now so as not to deprive Yadwiga of the whole day. He sat in the cab and the turmoil within him erupted in laughter. Yes, Tamara was here; it was no hallucination.

The taxi stopped and Herman paid his fare and tipped the driver. He rang the bell and Tamara opened the door. The first thing he observed was that she had removed the red polish from her nails. She was wearing a different dress of a dark color and her hair was slightly disheveled. He even noticed a few white strands. She had sensed his displeasure at seeing her dolled up in American fashion and reverted to her Old World style. She looked older now, and he noticed wrinkles at the corners of her eyes.

"My aunt has just left," she said.

Herman hadn't kissed Tamara at their first meeting. He made a gesture to do so now, but she moved away.

"I'll make some tea."

"Tea? I just had lunch."

"I think I've earned the right to invite you to have a glass of tea with me," she said with Nalenczew coquetry.

He followed her into the living room. The kettle in the kitchen began to whistle, and Tamara left to brew tea. Soon she carried in a tray with tea, lemon, and a plate of cookies—surely baked by Sheva Haddas. They were not uniform in shape, but crooked and twisted like the homebaked cakes in Tzivkev. They smelled of cinnamon and almonds. Herman chewed on a cookie. His tea glass was full and extremely hot and contained a tarnished silver spoon. In some odd way all the mundane characteristics of the Polish-Jewish past, down to the smallest details, had been transplanted to this place.

Tamara seated herself at the table, not too close to Herman and not too far away, just the proper distance for a woman when sitting with a man who was not her husband, but a relative nevertheless. "I keep looking at you and I can't believe it really is you," she said. "I can't allow myself to believe anything. Everything has lost perspective since I've come here."

"In what way?"

"I've almost forgotten what it was like there. You won't believe me, Herman, but I lie awake at night and can't remember how we first met or how we grew close. I know that we quarreled often, but I don't know why. My life seems to have been peeled away like the skin of an onion. I'm beginning to forget what happened in Russia and even more recently in Sweden. We were shunted about from place to place, God knows why. They gave us papers and they took them away again. Don't ask me how many times I had to sign my name those last few weeks! Why did they need so many signatures? And everything in my married name—Broder. To the officials, I'm still your wife, Tamara Broder."

"We can never be strangers."

"You don't mean that, you're only saying it. You consoled yourself very quickly with your mother's maid. But my children—your children—still come to me. Let's not talk about it any more! Better, tell me how you live. Is she a good wife, at least? You had a thousand complaints about me."

"What can I expect of her? She does the same things she did when she was our servant."

"Herman, you can tell me everything. In the first place, we were once together. In the second, as I've told you before, I really no longer think of myself as being part of this world. Perhaps I can even help you."

"How? When a man hides in an attic for years, he ceases to be a part of society. The truth is that I'm still hiding in an attic right here in America. You said so yourself the other day."

"Well, two dead people certainly needn't have any secrets from one another. So long as you've done what you've done, why don't you find a decent job for yourself? Writing for a rabbi is no way to spend one's life."

"What else can I do? In order to press pants, you have to be strong and belong to a union. That's what they call workers' organizations here, and it's very difficult to get into one. Other than that—"

"Your children are gone. Why don't you have a child by her?"

"Perhaps *you* can still have children."

"What for? So that the Gentiles will have someone to burn? But it's terribly empty here. I've met a woman who was also in the camps. She lost everyone, but now she has a new husband, a new set of children. Many people have started all over again. My uncle kept nagging me until late in the night to have a talk with you and come to a decision. They are fine people, but a bit too outspoken. He says you should divorce the other one; if not, you should divorce me. He even hinted that he intended to leave me some inheritance. They have one answer for everything: it's God's will. And because they believe this, they go through every hell and remain healthy and whole.''

"I can't get a Jewish divorce from Yadwiga, because we weren't married according to Jewish law,'' Herman said.

"Are you at least faithful to her, or do you have six others?'' Tamara asked.

Herman paused. "Do you want me to confess everything?''

"I might as well know the truth.''

"The truth is, I have a mistress.''

Tamara smiled fleetingly. "I thought so. What can you talk about with Yadwiga? She's a right shoe on a left foot. Who is your mistress?''

"From over there, from the camps.''

"Why didn't you marry her instead of the peasant?''

"She has a husband. They don't live together, but he won't give her a divorce.''

"I see, nothing's changed with you. At any rate, you're telling me the truth. Or are you still hiding something?''

"I'm not hiding anything.''

"It's all the same to me whether you have one or two, or a dozen. If you were unfaithful to me even though I was young and pretty—at least not ugly— why should you be faithful to a peasant, and an unattractive one at that? Well, and the other one, your sweetheart, does she accept this arrangement?''

"She has no choice. Her husband won't divorce her. And she's in love with me.''

"Do you love her too?''

"I can't live without her.''

"Well, well, to hear such words fom you! Is she beautiful? Intelligent? Charming?''

"She is all three.''

"How do you manage it? Do you rush from one to the other?''

"I do the best I can.''

"You haven't learned a thing. Absolutely nothing. I might have remained the same myself if I hadn't seen what they did to our children. Everyone tried to console me by telling me that time heals. It's been just the opposite: the further away it is, the more the wound festers. I must get a room somewhere, Herman. I can't live with anyone any more. It was easier with my fellow prisoners. When I didn't want to listen to them, I simply told them to go and bother someone else. But I can't talk that way to my uncle. He is like a father to me. I don't need a divorce; I will never live with anyone again. Unless, of course, you want one. In that case—''

"No, Tamara, I don't want a divorce. The feelings I have for you cannot be taken away by someone else.''

"What feelings? You've deceived others—well, you can't change that—but you're deceiving yourself. I don't want to preach to you, but no good can come from such a mess. I looked at you and thought, 'This is the way an animal looks when it's surrounded by hunters and cannot escape.' What sort of person is your mistress?''

"A little crazy, but tremendously interesting."

"She hasn't any children?"

"No."

"Is she young enough to have a child?"

"Yes, but she doesn't want children either."

"You're lying, Herman. If a woman loves a man, she wants to have his child. She wants to be his wife too and not have him run off to another woman. Why didn't she get along with her husband?"

"Oh, he's a faker, a parasite, an outcast. He's given himself the title of Doctor and takes money from old women."

"Forgive me, but what did she get in exchange? A man who has two wives and writes sermons for some fake rabbi. Have you told your mistress about me?''

"Not yet. But she read the notice in the newspaper and is suspicious. She may call here at any time. Or has she already?"

"No one has called me. What shall I say if she does ring up? That I'm your sister? That's what Sarah said to Abimelech about Abraham.''

"I told her that a cousin of mine had showed up, a man called Feivl Lemberger."

"Shall I tell her that I'm Feivl Lemberger?" Tamara burst into laughter. Her whole appearance was altered. Her eyes lighted up with a gaiety Herman had never noticed before, or had perhaps forgotten. A dimple appeared in her left cheek. For a moment, she looked girlishly mischievous. He rose from his chair and she too stood up.

"Are you going so soon?"

"Tamara, it's not our fault the world went to pieces."

"What do I have to hope for? To be the third wheel on your broken wagon? Let's not spoil the past. We shared many years. With all your carryings on, those were still my happiest years."

They continued to talk, standing in the foyer, near the door. Tamara had heard that the wife of the son of the rebbitzin of Old Dzikow was alive and was about to remarry. But as a religious woman, she would need to be released from the obligation of levirate marriage. There was a brother who was a freethinker, living somewhere in America. "At least I had the privilege of knowing these saints," Tamara said. "Perhaps that was God's purpose in my miserable adventures." Suddenly she moved close to Herman and kissed him on the mouth. It happened so quickly that he didn't even have a chance to return her kiss. He tried to embrace her, but she moved quickly away, indicating that she wanted him to go.

4

Friday in Brooklyn was not unlike Friday in Tzivkev. Although Yadwiga hadn't converted, she tried to observe traditional Judaism. She remembered the Jewish rituals from the time she had worked for Herman's parents. She bought a challah and baked the special little Sabbath cakes. Here in America she didn't have the right oven for making cholent, but a neighbor taught her to cover the gas burners with asbestos pads, so that the food would not burn and would stay hot through Saturday.

On Mermaid Avenue, Yadwiga bought the wine and candles needed for the blessing. She had at some point acquired two brass candlesticks, and although she didn't know how to pronounce the benediction, she would cover her eyes with her fingers for a moment after lighting the Sabbath candles and mumble something, just as she had seen Herman's mother do.

But Herman the Jew ignored the Sabbath. He turned on the lights and shut them off, even though it was forbidden. After the Sabbath meal of fish, rice and beans, chicken and carrot stew, he sat down to write, though this too was proscribed. When Yadwiga asked him why he was breaking God's commandment, he said, "There is no God, do you hear? And even if there were, I would defy Him."

In spite of having been paid, Herman seemed more worried than ever this Friday. Several times he asked Yadwiga whether anyone had telephoned. Between the fish and soup courses, he took a notebook and pen from his breast pocket and jotted something down. Sometimes on Friday evenings, when he was in the mood, he would sing his father's table chants as well as "Sholom Aleichem" and "A Worthy Woman," songs he translated into Polish for Yadwiga. The former was a greeting to the angels who escorted Jews on the Sabbath home from the synagogue. The latter was in praise of the virtuous wife, rarer than a pearl. Once, he had translated for her a hymn about an apple orchard, a loving bridegroom, and a bride bedecked with jewelry. It described caresses that, according to Yadwiga, did not belong in a holy chant. Herman explained that the hymn was written by a cabalist known as the Holy Lion, a miracle worker to whom the prophet Elijah had revealed himself. The wedding of the song took place in the heavenly mansions.

Yadwiga's cheeks would become flushed when he sang these holy songs, and her eyes would become brighter, full of joy in the Sabbath. But tonight he was taciturn and irritable. Yadwiga suspected that he sometimes spent time with other women on his trips. After all, he might occasionally want a woman who could read those tiny letters. Could a man really know what was best for him? How easily men were deluded by a word, a smile, a gesture.

During the week, Yadwiga covered the parakeets' cage as soon as evening came. But on Sabbath eve she let them stay up late. Woytus, the male, would sing along with Herman. The bird would fall into a sort of trance, twitter, trill, and fly around. Tonight Herman wasn't singing, and Woytus perched on the roof of the cage and preened his feathers.

"Has anything happened?" Yadwiga asked.

"Nothing, nothing," Herman said.

Yadwiga left the room and went to turn down the bed. Herman looked out the window. Generally Masha called him on Friday nights. She never used the telephone in her house on the Sabbath, in order not to offend her mother. She would go out for cigarettes and call from a neighborhood store. But tonight the telephone remained silent.

Since Masha had read the notice in the newspaper, he expected the scandal to break at any moment. The lie he had concocted was too obvious. It was inevitable that Masha would soon discover he had not been joking about Tamara's return. Several times yesterday in a tone of jealous triumph, winking ironically, she had repeated the name of his sham cousin, Feivl Lemberger. She was apparently delaying the blow—perhaps so as not to spoil their week's vacation together that was to begin on Monday.

As secure as Herman felt about Yadwiga, he was completely uncertain of Masha. She had never accepted the fact that he lived with another woman. She taunted him by saying that she would go back to Leon Tortshiner. Herman knew that men pursued her. He had often observed them in the cafeteria trying to engage her in conversation, asking for her address and phone number and leaving their cards. The cafeteria personnel, from the proprietor to the Puerto Rican dishwasher, looked her over greedily. Even women admired her graceful figure, long neck, narrow waist, slender legs, the whiteness of her skin. What power did he have that held her? How long would it last? He had tried countless times to prepare himself for the day Masha would break with him.

Now he stood looking out into the dimly lighted street, at the motionless leaves on the trees, at the sky which reflected the lights of Coney Island, at the elderly men and women who had set up chairs around the doorway and were carrying on the long-drawn-out conversations of those with nothing more to hope for.

Yadwiga put her hand on his shoulder. "The bed is ready. The bedding is fresh."

Herman turned off the lights in the living room, leaving the dim glow of the flickering candles. Yadwiga went into the bathroom. From the village, she had brought with her feminine rituals which she never failed to perform. She rinsed her mouth before going to bed, washed herself, and combed her hair. Even in Lipsk she had kept herself immaculate. Here in America, on the Polish radio station, she had picked up all sorts of hygienic advice. Woytus uttered one last protest when it grew dark, and flew into the cage with Marianna. He placed himself firmly next to her on the perch, where they remained motionless till sunup, perhaps getting a taste of the great rest that comes with death, the redeemer of men and animals.

Herman undressed slowly. He imagined Tamara lying awake on the sofa in her uncle's house, her eyes glaring into the darkness. Masha was probably standing near Crotona Park or on Tremont Avenue, smoking her cigarettes. Boys who passed by whistled at her. Perhaps a car had stopped and someone was trying to pick her up. Maybe she was actually driving with someone.

The telephone rang and Herman hurried to answer it. One Sabbath candle had gone out, but the other still sputtered. He picked up the receiver and whispered, "Masha!"

There was silence for a moment. Then Masha said, "Are you lying in bed with your peasant?"

"No, I'm not lying in bed with her."

"Where then? Under the bed?"

"Where are you?" Herman asked.

"What difference does it make to you where I am? You could be with me. Instead, you spend your nights with an imbecile from Lipsk. And you have others too. Your cousin Feivl Lemberger is a fat whore, the kind you like. Have you slept with her too?"

"Not yet."

"Who is she? You might just as well tell me the truth."

"I told you: Tamara is alive and she's here."

"Tamara is dead and rotting in the earth. Feivl is one of your sweethearts."

"I swear by the bones of my parents that it isn't a sweetheart!"

There was a tense silence at the other end of the line.

"Tell me who she is," Masha insisted.

"A relative of mine. A broken woman who has lost her children. The 'Joint' brought her to America."

"Then why did you say Feivl Lemberger?" Masha asked.

"Because I know how suspicious you are. If you hear a woman mentioned, you immediately think that—"

"How old is she?"

"Older than I—a shattered remain. Do you really believe Reb Abraham Nissen Yaroslaver would put a notice in the paper for a sweetheart of mine? They're pious people. I told you to call them and find out for yourself."

"Well, maybe this time you're innocent. You'll never know what I've been through these last few days."

"Little idiot, I love you! Where are you now?"

"Where am I? In a candy store on Tremont Avenue. I walked along on the street, smoking, and every few minutes a car stopped and some ruffian wanted to pick me up. The boys whistled as if I were a girl of eighteen. What they see in me, I'll never know. Where are we going on Monday?"

"We'll find some place."

"I'm afraid to leave my mother alone. What will happen if she has an attack? She can die and not a cock will crow."

"Ask one of the neighbors to take care of her."

"I avoid the neighbors. I can't suddenly drop in and ask them for favors. Besides, my mother is afraid of people. If someone knocks at the door, she thinks it's a Nazi. The enemies of Israel should enjoy life as much as I'm enjoying the prospect of this trip."

"If that's the case, we can stay here in the city."

"I miss the sight of green grass, a breath of fresh air. Even in the camps the air wasn't as polluted as it is here. I would take my mother along, but in her eyes I'm a harlot. God inflicts every form of misery on her and she trembles for fear lest she isn't doing enough for Him. The truth is that what He wanted, Hitler did."

"Then why do you light Sabbath candles? Why do you fast on Yom Kippur?"

"Not for Him. The true God hates us, but we have dreamed up an idol who loves us and has made us His chosen people. You said it yourself: 'The Gentile makes gods of stone and we of theories.' What time will you be here on Sunday?"

"Four o'clock."

"You're also a god and a murderer. Well, have a good Sabbath."

5

Herman and Masha took a bus to the Adirondacks. They got off at Lake George after a six-hour trip. There they found a room for seven dollars and decided to stay the night. They had started without any plan at all. Herman had found a map of New York State on a park bench and this was his guide. The window of their room overlooked a lake and hills. The breeze that came in carried the fragrance of pines. There was a distant sound of music. Masha had brought along a basketful of food that she and her mother had prepared—pancakes, pudding, a compote of apples, prunes, and raisins, and a home-baked cake.

Masha, smoking, stood looking out the window at the rowboats and motorboats on the lake and said playfully, "Where are the Nazis? What kind of a world is this without Nazis? A backward country, this America."

Before leaving, she had bought a bottle of cognac with some of her vacation pay. She had learned to drink in Russia. Herman took only one sip from the paper cup, but Masha kept refilling hers, becoming more and more cheerful, singing and whistling.

From early childhood, Masha had taken dancing lessons in Warsaw. Her calves were as muscular as a dancer's. Now she raised her arms and began to dance. In her slip and nylon stockings, a cigarette dangling from her lips, her hair loose, she reminded Herman of the girl performers in the circus that used to come to Tzivkev. She sang in Yiddish, Hebrew, Russian, Polish. She asked Herman to dance with her, urging him in a drunken voice, "Come, yeshiva boy, let's see what you can do."

They went to bed early, but their night was full of interruptions. Masha slept an hour and woke up. She wanted to do everything at once: to make love, smoke, drink, talk. The moon hung low over the water. Fish splashed about. The stars shook like tiny lanterns. Masha told Herman stories that aroused both anger and jealousy in him.

In the morning, they packed up and again boarded a bus. They spent the following night at Schroon Lake in a bungalow near the water. It was so cold that they had to put their clothing over their blankets to keep warm. After breakfast next morning, they rented a boat. Herman rowed while Masha stretched out to warm herself in the sun. Herman imagined he could read her thoughts through the skin of her forehead, through her closed eyelids.

He mused on how fantastic it was to be in America, in a free country, without fear of Nazis, the NKVD, border guards, informers. He hadn't even brought his "first papers" with him. In the United States no one was asked for documents. But he could never quite forget that, on a street between Mermaid and Neptune Avenues, Yadwiga waited for him. On East Broadway, in Reb Abraham Nissen Yaroslaver's house, was Tamara, who had come back and was waiting for any crumb he might throw her way. He would never be totally free of the claims these women had on him. Even Rabbi Lampert had the right to complain about him. Herman had refused to accept the friendship the rabbi wanted to impose on him.

Surrounded by the light-blue sky, the yellow-green water, he nevertheless felt less guilty. The birds had announced the new day as if it were the morning after creation. Warm breezes carried the scent of the woods and the smell of food being prepared in the hotels. Herman imagined that he heard the screech of a chicken or a duck. Somewhere on this lovely summer morning, fowl were being slaughtered; Treblinka was everywhere.

Masha's food supply had given out, but she refused to eat in a restaurant. She went to a market and bought bread, tomatoes, cheese, and apples. She came back laden with enough groceries to feed an entire family. Along with her playful frivolity, she had the instincts of a mother. She didn't squander money as loose women do. In the bungalow, Masha found a little naphtha stove and she made coffee. The smell of naphtha and smoke reminded Herman of his student years in Warsaw.

Flies, bees, and butterflies flew in through the open window. The flies and bees settled on some spilled sugar. A butterfly hovered over a slice of bread. It didn't eat, but seemed to savor the odor. To Herman these were not parasites to be driven away; he saw in each of these creatures the manifestations of the eternal will to live, experience, comprehend. As the fly's antennae stretched out toward the food, it rubbed its hind legs together. The wings of the butterfly reminded Herman of a prayer shawl. The bee hummed and buzzed and flew out again. A small ant crawled about. It had survived the cold night and was creeping across the table—but where to? It paused at a crumb, then continued on, zigzagging back and forth. It had separated itself from the anthill and now had to make out on its own.

From Schroon Lake, Herman and Masha went to Lake Placid. There they found a room in a house on a hill. Everything in the house was old but spotless: the parlor, the stairs, the pictures and ornaments hanging on the walls, the towel with its embroidered emblem, imported from Germany, a leftover from pre-World War I days. On the wide bed lay thick pillows, like the ones in European inns. The window here looked out on the mountains. The sun had set, casting purple squares on the walls.

After a while Herman went downstairs to telephone. He had taught Yadwiga how to receive a collect phone call. Yadwiga asked him where he was and he mentioned the first name that came to mind. Generally Yadwiga didn't complain, but this time she talked excitedly: she was afraid at night, the neighbors laughed at her and pointed their fingers at her. Why did Herman need so much money? She was more than willing to go to work and help out so that he could stay at home like other men. Herman quieted her, apologized, and promised not to stay away too long. She sent him a kiss through the telephone and he made a kissing sound in return.

When he came upstairs, Masha wouldn't speak to him. She said, "Now I know the truth."

"What truth?"

"I heard you. You miss her, you can hardly wait till you're back with her again."

"She's all alone. Helpless."

"And what about me?"

They ate supper in silence. Masha didn't turn on the lights. She handed him a hard-boiled egg and he was suddenly reminded of the evening before Tisha Ba'av, the last meal before fasting, when one partakes of a hard-boiled egg sprinkled with ashes, a sign of mourning, a symbol that one's luck can roll like an egg and turn bad. Masha alternately chewed and smoked. He tried to talk to her, but she would not reply. Soon after the meal, she flung herself on the bed in her clothes, curling herself up so that it was difficult to know whether she was asleep or sulking.

Herman went outside. He walked down an unknown street, stopped to look into the windows of souvenir shops: Indian dolls, gold-laced sandals with wooden soles, amber beads, Chinese earrings, Mexican bracelets. He came to a lake which reflected a copper sky. Refugees from Germany strolled by—broad-backed men and portly women. They were talking about houses, shops, the stock market. "In what way are they my brothers and sisters?" Herman asked himself. "What does their Jewishness consist of? What is my Jewishness?" They all had the same wish: to assimilate as quickly as possible and get rid of their accents. Herman belonged neither to them nor to the American, Polish, or Russian Jews. Like the ant on the table that morning, he had torn himself away from the community.

Herman walked around the lake, past patches of woods, past a hotel built like a Swiss chalet. Fireflies glimmered, crickets chirped, a sleepless bird screeched among the treetops. The moon rose—the head of a skeleton. What was above? What was the moon? Who had created it? For what purpose? Perhaps an answer as simple as gravitation was waiting for someone to discover, as Newton was said to have done the instant he saw an apple falling from a tree. Perhaps the all-embracing truth could be contained in a single sentence. Or were the words that could define it still to be created?

It was late when he returned to the rooming house. He had walked miles. The room was dark. Masha was lying in the same position in which he had left her. He went up close to her and touched her face as if to make sure she was alive. "What do you want?" she said, startled.

He undressed and lay down beside her. He lay there until he fell asleep. When he opened his eyes, the moon was shining. Masha stood in the center of the room, drinking from the flask of cognac.

"Masha, this is not the way!"

"What is the way?"

She took her nightdress off and came to him. They kissed silently and made love. Afterward she sat up and lighted a cigarette. Suddenly she said, "Where was I five years ago at this time?" She searched her memory for a long while. Then she said, "Still among the dead."

6

Herman and Masha traveled on, stopping at a hotel not far from the Canadian border. They had only a few days of vacation left, and the hotel was inexpensive.

A row of bungalows belonging to the hotel fronted a lake. Women and men in bathing costumes were playing cards outdoors. On a tennis court a rabbi, wearing a skullcap and shorts, played tennis with his wife, who was wearing the wig of an Orthodox woman. In a hammock between two pine trees lay a young boy and girl, giggling incessantly. The boy had a high forehead, a head of disheveled hair, and a hairy, narrow chest. The girl wore a tight bathing suit and a Star of David around her neck.

The proprietress had told Herman that the kitchen was "strictly kosher" and that the guests were all "one happy family." She escorted him and Masha to a bungalow with unpainted walls and a bare-beamed ceiling. The guests ate together at long tables in the hotel dining room. At lunchtime scantily clad mothers stuffed food into their children's mouths, determined to bring up tall Americans, six-footers. The little ones cried, gagged, and spat up the vegetables that had been forced down. Herman imagined that their angry eyes were saying, "We refuse to suffer just to satisfy your vain ambitions." The tennis-playing rabbi poured forth witticisms. The waiters—college or yeshiva students—joked with the older women and flirted with the girls. They immediately started questioning Masha as to where she came from and showered her with insinuating compliments. Herman's throat tightened. He could swallow neither the chopped liver and onions, the kreplach, the fatty piece of beef, nor the stuffed derma. The women at the table complained, "What kind of a man is he? He doesn't eat."

Since his stay in Yadwiga's hayloft, in the DP camp in Germany and in the years of struggle in America, Herman had lost contact with this kind of modern Jewry. But here they were again. A Yiddish poet with a round face and curly hair was carrying on a discussion with the rabbi. The poet, who referred to himself as an atheist, talked about worldliness, culture, the Jewish territory in Bira Bidjan, anti-Semitism. The rabbi performed the ritual washing of the hands after the meal and mumbled the blessing as the poet continued to spout phrases. At moments the rabbi's eyes took on a glazed expression and he intoned a few words aloud. A fat woman argued that Yiddish was a jargon, a mishmash without grammar. A bearded Jew, wearing gold-rimmed spectacles and a velvet skullcap, stood up and delivered a speech about the newly established State of Israel and solicited contributions.

Masha was engaged in conversation with the other women. They called her Mrs. Broder, and wanted to know when she and Herman had been married, how many children they had, what Herman's business was. Herman lowered his head. Every contact with people evoked terror in him. There was always the possibility that someone might know him and Yadwiga from Brooklyn.

An elderly man from Galicia had latched on to the name Broder and began to cross-examine Herman about whether or not he had family in Lemberg, in Tarnow, in Brody, in Drohobitch. He himself had a relative of that name, a second or third cousin, a man ordained as a rabbi, who had become a lawyer and was now an important figure in the Orthodox Party in Tel Aviv. The more answers Herman gave, the more the other probed. He seemed determined to prove that he and Herman were related.

The women at the table all commented on Masha's beauty, her slender figure, her clothes. When they learned that Masha had made the dress she was wearing, they wanted to know if she would sew for others. They all had items of clothing that needed to be let out, taken in, lengthened, or shortened.

Although Herman had eaten little, he rose from the table with a heavy feeling in his stomach. He and Masha went for a walk. He had not realized how impatient he had become during his years of solitude, how removed from all human involvement. He had one desire: to get away as quickly as possible. He walked so rapidly that Masha fell behind.

"Why are you running? No one is chasing you."

They walked uphill. Herman kept looking back. Would one be able to hide from the Nazis here? Would there be anyone to hide him and Masha in a hayloft? He had only just finished lunch and was already worrying about how he would face these people at suppertime. He would not be able to sit among them, watch the children being forced to eat, making a mess of the food. He could not listen to all those empty words. In the city, Herman never stopped longing for nature, the out-of-doors, but actually he was not suited for this tranquillity. Masha was afraid of dogs. Every time she heard one barking, she grasped Herman's arm. She soon said she could walk no farther in her high-heeled shoes. The farmers they passed eyed the strolling couple with dislike.

When they returned to the hotel, Herman suddenly decided to take out one of the rowboats supplied for the use of the guests. Masha attempted to dissuade him. "You'll drown us both," she said. But in the end she seated herself in the boat and lighted a cigarette. Herman knew how to row, but neither he nor Masha could swim. The sky was clear and light blue and a wind was blowing. Waves rose and fell, slapping against the sides of the boat, rocking it like a cradle. At times, Herman heard a splash, as if some monster were lurking in the water, silently swimming after them, ready to capsize the boat at any moment. Masha watched him with a worried expression, instructing him, criticizing him. She had little faith in his physical prowess. Or perhaps it was her own luck she mistrusted.

"Look at that butterfly!"

Masha pointed with her finger. How on earth had it flown so far from the shore? Would it be able to fly back? It fluttered in mid-air. It zigzagged, flying in no particular direction, and suddenly vanished. The waves, an alternating pattern of gold and shadow, turned the lake into a giant fluid chessboard.

"Careful! There's a rock!"

Masha sat bolt upright, and the boat wobbled. Herman quickly rowed backward. A rock was sticking out of the water, jagged and pointed, covered with moss— a remnant of the Ice Age and of the glacier that had once gouged out this basin in the earth. It had withstood the rains, the snows, the frost, the heat. It was afraid of no one. It did not need redemption, it had already been redeemed.

Herman rowed the boat to the shore and he and Masha got out. They went to their bungalow, got into bed, and covered themselves with the woolen blanket. Masha's closed eyes seemed to be smiling behind their lids. Then her lips started to move. Herman stared at her. Did he know her? Even her features seemed unfamiliar to him. He had never really considered the structure of her nose, chin, forehead. And what was going on in her mind?

Masha trembled and sat up. "I just saw my father."

She was silent awhile. Then she asked, "What day of the month is it?"

Herman figured out the date.

"It's been seven weeks since I've had my visitor," Masha said.

At first, Herman didn't understand what she was talking about. The women in his life each referred to their menstrual period by a different name: the holy day, the guest, the monthly. He became alert and calculated the time along with her.

"Yes, it's late."

"It's never late with me. As abnormal as I may be in other ways, I'm one hundred percent normal in this one."

"See a doctor."

"They can't tell so soon. I'll wait another week. An abortion in America costs five hundred dollars." Masha changed her tone of voice. "And it's dangerous too. A woman who worked in the cafeteria had one. She got blood poisoning and that was the end of her. What an ugly way to die! And what would my mother do if anything happened to me? I'm sure you would let her starve.''

"Don't get melodramatic. You're not dying yet.''

"How far is living from dying? I've seen people die and I know.''

7

The rabbi had apparently prepared a new set of jokes for the evening meal; his store of anecdotes seemed inexhaustible. The women giggled. The student-waiters served the food noisily. Sleepy children didn't want to eat and their mothers slapped them on the hands. One woman, a recent arrival in America, sent back her serving and the waiter asked, "By Hitler you ate better?''

Afterward they all gathered in the casino, a remodeled barn. The Yiddish poet gave a speech, lauding Stalin, and recited proletarian poetry. An actress did impersonations of celebrities. She cried, laughed, screamed, and made faces. An actor who had played in a Yiddish vaudeville theater in New York told bawdy jokes about a betrayed husband, whose wife had hidden a Cossack under her bed, and about a rabbi who had come to preach to a loose woman and had left her house with his fly open. The women and young girls doubled over with laughter. "Why is it all so painful to me?'' Herman asked himself. The vulgarity in this casino denied the sense of creation. It shamed the agony of the holocaust. Some of the guests were refugees from Nazi terror. Moths flew in through the open door, attracted by the bright lights, deceived by a false day. They fluttered about awhile and fell dead, having beaten themselves against the wall, or singed themselves on the lightbulbs.

Herman glanced around and saw that Masha was dancing with an enormous man in a plaid shirt and green shorts that exposed his hairy thighs. He held Masha by the waist; she barely reached his shoulder with her hand. One of the waiters was blowing a trumpet and another was banging a drum. A third blew on a home-made instrument that looked like a pot with holes in it.

Since Herman had left New York with Masha, he had had little chance to be alone. After some hesitation, he walked out without letting Masha see him leave. The night was moonless and chilly. Herman passed by a farm. A calf stood in a pen. It gazed into the night with the bewilderment of a mute creature. Its large eyes seemed to ask: Who am I? What am I here for? Cool breezes blew from the mountains. Meteors streaked across the sky. The casino grew smaller in the distance and lay down below like a firefly. With all her negativism, Masha had retained the normal instincts. She wanted a husband, children, a household. She loved music, the theater, and laughed at the actors' jokes. But in Herman there resided a sorrow that could not be assuaged. He was not a victim of Hitler. He had been a victim long before Hitler's day.

He came to the shell of a burned-out house and stopped. Attracted by the pungent smell, the holes that had been windows, the sooty entrance, the black chimney, he went inside. If demons did exist, they would be at home in this ruin. Since he could not stand humans, perhaps ghosts were his natural companions. Could he remain in this rubble for the rest of his life? He stood among the charred walls, inhaling the smell of the long-extinguished fire. Herman could hear the night breathing. He even imagined that it snored in its sleep. The silence rang in his ears. He stepped on coals and ashes. No, he could not be a part of all that acting, laughing, singing, dancing. Through a hole that had once been a window, he could see the dark sky—a heavenly papyrus filled with hieroglyphics. Herman's gaze fixed upon three stars whose formation resembled the Hebrew vowel "segul." He was looking at three suns, each probably with its planets, comets. How strange that a bit of muscle fitted into a skull should be capable of seeing such distant objects. How peculiar that a panful of brains should be constantly wondering and not able to arrive at any conclusion! They were all silent: God, the stars, the dead. The creatures who *did* speak revealed nothing . . .

He turned back toward the casino, which by now was dark. The building, so recently filled with noise, was quiet and abandoned, sunk in the self-absorption of all inanimate objects. Herman started to look for his bungalow, but he knew he would have difficulty finding it. He got lost wherever he went—in cities, in the country, on ships, in hotels. A single light was burning at the entrance of the house where the office was located, but there was no one there.

The thought ran through Herman's mind: perhaps Masha had gone to bed with that dancer in the green shorts. It was unlikely, but anything was possible among modern people stripped of all faith. What did civilization consist of if not murder and fornication? Masha must have recognized his footsteps. A door opened and he heard her voice.

8

Masha took a sleeping pill and fell asleep, but Herman remained awake. First he waged his usual war with the Nazis, bombed them with atomic bombs, blasted their armies with mysterious missiles, lifted their fleet out of the ocean and placed it on land near Hitler's villa in Berchtesgaden. Try as he might, he could not stop his thoughts. His mind worked like a machine out of control. He was again drinking that potion which enabled him to fathom time, space, "the thing in itself." His pondering always brought him to the same conclusion: God (or whatever He may be) was certainly wise, but there was no sign of His mercy. If a God of mercy did exist in the heavenly hierarchy, then he was only a helpless godlet, a kind of heavenly Jew among the heavenly Nazis. As long as one does not have the courage to leave this world, one can only hide and try to get by, with the help of alcohol, opium, a hayloft in Lipsk, or a small room at Shifrah Puah's.

He fell asleep and dreamed of an eclipse of the sun and funeral processions. They followed one after another, long catafalques, pulled by black horses, ridden by giants. They were both the dead and the mourners. "How can this be?" he asked himself in his dream. "Can a condemned tribe lead itself to its own burial?" They carried torches and sang a dirge of unearthly melancholy. Their robes dragged along the ground, the spikes of their helmets reached into the clouds.

Herman started and the rusty springs of the bed jangled. He awoke frightened and perspiring. His stomach was distended and his bladder full. The pillow under his head was wet and twisted like a piece of wrung-out washing. How long had he slept? One hour? Six? The bungalow was pitch black and wintery cold. Masha was sitting up in bed, her pale face like a spot of light in the dark. "Herman, I'm afraid of an operation!" she cried out hoarsely, her voice not unlike Shifrah Puah's. It was a few moments before Herman realized what she was talking about.

"Well, all right."

"Perhaps Leon will divorce me. I'll speak frankly to him. If he won't divorce me, the child will bear his name."

"I can't divorce Yadwiga."

Masha fell into a rage. "You can't!" she shouted. "When the king of England wanted to marry the woman he loved, he gave up his throne, and you can't get rid of a stupid peasant! There's no law that can force you to live with her. The worst that can happen is that you'll have to pay alimony. I'll pay the alimony. I'll work overtime and pay!"

"You know that a divorce would kill Yadwiga."

"I know nothing of the sort. Tell me, were you married to the bitch by a rabbi?"

"By a rabbi? No."

"How then?"

"A civil marriage."

"That's not worth a thing according to Jewish law. Marry me in a Jewish ceremony. I don't need their Gentile papers."

"No rabbi will perform a marriage without a license. This is America, not Poland."

"I'll find a rabbi who will."

"It would still be bigamy—worse, polygamy."

"No one will ever know. Only my mother and I. We'll move out of the house and you can use whatever name you like. If your peasant is so dear to you that you can't live without her, then go spend one day a week with her. I'll make my peace with that."

"Sooner or later, they'll arrest me and deport me."

"As long as there is no marriage certificate, no one can prove that we're man and wife. You can burn the ketuba right after the wedding ceremony."

"You have to register a child."

"We'll work something out. It's enough that I'm prepared to share you with such an idiot. Let me finish." Masha changed her tone. "I've been sitting here and thinking a full hour. If you won't agree, you can leave this minute and not come back. I'll find a doctor who will perform the operation, but don't you ever show your face to me again. I'll give you one minute to answer. If it's no, get dressed and get out. I don't want you here another second."

"You're asking me to break the law. I'll be afraid of every policeman in the street."

"You're afraid anyhow. Answer me!"

"Yes."

Masha was silent for a long time.

"Are you just saying that?" she said finally. "Or will I have to start all over again tomorrow?"

"No, it's settled."

"It takes an ultimatum to get you to decide anything. First thing tomorrow morning I'll telephone Leon and tell him he must give me a divorce. If he won't, I'll destroy him."

"What will you do? Shoot him?"

"I'm capable of doing that too, but I have other ways of getting at him. Legally he's as unkosher as pork. If I wanted to report him, he could be deported tomorrow."

"According to Jewish law, our baby will be a bastard anyhow. It was conceived before the divorce."

"Jewish law and all the other laws mean as much to me as last year's frost. I'm only doing it for my mother, only for her."

Masha got out of bed and moved about in the dark. A rooster crowed; other roosters answered him. A bluish light shone in through the window. The summer night was over. The birds started chirping and whistling all at the same time. Herman could no longer stay in bed. He got up, put on his trousers and shoes, opened the door.

The outdoors was occupied with its early-morning tasks. The rising sun had executed a childish painting on the night sky—spots, smears, a mess of colors. Dew had settled on the grass and a milky-white mist hung over the lake. Three young birds perched on the branch of a tree near the bungalow, kept their soft beaks wide open while the mother bird fed them little bits of stems and worms from her beak. She flew back and forth, with the single-minded diligence of those who know their duties. The sun rose behind the lake. Flames ignited the water. A pine cone fell, ready to fructify the earth, to bring forth a new pine.

Masha went out barefoot in her long nightgown, a cigarette between her lips.

"I've wanted your child since the day we met."

PART TWO

■

CHAPTER FIVE

———————

1

Herman was again getting ready for one of his trips. He had invented a new lie
about going on the road to sell the Encyclopedia Britannica, and had told Yadwiga
that he would have to spend a whole week in the Middle West. Since Yadwiga
hardly knew the difference between one book and another, the lie was superfluous.
But Herman had got into the habit of making up stories. Besides, lies wore thin
and had to be repaired constantly, and recently Yadwiga had been grumbling
about him. He was away the first day of Rosh Hashanah and half of the second.
She had prepared carp's head, apple and honey, and had baked the special New
Year challah exactly as her neighbor had taught her to, but apparently Herman
sold books even on Rosh Hashanah.

The women in the house were now trying to convince Yadwiga—speaking
half in Yiddish, half in Polish—that her husband must have a mistress somewhere.
One old woman had advised her to consult a lawyer, get a divorce from Herman,
and demand alimony. Another had taken her to the synagogue to hear the blowing
of the ram's horn. She stood among the wives and at the horn's first wailing
sound had burst into tears. It had reminded her of Lipsk, of the war, of her
father's death.

Now after only a few days with her, Herman was leaving again, to join not
Masha but Tamara, who had rented a bungalow in the Catskill Mountains. He
had had to lie to Masha too. He had told her that he was going with Rabbi
Lampert to Atlantic City to attend a two-day rabbinical conference.

It was a lame excuse. Even Reformed rabbis did not hold conferences during
the Days of Awe. But Masha, who had succeeded in getting Leon Tortshiner to
give her a divorce and expected to marry Herman when the ninety-day waiting
period was over, had stopped making jealous scenes. The divorce and her pregnancy
seemed to have changed her outlook. She behaved toward Herman as a wife.
And she showed more devotion than ever to her mother. Masha had found a
rabbi, a refugee, who had agreed to perform the wedding ceremony without a
license.

When Herman told her that he would be back from Atlantic City before Yom
Kippur, she didn't question him. He also told her that the rabbi would pay him
a fee of fifty dollars—and they needed the money.

The entire adventure was fraught with danger. He had promised to phone
Masha and he knew that the long-distance operator might mention where the

call was coming from. Masha might decide to phone Rabbi Lampert's office and discover that the rabbi was in New York. But since Masha had not called Reb Abraham Nissen Yaroslaver to check on him, she probably would not call Rabbi Lampert. One additional danger did not make that much difference. He had two wives and was about to marry a third. Even though he feared the consequences of his actions and the scandal that would follow, some part of him enjoyed the thrill of being faced with ever-threatening catastrophe. He both planned his actions and improvised. The "Unconscious," as von Hartmann called it, never made a mistake. Herman's words seemed to issue from his mouth of their own accord and only later would he realize what stratagems and subterfuges he had managed to invent. Behind this mad hodgepodge of emotions, a calculating gambler throve on daily risk.

Herman could easily free himself from Tamara. She had said several times that if he needed a divorce, she would give him one. But this divorce would not be of much help to him. There was probably little difference in the eyes of the law between a bigamist and a polygamist. Furthermore, a divorce would cost money and Herman would have to produce his papers. But there was something more: Herman saw in Tamara's return a symbol of his mystical beliefs. Whenever he was with her, he re-experienced the miracle of resurrection. Sometimes, as she spoke to him, he had the feeling he was at a séance at which her spirit had materialized. He had even played with the thought that Tamara wasn't really among the living, but that her phantom had returned to him.

Herman had been interested in occultism even before the war. Here in New York, when he could spare the time, he would go to the public library on Forty-second Street and look up books on mind-reading, clairvoyance, dybbuks, poltergeists—anything pertaining to parapsychology. Since formal religion was as good as bankrupt and philosophy had lost all meaning, occultism was a valid subject for those who still sought the truth. But souls existed on various levels. Tamara behaved—at least on the surface—like a living person. The refugee organization gave her a monthly allowance, and her uncle, Reb Abraham Nissen Yaroslaver, helped her as well. She had rented a bungalow at a Jewish hotel in Mountaindale. She didn't want to stay in the main building and eat in the dining room. The proprietor, a Jew from Poland, had agreed to have two meals a day brought to her bungalow. Her two weeks were almost over and Herman had not yet kept his promise to spend a few days with her. He had received a letter from her at his Brooklyn address chiding him for not keeping his word. She said at the end, "Make believe I'm still dead and come to visit my grave."

Before he left, Herman accounted for all eventualities. He gave money to Yadwiga; he paid the rent in the Bronx; he bought a gift for Tamara. He also put into his suitcase one of Rabbi Lampert's manuscripts to work on.

Herman arrived at the terminal too early and sat on a bench, his suitcase at his feet, waiting for the Mountaindale bus to be announced. It would not take him directly to where Tamara was stopping and he would have to change at some point along the route.

He had bought a Yiddish newspaper, but read only the headlines. The sum total of the news was always the same: Germany was being rebuilt; the Nazis' crimes were being forgiven by both the Allies and the Soviets. Each time Herman read such news, it awakened in him fantasies of vengeance in which he discovered methods for destroying whole armies, for ruining industries. He managed to bring to trial all those who had been involved in the annihilation of the Jews. He was ashamed of these reveries, which filled his mind at the slightest provocation, but they persisted with childish stubbornness.

He heard them call out Mountaindale and hurried to the exit where the buses were waiting. He lifted his suitcase up onto the rack and for the moment felt light-hearted. He was barely aware of the other passengers who had boarded the bus. They were speaking Yiddish and carrying packages wrapped in Yiddish newspapers. The bus started, and after a while a breeze smelling of grass, trees, and gasoline blew in through the partially opened window.

The ride to Mountaindale, which should have taken five hours, took almost a whole day. The bus halted at some terminal where they had to wait for another bus. It was still summery weather outside, but the days were already growing shorter. After sunset, a quarter moon came out and soon disappeared behind clouds. The sky became dark and starry. The driver of the second bus had to shut off the inside lights, because they disturbed his vision on the narrow, winding road. They drove through woods and suddenly a brightly lighted hotel materialized. On the veranda, men and women were playing cards. It had the insubstantiality of a mirage as they drove quickly by.

Gradually the other passengers got off at various stops and vanished into the night. Herman remained alone on the bus. He sat with his face pressed against the windowpane and tried to memorize each tree, shrub, stone along the way, as if America were destined for the same destruction as Poland, and he must etch every detail on his memory. Would not the entire planet disintegrate sooner or later? Herman had read that the whole universe was expanding, and was actually in the process of exploding. A nocturnal melancholy descended from the heavens. The stars gleamed like memorial candles in some cosmic synagogue.

The lights in the bus went on as it pulled up in front of the Hotel Palace, where Herman was to get off. It was exactly like the one they had already passed: the same veranda, the same chairs, tables, men, women, the same absorption in cards. "Had the bus been traveling in a circle?" he wondered. His legs felt stiff from having sat for so long, but he bounded up the wide steps of the hotel with vigor.

Suddenly Tamara appeared, wearing a white blouse, dark skirt, and white shoes. She looked tanned and younger. She had combed her hair differently. She ran toward him, took his suitcase, and introduced him to some women at a card table. One woman, who was wearing a bathing suit, with a jacket over her shoulders, threw a quick glance at her cards before saying in a hoarse voice, "How can a man leave such a pretty wife alone for such a long time? The men buzz around her like flies around honey."

"Why did it take so long?" Tamara asked, and her words, her Polish-Yiddish accent, the familiar intonations, shattered all his occult fantasies. This was no specter from the other world. She had put on some weight.

"Are you hungry?" she asked. "They've kept supper for you." She took him by the arm and led him into the dining room, where a single light was burning. The tables were already set for breakfast. Someone was still puttering about in the kitchen and the sound of running water could be heard. Tamara went into the kitchen and returned with a young man who carried Herman's supper on a tray: a half melon, soup with noodles, chicken with carrots, compote and a slice of honey cake. Tamara joked with the man and he answered her familiarly. Herman noticed that he had a blue number tattooed on his arm.

The waiter left and Tamara became silent. The youthfulness and even the suntan Herman had noticed upon his arrival seemed to fade. Shadows and the hints of pouches appeared under her eyes.

"Did you see that boy?" she said. "He was at the very doors of the ovens. In another minute, he would have been a heap of ashes."

2

Tamara lay in her bed and Herman rested on the rollaway cot that had been brought into the bungalow for him, but neither of them could sleep. Herman had dozed off for a moment, but awakened with a start. The cot creaked under him.

"You aren't sleeping?" Tamara said.

"Oh, I'll fall asleep."

"I have some sleeping pills. If you like, I'll give you one. I take them, but I stay wide awake. And if I do fall asleep, it really isn't a sleep at all, but a sinking into emptiness. I'll get you a pill."

"No, Tamara, I'll get along without one."

"Why should you toss and turn all night?"

"If I were lying with you, I would sleep."

Tamara didn't speak for a time.

"What's the sense of it? You have a wife. I'm a corpse, Herman, and one doesn't sleep with a corpse."

"And what am I?"

"I thought you were faithful to Yadwiga, at least."

"I told you the whole story."

"Yes, you did tell me. It used to be that when someone told me something, I knew exactly what he was talking about. Now I hear the words clearly, but they don't seem to get through to me. They roll off me like water on oilcloth. If you aren't comfortable in your bed, come into mine."

"Yes."

Herman got out of the cot in the dark. He crawled under the covers and felt the warmth of Tamara's body and something he had forgotten over the years of separation, something both maternal and utterly strange. Tamara lay on her back, motionless. Herman lay on his side with his face toward her. He didn't touch her, but he noticed the fullness of her breasts. He lay still, as embarrassed as a bridegroom on his wedding night. The years separated them as effectively as a partition. The blanket was tightly tucked under the mattress, and Herman wanted to ask Tamara to loosen it, but he hesitated.

Tamara said, "How long has it been since we've lain together? It seems like a hundred years to me."

"It's less than ten."

"Really? To me it's been an eternity. Only God can cram so much into such a short time."

"I thought you didn't believe in God."

"After what happened to the children, I stopped believing. Where was I on Yom Kippur in 1940? I was in Russia. In Minsk. I sewed burlap sacks in a factory and somehow earned my ration of bread. I lived in the suburbs with Gentiles. When Yom Kippur came, I decided I was going to eat. What was the sense of fasting there? Also, it wasn't wise to show the neighbors you were religious. But when evening came and I realized that somewhere Jews were reciting *Kol Nidre*, the food wouldn't go down."

"You said that little David and Yocheved come to you."

Herman regretted his words immediately. Tamara didn't move, but the bed itself started to groan as if it had been shocked by his words. Tamara waited for the scraping sounds to stop before she said, "You won't believe me. I'd better not say anything."

"I believe you. Those who doubt everything are also capable of believing everything."

"Even if I wanted, I couldn't tell you. There's only one way to explain it—that I'm crazy. But even insanity has to have an origin."

"When do they come? In your dreams?"

"I don't know. I told you, I don't sleep but sink into an abyss. I fall and fall and never reach bottom. Then I hang suspended. That's only one example. I experience so many things I can neither remember nor tell anyone about. I get through the days all right, but my nights are filled with terror. Perhaps I should go to a psychiatrist, but how can he help me? All he can do is give these things a Latin name. When I do go to a doctor, it's for only one thing: a prescription for sleeping pills. The children—yes, they come. Sometimes they visit till morning."

"What do they say?"

"Oh, they talk all night, but when I wake up, I don't remember any of it. Even if I do remember a few words, I soon forget them. But a feeling remains: that they exist somewhere and want to be in contact with me. Sometimes I go with them or I fly, I'm not sure which. I also hear music, but it's a kind of music without sound. We come to a border and I can't cross. They tear themselves away from me and float over to the other side. I can't remember what it is—a hill, some barrier. Sometimes I imagine I see stairs and someone is coming to meet them—a saint or a spirit. Whatever I say, Herman, it won't be accurate because there are no words to describe it. Naturally, if I'm mad, then it's all part of my madness."

"You aren't mad, Tamara."

"Well, that's nice to hear. Does anyone really know what madness is? Since you're here, why don't you move a bit closer? It's all right. For years I've lived with the conviction that you were no longer among the living, and one has different accounts to settle with the dead. When I found out you were alive, it was too late to change my attitude."

"The children never talk about me?"

"I think they do, but I'm not sure."

For a moment the silence was total. Even the crickets grew still. Then Herman heard the gushing sound of water like a running brook, or was it a drainpipe? A stomach rumbled, but he wasn't sure whether it was his or Tamara's. He felt an itch and had the urge to scratch, but restrained himself. He wasn't exactly thinking. Nevertheless, some thought process was going on in his brain. Suddenly he said, "Tamara, I want to ask you something." Even as he spoke, he didn't know what he was going to ask.

"What?"

"Why did you remain alone?"

Tamara didn't answer. He thought she might have dozed off, but then she spoke, wide awake and clearly. "I've already told you that I don't consider love a sport."

"What does that mean?"

"I can't have to do with a man I'm not in love with. It's as simple as that."

"Does that mean you still love me?"

"I didn't say that."

"During all these years you've never had one single man?" Herman asked with a tremor in his voice, ashamed of his own words and the agitation they evoked in him.

"Supposing there had been someone? Would you jump out of bed and walk back to New York?"

"No, Tamara. I wouldn't even consider it wrong. You may be perfectly honest with me."

"And later you'll call me names."

"No. As long as you didn't know I was alive, how could I demand anything? The most devout widows remarry."

"Yes, you're right."

"Then what is your answer?"

"Why are you shaking? You haven't changed one bit."

"Answer me!"

"Yes, I did have someone."

Tamara spoke almost angrily. She turned on her side, with her face toward him, thereby moving somewhat closer to him. In the dark he saw the glint of her eyes. As she turned, Tamara touched Herman's knee.

"When?"

"In Russia. Everything happened there."

"Who was it?"

"A man, not a woman."

There was suppressed laughter in Tamara's reply, mixed with resentment. Herman's throat tightened. "One? Several?"

Tamara sighed impatiently. "You don't have to know every detail."

"If you've told me this much, you might as well tell me everything."

"Well—several."

"How many?"

"Really, Herman, this isn't necessary."

"Tell me how many!"

It was quiet. Tamara seemed to be counting to herself. Herman became filled with grief and lust, amazed by the caprices of the body. One part of him mourned for something irrevocably lost: this betrayal, no matter how trivial compared to the world's iniquity, was a blot forever. Another part of him yearned to plunge himself into this treachery, to wallow in its degradation. He heard Tamara say, "Three."

"Three men?"

"I didn't know you were alive. You had been cruel to me. You made me

suffer all those years. I knew that if you were alive, you would do the same.
In fact, you married your mother's servant.''

"You know why."

"There were 'whys' in my case, too."

"Well, you're a whore!"

Tamara made a sound like a laugh. "Didn't I tell you."

And she stretched out her arms to him.

3

Herman had fallen into a deep sleep, out of which someone was waking him.
He opened his eyes in the dark and didn't know where he was. Yadwiga? Masha?
"Have I gone off with another woman?" he wondered. But his confusion lasted
only a few seconds. Of course it was Tamara. "What is it?" he asked.

"I want you to know the truth." Tamara spoke with the trembling voice of
a woman barely holding back her tears.

"What truth?"

"The truth is that I had no one—not three men, not one, not even half a
man. No one so much as touched me with his little finger. That is God's truth.''

Tamara was sitting up, and in the dark he sensed her intensity, her determination
not to let him go to sleep again until he heard her out.

"You're lying," he said.

"I'm not lying. I told you the truth the very first time when you asked me.
But you seemed disappointed. What's wrong with you—are you perverse?"

"I'm not perverse."

"I'm sorry, Herman, I'm as pure as the day you married me. I say I'm sorry
because, if I had known that you would feel so cheated, I might have tried to
accommodate you. There was certainly no lack of men who wanted me."

"Since you talk out of both sides of your mouth so easily, I'll never be able
to believe you again."

"Well, then, don't believe me. I told you the truth when we met in my
uncle's house. Perhaps you'd like me to describe some imaginary lovers just to
satisfy you. Unfortunately, my imagination isn't good enough. Herman, you
know how sacred the memory of our children is to me. I would sooner cut out
my tongue than desecrate their memories. I swear by Yocheved and David that
no other man has touched me. Don't think it was such an easy thing to accomplish.
We slept on floors, in barns. Women gave themselves to men they hardly knew.
But when someone tried to get close to me, I pushed him away. I always saw
the faces of our children before me. I swear by God, by our children, by the
blessed souls of my parents, that no man so much as kissed me all those years!
If you don't believe me now, then I beg you to leave me alone. God himself
couldn't force a stronger vow from me.''

"I believe you."

"I told you—it could have happened, but something didn't allow it. What
it was I don't know. Though reason told me that there wasn't a trace left of
your bones, I felt that you existed somewhere. How can one understand it?"

"It isn't necessary to understand it."

"Herman, there is something else I want to say to you."

"What?"

"I beg you, don't interrupt me. Before I came here, the American doctor at the consulate examined me and told me that I was in perfect health. I had survived everything—the hunger, the epidemics. I worked hard in Russia. I sawed logs, dug ditches, dragged wheelbarrows filled with rocks. At night, instead of sleeping, I often had to tend the sick who lay near me on planks. I never knew that I possessed so much strength. I'll soon get a job here, and no matter how hard it may be, it will be easier than what I had to do there. I don't want to go on accepting money from the 'Joint,' and I want to return the few dollars my uncle insisted on giving me. I'm telling you this so that you will know that I won't, God forbid, have to come to you for help. When you told me that you made your living by writing books for some rabbi who published them under his own name, I understood your situation. That's no way to live, Herman. You're destroying yourself!"

"I'm not destroying myself, Tamara. I've been a ruin for a long time."

"What will become of me? I shouldn't say this, but I can't ever be with anyone else. I know it as surely as I know that it's night now."

Herman didn't answer. He closed his eyes as if to get another moment of sleep.

"Herman, I have nothing to live for any more. I've wasted almost two weeks, eating, strolling, bathing, talking with all kinds of people. And all the while I've been saying to myself: 'Why am I doing this?' I try to read, but the books have no appeal for me. The women keep making suggestions about what I should do with myself, but I change the subject with jokes and meaningless banter. Herman, there's no other way out for me—I must die."

Herman sat up. "What do you want to do? Hang yourself?"

"If a piece of rope would make an end of it, then God bless the ropemaker. Over there I still had some hope. Actually, I had planned to settle in Israel, but when I found out you were alive, everything changed. Now I'm entirely without hope, and one dies of that more quickly than of cancer. I've observed it many times. I saw the opposite too. A woman in Jambul was lying on her deathbed. Then she received a letter from abroad and a package of food. She sat up and instantly became well. The doctor wrote a report about it and sent it to Moscow."

"And she's still alive?"

"She died of dysentery a year later."

"Tamara, I too am without hope. My only prospects are imprisonment and deportation."

"Why should you be imprisoned? You haven't robbed anyone."

"I have two wives and soon I'll have a third."

"Who is the third one?" Tamara asked.

"Masha, the woman I told you about."

"You said she already had a husband."

"He divorced her. She's pregnant."

Herman didn't know why he was revealing this to Tamara. But apparently he needed to confide in her, perhaps to shock her with his entanglements.

"Well, congratulations. You're going to be a father again."

"I'm going crazy, that's the bitter truth."

"Yes, you can't be in your right mind. Tell me, what sense does it make?"

"She's afraid of an abortion. When it comes to such things, a person can't be forced. She doesn't want the child to be illegitimate. Her mother is pious."

"Well, I must promise myself never to be surprised again. I'll give you a divorce. We can go to the rabbi tomorrow. You shouldn't have come to me under these circumstances, but talking consistency to you is like discussing colors with a blind man. Were you always like this? Or did the war do it? I don't really remember what kind of human being you used to be. I told you, there are periods of my life about which I've forgotten almost everything. And you? Are you just frivolous, or is it that you enjoy suffering?"

"I'm caught in a vise and can't free myself."

"You'll soon be free of me. You can also get rid of Yadwiga. Give her her fare and send her home to Poland. She sits there alone in the apartment. A peasant has to work, have children, go out into the fields in the morning, not stay cooped up like an animal in a cage. She can go out of her mind that way, and if, God forbid, you are arrested, what will become of her?"

"Tamara, she saved my life."

"Is that why you want to destroy her?"

Herman didn't reply. It had begun to grow light. He could make out Tamara's face. It was taking shape out of the darkness—a patch here, a patch there, like a portrait in the process of being painted. Her eyes stared at him wide open. On the wall opposite the window, the sunlight suddenly cast a spot that resembled a scarlet mouse. Herman became aware of how cold it was in the room. "Lie down. You'll catch your death," he said to Tamara.

"The devil isn't taking me away so soon."

Nevertheless, she lay down again and Herman covered them both with the blanket. He embraced Tamara and she didn't resist him. They lay together without speaking, overcome by both the complexities and the contradictory demands of the body.

The fiery mouse on the wall grew paler, lost its tail, and soon vanished altogether. For a while, night returned.

4

Herman spent the day and night before Yom Kippur eve at Masha's house. Shifrah Puah had bought two sacrificial hens, one for herself and one for Masha; she had wanted to buy a rooster for Herman but he had forbidden it. For some time now he had been thinking of becoming a vegetarian. At every opportunity, he pointed out that what the Nazis had done to the Jews, man was doing to animals. How could a fowl be used to redeem the sins of a human being? Why should a compassionate God accept such a sacrifice? This time Masha agreed with Herman. Shifrah Puah swore that if Masha didn't go through with the ceremony, she would leave the house. After reluctantly agreeing and twirling the hen above her head, uttering the prescribed prayers, Masha refused to take the fowl to the ritual slaughterer.

The two hens, one white, one brown, lay on the floor, their feet bound, their golden eyes looking sideways. Shifrah Puah had to take the hens to the slaughterer herself. As soon as her mother left the house, Masha burst into tears. Her whole face became contorted and wet. She fell into Herman's arms and cried out, "I can't take any more of this! I can't! I can't!"

Herman gave her a handkerchief to blow her nose. Masha went into the bathroom and he could hear her muffled crying. Afterward, she came into the room with a flask of whiskey in her hand. She had already drunk part of it. She was half laughing, half crying, with the mischievousness of a spoiled child. It occurred to Herman that as her pregnancy progressed she was becoming inappropriately babyish. She was full of little-girl mannerisms, giggly, even playfully naïve. He remembered Schopenhauer's statement that the female never really becomes fully mature. The bearer of children remains a child herself.

"In this kind of a world, there is only one thing left—whiskey. Here, have a drink!" Masha said, putting the flask to his lips.

"No, it's not for me."

Masha didn't come to him that night. She fell asleep right after supper, having taken a sleeping pill. Fully clothed, she lay on her bed in a drunken stupor. Herman turned off the light in his room. The hens, about which Shifrah Puah and Masha had quarreled, were already soaked, rinsed, and in the icebox. A not quite three-quarter moon shone in through the window. It cast its glow on the evening sky. Herman fell asleep and dreamed of things that had nothing to do with his mood. Somehow he was sliding down a hill of ice, using a contraption that was a combination of skates, a sled, and skis.

The next morning after breakfast, Herman said goodbye to Shifrah Puah and Masha and went to Brooklyn. On the way, he telephoned Tamara. Sheva Haddas had bought a seat for her in the women's section of their synagogue so that she might attend the midnight prayers. Tamara, after wishing Herman well like a pious wife, added, "No matter what happens, there is no one closer to me than you."

Yadwiga hadn't performed the ritual hen-twirling ceremony, but she had, on the day before Yom Kippur, prepared challah, honey, fish, kreplach, and chicken. Her kitchen smelled exactly the same as Shifrah Puah's. Yadwiga fasted on Yom Kippur. She paid for a ticket at the synagogue with ten dollars that she had managed to save out of her household money. She now poured out her resentment at Herman, accused him of running around with other women. He tried to defend himself, but couldn't conceal his annoyance. Finally he even pushed and kicked her, knowing that in her village in Poland, for wives to be beaten by their husbands was an affirmation of love. Yadwiga began to wail: she had saved his life and he was repaying her by a beating on the eve of the holiest day of the year.

The day was over and night fell. Herman and Yadwiga ate the last meal before fasting. Yadwiga drank eleven gulps of water as her neighbors advised her to—a prevention against thirst during the fast.

Herman fasted but did not go to the synagogue. He couldn't bring himself to be like one of those assimilated Jews who only prayed on the High Holy Days. He sometimes prayed to God when he was not fighting with Him, but to stand in a House of God with a holiday prayer book in his hands and praise Him according to the prescribed custom—this he couldn't do. The neighbors knew that Herman the Jew stayed at home while his Gentile wife went to pray. He could visualize them spitting at the mention of his name. In their own way, they had excommunicated him.

Yadwiga had dressed in a new frock that she had bought cheaply at a close-out sale. She had wrapped her hair in a kerchief, put a necklace of false pearls around her neck. The wedding ring Herman had bought for her, even though he had not stood beneath the wedding canopy with her, shone on her finger. She took a holiday prayer book with her to the synagogue. It was printed in Hebrew and English on facing pages: Yadwiga couldn't read either language.

Before leaving she kissed Herman and said maternally, "Ask God for a happy year."

Then she burst into tears like a good Jewish woman.

The neighbors were waiting for Yadwiga downstairs, eager to include her in their circle, to teach her the Judaism that remained from their mothers and grandmothers and which the years in America had diluted and distorted.

Herman paced back and forth. Generally, when he found himself alone in Brooklyn, he would immediately phone Masha, but on Yom Kippur Masha didn't talk on the phone, nor did she smoke. Nevertheless, he did try to call her, because he noticed that there were not yet three stars in the sky. But there was no reply.

Alone in the apartment, Herman felt as if he were with all three women: Masha, Tamara, Yadwiga. Like a mind reader, he could read their thoughts. He knew, or at least he thought he knew, how the mind of each one of them functioned. Their grudges against God blended with their grudges against him. His women prayed for his health, but they also asked the omnipotent God that He reform Herman's ways. On this day, when God received so much homage, Herman was in no mood to bare his soul to Him. He went to the window. The street was empty. The leaves were beginning to turn and fell with each gust of wind. The Boardwalk was deserted. On Mermaid Avenue, all the shops were boarded up. It was Yom Kippur and quiet in Coney Island—so quiet that from his apartment he could hear the roar of the waves. Perhaps it was always Yom Kippur for the sea and it also prayed to God, but its God was like the sea itself—flowing eternally, infinitely wise, boundlessly indifferent, awesome in its unlimited power, bound by unchangeable laws.

Standing there, Herman tried to send telepathic messages to Yadwiga, Masha, and Tamara. He comforted them all, wished them a good year, promised them love and devotion.

Herman went into the bedroom and stretched out on the bed in his clothes. He didn't want to admit it, but of all his fears, the greatest was his fear of again becoming a father. He was afraid of a son and more afraid of a daughter, who would be an even stronger affirmation of the positivism he had rejected, the bondage that had no wish to be free, the blindness that wouldn't admit it was blind.

Herman fell asleep and Yadwiga awakened him. She told him that at the synagogue the cantor had sung *Kol Nidre* and that the rabbi had delivered a sermon soliciting funds for the yeshivas of the Holy Land and for other Jewish causes. Yadwiga had pledged five dollars. She told Herman in an embarrassed way that she didn't want him to touch her that night. It was forbidden. She bent over him and he saw in her eyes an expression that he used to see on the face of his mother during the high holidays. Yadwiga's lips trembled as if she were about to speak, but no sound came from them. Then she whispered, "I'm going to become Jewish. I want to have a Jewish child."

CHAPTER SIX

1

Herman had spent the first two days of Succoth with Masha and had returned for Chol Hamoed, the intermediary days, to his apartment in Brooklyn.

He had eaten breakfast and was sitting at a table in the living room, working on a chapter of a book entitled *Jewish Life as Reflected in the Shulcan Aruch and the Responsa*. It had already been accepted by publishers in America and in England, and Rabbi Lampert was about to sign a contract with a French firm as well. Herman was to receive a percentage of the royalties. It was to be approximately fifteen hundred pages long, and had originally been planned for several volumes. But Rabbi Lampert had arranged that the work appear first as a series of monographs, each allegedly complete in itself, but prepared in such a way that they could later, with minor alterations, be bound into one large volume.

Herman wrote a few lines and paused. As soon as he sat down to work, his "nerves" began to sabotage him. He grew sleepy and could hardly keep his eyes open. He had to have a drink of water, he needed to urinate, he became conscious of a crumb between two loose teeth and tried to get it out first with the tip of his tongue and then with a thread drawn from the notebook binding.

Yadwiga had gone to the basement to do the laundry, having taken a quarter from Herman to put in the washing machine. In the kitchen, Woytus was delivering an avian lecture to Marianna, who was perched near him on the stand. Her head was bowed guiltily, as if she were being reprimanded for some inexcusable misdeed.

The telephone rang.

"What does she want now?" Herman wondered. He had talked to Masha just a half hour before and she had told him that she was going down to Tremont Avenue to shop for the remaining days of the holiday—Shmini Atzeres and Simchas Torah.

He lifted the receiver and said, "Yes, Mashele."

Herman heard a deep masculine voice, making the kind of hesitant, throaty sound a man makes when he is about to speak but is interrupted and loses his train of thought. Herman started to say that the caller had the wrong number, when the voice asked for Herman Broder. Herman couldn't decide whether or not to hang up. Was it a police detective? Had his bigamy been discovered? "Who is it?" he said finally.

The person at the other end of the line coughed, cleared his throat, and coughed again, like a speaker preparing for a speech. "I beg you to listen to me," he said, speaking in Yiddish. "My name is Leon Tortshiner. I'm Masha's former husband."

Herman's mouth became dry. It was the first direct contact he had ever had with Tortshiner. The man's voice was deep and his Yiddish was different from Herman's and Masha's. He spoke in an accent that was typical of a small area of Poland, somewhere in the provinces between Radom and Lublin. Each word ended in a slight vibrato, like the sound made by the bass notes of a piano.

"Yes, I know," Herman said. "How did you get my phone number?"

"What's the difference? I have it and that's what counts. If you must know, I saw it in Masha's address book. I have a good memory for numbers. I didn't know whose number it was, but eventually, as they say, I figured it out."

"I see."

"I hope I didn't wake you."

"No, no."

Tortshiner paused before he continued and Herman surmised from this pause that Tortshiner was a deliberate person, someone who thought ponderously and reacted slowly. "Can we get together?"

"For what reason?"

"It's a personal matter."

"He's not very clever," ran through Herman's mind. Masha had often said that Leon was a fool. "I'm sure you understand that this is extremely unpleasant for me," Herman heard himself stammer. "I can't see why it should be necessary. As long as you're divorced and—and—"

"My dear Mr. Broder, I wouldn't ring you up if it weren't necessary—for both of us."

He half chortled, half coughed, making a sound that was a combination of good-humored annoyance and the triumphant joviality of someone who has outsmarted his opponent. Herman felt the tips of his ears growing hot. "Perhaps we can talk about it over the phone?"

"There are things that have to be discussed face-to-face. Tell me where you live and I'll come over to your place, or we can meet in a cafeteria. You'll be my guest."

"At least give me an idea what it's about," Herman insisted.

It sounded as if Leon Tortshiner was smacking his lips together and struggling with words that were escaping his control.

The sounds finally became words. "What else can it be but about Masha?" Tortshiner was saying. "She is the link between us, so to speak. It's true Masha and I are divorced, but we were once man and wife, no one can deny that. I knew all about you even before she told me. Don't ask me how. I have, as they say, my sources of information.

"Where are you now?"

"I'm in Flatbush. I know you live somewhere in Coney Island, and if it's inconvenient for you to come to my place, then I'll come to yours. What is the saying? If Mohammed won't come to the mountain, then the mountain must come to Mohammed."

"There's a cafeteria on Surf Avenue," Herman said. "We can meet there." It was an effort for him to speak. He gave Tortshiner the exact location of the cafeteria and told him what subway would get him there. Tortshiner made him repeat the directions several times. He elaborated on everything and repeated phrases as if the very act of talking gave him pleasure. It was not actual dislike that he aroused in Herman so much as irritation at being forced into such an embarrassing situation. Herman was also suspicious. Who knows? It was not impossible that such a low character might be carrying a knife, or a revolver. Herman bathed and shaved hastily. He decided to wear his better suit; he didn't want to look shabby before this man. "One must please everyone," Herman thought ironically, "even the former husband of one's mistress."

He went to the basement and saw his underwear whirling wildly about through the window of the washing machine. The water foamed and splashed. Herman had the odd thought that these inanimate objects—the water, the soap, the bleach—were angry at man and the power he used to control them. Yadwiga was frightened at the sight of Herman. He had never before come down to the basement.

"I have to meet someone at a cafeteria on Surf Avenue," he told her. And though Yadwiga didn't question him, he described in detail where the cafeteria was located, thinking that if Leon Tortshiner were to attack him, Yadwiga would know where he was, or if necessary she would be able to appear as a witness in court. He even repeated Leon Tortshiner's name several times. Yadwiga gaped at him with the submission of the peasant who has long since given up trying to understand the city dweller and his ways. Still, her eyes betrayed a trace of distrust. Even on the days that belonged to her, he found reasons for getting away.

Herman looked at his wristwatch and timed himself so that he would not arrive at the cafeteria too early. He felt certain that a man like Leon Tortshiner would be at least half an hour late, and he decided to take a walk on the Boardwalk.

The day was sunny and mild, but the amusements had all been shut down. Nothing remained except boarded-up doors, faded and peeling posters. The performers had all left: the girl who was half snake, the strong man who ripped chains apart, the swimmer without hands and feet, the medium who called forth the spirits of the dead. The billboard announcing that the High Holy Days' services would be held in the auditorium of the Democratic Club was already ragged and weather-stained. Seagulls flew and shrieked above the ocean.

The waves surged toward the shore, hissing and foaming, receding again as they always had—barking packs of dogs, powerless to bite. In the distance, a ship with a gray sail rocked on the water. Like the ocean itself, it both moved and remained stationary—a shrouded corpse walking upon the water.

"Everything has already happened," Herman thought. "The creation, the flood, Sodom, the giving of the Torah, the Hitler holocaust." Like the lean cows of Pharaoh's dream, the present had swallowed eternity, leaving no trace.

2

Herman entered the cafeteria and saw Leon Tortshiner sitting at a table next to the wall. He recognized him from a photograph he had seen in Masha's album, though Tortshiner was now considerably older. He was a man of about fifty, large-boned, with a square-shaped head and thick dark hair that one could tell at a glance was dyed. His face was broad, with a prominent chin, high cheekbones, and a wide nose with large nostrils. He had thick eyebrows and his brown eyes were slanted like a Tartar's. There was a scar on his forehead that looked like an old knife wound. His somewhat coarse appearance was softened by the aura of Polish-Jewish affability. "He won't murder me," Herman thought. It seemed unbelievable that this boor had once been Masha's husband. The mere thought of it was ridiculous. But that was the way with facts. They punctured every bubble of conceit, shattered theories, destroyed convictions.

A cup of coffee was set in front of Tortshiner. A cigar with an inch of ash at its tip rested on an ashtray. At his left was a dish holding a partially eaten egg cake. Catching sight of Herman, Tortshiner made as if to rise, but fell back in his chair again.

"Herman Broder?" he asked. He stretched out a large, heavy hand.

"Sholom aleichem."

"Sit down, sit down," said Tortshiner. "I'll bring you some coffee."

"No, thanks."

"Tea?"

"No. Thanks."

"I'll get you some coffee!" Leon Tortshiner said decisively. "Since I invited you, you're my guest. I have to watch my weight, that's why I'm only eating an egg cake, but you can afford to eat a piece of cheesecake."

"Really, it's not necessary."

Tortshiner stood up. Herman watched him as he picked up a tray and took his place in the line at the counter. For his broad build, he was too short, with overly large hands and feet and with the shoulders of a strong man. This was how they grew in Poland: more in breadth than in height. He wore a brown striped suit, obviously chosen in an effort to look younger. He returned with a cup of coffee and a piece of cheesecake. He picked up the almost extinguished cigar quickly, puffed at it vigorously, and blew out a cloud of smoke.

"I pictured you altogether differently," he said. "Masha described you as a regular Don Juan." He obviously didn't intend the description to be derogatory.

Herman lowered his head. "Women's notions."

"I debated whether or not to call you for a long time. One doesn't do a thing like this easily, you know. I have every reason to be your enemy, but I'll tell you right off that I'm here for your sake. Whether you believe me or not— that's, as they say, another matter."

"Yes, I understand."

"No, you don't understand. How can you understand? You are, as Masha told me, something of a writer, but I'm a scientist. Before one can understand, one must have the facts, all the information. *A priori* we know nothing, only that one and one make two."

"What *are* the facts?"

"The facts are that Masha bought the divorce from me at a price that no honest woman should pay, even if her life depended on it." Leon Tortshiner spoke in his deep voice, without hurry, seemingly without anger. "I think you should know this, because if a woman is capable of paying such a price, one can never be altogether sure of her integrity. She had lovers before she knew me and also while she lived with me. That is the absolute truth. That's the reason we separated. I'll be frank with you. Normally, I would have no reason to take this interest in you. But I struck up an acquaintance with a person who knows you. He doesn't know our connection, if you want to call it a connection, and he happened to tell me about you. Why make a secret of it? His name is Rabbi Lampert. He told me that you suffered during the war, that you spent years lying in a loft filled with hay, and all that. I know you do some work for him. He calls it 'research,' but you don't have to draw any diagrams for me. You're a Talmudist, I specialized in bacteriology.

"As you know, Rabbi Lampert is working on a book to prove that all knowledge stems from the Torah and he wanted me to help him with the scientific part. I told him plainly that modern knowledge is not to be found in the Torah and there was no point looking for it there. Moses knew nothing about electricity or vitamins. What's more, I don't want to waste my energy for a few dollars. I'd rather manage with less. The rabbi didn't actually mention your name, but when he spoke of a man who had hidden in a hayloft, I put two and two together, as they say. He praises you to the skies. But naturally he doesn't know what I know. He's a strange character. He immediately called me by my first name and that's not my style. Things must take their natural course. There has to be an evolution even in personal relationships. It's impossible to talk to him, because the telephone keeps ringing. I'll wager he has a thousand deals going on at the same time. Why does he need so much money? But I'll come to the point.

"I want you to know, Masha is a bum. Pure and simple. If you want to marry a bum, that's your privilege, but I thought I should warn you before she catches you in her net. Our meeting will, of course, remain a secret. That is the assumption on which I phoned you." Leon Tortshiner picked up his cigar and drew on it, but it had gone out.

While Tortshiner talked, Herman had been sitting with his head bent over the table. He was hot and wished he could open his collar. He felt a burning sensation behind his ears. A trickle of perspiration ran down his back, along his spine. When Tortshiner started to fuss with his cigar, Herman asked in a choked voice, "What price?"

Leon Tortshiner cupped his ear. "I can't hear. Speak a little louder."

"I said, 'What price?' "

"You know what price. You're not so naïve. You probably think I'm no better than she is and in a sense I can understand that. First of all, you're in love with her and Masha is a woman with whom one can fall in love. She drives men crazy. She almost drove me crazy. As primitive as she is, she has the perceptiveness of a Freud, Adler, and Jung put together, plus a little bit more. She's a brilliant actress too. When she wants to laugh, she laughs; and when she wants to cry, she cries. I told her straight out that if she stopped wasting her talents on foolishness, she could be a second Sarah Bernhardt. So, you see, it's no surprise to me that you're tangled up with her. I won't try to deny it— I still love her. Even a first-year student in psychology learns that one can love and hate at the same time. You're probably asking yourself, why should I tell you these secrets? What do I owe you? To understand, you'll have to hear me out with patience."

"I'm listening."

"Don't let the coffee get cold. Eat a piece of cheesecake. There. And don't be so upset. After all, the whole world is living through a revolution, a spiritual revolution. Hitler's gas chambers were bad enough, but when people lose all values, it's worse than torture. You undoubtedly come from a religious home. Where else did you learn Gemara? My parents weren't fanatics, but they were believing Jews. My father had one God and one wife, and my mother had one God and one husband.

"Masha probably told you that I studied at Warsaw University. I specialized in biology, worked with Professor Wolkowki, and helped him with an important discovery. Actually I made the discovery myself, though he received the credit. The truth is, they didn't reward him either. People think that thieves are to be found only on Krochmalna Street in Warsaw or the Bowery in New York. There are thieves among professors, artists, among the greatest in all fields. Ordinary thieves generally don't steal from one another, but plenty of scientists literally live by theft. Do you know that Einstein stole his theory from a mathematician who was helping him and no one really knows his name? Freud also stole, and so did Spinoza. This really has no connection with the subject, but I'm a victim of this sort of thievery.

"When the Nazis occupied Warsaw, I could have worked for them because I had letters from the greatest German scientists, and they would even have overlooked the fact that I was Jewish. But I didn't want to take advantage of such privileges and went through the whole Gehenna. Later I escaped to Russia, but our intellectuals there did an about-face and even started informing on one another. That's all the Bolsheviks needed. They sent them away to the camps. I myself had once been sympathetic to Communism, but actually, at the time when it would have paid me to be a Communist, I became fed up with the whole system and told them so openly. You can imagine how they treated me.

"In any case, I lived through the war, the camps, the hunger, the lice, and in 1945 I wound up in Lublin. There I met your Masha. She was the mistress, or the wife, of some Red Army deserter who had become a smuggler and a black marketeer in Poland. She apparently got enough to eat from the smuggler. I don't know exactly what happened between them. He accused her of being unfaithful and God knows what else. I don't have to tell you that she's an attractive woman—a few years ago she was a beauty. I had lost my whole family. When she heard I was a scientist, she became interested in me. The smuggler, I suppose, had another woman or half a dozen others. You must keep in mind that in all walks of life there is more chaff than wheat.

"Masha had found her mother and we all left for Germany. We had no papers and had to smuggle ourselves in. Every step of the way was fraught with peril. If you wanted to live, you had to break the law, because all laws sentenced you to death. You were a victim yourself, so you know how it was, though everyone has a different story to tell. It's impossible to talk sensibly to refugees, because no matter what you have to tell, someone will say that it happened just the other way around.

"But let's get back to Masha. We reached Germany and they 'respectfully' interned us in a camp. Generally, couples lived together without the benefit of a marriage ceremony. Who needed such ceremonies at a time like that? But Masha's mother insisted that we get married according to the laws of Moses and Israel. The smuggler probably gave her a divorce, or she hadn't been married to him in the first place. I couldn't care less. I wanted to get back to my scientific work as soon as I could, and I'm not religious. She wanted a wedding; I agreed to a wedding. Others in the camp started to do business immediately—smuggling. The American Army brought all kinds of goods to Germany and they handled it. Jews did business everywhere, even in Auschwitz. If there is a hell, they'll do business there too. I don't say this with malice. What else could they do? The relief organizations provided barely enough to exist on. After all those years of starvation, people wanted to eat well and to wear decent clothes too.

"But what could I do if by nature I'm not a businessman? I stayed at home and lived on what the 'Joint' rationed out to me. The Germans didn't allow me near a university or laboratory. There were a few other loafers like me around and we read books or played chess. This didn't please Masha. Living with her smuggler, she had grown accustomed to luxury. When she met me, she had been impressed because I was a scientist, but that didn't satisfy her for long. She began to treat me like dirt; she made terrible scenes. Her mother, I must tell you, is a saint. She suffered every hell and remained pure. I loved her mother dearly. How often does one find a holy person? Masha's father had also been a fine man, something of a writer, a Hebraist. Who she takes after, I don't know. She just couldn't resist gaiety wherever it was. The smugglers were always giving parties, dances. In Russia they had gotten used to vodka and all its glories.

"When I met Masha in Lublin, it was my impression that she was faithful to the smuggler. But soon it was obvious that she was having all kinds of affairs. The feeble Jews had been killed off and those who were left had iron constitutions, though, as it turns out, they were broken people too. Their troubles are coming to the surface now. In a hundred years, the ghettos will be idealized and the impression created that they were inhabited only by saints. There could be no greater lie. First of all, how many saints are there in any generation? Second of all, most of the really pious Jews perished. And among those who managed to survive, the great drive was to live at any cost. In some of the ghettos, they even ran cabarets. You can imagine what cabarets! You had to step over dead bodies to get in.

"My theory is that the human species is getting worse, not better. I believe, so to speak, in an evolution in reverse. The last man on earth will be both a criminal and a madman.

"I imagine that Masha told you the worst about me. As a matter of fact, it was she who broke up the marriage. While she was running around, I, like an idiot, sat home with her mother. Her mother suffered from an eye disease, and I would read the Pentateuch and the American-Yiddish newspapers out loud to her. But how long could I lead such a life? I'm not old now, and in those days I was in my prime. I was also beginning to meet people and make contact with the scientific world. Women professors used to visit from America—there are quite a number of educated women here—and they became interested in me. My mother-in-law, Shifrah Puah, told me openly that as long as Masha left me alone all day and half the night, I didn't owe her a thing. Shifrah Puah loves me to this day. Once I met her in the street and she embraced me and kissed me. She still calls me 'my son.'

"When my visa for America came through, all of a sudden Masha made up with me. I was granted the visa not as a refugee but as a scientist. I got the visa, not she. She was supposed to have gone to Palestine. Two famous American universities were competing for me. Later I was pushed out of one and then the other by intrigues. I won't go into that now because it has no bearing on the subject. I established theories and made discoveries that the big companies didn't appreciate. The president of one university told me frankly, 'We can't afford to have a second Wall Street crash.' What I had discovered was nothing more or less than new sources of energy. Atomic energy? Not exactly atomic. I would call them biological. The atomic bomb would also have been ready years before it was if Rockefeller hadn't butted in.

"American billionaires hired thieves to rob the man you see before you. They were after an apparatus I had spent years building with my own hands. If this apparatus had been put into operation—and it was only one step from it— the American oil companies would have gone bankrupt. But without me the machinery and chemicals were of no value to the thieves. The companies tried to buy me off. I've been having difficulties getting my citizenship, and I'm sure they're behind it. You spit in Uncle Sam's face ten times a day and he'll grin and bear it. But try to touch his investments and he turns into a tiger.

"Where was I? Oh, yes, America. What would Masha have done in Palestine? She would have landed in a refugee camp, which would not have been much better than the camp in Germany. Her mother was sick and the climate there would have finished her. I'm not making myself out to be a saint. Soon after we got here, I became involved with another woman. She wanted me to divorce Masha. She was an American, the widow of a millionaire, and she was prepared to set me up in a laboratory so that I wouldn't have to be dependent on a university. But somehow I wasn't ready for a divorce. Everything must ripen, even a cancer. True, I no longer trusted Masha, and as a matter of fact, no sooner did we get here than she started all over again. But it seems that it is possible to love without trust. I once ran into an old schoolmate who told me openly that his wife was living with other men. When I asked him how he could stand it, he answered simply, 'One can overcome jealousy.' One can overcome anything but death.

"How about another cup of coffee? No? Yes, one can overcome anything. I don't know exactly how she met you and I don't care. What difference does it make? I don't blame you. You never swore any loyalty to me, and besides in this world we grab what we can. I grab from you, you grab from me. That there was someone before you, here in America, I know for sure, because I met him and he didn't make a secret of it. It was after she met you that she started asking me for a divorce, but since she ruined my life I didn't feel that I had any obligation to her. She could easily get a civil divorce, because we've been separated for some time. But no one could force me to give her a Jewish divorce, not even the greatest of rabbis. It's her fault that I'm still at loose ends. After the wreck of our marriage, I tried to pick up the threads of my career, but I was so wound up I couldn't concentrate on serious work. I began to hate her, though it isn't in my nature to hate. I sit here with you as a friend and wish you only well. My reasoning is simple: if it hadn't been you, it would have been someone else. If I were as guilty as Masha tries to make me appear, would her mother send me a New Year's card on Rosh Hashanah with a personal note?

"Now I come to the point. A few weeks ago, Masha called me up and asked me to meet her. 'What's happened?' I asked. She hemmed and hawed until finally I told her to come to my place. She came, all dressed up, fit to kill, as they say. I had heard about you, but she began to tell me the whole story, as if it had only happened yesterday. All the details. She'd fallen in love with you;

she was pregnant. She wanted to have the baby. She wanted a rabbi to perform the wedding ceremony because of her mother. 'Since when have you become so concerned about your mother?' I asked. I was in a bitter mood. She sat down and crossed her legs like an actress posing for a photograph. I said to her, 'You behaved like a prostitute when you were with me, now pay the price.' She hardly protested. 'We're still man and wife,' she said. 'I guess it's permitted.' To this day I don't know why I did it. Vanity, perhaps. Then I met Rabbi Lampert and he told me about you, your learning, the years of hiding in that attic, and everything became clear, painfully clear. I realized that she'd caught you in her net just as she had me. Why she's attracted to intellectuals is a good question, though undoubtedly she's been mixed up with roughnecks as well.

"That, in short, is the story. I hesitated a long time before deciding to tell it to you. But I came to the conclusion that you had to be warned. I hope, at least, that the child is yours. It looks as if she really loves you, but with such a creature one never can know."

"I won't marry her," Herman said. He spoke the words so quietly that Leon Tortshiner cupped his ear.

"What? Look, there's one thing I want to make sure. Don't tell her about our meeting. I really should have gotten in touch with you sooner, but as you see I am an impractical person. I do things and get myself into all kinds of trouble. If she knew that I told you what had happened, my life would be in danger."

"I won't tell her."

"You know you're not obliged to marry her. She's just the type to have a bastard. If there's someone to be pitied, it's you. Your wife—did she die?"

"Yes, she died."

"Your children too?"

"Yes."

"The rabbi told me that you live with a friend and that you don't have a telephone, but I remembered seeing your phone number in Masha's little book. She has a habit of outlining important phone numbers with circles and little drawings of flowers and animals. She drew a whole garden of trees and snakes around your number."

"How did you happen to be in Brooklyn today if you live in Manhattan?" Herman asked.

"I have friends here," Leon Tortshiner said, obviously lying.

"Well, I must go now," Herman said. "Thanks very much."

"What's your hurry? Don't go yet. I was only thinking of your own good. In Europe, people were accustomed to live secret lives. Maybe it made some sense there, but this is a free country and you don't have to hide from anyone. Here you can be a Communist, an anarchist, whatever you want. There are certain religious sects who hold venomous snakes when they pray, because of some verse in the Book of Psalms. Others go around naked. Masha, too, carries around a whole pack of secrets. The trouble is that those who have secrets betray themselves. Man is his own betrayer. Masha told me things that she didn't have to tell me and that I never would have found out otherwise."

"What did she tell you?"

"Whatever she told me she'll tell you. It's just a matter of time. People like to show off about everything, even a hernia. I don't need to tell you that she doesn't sleep at night. She smokes and talks. I used to plead with her to let me sleep. But the demon in her won't let her rest. If she had lived in the Middle Ages, she would surely have been a witch and flown a broomstick Saturday night to keep a date with the devil. But the Bronx is one place where the devil would have died of boredom. Her mother is also a witch in her own way, but a good witch: half rebbetzin, half fortuneteller. Every female sits in her own net weaving like a spider. When a fly happens to come along, it's caught. If you don't run away, they'll suck the last drop of life out of you.''

"I'll manage to run away. Goodbye.''

"We can be friends. The rabbi is a savage, but he loves people. He has unlimited connections and he can be of use to you. He's angry at me because I won't read electronics and television into the first chapter of Genesis. But he'll find someone who will. Basically he's a Yankee, although I think he was born in Poland. His real name isn't Milton but Melech. He writes a check for everything. When he arrives in the next world and has to give an accounting, he'll take out his checkbook. But, as my grandmother Reitze used to say, 'Shrouds don't have pockets.' ''

3

The telephone rang, but Herman didn't answer it. He counted the rings and went back to the Gemara. He sat at the table, which was covered with a holiday cloth, studying and intoning as he used to do in the study house in Tzivkev.

Mishnah: "And these are the duties the wife performs for the husband. She grinds, bakes, washes, cooks, nurses her child, makes the bed, and spins wool. If she has brought one servant with her, she doesn't grind, bake, or wash. If she has brought two, she doesn't cook or nurse the child; three, she doesn't make the bed or spin wool; four, she sits in the salon. Rabbi Eliezer says: Even if she brought him a houseful of servants, he should force her to spin wool, because idleness leads to insanity.''

Gemar: "She grinds? But the water does that—the intention is that she prepares the grain to be ground. Or it can mean a hand mill. This Mishnah doesn't concur with Rabbi Chiyah, because Rabbi Chiyah said: A wife is solely for beauty, for children. Rabbi Chiyah said further: Whoever wishes his daughter to be fair should feed her young chickens and make her drink milk during the time before she becomes ripe—''

The telephone began to ring again and this time Herman didn't count the rings. He was through with Masha. He had sworn to renounce all worldly ambitions, to give up the licentiousness into which he had sunk when he had strayed from God, the Torah, and Judaism. He had stayed up the previous night trying to analyze the modern Jew and his own way of life. He had once again arrived at the same conclusion: if a Jew departed in so much as one step from the Shulcan Aruch, he found himself spiritually in the sphere of everything base—Fascism, Bolshevism, murder, adultery, drunkenness. What could stop Masha from being what she was? What could change Leon Tortshiner? Who and what could have controlled the Jewish members of the GPU, the Capos, the thieves, speculators, informers? What could save him, Herman, from sinking even deeper into the mire in which he was caught? Not philosophy, not Berkeley, Hume, Spinoza, not Leibnitz, Hegel, Schopenhauer, Nietzsche, or Husserl. They all preached some sort of morality but it did not have the power to help withstand temptation. One could be a Spinozaist and a Nazi; one could be versed in Hegel's phenomenology and be a Stalinist; one could believe in monads, in the *Zeitgeist*, in blind will, in European culture, and still commit atrocities.

At night he had taken stock of himself. He was deceiving Masha, Masha was deceiving him. Both had the same goal: to get as much pleasure as possible out of life in the few years left before darkness, the final end, an eternity without reward, without punishment, without will, would be upon them. Behind this *Weltanschauung* festered deception and the principle of "might is right." One could escape from this only by turning to God. And to what faith could he repair? Not to a faith which had, in the name of God, organized inquisitions, crusades, bloody wars. There was only one escape for him: to go back to the Torah, the Gemara, the Jewish books. What about his doubt? Even if one were to doubt the existence of oxygen, one would still have to breathe. One could deny gravity, but one would still have to walk on the ground. Since he was suffocating without God and the Torah, he must serve God and study the Torah. He rocked back and forth, intoning, "And she nurses her child. So I would say that the Mishnah does not agree with the School of Shamai. 'If she made an oath not to nurse her child,' the School of Shamai says, 'she removes the breast from its mouth,' and the School of Hillel says, 'The husband forces her and she must nurse it.' "

The telephone rang again. Yadwiga came in from the kitchen, holding an iron in one hand and a pan of water in the other.

"Why don't you answer the telephone?"

"I'll never answer the phone again on a holiday. And if you want to become Jewish, don't iron on Shmini Atzeres."

"You write on the Sabbath, not I."

"I won't write on the Sabbath any more. If we don't want to become like the Nazis, we must be Jews."

"Will you go to Kuffoth with me today?"

"Say Hakaffoth, not Kuffoth. Yes, I'll go with you. You'll have to go to the ritual bath too, if you want to become a Jewish woman."

"When will I become Jewish?"

"I'll talk to the rabbi. I'll teach you how to say the prayers."

"Will we have a child?"

"If God wills it, we'll have one."

Yadwiga's face turned red. She seemed overcome with joy.

"What shall I do with the iron?"

"Put it away till after the holidays."

Yadwiga stood there a while longer, then she returned to the kitchen. Herman grasped his chin. He hadn't shaved and his beard was beginning to grow. He had decided that he could no longer work for the rabbi, since the work was a deception. He would have to find a position as a teacher or do something else. He would divorce Tamara. What hundreds of generations of Jews before him had done, he would do. Repent? Masha would never repent. She was a modern woman through and through, with all the modern woman's ambitions and delusions.

The wisest thing for him to do would be to leave New York, settle in a distant state. If not, he would always be tempted to go back to Masha. Even the thought of her name excited him. In the repeated ringing of the phone, he could hear her anguish, her wantonness, her attachment to him. Reading Rashi's annotations to the Talmud, he still couldn't keep her peppery words from intruding— her teasing remarks, her contempt for those who desired her, running after her like hounds after a bitch. Without question, she would have an explanation for her behavior. She was capable of declaring a pig kosher and propounding a plausible theory to prove it.

He sat over his Gemara, staring at the letters, at the words. These writings were home. On these pages dwelt his parents, his grandparents, all his ancestors. These words could never be adequately translated, they could only be interpreted. In context, even a phrase such as "a woman is for her beauty's sake" had a deep religious significance. It brought to mind the study house, the women's section of the synagogue, penetential prayers, lamentations for martyrs, sacrifice of one's life in the Holy Name. Not cosmetics and frivolity.

Could this be explained to an outsider? The Jew took words from the marketplace, from the workshop, from the bedroom, and sanctified them. In the Gemara the words for thief and robber had another flavor, different associations from those they had in Polish or English. The sinners in the Gemara stole and cheated solely so that Jews would have a lesson to learn—so that Rashi could make a commentary, so that Tosafoth could write the great super-commentaries on Rashi; so that the learned teachers such as Reb Samuel Idlish, Reb Meir of Lublin, and Reb Shlomo Luria could seek even clearer answers and ferret out new subtleties and new insights. Even the idol-worshippers that are mentioned worshipped the gods so that a Talmudic tractate would set forth the perils of idolatry.

The phone rang again and Herman imagined that he heard Masha's voice through the ringing: "At least hear my side!" According to all the laws of justice, both sides were entitled to be heard. Although Herman knew that he was breaking his vows again, he could not prevent himself from getting up and lifting the receiver.

"Hello."

There was silence at the other end of the line. Apparently Masha could not speak.

"Who is it?" Herman asked.

No one answered.

"You whore!"

Herman heard the sound of a gasp. "Are you still alive?" Masha asked.

"Yes, I'm alive."

There was another long silence.

"What's happened to you?"

"What's happened is that I've found out you are a despicable creature!" Herman was shouting. He couldn't catch his breath.

"I believe you've gone out of your mind!" Masha replied.

"I curse the day I met you! Slut!"

"My God! What have I done?"

"Paid for your divorce with prostitution!" It seemed to Herman that it wasn't his voice shouting. This was the way his father used to scold a faithless Jew:

Goy, fiend, apostate! It was the ancient Jewish outcry against those who broke the commandments. Masha began to cough. It sounded as if she were choking. "Who told you this? Leon?"

Herman had promised Leon Tortshiner not to mention his name. Just the same, he couldn't lie now. He didn't answer.

"He is a vicious devil and—"

"He may be vicious, but he spoke the truth."

"The truth is that he asked me, but I spat in his face. If I'm lying, may I not live to wake up in the morning and may I never have any rest in my grave. Bring us face to face. If he dares to repeat this ugly lie, I'll kill him and myself. Oh, Father in heaven!"

Masha was screaming, and her voice too was not like her own; it was like that of a Jewish woman of olden times who had been falsely accused of evil-doing. It seemed to Herman as if he were hearing a voice from generations past. "He isn't a Jew, he's a Nazi!"

Masha wailed so loudly that Herman had to hold the receiver away from his ear. He stood listening to her weeping. Instead of becoming less intense, it grew louder. Herman's anger was rekindled.

"You had a lover here in America!"

"If I had a lover in America, may I get cancer. May God hear my words and punish me. If Leon made it up, may the curse fall on him. Father in heaven, see what they're doing to me! If he's telling the truth, may the child in my womb die!"

"Stop it! You're swearing like a fishwife."

"I don't want to live any more!"

Masha was convulsed with sobs.

CHAPTER SEVEN

1

All night the snow fell—dry and coarse as salt. On the street where Herman lived, one could barely make out the contours of the few cars buried beneath it. Herman imagined that this was the way the Pompeiian chariots had looked covered over with ash after the eruption of Vesuvius. The night sky turned violet as if, through some miracle or transformation in the heavens, the earth had entered an unknown constellation. Herman thought about his boyhood: Hanukkah, the rendering of chicken fat for the coming Passover, playing games with a dreidl, skating in the frozen gutters, reading the weekly portion of the Torah which begins with "And Jacob dwelt in the land of his fathers." The past existed! Herman spoke to himself. Granted that time is nothing more than a mode of thinking, as maintained by Spinoza, or a form of perception, as Kant thought, still the fact cannot be denied that in Tzivkev in wintertime the stove was heated with firewood; his father, blessed be his memory, studied the Gemara and its commentaries, while his mother cooked a barley stew of pearl kasha, beans, potatoes, and dried mushrooms. Herman could taste the flavor of the grits, hear his father mumbling as he read, his mother talking to Yadwiga in the kitchen, the tinkling of a bell on a sled carrying logs that a peasant was bringing in from the forest.

Herman, in his robe and slippers, was sitting in his apartment. Though it was winter, the window was opened slightly, letting in a sound like countless crickets chirping under the snow. It was too warm in the house. The janitor had provided heat all night long. The steam in the radiator whistled its one-note tune full of inarticulate longing. Herman imagined that the sound of the steam in the pipes was a lament: bad, bad, bad; grief, grief, grief; sick, sick, sick. There was no light on, but the room was filled with the snow-reflected glow that suffused the sky. It was a light, Herman imagined, similar to the Northern Lights he had read about in books. For a while he stared at the bookcase and at the volumes of the Gemara which again stood neglected and dusty. Yadwiga never dared to touch these sacred books.

Herman had been unable to sleep. He had been married to Masha by a rabbi, and she was, according to his calculations, in her sixth month, although it certainly wasn't apparent. Yadwiga had also missed her period.

Herman thought of the Yiddish saying that ten enemies can't harm a man as much as he can harm himself. Yet he knew he wasn't doing it all by himself; there was always his hidden opponent, his demon adversary. Instead of destroying him with dispatch, his enemy continued to invent new and baffling tortures for him.

Herman breathed the cold air that blew in from the ocean and the snowfall. He looked outside and had the desire to say a prayer, but to whom? How could he dare to speak to the higher powers now? And what should he pray for? After a while he returned to bed and lay down next to Yadwiga. It was their last night together. In the morning, he was leaving on one of his trips, which meant he would be going to stay with Masha.

Since their wedding, when he had placed the ring on Masha's index finger, she had busied herself improving the apartment and redecorating his room. At night she no longer had to come to him secretly because of her mother. She had promised not to quarrel with him about Yadwiga, but she broke her word. She cursed Yadwiga at every opportunity, even blurting out that she would like to kill her. Masha's hope that the marriage would still her mother's reproaches proved false. Shifrah Puah complained that Herman's idea of marriage was a mockery. She forbade him to call her "mother-in-law." Only the most necessary words passed between them. Shifrah Puah became even more engrossed in her prayers, in leafing through books, reading the Yiddish newspapers and the memoirs of Hitler victims. She spent a great deal of time in her darkened bedroom and it was difficult to know whether she was thinking or napping.

Yadwiga's pregnancy was a new catastrophe. The rabbi of the synagogue Yadwiga had attended on Yom Kippur had accepted her ten dollars, a woman had led her to the ritual bath, and now Yadwiga was a convert to Judaism. She observed the laws of purification and Kashruth. She asked Herman questions continually. Was it permitted to keep meat in the refrigerator when there was a bottle of milk in it? Was it all right to eat dairy food after fruit? Was she permitted to write to her mother, who, according to Jewish law, was no longer her mother?

Her neighbors confused her with their conflicting suggestions, often based on shtetl superstitions. An elderly Jew, an immigrant peddler, tried to teach her the Yiddish alphabet. Yadwiga no longer tuned in to the Polish radio programs, but listened only to those in Yiddish. One always heard weeping and sighing on these stations; even the songs had a sobbing quality. She asked Herman to speak Yiddish to her, though she understood little. She reprimanded him more and more for not conducting himself like other Jews. He didn't go to synagogue, nor did he own a prayer shawl and phylacteries.

He would tell her to mind her own business, or say, "You won't have to lie on my bed of nails in Gehenna," or, "Do me a favor, and leave the Jews alone. We have enough trouble without you."

"May I wear the medallion Marianna gave me? It has a crucifix on it."

"You may, you may. Stop bothering me."

Yadwiga no longer kept her neighbors at a distance. They visited, shared secrets, and gossiped with her. These women, with little else to do, instructed Yadwiga in Judaism, showed her how to buy bargains, warned her about being exploited by her husband. An American housewife must have a vacuum cleaner, an electric mixer, an electric steam iron, and, if possible, a dishwasher. The apartment must be insured against fire and theft; Herman must take out a life-insurance policy; she must dress better and not go around in peasant's rags.

There was a controversy among the neighbors on what kind of Yiddish to teach Yadwiga. The women from Poland tried to teach her Polish Yiddish, and the Litvaks that of Lithuania. Continuously, they pointed out to Yadwiga that her husband spent too much time on the road and that, if she wasn't watchful, he might run off with another woman. In Yadwiga's mind, the insurance policy and the dishwasher were both necessary aspects of Jewish observances.

Herman fell asleep, woke up, dozed off, and woke again. His dreams were as intricate as his waking life. He had discussed the possibility of an abortion with Yadwiga, but she wouldn't hear of it. Wasn't she entitled to have at least one child? Must she die and have no Kaddish? (She had learned the word from her neighbors.) Well, and what about him? Why should he remain like a withered tree? She would be a good wife to him; she was willing to go to work till the ninth month, to wash clothes for the neighbors, scrub floors, to help contribute toward the expenses. A neighbor, whose son had just opened a supermarket, offered Herman a job, so that he wouldn't have to travel around the country selling books.

Herman was supposed to have phoned Tamara at the furnished room into which she had moved, but days passed and he hadn't called. He was, as usual, behind in his work for the rabbi. Every day he was afraid of receiving a letter from the Department of Internal Revenue imposing heavy penalties on him for non-payment of taxes. Any investigation might expose all his involvements. He shouldn't continue living in this apartment now that Leon Tortshiner had his phone number. Tortshiner was capable of paying a visit unannounced. Herman considered it possible that Tortshiner was scheming to bring about his downfall.

Herman laid his hand on Yadwiga's hip. Her body gave off an animal warmth. His was cold by comparison. Yadwiga seemed to sense in her sleep that Herman desired her and responded mutteringly without waking up altogether. "There is no such thing as sleep," Herman thought. "It's all a sham and make-believe."

He again dozed off, and when he opened his eyes, it was broad daylight.

The snow was dazzling in the sunshine. Yadwiga was in the kitchen—he could smell coffee. Woytus whistled and trilled. He was surely serenading Marianna, who rarely sang at all, but groomed herself all day plucking at the down under her wings.

For the hundredth time, Herman calculated his expenses. He owed rent here and in the Bronx, he had to pay the phone bills in the names of Yadwiga Pracz and Shifrah Puah Bloch. He hadn't paid the utilities for either apartment and the gas and electricity might be shut off. He had misplaced the bills. His papers and documents had a way of vanishing; perhaps he had even lost money, "Well, it's just too late to do anything," he thought.

After a while he went into the bathroom to shave. He looked at his lathered face in the mirror. The soap on his cheeks resembled a white beard. A pale nose and a pair of light-colored eyes, tired yet youthfully eager, could be seen peering out of the suds.

The phone rang. He went to it, lifted the receiver, and heard the voice of an older woman. She stammered and had trouble speaking. He was about to hang up when she said, "This is Shifrah Puah."

"Shifrah Puah? What has happened?"

"Masha—is sick—" And she began to sob.

"Suicide," ran through Herman's mind. "Tell me what has happened!"

"Come quickly—please!"

"What is it?"

"Please come!" Shifrah Puah repeated. And she hung up.

Herman had the impulse to call back to get more details, but he knew it was difficult for Shifrah Puah to speak over the phone and that her hearing was poor. He returned to the bathroom. The lather on his cheeks had dried up and was flaking off in bits. No matter what happened, he had to shave and shower. "As long as you're alive, you mustn't stink." He started to apply fresh lather to his face.

Yadwiga came into the bathroom. Usually she would open the door slowly and ask permission to come in, but this time she came without courtesy. "Who just phoned? Your mistress?"

"Leave me alone!"

"The coffee's getting cold."

"I can't have breakfast. I must go right away."

"Where to? To your mistress?"

"Yes, to my mistress."

"You made me pregnant and you go running to whores. You're not selling books. Liar!"

Herman was astonished. She had never spoken in such a venomous tone. Anger seized him. "Go back into the kitchen, or I'll throw you out of here!" he shouted.

"You have a mistress. You spend nights with her. You dog!"

Yadwiga shook her fist at him, and Herman pushed her out of the doorway. He heard her cursing at him in her peasant tongue: "*Szczerwa, cholera, lajdak, parch.*" He hurried into the shower, but only cold water sprayed out. He dressed clumsily but as quickly as he could. Yadwiga had left the apartment, probably to tell the neighbors that he had beaten her. Herman took one gulp of coffee from the cup on the kitchen table and hurried out. He returned in a moment; he had forgotten his sweater and rubbers. Outside, the snow blinded him. Someone had dug a path between two walls of snow. He walked down to Mermaid Avenue, where the shopkeepers were clearing away the snow, shoveling it into heaps. He was engulfed by a cold wind from which no amount of clothing could protect him. He hadn't had enough sleep, he felt light from hunger.

He climbed up the stairs to the open station to wait for a train. Coney Island, with her Luna Park and Steeplechase, lay desolate in the winter snow and frost. The train rolled up to the platform and Herman stepped inside. Briefly, he could see the ocean from the window. The waves leaped and foamed with wintry fury. A man moved slowly along the beach, but it was impossible to imagine what he was doing there in the cold, unless he was trying to drown himself.

Herman took a seat over hot pipes. He felt a warm blast of air through the cane seating. The car was half empty. A drunk had stretched himself out on the floor. He wore summer clothes, and no hat. From time to time, he uttered a growl. Herman picked up a muddy newspaper from the floor and read an item about a maniac who had murdered his wife and six children. The train was slower than usual. Someone said that the tracks were covered with snow. It speeded up when it went underground, and finally pulled into Times Square, where Herman changed for a Bronx express. The trip took almost two hours, during which Herman read through the muddy newspaper: the columnists, the ads, even the horse-racing page and the obituaries.

2

When he entered Masha's apartment, he saw Shifrah Puah, a stocky young man who was a doctor, and a dark-complexioned woman, probably a neighbor. Her head with its frizzly hair was too large for her small body.

"I thought you would never come," Shifrah Puah said.

"It's a long ride by subway."

Shifrah Puah was wearing a black kerchief on her head. Her face looked yellow and more wrinkled than usual.

"Where is she?" Herman asked. He didn't know whether he was asking about a living person or a dead one.

"She is asleep. Don't go in."

The doctor, round-faced, with moist eyes and curly hair, motioned toward Herman, and in a mocking tone asked, "The husband?"

"Yes," Shifrah Puah said.

"Mr. Broder, your wife wasn't pregnant. Who told you she was pregnant?"

"She did."

"She had a hemorrhage, but there was no baby. Did a doctor examine her?"

"I don't know. I'm not even sure she saw a doctor."

"Where do you people think you're living—on the moon? You're still in your little shtetl in Poland." The doctor spoke half in English, half in Yiddish. "In this country when a woman is pregnant, she is under the continuous care of a doctor. Her whole pregnancy was here!" the doctor said, pointing his index finger to his temple.

Shifrah Puah had already heard his diagnosis, but she clasped her hands together as if she were hearing it for the first time.

"I don't understand it, I don't understand. Her belly grew. The child kicked her."

"All nerves."

"Such nerves! Defend and protect us against such nerves. Father in heaven, she started to scream and go into labor. Oh, my wretched life!" Shifrah Puah wailed.

"Mrs. Bloch, I once heard of such a case," the neighbor said. "Everything happens to us refugees. We suffered so much under Hitler, we're half crazy. The woman I heard about got a huge stomach. Everybody said she was carrying twins. But in the hospital they found it was only gas."

"Gas?" Shifrah Puah asked, putting her hand to her ear as if she were deaf. "But I tell you, she didn't have her period all these months. Well, evil spirits are playing with us. We came out of Gehenna, but Gehenna followed us to America. Hitler has run after us."

"I'm leaving now," the doctor said. "She'll sleep till late tonight—maybe even tomorrow morning. When she wakes up, give her the medicine. You can give her some food too, but no cholent."

"Who eats cholent in the middle of the week?" Shifrah Puah asked. "We don't even have cholent on the Sabbath. The cholent that you have to cook in a gas oven has no taste."

"I was just kidding."

"You'll come again, Doctor?"

"I'll drop in tomorrow morning on the way to the hospital. You'll be a grandmother a year from now. She's completely normal inside."

"I won't live that long," Shifrah Puah said. "Only God in heaven knows what strength and life these few hours have cost me. I thought she was in her sixth month—her seventh month, at most. Suddenly she starts screaming that she has cramps and blood gushes out of her. That I'm still alive and standing on my feet is a miracle from above."

"Well, it was all up here." Again the doctor pointed to his forehead. He went out but paused at the doorway to beckon to the neighbor, who followed him. Shifrah Puah was silent, waiting suspiciously in case the woman might be listening at the door. Then she said, "I wanted so much to have a grandchild. At least someone to name after the murdered Jews. I'd hoped it would be a boy and he would be called Meyer. But with us nothing works because our luck is black. Oh, I shouldn't have saved myself from those Nazis! I should have stayed there with the dying Jews, and not run away to America. But we wanted to live. What use is my life to me? I envy the dead. All day I envy them. I can't even earn my death. I hoped my bones would be buried in the Holy Land, but it's fated that I should lie in an American cemetery."

Herman didn't answer. Shifrah Puah went over to the table and picked up the prayer book that was lying there. Then she put it down again. "Would you like something to eat?"

"No, thanks."

"Why did it take you so long? Well, I guess I'll say my prayers." She put on her eyeglasses, sat down on a chair, and began mumbling with her pale lips.

Herman opened the door to the bedroom carefully, Masha was sleeping in the bed in which Shifrah Puah usually slept. She looked pale and serene. He gazed at her for a long time. He was overcome with love for her as well as shame at himself. "What can I do? How can I repay her for all the pain I've caused her?" He closed the door and went to his room. Through the partially frosted-over window he could see the tree in the courtyard that not long ago had been covered with green leaves. It was laden with snow and icicles. Over the bits of scrap iron and metal grates that were strewn about, there lay a thick, bluish-white covering. The snow had made a graveyard of man's trash.

Herman lay down on the bed, and fell asleep. When he opened his eyes, it was evening and Shifrah Puah was standing over him, trying to wake him up.

"Herman, Herman. Masha's up. Go and see her."

It took a moment for him to realize where he was and to remember what had happened.

A single light was on in the bedroom. Masha lay in the same position as before, but her eyes were open. She looked at Herman and said nothing.

"How do you feel?" he asked.

"I have no feelings left."

3

It was snowing again. Yadwiga was making a stew as it used to be cooked in Tzivkev—a mixture of groats, lima beans, dried mushrooms, and potatoes, sprinkled with paprika and parsley. A song from a Yiddish operetta, which Yadwiga took to be a religious chant, came from the radio. The parakeets reacted to the music in their own fashion. They screeched, whistled, tweeted, and flew around the room. Yadwiga had to put lids on the pots, so the birds wouldn't—God forbid—fall in.

In the midst of writing, Herman was overcome with fatigue. He put down the pen, leaned his head back against the armchair, and tried to take a little nap. In the Bronx, Masha had not yet returned to work, because she was still weak. She had fallen into a state of apathy. When he spoke to her, she replied briefly and to the point, but in such a way that they were left with nothing to talk about. Shifrah Puah prayed all day as if Masha were still dangerously ill. Herman knew that without Masha's earnings, they did not have enough money even for essentials, but he too was without funds. Masha had suggested the name of a loan association where he could borrow a hundred dollars at a high rate of interest, but how far would such a loan go? He might also need a co-signer.

Yadwiga came in from the kitchen. "Herman, the stew is finished."

"So am I, financially, physically, spiritually."

"Speak so that I can understand you."

"I thought you wanted me to speak Yiddish to you."

"Talk the way your mother did."

"I can't talk the way my mother did. She believed and I am not even an atheist."

"I don't know what you're babbling about. Come eat. I've made a Tzivkev barley stew."

Herman was about to get up, when the doorbell rang.

"One of your ladies has probably come to give you a lesson," Herman said.

Yadwiga went to open the door. Herman crossed out the last half page he had written, and muttered, "Well, Rabbi Lampert, the world will do with a somewhat shorter sermon." He suddenly heard a suppressed cry. Yadwiga ran back into the room, slamming the door shut. Her face was white and her eyes seemed to turn upward. She stood there trembling, with her hand holding the doorknob, as if someone were trying to force his way in. "A pogrom?" ran through Herman's mind. "Who is it?" he asked.

"Don't go! Don't go! Oh, God!" Spittle appeared on Yadwiga's lips as she tried to block his way. Her face became distorted. Herman glanced at the window. The fire escape was not off this room. He took a step toward Yadwiga and she grabbed him by the wrists. At that moment the door opened and Herman saw Tamara in a shabby fur coat, hat, and boots. He understood instantly.

"Stop shaking, idiot!" he screamed at Yadwiga. "She's alive!"

"Jesus, Maria!" Yadwiga's head jerked convulsively. She pushed herself against Herman with all her strength, almost knocking him over.

"I didn't think she would recognize me," Tamara said.

"She's alive! She's alive! She isn't dead!" Herman shouted. He began wrestling with Yadwiga, trying both to calm her and to push her away. She clung to him, wailing. It was like the howling of an animal.

"She's alive! She's alive!" he shouted once again. "Calm down! Foolish peasant!"

"Oh, Holy Mother! My heart!" Yadwiga crossed herself. At once she realized that a Jewish woman doesn't make the sign of a cross and clasped her hands together. Her eyes bulged from their sockets, her mouth became twisted with cries she couldn't utter.

Tamara took a step backward. "It never occurred to me she would recognize me. My own mother wouldn't know me. Calm down, Yadzia," she said in Polish. "I'm not dead and I haven't come to haunt you."

"Oh, Little Father!"

And Yadwiga beat her head with both fists. Herman said to Tamara, "Why did you do this? She might have died of fright."

"I'm sorry, I'm sorry. I thought I was so changed. No resemblance. I wanted to see how and where you live."

"You could at least have telephoned."

"O God, O God! What will happen now?" Yadwiga cried. "And I'm pregnant." Yadwiga laid her hand on her belly.

Tamara looked surprised but also as if she were about to burst out laughing. Herman stared at her. "Are you crazy or drunk?" he asked.

As soon as he said the words, he became aware of the odor of alcohol. A week earlier Tamara had told him she was scheduled to go to the hospital to have the bullet removed from her hip. "Have you taken to hard liquor?" he said.

"When a person can't have the soft things of life, he takes to the hard ones. You're settled here quite comfortably." Tamara's tone changed. "When you lived with me, there was always a mess. Your papers and books were everywhere. Here it's spic and span."

"She keeps the place clean, and you ran around giving speeches to the Poalay Zion."

"Where's the crucifix?" Tamara asked in Polish. "Why isn't there a crucifix hanging here? Since there isn't a mezuzah, there must be a crucifix."

"There is a mezuzah," Yadwiga answered.

"There has to be a crucifix too," Tamara said. "Don't think I've come here to disturb your bliss. I learned how to drink in Russia, and when I have a glassful I become curious. I wanted to see for myself how you live. After all, we still have something in common. Both of you remember me when I was alive."

"Jesus! Maria!"

"I'm not dead, I'm not dead. I'm not alive and I'm not dead. The truth is that I have no claims on him," Tamara said, pointing to Herman. "He didn't know I was struggling to survive somewhere, and he probably always loved you, Yadzia. He surely slept with you before he did with me."

"No, no! I was an innocent girl. I came to him a virgin," Yadwiga said.

"What? Congratulations. Men love virgins. If men had their way, every woman would lie down a prostitute and get up a virgin. Well, I see that I'm an uninvited guest and I'll go now."

"Pani Tamara, sit down. You frightened me and that's the reason I screamed so. I'll bring coffee. God is my witness that if I had known that you were alive I would have kept away from him."

"I bear you no grudge, Yadzia. Our world is a greedy place. You didn't get much of a bargain in him, though," Tamara said, indicating Herman, "but anything is better than being alone. It's a nice apartment too. We never had such an apartment."

"I'll bring coffee. Would you, Pani Tamara, like something to eat?"

Tamara didn't answer. Yadwiga went to the kitchen, her house slippers clumsily slapping the floor. She left the door open. Herman noticed that Tamara's hair was mussed. There were yellowish pouches under her eyes.

"I didn't know you drank," he said.

"There's a lot you don't know. You think one can go through hell and come out unscathed. Well, one can't! In Russia, there was one cure for every illness—vodka. You drank your fill, lay down in the straw or on the bare earth, and stopped caring. Let God and Stalin do as they pleased. Yesterday I went to visit some people who own a liquor store—here in Brooklyn, but in another neighborhood. They gave me a whole shopping bag full of whiskey."

"I thought you were going to the hospital."

"I was supposed to go tomorrow, but I'm not sure I want to now. This bullet," Tamara said, placing her hand on her hip, "is my best souvenir. It reminds me that I once had a home, parents, children. If they take it away from me, I won't have anything left at all. It was a German bullet, but after lying in a Jewish body for so many years, it has become Jewish. It may decide to explode one day, but meanwhile it lies there quietly and we get along fine. Come, touch it, if you like. You're a partner in this too. The same revolver may have killed your children—"

"Tamara, I beg you—"

Tamara made a spiteful face and stuck her tongue out at him.

"Tamara, I beg you!" she mimicked him. "Don't be afraid. She won't divorce you. If she does, you can always go to the other one. What's her name again? And if she throws you out too, then you can come to me. Here's Yadzia with the coffee!"

Yadwiga came in, carrying a tray with two cups of coffee, cream, sugar, and a plate of home-made cookies. She had put on an apron and looked just like the servant she had once been. This was how she had served Herman and Tamara before the war, when they had come from Warsaw to visit. Yadwiga's face, which a while ago had been pale, was now red and moist. Beads of perspiration stood out on her forehead. Tamara looked at her with both astonishment and laughter.

"Set it down. Bring a cup for yourself," Herman said.

"I'll drink mine in the kitchen."

And again Yadwiga's slippers slapped back to the kitchen. This time she shut the door behind her.

4

"I seem to have blundered in like a bull into a china shop," Tamara said. "When things go wrong, it's hard to do anything right. It's true I did have a drink, but I'm far from drunk. Please call her in. I must explain to her."

"I'll explain it to her myself."

"No, call her in. She probably thinks I've come to take her husband away."

Herman went into the kitchen, closing the door behind him. Yadwiga was standing at the window with her back to the room. His footsteps startled her and she turned around quickly. Her hair was mussed up, her eyes were filled with tears, her face was red and puffy. She seemed to have aged. Before Herman could say anything, she raised her fists to her head and began to wail, "Where will I go now?"

"Yadzia, everything will be just as it was."

A cry like the hissing of a goose tore from Yadwiga's throat. "Why did you tell me she was dead? You weren't selling books, you were staying with her!"

"Yadzia, I swear by God that it isn't so. She only recently came to America. I had no idea she was alive."

"What shall I do now? She's your wife."

"You're my wife."

"She came first. I'll go away. I'll go back to Poland. If only I weren't carrying your child." Yadwiga began rocking from side to side, in the keening gesture of peasants mourning their dead: "Ay-ay-ay."

Tamara opened the door. "Yadzia, don't cry like that. I haven't come to take your husband away. I just wanted to see how you were living."

Yadwiga lurched forward as if to fall at Tamara's feet.

"Pani Tamara, you are his wife and that's how it will remain. If God granted you life, it's a gift. I'll step aside. It's your house. I'll go home. My mother won't turn me away."

"No, Yadzia, you don't need to do that. You're carrying his child and I'm already, as they say, a barren tree. God took my children Himself."

"Oh, Pani Tamara!" Yadwiga dissolved into tears, slapping her cheeks with both palms. She rocked back and forth, bending over as if she were looking for a place to fall down. Herman glanced at the door, afraid that the neighbors might hear her.

"Yadzia, you must calm yourself," Tamara said firmly. "I'm alive but I am as good as dead. They say dead people sometimes come back to pay a visit and in a way I'm that kind of visitor. I came to see how things are, but don't worry, I won't come again."

Yadwiga took her hands away from her face, which had turned the color of raw flesh.

"No, Pani Tamara, you stay here! I'm a simple peasant, uneducated, but I have a heart. It's your husband and your home. You suffered long enough."

"Be still! I don't want him. If you want to go back to Poland, go back, but not because of me. I wouldn't live with him even if you were to go away."

Yadwiga quieted down. She peered sideways at Tamara, doubtful and suspicious. "Where will you go? Here there's a home and a household for you. I'll cook and clean. I'll be a servant again. That's the way God wants it."

"No, Yadwiga. You have a good heart, but I can't accept such a sacrifice. A slit throat cannot be sewn together again."

Tamara, preparing to go, adjusted her hat and tidied some loose strands of hair. Herman took a step toward her. "Don't go. Since Yadwiga knows, we can all be friends. I'll have a few less lies to tell."

At that moment, they heard the doorbell. It was a long, loud ring. The two parakeets, who had been perched on the roof of the cage listening to the conversation, were startled and began to fly about. Yadwiga ran from the kitchen into the living room. "Who is it?" Herman called.

He heard muffled talk, but couldn't make out whether the voice was a man's voice or a woman's. He opened the door. Standing in the hall were a small couple. The woman had a sallow, wrinkled face, yellowish eyes, and carrot-colored hair. The lines in her forehead and cheeks looked as if they had been sculpted in clay. Nevertheless, she didn't seem old, not more than in her forties. She wore a house dress and slippers. She had brought some knitting along and was working the needles as she waited at the door. Next to her stood a tiny man wearing a felt hat with a feather in it, a checked jacket that was too light for a cold winter day, a pink shirt, striped trousers, tan shoes, and a tie that was a mixture of yellow, red, and green. He appeared outlandishly comical, as if he had just flown in from a hot climate and hadn't had time to change his clothes. His head was long and narrow and he had a hooked nose, sunken cheeks, and a pointed chin. His dark eyes had a humorous expression, as if the visit he was making was nothing more than a joke.

The woman spoke in a Polish-accented Yiddish. "You don't know me, Mr. Broder, but I know you. We live downstairs. Is your wife at home?"

"She's in the living room."

"A dear soul. I was with her when she was converted. It was I who took her to the ritual bath and told her what to do. Women who were born Jewish should love Jewishness the way she does. Is she busy?"

"Yes, a little."

"This is my friend, Mr. Pesheles. He doesn't live here. He has a house in Sea Gate. He has, may no evil eye befall him, houses in New York and Philadelphia too. He came to visit us, and we told him about you, that you sell books and write, and he would like to talk to you about some business.''

"Not business! Not business at all!" Mr. Pesheles interrupted. "My business isn't books but real estate and I don't do that any more either. After all, how much business does a person need? Even Rockefeller can't eat more than three meals a day. It's just that I love to read, whether it's a newspaper, a magazine, a book, whatever I can lay my hands on. If you have a few minutes, I'd like to have a chat with you.''

Herman hesitated. "I'm terribly sorry, but I'm really very busy.''

"It won't take long—ten or fifteen minutes," the woman urged. "Mr. Pesheles only comes to see me once every six months and sometimes not that often. He's a rich man, may no evil eye befall him, and if you're ever looking for an apartment, he may be able to do you a favor.''

"What kind of favor? I don't do any favors. I myself have to pay rent. This is America. But if you need an apartment, I can recommend you and it won't do you any harm.''

"Well, come in. Forgive me for receiving you in the kitchen. My wife is indisposed.''

"What's the difference where? He didn't come here to be honored. He gets, may no evil eye befall him, plenty of honors. They just made him president of the biggest home for the aged in New York. All over America they know who Nathan Pesheles is. And he just built two Yeshivas in Jerusalem—not one yeshiva, but two yeshivas—where hundreds of boys will be able to study Torah, at his expense—''

"Please, Mrs. Schreier, I don't need any publicity. If I need a publicity agent, I'll hire one. He doesn't have to know about all that. It's not for praise that I do it." Mr. Pesheles spoke quickly. He spat out his words like dried peas. His mouth was sunken, with almost no lower lip. He smiled knowingly and had the ease of a rich man visiting the poor. The two of them had continued standing at the door, but now they moved into the kitchen. Before Herman had a chance to introduce Tamara, she said, "I'd better go now.''

"Don't run away. No need to go because of me," Mr. Pesheles said. "You're a pretty woman, but I'm not a bear and I don't swallow people.''

"Sit down, sit down," Herman said. "Don't go, Tamara," he added. "I see there aren't enough chairs, but we'll soon go into the other room. One second!''

He went into the living room. Yadwiga was no longer crying. She stood there, staring at the door apprehensively with a peasant's fear of strangers. "Who is it?''

"Mrs. Schreier. She brought a man with her.''

"What does she want? I can't see anyone now. Oh, I'm going out of my mind!''

Herman returned to the kitchen with a chair. Mrs. Schreier was already seated next to the kitchen table. Woytus was perched on Tamara's shoulder, pulling at an earring. Herman heard Mr. Pesheles saying to Tamara, "Only a few weeks? But you're not like a greenhorn at all. In my time you could spot an immigrant from a mile away. You look like an American. Absolutely.''

5

"Yadwiga doesn't feel well. I don't think she'll join us," Herman said. "I'm sorry, it's not very comfortable here."

"Comfortable!" Mrs. Schreier interrupted. "Hitler taught us how to get along without comfort."

"You come from there too?" Herman asked.

"Yes, from there."

"From the concentration camps?"

"From Russia."

"Where were you in Russia?" Tamara asked.

"In Jambul."

"In the camp?"

"In the camp too. I lived on Nabroznaya Street."

"God in heaven, I also lived on the Nabroznaya," Tamara cried, "with a rebbetzin from Dzikow and her son."

"Well, it's a small world, a small world," Mr. Pesheles said, clapping his hands together. He had pointed fingers and freshly manicured fingernails. "Russia is a vast country, but no sooner do two refugees meet than they are either related or were in the same camp together. You know what? Let's all go down to your place," he said, addressing Mrs. Schreier. "I'll send out for bagels, lox, and maybe even some cognac. Since both of you are from Jambul, you'll have a lot to talk about. Come down, Mr. er-er-Broder. I remember people, but I forget names. Once I forgot my own wife's name—"

"That's something all men forget," Mrs. Schreier said with a wink.

"Unfortunately, it's not possible," Herman said.

"Why not? Bring your wife and come on down. Nowadays a Gentile converting to Judaism is no small matter. I heard she hid you for years in a loft. What kind of books do you sell? I'm interested in old books. I once bought a book with Lincoln's signature in it. I like to go to auctions. I was told you do some writing too. What do you write?"

Herman was about to answer, but the telephone rang. Tamara looked up and Woytus began flying around again. The phone was located near the kitchen, in a small foyer that led to the bedroom. Herman became angry at Masha. Why was she calling? She knew he was coming. Perhaps he shouldn't answer it? He picked up the receiver and said, "Hello."

It occurred to him that it might be Leon Tortshiner. Herman had expected a call from him ever since their meeting in the cafeteria. Herman heard a man's voice, but it wasn't Leon Tortshiner's. It was a deep bass voice asking in English, "Is this Mr. Herman Broder?"

"Yes."

"This is Rabbi Lampert." It was quiet. In the kitchen, they had stopped talking.

"Yes, Rabbi."

"So you do have a telephone, and not in the Bronx, but in Brooklyn. Esplanade 2 is somewhere in Coney Island."

"My friend moved," Herman mumbled, knowing the lie would only lead to new complications.

The rabbi cleared his throat. "He moved and had a phone installed? Sure, sure. I really am a damn fool, but not such a damn fool as you think." The rabbi's voice rose a pitch. "Your whole comedy is altogether superfluous. I know everything, absolutely everything. You got married and you didn't even tell me so I could congratulate you. Who knows? I might even have given you a nice wedding present. But if this is the way you want it, it's your privilege. I'm calling you because in your cabala article you made several serious errors which do neither of us any credit."

"What errors?"

"I can't tell you now. Rabbi Moscowitz called me up—something about the Angel Sandalphon or Metatron. The article is in type. When he caught the mistakes, they were going to press. They'll have to take out the pages and rearrange the whole magazine. That's what you've done to me."

"I'm very sorry, but in that case I resign, and you don't have to pay me for the work I've done."

"How will that help me? I depend on you. Why didn't you check? That's why I hired you, to do research so I wouldn't look like a simpleton in the eyes of the world. You know I'm busy and—"

"I don't know what errors I made, but if there are errors, I shouldn't be doing this work."

"Where will I get someone else now? You kept secrets from me. Why? If you love a woman, that's no sin. I treated you like a friend and opened my heart to you, but you made up some story about a landsman from the old country, a Hitler victim. Why can't I know that you have a wife? At least I have the right to wish you mazel tov."

"Certainly. Thank you very much."

"Why are you speaking so quietly? Do you have a sore throat or something?"

"No, no."

"I told you all along that I can't work with a man who won't give me his address and phone number. I must see you right away, so tell me where you live. If we make the corrections, they'll hold the presses till tomorrow."

"I don't live here, but in the Bronx."

Herman was practically whispering into the phone.

"Again in the Bronx? Where in the Bronx? Honestly, I can't figure you out."

"I'll explain everything to you. I'm just here temporarily."

"Temporarily? What's the matter with you? Or do you have two wives?"

"Maybe."

"Well, when will you be there in the Bronx?"

"Tonight."

"Give me the address. Once and for all! Let there be an end to this muddle!"

Reluctantly, Herman gave him Masha's address. He covered his mouth with his hand so he wouldn't be heard in the kitchen.

"What time will you be there?"

Herman told him the time.

"Is this definite, or are you bluffing again?"

"No, I'll be there."

"Well, I'll come over. You don't have to be so nervous. I won't steal your wife."

Herman returned to the kitchen and saw Yadwiga. She had come out of the living room. Her face and eyes were still red and she stood with her fists on her hips, looking over to where he had been standing. She had apparently been listening to his conversation. Herman heard Mrs. Schreier asking Tamara, "How did they send you to Russia, with the echelons?"

"No, we were smuggled across the border," Tamara answered.

"We rode in cattle cars," Mrs. Schreier said. "Three weeks we rode, packed in like herring in a barrel. If we needed to eliminate—you should excuse me— we had to do it through a small window. Picture it, men and women together. How we survived, I'll never be able to understand. And some didn't survive. They died standing up. They simply threw the dead bodies out of the train. We came to a forest in a terrible frost and first we had to chop down the trees with which to build the barracks. We dug ditches in the frozen earth and that's where we slept—"

"I know it only too well," Tamara said.

"Do you have relatives here?" Mr. Pesheles asked Tamara.

"An uncle and aunt. They live on East Broadway."

"East Broadway? And what is he to you?" Mr. Pesheles asked, indicating Herman.

"Oh, we're friends."

"Well, come down to Mrs. Schreier's and we'll all become friends. With all this talk about starvation, I'm feeling hungry. We'll eat, drink, and have a talk. Come on, Mr. er-er-Broder. On such a cold day, it's good to pour out one's heart."

"I'm afraid I must leave now," Herman said.

"I have to go too," Tamara added.

Yadwiga seemed suddenly to wake up.

"Where is Pani Tamara going? Please stay here. I'll make supper."

"No, Yadzia, another time."

"Well, it looks as if you're not going to accept my invitation," Mr. Pesheles said. "Come, Mrs. Schreier, we didn't succeed this time. If you have any old volumes, we can do a little business another time. I am, as I've mentioned, a bit of a collector. Other than that—"

"We'll talk later," Mrs. Schreier said to Yadwiga. "Maybe Mr. Pesheles won't be such an infrequent guest in the future. What that man did for me, only God knows. Others were content to moan about the fate of the Jews, but he sent visas. I wrote him a letter, a total stranger—only because his father had been my father's partner, they both handled produce—and four weeks later an affidavit arrived. We went to the consulate and they already knew about Mr. Pesheles. They all knew."

"Well, enough. Don't praise me, don't praise me. What's an affidavit? A piece of paper."

"With such pieces of paper, they could have rescued thousands of people."

Pesheles stood up. "What's your name?" he asked Tamara. She looked questioningly at him, at Herman, at Yadwiga.

"Tamara."

"Miss? Missus?"

"Whatever you like."

"Tamara what? Surely you have a last name."

"Tamara Broder."

"Also Broder? Are you brother and sister?"

"Cousins," Herman answered for Tamara.

"Well, it's a small world. Extraordinary times. Once I read a story in the paper about a refugee who was eating supper with his new wife. Suddenly the door opened and in walked his former wife, who he thought had died in the ghetto. That's the kind of mess Hitler and Stalin and the rest of their gangs cooked up."

Mrs. Schreier's face broke into a smile. Her yellow eyes sparkled with flattering laughter. The creases of her face grew even deeper, becoming like the tattoo lines sometimes seen on the faces of primitive tribes.

"What's the point of the story, Mr. Pesheles?"

"Oh, nothing really. In life, anything can happen. Especially nowadays, when everything is turned upside down."

Mr. Pesheles lowered the lid of his right eye and puckered his lips as if about to whistle. He put his hand in his breast pocket and handed Tamara two calling cards.

"Whoever you are, let's not be strangers."

6

No sooner did the guests leave than Yadwiga burst into tears. In a moment, her face was once again contorted. "Where are you going now? Why are you leaving me? Pani Tamara! He doesn't sell books. It's a lie. He has a mistress and he goes to her. Everyone knows it. The neighbors laugh at me. And I saved his life! I took the last bite of food out of my mouth and brought it to him in the hayloft. I carried out his excrement."

"Please, Yadwiga, stop!" Herman said.

"Herman, I must go! I just want to tell you one thing, Yadzia. He didn't know that I was alive. I came here from Russia only a short time ago."

"She telephones every day, his sweetheart. He thinks I don't understand, but I understand. He spends days with her and comes home exhausted and penniless. The old landlady comes every day to ask for the rent and threatens to throw us out in the middle of winter. If I weren't pregnant, I could work in a factory. Here you have to reserve a hospital and a doctor. Here nobody gives birth at home—I won't let you go, Pani Tamara." Yadwiga ran to the door and spread her arms out, barring it.

"Yadzia, I have to go," Tamara said.

"If he wants to go back to you, I'll give the baby away. Here you can give children away. They even pay—"

"Stop talking nonsense, Yadzia. I won't go back to him and you don't need to give your baby away. I'll find you a doctor and a hospital."

"Oh, Pani Tamara!"

"Yadzia, let me out!" Herman said. He had put on his coat.

"You're not going!"

"Yadzia, a rabbi's waiting for me. I work for him. If I don't meet him now, we'll remain without a crust of bread."

"It's a lie! A whore's waiting for you, not a rabbi."

"Well, I see what's going on here," Tamara said, half to herself and half to Yadwiga and Herman. "I really have to leave now. If I change my mind and decide to go to the hospital, I must wash some things and get ready. Let me out, Yadzia."

"You've decided to go, after all? Which hospital are you going to? What's the name of it?" Herman asked.

"What difference does it make? If I live, I'll come out, and if I don't, they'll bury me somehow. You don't have to visit me. If they find out you're my husband, they'll make you pay. I told them I have no relatives and that's the way it must remain."

Tamara went over to Yadwiga and kissed her. For a moment Yadwiga laid her head on Tamara's shoulder. She cried loudly and kissed Tamara on the forehead, cheeks, both hands. She almost sank to her knees, mumbling in her peasant dialect, but it was impossible to make out what she was saying.

As soon as Tamara left, Yadwiga placed herself in front of the door again. "You won't leave today!"

"We'll soon see."

Herman waited till he could no longer hear Tamara's footsteps. Then he grabbed Yadwiga by the wrists and wrestled with her in silence. He pushed her and she fell to the floor with a thud. He unlocked the door and ran out. He hurried down the uneven stairs two at a time and heard a sound that was both a cry and a groan. He remembered something he had once learned: when you break one of the Ten Commandments, you break them all. "I'll end up a murderer," he said to himself.

He hadn't noticed that dusk had fallen. The stairway was already dark. Doors opened, but he didn't turn around. He went outside. Tamara stood in the snowdrifts, waiting for him.

"Where are your rubbers? You can't go like that!" she shouted.

"I must."

"Are you trying to commit suicide? Go get your rubbers, unless you want to catch pneumonia."

"What I'll catch is no concern of yours. Go to the devil—the lot of you!"

"Well, it's the same Herman. Wait here, I'll go up and bring your rubbers down to you."

"No, you're not going!"

"So we'll have one idiot less in the world."

Tamara picked her way through the snowdrifts. They looked blue and crystalline. The street lights had gone on, but it was still twilight. The sky was overcast with yellowish, rust-red clouds, stormy and threatening. A cold wind blew in from the bay. Suddenly an upper-story window opened and one rubber fell down, then another. Yadwiga was throwing Herman his rubbers. He looked up at the window, but she closed it immediately and drew the curtains. Tamara turned back toward him and laughed. She winked and shook her fist at him. He managed to put on the rubbers, but his shoes were filled with snow. Tamara waited until he caught up with her.

"The worst dog gets the best bone. Why is it?"

She took him by the arm and together they made their way through the snow, carefully and slowly like an elderly couple. Chunks of snow and ice fell from the roofs. Mermaid Avenue was covered with high drifts. A dead pigeon lay in the snow, its red feet protruding. "Well, holy creature, you've already lived your life," Herman addressed it in his thoughts. "You're lucky." He was gripped with sorrow. "Why did you create her, if this was to be her end? How long will you be silent, Almighty sadist?"

Herman and Tamara walked to the station, where they boarded a train. Tamara was going only as far as Fourteenth Street, and Herman to Times Square. All the seats were occupied except for a small corner bench, and Herman and Tamara squeezed into it.

"So you've decided to go through with the operation," Herman said.

"What have I got to lose? Nothing more than my wretched life."

Herman bowed his head. As they approached Union Square, Tamara took leave of him. He stood up and they kissed.

"Think of me once in a while," she said.

"Forgive me!"

Tamara hurried out of the train. Herman sat down again in the dimly lighted corner. It seemed to him that he heard his father's voice saying, "Well, I ask you, what have you accomplished? You've made yourself and everyone else wretched. We're ashamed of you here in heaven."

Herman got off at Times Square and crossed over to the IRT subway. He walked to Shifrah Puah's street from the station. The rabbi's Cadillac practically filled the snow-covered street. All the lights in the house had been turned on and the car seemed to glow in the dark. Herman was ashamed to enter this brightly lighted house with his pale face, frozen, red nose, and shabby clothes. In the dark entryway, he shook off the snow and rubbed his cheeks to give them color. He fixed his tie and wiped the moisture from his forehead with a handkerchief. It occurred to Herman that the rabbi might not have found any mistakes in the article at all. His call might simply have been an excuse to interfere in Herman's affairs.

The first thing Herman noticed when he entered the door was a huge bouquet of roses in a vase on the dresser. On the cloth-covered table, between the cookies and oranges, stood a magnum of champagne. The rabbi and Masha were clicking their glasses together; they obviously hadn't heard Herman come in. Masha was already tipsy. She spoke in a loud voice and laughed. She had put on a party dress. The rabbi's voice thundered. Shifrah Puah was in the kitchen, frying pancakes. Herman heard the sound of sizzling oil and smelled the browning potatoes. The rabbi was wearing a light-colored suit and seemed strangely tall and broad in this crowded apartment with its low ceilings.

The rabbi got up and reached Herman in one long stride. Clapping his hands, he called out loudly, "Mazel tov, bridegroom!"

Masha set down her glass. "He's here at last!" And she pointed at him and shook with laughter. Then she too got up and went to Herman. "Don't stand at the door. It's your home. I'm your wife. Everything here is yours!"

She threw herself into his arms and kissed him.

CHAPTER EIGHT

1

The snow was falling for the second day. There was no heat in Shifrah Puah's apartment. The janitor, who lived in the basement, lay in his room in a drunken stupor. The furnace had broken down and there was no one to repair it.

Shifrah Puah wandered about the house in heavy boots, huddled in a ragged fur coat which she had brought from Germany, her head wrapped in a woolen shawl. Her face was sallow with cold and vexation. She put on her eyeglasses and paced up and down as she read her prayer book. She alternately prayed and cursed the swindling landlords who allowed poor tenants to freeze in winter. Her lips had turned blue. She read a verse aloud and said, "As if we didn't have enough trouble before coming here. Now we can add America to the list. It's not so much better than the concentration camps. All we need is a Nazi to come in and beat us up."

Masha, who had skipped work that day because she was getting ready to go to a party at Rabbi Lampert's, scolded her mother. "Mama, you should be ashamed of yourself! In Stutthoff, if you had had what you have now, you would have gone out of your mind with joy."

"How much strength does a person have? There we at least had hope to sustain us. There isn't a part of my body that isn't frozen. Maybe you can buy a fire pot. My blood is congealing."

"Where can you get a fire pot in America? We'll move out of here. Just wait till spring comes."

"I won't last till spring."

"Old witch, you'll outlive us all!" Masha's voice was shrill with impatience.

The party to which the rabbi had invited Masha and Herman had driven her into a frenzy. At first she had refused to go, arguing that Leon Tortshiner was probably behind the invitation and had some trick in mind. Masha suspected that the rabbi's visit to her house, his getting her drunk on champagne, were all part of a plot on Leon Tortshiner's part to separate her from Herman. Masha kept belittling the rabbi, calling him a spineless creature, a braggart, a hypocrite. And when she finished with him, she reviled Leon Tortshiner as a maniac, impostor, provocateur.

Since her false pregnancy, Masha had not been able to sleep at night, even with the help of pills. When she finally fell asleep, nightmares awakened her. Her father appeared to her in his shrouds, shouting verses from the Bible in her ear. She saw fantastic beasts with coiled horns and pointed snouts. They had pouches, teats, and were covered with sores. They barked, roared, and drooled over her. She was menstruating painfully every two weeks and passing blood clots. Shifrah Puah urged her to go to the doctor, but Masha said she didn't believe in doctors and swore that they poisoned their patients.

But suddenly Masha had changed her mind and decided to go to the party. Why should she be afraid of Leon Tortshiner? She had got both a civil and a rabbinical divorce from him. If he greeted her, she would turn her back on him; if he tried any tricks, she would simply spit in his face.

Herman observed once again how Masha went from one extreme to the other. She began to get ready for the party with growing enthusiasm. She flung open closets, dresser drawers, dragged out dresses, blouses, shoes, most of which she had brought from Germany. She decided to remodel a dress. She sewed, ripped out the basting, smoked cigarette after cigarette, pulled out heaps of stockings, lingerie. She chattered all the while, telling stories of how men had pursued her—before the war, during the war, after the war, in the camps, the offices of the "Joint"—and insisted that Shifrah Puah verify her words. For a moment she abandoned her sewing to dig up old letters and photographs as proof.

Herman understood that what she craved was to be a success at the party, to outshine all the other women with her elegance, her good looks. He had known from the beginning that, despite Masha's initial opposition, she would eventually decide to go. With Masha, everything had to be made into drama.

The radiator began to hiss unexpectedly—the furnace had been repaired. The apartment became steamy and Shifrah Puah complained that the drunken janitor was surely trying to set the house on fire. They would have to leave the apartment and run out into the frost. It smelled of smoke and coal fumes. Masha filled the tub with hot water. She did everything at once: prepared her bath, sang songs in Hebrew, Yiddish, Polish, Russian, and German. With amazing speed, she had turned an old dress into a new one, found a pair of matching high-heel shoes and a stole that someone had given her as a gift in Germany.

By evening it had stopped snowing, but the air was icy cold. The streets in the east Bronx might have been the winter streets of Moscow or Koybishev.

Shifrah Puah, who deprecated the idea of the party, mumbled about Jews not having the right to celebrate after the holocaust, but she inspected Masha's appearance and suggested improvements. In her preoccupation, Masha had forgotten to eat, and her mother prepared some rice and milk for her and Herman. The rabbi's wife had phoned Masha and told her how to get to West End Avenue in the Seventies, where they lived. Shifrah Puah insisted that Masha wear a sweater, or a pair of warm underpants, but Masha wouldn't hear of it. Every few minutes, she took a swig from a bottle of cognac.

Night was already falling when Herman and Masha left. A freezing wind gripped his shoulders and ripped his hat from his head; he caught it in mid-air. Masha's party dress fluttered and filled up like a balloon. The deep snow gripped one of her boots as she tried to walk, and her stockinged foot got wet. Her carefully set hair, only partially protected by her hat, became white with snow, as if she had aged in a second. She held on to her hat with one hand and with the other held down the hem of her dress. She shouted something to Herman, but the wind carried her voice away.

The walk to the El, which normally took a few minutes, now became a major undertaking. When they finally got there, a train had just pulled out. The cashier, who sat in a booth heated by an iron stove, told them that trains were stalling on the snow-covered tracks and there was no telling when the next one would come. Masha shivered and hopped up and down to warm her feet. Her face was sickly pale.

Fifteen minutes passed and no train arrived. A large group of waiting passengers had collected: men wearing rubber boots, galoshes, and carrying lunch boxes;

women clad in heavy jackets, with kerchiefs on their heads. Each face in its own way seemed to express dullness, greed, anxiety. The low foreheads, the troubled gazes, the broad noses with large nostrils, the square chins, the full breasts and wide hips refuted all visions of Utopia. The caldron of evolution was still simmering. One scream could instigate a riot here. The right bit of propaganda could rouse this group into a pogrom-making rabble.

A whistle blew and the train rushed in. The cars were half empty. Their windows were white with frost. It was cold in the car, and the floor was covered with slush, soiled newspapers, chewing gum. "Can there be anything uglier than this train?" Herman wondered. "Everything here is as dismal as if it were made to order for the purpose." A drunkard began making a speech, prattling about Hitler and the Jews. Masha took a little mirror out of her bag and strained to see her reflection in the fogged-up glass. She moistened her fingertips and tried to smooth her hair, which the wind would only disarrange again when they got out.

As long as the train ran aboveground, Herman looked out through a bit of window he had wiped clear of mist. Newspapers fluttered in the wind. A grocer was throwing salt on the sidewalks near his store. An automobile was trying to get out of a ditch, but its wheels spun helplessly in one spot. Herman was suddenly reminded of his resolution to become a good Jew, to return to the Shulchan Aruch, the Gemara. How many times had he made such resolutions! How many times had he tried to spit in the face of worldliness, and each time been tricked away. Yet here he was on his way to a party. Half of his people had been tortured and murdered, and the other half were giving parties. He was overcome with pity for Masha. She looked underweight, wan, sick.

It was late when Herman and Masha stepped out of the train into the street. A wild wind was blowing from the frozen Hudson River. Masha clung to Herman. He had to lean into the wind with all his weight in order not to be blown back. Snow covered his eyelids. Masha, gasping, shouted something to him. His hat tried to tear itself off his head. His coattails and trousers whipped about his legs. It was a miracle that they were able to make out the number on the rabbi's house. He and Masha ran breathlessly into the lobby. Here it was warm and tranquil. Gold-framed pictures hung on the walls; carpets covered the floors; chandeliers diffused soft light; sofas and easy chairs awaited guests.

Masha went up to a mirror to try to repair some of the damage inflicted on her dress and appearance. "If I can survive this, I'll never die," she said.

2

She twisted a last lock into place and walked toward the elevator. Herman straightened his tie. His collar felt loose around his neck. A full-length mirror reflected all the defects of his figure and attire. His back was stooped and he looked haggard. He had lost weight: his overcoat and his suit seemed too big for him. The elevator man hesitated an instant before opening the elevator door. When he stopped at the rabbi's floor, he watched suspiciously as Herman rang the bell.

No one came. Herman could hear noise, the sound of talking, and the rabbi's loud voice within the apartment. After a while, a black maid in white apron and white cap opened the door. Behind her was the rabbi's wife, the rebbetzin. She was a tall, statuesque woman, even taller than her husband. She had wavy, blond hair, a turned-up nose, and wore a long, gold-colored dress. She was bedecked with jewelry. Everything about this woman appeared bony, pointed, long, Gentile. She looked down on Herman and Masha and her eyes lighted.

Suddenly the rabbi appeared.

"Here they are!" he bellowed. And he stretched out both hands, one to Herman and one to Masha, at the same time kissing Masha.

"She's really a beauty!" he shouted. "He's nabbed the prettiest woman in America. Eileen, look at her!"

"Give me your coats. It's cold, isn't it? I was afraid you might not be able to make it. My husband has told me so much about you. I'm really happy that—"

The rabbi put his arms around Masha and Herman and led them into the living room. He pushed his way through the crowd, introducing them as they went along. Through the haze, Herman saw clean-shaven men with tiny skullcaps perched on top of their thick hair, as well as men without skullcaps, and men with goatees or with full beards. There was as much variety in the women's hair coloring as there was in the shades of their dresses. He heard English, Hebrew, German, even French. There was a smell of perfume, liquor, chopped liver.

A butler approached the new guests and asked what they wanted to drink. The rabbi led Masha to the bar, leaving Herman behind. He put his hand around Masha's waist, leading her as if they were dancing. Herman wished he could sit down somewhere, but he didn't see an empty chair. A maid offered him a tray of assorted fish, cold cuts, eggs, crackers. He tried to spear a half egg with a toothpick, but it slipped away. People were speaking so loudly that he was deafened by the noise. A woman shrieked with laughter.

Herman had never been to an American party. He had anticipated that the guests would be seated and that dinner would be served. But there was neither room to sit down nor was a meal served. Someone spoke to him in English, but in all the din he couldn't make out the words. Where on earth was Masha? She seemed to have been swallowed up in the throng. He stopped in front of a painting and stood looking at it for no particular reason.

He walked into a room with several armchairs and couches. The walls were lined with books from floor to ceiling. Some men and women were sitting around, holding drinks in their hands. A vacant chair stood in a corner and Herman sank into it. The group was discussing a professor who had received a five-thousand-dollar grant to write a book. They were ridiculing him and his writing. Herman heard the names of universities, foundations, scholarships, grants, publications on Judaica, socialism, history, psychology. "What kind of women are these? How is it they are so well informed?" Herman thought. He was self-conscious about his shabby clothing, apprehensive that they might try to draw him into their conversation. "I don't belong here. I should have remained a Talmudist." He angled his chair still farther away from the group.

For the sake of something to do, he took a copy of Plato's *Dialogues* from the bookcase. He opened it at random to "Phaedo" and read these words: "It may seem unlikely that those who are sincerely concerned with philosophy actually are merely studying how to die and how to be dead.'' He leafed back a few pages to the ''Apologia'' and his eye fell on the words, ''Because I believe it is against nature that a better man should be hurt by a lesser one.'' Was this really so? Was it against nature that the Nazis should have murdered millions of Jews?

A servant came to the door and announced something which Herman didn't understand. Everyone got up and left the room. Herman remained alone. He imagined that the Nazis were in New York, but someone—perhaps even the rabbi—had boarded him up in this library. His food was served through an opening in the wall.

A person who looked familiar appeared in the doorway. He was a small man wearing a dinner jacket; his laughing eyes expressed recognition and irony. ''Whom do I see?'' he said in Yiddish. ''Well it's really, as they say, a small world.''

Herman stood up.

''You don't recognize me?''

''I'm so confused here, that—''

''Pesheles! Nathan Pesheles! I came to your apartment a few weeks ago—''

''Yes, of course.''

''Why are you sitting here by yourself? Did you come here to read books? I didn't know that you know Rabbi Lampert. But who doesn't know him? Why don't you get something to eat? They're serving food in the other room cafeteria-style. You take it yourself from a buffet. Where is your wife?''

''She's here somewhere. I've lost her.''

As soon as Herman uttered these words, he realized that Pesheles was talking not about Masha but about Yadwiga. The catastrophe Herman had dreaded was upon him. Pesheles took him by the arm.

''Come, let's find her together. My wife couldn't come tonight. She has the grippe. There are women who get sick whenever they have to go somewhere.''

Pesheles led Herman into the living room. The crowd was standing with plates in hand, eating and chatting. Some sat on windowsills, on the radiator, wherever they could find a spot. Pesheles drew Herman toward the dining room. A large group of people were clustered around a long table covered with food. Herman caught sight of Masha. She was with a short man, who held her by the arm. He was obviously saying something very amusing to her, because Masha laughed out loud and clapped her hands together. When she saw Herman, she squirmed out of the man's grip and made her way to his side. Her companion followed. Masha's face was flushed and her eyes shone with high spirits.

''Here is my long-lost husband!'' she called out. She threw her arms around Herman's neck and kissed him as if he had just returned from a journey. Her breath reeked of alcohol.

''This is my husband; this is Yasha Kotik,'' Masha said, indicating the man to whom she had been talking. He was wearing a European tuxedo with worn lapels; a broad satin stripe adorned each side of his trousers. His black hair was parted and glossy with pomade and he had a crooked nose and cleft chin. His youthful figure contrasted oddly with his wrinkled forehead and lined mouth, which revealed a set of false teeth when he smiled. There was something mocking and shrewd in his gaze, in his smile, in his mannerisms. He stood with his arm bent, as if waiting to escort Masha off again. He puckered his lips, creating more creases in his face.

"So this is your husband?" he asked, clownishly lifting one eyebrow.

"Herman, Yasha Kotik is the actor I told you about. We were together in the camp. I didn't know he was in New York."

"Someone told me that she went to Palestine," Yasha Kotik said to Herman. "I thought she was somewhere near the Wailing Wall, or at Rachel's Tomb. I look around—she's standing and drinking whiskey in Rabbi Lampert's living room. That's America for you, crazy Columbus, ha!"

Simulating a gun with his thumb and index finger, he made a shooting gesture. Everything about him moved with acrobatic agility. His face was in constant motion, grimacing and mimicking simultaneously. He raised one eye in mock surprise while the other one drooped as if crying. He inflated his nostrils. Herman had heard a great deal about him from Masha. It was said he told jokes while digging his own grave and the Nazis had been so amused by him that they let him go. Similarly, his buffoonery also stood him in good stead with the Bolsheviks. He had been able to overcome countless perils with his gallows humor and comic antics. Masha had boasted to Herman that Yasha had been in love with her but she had discouraged him.

"That means you are the husband and she's the wife?" Kotik said to Herman. "How did you catch her? I've been searching for her through half the world, and you marry her just like that. Who gave you the right? It's, you should pardon me, rank imperialism—"

"You're still a buffoon," Masha said. "It seems to me I heard you were in Argentina."

"I was in Argentina. Where haven't I been? Blessed be the airplane. You sit down, knock off a glass of schnapps, and before you start snoring and dreaming about Cleopatra, you're in South America. Here it's Shevuot and people are swimming in Coney Island and there it's Shevuot and you shudder in an apartment without heat. How delicious can a Shevuot dairy meal taste when it's freezing outside? Hanukkah you melt from the heat, and everyone goes to cool off at Mar-del-Plata. But just duck into the casino and lose your few pesos, and it's hot again. What did you see in him that made you marry him?" Yasha Kotik said to Masha, underscoring his question with an exaggerated raising of his shoulders. "What, for example, does he have that I don't? I want to know."

"He's a serious person and you're a pain in the neck," Masha replied.

"Do you know what you have here?" Yasha Kotik said, addressing Herman and pointing to Masha. "She's not just a woman. She's a firebrand, whether from heaven or hell I still can't decide. Her wit kept us all alive. She could have convinced Stalin himself if he had paid a visit to the camp. Whatever happened to Mosheh Feifer?" Yasha asked, turning to Masha. "I thought you went away with him—"

"With him? What are you jabbering about? Are you drunk, or do you just want to make trouble between my husband and me? I don't know a thing about Mosheh Feifer, nor do I want to. The way you talk, someone might think he and I were lovers. He had a wife and everyone knew it. If they're both alive, they're surely together."

"Well, I didn't say a thing. You don't have to be jealous, Mr.—what's your name? Broder? Let it be Broder. During the war, none of us was human. The Nazis made soap out of us, kosher soap. And to the Bolsheviks we were manure for the revolution. What can you expect from manure? If it were up to me, I would just wipe those years from the calendar.''

"He's as drunk as Lot," Masha muttered.

3

Pesheles had been standing one step behind the group throughout their conversation. He had raised his eyebrows in astonishment, waiting with the patience of a card player who knows he has an ace in the hole. A smile was frozen on his lipless mouth. Herman in his consternation had forgotten about him and he now turned to him. "Masha, this is Mr. Pesheles."

"Pesheles? Seems to me I once met a Pesheles. In Russia or Poland—I don't remember where now," Masha said.

"I come from a small family. We probably had a grandmother named Peshe or Peshele. I met Mr. Broder in Coney Island, in Brooklyn—I didn't know—"

Pesheles blurted out the last words with a cackle. Masha looked questioningly at Herman. Yasha Kotik roguishly scratched his head with the nail of his pinky.

"Coney Island? I played there once, or tried to—what's it called? Oh, yes, Brighton. A whole theater full of old women. Where do they get so many old women in America? They're not only deaf, they've forgotten Yiddish. How can you be a comedian to an audience that doesn't hear you and couldn't understand if they did? The manager, or whatever he called himself, kept bending my ear about success. Go be a success in an old-age home! As you see me, I've been in Yiddish show business for forty years. I started when I was eleven. When they didn't let me perform in Warsaw, I went to Lodz, Vilna, Ishishok. I performed in the ghetto too. Even a hungry audience is better than a deaf audience. When I got to New York, the actors' union made me audition. They asked me to play Cuny Leml while the union experts played cards as they watched. I didn't make it—diction, schmiction. In short, I met a man who ran a Rumanian restaurant in a cellar. He called it Night-Spot Cabaret. Jewish ex-truck drivers go there with their shiksehs. Every one of the men is over seventy. They all have wives and grandchildren who are already professors. The women wear expensive mink coats and Yasha Kotik has to amuse them. My specialty is that I speak a bad English and throw in Yiddish words. And that's what I get for saying no to the gas chambers, for refusing to lie down and die for Comrade Stalin in Kazakhstan. Just my luck, I've developed arthritis here in America and my heart is beginning to act up. What do you do, Mr. Pesheles? Are you a businessman?''

"What's the difference? I don't take anything away from you."

"Take!"

"Mr. Pesheles deals in real estate," Herman said.

"Maybe you have a house for me?" Yasha Kotik asked. "I'll give you a written guarantee that I won't eat the bricks."

"What are we standing here for?" Masha interrupted. "Let's get something to eat. Honestly, Yashele, you haven't changed one bit. Still the same square peg in a round hole."

"You've become extremely pretty."

"How long have you two been married?" Pesheles asked Masha.

Masha frowned. "Long enough to start thinking about a divorce."

"Where do you live? Also in Coney Island?"

"What's all this talk about Coney Island? What happened in Coney Island?" Masha asked suspiciously.

"Well, here it is!" Herman said to himself. It surprised him that his anticipation of the catastrophe had been much worse than the actuality. He was still on his feet. He hadn't fainted away. Yasha Kotik closed one eye and wiggled his nose. Pesheles took a step closer.

"I'm not making it up, Mrs.—what shall I call you? I was in Mr. Broder's home in Coney Island. What street is it on? Between Mermaid and Neptune? I thought the woman who was converted was his wife. It turns out he has a pretty little wife here. I tell you, these greenhorns know how to live. With us Americans, when you get married, you stay that way, whether you like it or not. Or you get divorced and pay alimony, and if you don't pay, you go to prison. What happened to that other pretty little woman—Tamara? Tamara Broder? I even wrote her name down in my notebook."

"Who is this Tamara? Your dead wife was called Tamara, wasn't she?" Masha asked.

"My dead wife is in America," Herman replied. As he spoke, his knees trembled and he felt sick to his stomach. Was he going to faint after all, he asked himself.

Masha's face became angry. "Has your wife risen from the dead?"

"So it seems."

"Is it the one you went to see at her uncle's on East Broadway?"

"Yes."

"You told me she was old and ugly."

"That's what all men tell all wives," Yasha Kotik said, laughing. He stuck out the tip of his tongue and rolled one eye. Pesheles stroked his chin.

"I'm not sure now who's mixed up—I or everyone else." He turned to Herman. "I visited Mrs. Schreier in Coney Island and she told me about a woman upstairs who had converted to Judaism and that you were her husband. She described you as an author, a rabbi or whatever you are, and said you sold books. I have a weakness for literary matters, whether Yiddish, Hebrew, or Turkish. She praised you to the skies, saying this and that, and since I have a library and collect odds and ends, I thought I might be able to buy something from you. Now who is Tamara?"

"I don't know, Mr. Pesheles, what you want or why you're interfering in other people's business," Herman said. "If you think there's something wrong, why not call the police."

Fiery rings appeared before his eyes as he spoke. They oscillated slowly in his line of vision. It was a phenomenon he remembered experiencing ever since childhood. It seemed the little rings lurked behind his eyes, ready to appear at times of stress. One ring swung off to the side, but floated back. Can one faint and remain standing, Herman wondered.

"What police? What are you talking about? I'm not, as they say, God's cossack. As far as I'm concerned, you can have a whole harem. You don't live in my world. I thought I might be able to help you. After all, you're a refugee, and a Polish Gentile who becomes Jewish is nothing to sneeze at. They told me you travel around selling encyclopedias. It happened that a few days after I saw you I had occasion to visit a woman in the hospital who had undergone an operation for female troubles. She is the daughter of an old friend. I come in and see your Tamara; they were sharing a room. She had a bullet removed from her hip. New York is such a vast city, a whole world, but it is also a little village. She told me she was your wife—perhaps she was talking in a state of delirium."

Herman opened his mouth to answer, but just then the rabbi joined them. His face glowed with the liquor he had drunk.

"I've been looking all over for them and here they are!" he shouted. "You all know each other? My friend Nathan Pesheles knows everyone and everyone knows him. Masha, you're the most beautiful woman at the party! I never knew there were such lovely women left in Europe. And here's Yasha Kotik too!"

"I knew Masha before you did," Yasha Kotik said.

"Well, my friend Herman hid her from me."

"He's hiding more than one," Pesheles added insinuatingly.

"You think so? You must know him well. With me he plays the role of an innocent lamb. I began to think he was a eunuch and—"

"I wish I were such a eunuch," Pesheles interrupted.

"You can't hide from Mr. Pesheles." The rabbi laughed. "He has his spies everywhere. What do you know? Let me in on it."

"I don't reveal other people's secrets."

"Come eat. Come into the dining room. We'll stand on line with all the others."

"Excuse me, Rabbi, I'll be right back," Herman said abruptly.

"Where are you running to?"

"I'll be right back."

Herman walked away quickly and Masha hurried after him. They had to push their way through the crowd.

"Don't follow me. I'll be right back," Herman insisted.

"Who is this Pesheles? Who is Tamara?" Masha grabbed Herman's sleeve.

"I beg you, let go of me!"

"Give me a straight answer!"

"I have to vomit."

He tore himself away from Masha and ran to find a bathroom. He bumped into people and they pushed him back. A woman yelled at him because he had stepped on her corns. He went out into the hallway and saw a number of doors through the smoke-filled air, but he couldn't tell which one led to a bathroom. His head began to spin. The floor rocked beneath him like a ship. A door opened and someone came out of a bathroom. As Herman hurried in, he became entangled with another man coming out, who scolded him.

He ran to the toilet bowl and vomit poured from his mouth. There was a ringing in his ears, a hammering in his temples. Spasmodically, his stomach brought up acids, bitter tastes, and stenches he had forgotten existed. Each time he thought his stomach was emptied and he started to wipe his mouth with paper, he was gripped by another spasm. He groaned and retched, bending lower and lower. He vomited one last time and stood up, feeling drained. Someone banged on the door and tried to push it open. He had soiled the floor tiles, splattered the walls, and he had to clean up. He looked in the mirror which reflected his pale face. He removed a hand towel from the rack and wiped off his jacket lapels. He tried to open the window to let the smell out, but he didn't have the strength to raise it. He made one last effort and the window opened. Hardened snow and icicles hung from the frame. Herman breathed in deeply and the fresh air revived him. Again he heard the door being pounded on, the knob rattling. He opened it and saw Masha.

"Are you trying to break the door?"

"Shall I call a doctor?"

"No doctor. We have to get out of here."

"You're all dirty."

Masha took a handkerchief from her purse. As she wiped him off, she asked, "How many wives do you have? Three?"

"Ten."

"May God shame you as you've shamed me."

"I'm going home," Herman said.

"Go ahead, but to your peasant, not to me," Masha answered. "Everything is over between us."

"Over is over."

Masha returned to the living room and Herman went in search of his coat, hat, and rubbers, but he didn't know where to look. The rabbi's wife, who had taken them from him, had disappeared. The maid was nowhere to be seen. He wandered among the crowd in the foyer. He asked a man where the coats were, but the man just shrugged his shoulders. Herman went into the library and dropped into an armchair. Someone had left half a glass of whiskey and part of a sandwich on an end table. Herman ate the bread and the smelly cheese and drank the remains of the whiskey; the room spun round him like a carousel. A network of spots and lines swung before his eyes, the blazing colors he sometimes saw when he pressed his eyelids with his fingertips. Everything seemed to shimmer, quiver, change form. People stuck their heads in the door, but Herman didn't really see them. Their faces swam around indistinctly. Someone spoke to him, but Herman's ears felt as if they were full of water. He was being rocked on a stormy sea. How strange that there was any order at all in this chaos. The forms he saw were all geometrical, though distorted. The colors changed rapidly. He recognized Masha when she came in. She came up to him with a drink in her hand and said, "You're still here?"

He heard her words as if from a distance, astonished at the change in his sense of hearing and at his feeling of indifference to himself. Masha pulled up a chair and sat down, almost touching his knee with hers.

"Who is this Tamara?"

"My wife is alive. She's in America."

"We're through, but I think you owe it to me to be honest with me for the last time."

"It's the truth."

"Who is Pesheles?"

"I don't know."

"Rabbi Lampert has offered me a job—supervisor in a convalescent home. The pay is seventy-five dollars a week."

"What will you do with your mother?"

"There will be a place for her there too."

Herman fully understood what all this meant, but it no longer mattered. He seemed to be experiencing the "disintegration of the limbs," the Hasidic description for the achievement of a state of selflessness. "If only I could always be this way!" he thought.

Masha waited. Then she said, "You wanted all this to happen. You planned it this way. I'll lock myself up with the old and sick people. Since there is no nunnery for Jewish women, that will be my nunnery—until my mother dies. After that, I'll make an end to the whole comedy. Can I get you something? It's not your fault you were born a charlatan."

Masha left. Herman leaned his head against the back of the chair. His one desire was to be able to lie down somewhere. He heard talking, laughter, footsteps, the clatter of dishes and glassware. Then gradually the fuzziness in his brain diminished; the room stopped spinning; the chair stood on firm ground again. His mind reintegrated itself. All that remained was the weakness in his knees and the bitter aftertaste in his mouth. He even felt a slight pang of hunger.

Herman thought of Pesheles and Yasha Kotik. It was clear that if he survived this ordeal he would never be able to work for Rabbi Lampert again. In all the turmoil there existed a plan engineered by the Powers who controlled human affairs. The rabbi was clearly trying to take Masha away from him. He would never pay seventy-five dollars a week to a woman without training or experience for such a job. Nor would he take care of her mother in addition, at the cost of another seventy-five dollars a week, if not more.

Herman suddenly remembered what Yasha Kotik had said about Mosheh Feifer. The party had destroyed once and for all the few illusions about Masha to which he had clung. He waited a long time, but Masha hadn't returned. "Who knows? She may have gone to call the police," he fantasized. He pictured how they would arrive, arrest him, send him to Ellis Island, and then deport him to Poland.

Mr. Pesheles stood before him. He looked at Herman, his head cocked to one side, and said mockingly, "Oh, so here you are! They're looking for you."

"Who?"

"The rabbi, the rebbetzin. Your Masha is a pretty woman. Piquant. Where do you find them? No offense, but to me you look like a nothing."

Herman didn't answer.

"How do you do it? I too would like to know how."

"Mr. Pesheles, you don't need to envy me."

"Why not? In Brooklyn, a Gentile woman has herself converted for your sake. You have here a woman as pretty as a picture. And Tamara is nothing to sneeze at either. I didn't mean any harm, but I told Rabbi Lampert about the Gentile woman who was converted because of you, and now he's totally confused. He told me that you're writing a book for him. Who is this Yasha Kotik? I don't know him at all."

"I don't know him either."

"He seems to be quite friendly with your wife. It's a crazy world, isn't it? The more you live, the more you see. Still and all, you must be a little bit more careful here in America. For years nothing happens and then the fat is in the fire. There was once a racketeer who associated with the top people: governors, senators—you name it. Suddenly someone started to make trouble and now he's cooling his heels in prison and they'll soon send him back to Italy where he came from. I'm not making any comparisons, God forbid, but for Uncle Sam the law is the law. My advice to you is, at least don't keep them in the same state. Tamara is a woman who's suffered. I tried to arrange a match for her and she told me that she was married to you. Naturally it's a secret and I won't tell anyone.''

"I didn't know she was alive."

"But she told me that from Europe she sent an announcement to the 'Joint' or Hias to be printed in the newspapers here. You probably don't read the papers?''

"Perhaps you know where I can find my coat?" Herman said. "I want to leave, but I can't find it."

"Is that so? All these women you could find, and your coat you can't find? I'll bet you're quite an actor yourself. Don't worry, no one will steal your coat. I imagine that the wraps are in the bedroom. Nobody in New York has enough closets to hang all the coats at a party. But what's the rush? You certainly won't leave without your wife. I hear our rabbi has just offered her a good job. Do you smoke?''

"Occasionally."

"Here, have a cigarette. It relaxes the nerves." Mr. Pesheles produced a gold cigarette case and a lighter also made of gold. The cigarettes were imported ones, shorter than American cigarettes, with gilded tips. "Then again, why worry about the future?" he said. "No one knows what tomorrow will bring. Whoever doesn't take what he can today has nothing. What happened to all the fortunes in Europe? A heap of ashes." Mr. Pesheles inhaled and blew smoke rings. In a minute, his face became aged, melancholy. He looked as if he were reflecting upon some inner sorrow for which there could be no comfort.

"I'd better see what's doing out there," he said, pointing toward the door.

4

Herman, left alone, sat with his head bowed. He had noticed a copy of the Bible on the shelf near his chair and he leaned over and took it out. He leafed through the pages and found Psalms: "Be gracious unto me, O Lord, for I am in distress. Mine eye wasteth away with vexation, yea, my soul and my body. For my life is spent in sorrow, and my years in sighing. My strength faileth because of mine iniquity and my bones are wasted away. Because of mine adversaries, I am become a reproach, yea, unto my neighbors exceedingly, and a dread to mine acquaintances.''

Herman read the words. How was it that these sentences fitted all circumstances, all ages, all moods, while secular literature, no matter how well written, in time lost its pertinence.

Masha staggered in, obviously drunk. She was carrying a plate and a glass of whiskey. Her face was pale, but her eyes shone with derision. Unsteadily, she set the plate on the arm of Herman's chair.

"What are you doing?" she asked. "Reading the Bible? You lousy hypocrite!"

"Masha, sit down."

"How do you know I want to sit down? Maybe what I really want to do is lie down. On second thought, I think I'll sit right in your lap."

"No, Masha, not here."

"Why not? I know he's a rabbi, but his apartment isn't a temple. During the war, even the temple didn't stop anyone. They drove Jewish women into the temple and—"

"Nazis did that."

"And who were the Nazis? Also men. They wanted the same thing you, Yasha Kotik, even the rabbi, want. Maybe you would have done exactly the same. They slept with plenty of Nazi women in Germany. They bought them for a pack of American cigarettes, for a bar of chocolate. You should have seen how the daughters of the master race went to bed with the ghetto boys, and how they hugged and kissed them. Some even married them. So why make so much of the word Nazi? We're all Nazis. The whole human race! You're not only a Nazi but a coward afraid of his own shadow."

Masha tried to laugh, but she soon became serious again. "I've had too much to drink. There was a bottle of whiskey and I kept pouring it out. Go ahead and eat if you don't want to drop dead from hunger." Masha fell into a chair. She took a pack of cigarettes out of her bag, but she couldn't find any matches. "Why are you looking at me like that? I won't sleep with the rabbi."

"What went on between you and Yasha Kotik?"

"My lice slept with his lice. Who is Tamara? Tell me once and for all."

"My wife is alive, as I've tried to tell you."

"Is that the truth or are you still leading me on?"

"It's the truth."

"But they shot her."

"She's alive."

"The children too?"

"No, not the children."

"Well. There is a hell that is even too much for Masha. Does your shikseh know about her?"

"She paid us a visit."

"It's all the same to me. I believed that when I came to America I'd get out of all the filth, but I seem to have landed in the thickest muck of all. This may be the last time I talk to you and I want to tell you that you're the worst fraud I've known in my life. And believe me, I've known plenty of rats. Where is your resurrected wife? I'd like to meet her, at least take a look at her."

"She lives in a furnished room."

"Give me her address and phone number."

"What for? All right, I'll give it to you, but I don't have my address book with me."

"If you hear that I'm dead, don't come to my funeral."

5

When Herman got outside and realized how fiercely cold it was, something in him began to laugh—the laughter that sometimes accompanies total misery. A biting wind blew from the Hudson, whistling and whining. The cold penetrated Herman's body in a few seconds. It was one o'clock in the morning. He hadn't the strength to undertake the long trip to Coney Island. He clung to the door, afraid to move. If only he had enough money for a hotel. But he had less than three dollars in his pocket, and there was not a room to be had for three dollars anywhere except perhaps on the Bowery. Should he go back and borrow some money from the rabbi? There were guests upstairs with cars who would undoubtedly take Masha home. "No, I'd rather die!" he muttered. He started walking toward Broadway. The wind was calmer there. Even the frost wasn't as piercing and it was more brightly lighted than West End Avenue. The snow had stopped, but once in a while a single flake fluttered down either from the sky or from a roof. Herman noticed a cafeteria. He hurried across the street and a taxicab almost ran him down. The driver shouted at him. Herman shook his head and waved his hand in a sign of apology.

He stumbled into the cafeteria, breathless and stiff with cold. Here in the light and warmth, breakfast was already being served. There was a clattering of dishes. People were reading morning newspapers, eating French toast with syrup, oatmeal with cream, wheat cereal with milk, waffles with sausages. The mere smell of food made Herman feel faint. He found a table next to the wall and hung up his hat and coat. He realized that he hadn't picked up a check and went back to the cashier to explain.

"Yes, I saw you come in," the cashier said. "You looked frozen through and through."

Herman ordered oatmeal, eggs, a roll, and coffee at the food counter. The whole meal came to fifty-five cents. As he carried the tray back to his table, his legs trembled and he could hardly bear up under its weight. But as soon as he started to eat, his vitality returned. The aroma of coffee was intoxicating. He now had only one wish—that the cafeteria remain open all night.

A Puerto Rican came to the table to clear away the dishes. Herman asked when the cafeteria closed, and the man said, "Two o'clock."

In less than an hour, he would be out in the snowy cold again. He had to make some plan, come to some decision. There was a phone booth opposite him. Maybe Tamara was still awake. She was now the only one who wasn't at war with him.

He went into the phone booth, inserted a coin, and dialed Tamara's number. A woman answered the phone and went to call her. In less than a minute, he heard her voice.

"I hope I didn't wake you. It's me, Herman."

"Yes, Herman."

"Were you asleep?"

"No, I was reading the newspaper."

"Tamara, I'm in a cafeteria on Broadway. They close at two o'clock. I have nowhere to go."

Tamara hesitated a moment. "Where are your wives?"

"They're both not speaking to me."

"What are you doing on Broadway at this hour?"

"I was at a party at the rabbi's."

"I see. Would you like to come here? It's bitter cold. I've pulled the sleeves of a sweater over my legs. There's a wind whistling through the house as if there wasn't a pane in the windows. Why are your wives fighting with you? On second thought, why don't you come right over? I was thinking of calling you tomorrow. There's something I have to talk to you about. The only problem is that they lock the outside door. You can ring the bell for two hours and the janitor won't come to open it. When will you be here? I'll go down and open it myself."

"Tamara, I'm ashamed to be bothering you like this. It's just that I've no place to sleep and don't have the money to pay for a hotel."

"Now, when she's pregnant, she's started a campaign against you?"

"She's being egged on from all sides. I don't want to blame you, but why did you have to tell Pesheles about us?"

Tamara sighed. "He came to the hospital and descended on me with a thousand questions. I still can't figure out how he got there. He sat down next to my bed and cross-examined me like a prosecutor. He tried to make a match for me too. It was soon after the operation. What kind of people are these?"

"I've got myself into such a mess that everything is hopeless," Herman said. "I'd better go back to Coney Island."

"At this hour? It will take you all night. No, Herman, come to my place. I can't sleep. I'm up all night anyhow."

Tamara was about to say something else, but the operator interrupted to ask for another coin, which Herman didn't have. He told Tamara he would be over as soon as he could, and hung up. He left the cafeteria and walked to the subway station on Seventy-ninth Street. An empty Broadway stretched out before him. The street lights, burning brightly, somehow created a wintry, holiday mood, mysterious and fairy-like. Herman descended the stairs to the station and stood waiting for a local train. The only other person on the platform was black. He wasn't wearing a coat despite the icy weather. Herman waited for fifteen minutes and still no train appeared, nor did any other person. The lights glared. Snow as fine as flour began to sift down through a grate in the ceiling.

Now he regretted having phoned Tamara. It might have been wiser for him to go to Coney Island. At least he might have got a few hours of warm sleep—that is, if Yadwiga would have left him in peace. He realized that in order to hear the doorbell Tamara would have to get dressed and wait downstairs in the cold entryway.

The tracks started to vibrate and a train roared in. There were only a few men sitting in the car—a drunk who mumbled and made faces; a man with a broom and a box of signal lights used by track workers; a laborer carrying a metal lunch box and a wooden last. Muddy puddles surrounded the men's shoes, their noses were red and shiny from the cold, their fingernails were ragged and dirty. A restlessness peculiar to people who turn the night into day hung in the air. Herman imagined that the walls, the lights, the windowpanes, the advertisements were tired of the cold, the noise, the harsh light. The train kept whistling and howling its warning siren, as if the motorman had lost control or had gone through a red signal light and realized his mistake. On Times Square Herman made the long walk to the shuttle that went to Grand Central Station.

Again Herman had to wait a long time for a local train to Eighteenth Street. The other people waiting seemed to be in situations similar to his: men separated from their families, drifters whom society could neither assimilate nor reject, whose faces expressed failure, regret, guilt. Not one of these men was properly shaved or dressed. Herman observed them, but they ignored him and each other. He got off at Eighteenth Street and walked the block to Tamara's house. The office buildings stood unlighted, abandoned. It was difficult to believe that, just a few hours ago, swarms of people were doing business there. Above the rooftops, the sky glowed somberly, starless. Herman walked up the few slippery steps to the glass door of Tamara's house. He saw Tamara in the dim light of a single electric bulb. She was waiting for him in an overcoat, the bottom of her nightgown showing below the hem, her face gray with sleeplessness, her hair uncombed. She opened the door silently and they shuffled up the stairs, because the elevator wasn't in operation.

"How long have you been waiting?" Herman asked.

"What's the difference? I'm used to waiting."

It seemed incredible to him that this was his wife, the same Tamara whom he had met for the first time almost twenty-five years ago at a lecture where the subject under discussion had been "Can Palestine Solve the Jewish Question?" On the third floor, Tamara paused and said, "Oh, my legs!"

His calves, too, felt strained.

Tamara caught her breath, and now asked, "Does she have a hospital yet?"

"Yadwiga? The neighbors have taken over completely."

"But it's your child, after all."

He wanted to say, "So what?" but he kept silent.

6

Herman had slept an hour and had awakened. He hadn't undressed, but lay in bed wearing his jacket, trousers, shirt, and socks. Tamara had again pulled the sleeves of a sweater over her feet. She had thrown her mangy fur coat and Herman's overcoat on top of the blanket.

She was saying: "Thank God, my time of suffering isn't over. I'm still right in the midst of it. This, more or less, is the way we had to struggle in Jambul. You won't believe me, Herman, but I find some comfort in it. I don't want to forget what we went through. When it's warm in the room, I imagine that I've betrayed all the Jews in Europe. My uncle feels that Jews should observe an eternal shiva. The entire people should squat on low stools and read from the Book of Job."

"Without faith, one can't even mourn."

"That in itself is reason enough to mourn."

"You said on the phone that you had been planning to call me. What about?"

Tamara was thoughtful. "Oh, I don't know how to begin. Herman, it isn't in me to lie continually the way you do. My aunt and uncle confronted me about us. Since I had already confessed the truth to a nobody like Pesheles, how could I keep the facts from the only relatives I have left in the world? I didn't mean to complain about you, Herman. It's my shame too, but I felt I had to tell them. I thought they would die of shock when I told them that you're married to a Gentile. But my uncle just sighed and said, 'If you perform an operation on someone, there are afterpains.' Who knows that better than I? The suffering only started the morning after the operation. Naturally, he wants us to get a divorce. He has in mind not one but ten matches for me—learned men, fine Jews, all refugees who have lost their wives in Europe. What am I to say? I have as much desire to get married as you have to dance on the roof. But my uncle and aunt both insisted that either you divorce Yadwiga and come back to me or I divorce you. From their point of view, they're right. My mother, blessed be her memory, once told me a story about dead people who don't know they've died. They eat, drink, even get married. So, since we once lived together, had children together, and now are roaming about the World of Delusion, why do we need a divorce?"

"Tamara, they can put a corpse in prison too."

"No one is going to imprison you. And why are you so afraid of prison? You might be better off than you are now."

"I don't want them to deport me. I don't want to be buried in Poland."

"Who will inform on you? Your mistress?"

"Maybe Pesheles."

"Why should he inform on you? And what proof does he have? You didn't marry anyone in America."

"I gave Masha a Jewish marriage contract."

"What will she do with it? My advice is, go back to Yadwiga and make peace with her."

"Is this what you wanted to tell me? I can't work for the rabbi any more. It's out of the question now. I owe rent. I hardly have enough to get through tomorrow."

"Herman, I want to say something, but don't be angry with me."

"What is it?"

"Herman, people like you are incapable of making decisions for themselves. It's true, I'm not very good at it either, but sometimes it's easier to deal with others' problems than with one's own. Here in America, some people have what is called a manager. Let me be your manager. Put yourself entirely in my hands. Pretend that you're in a concentration camp and must do whatever you're told to do. I'll tell you what to do and you do it. I'll find you a job too. In your state, you're in no position to help yourself."

"Why should you do this? And how?"

"That's not your concern. I'll do something. Beginning tomorrow, I'll take care of all your needs and you must be ready to do whatever I ask. If I tell you to go out and dig ditches, you must go and dig ditches."

"What will happen if they put me in jail?"

"Then I'll send you packages in jail."

"Really, Tamara, this is just a way of giving me your few dollars."

"No, Herman. You won't be taking anything away from me. Starting tomorrow, I'm taking over all your affairs. I know I'm a greenhorn, but I'm used to living in strange places. I can see that things have become too much for you and you're about to fall under the burden."

Herman was silent. Then he said, "Are you an angel?"

"Maybe. Who knows what angels are?"

"I told myself it was madness to phone you so late at night, but something made me do it. Yes, I'll put myself in your hands. I have no strength left—"

"Get undressed. You're ruining your suit."

Herman got out of bed and took off his jacket, trousers, and tie, keeping on only his underwear and socks. In the dark, he laid his clothes over the chair. While undressing, he heard steam hissing in the radiator.

He got into bed again and Tamara moved closer to him, laying her hand on his ribs. Herman dozed. Every once in a while he opened an eye. Slowly the darkness lifted. He could hear noises, footsteps, the opening and closing of doors in the hallway. The roomers must be working people who got up early to go to work. Even to live in these miserable rooms, one had to earn money. After some time, Herman fell asleep. When he woke up, Tamara was already dressed. She told him she had taken a bath in the hall bathroom. She looked at him appraisingly, and her face took on a decisive expression.

"Do you remember our agreement? Go wash up. Here's a towel."

He put his coat around his shoulders and went out in the hallway. All morning, people had been waiting to get into the bathroom, but now the door stood open. Herman found a piece of soap which someone had left behind, and washed himself at the sink. The water was lukewarm. "Where does her goodness come from?" Herman wondered. He remembered Tamara as stubborn and jealous. But now, despite the fact that he had exchanged her for others, she alone was prepared to help him. What did it mean?

He returned to the room and dressed. Tamara told him to walk down to the floor below and ring for the elevator there. She didn't want people in the house to know that a man had spent the night with her. She told him to wait for her outside. Outdoors the morning light blinded him for an instant. Nineteenth Street was jammed with trucks unloading packages, boxes, crates. On Fourth Avenue huge machines were shoveling the snow. The sidewalks were swarming with passers-by. Pigeons that had survived the night were scavenging in the snow; sparrows hopped after them. Tamara took Herman to a cafeteria on Twenty-third Street. The smells were the same as they had been the previous night on Broadway, but here they were combined with a disinfectant used to wash the floors. Tamara didn't even ask what he wanted to order. She seated him at a table and brought him orange juice, a roll, an omelet, and coffee. She watched him eat for a moment, then went to get breakfast for herself. Herman held his cup of coffee in both hands, not drinking, but warming himself with it. His head bent lower and lower. Women had ruined him, but they had also showed him compassion. "I'll manage to live without Masha too," he consoled himself. "Tamara is right—we're not really alive any more."

CHAPTER NINE

1

Winter was over. Yadwiga was walking about with a pointed belly. Tamara had reserved a bed for her in a clinic and talked to her every day on the phone in Polish. The neighbors hovered over her. Woytus sang and warbled from early morning till evening. Marianna had laid a little egg. Though Yadwiga had been cautioned not to do too much physical work, she never stopped cleaning and scrubbing. The floors gleamed. She bought paint and with the help of a neighbor who had been a painter in Europe redecorated the walls. In New Jersey, Masha and Shifrah Puah celebrated the Passover seder with the aged and infirm at the rabbi's convalescent home. Tamara helped Yadwiga prepare for the holiday.

The neighbors were told that Tamara was Herman's cousin. They had something new to wag their tongues about, but if a man chooses to be an outcast and has found a woman who will tolerate his ways, there was little to be done about it. The older tenants were eager to chat with Tamara, to question her about the concentration camps, about Russia and the Bolsheviks. Most of these people were anti-Communists, but among them was a former peddler, who insisted everything the newspapers reported about Russia was untrue. He accused Tamara of lying. The slave-labor camps, the starvation, the black market, the purges— all were figments of her imagination. Whenever he listened to Tamara's accounts, he would comment, "I still say, blessed be Stalin!"

"Why don't you go to him then?"

"They will come here." He complained because his wife, who kept a strictly kosher kitchen, forced him to say the blessing over the wine each Friday evening and insisted that he go to synagogue. Before Passover, the whole building smelled of matzo and borscht, which the women prepared themselves, of sweet wine, horse-radish, and other foods that had immigrated from the old country and now blended their odors with the smell of the bay and the ocean.

Herman could barely believe it himself, but Tamara had found him a job. Reb Abraham Nissen Yaroslaver and his wife Sheva Haddas had decided to go on a long visit to Israel. Reb Abraham Nissen even hinted that he might settle there permanently. He had saved several thousand dollars and was receiving Social Security payments. He wanted to be buried in Jerusalem on the Mount of Olives, not among the shaved Jews in a New York cemetery. He had been wanting to sell his bookstore for some time, but to sell it for the low prices he had been offered would have shown a lack of respect for the books he had so carefully accumulated. Besides, there was always the possibility that he might not want to remain in Israel. Tamara had talked her uncle into leaving the store in her hands. Herman would help her run it. Whatever else Herman might be, he was honest in money matters. Tamara would live in her uncle's apartment and pay the rent.

Reb Abraham Nissen sent for Herman and showed him the stock—all old books. Reb Abraham Nissen had never been able to organize them. Books lay about in dusty heaps on the floor, many of them with torn bindings and peeling covers. Somewhere he had an inventory, but it was not to be found. He never bargained with a customer: whatever was offered, he accepted. What did he and Sheva Haddas need? The old building on East Broadway where they lived was rent-controlled.

Though he knew about Herman's behavior and kept urging Tamara to divorce him, the old man nevertheless managed to find excuses for him. Why should these young people be expected to have faith when he himself was plagued by doubts? How could those who had lived through the destruction believe in the Almighty and in His mercy? Deep in his heart, Reb Abraham Nissen had no sympathy for those Orthodox Jews who tried to pretend that the holocaust in Europe had never taken place.

Reb Abraham Nissen expressed these thoughts to Herman during their long talk before he left for Israel. He wanted to settle in the Holy Land to save himself the arduous journey through the underground caverns which the dead must traverse before reaching the Holy Land, there to be resurrected when the Messiah came. The old man made no written contract with Herman. They agreed verbally that Herman was to take out of the business whatever he needed to live on.

Since Masha had accepted the job at the convalescent home, Herman no longer felt that he was in control of things, nor did he want to be. He had become a fatalist in practice as well as in theory. He was willing to let the Powers lead him, whether they were called Chance or Providence or Tamara. His only problem was this matter of hallucinations: in the subway he would see Masha in a train on the opposite track. The telephone in the store would ring and he would hear Masha's voice. It would be several seconds before he realized that it was not she. The most frequent calls came from young Americans asking whether they could sell or give away books left to them by fathers who had died. How they knew about Reb Abraham Nissen's bookstore Herman had no idea, since the old man had never advertised anywhere.

It was all one great riddle to Herman: Reb Abraham Nissen's trust in him, Tamara's readiness to help him, her devotion to Yadwiga. Since that night in the Catskill Mountains, Tamara would have nothing to do with him physically. Their relationship was entirely platonic.

A latent business sense had awakened in Tamara. With Herman's help, she catalogued the books, set prices, and sent the torn books out to a bindery to be repaired. Before Passover, Tamara had stocked up on Haggadahs, seder trays, matzo covers, skullcaps of all styles and colors, even candles and matzo plates. She acquired a supply of prayer shawls, phylacteries, prayer books printed in both English and Hebrew, as well as texts boys used in studying for their bar mitzvahs.

The lie about selling books that Herman had so often repeated to Yadwiga had become a reality. One morning he took Yadwiga downtown with him to see the store. Tamara later took her home, because Yadwiga was still afraid to travel alone by subway, especially now that she was in the last months of pregnancy.

How strange it was to be sitting at the seder table with Tamara and Yadwiga and to be reciting the Haggadah with the two of them. They had insisted that he wear a skullcap and go through the entire ceremony—the blessing over the wine, the symbolic partaking of parsley, chopped apples with nuts and cinnamon, the eggs and salt water. Tamara asked the Four Questions. For him, and probably for Tamara too, it was all a game, an expression of nostalgia. But then, what wasn't a game? Nowhere could he find anything that was "real," not even in the so-called "exact sciences."

In Herman's private philosophy, survival itself was based on guile. From microbe to man, life prevailed generation to generation by sneaking past the jealous powers of destruction. Just like the Tzivkever smugglers in World War I, who stuffed their boots and blouses with tobacco, secreted all manner of contraband about their bodies, and stole across borders, breaking laws and bribing officials—so did every bit of protoplasm, or conglomerate of protoplasm furtively traffic its way from epoch to epoch. It had been so when the first bacteria appeared in the slime at the ocean's edge and would be so when the sun became a cinder and the last living creature on earth froze to death, or perished in whichever way the final biological drama dictated. Animals had accepted the precariousness of existence and the necessity for flight and stealth; only man sought certainty and instead succeeded in accomplishing his own downfall. The Jew had always managed to smuggle his way in through crime and madness. He had stolen into Canaan and into Egypt. Abraham had pretended that Sarah was his sister. The whole two thousand years of exile, beginning with Alexandria, Babylon, and Rome and ending in the ghettos of Warsaw, Lodz, and Vilna had been one great act of smuggling. The Bible, the Talmud, and the Commentaries instruct the Jew in one strategy: flee from evil, hide from danger, avoid showdowns, give the angry powers of the universe as wide a berth as possible. The Jew never looked askance at the deserter who crept into a cellar or attic while armies clashed in the streets outside.

Herman, the modern Jew, had extended this principle one step: he no longer even had his faith in the Torah to depend on. He was deceiving not only Abimelech but Sarah and Hagar as well. Herman had not sealed a covenant with God and had no use for Him. He didn't want to have his seed multiply like the sands by the sea. His whole life was a game of stealth—the sermons he had written for Rabbi Lampert, the books he sold to rabbis and yeshiva boys, his acceptance of Yadwiga's conversion to Judaism, and Tamara's favors.

Herman read the Haggadah and yawned. He raised his wineglass and poured off ten drops to indicate the ten plagues visited on Pharaoh. Tamara praised Yadwiga's dumplings. A fish from the Hudson River or some lake had paid with its life so that Herman, Tamara, and Yadwiga should be reminded of the miracles of the exodus from Egypt. A chicken had donated its neck to the commemoration of the Passover sacrifice.

In Germany and even in America, neo-Nazi parties were being organized. In the name of Lenin and Stalin, Communists had tortured elderly teachers, and annihilated whole villages in China and Korea in the name of "cultural" revolution. In the Munich taverns, murderers who had played with the skulls of children sipped beer from tall steins and sang hymns in church. In Moscow they had liquidated all the Jewish writers. Yet Jewish Communists in New York, Paris, and Buenos Aires praised the murderers and reviled yesterday's leaders. Truth? Not in this jungle, this saucer of earth perched over hot lava. God? Whose God? The Jews'? Pharaoh's?

Both Herman and Yadwiga begged Tamara to stay overnight, but she insisted on going home, promising to return in the morning to help prepare the second seder. She and Yadwiga washed the dishes. Tamara wished Yadwiga and Herman a happy holiday and left for home.

Herman went into the bedroom and lay down on the bed. He didn't want to think about Masha, but his thoughts kept returning to her. What was she doing? Did she ever think of him?

The telephone rang and Herman ran to pick up the receiver, hoping that it was Masha and afraid that she would change her mind. He almost tripped and shouted a breathless hello into the phone.

There was no answer.

"Hello! Hello! Hello!"

It was an old trick of Masha's to call and not say a word. Perhaps she just wanted to hear his voice.

"Don't be an idiot, say something!" he said.

There was still no answer.

"You left, not I," he found himself saying.

No one replied. He waited a moment and said, "You can't make me more miserable than I am."

2

Weeks went by. Herman had fallen asleep and had dreamed about Masha. The telephone rang, he threw off his blankets and bolted out of bed. Yadwiga continued snoring. He ran into the hall, bruising his knee in the dark. He lifted the receiver and called hello, but there was no answer.

"If you don't answer, I'm going to hang up," he said.

"Wait!" It was Masha's voice. It sounded choked, and she was swallowing her words. After a time, her speech became clearer. "I'm in Coney Island," she said.

"What are you doing in Coney Island? Where are you?"

"At the Manhattan Beach Hotel. I've been trying to reach you all evening. Where have you been? I decided to try once more, but then I fell asleep."

"What are you doing at the Manhattan Beach Hotel? Are you alone?"

"I'm alone. I've come back to you."

"Where's your mother?"

"In the home in New Jersey."

"I don't understand."

"I've arranged for her to stay there. The rabbi will get her a stipend or something. I told him everything—that I couldn't live without you and that my mother was the only obstacle. He tried to talk me out of it, but logic doesn't help."

"You know Yadwiga's about to give birth."

"He'll take care of her too. He's a great man, though he's mad. He has more heart in his fingernail than you have in your whole being. How I wish I could love him! But I can't. When he so much as touches me, I shudder with disgust. He'll be talking to you himself. He wants you to finish the work you started for him. He loves me and would divorce his wife if I agreed to marry him, but he understands my feelings. I never believed he could have so much heart.''

Herman waited a moment before speaking.

''You could have told me all this from New Jersey,'' he said with a tremor in his voice.

''If you don't want me, I won't force myself on you. I swear that if you turn me away this time, I'll never look at your face again. Everything has come to a climax. I want to know once and for all: yes or no?''

''You gave up your job?''

''I've given up everything. I've packed a suitcase and I've come back to you.''

''What will happen to your apartment? Have you given that up too?''

''We'll liquidate everything. I don't want to stay in New York. Rabbi Lampert gave me a wonderful reference and I can get a job anywhere. The people at the home were crazy about me. I literally brought people back to life. The rabbi has a convalescent home in Florida, and if I want to work for him there, I can start right away at a hundred a week. If you don't like Florida, he also has a home in California. You can work for him too. He's as good as an angel from heaven.''

''I can't leave her now. She may go into labor any day.''

''And after she gives birth, you'll have other reasons. I've made up my mind. Tomorrow I'm flying to California and you'll never hear from me again. I swear by the bones of my father.''

''Wait a minute!''

''For what? For new excuses? I'll give you one hour to pack and get here. Rabbi Lampert will take care of your peasant's hospital bills and everything else. He's the president of some lying-in hospital—I've forgotten the name of it. I didn't hide anything from him. He was shocked, but he understands. He may be vulgar but he's a saint just the same. Or have you found a new lover?''

''I don't have a new lover, but I do have a bookstore.''

''What? You have a store?''

Herman told her the story briefly.

''You've gone back to your Tamara?''

''Absolutely not. But she's also an angel.''

''Introduce her to the rabbi. Two angels may bring forth a new God. We're both devils, and we only hurt each other.''

''I can't start packing my things now in the middle of the night.''

''Don't pack anything. What do you have anyway? The rabbi gave me a loan, or an advance, depending on what I do. Leave everything, like that slave in the Bible.''

''What slave? This will kill her.''

''She's a strong peasant. She'll find somebody and be happy. She can give the child up for adoption. The rabbi is connected with such an agency too. He has a hand in everything. If you like, we'll have a child. But the time for talking is over. If Abraham could sacrifice Isaac, you can sacrifice Esau. Maybe later we can take her child to live with us. What's your answer?''

''What exactly do you want me to do?''

''Get dressed and come here. Such things are done every day.''

''I'm afraid of God.''

"If you're afraid, stay with her. Good night forever!"

"Wait, Masha, wait!"

"Yes or no?"

"Yes."

"I'll give you my room number."

Herman hung up. He listened attentively. Yadwiga was still snoring. He remained beside the phone. He hadn't realized how intensely he had longed for Masha. He stood there in the darkness with the mute submissiveness of one who has surrendered his will. It was a while before he could act. He remembered that he had a flashlight somewhere in a drawer. He found it and focused it on the telephone, so that he could make a call. He had to talk to Tamara. He dialed Reb Abraham Nissen Yaroslaver's number. It rang for minutes until at last he heard Tamara's sleepy voice.

"Tamara, forgive me," he said. "This is Herman."

"Yes, Herman, what's the matter?"

"I'm leaving Yadwiga. I'm going away with Masha."

Tamara did not speak for a time. "Do you know what you're doing?" she asked finally.

"I know and I'm doing it."

"A woman who demands such sacrifices doesn't deserve them. I didn't think you'd lost your grip on yourself so completely."

"These are the facts."

"What about the store?"

"It's all in your hands. The rabbi for whom I used to work wants to do something for Yadwiga. I'll give you his address and phone number. Get in touch with him."

"Wait, I'll get a pencil and paper."

It was quiet as he held the receiver and waited. Yadwiga's snoring had stopped.

"I wonder what time it is," Herman thought. Usually he had a keen sense of time. He could often guess the time exactly to the minute. But now he seemed to have lost the knack. He begged the very God against whom he was sinning to keep Yadwiga from wakening. Tamara returned to the phone. "What's the number?"

Herman gave her Rabbi Lampert's name and phone number.

"Couldn't you at least wait till she has the baby?"

"I can't wait."

"Herman, you have the keys to the store. Can you open up in the morning? I'll be there at ten o'clock."

"I'll be there."

"Well, you've made your bed, and you'll have to sleep in it," Tamara said, and hung up.

He stood in the dark, listening to his inner self. Then he went to look at the clock in the kitchen. He was surprised to find it was only fifteen minutes past two. He hadn't slept more than an hour, though it seemed as if he had slept through the night. He looked for a suitcase in which to pack shirts and underwear. He carefully opened a drawer and removed a few shirts, some underwear and pajamas. He sensed that Yadwiga was awake and only pretending to be asleep. Who knows? Could it be that she wanted to get rid of him? Maybe she was tired of it all? She might also be waiting to make a scene at the last moment. As he crammed his clothes into the suitcase, he remembered the rabbi's manuscript. Where was it? He heard Yadwiga getting up.

"What's the matter?" she called.

"I must go somewhere."

"Where? Oh, never mind." Yadwiga lay down again. He heard the bed creak.

He dressed in the dark, perspiring although he felt cold. Loose change fell out of his trouser pockets. He kept bumping into furniture.

The telephone rang and he hurried to answer it. It was Masha again. "Are you coming or aren't you?"

"Yes. You've given me no choice."

3

Herman was afraid that at any moment Yadwiga might change her mind and try to prevent him from leaving by force, but she lay quietly. She had been awake throughout his preparations. Why wasn't she saying anything? For the first time since he had known her, she was behaving unpredictably. It was as if she had become part of a plot against him and knew something that was unknown to him. Or had she really achieved the ultimate stage of resignation? It was a riddle that made him uneasy. She might still spring at him with a knife at the last moment. Before he left, he went into the bedroom and said, "Yadwiga, I'm going now."

She didn't reply.

He wanted to close the door without a sound, but it shut with a bang. He descended the stairs quietly so as not to waken the neighbors. He crossed Mermaid Avenue and walked down Surf Avenue. How quiet and dark Coney Island was in the early morning! The amusement concessions were closed and the lights were out. The avenue stretched out before him as empty as a country road. He could hear the rush of the waves from beyond the Boardwalk. It smelled of fish and other sea things. Herman could make out a few stars in the sky. He saw a taxi and hailed it. All he had was ten dollars. He opened a window of the taxi to clear out the cigarette smoke. A breeze was blowing, but his forehead remained damp. He took a deep breath of air. Despite its nighttime coolness, it already held the promise of a warm day to come. The thought flashed through his mind that this must be the way a murderer felt when he was about to kill someone. "She's my enemy! My enemy!" he muttered, meaning Masha. He had the uncanny feeling that he had already experienced this event at some other time. But when? Could he have dreamed it? He had a strong sensation of thirst, or was it yearning for Masha?

The taxi stopped at the Manhattan Beach Hotel. Herman was concerned that the driver might not have change for ten dollars, but the man silently counted out the money for him. It was quiet in the lobby. The clerk was dozing behind the counter in front of the key boxes. Herman was sure that the elevator man would ask him where he was going at that hour, but the man took him up to the floor he asked for, without a word. Herman soon found the room. He knocked at the door and Masha opened it immediately. She was wearing a negligee and slippers. The only illumination came from the street lights. They fell into each other's arms and clutched each other wordlessly, locked together in grim silence. The sun rose and Herman hardly noticed it. Masha tore herself away from him and went to lower the shades.

They had fallen asleep having hardly spoken. He slept deeply and awoke with renewed desire and a fear that was bound with a forgotten dream. All he could remember was disorder, screaming, and something derisive. Even this confused memory soon faded away. Masha opened her eyes. "What time is it?" she asked, and fell asleep again.

He woke her up to explain that he had to be at the bookstore at ten o'clock. They went into the bathroom to wash up. Masha began to speak. "The first thing we must do is go to my apartment. I still have some things there, and I have to close it up. My mother won't be coming back there."

"That can take days."

"No, a few hours. We can't stay here any longer."

Although he had just satisfied himself with her body, he couldn't imagine how he had been able to stand such a long separation from her. In those weeks she had become somewhat fuller; she looked more youthful.

"Did your peasant make a fuss?" she asked.

"No, she didn't say a word."

They dressed quickly and Masha checked out of the hotel. They walked to the subway station at Sheepshead Bay. The bay was sunlit and filled with boats, many of them just returned from early-dawn trips to the open sea. Fish that a few hours before had been swimming in the water now lay on the boat decks with glassy eyes, wounded mouths, bloodstained scales. The fishermen, well-to-do sportsmen, were weighing the fish and boasting about their catches. As often as Herman had witnessed the slaughter of animals and fish, he always had the same thought: in their behavior toward creatures, all men were Nazis. The smugness with which man could do with other species as he pleased exemplified the most extreme racist theories, the principle that might is right. Herman had repeatedly pledged himself to become a vegetarian, but Yadwiga wouldn't hear of it. They had starved enough in the village and later in the camp. They hadn't come to rich America to starve again. The neighbors had taught her that ritual slaughter and Kashruth were the roots of Judaism. It was meritorious for the hen to be taken to the ritual slaughterer, who recited a benediction before cutting its throat.

Herman and Masha stopped at a cafeteria to eat breakfast. He explained again that he couldn't go directly to the Bronx with her, because he had to meet Tamara and give her the keys to the store. Masha listened to him suspiciously. "She'll talk you out of it."

"Then come with me. I'll give her the keys and we can go home together."

"I have no energy left. The weeks in the home were one long hell. Every day my mother insisted that she wanted to go back to the Bronx, though she had a comfortable room, nurses, a doctor, and everything a sick person could wish for. They had a synagogue where men and women prayed. Each time the rabbi paid a visit, he brought her a gift. She couldn't have it better in heaven. But she never stopped accusing me of driving her into an old-age home. The other old people soon realized that there was no way of making her happy. There was a garden where everybody would sit to read the newspapers, or play cards—but she locked herself in her room. The old people were sorry for me. What I told you about the rabbi was the truth: he offered to leave his wife for me. All I had to do was say the word.''

Once in the subway, Masha became silent. She sat with her eyes shut. Whenever Herman spoke to her, she would start as if he had awakened her from sleep. Her face, which that morning had looked so full and youthful, had again become drawn. Herman noticed a white hair on her head. Masha had finally brought their drama to a climax. With her, things always came out twisted, wild, theatrical. Herman kept looking at his watch. He was to have met Tamara at the store at ten o'clock, but it was already twenty minutes past and the train was still far from his station. At last the train stopped at Canal Street and Herman rose quickly. He promised to phone Masha and come to the Bronx as soon as he could. He ran up the stairs two at a time. He rushed to the store, but Tamara wasn't there. She must have gone home. He unlocked the door and went in to call Tamara and to tell her that he had arrived. He dialed the number, but there was no answer.

Herman thought that Masha might have reached home by this time and he phoned her. The phone rang many times, but no one answered there either. He called again and was about to hang up when he heard Masha's voice. She was both shouting and crying, and at first he couldn't make out what she was saying. Then he heard her wail, ''I've been robbed! They've taken all our things! They've left nothing but the bare walls!''

''When did it happen?''

''Who knows? Oh, God, why wasn't I cremated like all the other Jews?'' She burst into hysterical weeping.

''Have you called the police?''

''What can the police do? They're thieves themselves!'' Masha hung up. It seemed to Herman he could still hear her crying.

4

Where was Tamara? Why hadn't she waited? He called her number again and again. Herman opened a book to quiet his anxiety. It was *The Sanctity of Levi.* ''The fact is,'' he read, ''that all the angels and sacred animals trembled before the Day of Judgment. And also in men, each limb fears the Day of Reckoning.''

The door opened and Tamara entered the store. She was wearing a dress that seemed too long and too wide for her. She looked pale and haggard. She spoke loudly in a hoarse voice, barely restraining herself from shouting. ''Where were you? I waited from ten to half past ten. We had a customer. He wanted to buy a set of the Mishnah, but I couldn't open the door. I telephoned you at Yadwiga's and no one answered. She may have killed herself.''

''Tamara, I'm no longer in my own hands.''

''Well, you're digging your own grave. That Masha is worse than you are.

You don't take a man away from a woman who is in the last weeks of pregnancy. You have to be a bitch to do that.''

"She has no more control over her actions than I have over mine.''

"You always talked about 'free choice.' I read the book you wrote for the rabbi and it seemed to me that every second phrase was 'free choice.' ''

"I gave him as much free choice as he ordered.''

"Stop it! You make yourself sound worse than you are. A woman can drive a man insane. While we were fleeing from the Nazis, a man prominent in the Poalay Zion stole his best friend's wife. Later we were all forced to sleep in one room, about thirty people, and she had the chutzpa to lie with her lover two steps away from her husband. All three are dead now. Where are you planning to go? God has granted you a child after all this destruction—isn't that enough?''

"Tamara, this kind of talk is useless. I can't live without Masha, and I don't have the guts to kill myself.''

"You don't have to kill yourself. We will bring up the baby. The rabbi will work out something, and I'm not exactly helpless. If I live, I'll be a second mother to it. You probably have no money?''

"I won't take another penny from you.''

"Don't rush away. If she's waited this long, she'll wait another ten minutes. What are you going to do?''

"We haven't decided. The rabbi has offered her a job in Miami or California. I'll find work too. I'll send money for the baby.''

"That's not the problem. I could move in with Yadwiga, but it's too far from the store. Perhaps I should bring her here to live with me. My uncle and aunt write such enthusiastic letters, I doubt that they'll be coming back. They've already visited all the holy graves. If Mother Rachel still has some pull with the Almighty, she'll surely intercede for them. Where does your Masha live?''

"I told you, in the East Bronx. She's just been robbed. They took everything.''

"New York is full of thieves, but I don't have to worry about the store. A few days ago when I locked up, my neighbor, the one who has the yarn shop, asked me if I wasn't afraid of thieves and I said my only fear is that some Yiddish author might break in at night and put in some more books.''

"Tamara, I must go. Let me kiss you. Tamara, it's the end for me.''

Herman grabbed his valise and hurried out of the store. At this time of day, the subway was almost empty. He got off at his station and walked to the little side street where Masha lived. He still had the key to her apartment. He opened the door and saw her standing in the middle of the room. She seemed to have calmed down. All the closets were open, the dresser drawers pulled out. The apartment looked as if it were in the midst of being vacated, with the personal belongings packed and only the furniture still waiting to be moved. Herman noticed that the thieves had even unscrewed the electric lightbulbs.

Masha locked the door behind Herman so that the neighbors wouldn't come in. She went into Herman's room and sat down on the bed. Both the pillow and the spread had been stolen. She lighted a cigarette.

"What did you tell your mother?'' Herman asked.

"The truth.''

"What did she say?''

"The same old phrases: I'd be sorry. You would leave me, and all the rest of it. If you leave me, you'll leave me. Only the present counts for me. This robbery is no ordinary thing. It's a warning that we mustn't stay here any longer. In the Bible it says, 'Naked I came out of my mother's womb and naked will I return there.' Why 'there'? We don't return to our mothers' wombs.''

"The earth is the mother.''

"Yes. But until we return to her, let's try to live. We must decide right now where to go—California or Florida. We can go by train or bus. The bus is cheaper, but it takes a week to go to California and you get there more dead than alive. I think we should go to Miami. I'll be able to start working at the home right away. It's off-season and everything is half-price. It's hot, but as my mother says, 'In hell it will be hotter.' ''

"When does the bus leave?''

"I'll call and find out. They didn't steal the telephone. They left an old valise too, and that's all we need. This is how we wandered across Europe. I didn't even have a valise, just a pack. Don't look so miserable! You'll find a job in Florida. If you don't want to write for the rabbi, you can teach. The old people need someone who will help them study the Pentateuch or some of the Commentaries. I'm sure you can earn at least forty dollars a week, and with the hundred I make we can live like kings.''

"Well, then, it's decided.''

"I wouldn't have taken all this junk along anyhow. Maybe it's a blessing in disguise that we were robbed!''

Masha's eyes became gay with laughter. The sun shone on her head, turning her hair a fiery color. The tree outside, which all winter long had stood blanketed with snow, was again adorned with glossy leaves. Herman looked at it in wonder. Each winter Herman had been convinced that the tree, which stood amid garbage and tin cans, had finally shriveled and died. The wind would snap off some of its branches. Stray dogs urinated on its trunk, which seemed to grow thinner and more gnarled with time. Neighborhood children carved their initials, hearts, and even obscenities into its bark. But when summer came, it was covered with foliage. Birds chirped in the thick growth. The tree had carried out its mission, never worrying that a saw, ax, or even one of the burning cigarette butts that Masha habitually threw out of the window might end its existence.

"Does the rabbi have a home in Mexico, by any chance?'' Herman asked Masha.

"Why Mexico? Wait here, I'll be right back. Before I left, I gave some clothes to be dry-cleaned, and I took some of your things to the Chinese laundry. I still have a few dollars in the bank that I want to withdraw. It'll take about half an hour.''

Masha left. Herman heard her lock the door. He began rummaging through his books and picked up a dictionary he would need if he were to continue working for the rabbi. He found all kinds of notebooks lying in a drawer, even an old fountain pen that the thieves had overlooked. Herman opened his valise and crammed the books into it, but then he couldn't shut it. He had an impulse to phone Yadwiga, but he knew it didn't make sense. He stretched out on the bare bed. He slept and dreamed. When he awakened, Masha still hadn't returned. The sun had disappeared and the room had darkened. Suddenly Herman heard noises outside the door, footsteps and shouts. It sounded as if something heavy was being dragged along. He got up and opened the outside door. A man and a woman held Shifrah Puah between them, half carrying, half leading her. Her face was sick and altered. The man called out, "She passed out in my taxi. Are you her son?"

"Where is Masha?" the woman asked. Herman recognized her as a neighbor. "She's not at home."

"Call a doctor!"

Herman ran down the few steps separating him from Shifrah Puah. She stared at him with a stern expression when he tried to help her.

"Shall I call a doctor?" he asked.

Shifrah Puah shook her head. Herman backed into the apartment. The cab driver handed him Shifrah Puah's purse and overnight bag, which Herman hadn't noticed before. Herman paid the cab driver out of his own money. They led Shifrah Puah into the shadowy bedroom. Herman pushed the light switch, but the thieves had also removed these bulbs. The cab driver asked why no one turned on a light, and the woman went out to bring a lightbulb from her apartment. Shifrah Puah started to whimper, "Why is it so dark here? Where is Masha? Woe on my miserable life!"

Herman held Shifrah Puah by the arm and shoulder. Meanwhile, the woman returned and screwed in the lightbulb. Shifrah Puah looked at her bed. "Where is the bedding?" she asked in an almost healthy tone of voice.

"I'll get her a pillow and sheet," the neighbor said. "Lie down on it as it is for now."

Herman led Shifrah Puah to the bed. He could feel her body shaking. She clung to him as he lifted her and then lowered her onto the mattress. Shifrah Puah groaned and her face grew even more shriveled. The woman came in with a pillow and sheet. "We must call an ambulance immediately."

Again there was the sound of footsteps on the stairs and Masha entered. In one hand she carried clothes on hangers, and in the other a bundle of laundry. Before she could come into the room, Herman said through the open door, "Your mother is here!"

Masha stopped in her tracks. "She's come running back, has she?"

"She's sick."

Masha handed Herman the clothes and the bundle, which he laid on the kitchen table. He heard Masha shouting angrily at her mother. He knew he should call a doctor, but he didn't know one to call. The neighbor came out of the bedroom with her hands spread out in a questioning gesture. Herman went to his own room. He heard the woman complaining to someone on the phone.

"A policeman? Where will I get a policeman? The woman can die in the meantime!"

"A doctor! A doctor! She's dying!" Masha screamed. "She's killed herself, the bitch, just for spite!"

And Masha let out a wail similar to the one he had heard over the phone a few hours earlier, when she had told him about the robbery. It was a sound unlike her own voice—catlike and primitive. Her face became contorted, she tore her hair, stamped her feet, leaped at Herman as if to attack him. The neighbor held the phone to her breast, stunned.

Masha screamed, "This is what you wanted! Enemies! Bloody enemies!"

She gasped for breath and doubled over as if she were about to fall. The neighbor dropped the receiver and grabbed Masha by the shoulders. She shook her, as one would to relieve a child who was choking.

"Murderers!"

CHAPTER TEN

1

A doctor arrived, the one who had attended Masha when she thought she was pregnant, and gave Shifrah Puah a shot. Then the ambulance came and Masha went with her to the hospital. A few minutes later a policeman knocked at the door. Herman told him that Shifrah Puah had already been taken to the hospital, but he said that his visit had to do with the robbery. The policeman asked Herman his name and address and what his connection was with the family. Herman stammered and turned pale. The policeman eyed him suspiciously and asked when he had come to America and whether he was a citizen. He wrote down something in a notebook and left. The woman next door had taken back her pillow and sheet. Herman was expecting Masha to phone from the hospital, but two hours passed and the phone was silent.

Evening came and, except for the bedroom, the apartment was without light. Herman unscrewed the lightbulb from the bedroom fixture to take it to his own room, but he bumped into a doorpost and heard the bulb filament rattle. He screwed the bulb into his bedside lamp, but it no longer worked. He went to the kitchen to look for matches and candles, and couldn't find any. He stood at the window, looking out into the night. The tree, whose every leaf had reflected the play of sunlight a few hours earlier, now stood black against the darkness. A single star twinkled in the reddish, glowing sky. A cat walked across the yard with cautious steps and crawled into a space between the scrap iron and the trash. Shouts, traffic noises, and the muffled roar of the El echoed in the distance. Herman experienced a melancholy more intense than he had ever felt before. He couldn't remain in this vandalized, unlighted house alone all night. If Shifrah Puah had died, her spirit might come to haunt him.

He decided to go out and get some bulbs. Besides, he hadn't eaten anything since breakfast. He left the apartment, realizing the moment the door closed behind him that he had forgotten his key. He searched through his pockets, knowing he wouldn't find it. He must have put it down on the table. The phone began to ring inside the apartment. Herman pushed at the door, but it was securely locked. The ringing didn't stop. Herman pushed with all his might, but the door would not budge and the phone continued to ring.

"It's Masha! Masha!" He couldn't even remember to which hospital they had taken Shifrah Puah.

The telephone stopped ringing, but Herman remained standing at the door. He wondered if he should try to break it down. He was sure that the phone would soon ring again. He waited a full five minutes before he went down the stairs. Just as he reached the street door, the ringing started again and went on for many minutes. Herman imagined that he could hear Masha's fury in the insistent ringing. He could see her face distorted in agony.

There was no sense in turning back. He walked in the direction of Tremont Avenue and came to the cafeteria where Masha had worked as a cashier.

He decided to get a cup of coffee and then go back and wait on the stairs until Masha returned. He went up to the counter. He touched his vest pocket and felt a key, but it was the key to his apartment in Brooklyn.

Instead of ordering coffee, he thought he would phone Tamara, but all the booths were occupied. He tried to be patient. "Even eternity doesn't last forever," ran through his mind. "If the cosmos had no beginning, then one eternity has already passed." Herman smiled to himself. Back to Zeno's paradoxes! One of the three conversationalists at the telephones hung up. Herman quickly took his place in the booth. He dialed Tamara's number, but no one answered. He got his dime back and without thinking dialed the number of his Brooklyn apartment. He needed to hear a familiar voice, even a hostile one. Yadwiga wasn't at home either. He let the phone ring ten times.

Herman sat down at an empty table and decided to wait half an hour and then call Masha's apartment. He took a piece of paper out of his pocket and tried to calculate how long he and Masha could exist on the money they had. It was a futile effort since he did not know the price of the bus tickets. He figured, doodled, and every few minutes looked at his wristwatch. How much would he get for it if he were to sell it? Not more than a dollar.

He sat there, trying to sum things up. In the hayloft, he had had the illusion that some basic change would take place in the world, but nothing had changed. The same politics, the same phrases, the same false promises. Professors continued to write books about the ideology of murder, the sociology of torture, the philosophy of rape, the psychology of terror. Inventors created new deadly weapons. The talk about culture and justice was more revolting than the barbarism and injustice. "I am sunk in offal and I am myself offal. There is no way out," Herman muttered. "Teach? What is there to teach? And who am I to teach it? He felt nauseated in the same way that he had on the evening of the rabbi's party. After twenty minutes, Herman dialed Masha's number and she answered.

He knew from her voice that Shifrah Puah had died. It was toneless, the exact opposite of the overdramatic style in which she related the most ordinary things.

"How is your mother?" he nevertheless asked.

"I have no mother," Masha said.

Both were silent.

"Where are you?" Masha asked after a moment. "I thought you'd be waiting for me."

"God in heaven, when did it happen?"

"She died before she got to the hospital. Her last words were, 'Where is Herman?' Where *are* you? Come right back."

He rushed out of the cafeteria, forgetting to give the check back to the cashier, who shouted after him. He threw it to her.

2

Herman had expected to find the neighbors with Masha, but no one was there. The apartment was as dark as when he had left it. They stood close together in silence.

"I went down to buy lightbulbs, and locked myself out," he said. "Do you have a candle somewhere?"

"What for? No, we don't need one."

He led her to his room. It was a little lighter there. He sat down on a chair and Masha seated herself on the edge of the bed.

"Does anyone know yet?" Herman asked.

"No one knows and no one cares."

"Shall I call the rabbi?"

Masha didn't reply. He was beginning to think that in her grief she hadn't heard him, but suddenly she said, "Herman, I can't stand any more. These things involve formalities and require money too."

"Where is the rabbi? Still at the home?"

"I left him there, but he was supposed to fly some place. I don't remember where."

"I'll try to reach him at home. Do you have a match?"

"Where's my bag?"

"If you brought it home, I'll find it."

Herman got up and went to look for it. He had to feel his way like a blind man. He felt the surface of the table and chairs in the kitchen. He wanted to go into the bedroom, but was afraid. Could it be that Masha had left her bag at the hospital? He went back to Masha.

"I can't find it."

"I had it here. I took the doorkey out of it."

Masha got up and both of them fumbled around in the dark. A chair fell over and Masha picked it up. Herman felt his way into the bathroom and, out of habit, turned the light switch. The light went on, and he saw Masha's bag on the laundry hamper. The thieves had missed the bulb over the medicine cabinet.

Herman picked up the bag, surprised at its weight, and called to Masha that he had found it and that the bathroom light was working. He glanced at his wristwatch, but he had forgotten to wind it and it had stopped.

Masha came to the bathroom door, her face changed, her hair disordered; she squinted. Herman handed her the bag. He could not look at her directly. He spoke to her, his face averted, like a pious Jew who may not look at a woman.

"I must put this bulb in the lamp near the phone."

"What for? Well—"

Herman unscrewed the bulb carefully and held it close to his body. He was grateful that Masha wasn't scolding him, crying, or making a scene. He screwed the bulb into the floor lamp and experienced a moment of satisfaction when it lighted. He phoned the rabbi, and a woman answered. "Rabbi Lampert has gone to California."

"Do you have any idea when he'll be back?"

"Not sooner than a week."

Herman knew what that implied. If he were here, the rabbi would take care of the formalities, probably assume the funeral expenses. Herman hesitated and then asked where the rabbi could be reached.

"I cannot tell you," the woman said officiously.

Herman turned off the light, not knowing why he did so. He went back to his room. Masha was sitting there with her bag on her knees.

"The rabbi left for California."

"Well—"

"Where do we begin?" Herman asked both Masha and himself. Masha had once mentioned that neither she nor her mother belonged to any organization or synagogue that handled its members' burials. Everything would have to be paid for: the funeral, the cemetery plot. Herman would have to see officials, request favors, credit, give guarantees. But who knew him? His thoughts turned to animals. They lived without complications and burdened no one when they died.

"Masha, I don't want to live," he said.

"You once promised me we would die together. Let's do it now. I have enough sleeping pills for both of us."

"Yes, let's take them," he said, not knowing whether he really meant it.

"I have them in my bag. All we need is a glass of water."

"That we have."

His throat constricted and he could hardly say the words. The way it had happened and the swiftness with which everything had come to a climax baffled him. He could hear the noisy clinking and scraping of keys, coins, lipstick, as Masha rummaged through her bag. "I always knew she was my Angel of Death," he thought.

"Before we die, I'd like to know the truth," he heard himself saying.

"About what?"

"Whether you've been faithful to me since we've been together."

"Have you been faithful to me? If you tell the truth, I will too."

"I'll tell the truth."

"Wait, I want to get a cigarette."

Masha took a cigarette out of a pack. She did everything slowly. He could hear her rolling the tip of the cigarette between her thumb and forefinger. She struck a match and in the glow of the flame her eyes looked at him questioningly. She inhaled, blew out the flame, and the match head glowed for an instant, illuminating her fingernail. "Well, let's hear," she said.

Herman had to make an effort to speak. "Only with Tamara. That's all."

"When?"

"She was at a hotel in the Catskills."

"You never went to the Catskills."

"I told you I was going to Atlantic City with Rabbi Lampert to attend a convention. Now it's your turn," Herman said.

Masha laughed a short laugh.

"What you did with your wife, I did with my husband."

"So that means he told the truth?"

"That time, yes. I went to ask him for the divorce and he insisted. He told me it was the only way I could get it."

"You swore a holy oath that he lied."

"I swore falsely."

They sat silently, each with his own thoughts.

"There isn't any point in dying now," Herman said.

"What do you want to do? Leave me?"

Herman didn't answer. He sat there, his mind blank. Then he said, "Masha, we must go tonight."

"Even the Nazis allowed the Jews to bury their dead."

"We're not Jews any more and I can't stay here any longer."

"What do you want me to do? I'll be damned for ten generations to come."

"We're damned already."

"At least let's wait till after the funeral." Masha barely managed to say the last word.

Herman stood up. "I'm leaving now."

"Wait, I'll go with you. Let me go into the bathroom a moment."

Masha rose. She dragged her feet as she walked. The heels of her shoes scraped along the floor. Outside, the tree stood motionless in the night. Herman bade it farewell. He tried one last time to fathom its mystery. He heard water splashing; Masha was apparently washing up. He stood quietly, listening intently, amazed at himself and at Masha's willingness to go with him.

Masha came out of the bathroom. "Herman, where are you?"

"Here I am."

"Herman, I can't leave my mother," Masha said quietly.

"You have to leave her anyhow."

"I want a grave next to hers. I don't want to lie among strangers."

"You'll lie near me."

"You're a stranger."

"Masha, I *must* go."

"Wait a second. As long as it is this way, go back to your peasant. Don't leave your child."

"I will leave everybody," Herman said.

EPILOGUE

The night before Shevuot, Yadwiga gave birth to a daughter. The rabbi had suggested that if the child were a girl, she should be called Masha. He had taken care of everything: Shifrah Puah's and Masha's burials, Yadwiga's hospital costs. He had bought a baby carriage, blankets, a layette—even toys. Reb Abraham Nissen and Sheva Haddas had decided to remain in Israel, and Tamara had permanently taken over her uncle's apartment and bookstore.

Since Tamara did not want Yadwiga to live alone, she had arranged for Yadwiga and the baby to move in with her. Tamara worked in the store all day, and Yadwiga took care of the household.

Masha had left the usual note: no one was responsible for her death. She asked to be buried beside her mother. With the rabbi in California, they came close to being buried in the paupers' cemetery. Two days passed without anyone knowing what had happened. According to a story that was published in a Yiddish newspaper, Masha had appeared to Yasha Kotik, the actor, in a dream and had told him that she was dead. The following morning Yasha Kotik telephoned Leon Tortshiner. Tortshiner, who still had a key to Masha's apartment, went there and found her body. It was Tortshiner who got in touch with the rabbi in California. This story was later refuted in a letter to the paper written by a neighbor of Masha's. The neighbor maintained that she had called the hospital, learned that Shifrah Puah had died and that no one had claimed the body. She had then called the janitor, who opened the apartment, and they had found Masha dead.

The rabbi became a frequent visitor to Tamara and to little Masha. He often parked his car in front of Tamara's store and came in to browse through the books. He sent her customers, and people who either gave her books free or charged little for them. The rabbi ordered a joint headstone for mother and daughter from a monument-maker on Canal Street, whose shop was located one block from Tamara's store.

Tamara had several times listed Herman's name in the missing-persons columns published in the Yiddish press, but without results. Tamara believed that Herman had either killed himself or was hiding somewhere in an American version of his Polish hayloft. One day the rabbi informed Tamara that, because of the holocaust, the rabbinate had eased restrictions so that deserted wives could be married a second time.

And Tamara had replied, "Perhaps, in the next world—to Herman."

Shosha

AUTHOR'S NOTE

This novel does not represent the Jews of Poland in the pre-Hitler years by any means. It is a story of a few unique characters in unique circumstances. It appeared in the *Jewish Daily Forward* in 1974 under the title *Soul Expeditions*. A great part of it was translated into English by my nephew Joseph Singer. A number of chapters I dictated to my wife, Alma, and to my secretary, Dvorah Menashe. The entire work was edited by Rachel MacKenzie and Robert Giroux. My gratitude and love to all of them.

I.B.S.

PART ONE

███████

CHAPTER ONE

───────────

1

I was brought up on three dead languages—Hebrew, Aramaic, and Yiddish (some consider the last not a language at all)—and in a culture that developed in Babylon: the Talmud. The cheder where I studied was a room in which the teacher ate and slept, and his wife cooked. There I studied not arithmetic, geography, physics, chemistry, or history, but the laws governing an egg laid on a holiday and sacrifices in a temple destroyed two thousand years ago. Although my ancestors had settled in Poland some six or seven hundred years before I was born, I knew only a few words of the Polish language. We lived in Warsaw on Krochmalna Street, which might well have been called a ghetto. Actually the Jews of Russian-occupied Poland were free to live wherever they chose. I was an anachronism in every way, but I didn't know it, just as I didn't know that my friendship with Shosha, the daughter of our neighbor Bashele and her husband, Zelig, had anything to do with love. Love affairs took place between worldly young men who shaved their beards and smoked cigarettes on the Sabbath and girls who wore blouses with short sleeves and dresses with a décolleté. Such follies did not touch a cheder boy of seven or eight from a Hasidic house.

Still, I was drawn to Shosha and I passed through the dark hall that led from our apartment to Bashele's as often as I could. Shosha was about my age, but while I was considered a prodigy, knew several pages of the Gemara and chapters of the Mishnah by heart, could write in Yiddish as well as in Hebrew, and had already begun to ponder God, providence, time, space, and infinity, Shosha was considered a little fool in our building, No. 10. At nine, she spoke like a child of six. She was left behind two years in a class in the public school to which her parents sent her. Shosha had blond hair that fell to her shoulders when she undid her braids. Her eyes were blue, her nose straight, her neck long. She took after her mother, who had been known as a beauty in her youth. Her sister Yppe, two years younger than Shosha, was dark, like her father. She wore a brace on her left leg and limped. Teibele, the youngest, was still a baby when I began to visit at Bashele's. She had just been weaned and slept in a cradle.

One day Shosha came home from school crying—the teacher had dismissed her, with a letter saying there was no place there for her. She brought home two books—one in Russian, one in Polish—as well as some exercise books and a box with pens and pencils. She had not learned any Russian but could read Polish slowly. The Polish schoolbook had pictures of a hut in a village, a cow,

295

a rooster, a cat, a dog, a hare, and a mother stork feeding her newly hatched offspring in their nest. Shosha knew some of the poems in the book by heart.

Her father, Zelig, worked in a leather store. He left home early in the morning and returned late in the evening. His black beard was always short and round, and the Hasidim in our building said that he had it trimmed—a violation of Hasidic practice. He wore a short gaberdine, a stiff collar, a tie, and kid shoes with rubber tops. Saturday he went to a synagogue frequented by tradesmen and workers.

Though Bashele wore a wig, she did not shave her head as did my mother, the wife of Rabbi Menahem Mendl Greidinger. Mother often told me it was wrong for a rabbi's son, a student of the Gemara, to be the companion of a girl, and one from a common home at that. She warned me never to taste anything there, since Bashele might feed me meat that was not strictly kosher. The Greidingers came from generations of rabbis, authors of sacred books, while Bashele's father was a furrier and Zelig had served in the Russian Army before they married. The children in our house mimicked Shosha's speech. Shosha made silly mistakes in her Yiddish; she began a sentence and rarely finished it. When she was sent to the grocery store to buy food, she lost the money. Bashele's neighbors told her she ought to take Shosha to a doctor because her brain didn't seem to be developing, but Bashele had neither time nor money for doctors. And how could they help? Bashele herself was as naïve as a child. Michael the shoemaker said about her that you could make her believe she was pregnant with a kitten and that a cow flew over the roof and laid brass eggs.

How different Bashele's apartment was from ours! We had almost no furniture. The walls were lined with books from floor to ceiling. My brother, Moishe, and I did not have toys. We played with my father's volumes, with a broken pen, an empty ink bottle, or pieces of paper. Our living room had no sofa, no upholstered chairs, no chest of drawers—only an ark for scrolls, a long table, and benches. People prayed there on the Sabbath. My father stood at a lectern all day long and looked into large books that lay open in a great pile. He wrote commentaries, trying to answer the contradictions that one commentator found in the works of another. He was short, had a red beard and blue eyes, and he smoked a long pipe. From the time I can first remember, I heard him repeat the phrase "It is forbidden." Everything I wanted to do was a transgression. I was not allowed to draw or paint a person—that violated the Second Commandment. I couldn't say a word against another boy—that was slander. I couldn't laugh at anyone—that was mockery. I couldn't make up a story—that represented a lie.

On Sabbaths we weren't allowed to touch a candlestick, a coin, any of the things we amused ourselves with. Father reminded us constantly that this world was a corridor in which one had to study the Torah and perform virtuous deeds, so that when one made one's way to the palace that was the next world, rewards would be waiting to be collected. He used to say, "How long does one live, anyhow? Before you turn around it's all over. When a person sins, his sins turn into devils, demons, hobgoblins. After death they chase the corpse and drag it through forsaken forests and deserts where people do not go or cattle tread."

Mother occasionally got angry at Father for talking so depressingly to us, but she was a moralizer herself. She was lean, with sunken cheeks, a pointed chin, and large gray eyes that expressed both sharpness and melancholy. My parents had lost three children before I was born.

At Bashele's, before I even opened the door, I could smell her stews, roasts, and desserts. Her kitchen contained rows of copper and brass pots and pans, painted and gold-rimmed plates, a mortar and pestle, a coffee mill, all kinds of pictures and knickknacks. The children had a crate filled with dolls, balls, colored pencils, paints. The beds were covered with pretty bedspreads. Embroidered cushions lay across the sofa.

Yppe and Teibele were too young for me, but Shosha was just right. Neither of us went down to play in the courtyard, which was controlled by rough boys with sticks. They bullied any child younger or weaker than they. Their talk was mean. They singled me out in particular because I was the rabbi's son and wore a long gaberdine and a velvet cap. They taunted me with names like "Fancypants," "Little Rabbi," "Mollycoddle." If they heard me speak to Shosha, they jeered and called me "Sissy." I was teased for having red hair, blue eyes, and unusually white skin. Sometimes they flung a rock at me, a chip of wood, or a blob of mud. Sometimes they tripped me so that I fell into the gutter. Or they might sic the house watchman's dog on me because they knew I was afraid of it.

But inside Bashele's I received neither teasing nor roughness. The moment I arrived Bashele offered me a plate of groats, a glass of borscht, a cookie. Shosha took down her toy box with her dolls, doll-sized dishes and cooking things, her collection of human and animal figurines, shiny buttons, gaudy ribbons. We played jacks, knucklebones, hide-and-seek, husband and wife. I made believe I went to the synagogue and when I returned Shosha prepared a meal for me. Once I played the role of a blind man and Shosha let me touch her forehead, cheeks, mouth. She kissed the palm of my hand and said, "Don't tell Mama."

I repeated to Shosha stories I had read or heard from my mother and father, embellishing them freely. I told her of the wild forests of Siberia, of Mexican bandits, and of cannibals who ate their own children. Sometimes Bashele would sit with us and listen to my chatter. I boasted to them that I was familiar with the cabala and knew expressions so sacred they could draw wine from the wall, create live pigeons, and let me fly to Madagascar. One such name I knew contained seventy-two letters, and when it was uttered the sky would turn red, the moon topple, and the world be destroyed.

Shosha's eyes filled with alarm. "Arele, don't ever say the word!"

"No, Shoshele, don't be afraid. I will make it so that you'll live forever."

2

Not only could I play with Shosha, but I could also tell her things I dared not speak of to anyone else. I could describe all my fantasies and daydreams. I confided that I was writing a book. I often saw this book in my dreams. It was written by me and also by some ancient scribe in Rashi script on parchment. I imagined that I had done it in a former life. My father had forbidden me to look into the cabala. He admonished me that anyone who indulges in the cabala before the age of thirty is in danger of falling into heresy or insanity. But I believed that I was a heretic and half mad anyhow. There stood on our shelves volumes of the Zohar, *The Tree of Life, The Book of Creation, The Orchard of Pomegranates,* and other cabalistic works. I found a calendar where many facts about kings, statesmen, millionaires, and scholars were set down. My mother often read *The Book of the Covenant,* which was an anthology packed with scientific information. There I could read about Archimedes, Copernicus, Newton, and about the philosophers Aristotle, Descartes, Leibnitz. The author, Reb Elijah from Wilna, engaged in long polemics with those who denied the existence of God, and so I learned their opinions. Though the book was forbidden to me, I used every opportunity to read it. Once my father mentioned the philosopher Spinoza—his name should be blotted out—and his theory that God is the world and the world is God. These words created turmoil in my mind. If the world is God, I, the boy Aaron, my gaberdine, my velvet cap, my red hair, my shoes were part of the Godhead. So were Bashele, Shosha—even my thoughts.

That day, I lectured to Shosha about Spinoza's philosophy as if I had studied all his works. Shosha listened while she laid out her collection of gilded buttons. I was sure that she didn't grasp a single word, but then she asked, "Is Leibele Bontz also God?"

Leibele Bontz was known in our courtyard as a hoodlum and a thief. When he played cards with the boys, he cheated. He had all kinds of tricks and excuss to beat up a weaker boy. He would approach a little boy and say, "Someone told me that my elbow stinks. Do me a favor and smell it." When the little boy obliged, Leibele Bontz punched him in the nose. The idea that he could be part of God destroyed my enthusiasm for Spinoza's philosophy and I immediately developed a theory that there were two Gods—a good one and a bad one—and Leibele Bontz belonged with the bad one. Shosha accepted my new version of Spinoza willingly.

Every day there used to come to the Radzymin studyhouse, where my father prayed, a man called Joshua the herring merchant. He also had a nickname—Joshua the philosopher. He was short, slight, with a beard that had all colors: yellow, gray, brown. He sold marinated herring and smoked herring, and his wife and daughters pickled cucumbers. He prayed late and with great speed after the other worshippers had left. One minute he put on his prayer shawl and phylacteries; a minute later—or so it seemed to me—he took them off. I had stopped going to cheder because my father could not afford the tuition; besides, I was now able to read a page of the Gemara by myself. I often went to the Radzymin studyhouse to converse with this man. He dabbled in logic and told me about the paradoxes of the Greek philosopher Zeno. He also told me that even though the atom was supposed to be the smallest particle of matter, from a mathematical point of view it could be divided infinitely. He explained the meaning of the words "microcosm" and "macrocosm."

The next day I spoke about all this to Shosha. I told her that each atom is a world in itself, with myriads of tiny human beings, animals, and birds. There are Gentiles there and Jews. The men build houses, towers, towns, bridges, without realizing how infinitely small they are. They speak many languages. "In one drop of water there may be myriads of such worlds."

"Don't they get drowned?" Shosha asked.

In order not to make things too complicated, I said, "They all know how to swim."

A day did not pass without my coming to Shosha with new stories. I had discovered a potion that, if you drank it, made you as strong as Samson. I had drunk it already and I was so strong I could drive the Turks from the Holy Land and become King of the Jews; I had found a cap that, if you put it on your head, made you invisible. I was about to grow as wise as King Solomon, who could speak the language of birds. I told Shosha about the Queen of Sheba, who came to learn wisdom from King Solomon and brought with her many slaves, as well as camels and donkeys bearing gifts for the ruler of Israel. Before she came King Solomon ordered that the palace floor be replaced with glass. When the Queen of Sheba entered, she mistook the glass for water and lifted up her skirt. King Solomon sat on his golden throne, and when he saw the queen's legs, he said, "You are famous for your great beauty, but you have hair on your legs like a man."

"Was this true?" Shosha asked.

"Yes, true."

Shosha lifted up her skirt to look at her own legs, and I said, "Shosha, you are more beautiful than the Queen of Sheba." I promised her that when I was anointed and sat on Solomon's throne, I would take her for a wife. She would be the queen and wear on her head a crown of diamonds, emeralds, rubies, and sapphires. The other wives and concubines would bow before her with their faces to the earth.

"How many wives will you have?" Shosha asked.

"Together with you, a thousand."

"Why so many?"

"King Solomon had a thousand wives. It is written so in the Song of Songs."

"Is this allowed?"

"A king may do anything."

"If you have a thousand wives, you will have no time for me."

"Shoshele, for you I will always have time. You will sit near me on the throne and rest your feet on a footstool of topaz. When the Messiah comes, all Jews will mount a cloud and fly to the Holy Land. The Gentiles will become slaves to the Jews. The daughter of a general will wash your feet."

"Oh, it will tickle." Shosha began to laugh, showing her white teeth.

The day that Zelig and Bashele moved from No. 10 to No. 7 Krochmalna Street was like Tisha Bov for me. It happened suddenly. One day I stole a groschen from my mother's purse and bought a piece of chocolate for Shosha in Esther's candy store; a day later movers opened the door of Bashele's apartment and carried out the wardrobes, the sofa, the beds, the Passover dishes, the all-year-round dishes. I didn't even have a chance to say goodbye to the family. Actually, I had become too old to have a girl for a friend. I was studying not only Gemara now but also Tosaphot. The morning they moved, I was reading with my father *Rabbi Chanina, the Assistant of Priests*. From time to time I glanced out the window. Bashele's possessions were loaded on a platform harnessed to two Belgian horses. Bashele carried Teibele. Shosha and Yppe walked behind the wagon. The distance from No. 10 to No. 7 was only two blocks, but I knew that this meant the end. It was one thing to sneak out of the apartment, pass quickly through a dark hall, and knock on Shosha's door, and quite another thing to pay a visit in a strange building. The members of the community that paid my father his weekly remuneration were watchful, always ready to find some sign of misconduct in his children.

It was summer 1914. A month later, a Serbian assassin shot the Austrian Crown Prince and his wife. Soon the Czar mobilized all the armed forces. I saw men who worshipped in our living room on the Sabbath pass by our house with round shiny buttons on their lapels as a sign that they had been called up and would have to fight against the Germans, the Austrians, and the Italians. Policemen entered Elozar's tavern at No. 17 and poured all his vodka into the gutter—in time of war, citizens should be sober. The storekeepers refused to sell merchandise for paper money; they demanded silver coins or gold pieces. The doors of the stores were kept half closed, and only customers with such coins were allowed in.

At home we soon began to go hungry. In the time between the assassination in Sarajevo and the outbreak of the war, many wealthy housewives had stocked their larders with flour, rice, beans, and groats, but my mother had been busy reading morality books. Besides, we had no money. The Jews on our street stopped paying my father. There were no more weddings, divorces, or lawsuits in his courtroom. Long lines formed at the bakeries for a loaf of bread. The price of meat soared. In Yanash's Bazaar the slaughterers stood with knives in their hands, looking out for a woman with a chicken, a duck, or a goose. The price of fowl went up from day to day. Herring could not be bought at all. Many housewives began to use cocoa butter instead of butter. There was a lack of kerosene. After the Succoth holiday the rains, the snow, the frosts began, but we couldn't afford coal for heating the oven. My brother Moishe stopped going to cheder because his shoes were torn. Father became his teacher. Weeks passed by and we never tasted meat, not even on the Sabbath. We drank watery tea without sugar. We learned from the newspapers that the Germans and Austrians had invaded many towns and villages in Poland, among them those where our relatives lived. The Czar's great-uncle Nikolai Nikolaievitch, the chief commander, decreed that all Jews be driven from the regions behind the front; they were considered German spies. The Jewish streets in Warsaw teemed with thousands of refugees. They slept in the studyhouses, even in synagogues. It wasn't long before we began to hear the shooting of heavy guns. The Germans attacked at the river Bzura, and the Russians launched a counterattack. In our apartment the windowpanes rattled day and night.

3

Our family left Warsaw in the summer of 1917. My parents moved to a village occupied by the Austrians. Food was cheaper there. Mother had relatives in that part of the country. The city seemed on the verge of destruction. The war had already lasted three years. The Russians had evacuated Warsaw and in their retreat they had blown up the Praga Bridge. The Germans who ruled Poland were losing on the western front and they let the population starve. We never had enough to eat. Before we left, Moishe fell ill and was taken to the Hospital for Epidemic Diseases on Pokorna Street. Mother and I were taken to the disinfecting station on Szczesliwa Street near the Jewish cemetery. There they shaved off my earlocks and fed me soup flavored with pork. For me—the son of a rabbi— these were spiritual calamities. A Gentile nurse ordered me to strip naked and gave me a bath. When she lathered me, her fingers tickled and I felt like both laughing and crying. It must be that I had fallen into the hands of the demonic Lilith dispatched by her husband, Asmodeus, to corrupt yeshiva students and drag them down into the abyss of defilement. Later when I saw myself in a mirror and caught a glimpse of my image minus earlocks and ritual garment, and wearing some kind of bathrobe I had never seen on a Jewish lad and slippers with wooden soles, I didn't recognize myself. I was no longer formed in the image of God.

I told myself that what had happened to me this day was no mere consequence of the war and German decrees but rather a punishment for my sins—for doubting my faith. I had already read on the sly the works of Mendele Mocher Sforim, Sholem Aleichem, and Peretz, as well as Yiddish or Hebrew translations of Tolstoy, Dostoevsky, Strindberg, Knut Hamsun. I had glanced into Dr. Shlomo Rubin's Hebrew translation of Spinoza's *Ethics* and had gone through a popular history of philosophy. I had taught myself to read German—so similar to Yiddish— and had read in the original the Brothers Grimm, Heine, and whatever I could lay my hands on. I had kept secrets from my parents.

Simultaneously with the German soldiers, Enlightenment had invaded Kroch-malna Street. I had heard of Darwin and was no longer sure that the miracles described in *The Assembly of Saints* had really occurred. Ever since war had broken out on the Ninth Day of Ab, the Yiddish newspaper was brought daily into our house and I read there about Zionism, socialism, and, following the Russian evacuation of Poland when the Russian censorship ceased, a series of articles about Rasputin.

Now revolution had taken over Russia, and the Czar had been deposed. The news was full of the fights and disputes among the Social Revolutionaries, the Mensheviks, the Bolsheviks, the Anarchists—new names and concepts had emerged. I absorbed all this with an eagerness that couldn't be sated. In the years between 1914 and 1917, I didn't see Shosha and I never once met her in the street, not her or Bashele or the other children. I had grown up and had studied one semester in the Sochaczów yeshiva and another semester in Radzymin. Father became the rabbi of a hamlet in Galicia and I had to start to earn my own livelihood.

But I never forgot Shosha. I dreamed of her at night. In my dreams she was both dead and alive. I played with her in a garden which was also a cemetery. Dead girls joined us there, wearing garments that were ornate shrouds. They danced in circles and sang songs. They swung, skated, occasionally hovered in the air. I strolled with Shosha in a forest of gigantic trees that reached the sky. The birds there were different from any I knew. They were as big as eagles, as colorful as parrots. They spoke Yiddish. From the thickets surrounding the garden, beasts with human faces showed themselves. Shosha was at home in this garden, and instead of my pointing out and explaining to her as I had done in the past, she revealed to me things I hadn't known and whispered secrets in my ear. Her hair had grown long enough to reach her loins, and her flesh glowed like mother-of-pearl. I always awoke from this dream with a sweet taste in my mouth and the impression that Shosha was no longer living.

During the years I wandered through the villages of Poland trying to support myself by teaching Hebrew, I seldom thought of Shosha when I was awake. I had fallen in love with a girl whose parents wouldn't permit me to go near her. I began to write in Hebrew and later switched to Yiddish, and the editors rejected everything I submitted to them. I couldn't seem to find a style that might create a literary domain for myself. Discouraged, I gave up literature and concentrated on philosophy, but what I was seeking I did not find there. I knew I must return to Warsaw, but again and again the forces that direct the fate of man hurled me back to the muddy villages. I often considered suicide. When finally I managed to get to the city to find work as a proofreader and a translator, and to be invited to the Writers' Club, first as a guest, then as a member, I felt like one recovered from a state of coma.

Years had gone by, and I didn't know where. Writers my age had achieved fame and immortality, but here I was, still a beginner. My father had died. His manuscripts, like mine, had been scattered and lost, though he had managed to publish one small book.

In Warsaw, I began an affair with Dora Stolnitz, a girl whose goal was to settle in Soviet Russia, the land of socialism. I learned later that she was a functionary of the Communist Party. She had been arrested several times and had spent months in Pawiak and other prisons. I was anti-Communist—anti all "isms"—but I lived in constant fear of being arrested and imprisoned because of my connection with this girl, whom I later began to dislike for her hollow slogans and bombastic clichés about the "happy future," the "bright tomorrow."

The Jewish streets in which I now wandered were close to Krochmalna, but I never went near it. I told myself that I imply had no occasion to go into that section of the city, but there had to be other reasons. I had heard that half the residents of the street had died in the typhus epidemics, of influenza, of starvation. Boys with whom I attended cheder had served in the Polish Army and been killed in the 1920 Polish-Bolshevik War. Later, Krochmalna Street had become a hotbed of Communism. There were always Communist demonstrations in the neighborhood. Young Communists draped red flags over telephone and streetcar wires—even on the windows of the police station. On the Place, an area between No. 9 and No. 13, and in the den where the thieves, pimps, and whores hung out, they now planned the dictatorship of Comrade Stalin. The police were forever conducting raids. This was no longer my street. No one would remember me or my family. When I thought of it, I had the strange feeling that my experience there constituted something removed from the world. I was in my twenties, but it seemed as if I were already an old man. Krochmalna Street was like a deep stratum of an archaeological dig which I would never uncover. At the same time, I recalled every house, courtyard, cheder, Hasidic studyhouse, store; every girl, street loafer, housewife—their voices, gestures, manners of speaking, their peculiarities.

I believed that the aim of literature was to prevent time from vanishing, but my own time I had thrown away. The twenties had passed and the thirties had come. Hitler was fast becoming the ruler of Germany. In Russia, the purges had commenced. In Poland, Pilsudski had created a military dictatorship. Years earlier, America had established an immigration quota. The consulates of nearly all nations refused to issue visas to Jews. I was stranded in a country squeezed between two mighty foes, stuck with a language and culture no one recognized outside of a small circle of Yiddishists and radicals. Thank God, I found friends among members of the Writers' Club and its periphery. The greatest of them all was Dr. Morris Feitelzohn, who was considered by many to be a genius.

CHAPTER TWO

1

Dr. Morris Feitelzohn wasn't widely known. His philosophical works, some written in German and some in Hebrew and Yiddish, were not translated into English or French. To this day I haven't found his name in any philosophical lexicon. His book *Spiritual Hormones* got bad reviews in Germany and in Switzerland. Dr. Feitelzohn was my friend, even though he was some twenty-five years older than I. He could have become famous if he hadn't squandered his energies. His erudition was monumental. For a time he was a lecturer at the University of Berne. He literally invented the Hebrew terminology for modern philosophy. If Feitelzohn was the dilettante one reviewer labeled him, his dilettantism was of the highest order. As a person, he was a brilliant conversationalist and he enjoyed fantastic success with women.

But this same Dr. Morris Feitelzohn often borrowed five zlotys from me at the Writers' Club. Nor did he have any luck with the Yiddish press in Warsaw, where articles that had been accepted were delayed for weeks while the editors changed and corrupted his style. They kept on finding defects in his work. There was much gossip about him. He was the son of a rabbi, but he had fled the house and became an agnostic. He divorced three wives and constantly changed lovers. Someone told me that Feitelzohn sold a sweetheart to a rich American tourist for five hundred dollars. The bearer of this tale called him a charlatan. But the one who slandered Feitelzohn most was Feitelzohn himself. He boasted of his adventures. I once observed that if one combined Arthur Schopenhauer, Oscar Wilde, and Solomon Maimon, one might end up with Morris Feitelzohn. I should have included the Kotzk rabbi, because in his own fashion Feitelzohn was a mystic and a Hasid.

Morris Feitelzohn was of medium height, broad-shouldered, with a square face, thick eyebrows that met over the bridge of his wide nose, and full lips from between which a cigar always jutted. In the Writers' Club they joked that he slept with the cigar in his mouth. His eyes were almost black, but occasionally I saw green glints in them. His dark hair had already begun to recede. Poor as he was, he wore English suits and expensive ties. In his conversation, he had praise for no one and derided world-famous figures. Yet severe critic that he was, he had detected talent in me, and when he told me this, it evoked in me a sense of friendship that bordered on idolization. It didn't prevent me from seeing his faults. At times, I dared to chide him, but he only said, "It won't do you any good. I'll die an adventurer."

Like all skirt-chasers, he had to report his successes. One time when I came to his furnished room, he pointed to the sofa and said, "If you only knew who lay here just yesterday, you'd faint."

"I soon will know," I said.

"How?"

"You will tell me."

"Ah, you're even more cynical than I am." And he told me.

Strangely, Morris Feitelzohn could speak with ardor about the wisdom found in *The Duty of the Hearts, The Path of the Righteous,* and in some of the Hasidic books. He had written a work about the cabala. In his own fashion, he loved the pious Jew and admired his faith and power to resist temptation. He once said to me, "I love the Jews even though I cannot stand them. No evolution could have created them. For me they are the only proof of God's existence."

One of Feitelzohn's admirers was Celia Chentshiner. Celia's husband, Haiml, was descended from the famous Reb Shmuel Zbitkower, the millionaire who during the Kosciusko uprising gave away a fortune to save the Jews of Praga from the Czar's Cossacks. Haiml's father, Reb Gabriel, owned houses in Warsaw and Lodz. Haiml was his only son. In his youth, Haiml had spent half of each day with a Talmud teacher at the Sochaczów studyhouse, and the other half trying to learn languages—Russian until 1915, German after the Germans occupied Warsaw, and Polish after 1919, when Poland was liberated. But he knew only one language—Yiddish. He liked to discuss Darwin, Marx, and Einstein with Feitelzohn. Haiml read about them all in Yiddish.

Haiml had never had to concern himself with a livelihood. He was a runt of a man and frail. I sometimes thought there wasn't a trade or business for which he would have been suited. Even drinking tea didn't come easy to him. He lacked the dexterity to cut a slice of lemon and Celia had to do this for him. Haiml was capable only of a childlike love for his father and for his wife. His mother was no longer living. Reb Gabriel had a second wife, whose name I didn't dare mention before Haiml. I asked him only once about his stepmother. He turned pale, put his little hand over my mouth, and exclaimed, "Don't talk! Don't talk! Don't talk! My mother is alive!"

Celia was short too, but taller than Haiml. She was related to him on his mother's side. An orphan, she had been raised in Reb Gabriel's house. Haiml fell in love with her while he was still in cheder. When Haiml didn't want to eat, Celia fed him. When he was studying Russian, German, and Polish, Celia studied with him, and while he learned none of these languages, she did. Their marriage took place when Haiml's mother lay on her deathbed.

By the time I met this couple, they were in their late thirties. Haiml looked like a cheder boy who had been dressed in a man's suit, stiff collar, and tie. He spoke in a piping voice, made childish gestures, laughed with a shriek, and when things didn't go his way he burst out crying. He had dark eyes, a small nose, and a wide mouth full of brackish teeth. The black ruff around his bald head hung down in tufts. He was afraid of barbers and Celia cut his hair. She also trimmed his nails. Celia considered herself an atheist, but traces of her Hasidic upbringing lingered. She chose dresses with long sleeves and high collars. She wore her long dark hair in an unfashionable bun. She was pale, with brown eyes, a straight nose, thin lips, and she moved with the lightness of a girl. Haiml used to call her "my empress." Celia had borne Haiml a daughter, who died at the age of two, and Feitelzohn once told her that the child's death contained a measure of divine logic, since Celia already had a child—Haiml. To Celia and Haiml, Feitelzohn represented the big world and European culture. Feitelzohn did not need to suffer want. They were always proposing that he move in with them in their big apartment on Zlota Street, but Feitelzohn refused.

He told me, "All my foibles and aberrations stem from my urge to be absolutely free. This alleged freedom has transformed me into a slave."

2

Because Feitelzohn praised me, the Chentshiners often invited me to dinner, lunch, or for a glass of tea. When Feitelzohn was present, no one else could speak. We were all content to listen. He had traveled throughout the world. He knew practically every important Jewish personality, as well as many non-Jewish scholars, writers, and humanists. Haiml used to say that he was a living encyclopedia. From time to time, Feitelzohn gave lectures in the Writers' Club in Warsaw and in the provinces, and also on short trips he made abroad. On those occasions, Haiml, Celia, and I had a chance to talk among ourselves. Haiml liked opera and was interested in art. He attended exhibitions and bought paintings. Cubism and expressionism had been in fashion many years, but Haiml liked pastoral landscapes of woods, meadows, streams, and huts half hidden behind trees, where, as he put it, one could hide from Hitler, who was threatening to invade Poland. I myself had fantasies about a house in the woods or on an island where I would be safe from Nazis.

Celia's passion was literature. She bought and read nearly every new book that came out in Polish and Yiddish, as well as translations from other languages, and she possessed a sharp critical taste. I often wondered how this woman who had had no formal education could so accurately appraise not only belles lettres but also scientific works. I paid attention to her opinions regarding my writing; invariably they were correct, tactful, and clever.

One time Celia invited me to the apartment on an evening when Haiml was away at a conference of the Poale Zion. We talked so long she revealed a secret to me: she was having an affair with Morris Feitelzohn. That evening I realized that Celia had the same need to confess as everyone else. She was quite frank about the fact that when it came to love, Haiml was as inexpert as a child. He needed a mother, not a wife, while she was hot-blooded. She said, "I like gentleness, but not in bed."

This remark coming from a woman who dressed and behaved so conservatively and who watched her every word astounded me more than the fact that she was unfaithful to Haiml. Our conversation became nakedly intimate. The essence of what she said was that literature, theater, music, even accounts in the newspapers roused her erotically, yet at the same time her nature was such that she could give herself only to someone to whom she looked up. For a man to utter some foolishness or demonstrate weakness was enough to repel her.

She said, "I could be happy with Feitelzohn, but he's the worst liar I've ever met. He has hoodwinked me so many times that I've lost all respect for myself for still believing him once in a while. He possesses hypnotic powers. He could be the Mesmer or Svengali of our time. If you're convinced that you know him, you're only deluding yourself. Each time I tell myself that the man can no longer surprise me, I get a new shock. Do you know that Morris is superstitious to the point of absurdity? He is terrified of black cats. When he is on his way to a lecture and meets someone holding an empty vessel, he runs back. He carries around all kinds of amulets. When he sneezes he pulls his ear. There are certain words you can't use in his presence. Did you ever try to discuss death with him? He has more idiosyncrasies than a pomegranate has seeds. He considers all women witches. He goes to fortune-tellers who for a zloty tell him he will take a long trip and meet a dark woman. And his contradictions! He breaks every law of the Shulchan Aruch, yet at the same time he preaches Jewishness. He has a wife whom he's never divorced and a daughter he hasn't seen in years. When his mother died he didn't go to her funeral."

I remember that evening and the things Celia said to me, because this was the beginning of our intimacy. I suspected that she had decided to revenge herself upon Feitelzohn through me for his affairs with other women. There was a minute when I was ready to embrace her and whisper those smooth lies that come to the lips on such occasions. But I was sure that Feitelzohn possessed clairvoyant powers. Often when I was about to say something, he plucked the words right out of my mouth. I switched the conversation with Celia to a different topic and her eyes seemed to ask, "You're scared, eh? Yes, I understand."

A while later the doorbell rang. It was Haiml. The conference had been canceled because a quorum wasn't present. Winter had set in and Haiml wore a fur coat, fur boots, and a fur hat resembling a rabbinical *shtreimel*. He looked so funny I barely kept from laughing.

Celia said, "Haiml, our young friend here is as bashful as if he had left the yeshiva only yesterday. I tried to seduce him but he wouldn't cooperate."

"What is there to be bashful about?" Haiml said. "We're all created from the same protoplasm, we all feel the same urges. Don't you find Celia attractive?"

"Both attractive and intelligent."

"So what's the problem? You may kiss her."

"Come here, yeshiva boy!" Celia said, and she gave me a mighty kiss. She said, "He writes like a grown-up but he's still a child. Truly a mystery." After a while she added, "I have a name for him—Tsutsik. That's what I'll call him from now on."

3

Dr. Morris Feitelzohn had spent the years between 1920 and 1926 in America, where he had been on the staff of a Yiddish newspaper in New York and had given courses at some local college. I never found out exactly why he left the Golden Land. Each time I questioned him about it, he gave me a different answer. He said that he couldn't stand the New York climate because he suffered there from hay fever, rose fever, and other allergies. Or he said that he couldn't bear American materialism and reverence for the dollar. He hinted at romantic entanglelments. I had heard that the writers at the newspaper conspired against him and got him fired. Also, he had problems at the college where he lectured. In his conversations with me, he often referred to the Yiddish theater in New York, to the Café Royal where the Yiddish intellectuals of the city gathered, and to such Zionist leaders there as Stephen Wise, Louis Lipsky, and Shemaryahu Levin.

In spite of his frequently expressed antipathy toward America and Americans, Morris Feitelzohn never severed his connections with them. He was a friend of the director of HIAS in Warsaw and was known at the American consulate. From time to time, tourists who had either known Feitelzohn in New York or to whom one of his American friends had recommended him came to Poland and Feitelzohn brought them up to the Writers' Club and played the role of guide. He assured me he never took any money from these Americans, but I knew that he went with them to first-class restaurants, to the theater, to museums, and to concerts, and they often left him ties and other gifts. He confided to me that one of the higher officials at the Warsaw American consulate could be bribed to help obtain visas for alleged rabbis, professors, and bogus relatives beyond the quota. The way of transmitting the bribe was to play poker and allow the official to win a large amount. The intermediary was a foreign correspondent in Warsaw who took a percentage for himself. The fact that despite all these contacts Feitelzohn remained a pauper who had to borrow a few zlotys from a poor slob like me seemed proof that he himself was basically honest.

For me that winter in the 1930's was one of the hardest I had known since I left my parents' house. The literary magazine where I read proof two days a week was on the verge of folding. The publisher who printed my translations was facing bankruptcy. I had sublet a room from a family who now wanted to be rid of me. More than once when people telephoned me they were told that I was out, even though I was right there in my room. In order to go to the bathroom I had to walk through the living room, and the door to this room was often locked at night. I had been planning to move for weeks but hadn't found a room for the little rent I could pay. I was still involved with Dora Stolnitz—I didn't want to marry her, yet wasn't willing to let go.

When I met Dora she had said that she considered marriage a vestige of religious fanaticism. How could you sign a contract for lifelong love? Only capitalists and clerics were dedicated to perpetuating such a hypocritical institution. Although I had never been a leftist, in this I concurred with her. Everything I saw and read bore witness to the fact that modern man didn't take family responsibility seriously. Dora's father, a widower, had gone bankrupt in Warsaw and, to avoid imprisonment, had fled to France with a married woman. Dora had a sister who lived with a journalist, a married man who used to frequent the Writers' Club. Through him I came to know Dora. But in the very first months of our affair she began to insist that we marry. She said she wanted this for the sake of some aunt, a sister of her deceased mother, who was a pious woman.

On that winter day I looked for a room from ten in the morning until nightfall. The rooms I liked cost too much. Others were too small or stank of insecticide and bedbugs. The truth was that the way my affairs were going I couldn't afford even a cheap room. Around five o'clock, I headed for the Writers' Club. It was warm there and I could have a meal on credit. Going to the club gave me a feeling of shame. What kind of writer was I? I hadn't published a single book. It was a cold, wet day. Around evening, snow began to fall. I walked along Leszno Street, shivering under my thin coat, and imagined I had written a work that would startle the world. But what could startle the world? No crime, no misery, no sexual perversion, no madness. Twenty million people had perished in the Great War, and here the world was preparing for another conflagration. What could I write about that wasn't already known? A new style? Every experiment with words turned quickly into a collection of mannerisms.

I opened the door to the club and saw Morris Feitelzohn with an American couple. The man was short and stout, with a wide, ruddy face, a headful of hair white as foam, and a bulging belly. He wore a light-colored coat—a shade of yellow not seen in Poland. The woman was no taller, but young, slim, and dressed in a short fur coat I guessed to be sable. She wore a black velvet beret over her red hair. I wasn't in a mood to meet the Americans and tried to avoid them, but Feitelzohn had already seen me and called out, "Tsutsik, where are you going?"

He had never called me Tsutsik before—obviously he had talked with Celia. I stopped, my eyes bleary from the cold. I tried to dry my palms on the soaked tails of my overcoat.

Feitelzohn said, "Where are you running? I want you to meet my American friends. This is Mr. Sam Dreiman and this is Betty Slonim, an actress. This young man is a writer."

Sam Dreiman's face seemed to have been pasted together from clay. He had a broad nose, thick lips, high cheekbones, and small, boring eyes beneath thick white brows. His tie was yellow, red, and gold, pierced with a diamond stickpin. He held a cigar between two fingers and spoke in a loud, grating voice. "Tsutsik?" he bellowed. "What kind of name is that? A pet name, what?"

Betty Slonim might have had the figure of a schoolgirl, but behind the makeup her face revealed maturity. She had hollow cheeks, a narrow chin, and eyes that by the dim glow of the overhead lamps seemed to be yellowish. She reminded me of trapeze artists in the circus. Her voice was that of a boy.

Sam Dreiman shouted at me as if I were deaf. "You write for the papers, eh?"

"For magazines, from time to time."

"What's the difference? In this world we need everything. On the ship I met a man and we played a little pinochle—that's a kind of card game. We got to talking and I asked him, 'What do you do?' and he told me he was going to Africa to capture lions and other wild animals for the zoos in the States. He had a group of hunters with him, and cages, nets, and the devil knows what. This lady, Betty Slonim, is a great actress who has come to Poland to appear in the Yiddish theater. If you have a play, we can do business immediately—"

"Sam, don't talk nonsense," Betty Slonim interrupted him.

"A young man like this could have just the play you're looking for. But before we get down to business, let's first go somewhere for a bite. Come along, young man. What's your real name?"

"Aaron Greidinger."

"Aaron what? That's a hard name. In America we don't go for long European names. There, time is money. A Russian came into our office and his name was Sergei Ivanovich Metropolitansky. You could get asthma just from trying to pronounce a name like that. We called him Met, and that's how it stuck. He's a plumber, a specialist. He puts an ear to a pipe in the basement and he knows what's going on on the top floor. I didn't have any lunch today, and I'm hungry as a dog.''

"You can get a bite here," Feitelzohn said, pointing to the lunch counter.

"I'll tell you something. I never trust a writers' restaurant. I ordered dinner at the Café Royal and they gave me a steak as tough as leather. I noticed two restaurants down the street and they both looked pretty good to me. Come, young man, come along with us. May I call you Tsutsik?''

"Yes, of course. But I'm not hungry. I ate not long ago," I lied.

"What did you eat? You don't look like somebody who's overeaten. We'll have a drink of whiskey, too—maybe even champagne.''

"Really, I'm not—''

"Don't be so stubborn," Feitelzohn interjected. "Come with us. I think you told me you'd written a play?" he went on, changing his tone.

"I only have the first act and it's just a first draft.''

"What kind of play is it?" Betty Slonim asked.

I had stopped blushing when a woman addressed me, but now I felt the blood rush to my face. "Oh, it's not for the theater.''

"Not for the theater?" Sam Dreiman shouted. "For who is it then—King Tut?''

"It wouldn't draw an audience.''

"What's the subject?" Feitelzohn asked.

"The Maiden from Ludmir. She was a girl who wanted to live like a man. She studied the Torah, wore ritual fringes, a prayer shawl, and even put on phylacteries. She became a rabbi and held court for Hasidim. She covered her face with a veil and preached the Torah.''

"If it's well written, it's exactly what I'm looking for," Betty Slonim said. "Can I see the first act?''

"Something will come of this meeting," Feitelzohn observed as if to himself. "Come along; we'll eat, drink, and talk business, as they say in America.''

"Yes, come, young man!" Sam Dreiman shouted. "Keep your wits about you and you'll be swimming in gravy.''

4

We sat in Gertner's Restaurant and Sam Dreiman spoke of his and Betty Slonim's plans. He had lost over a million dollars in the Wall Street crash, he said, but only on paper. Sooner or later the stocks would rise again. The economy in Uncle Sam's land was healthy. A good many of the stocks still paid dividends. Besides, he owned houses and was a partner in a factory. The manager was his brother's grandson, Bill, a lawyer. He himself was far from being a young man, so what need was there to worry? God had blessed him with a great love in his late years—he indicated Betty—and what he wanted was to enjoy himself and to provide her with enjoyment. She was a marvelous actress, but the hams on Second Avenue were jealous of her talent. They wouldn't even accept her in the Hebrew Actors Union, but the few times she managed to perform in spite of them, her reviews were sensational—not only from the Yiddish but from the English press as well. She could have appeared on Broadway, but she preferred to act in Yiddish. That was the language that really brought out her talent. Money was no problem. He would rent a theater for her here in Warsaw. The main thing was to find a play that suited her. Betty required dramatic roles. Her first choice was tragedy. She was no comedienne and despised the "dance, song, and strut" of the Yiddish theater in America.

He turned to me. "If you come up with the right goods, young man, I'll give you a five-hundred-dollar advance. If the play goes well, you'll get royalties. If it becomes a hit in Warsaw, I'll take it over to America. The first act is ready, you say? Have you started the second? Betty, you talk to him. You know better what to ask."

Betty was about to speak but Feitelzohn beat her to it: "Aaron, you'll be a millionaire. You'll become my patron and my publisher. Don't forget that I was the broker who brought it all about."

"If it comes to anything, you'll get your broker's fee from *me!*" Sam Dreiman bellowed. Each time he spoke he spread his hands, and I noticed a big diamond ring on his finger. He also wore a gold-banded wristwatch and jeweled studs.

Now that Betty had taken off her fur coat and sat there in a sleeveless black dress, I could see how thin she was. She had an Adam's apple like a boy's; her arms were like sticks. Warsaw was already talking about how healthy and fashionable it was to be thin, but this Betty seemed to me emaciated. It had become the style for Warsaw women to let their nails grow and cover them with red polish, but Betty's fingernails were uncolored and it was obvious that she bit them. Hair cut *à la garçon* was passé, but Betty still wore hers short. She barely tasted the food before her, and between bites she puffed on a cigarette. She wore a huge diamond bracelet on her left wrist and around her throat a necklace with smaller diamonds.

She leaned toward me and asked, "When did this girl live? In what century?"

"In the nineteenth. She died only a short while ago in Jerusalem. She may have been a hundred years old."

"I never heard of her. Was she that pious?"

"Yes, very pious. Many Hasidim felt that she had been possessed by the dybbuk of an ancient rabbi who uttered the Torah through her lips."

"What else did she do? Is there any action in this play?"

"Very little."

"A drama has to have action. The heroine can't just spout Torah through three or four acts. Something has to happen. Did she have a husband?"

"If I'm not mistaken, she married later on, but it seems she divorced her husband."

"Why don't you write in an affair for her? If a woman like that fell in love, it could create a strong conflict."

"Yes, that's an idea worth considering."

"Have her fall in love with a non-Jew, a Christian."

"A Christian? That couldn't be."

"Why not? Love knows no restrictions. Suppose she were to get sick and go to a Christian doctor. A love might very well develop between them."

"Why couldn't she fall in love with one of her own kind?" Feitelzohn asked. "I'm sure that the Hasidim who sat around her table and swallowed her leavings and listened to her Torah were all mad about her."

"Absolutely!" Sam Dreiman roared. "If I was one of those Hasidim and didn't have my Betty—may she outlive me—I would be mad about her myself! I admit to being an ignoramus, but I love educated women! Betty studied at the Gymnasium. She reads books by the hundreds. She performed in Stanislavsky's theater. Tell them, Betty, who you played with. Let them know who you are!"

Betty shook her head. "There's nothing to tell. I did perform in Russia in Yiddish and in Russian too, but it's just my luck that even before I got going, a whole network of intrigue formed around me. I'll never know why. I don't want power, I'm not rich, I've never tried to steal anyone's husband or lover. The men were attentive to me at first, but when I kept them at a distance, they became my enemies overnight. The women were all ready to drown me in a spoonful of warm water, as the saying goes. That's how it was in Russia and that's how it was in America, and it will be the same here, too—unless there's no competition to conspire against me."

"If anyone dares say a word against my Betty, I'll poke his eyes out!" Sam Dreiman shouted. "Here, they'll kiss your feet!"

"I don't want anyone to kiss my feet. All I want is to be left alone so that I can play with peace of mind."

"You'll play, Betty darling, and the whole world will learn how great you are. They kept all the great ones down. You think Sarah Bernhardt's path was strewn with roses? Well, and what about the others? That one from Italy—whatever her name was. And Isadora Duncan, you think she didn't have trouble? Even Pavlova had it. When people sense the presence of a talent they turn into wolves. I once read in the paper—I forget the writer's name—about Rachel and how the anti-Semites in Paris tried to push her out of—"

"Sam, I want to talk about the play with the young man."

"Talk, darling. I like this play even before I've read it. I feel it was made for you. I bet a dybbuk sits inside you too, Betty darling." He turned to me. "At times when she begins to yell at me, she acts possessed herself—"

"Will you stop or not? Stop it."

"I'll stop. I'll only say one thing more to this young man. I'll give you a few hundred dollars so you can work without worrying where your next meal is coming from. Just make the play so that things happen. Let her fall in love with a doctor or a Hasid or a dogcatcher, you name it. The main thing is, the audience should be curious to know what's going to happen next. I'm no writer, but I would have her get pregnant and—"

"Sam, if you don't stop talking like a clown, I'm leaving."

"So be it. You won't hear another peep from me till we go home."

"I wanted to say something, but he's mixed me up to the point that I hardly know where I am," Betty complained. "Oh, yes—there has to be action. But you're the writer, not I."

"Really, I'm no playwright. I started to write the thing for myself. I wanted to show the tragedy of the intellectual woman, particularly among Jews who—"

"I don't consider myself an intellectual but that is *my* tragedy. Why do you think they conspired against me? Because I had no patience with their gossip, intrigues, and stupidity. Ever since childhood I've been like a foreign element around women. My own sisters didn't understand me. My mother looked at me like a hen that had sat on a duck's egg and hatched a creature drawn to the water. My father was a scholar—a Hasid, a follower of the Husiatiner rabbi—and the Bolsheviks shot him. Why? He was rich once, but the war had ruined him. People fabricated stories and made false accusations against him. My whole family stayed on in Russia, but I couldn't remain among the murderers of my father. The truth is that the whole world is full of evildoers."

"Bettyle, stop talking like that. If I had a million for every good person, Rockefeller would be heating my stove."

"You're the first pessimistic woman I've ever met," Feitelzohn observed. "Pessimism is usually a male trait. I can envision a woman with masculine characteristics and gifts—a female Mozart, say, or even an Edison. But a female Schopenhauer is beyond the stretch of imagination. Blind optimism is essential to the concept of woman. All of a sudden, to hear such words from a female!"

"Maybe I'm not a woman?"

"That's for me to decide!" Sam shouted. "You are one hundred percent a woman—no, not one hundred percent, but a thousand! I've had many women in my life, but what she is—"

"Sam!"

"Well, I'll shut up. Start on the play first thing tomorrow, young man, and don't worry about the money. Betty sweetheart, stop smoking so much. You're on your third pack today."

"Sam, mind your own business."

5

By the time Feitelzohn and I said goodbye to Sam Dreiman and Betty, it was midnight. While shaking hands, Betty squeezed my palm once and then again. She tilted her face toward mine and I caught a whiff of liquor and tobacco. Betty had eaten little, but she had finished several glasses of cognac. She and Sam were staying at the Hotel Bristol and they took a taxi there. Feitelzohn had a room on Dluga Street, but he walked me to Nowolipki Street, where Dora Stolnitz lived. He knew about my affairs. He seldom went to bed before two.

He took my arm and said, "My boy, you caught Betty's eye for sure—hoo hah! If that play of yours has anything to it, you're a made man. Sam Dreiman is loaded and he's crazy about Betty. Get out your manuscript and pack it with all the love and sex it can take."

"I don't want to turn it into a piece of trash."

"Don't be an ass. Theater is trash by definition. There's no such thing as a sustaining literary play. Literature must consist of words, just as music must consist of sounds. Once you perform the words on stage or even recite them, they're already secondhand goods."

"The audiences won't come."

"They'll come, they'll come. A guy like Sam Dreiman would think nothing of bribing critics. He may even bribe audiences. The main thing is, don't spare the schmaltz. Today's Jews like three things—sex, Torah, and revolution, all mixed together. Give them those and they'll raise you to the skies. Maybe you have a zloty?"

"Two."

"Well, you're already acting like a millionaire. What do you think about Betty?"

"She seems to be suffering from a persecution complex."

"Probably a lousy actress, too. But I'm having strange fantasies lately. We spoke of dybbuks today—I've been possessed by a dybbuk. He tells me to found an institute of pure hedonism."

"Isn't life itself such an institute?"

"Yes and no. All people are hedonists, yes. From cradle to grave, man thinks only of pleasure. What do the pious want? Pleasure in the other world. And what do ascetics want? Spiritual pleasure or whatever. I go even further. For me, pleasure takes in not only life but the whole universe. Spinoza says that God has two attributes known to us—thought and extension. I say that God is pleasure. If pleasure is an attribute, then it must consist of infinite modes. This would mean that there are myriads of unknown pleasures still to be discovered. Of course, if God happens to have an attribute of evil, woe to us. Maybe He isn't so almighty after all and needs our cooperation. My dybbuk tells me that since we are all parts of Him and since men are the greatest egotists among all creatures—Spinoza says that man's love of himself is God's love for man—the pursuit of pleasure is man's only goal. If he fails here, he must fail in everything else."

"Doesn't your dybbuk know that man has already failed? Isn't the Great War proof enough?"

"It may be proof to me, but not to my dybbuk. He tells me that God suffers from a kind of divine amnesia that made Him lose the purpose of His creation. My dybbuk suspects that God tried to do too much in too short an eternity. He has lost both criterion and control and is badly in need of help."

"Really, you are joking."

"Of course I'm joking, but in some foolish way I am also serious. I see Him as a very sick God, so bewildered by His galaxies and the multitude of laws He established that He doesn't know what He aimed for to start with. Sometimes I look into my own scribblings and discover that I began one kind of work and it turned out to be the opposite of what I intended. Since we are supposed to have been formed in His image, why couldn't such a thing have happened to Him?"

"So you are going to refresh His memory. Is this the topic of your next article?"

"It could be, but these idiotic editors will not take anything from me. Lately they send everything back. They don't even bother to read it. By the way, your memory must also be refreshed. You promised me two zlotys."

"You're right. Here they are. I'm sorry."

"Thank you. Please don't laugh at me. First of all, this crazy Sam gave me too much to drink. Second, after midnight I let go of what is left of my mind. I am not responsible for anything I babble or even think. Since I cannot sleep

I must dream with open eyes. Perhaps like me He suffers from insomnia. As a matter of fact, the Good Book tells us He doesn't doze or sleep but watches over the children of Israel. What a watchman! Good night.''

"Good night. It was a great pleasure. Thank you."

"Try to write this lousy play. I have lost respect for everything, but I absolutely worship money. If we ever return to idolatry, my temple will be a bank. Here you are.''

At Nowolipki Street, Feitelzohn held out a warm hand to me and headed home. I rang and the janitor let me in. All the windows in the courtyard were dark but for one on the third floor. For me, spending the night at Dora's was both a danger (they might raid the apartment and find illegal literature) and a humiliation (we had broken up). She was about to smuggle herself into Russia to take a course in propaganda. Although she denied it heatedly, almost every Communist who crossed the border from Poland was arrested by the Soviets— they were accused of espionage, sabotage, and Trotskyism. More than once I warned her that such a trip was sure suicide, but she said, "Those who have been arrested deserved it richly. Fascists, social Fascists, and all the other capitalist lackeys should be liquidated, the quicker the better."

"Was Hertzke Goldshlag a Fascist? Was Berel Guttman a Fascist? Was your friend Irka a Fascist?" I demanded.

"Innocent people aren't jailed in the Soviet Union! That's done in Warsaw, in Rome, and in New York.''

No facts or arguments would convince her. She had hypnotized others and was herself under the spell. In my mind I could see her cross the border at Nieświez, fall to the ground to kiss the soil of the land of socialism, and promptly be dragged off to jail by the Red guards. There she would sit among dozens like her—hungry and thirsty beside a bucket of slops—and keep on asking herself, "Is this possible? What was my crime? I who gave my best years to the socialist ideal.''

I walked slowly. I had vowed solemnly not to come here again, but I needed her body. I knew that we would be parting forever. Perhaps she was perplexed by doubts herself. Even the most pious experience occasional heretical thoughts. I stopped for a moment on the dark stairs and indulged in a brief introspection. What if I should be arrested with her this night? What kind of justification could I offer myself? Why, as the saying goes, did I crawl with a healthy head to a sickbed? Well, and should I try to refashion my play to suit Betty Slonim's whims? And what was it Feitelzohn actually wanted? How strange, but during the last few months I heard time and again at the Writers' Club that someone was arranging an orgy. There was a table at the club that young writers had dubbed the "Table of the Impotent." Each night after the theater and movies, the older writers—the classicists, newspaper editors, old journalists, and their ladies—gathered there to discuss politics, Jewish topics, and the eroticism that had come into fashion with Freud and the sexual upheavals in Russia, Germany, and the whole Western world. A famous actor, Fritz Bander, had come to Poland from Germany. The Nazi and conservative newspapers had for a time waged a campaign against Bander for corrupting the German language (''Moischeling,'' they called it), for making insulting remarks about Ludendorff, and for seducing a German aristocratic young lady and driving her to suicide. Bander, a Galician Jew, fell into such a rage from these attacks, as well as from the poor reviews he had been receiving, that he abandoned Berlin for Warsaw. He wanted to do penance and return to the Yiddish theater. He had brought along his Christian sweetheart, Gretel, the wife of a German film director. Her husband had challenged Bander to a duel and threatened him with a gun. Bander now sat every night with his sweetheart at the Table of the Impotent and told jokes in Galician-accented Yiddish. He had been notorious in Berlin for his sexual prowess. In the Romanisches Café on Grenadierstrasse queer tales were told of his adventures. It was the joke at the Warsaw Writers' Club that Bander's boastings had sparked the ambitions of the old, sick writer, Roshbaum, to become another Casanova.

Before knocking on Dora's door, I stopped to listen. Maybe a meeting of the District Committee was going on inside? Maybe the police were conducting a raid? In this compromised apartment, anything was possible. But no, all was quiet. I knocked three times—a signal between Dora and me—and waited. Soon I heard her footsteps. I never learned why there was no telephone in the apartment, but guessed it was so that the police couldn't tap the wire.

Dora was small, broad in the hips and with a huge bosom. She had a crooked nose. Her big, fluttering eyes were her only attractive feature. They reflected a blend of cunning and the solemnity of one who has assumed the mission of saving mankind. She stood at the door now in her nightgown, with a cigarette stuck between her lips. "I thought you'd left Warsaw," she said.

"Where to? Without saying goodbye?"

"I wouldn't put anything past you."

6

Although a Communist is forbidden to reveal Party secrets to a member of the enemy class, Dora told me that everything was ready for her departure. It was a matter of a few days. She had already sold pieces of her furniture to neighbors. A Party functionary was scheduled to take over the apartment. I had stored a bundle of manuscripts with her and she reminded me that I must take them away when I left in the morning. Although I had eaten a heavy dinner, Dora insisted I join her for rolls with marinated herring and tea.

"You brought this situation about yourself," she said accusingly. "If we had lived together like a normal couple, I wouldn't be going away. The Party doesn't compel a husband and wife to part, especially when there is a child. We could have had a couple of children by now."

"And who would support them? Comrade Stalin? I've been left without work. I owe two months' rent."

"Our children wouldn't have starved. Well, it's foolish and too late for such talk. You'll have your children with someone else."

"I don't want children with anyone," I said.

"The typical degenerate psychology of capitalist stooges. It's the collapse of the West, the end of civilization. There's nothing left but to lament the catastrophe. However, Mussolini and Hitler will bring order. Mother Rachel will rise from her grave and lead her children back to Zion. Mahatma Gandhi and his goat will triumph over English imperialism."

"Dora—enough!"

"Come to bed. This may well be the last time for us."

The wire springs of the bed had a depression in the middle and we couldn't lie apart even if we wanted to. We rolled toward each other and listened in on our own desire. Her flesh was plump, smooth, warm. Her enormous breasts amazed me each time we were together—how could she carry around such a load? She pressed her plump knees against mine and complained that I was hurting her. Our souls (or whatever they may be called) were battered and at odds, but our bodies had remained friendly. I had learned to curb my lust. We indulged in some foreplay, some during-play, and sometimes even some afterplay.

Dora put a hand on my loin. "Do you have my replacement standing by yet?"

"Well, and what about you?"

"There'll be so much to do there, I won't have time to think of such things. It's a hard course. It's not so easy to adjust to new circumstances. To me love is no game. I have to respect the person first, believe in him, have faith in his thoughts and character."

"A Russky with all these qualities is awaiting you there."

"Look who's talking! You were always ready to trade me for the first available yenta."

We kissed and bickered. I listed all her former lovers while she counted off all those with whom I might have betrayed her. "You don't even know the meaning of the word faithful!" she said. She kissed and bit me. We went to sleep sated and I woke up with lust renewed.

Dora spoke in a crooning chant, "I'll never forget you, never! My last thoughts on my deathbed will be of you, you reprobate!"

"Dora, I'm worried about you."

"What are you worried about, you lousy egotist?"

"Your Comrade Stalin is a madman."

"You're not even worthy to mention his name. Put your arms around me! It's better to die in a free land than to live among Fascist dogs."

"Will you write me?"

"You don't deserve it, but my first letter will be to you."

I dozed off again, and I was in Warsaw and in Moscow at the same time. I came to a square filled with graves. I knocked on a door and a huge Russian answered. He was mother-naked and uncircumcised. I asked for Dora and he replied, "Rotting in Siberia." A wild party was going on inside. Men played accordions, guitars, balalaikas; nude women danced. A yellow dog came out from the crowd and I recognized her—Jolka, who belonged to the Soltys of Miedzeszyn. But Jolka had died. What was she doing in Moscow? Oh, these trivial dreams, they have no meaning whatsoever, I said in my dream.

I opened my eyes and beyond the window a murky dawn seemed to be pondering its eternal return. Dora was banging pots in the kitchen. She drew water from the tap and mumbled a song about Charlie Chaplin. I lay still, dazed by the world and its absurdities. She appeared in the doorway. "I'm making your breakfast."

"How is it outside?"

"Snowing."

I washed at the kitchen sink. The water was icy.

Dora said, "A pair of your drawers was knocking around here. I washed them."

"Well, thank you."

"Put them on. And don't forget to take your Fascist manuscripts."

She brought me the drawers and from under the bed pulled a bundle of manuscripts tied with a string.

While I ate, Dora preached: "It's never too late to accept the truth. Spit on all this slime and come with me. Stop writing about those rabbis and spirits and see what the real world looks like. Everything here is corrupt. Over there life is beginning."

"It's corrupt all over."

"Is that your world concept? This could be our last breakfast together. Would you happen to have three zlotys?"

I counted out three zlotys and gave them to her. It left me with three zlotys and change. The magazine and the publisher owed me some money, but it was impossible to get so much as a groschen out of them. My only hope was an advance from Sam Dreiman. I said goodbye to Dora and promised to come back that evening. I took the bundle of manuscripts and went out into the cold courtyard. A dry snow was falling. On the top of the garbage bin a cat stood poised. She fixed her gooseberry-green eyes on me and meowed. Was she hungry? Forgive me, pussy, I have nothing for you. Dun the malefactor who created you. I went out the gate. There was an infirmary in the building, where the sick came to buy chits to see doctors. Some elderly women wrapped in shawls entered the gate. I imagined that they smelled of toothache and iodine. They spoke at the same time, each about her own sickness. The clouds hovered low. An icy wind blew. I headed for the street and my furnished room. It was just big enough to hold the bed and a single chair and almost as cold as outside. I opened the bundle of manuscripts and to my amazement saw the beginning of a second act of my play. Had Providence ordained this? Somewhere causality and purpose were firmly bonded. I began to read. The Ludmir Maiden bewailed the fact that God had granted all the favors to men and only the leavings to women—the laws connected with childbirth, ablutions in the mikvah, the lighting of the Sabbath candles. She accused Moses of being antifeminist and blamed the evils of the world upon the fact that God was a male. Should I add love and sex to this play? Whom should she love—a doctor, a Cossack? She could be a lesbian, but the Warsaw Jews weren't ready for this theme. Suddenly I had an idea: she would fall in love with the dybbuk who possessed her. The dybbuk was a man— I'd make him a musician, a cynic, a lecher, an atheist. She would talk in his voice as well as her own. There was a chance that Betty Slonim could play this. She would portray a split personality. She would supposedly wed the dybbuk inside her; he would mistreat her, disappoint her, and she would demand a divorce.

I felt an urge to tell Betty Slonim my idea that very moment. I knew she was staying at the Hotel Bristol, but I couldn't bring myself to drop in on a lady at a hotel unexpectedly. I lacked even the courage to telephone her. I decided to go to the Writers' Club. Feitelzohn might be there and I could describe my plot to him. Although I was tired, a spark of interest in Betty Slonim kindled in me. I had already indulged in a fantasy in which we enjoyed fame together— she as an actress, and I as a playwright. But Feitelzohn wasn't at the club. In the first room two unemployed journalists played chess and I stopped for a while to look on. The one who was winning—Pinie Machtei, a little man who had only one leg—swayed over the chess board, pulled at his goatee, and sang a Russian song:

> *"Happy or not happy*
> *As long as there is vodka and wine*
> *Let us not whine."*

He said to me, "You may look, but don't kibitz."

He had put his knight in such a situation that his opponent, Zorach Leibkes, had to give up his queen for a castle. If not, he would have been checkmated in two moves. Zorach Leibkes was a temporary replacement in the Yiddish press when the proofreaders were on vacation. He was small and round like a barrel. He too swayed, and he was saying, "Machtei, stop singing. Your castle is nothing but an idiot. I'm afraid of him as much as I'm afraid of last year's frost. You have been a botcher and a botcher you'll remain until the tenth generation."

"Where does the queen go?" Machtei asked.

"She will go. She will go. Don't worry your silly head over it. Once she goes she will shatter your pieces to smithereens."

I went into the main room. There were only three writers there. At a small table sat Shloimele, a folk-poet who signed his poems only with his first name. He was writing a poem in a ledger like those used in grocery stores. He was known to write in almost microscopic letters that only he could decipher. While he wrote, he chirped a monotonous tune. At another table sat Daniel Liptzin, nicknamed the "Messiah." In 1905 he had taken part in the revolution against the Czar and was sent to Siberia. But there he became religious and began to write mystic stories. Nahum Zelikowitz—tall, thin, black like a gypsy, a pipe in his mouth—was pacing back and forth. He belonged to a minority in the Writers' Club that believed Hitler was bluffing and there would be no war. He had published twenty novels and all on the same subject: his love for the actress Fania Ephros, who betrayed him and married a union leader. Fania Ephros had been dead for ten years, but he continued to brood about her many treacheries. Zelikowitz had a continuing war with the Warsaw critics, who all put him down. He had slapped one of them across the face. I greeted him, but he didn't answer me. He was angry with young writers and considered them intruders.

I went back to the first room. Perhaps the Maiden should be possessed by *two* dybbuks, I thought, one a slut, the other a whoremonger? I had written a story of a girl possessed by both a whore and a blind musician. I was seized with boldness. From a phone booth I called information for the number of the Hotel Bristol, and when the hotel answered, I asked to be connected with Miss Betty Slonim. The telephone rang once and I heard her voice: "Hello?"

I was momentarily speechless. Then I said, "I'm the young man who had the honor of being with you at Gertner's Restaurant last night."

"Tsutsik?"

"Yes."

"I've been sitting here thinking about you. What's new with the play?"

"I have an idea I would like to talk over with you and Mr. Dreiman."

"Sam has gone to the American consulate, but come over, and you and I can discuss it."

"I won't be disturbing you?"

"Come right over!" She gave me her room number. I thanked her and hung up. I was tingling with delight over my own courage. Forces stronger than I propelled me. I wanted to take a cab but three zlotys might be too little to pay for it. Suddenly I remembered that I hadn't shaved, and fingered my stubble. I would have to visit a barber. I couldn't call on an American lady unshaven.

7

A doorman in livery guarded the entrance of the Hotel Bristol, and going inside felt almost like entering a police station or a courtroom. But everything went off without a hitch. Although there was an elevator, I climbed the stairs to the fourth floor. The steps were made of marble and along the middle ran a carpet. Betty answered my knock at once. Her room had a huge window and was brighter than any room I had ever seen. The snow had stopped and the sun shone in. I seemed to have been transported to a different climate.

Betty wore a long houserobe and slippers with pompons. Having red hair and having been tormented by nicknames through my childhood—red dog, red cheater, red carrot—I had an aversion to redheads, but Betty's hair didn't repel me. In the sun it seemed a blend of fire and gold. Only now did I observe how white her skin was—as white as my own. Her eyebrows were brown.

A moment after I came in, the telephone rang and she conversed for a few minutes in English. How grand and worldly this language sounded! Betty was shorter than I but she carried herself with pride. She hung up and invited me to take off my coat and make myself comfortable. Even her Yiddish smacked of sophistication. She took my coat and hung it on a wooden hanger. This struck me as novel—so much respect for an old rag that was missing a button. When I was with Dora I felt like a mature man, but here I reverted to a youth. Betty waved me to a sofa and sat down in an easy chair facing me. Her robe parted, and for a fraction of a second I saw her dazzling legs. She offered me a cigarette. I didn't smoke but I wouldn't think of refusing her. She brought me a lighter. I took one puff and became intoxicated by the aroma.

She said, "Now tell me more about the play."

I began to talk and she listened. The expression in her eyes kept changing from anticipation to amazement. "This means I'll have to conduct a love affair with myself?"

"Yes, but in a sense we all do."

"True. I could easily play a man and a woman. Why didn't you bring the script along?"

"Everything is too rough to show."

"Couldn't you recall a few lines for me? I'd like to try it out right now. I'll give you paper and pen and you can write a few lines—some words for the musician and some for the harlot. Wait!" She stood up and from her purse that lay on the dresser took out a lady's fountain pen and a notebook.

I began to write as if automatically:

MUSICIAN

Come, girl, be mine. You're a corpse and I'm a corpse, and when two corpses dance the bedbugs prance. I'll make you a present of a pouch of earth from the Land of Israel and the shards that covered my eyelids. With the myrtle between my fingers I'll dig you a pit reaching from Tishevitz to the Mount of Olives. On the way, we'll do like Zimri the son of Solu, and Cozby the daughter of Zur.

HARLOT

Hold your tongue, foul whelp of a musician! I left the world a pure virgin while you wallowed with every whore from Lublin to Leipzig. A band of angels awaits me, while myriads of demons lie in ambush for you.

I handed Betty the pen and notebook and she began to read slowly. Her thin eyebrows lifted and remained raised. Her lips formed an inquisitive smile. She read through to the end, then asked, "Is this taken from your play?"

"Not really."

"You composed it right here and now?"

"More or less."

"Well, you're a strange young man. You have an exceptional imagination."

"That's about all I do have."

"What else do you need? Wait, I'll try to play this."

She began to mumble into the notebook, halting here and there over some word. Suddenly she began acting out the parts in two voices. I clenched my teeth to stop them from chattering. The powers that ruled the world had brought me together with a superb actress. It was hard to conceive that talent like this spent night after night in bed with Sam Dreiman. My cigarette had gone out. Betty walked up and down the room, repeating the dialogue over and over. It struck me that she was better as the musician than as the girl. The girl's voice sounded half masculine. Each time Betty concluded, she glanced at me and I nodded.

Finally she came up and said, "This is good to recite, but a play must have a plot. One of the Hasidim, a rich one, must be in love with me."

"I'll write it in."

"He should have a wife and children."

"Definitely."

"Let him offer to divorce his wife and marry the girl."

"Surely."

"But she won't be able to decide between the dead musician and the live Hasid."

"Right."

"What then?" she asked.

"She'll marry the Hasid."

"Aha."

"But on her wedding night the musician won't let her be with her husband."

"Yes."

"And she'll go off with the musician."

"Where to?"

"To be with him in the grave."

"How long will it take you to write the play? Mr. Dreiman is ready to rent a theater. You could become a famous playwright overnight."

"As it is fated, so shall it be," I said.

"You believe in fate?"

"Absolutely."

"So do I. I'm not religious—you see how I live—but I do believe in God. Before I go to sleep I say a prayer. On board ship I prayed to God each night to send me the right play. All of a sudden, along comes a young fellow, a Tsutsik, with a play that can express my soul. Isn't that miraculous?"

"Let's hope so."

"Don't you have faith in yourself?"

"How can one have faith in anything?"

"You must believe in yourself. That's my tragedy—I never have had that belief. As soon as something good begins to happen, I foresee nothing but difficulties and mishaps and I spoil whatever there is. That's how it's been in love and that's how it's been in my career. Do you have a director to suggest?"

"There's no point looking for a director until the play is finished."

"You're still doubtful, eh? This time I won't allow doubt. The play has to turn out well. Stick to the outline we put together just now. Sam Dreiman will give you a five-hundred-dollar advance and that's a lot of money here in Poland. Are you married?"

"No."

"You live alone?"

"I had a girl, but we've broken up."

"May I ask why?"

"She's a Conmmunist and is going away to Stalin's land."

"Why didn't you marry?"

"I don't believe two people can make a contract to love each other forever."

"Do you have a comfortable apartment?"

"I have to move. I'm being dispossessed."

"Rent a nice room. Put aside any other work you're doing and concentrate on our play. What do you intend to call it?"

"The Ludmir Maiden and Her Two Dybbuks."

"Too long. Leave it to me to decide on the title. How much time will the rewriting take?"

"If it goes well, three weeks—a week for each act."

"How do you see the three acts?"

"In the first act, the Ludmir Maiden will become what she is and the rich Hasid will fall in love with her. In the second act, the dead musician must emerge and establish the conflict."

"In my opinion, the dead musician should appear in the very first act," Betty said after some hesitation.

"You're absolutely correct."

"Don't agree with me so quickly. Think it over first. A playright shouldn't be so compliant."

"I'm no playwright."

"If you write a play, then you're a playwright. If you don't take yourself seriously, no one else will either. Forgive me for speaking to you this way, but I'm a few years older. Actually, everything I tell you I should tell myself as well. Sam Dreiman believes in me. He believes too much. He is perhaps the only person who believes in me and in my talent. That's why—''

"I believe in you, too."

"You do? Eh? Well, thank you. What did I do to deserve that? Apparently someone up there doesn't want my end just yet. Some sort of providence directed you to me."

CHAPTER THREE

1

Sam Dreiman offered me the five-hundred-dollar advance he had spoken of, but I refused to accept such a big sum. We agreed I would take two hundred dollars for now, and I traded them at a currency exchange for over eighteen hundred zlotys. This was a real windfall. I found a new place on Leszno Street that cost eighty zlotys a month. I put down three months' rent and got a wallpapered room with central heating, solid furniture, and an Oriental carpet. My landlord, Isidore Katzenberg, a former manufacturer, told me he had been ruined by exorbitant taxes. The apartment house lay close to Iron Street and was relatively new and modern. One floor was a Gymnasium, and there was an elevator at the front entrance, for which I was given a key.

Everything happened quickly. One evening Sam Dreiman handed me the money and the next day I moved into my new place. I had only to pack my possessions in two valises and carry them over. The maid, Tekla, a young country girl with brown hair and ruddy cheeks, had polished the floor until it gleamed. There was a bed in my room, a sofa, upholstered chairs, and in the long, wide corridor a telephone I was permitted to use at eight groschen a call. God in heaven, I had been thrown into the lap of luxury! I went to a tailor to be fitted for a suit. I lent Feitelzohn fifty zlotys. He demurred, but I forced them on him. I invited him to dinner at a café on Bielanska Street. I had told him the theme of the play and he offered suggestions. Feitelzohn was going to earn money from this venture as well—Sam had asked him to do the "publicity." I had never heard this word, and it had to be explained to me.

Feitelzohn sipped his tea, puffed his cigar, and said, "What kind of publicity man will I make, anyway? If I don't like the play, I won't praise it. But Sam Dreiman is apparently a multimillionaire. He is seventy or more, he has a nasty wife and estranged children who are rich in their own right—what else does he have to do with the money? He wants to spend it as long as he can. This Betty must have brought back his potency. I didn't know either of them in America, but I heard about him. It seems I even met him once at the Café Royal. He is a carpenter by trade. He went to America in the 1880's and became a builder in Detroit. When Ford built his automobile factories there and began to pay his workers five dollars a day, men came flocking from all over America—from the whole world, in fact. Sam Dreiman built houses and he built factories. In America when the money starts flowing toward someone, there is no limit to it. In 1929 he lost a fortune but enough remained. You should have taken the whole five hundred. To him that's a trifle. He'll think you're a shlemiel.''

"I can't accept money for goods that don't exist yet.''

"Well then, write a good play. The American believes in paying. You can give him mud, but if he pays a lot for it, in his mind it becomes gold.''

I was anxious to go home and get to work, but Feitelzohn had begun to expound on a "soul expedition" he was preparing to launch. Psychoanalysis wasn't the answer, he said. The patient comes to the analyst to be cured—that is, to become like everyone else. He wants to be rid of his complexes, and the analyst is supposed to help him in this effort. But where is it written that the cure is better than the disease? Those who would take part in his soul expedition wouldn't be bound by any restrictions. We would assemble in a room on an evening, with the lights off, and give our souls free rein. Man has to be granted the courage to reveal to himself and others what it is he truly desires. The real tyrants weren't those who repressed the body (which is confined anyhow) but those who enslaved the spirit. Alleged liberators, they have all been subjugators of the soul! Feitelzohn said, "Moses and Jesus, the author of the Bhagavad-Gita, and Spinoza, Karl Marx, and Freud. The spirit is a game uncontrolled by rules and laws. If Schopenhauer is right—if blind will is really the thing-in-itself, the essence of all—why not let the wanter want?''

"What's the purpose of only wanting?'' I asked.

"Where is it written that there must be a purpose? Maybe chaos *is* the purpose. You've glanced into the cabala, and you know that before Ain Sof created the world He first dimmed His light and formed a void. It was only in this void that the Emanation commenced. This divine absence may be the very essence of creation.''

Evening had fallen but still Feitelzohn talked. By the time we went outside, it was night. The street lights were on in Bielanska Street, and a thin snow was falling. As usual after speaking at length, Feitelzohn grew silent and cranky, ashamed of his own verbosity. He shook my hand and went off in the direction of Dluga Street. I walked toward Leszno. It felt strange to have a pocketful of money suddenly, an elegant room, even a maid who would make my bed and bring me breakfast. Feitelzohn's words had stirred me. Yes, what was it, actually, that I wanted? I felt drawn to Betty Slonim. Celia's kiss and confession presaged a new affair. I did not want Dora to leave. But was I in love with these women? Well, what else did I want? I had dreamed of writing a perfect book and now I wanted a perfect play, too. The snow grew denser. It made my eyelids blink and caused spearlike beams to radiate from lamp posts and show windows. Feitelzohn's constant insinuations that Celia desired me were puzzling. Was he trying to palm her off on me, or to share her with me? I had heard him say that man was on the verge of trading the instinct of jealousy for the instinct of participation.

I had resolved to work late into the night, but as I climbed the steps to my

room, weariness settled over me. Tekla let me in. She wore a short white apron
and a cap with lace over her hair, like a maid at a doctor's. She smiled familiarly
and showed me the curtains she had hung in my room. She had already made
my bed. She asked if I would like some tea. I thanked her and said not now.

I tried to overcome my weariness and sat down to rewrite the first act of
The Ludmir Maiden, but instead I started to write a play that was completely
new. I seemed to have lost control over my pen. It raced faster than my fingers.
Although the mistress of the house had installed a desk covered in green felt
and a desk lamp with a green shade, things glared before my eyes. Aha, that
inner antagonist and saboteur was launching a campaign against me. I knew his
tricks by now. I wanted to succeed, but he sought my downfall. I found I was
leaving out letters and whole words. I began to consult the books that were
supposed to serve as guides for my behavior: Payot's *The Education of the Will*
and Charles Baudouin's work on autosuggestion, the notebook in which I had
set down rules for living and means of maintaining spiritual hygiene, but fatigue
overcame me and I fell on my bed in my clothes.

At once the dreams and nightmares took over. When I opened my eyes, the
clock showed a quarter of two. I hardly managed to undress before drifting off
again into a deep sleep. In my dreams I was able to analyze what I was going
through. Yes, dreams were precisely what Dr. Feitelzohn sought to restore to
man—aimlessness, spiritual anarchy, the whims of idolators, the perversions of
madmen. In my sleep, Betty and Celia became one, although not altogether. I
mated with this plural female, and Haiml stood by and encouraged us. Even this
coupling had some connection with the play. *Is Celia the Ludmir Maiden? Is
Betty the dybbuk of the adulteress? And am I myself the blind musician?* But I
had never had any special feeling for music.

I had known Betty Slonim less than two days, but here she was participating
not only in my daytime fantasies but in my nocturnal visions as well. She was
somehow with me and part of me, my deeds and philosophizing. Feitelzohn
wanted to return the soul to that primeval chaos from which all things evolved,
but how could chaos create anything? Could it be that purpose, not causality
was the essence of being? Were the teleologists right after all?

2

I had planned to get up at seven, but when I wakened I heard the clock in the
living room toll nine times. Someone knocked on my door with the stippled
panes and Tekla came in carrying a tray covered with a napkin. She had brought
me eggs, rolls, cheese, and coffee. I had slept more than seven hours. I had
gone through a dreamy epoch I had forgotten except for one fragment—sliding
down a mountain as a band of wild people awaited below with clubs, spears,
poles, and axes. They half shouted, half chanted a melody, a remnant of which
still lingered in my ears—a dirge of passion and madness.

The girl started to apologize. "I thought you were up."

"Oh, I overslept."

"Shall I take the tray back to the kitchen?"

"No, I'll wash later."

"You have a pitcher of water and a basin right here. A towel, too."

"Thank you, Tekla. Thank you very much."

I was overcome by the feeling that I was being given more than I deserved. Why should this country girl be waiting on me? She had undoubtedly been on her feet since six that morning. Yesterday, I had seen her washing clothes. I would have liked to give her something, but I couldn't reach the chair where my jacket hung. She smiled, showing a mouthful of teeth without a blemish. She had muscular legs and firm breasts. She placed the tray carefully on the table. She studied me as if trying to fathom my thoughts. "A good appetite!"

"Thank you, Tekla. You're a fine girl."

A dimple showed in her left cheek. "Good health to you." She left the room slowly.

These are the real people, the ones who keep the world going, I thought. They serve as proof that the cabalists are right—not Feitelzohn. An indifferent God, a mad God couldn't have created Tekla. I felt temporarily enamored of this girl. Her cheeks were the color of ripe apples. She gave forth a vigor rooted in the earth, in the sun, in the whole universe. She didn't want to better the world as did Dora; she didn't require roles and reviews as did Betty; she didn't seek thrills as did Celia. She wanted to give, not to take. If the Polish people had produced even one Tekla, they had surely accomplished their mission. I poured a little water from the clay pitcher into the basin on my washstand. I moistened my hands and dried them on the towel. I took a drink of coffee and a bite of the fresh roll. I felt an urge to utter a benediction and thank the powers that made wheat and coffee beans grow, to offer thanks to the chickens that laid these eggs. I had gone to sleep in misery and risen almost happy.

Someone knocked on the door and opened it. It was my landlord's son, Wladek, who, his father had told me, had quit his law studies at Warsaw University and spent all day at home reading trash and listening to the music and chatter on the radio. Wladek was tall, lean, pale, with a high forehead, thin nose. To me, he appeared ill both physically and mentally. The father spoke Polish with a Yiddish accent but Wladek spoke it grammatically and with style. He said, "Excuse me, sir, for disturbing you in the midst of your meal, but you're wanted on the telephone."

I jumped up, nearly spilling my coffee. This was my first call here. I went out into the corridor and snatched up the receiver.

It was Celia. "I know that if Mohammed won't come to the mountain, the mountain must come to Mohammed," she said. "The trouble is, I have never considered myself a mountain. I've heard about your successes and I want to congratulate you. I thought we were friends, but if you prefer to remain aloof, of course that's your privilege. Still, I would like you to know I'm delighted for you."

"Not only am I your friend—I love you!" I exclaimed with the light-minded assurance of those who can afford to say whatever comes to their lips.

"Oh, really? Well, that's good to hear. But if that's the case, why haven't I heard from you? When you come to us you're like a friend, a brother. Then you go away—and silence. Is this your nature or is it a system you use?"

"No system. Nothing of any kind. I know how busy you are."

"Busy? With what am I busy? Our Marianna does everything. I sit and read, but how much reading can you do? Morris has been visited lately by hordes of Americans, so I see nothing of him. The second American ambassador to Poland I call him. Besides you two, there's no one in our circle to exchange a few words with. Haiml, God bless him, has gotten himself too involved with the Poale Zion. I believe in Palestine and all that, but England does what she pleases with her mandate. Days go by that I don't speak a word to anyone.''

"Madam Chentshiner, whenever you want to meet me, all you need do is call. I miss you too," my mouth said of its own volition.

Again Celia paused. "If you miss me, what's to keep you away? And call me Celia, not Madam Chentshiner. Come over and we'll talk. If you'd rather, we can meet at a confectionery. You're probably busy with the play. Morris told me all about it. But no writer writes ten hours a day. What kind of woman is this Betty Slonim? I expect you're in love with her already."

"No, not in love."

"I sometimes envy women like her. They go straight to the target. She picked out a rich old man for a lover and he'll do everything to make her famous. To me, this is prostitution, but when have women not sold themselves for money? If she gets two zlotys for it, she's a streetwalker, but when it's many thousands, along with diamonds and furs, she's a lady. I didn't know you wrote plays. Morris told me the theme. An interesting subject. When will you be over?''

"When shall I come?"

"Come for lunch today. Haiml went to his father's in Lodz. I'm all alone."

"At what time?"

"Three."

"Fine, I'll see you at three."

"Don't be late!"

I put down the receiver. She was lonely. I had suffered for years from loneliness; now suddenly my luck had changed. But for how long? An inner voice, that unconscious which Hartmann claims is never in error, told me that it wouldn't be for long. Everything would end in catastrophe. Then why not enjoy the moment? Sleep had calmed me somewhat, but now tension returned. I wouldn't make the first move with Celia, I decided. I'd leave all the initiative to her.

I went back to my interrupted breakfast. Yes, I had to find pleasure before I died and returned to nothing. I reminded myself that I hadn't checked the money I had left overnight in my jacket pocket. Someone might have robbed me while I was asleep. Even Tekla could have stuck in her hand and taken everything. I jumped up and tapped the pocket. No, no one had robbed me. Tekla was an honest girl. Still, I began to count the bills even as I felt ashamed of my mistrust.

There was another knock on the door. Tekla had come to see if I wanted more coffee.

"No, Tekla dear, I've had enough." I gave her a zloty and her cheeks turned red.

3

Exactly at three o'clock I arrived at Haiml's house on Zlota Street. To get there I walked down Iron Street to the juncture of Twarda and Zlota, then turned left. Zlota Street was almost always deserted—a residential street, without stores. Most of the residents were well off, with few or married children. The five-story building where Haiml lived was dark gray, with balconies supported on the shoulders of mythological figures. One had to ring a bell to get in the front entrance. The stairs were of marble but worn, and a spittoon stood on every landing. From the landings one looked out onto a square courtyard, a small enclosed garbage bin with snow on its deck, and a tiny garden where the branches of trees were glazed by the frost and reflected the colors of the rainbow. Celia answered when I rang. Marianna, the maid, had gone to visit her sister, Celia explained. She invited me in. The apartment glistened from cleanliness. In the dining room the table was set. A huge china closet sparkled with crystal and silver. Portraits of men with white beards and of women in wigs and jewelry hung on the walls.

Celia said, "I prepared your favorite dish—potatoes with borscht and meatballs."

She showed me to Haiml's place at the head of the table. From the way she had sounded on the telephone, I expected kisses the moment I came in, an immediate physical intimacy. But her expression told me that she was in no mood for this. She had turned formal. We sat facing each other, far apart. Celia served me. I suspected she had sent the maid away so that we could be alone. The cold walk had given me an appetite and I ate a lot. Celia questioned me about the play, and as I outlined the theme to her, I found myself making unexpected changes. This was a magical theme—like the Torah, it seemed to possess seventy different faces.

Celia said, "Where will you find the actors for such a play? And what about the director? If it doesn't come out absolutely right, it can turn into something terribly vulgar. Our Yiddish actors and actresses in Warsaw are of a low breed. You know this yourself. In all these years I haven't seen anything worthwhile on our stage."

"I'm afraid that I've fallen into a trap."

"Not if you don't hand the play over to them until you're satisfied it's just as you want it. That's my advice."

"Sam Dreiman is about to rent a theater and hire a cast."

"Don't let him do it. From what Morris tells me, he's a common man—a former carpenter. If the thing turns out badly it's *your* reputation that will suffer."

This was not the Celia I had seen on my earlier visit, but I was growing accustomed to abrupt changes both in myself and in others. Modern man may be ashamed of emotion, but he is all affect and temperament. He burns with love and turns cold as ice; he is intimate one moment and aloof the next. I was no longer astonished by these mysterious variations. In fact, I often suspected that I unwillingly hypnotized those with whom I came in contact and inflicted my moods upon them.

After lunch we went into the parlor and Celia offered me cherry liqueur and cookies. The walls were covered with paintings by Jewish artists—Liebermann, Minkowski, Glicenstein, Chagall, Rybak, Rubinlicht, Barlevi. Jewish antiques were displayed in a glass cabinet—spice boxes, a gold-plated wine benediction goblet, Hanukkah candelabra, a Passover bowl, the sheath of a Book of Esther, a Sabbath bread knife with a mother-of-pearl handle, an illuminated marriage contract, a pointer and crown from a Torah scroll. It was difficult for me to accept the fact that this intense Jewishness was merely decoration, its essence long since lost to many of us.

For a while we discussed painting—cubism, futurism, expressionism. Celia had recently attended an exhibition of modern art and been thoroughly disappointed. In what way was a square head and a nose like a trapeze indicative of man and his dilemmas? What could harsh colors that had neither harmony nor basis in reality say to us? As to literature, Celia had read Gottfried Benn, Trackl, Däubler, as well as translations from modern American and French poets. They left her cold. "All they want is surprise and shock," she said. "But we become shock-proof so quickly."

She began to look at me quizzically. It seemed that she was wondering, as I was, why we were behaving so conventionally. She said, "I'm sure that you're infatuated with that Betty Slonim. Tell me about her."

"What is there to tell? She wants the same thing we all do—to grab some pleasure before we vanish forever."

"What do you call pleasure? Sleeping, if you'll forgive me, with a seventy-year-old carpenter?"

"It's payment for other pleasures she's getting."

"What, for instance? I know women who would give up everything to perform on the stage. This seems to me a strange passion. Now, to write a good book, that's something I'd like to do, but I realized early that I hadn't the talent for it. It's the reason I admire writers so."

"What are writers? The same kind of entertainers as magicians. As a matter of fact, I admire someone who can balance a barrel on his feet more than I do a poet."

"Oh, I don't believe you. You play the cynic, but you're really a serious young man. Sometimes it seems to me that I can see right through you."

"What do you see?"

"That you're constantly bored. All people bore you except maybe Morris Feitelzohn. He is exactly like you. He can't find a place for himself anywhere. He wants to be a philosopher, but he's basically an artist. He's a child who breaks all its toys, then cries to have them put together again. Though I'm no artist, I suffer from the same sickness. We might have shared a great love, but he doesn't want this. He tells me how he carries on with servant girls. He continually douses me with cold water, enough to put out the hottest fire. You must give me your solemn word that you won't repeat my words to him. He is deliberately driving me into your arms, and he does this out of insanity. His game consists of igniting the fire in a woman, then leaving her to herself. But he has a heart too, and when he sees those close to him being hurt, it touches his conscience. He is also morbidly curious. He wants to try everything. He's afraid that somewhere there may remain an emotion he hasn't tasted.''

"He wants to establish a school of hedonism.''

"Foolish fantasies. For years I've been hearing about orgies but I'm sure they provide no satisfaction. They're a lark for fifteen-year-old boys and street-walkers, not for mature people. You have to be drunk or mad to take part in them. In Paris, for five francs tourists can watch acts of perversion. The few writers who babble about this at the Writers' Club are old and sick people. They can barely stand on their feet.''

We were still for a while; then Celia asked, "What about your Communist sweetheart? Has she gone to Stalin's land yet?''

"You know about her, too?''

"Morris speaks of you constantly.''

"She's due to go any day now. Everything between us is ended.''

"How do you end things? I never could end anything. I hear you finally have a nice room.''

"Yes, with Sam Dreiman's money.''

"Does it have a balcony?''

"No balcony.''

"You once told me that you liked a balcony.''

"One can't have everything.''

"I sometimes feel that the reason some people get nothing is that they never have the courage to reach out their hands. I am one of those.''

"What would happen if I reached out my hands to you now?'' I asked.

Celia rocked in her chair. "You can try.''

I went over and held out my hands to her.

She looked at me ironically. She stood up. "You may kiss me.''

I put my arms around her and we kissed silently for a long time. She moved her lips as if to say something. But no words came out.

Afterward she said, "Don't tell Feitelzohn. He's a jealous little boy.''

4

Dusk fell. The winter day—the like of which would never occur again, unless Nietzsche was right in his theory of perpetual repetition—flickered out like a candle. For a while, a purple pane reflected on the parlor wall, a sign that some part of the sky in the west had cleared preceding sunset. Celia didn't switch on the lights. Her face was in shadow and her eyes shone out of it as if casting their own glow. Then it darkened again. Through the window a star sparkled within a split in the clouds. From where I was sitting I tried to fix it in my memory before it vanished. I toyed with the notion of how it would be if the sky remained constantly overcast and parted for only one second each hundred years, when someone might catch a glimpse of a star. He would tell of his revelation, but no one would believe him. He would be called a liar or accused of having suffered an hallucination. Behind how many clouds does the truth lie concealed now? And what did I know about the star I was looking at? This was a fixed star, not a planet. It might be bigger than the sun. Who could know how many planets rotated around it, how many worlds drew sustenance from it? Who could conceive what kind of creatures lived there, what plants grew, what thoughts were thought there? Well, and there were billions of such fixed stars in our Milky Way alone. They couldn't be merely physical or chemical accidents. There had to be someone whose commands controlled the infinite universe. His orders traveled faster than light. So omnipotent and omniscient was he that he presided over every atom, every molecule, every mite and microbe. He even knew that Aaron Greidinger had just embarked on an affair with Celia Chentshiner.

The telephone rang and Celia, who had been sitting silently in the easy chair mulling over her own thoughts, lazily stretched out her hand to the small table on which it stood. She drawled in that singsong used in Warsaw exclusively for telephone conversations, "Haiml? Why so late? I thought you'd call earlier . . . What's that? . . . Everything is fine. Haiml, we have a guest—our young friend came for lunch . . . No, *I* called *him*. If he wants to put on airs, I'll be the one to give in. Who am I, a simple housewife, and he a writer, a playwright, and who knows what . . . Yes, we had lunch and I persuaded him to stay to dinner . . . Oh, he has a famous actress now, young and probably pretty, too. What does he need with a woman my age? How is your father? . . . So? Good, let him take his medicine . . . Tomorrow? When tomorrow? On the twelve o'clock train? . . . Good. I'll meet you at the station . . . What else do I have to do with myself. A whole day went by yesterday and no one rang me. So I swallowed my pride and called him . . . Who? To direct? Don't talk nonsense. He knows as much about theater as I do about astronomy . . . You mustn't laugh at me, but a Gentile director would understand the thing better than one of our boors. They at least have studied and seen theater . . . Morris? I haven't heard from him at all. He has forgotten us, too . . . Oy, Haiml, you're one of those types, all right . . . You want to talk to him? I'll give him the phone. Here he is!"

Celia handed me the receiver. The phone had a long cord. Everything in this room was arranged to avoid effort. I heard Haiml's voice, which sounded even more thin and shrill than when we talked directly.

"Tsutsik! How are you? I hear you're working on your play. Good, good. It's high time a young person wrote for our theater. The world goes forward, but we're still stuck with *Chinke Pinke,* and *Dos Pintele Yid.* Each time Celia and I go to the Yiddish theater we vow it's the last. Well, but not to go is no achievement, either. Our conservative Zionists have renounced the diaspora. All good fortune, they say, will come about in Palestine. But let's not forget that Palestine was only our cradle. We should have grown up in those two thousand years. By ignoring the exile they help bring about assimilation. You were kind to come spend time with Celia. Who can she entertain herself with? She has nothing to say to the women in our circle. With them, it's always the same— this dress, that dress, this hat or the other. All gossip. Don't be in any hurry to leave. Don't be bashful . . . Did you say jealous? Nonsense! Who was it said that when people rejoice in one another they exalt the creator, too. When I married Celia and even long before, while we were still engaged, I was terribly jealous. If she so much as spoke or smiled at another man I was ready to trample the two of them to dust. But I once read in a Hasidic volume that when one has a harmful trait and overcomes it, it can completely reverse itself. Today I know that if you really love a woman, her friend can be your friend, her pleasure your pleasure, her ecstasy your ecstasy. Tsutsik, I still want to say something to Celia. Be so good as . . .''

I turned the receiver over to Celia and went off to the room the Chentshiners designated as the library. It was dark there except for the reflection of light from a window across the street. I stood and asked myself, ''Are you happy now?'' I waited for an answer from that deep source called the inner being, the ego, the superego, the spirit—whatever its name—but no answer came.

Celia opened the door. ''What are you doing in the dark like a lost soul? We have no secrets from you.''

I could not find words to reply to her, and she said, ''How can I begin an affair when I'm seriously thinking about suicide? There are people who at a certain age come to a natural end—all words spoken, all deeds done, and nothing remaining but death. I used to get up each morning with hope. Today I no longer expect anything.''

''Why, Celia, why?''

''Oh, I don't fit in anywhere. Haiml is a decent person and I love him, but before he even opens his mouth I know what is going to come out of it. Morris is the very opposite, but you never know where you stand with him. He lives close to desperation. You're too young for me, and unstable. I have the feeling that you won't be staying here in Warsaw long. One day you'll simply pick up and disappear. Morris told me that Sam Dreiman wants to take you to America.''

''He's a big talker.''

''Such things happen fast. If you have a chance to escape from here, don't wait. We're caught between Hitler and Stalin. Whichever invades the country will bring a cataclysm.''

''Why don't *you* leave?''

''Where to? I don't see myself in America.''

''What about Palestine?''

''Somehow I don't see myself there, either. It's a place we'll be transported to on a cloud when the Messiah comes.''

''You believe this?''

''No, my dear.''

CHAPTER FOUR

1

Spring arrived early this year. By March, the trees were abloom in the Saxony Gardens. My play wasn't ready, but even if it had been, it was too late to present it. By May all the affluent families went off for the summer to Otwock, Świder, Michalin, and Jósefow. The play wasn't the only problem. Sam Dreiman had had trouble obtaining a theater. So the première was put off until Succoth, when the Yiddish theaters regularly commenced their season. Sam Dreiman had advanced me another three hundred dollars, which I reckoned would carry me through until fall. He was considering renting a summer home on the Otwock route and I would be assigned a room there to work on the play under Betty's supervision. Sam confided to me that even as he sat in Warsaw doing nothing, he was earning several thousand dollars each and every week.

He said, "Take as much as you need. I won't spend it all in any case."

By now, I was on a first-name basis with Sam and with Betty, and they both called me Tsutsik. Yet I knew that everything depended on the play. Sam Dreiman often used the word "success." He kept warning me that the play must reach audiences both in Warsaw and in New York, where he still planned to take it, along with me, its author.

He said, "I know the Yiddish theater in America like the back of my hand. What else did we immigrants have except the theater and the Yiddish paper? Each time I came from Detroit to New York, I never failed to enjoy an evening in the theater. I knew them all—the Adlers, Madam Liptzin, Kessler, and Thomashefsky, not to speak of his wife, Bessie. They spoke plain Yiddish—none of that gobbledygook you hear in the art theaters, where they bore the crowds to death with propaganda. People come to the theater to enjoy themselves, not to revolt against Rockefeller's millions."

Betty and I had already kissed, both in front of Sam and behind his back. When we sat over the manuscript, she would take my hand and put it on her knee. Feitelzohn's contention that the instinct of jealousy was becoming vestigial like the appendix, coccyx, and male breasts seemed to hold as true for this couple as for Haiml and Celia. Sam Dreiman smiled and kidded me good-naturedly when Betty kissed me. He often left us alone and went off to play cards with his acquaintance at the consulate.

Feitelzohn went there as well. Recently he had lectured on the subject "Spiritual Vitamins" at the Writers' Club, and he was preparing to launch a series of soul expeditions. A friend of his, the hypnotist Mark Elbinger, had come to Warsaw from Paris. Feitelzohn told me remarkable facts about this man. He could hypnotize his patients over the phone or merely by telepathy. He was also clairvoyant. He had held séances in Berlin, in London, Paris, New York, and South America. He was supposed to take part in the soul expeditions.

Since Sam preferred to play cards rather than to spend his time looking around for a summer place in the still empty resort villages in the Otwock region, he sent Betty and me to find a suitable villa. Sam planned to arrange that the rehearsals of the play take place there. Feitelzohn had promised to hold soul expeditions on "the loin of nature." At the Table of the Impotent there was even talk of an orgy to be organized by that famous master of revelry, Fritz Bander.

One day I met Betty at the Danzig Railroad station. She bought tickets for us, and we waited in line together. It smelled here of beer, sausages, coal smoke, and sweat. Soldiers carrying full field packs waited for a train and passed the time downing huge mugs of beer that a girl drew from a keg. Her cheeks were red and she wore a tight blouse over her bosom. The soldiers joked with her, talked smut, and her pale-blue eyes smiled half in arrogance, half in embarrassment, as if to say, "I'm only one—you can't all have me."

The newspapers talked of how modern the German Army had become, fully mobilized and equipped with the latest weapons, but these Polish soldiers looked just like the Russian soldiers in 1914. They wore heavy greatcoats and the sweat poured from their faces. Their rifles appeared too long and too bulky. All of them were doomed to be massacred, yet they made fun of the Jews in the long gaberdines. One even tugged at a Jew's beard, and they could be heard hissing, "*Żydy, Żydy, Żydy.*"

I hadn't been in a train for years. I never traveled second class, always third or even fourth. But here I sat on an upholstered bench with an American lady, an actress, and looked out at the brick-red buildings of the Citadel, whose roofs were covered with earth and overgrown with grass. This ancient fortress was supposed to defend Warsaw in case of attack. It also contained a prison. The train rode out onto the bridge. The Vistula gleamed, and a strong breeze blew in from it. The sun reflected large and red in the water, and although the hour was long before sunset, a pale moon appeared in the sky. We rode through Wawer, Miedzeszyn, Falenica, Michalin. There were memories connected with each of these stops. In Miedzeszyn I had slept with a girl for the first time— only slept and done nothing else, since she wanted to preserve her virginity for her husband. In Falenica I had delivered a lecture that turned out to be a fiasco.

We got off in Świder, one stop after Jósefow, where Haiml and Celia had their summer house. A real-estate broker was waiting for us at the station. We waded through the sand until we came to a villa that appeared to me the height of luxury, with verandas, balconies, flower beds, even hothouses, all surrounded by woods. Betty seemed so eager to get rid of the broker that almost immediately she handed him a deposit of two hundred zlotys. Only then did we learn that the house had no lights, there was no linen for the beds, and the nearest restaurant or coffee shop in the neighborhood was kilometers away. The summer hotels were not open. We had to return to Warsaw and wait for the contract to be drawn up and sent to Sam Dreiman. The broker, a little man with a yellow beard and yellow eyes, seemed suspicious of our intentions. He said to us, "It's too early. The nights are cold and dark. The summer is not here yet. Everything has its time."

From a hut a janitor came out with two barking dogs. He asked the broker to give back the keys to him. We were advised to go back to the station, because at this time of year the trains did not run frequently. But Betty insisted that she see the river Świderek and its waterfall, which the real-estate broker in Warsaw had spoken to her and Sam about. As we walked, a blast of icy wind brought winter back to us. In a matter of minutes the sky became overcast, the moon disappeared, and a mixture of driving rain and hail hit our faces. Betty spoke to me, but I could not hear her in the clamor of the wind. We had reached the Świderek River. The beach stretched before us wet and empty. The low waterfall tumbled with a thundering roar. The narrow stream shone strange and mysterious and two large winter birds flew along the surface, all the while screeching warnings, one to the other, not to get lost in the stormy twilight. Betty's straw hat lifted itself into the air and landed on the bank across. Then it started to roll and turn somersaults; it vanished in the shrubs. Betty clutched with both hands at her disheveled hair as if it were a wig, and she shrieked, "Let's go! The demons are after me. It's always like this when a spark of happiness lights up my life!"

She threw her purse on the sand, put her arms around me, and, pressing me to her, hollered, "Keep away from me! I'm cursed, cursed, cursed!"

2

Winter returned for a while, and Betty put on her sable coat once more. Then spring moved in for good. Warm breezes blew from the Praga woods through my open window, carrying with them the fragrance of grass, blossoms, and newly turned earth. In Germany, Hitler had solidified his power, but the Warsaw Jews had celebrated the festival of the exodus out of Egypt four thousand years ago. That day I didn't go to Betty at the Hotel Bristol. She came to me instead. Sam Dreiman had gone to Mlawa to attend the funeral of a cousin. Betty refused to go with him. She said to me, "I want to enjoy life, not mourn the death of some strange woman." She was again dressed in a summery outfit—a pale-blue suit and a straw hat. She brought me a bouquet, and Tekla took it and put it in a vase. I had never heard of a woman bringing a man flowers.

The spring wouldn't let us work. Birds flew past the open window with cries and twitters. We left the manuscript on the table and went to the window. The narrow sidewalks swarmed with pedestrians.

Betty said, "Spring in Warsaw makes me crazy. In New York there is no such thing as spring."

After a while we went down into the street. Betty took my arm with her gloved hand and we strolled aimlessly. She said, "You always speak of Krochmalna Street. Why haven't you ever taken me there?"

I didn't answer immediately. "That street is completely bound up with my youth. For you, it won't be anything more than a dirty slum."

"Just the same, I want to see it. We can go by cab."

"No, it's not so far. I can't believe myself that I haven't been back to visit Krochmalna Street since I left there in 1917."

We could have gone by way of Iron Street, but I preferred to walk to Prezejazd and there to turn south. On Bank Place we stopped momentarily before the gate of the old bank with its heavy columns. Just as in my boyhood, carts of money were being trundled in and out, guarded by armed police. Żabia Street was still the millinery center, with rows of windows showing hats that were modern and hats worn only by older women—hats with veils, nets, ostrich plumes, wooden cherries, grapes, and hats with crepe for those in mourning. Behind the iron fence of the Saxony Gardens the chestnut trees were scattering their blossoms.

There were benches on Iron Gate Square and weary passersby were sitting in the sunshine. God in heaven, this walk was wakening in me the enthusiasm of a boy. We stopped before the building called Vienna Hall, where wealthy men had weddings for their daughters catered. Below, among the columns, women still peddled handkerchiefs, needles, pins, buttons, and yard goods of calico, linen—even remnants of velvet and silk. We came out onto Gnoyna Street and my nostrils were assailed by the familiar odor of soap, oil, and horse manure. In this neighborhood were the cheders, studyhouses, and Hasidic prayer houses where I had learned Torah.

We reached Krochmalna Street and the stench I recalled from my childhood struck me first—a blend of burned oil, rotten fruit, and chimney smoke. Everything was the same—the cobblestone pavement, the steep gutter, the balconies hung with wash. We passed a factory with wire-latticed windows and a blind wall with a wooden gate I never saw open in all my youth. Every house here was bound up with memories. No. 5 contained a yeshiva in which I had studied for a term. There was a ritual bath in the courtyard, where matrons came in the evening to immerse themselves. I used to see them emerge clean and flushed. Someone told me that this building had been the home of Rabbi Itche Meir Alter, the founder of the Gur dynasty generations ago. In my time the yeshiva had been part of the Grodzisk house of prayer. Its beadle was a drunk. When he had a drop too much, he told tales of saints, dybbuks, half-mad squires, and sorcerers. He ate one meal a day and always (except on the Sabbath) stale bread crumbled into borscht.

No. 4 was a huge bazaar, Yanash's Court, which had two gates—one leading into Krochmalna and the other into Mirowska Street. They sold everything here—fruit, vegetables, dairy, geese, fish. There were stores selling secondhand shoes and old clothes of all kinds.

We came to the Place. It always swarmed with prostitutes, pimps, and petty thieves in torn jackets and caps with visors pulled down over their eyes. In my time, the Boss here had been Blind Itche, chief of the pickpockets, proprietor of brothels, a swaggerer and a knife carrier. Somewhere in No. 11 or 13 lived fat Reitzele, a woman who weighed three hundred pounds. Reitzele was supposed to conduct business with white slavers from Buenos Aires. She was also a procurer of servant girls. Many games were played in the Place. You drew numbers from a bag and you could win a police whistle, a chocolate cake, a pen with a view of Cracow, a doll that sat up and cried "Mama."

I stopped with Betty to gape. The same louts, the same flat pronunciation, the same games. I was afraid that all this would disgust her, but she had become infected by my nostalgia. "You should have brought me here the very first day we met!" she said.

"Betty, I'll write a play called *Krochmalna* and you shall play the leading role."

"You're a great promiser."

I didn't know what to show her next—the den in No. 6 where the thieves played cards and dominoes and where the fences came to buy stolen goods; the prayer house in No. 10 where we used to live, or the Radzymin studyhouse in No. 12, to which we later moved; the courtyards where I attended cheder or the stores where my mother used to send me to buy food and kerosene. The only change I could observe was that the houses had lost most of their plaster and grown black from smoke. Here and there, a wall was supported on logs. The gutters seemed even deeper, their stink even stronger. I stopped before each gate and peered in. All the garbage bins were heaped high with refuse. Dyers dyed clothing, tinsmiths patched broken pots, men with sacks on their shoulders cried, "Ole clo's, ole clo's, I buy rags, ole pants, ole shoes, ole hats; ole clo's, ole clo's." Here and there, a beggar sang a song—of the *Titanic*, which had gone down in 1911, of the striker Baruch Shulman, who had thrown a bomb in 1905 and been hanged. Magicians were performing the same stunts they had in my childhood—they swallowed fire, rolled barrels with their feet, lay down bareback on a bed of nails. I knew it couldn't be, but I imagined that I recognized the girl who went around shaking a tambourine hung with bells to collect coins from the watchers. She wore the same velvet breeches with silver sequins. Her hair was cut like a boy's. She was tall and slim, flat-chested, her eyes were shiny black. A parrot with a broken beak perched on her shoulder.

"If all this could only be transported to America!" Betty said.

I asked her to wait outside and opened the door to the Neustat prayer house— empty, but the holy ark with the two gilded lions on the cornice, the pulpit, the reading table and benches gave witness that Jews still came here to pray. On shelves the holy books lay and stood in black rows, old and ragged. Since no one was inside, I called Betty to join me. I shouted and an echo responded. I pulled apart the curtain before the ark, opened the door, and glanced at the scrolls in their velvet mantelets and the gold embroidery tarnished with the years. Betty and I thrust our heads inside. Her face was hot. We shared a sinful urge to desecrate the sacred and we kissed. At the same time I excused myself before the scrolls and reminded them that Betty was not a married woman.

We left the prayer house and I looked around the courtyard. Shmerl the shoemaker once lived and had his workshop here in a cellar. He had been given the nickname "Shmerl not today." If you came with shoes or boots to be soled or heeled, he always said, "Not today!" He died while we were still living in Warsaw. A cart drove into the courtyard and took him away to the Hospital for Epidemic Diseases. On Krochmalna Street it was believed that they poisoned patients there. The wags in the courtyard joked that when the Angel of Death with his thousand eyes and sharp sword came for him, Shmerl said, "Not today," but the Angel replied, "Yes, today."

At No. 10 the balcony of what had been our apartment was hung with wash. It had once seemed so high to me, but now I could almost reach it with my fingers. I glanced into the stores. Where were Eli the grocer and his wife, Zeldele? Just as Eli was tall, quick, agile, sharp, and argumentative, Zeldele was small, slow-moving, dull, and good-natured. Zeldele had to be told twice what it was a customer wanted. For her to put out her hand, take a piece of paper, slice off a chunk of cheese, and weigh it could take a quarter of an hour. If you asked her the cost, she began to mull it over and scratch under her wig with a hairpin. If the customer bought on credit and Zeldele marked down the amount, she couldn't make out later what she had written. When the war came and German marks and pfennigs came into use, she grew completely bewildered. Eli abused her in front of the customers and called her "Cow." She became sick during the war and they didn't manage to get her to a hospital. She lay down in bed and went off to sleep like a chick. Eli cried, wailed, and beat his head against the wall. Three months later, he married a plump wench who was just as slow and tranquil as Zeldele.

3

We entered Yanash's Court and went to the slaughterhouse. The same blood-spattered walls, the hens and roosters going to their deaths shrieking with the same voices: "What have I done to deserve this? Murderers!" Evening had fallen and the harsh light of the lamps reflected off the slaughterers' blades.

Women pushed forward, each with her fowl. Porters loaded baskets with dead birds and carried them off to the pluckers. This hell made mockery of all blather about humanism. I had long considered becoming a vegetarian and at that moment I swore never again to touch a piece of meat or fish.

Outside the slaughterhouse, the lamps used to illuminate the courtyard only intensified the darkness. We passed tubs and basins containing live carp, tench, and pike, which the housewives would clean and chop in honor of the Sabbath. We walked on straw, feathers, and slime. The storekeepers scolded and swore the familiar old curses: "A black plague on you!" "A fever in your guts!" "You should lead your daughter to a black wedding canopy!"

We left the bazaar and went into the street again. Before gates and lamp posts stood streetwalkers—some fat with huge bosoms and flowing hips; others slim, draped in shawls. Workers coming from factories and shops on Wola and Iron Streets stopped to talk to the whores and haggle over prices.

Betty said, "Let's get out of here! Besides, I'm hungry."

Suddenly I saw the No. 7 building, where Bashele and her three daughters had moved. Even if the family was still alive, they would have left their apartment years ago. Well, but suppose they hadn't moved out? And Shosha still remembered the tales I used to tell her, our playing house, hide-and-seek, tag? I stopped in front of the gate.

Betty asked, "Why are you standing there? Let's go."

"Betty, I have to find out if by any chance Bashele still lives here."

"Who is this Bashele?"

"Shosha's mother."

"And who is Shosha?"

"Wait, I will explain."

A woman walked into the gate and I asked her if Bashele lived in the courtyard.

"Bashele? Does she have a husband? What's her surname?" the woman asked.

I couldn't recall, or perhaps I had never known the family's last name. "Yes, her husband has a round beard," I answered. "He used to be a clerk at some store. She has a daughter, Shosha. I hope they're alive."

The woman clapped her hands. "I know the one you mean! Basha Schuldiener. They live on the first floor opposite the gate to the left. You're an American, eh?"

I pointed to Betty. "She is an American."

"Family?"

"Just friends. I haven't seen them for almost twenty years."

"Twenty years? Go straight ahead, but be careful. The kids dug a hole in the middle of the yard. You can fall and break a leg. It's dark there. The landlords grab the rent money but they don't believe in lighting a lamp at night."

Betty began to grumble, but I exclaimed, "It's a miracle! A miracle! Many thanks!" I called after the woman. I stood in the courtyard of No. 7 and looked across it into a window with a burning gaslight behind which I might possibly soon meet Bashele and Shosha. As if she finally realized what I was going through, Betty grew silent. I took her arm and led her along. Despite the darkness I spotted the hole and we avoided it. We came to the short flight of unlit stairs that led to the first-floor apartment, I felt about for a doorknob, pushed the door open, and a second miracle unfolded before me. I saw Bashele. She stood at the kitchen table peeling an onion. She had aged little in all this time. Her wig was still blond; her wide fair face had wrinkled slightly, but her eyes looked up with the amiable half smile I remembered from my childhood. Her dress might have come from those days, too. When she saw me, her upper lip lifted—she still had her broad teeth. Her mortar and pestle, the cooking utensils, the closet with the carved molding, the chairs, the table—all were familiar.

"Bashele! You don't recognize me, but I recognize you!" I said.

She put down the onion and knife. "I do recognize you. You're Arele."

In the Pentateuch, when Joseph recognized his brothers, they kissed and embraced, but Bashele wasn't a woman who would kiss a strange man, not even one she had known as a child.

Betty arched her brows. "Is it true that you haven't seen each other for almost twenty years?"

"Wait—yes, almost as long," Bashele said in a common woman's voice, kind, motherly, and yet unique. I would have known it out of a million other voices. "Many years," she added.

"But he was only a child," Betty protested.

"Yes. He and Shosha are the same age," Bashele said.

Betty asked, "How can you recognize someone who left here as a child?"

Bashele shrugged. "As soon as he started speaking, I knew him. I heard you became a writer for the papers. Don't stand there in the doorway. Come in and be welcome. This is probably your wife," she said, nodding toward Betty.

Betty smiled. "No, I'm not his wife. I'm an actress from America and he's writing a play for me."

"I know," Bashele said. "We have a neighbor who reads your things. Every time your name appears in the paper he comes and reads to us. Once it said that a piece by you will be played in the theater."

"Where is Shosha?" I asked.

"Went to the store for sugar. She'll be right back."

As Bashele spoke, Shosha came in. God in heaven—what surprises this day had brought, each greater than the other! Were my eyes deceiving me? Shosha had neither grown nor aged. I gaped at this mystery. After a while, I did observe a slight change in her face and in her height. She had grown perhaps an inch or two. She wore a faded skirt and sleeveless jacket that I could have sworn she wore twenty years ago. She stood holding a paper cone used by grocers to weigh out a quarter pound and looked at us. In her eyes was the same childish fascination I remembered from the times I told her stories.

"Shosha, do you know who this is?" Bashele asked.

Shosha didn't answer.

"It's Arele, the rabbi's son."

"Arele," Shosha repeated, and it was her voice, although not exactly the same.

"Put down the sugar and take off your jacket," Bashele said.

Slowly Shosha put the cone of sugar on the table and took off her jacket. Her figure had remained childlike, although I detected signs of breasts. Her skirt was shorter than those in style and it was hard to tell by the gaslight whether it was blue or black. This was how garments looked that had passed through the disinfection station during the war—shrunken, steamed, faded. Shosha's neck was long, her arms and legs thin. Everyone in Warsaw wore sheer, glossy, colored stockings, but Shosha's appeared to be made of coarse cotton.

Bashele began, "The war, the miserable war destroyed us. Yppe died shortly after you moved to the country. She caught a fever and took to bed. Someone snitched and the hospital wagon came for her. For eight days the fever consumed her. They let none of us into the hospital. On the last day I went to ask about her and the guard at the gate said, *'Bardzo kiepsko,'* and I knew that she was gone. Zelig wasn't in Warsaw. He didn't even go to his daughter's funeral. Four years went by before we could put up a tombstone. Teibele grew up a young lady, God spare her, smart, pretty, educated—everything you could want. She went to the Gymnasium. She is a bookkeeper now in a mattress business. They sell everything wholesale. On Thursdays she figures out what's coming to all the employees and gives the slips to the cashier. If she doesn't sign them, nobody gets paid. The boys run after her but she says, 'I've got plenty of time.' She doesn't live here with us, comes only on Sabbaths and holidays. She has an apartment with a roommate on Grzybowska Street. If you tell people you live on Krochmalna Street it ruins your chances for a good match. Shosha lives at home, as you can see for yourself. Arele, and you, young lady, take off your coats. Shosha, don't stand there like a clod! The lady is from America."

"From America," Shosha repeated.

"Have a seat. I'll make tea. Have you eaten supper?" Bashele asked.

"Thanks, we're not hungry." Betty winked at me.

"Sit down. Arele, your parents still live in the provinces?"

"Father is no longer living."

"He was a dear man, a saint. I used to consult him on questions of religious law. He wouldn't even look at a female. The moment I came in he turned away. He was always at the lectern. Such big books, like in a studyhouse. What did he die of? There are no such Jews any more. Even the Hasidim dress like dandies today—cutaway gaberdines, polished boots. Mother still living?"

"Yes."

"And your brother, Moishele?"

"Moishele is a rabbi."

"Moishele a rabbi? You hear, Shosha? He was such a tiny thing. Didn't even go to cheder then."

"He did go to cheder," Shosha said. "Here in the courtyard at the crazy teacher's."

"Eh? The years go by. Where is Moishele a rabbi?"

"In Galicia."

"In Galicia? Where is that? There are such faraway towns," Bashele said. "When we lived in No. 10, Warsaw was Russia. All the signs had to be in Russian. Then the Germans came, and with them the hunger. Later, the Polacks raised their heads and shouted, *'Nasza Polska!'* Some boys around here went to join Pilsudski's legion and were killed. Pilsudski went with his men to Kiev; then they were pushed back to the Vistula. The people thought the Bolsheviks were coming and the ruffians began to talk about knifing all the rich and taking their money. Then the Bolsheviks were driven back. They were driven here, driven there—the shortages grew. Zelig is never at home any more. Things happened I will tell you about some other time. People have become selfish. They stopped caring even for their nearest. The zloty is falling, the dollar rises.

Here they call dollars 'noodles.' And everything is dearer, dearer. Shosha, set the table.''

"With the tablecloth or the oilcloth?''

"Let it be the oilcloth.''

Betty signaled that she wanted to tell me something in private, I leaned toward her and she whispered, "I can't eat here. If you want to stay with them, I'll go back to the hotel alone.''

I said, "Bashele, Shosha, the fact that I lived to see you again is a great joy to me, but the lady has to leave and I can't let her go alone. I'll come back later. If not tonight, then tomorrow.''

"Don't go away," Shosha said. "You went away once and I thought you were never coming back again. One time, our neighbor—Leizer, his name is—said you were in Warsaw and showed us your name in the newspaper, but it didn't say your address. I thought you had forgotten all about us.''

"Shosha, a day didn't go by that I didn't think of you.''

"Then why didn't you come over? Something you wrote—it had your name on it—was printed in a paper. Not a paper but a book with green covers. Leizer reads everything. He's a watchmaker. He came and read it to us. You described Krochmalna Street accurately.''

"Yes, Shosha, I didn't forget anything.''

"We moved to No. 7 here and after that you never came over. You got big and you put on phylacteries. I saw you pass by a few times. I wanted to go over to you, but you were walking so fast. You became a Hasid and didn't look at girls. I was shy. Then they said you left the city. Yppe died and there was a funeral. I saw her lying there dead and she was all white.''

"Shosha, be quiet!" her mother snapped at her.

"White as chalk. I dreamed about her every night. They made her shroud from my shirt. I got sick and stopped growing. They took me to Dr. Kniaster and he gave me a prescription, but it didn't help. Teibele is tall and pretty.''

"You are pretty, too, Shosha," I said.

"I'm like a midget.''

"No, Shosha. You have a nice figure.''

"I'm grown up and I look like a child. I couldn't go to school. The books were too hard for me. When the Germans took over they began to teach us German. A boy is a *Knabe* to them and how could I remember all that? We were supposed to buy German books and Mama didn't have the money for it. Finally, they sent me home for the second time.''

"It's all from not getting enough to eat," Bashele added. "They mixed the bread with turnip or sawdust. It tasted like clay. That winter the potatoes froze and got so sweet you couldn't eat them. I cooked potatoes three times a day. Dr. Kniaster said that Shosha had no blood and he prescribed some brown medicine. She took it three times a day, but when you're hungry, nothing helps. How Teibele—the evil eye spare her—managed to grow up so pretty is God's miracle. When will you be back?''

"Tomorrow.''

"Come to lunch tomorrow. You used to be fond of noodles with beans. Come at two. You can bring the lady along. Shosha, this lady is an actress," Bashele said, indicating Betty. "Where do you perform? In the theater?''

"I played in Russia, I played in America, and I hope to appear here in Warsaw," Betty said. "It all depends on Mr. Greidinger."

"He always could write," Shosha said. "He bought a notebook and a pencil and filled three pages. He drew figures, too. One time he drew a house on fire. Flames shot out of every window. He drew the house with a black pencil and the fire with a red pencil. Fire and smoke poured from the chimney. Remember, Arele?"

"I remember. Good night. I'll be here tomorrow at two."

"Don't stay away so long again," Shosha said.

4

I wanted to walk but Betty hailed a droshky. She told the driver to take us to the restaurant on Leszno Street where we had had our first meal in company with Sam Dreiman and Feitelzohn.

In the droshky, Betty put her hand on my shoulder. "The girl is an idiot. She belongs in an institution. But you're in love with her. The moment you saw her, your eyes lit up in a strange way. I'm beginning to think you aren't in your right mind yourself."

"That may be, Betty."

"Writers are all slightly touched. I'm crazy, too. All talents are. I once read a book about this. I forget the author's name."

"Lombroso."

"Yes, maybe. Or maybe the book was about him. But since each of us is crazy in a different fashion, one can observe the other's madness. Don't start up with that girl. She is sick. If you promise her something and don't keep your word, she'll crack up altogether."

"I know."

"What do you see in her?"

"I see myself."

"Well, you'll fall into a net you'll never be able to untangle yourself from. I don't even believe that such a woman is capable of living with a man. She surely can't have a child."

"I don't need children."

"Instead of your raising her up, she'll drag you down to her level. I know of such a case—a highly intelligent man, an engineer, and he married some unbalanced woman who was older. She bore him a crippled child, a piece of flesh that could neither live nor die. Instead of placing it in an institution, they dragged it to all kinds of clinics, spas, and quacks. It died finally, but the man was ruined."

"I won't have such a freak with Shosha."

"It's typical that the moment something interesting presents itself to me, fate thumbs its nose in my face."

"Betty, you have a lover who is goodness himself, rich as Croesus, and ready to turn the world upside down for you."

"I know what I have. I hope this won't spoil our plans for the play."

"It won't spoil anything."

"If I hadn't seen it with my own eyes, I wouldn't have believed such a thing possible."

I leaned my head against the back of the droshky and looked up above the tin rooftops at the Warsaw sky. It seemed to me that the city had changed. There was something festive and Purim-like in the air. We passed Iron Gate Square again. All the windows of the Vienna Hall were illuminated and I could hear music. Someone must be getting married there this evening. I closed my eyes and put my hand on Betty's lap. The smells of spring came to my nostrils along with the stench of garbage wagons transporting the day's refuse to the fields.

The droshky stopped. Betty wanted to pay but I would not allow it. I helped her out and took her arm. Normally I would have been self-conscious about escorting such an elegant lady to a restaurant, but my encounter with Shosha had dazed me. In the restaurant an orchestra was playing American jazz and hits from Warsaw cabarets. All the tables seemed to be taken. Here they ate the chickens, ducks, geese, and turkeys that had been slaughtered earlier that day. It smelled of roasting, of garlic, horseradish, beer, and cigars. The older men had tucked the huge napkins into their stiff collars. Bellies protruded, necks were thick, and bald pates gleamed like mirrors. The women chattered vivaciously, laughed, and dug their red fingernails into the portions of fowl that couldn't be got at by a fork. Their rouged lips drank from foaming mugs of beer. The headwaiter offered us a table in a niche. They knew Betty here. Sam Dreiman left dollar tips. Skillfully waiters maneuvered among the tables, balancing trays from which steam rose. I sat not facing Betty but alongside her.

The menu didn't feature a single dish that wasn't fish or meat, and I had just vowed to become a vegetarian. After some deliberation I decided the vow would have to wait another day. I ordered broth and meatballs with farfel and carrots, but I had no desire for food. Betty ordered a cocktail and a steak, insisting that it be rare. She took little sips of her drink and looked at me sharply.

She said, "I don't intend to hang around this stinking world too long. Forty years is the maximum. I don't want to live a day longer. What for? If it works out that I can perform a few years the way I want, all the better. If not, I'll put an end to it sooner. Thank God for one gift—the choice to commit suicide."

"You'll live to ninety. You'll be a second Sarah Bernhardt."

"No. Also, I don't choose to be a second anything. It's first or nothing. Sam promises me a huge inheritance, but I'm convinced he'll outlive me, and I hope that he does with all my heart. They don't know how to mix a cocktail here. They try to copy America but imitations are always false. The music's a poor imitation, too. The whole world wants to copy America and America copies the whole world. Why should I be an actress? Actors are all monkeys or parrots. I tried to write once. I still have a bundle of poems lying around—some in Yiddish, some in Russian. Nobody wanted to publish them. I read the magazines and I see that they print the worst rubbish, but from me they demand that I be another Pushkin or Yesenin. Why are you looking at my steak like that? What you said about vegetarianism today is nonsense. If God created the world this way, then that is His will."

"The vegetarians only express a protest."

"How can a bubble protest against the sea? It's arrogant. If a cow lets herself be milked, she must be milked, and if she lets herself be slaughtered, she should be slaughtered. That's what Darwin said."

"Darwin didn't say that."

"No matter, someone said it. Since Sam gives me money, I must take it from him, and since he goes to Mlawa and leaves me alone, I must spend time with someone else."

"Since your father let himself be shot, then—"

"That's vile!"

"Forgive me."

"Basically, you're right. But man must have regard for his fellow man. Even animals don't devour their own species."

"In my uncle's house a tomcat killed his own kittens."

"A tomcat does what nature tells him. Or this could have been a mad tomcat. You're a mad tomcat yourself, and you too will devour somebody. You looked at that stunted girl today with the eyes of a tomcat looking at a canary. You'll give her a few weeks of happiness, then you'll abandon her. I know this as well as I know it's night now."

"All I did was promise her I'd come for lunch tomorrow."

"Go to her tomorrow and tell her you're married. Actually you do have a wife—that Communist you told me about. What's her name? Dora. Since you don't believe in marriage, then the woman you're with *is* your wife."

"In that case, every modern man has dozens of wives."

"Yes, every modern man has dozens of wives and every modern woman has dozens of husbands. If laws no longer have meaning, let the lawlessness apply to everybody."

The music stopped and we grew silent. Betty tasted a piece of her steak and pushed the plate away. The headwaiter noticed and came over to ask if he could bring her something else. She said that she was not hungry. She complained that the cook used too many spices. Our waiter came over and the two men began to discuss the chef. The headwaiter said, "He'll have to go."

"Don't fire him on my account," Betty said.

"It's not a question of only you. He's been told a hundred times not to use so much pepper, but it's like a madness in him. Because he likes pepper he'll end up without a job—isn't that madness?"

"Oh, every chef is half mad," the waiter said.

Both he and the headwaiter lingered around the table while we ate dessert. They were apparently afraid of losing their usual tip, but Betty took out two dollars and gave one to each of them. Both men began to bow and scrape. In Warsaw a family could have eaten for half a week on that sum. A millionaire's mistress apparently had to act like the millionaire himself.

"Come, let's go," Betty said.

"Where?"

"To my place.'

5

I got home at eight in the morning. On the way to catch my trolley I glanced in a mirror—a pale face, a bristly beard; I had had to leave the hotel early, before the maid brought breakfast. The trolley was full of men and young women going to factories and shops, with lunches under their arms. I yawned and tried to stretch, but there was no room to extend my legs. It had rained during the night and the sky hung overcast and dark as dusk; in the trolley the lights had been turned on. All the faces appeared grim and preoccupied. Everyone seemed to be taking account, wondering at the start of another day, what's the sense of all this effort, and where does it lead to? I imagined that by some common sensitivity they all realized the same mistake and were asking, "How could we have missed something so obvious and why is it too late to correct it?"

At home Tekla let me in. In the corridor her eyes expressed a reproof that seemed to say, "You wild man!" She asked if I wanted breakfast and I told her thanks, but later.

She said to me, "A glass of coffee would be good."

"So be it, dear Tekla." And I handed her a half zloty.

"No, no, no," she protested.

"Take it, Tekla, I like you."

Her cheeks flushed. "You are too good."

I opened the door to my room. My bed stood made and untouched, the shades were lowered—a bit of yesterday lingering and demanding its due. I stretched out on the bed and tried to snatch a few moments' rest. Never had a night seemed as long as this. Once my mother told me the story of a bewitched yeshiva boy who bent down over a water tub to wash his hands before supper and in the second it took him to obtain a pitcher of water lived through a reincarnation of seventy years. Something of this kind had happened to me. During one night I had found my lost love and then succumbed to temptation and betrayed her. I had stolen the concubine of my benefactor, lied to her, aroused her passion by telling her all my lusty adventures, and made her confess sins that filled me with disgust. I had been impotent and then turned into a sexual giant. We got drunk, quarreled, kissed, insulted one another. I had acted like a shameless pervert and an ardent repentant. At dawn, some drunkard tried to break open our door and we were both convinced that Sam Dreiman had come back to surprise us, punish us, perhaps even put us to death. I dozed off and Tekla wakened me with a tray of coffee, fresh rolls, and fried eggs. She no longer paid attention to my wishes but, like a sister or wife, acted on her own initiative. She looked at me knowingly. When she put the tray on the table, I took her around from behind and kissed her nape. She made no move for a moment. Then she turned and murmured, "What are you doing?"

"Give me your mouth."

"Oh, it's forbidden!" She brought her lips to mine.

I kissed her long. She kissed back and her breasts pressed against me. She kept glancing at the door. She risked her reputation, her job. She tore from my arms, panting. She seized my wrists, held them with a peasant's strength, and hissed like a goose, "The mistress could come in!" She shuffled toward the door, dragging her legs with their broad calves. I recalled the phrase from the *Ethics of the Fathers:* "One sin drags another." I sipped the coffee, bit into a roll, tasted the eggs, and took off my shoes. The play lay on my desk, but I couldn't write now. I lay down on the bed and I neither slept nor stayed fully awake. In all the novels I had read, the heroes desired only one woman, but here I was, lusting after the whole female gender.

Finally I dropped off, and in my sleep I wrote the play. The writing became increasingly harder. The pen blotted, ran dry; it scratched the paper and I couldn't make out my own handwriting. I opened my eyes and glanced at my watch— ten past one. I had slept for hours. I was supposed to be at Shosha's at two, and I still must wash and shave. I had decided to take Shosha a box of candy. I no longer needed to steal a groschen or six from my mother to get Shosha chocolate—my pockets were stuffed with Sam Dreiman's banknotes.

I did everything in a hurry. It would take too long to walk to Krochmalna Street, and when I left the confectionary I hailed a droshky. As it pulled up before No. 7, my wristwatch showed five minutes past two. I could feel the mother's and daughter's anxiety. I rushed through the courtyard and nearly fell into the hole I had sidestepped in the dark the evening before. When I opened the door, I walked into a holiday household. The table was set with a tablecloth and china. Shosha wore a Sabbath dress and high-heeled shoes. She no longer looked like a midget, merely a short girl. Her hair was set differently—high, to make her appear taller. Even Bashele had fixed herself up in honor of my visit. I handed Shosha the candy and her blue eyes gazed at me in embarrassed bliss.

Bashele said, "Arele, you are a real gentleman."

"Mama, shall I open it?"

"Why not?"

I helped her. I had asked the confectioner for his best candy. The box was black with little gold stars. The chocolate lay in fluted paper cups, each of a different size and in its own niche.

The color changed on Shosha's face. "Mama, look!"

"You shouldn't have spent so much," Bashele protested.

"Remember, Shosha, how I used to steal money from my mother to buy you chocolate and was lashed for it at home?"

"I remember, Arele."

"Don't eat any chocolate before lunch. It'll spoil your appetite," Bashele said.

"Just one, Mama!" Shosha pleaded. She studied which piece to select, pointing to one and then another, but she couldn't make up her mind. She stopped, bewildered.

I had read in a book on psychiatry that the inability to decide about even small things was a symptom of a spiritual disorder. I picked out three pieces, one for each of us. Shosha held the candy between her thumb and index finger and lifted her pinky with the gesture of the poseurs of Krochmalna Street. She took a bite. "Mama, it melts in your mouth! How delicious!"

"Say thank you, at least."

"Oh, Arele, if you only knew—"

"Give him a kiss," Bashele told her.

"I'd be ashamed."

"What's to be ashamed of? You're a young lady—may the evil eye spare you."

"Not here, then. In the other room." She held out her hand. "Come with me," she said.

I followed her into the other room, which was crowded with bundles, sacks, and old furniture. There was a metal cot, with a straw mattress but no sheet. Shosha stood on tiptoe and I bent down toward her. She took my face in her childlike hands and kissed me on the lips, on both cheeks, on my forehead, and on the nose. Her fingers were hot. I took her in my arms and we stood there clinging to each other.

I asked, "Shosha, you want to be mine?"

"Yes," Shosha replied.

CHAPTER FIVE

1

It was early summer, the month of May, and Sam Dreiman had rented a cottage for himself and Betty in Świder, not far from Otwock. It wasn't the villa we had seen in March. He had hired a maid and a cook. Every morning, after breakfast, Sam went to bathe in the Świderek River. He stood under the low waterfall with his round shoulders, white-haired chest, swollen belly, and let the water pour over him. He screamed with pleasure, sneezed, gasped, and barked out his gratitude to the cool stream. Betty sat on the beach on a folding chair under a parasol and read a book. Like me, Betty avoided all sports. She could not swim. In the sun, her skin became sickly-red and developed blisters. In the attic, a room with a balcony had been set aside for me, and I used it several weekends. But I stopped going there. There were constant visitors from Warsaw or America—guests came even from the American consulate. The majority of the visitors spoke English, and then when Sam knew I was coming he invited actors and actresses who were scheduled to appear in our play and demanded that I read scenes to them. They were all old, but they dressed like young people—the men in narrow pants, the women in gaudy trousers over their broad hips. They kept praising me and I couldn't stand the excitement and even less the undeserved compliments. I had paid another two months' advance on my room on Leszno Street and wasn't about to let it stand empty. Besides, each time I went, Sam complained because I wouldn't bathe in the little river. I was embarrassed about undressing before strangers. I had never freed myself from a notion inherited from generations: the body is a vessel of shame and disgrace, dust in life and worse in death.

But what really kept me in Warsaw was Shosha. I went to see her now daily. I had laid out a program and tried desperately to stick to it. It required me to rise at eight and wash at the stand. The hours from nine to one were to be spent at my desk with the play. But I had also started a novel, which I shouldn't have done. Besides, the few hours of work were full of interruptions. Feitelzohn phoned every day. He had prepared the first soul expedition, which was to take place at Sam Dreiman's summer house. He was planning to read a paper there, to defend his theory that jealousy was about to vanish from human love and sex and be supplemented by a wish to share libidinous enjoyments with others. Celia called me every other day from Jósefow. Each time, she asked the same thing: "Why do you sit in hot Warsaw? Why not enjoy the fresh outdoors?" She and Haiml both described how balmy the air was in Jósefow, how cool the nights, how sweet the song of the birds. They begged me to come to them. Celia argued, "Let's snatch a little peace before another world war breaks out."

I admitted that they were right and promised them, as I promised Sam Dreiman and Betty, that I would come out that very day or the next, but the moment the clock showed one-thirty I headed for Krochmalna Street. I would enter the gate of No. 7 and see Shosha standing at her window watching for me—a blond girl, blue-eyed, with a short nose, thin lips, a slender neck, her hair braided in pigtails. Thank God, she had all her teeth. She spoke the Yiddish of Krochmalna Street. In her own fashion she denied death. Although they had all died, in Shosha's mind Eli and Zeldele still ran the grocery store, David and Mirale still sold butter, raw and boiled milk, as well as sour milk and cottage cheese, Esther still kept the candy store where you could buy chocolate, cheesecake, soda water, and ice cream. Each day Shosha surprised me with something. She got out her old school textbooks with the familiar pictures and poems. She had kept the notebooks in which I began my literary career and attempted to paint as well. I noticed that when it came to drawing I hadn't made the slightest progress.

Whenever I was with her, I asked myself, How can this be? How can it be explained? Had Shosha found a magical way to stop the advance of time? Was this the secret of love or the power of retrogression? Oddly, Bashele, like Shosha, showed no surprise at my reappearance. I had come back and I was here. I gave Bashele money to prepare meals for me, and when I arrived at two or a bit later, the house already smelled of new potatoes, mushrooms, tomatoes, cauliflower— whatever she had bought that day. She set the table and the three of us sat down and ate as if we had never been parted.

Bashele's dishes tasted as good as they had when I was a child. No one could give to the borscht such a sweet-and-sour zest as Bashele. She added spices to her dishes. She cooked cabbage with raisins and cream of tartar. She kept jars of cloves, saffron, crushed almonds, cinnamon, and ginger on her kitchen shelves.

Bashele took everything in stride. I told her I had just become a vegetarian, and she asked no questions but began to provide meals for me consisting of fruit, eggs, and vegetables. Shosha would go into the alcove to take out her old playthings and lay them out for me as she had done twenty years before. During the meal Bashele and Shosha related all kinds of things. The stone over Yppe's grave had tipped and was leaning on another tombstone. Bashele wanted to set it upright, but the cemetery watchman demanded fifty zlotys. Leizer the watchmaker had a clock with a brass bird that popped out every half hour and sang like a canary. He had a pen that wrote without being dipped in ink and a lens that could light a cigarette when held under the sun. Berl the furrier's daughter had fallen in love with the son of the proprietor of the tough guys' den at No. 6. The mother didn't want to go to the wedding, but the rabbi who came after my father, Joshua the preacher, said this would be a sin. In No. 8, a ditch was dug and they found a dead Russian sapper, with a sword and a revolver. The uniform wasn't yet ruined and medals were still pinned to its lapel. Each time I asked for a person on Krochmalna Street, Bashele knew all about him or her. Most had died. Of those who were still living, many had moved to the provinces or gone to America. One beggar who died in the street was found to be carrying a pouch with golden ducats dating back to the Russian occupation. A whore had been visited by a man from Cracow. He paid her one zloty and went with her to her cellar room. The next day he came again and the day after that, too, and so day after day. He had fallen in love with her. He divorced his wife and married the whore.

Shosha listened in silence. Suddenly she blurted, "She lives in No. 9. She became a decent woman."

It would seem that Shosha understood such things. I glanced at her and she blushed. "Tell me, Shosha," I asked, "did anyone ever propose a match to you?"

Shosha put down her spoon. "They offered me one with a tinsmith from No. 5. His wife died and a matchmaker came to see me."

Bashele shook her head. "Why not tell him about the store manager who wanted you?"

"Who was this manager?" I asked.

"Oh, he worked in a store on Mead Street. A short fellow with a lot of black hair. I didn't like him," Shosha said.

"Why not?"

"He had black teeth. When he laughed, it sounded like 'ech, ech, ech, hee, hee, hee.' "

As Shosha mimicked the man's laughter, she started laughing herself. Then she grew serious and said, "I can't marry without love."

2

No, Shosha hadn't remained completely a child. I kissed her when her mother went shopping and she kissed me back. Her face glowed. I put her on my lap and she kissed my lips and played with my earlobes.

She said, "Arele, I never forgot you. Mama laughed at me. 'He doesn't even know you exist any more,' she told me. 'He probably has a fiancée by now, or a wife and children.' Yppe died, and Teibele went to school. The frosts came, but Teibeie always got up early, washed her face, and took her books. She got good grades. Mama was kind to me but she didn't buy me a dress or shoes. When she got angry she said, 'Too bad you didn't die instead of Yppe!' Don't repeat this—she would kill me. During the war Mama began to sell crockery—glasses, ashtrays, saucers, and things like that. She took up a place between the First and the Second Market. She sat there every day and earned next to nothing—a few pfennigs or a mark. I was left alone. They think that I'm a child because I'm small, but I understand everything. Daddy has another woman. He lives with her on Nizka Street. He comes home maybe once every three months. He comes in, counts out some money, and starts right in to yell. He goes to Teibele's—to where she lives. He says, 'She is *my* daughter.' Sometimes he sends the money by her."

"What does your father do? How does he earn money?"

Shosha's face grew solemn. "It's not allowed to say."

"You can tell me."

"I can't tell anybody."

"Shosha, I swear by God I won't tell a soul."

Shosha sat down on a stool next to me and clasped my legs. "With the dead."

"In the burial society?"

"Yes, there. First he worked in a wine and spirits store. When the boss died, the sons pushed him out. On Grzybowska Street there is a society, The True Mercy, and they bury the dead. The boss there went to cheder with Papa."

"Your father drives a hearse?"

"No, a car. This is a kind of car that if someone dies in Mokotów or Szmulewizna, Papa goes and brings him to Warsaw. He has gotten a gray beard but he dyes it and it's black again. The sweetheart—that's what they call her—is with the society, too. Swear that you'll tell nobody."

"Shoshele, whom would I tell? Who of my friends knows you?"

"Mama thinks that no one knows, but they know. There was a lot of trouble about drying the wash in the attic. If you hang it out to dry in the courtyard, it's stolen. Also, a policeman comes and gives a ticket. Whenever it's wash time, a brawl breaks out. The women curse and sometimes hit each other. There isn't enough room for everybody. One woman who sells cracked eggs cut a line with wash hanging on it and all the shirts fell down. The others beat her and she ran to snitch to the cops. Oh, there was such a fuss I had to laugh. The woman got mad at Mama and she yelled, 'Go to the dead, with your husband's sweetheart, and rot with them together!' When Mama came home she got spasms. They had to call the barber-surgeon. If Mama knew that I told you, she'd scream terribly."

"Shosha, I'll tell no one."

"Why did he leave Mama? I saw her once, that sweetheart. She has a voice like a man. It was winter and Mama got sick. We were left without a groschen. You're sure you want to hear?"

"Yes, I do."

"We had to call a doctor, but there was no money for medicine. Or for anything else. Yechiel Nathan, the owner of the grocery store, was still in No. 13 then. You remember him, eh? We used to do all our shopping from them."

"I should say so. He used to pray in the Neustat prayer house."

"Oh, you remember everything! It's good to talk with you—the others know nothing. We were always in debt to them, and when Mama sent me for a loaf of bread, the wife looked into a long ledger and said, 'Enough credit.' I went home, and when I told Mama, she began to cry. She fell asleep and I didn't know what to do. I knew that the society was on Grzybowska Street and I thought maybe Papa would be there. So I went. The windowpanes were white as milk, and a black sign read THE TRUE MERCY. I was afraid to go inside—suppose corpses lay there? I'm a terrible coward. You remember when Yocheved died?"

"Yes, Shoshele."

"They lived on our floor and I was afraid to pass their door at night. During the day too, because it was dark in the hall. At night I dreamed of her."

"Shoshele, I dream about Yocheved till this day."

"You do? She was a little child. What was wrong with her?"

"Scarlet fever."

"You know it all! If you hadn't gone away I wouldn't have gotten sick. I had no one to talk to. Everyone laughed at me. Yes, white panes with black letters. I opened the door and no corpses were lying there. It was a nice room—an office they call it. There was a little window in a wall and people were talking and laughing behind it. An old man carried glasses of tea on a tray. Someone at the little window asked, 'What do you want?' and I told him who I was and that Mama was sick. A woman with yellow hair came in. Her face and hands were covered with freckles. The man said to her, 'This girl is asking about you.' She glared at me and said, 'Who are you?' And I told her. She yelled, 'If you ever come here and bother me again I'll tear out your guts, you little no-good!' She said some filthy words, too. She mentioned that which a girl has—you understand?''

"Yes."

"I wanted to run away, but she opened her purse and dug up some money. When Papa found out about it, he came here and hollered so loud the whole courtyard could hear. He grabbed me by my pigtail and dragged me through the house and spat on me. For three years, maybe, he didn't talk to me when he visited. Mama was angry at me, too. Everyone hollered at me and that's how the years went by. Arele, I could sit with you for a hundred years and not yet finish telling you all of it. Here in our courtyard it's worse than in No. 10. There were bad kids there, too, but they wouldn't beat a girl. They called me names, sometimes they tripped me, but that's all. Remember how we played with nuts on Passover?''

"Yes, Shosha."

"Where was the hole?"

"Inside the gate."

"We played and I won them all. I cleaned you out. I wanted to give you back your nuts, but you wouldn't take them. Velvel the tailor made me a new dress and Mama ordered a pair of shoes from Michael the shoemaker. Suddenly, pious Ytzchokl came out and began to yell at you, 'The rabbi's son plays with a girl! You dreadful boy, I'm going to tell your father this minute and he'll pull out your ears.' Do you remember this?''

"As it happens, this is something I don't remember."

"He chased you and you ran. In those days, Papa still came home all the time. A sheet of matzohs hung in our house. Mama had rendered chicken fat after Hanukkah and we ate so many scraps our bellies nearly burst. They had made you a new gaberdine. Oh, look how I've been chattering away! In No. 10 it wasn't so bad—here, the thugs throw such big rocks they once made a hole in a girl's head. One fellow dragged a girl down the cellar. She screamed, but if you scream in No. 7, no one bothers to see what's wrong. A lot of the hoodlums carry knives. Mama always says, 'Don't mix in.' Here, if you stick up for someone, you could get stabbed. He did, you know what, to the girl.''

"And he wasn't jailed for it?"

"A policeman came and wrote in a book and that was that. The fellow—Paysach is his name—ran away. They run away and the policeman forgets what he has written. Sometimes they send the policeman to another street, or to the higher numbers here. When the Germans came, they threw all the bullies and thieves in jail. Later, they let them all out again. People thought it would get better under the Poles, but they take bribes, too. You slip a zloty into the policeman's hand and he erases what he wrote down.''

Shosha stood up. "Arele, you must never go away again. When you are here, I become healthy."

3

We took a stroll and Shosha clung to my arm. Her fingers stroked my hand, each finger fondling me in a separate fashion. Warmth spread over me and a prickling hair zigzagged across my spine. I barely kept from kissing her in the street. We stopped before every store. Asher the dairyman was still living. His beard had turned gray. This man who rode each day to the train depot to fetch cans of milk was a charitable person, my father's good friend. When we left Warsaw, my father owed him twenty-five rubles. Father went to say goodbye to him and to apologize for his debt, but Asher took fifty German marks from his purse and gave them to Father.

I was supposed to be sitting polishing the play; instead, I was walking with Shosha through the narrow gate of No. 12 to seek out my chum, Berish's son, Mottel. Shosha didn't know him—he belonged to a later period of my life. In the courtyard, I passed by the Radzymin and the Novominsk prayer houses. Afternoon services were already in progress. I wanted to leave Shosha for a minute and look inside to see which of the Hasidim remained alive from among those I had known, but she held on to my arm and wouldn't let go. She was afraid to remain alone in the courtyard. She had not forgotten the old tales of pimps who rode around in carriages snatching girls to sell into white slavery in Buenos Aires. I didn't dare bring a girl into a Hasidic prayer house while the congregation was praying. Only on Simchas Torah were girls allowed inside a house of worship, or when a relative was deathly ill and the family gathered to pray before the holy ark.

A Gentile man carrying a long pipe at the end of which a flame flared went from lamp post to lamp post lighting the street lamps. A pale light fell over the crowds. They shouted, jostled, pushed. Girls laughed noisily. At every other gate stood streetwalkers, beckoning to the men.

I didn't find my friend Mottel. I climbed the dark stairs to where his father lived with his second wife and knocked on the door, but no one answered. Shosha began to shiver. I stopped with her on the landing and kissed her. I pressed her close and thrust my hand inside her blouse and felt her tiny breasts.

She began to tremble. "No, no, no!"

"Shoshele, when you love, such things are permitted."

"Yes, but—"

"I want you to be mine!"

"For real?"

"I love you."

"I'm so small. I can't write."

"I don't need your writing."

"Arele, people will laugh at you."

"I've longed for you all these years."

"Oh, Arele! Is this true?"

"Yes. As soon as I saw you, I knew that I really haven't loved anyone till now."

"Have you had many girls?"

"Not many, but I've slept with some."

Shosha seemed to think it over. "Did you do it with this actress from America?"

"Yes."

"When? Before you came to me?"

I should have answered yes. Instead, I heard myself say, "I slept with her the night after we met." I regretted my words immediately, but confessing and boasting had become a habit with me. Perhaps I learned it from Feitelzohn or in the Writers' Club. I've lost her, I thought. Shosha tried to move away from me, but I held her tight. I had the feeling of a gambler who risks all he possesses in a game, yet makes himself remain quiet. I could hear the pounding of Shosha's heart behind her little left breast.

"Why did you do it? You love her?"

"No, Shoshele. I can do it without love."

"This is what *they* do—you know who I mean."

"The whores and the pimps. That's what we're all becoming, but I'm still able to love you."

"Do you have others, too?" Shosha asked after a pause.

"It happens. I don't want to lie to you."

"No, Arele. You don't need to fool me. I love you as you are. But don't tell Mama. She would raise a fuss and spoil my happiness."

I had expected Shosha to demand details about my affair with Betty. I was ready to give them to her, as well as the fact that I made love to Tekla, though she had a fiancé in the army to whom I wrote letters for her. But Shosha seemed to have forgotten what I told her or to have dismissed it as of no importance. Was she born with the instinct for sharing Feitelzohn talked about? We continued our walk and we came out on Mirowska Street. The fruit stores had closed, but the sidewalk was littered with straw, slats from broken crates, and tissue paper used to wrap oranges. In the First Market, workers were hosing down the tiled floor. The merchants and customers had already dispersed, but the echoes of their shouts hung in the air. In my time, non-kosher sea creatures without scales or fins used to swim here in enormous tubs. The storekeepers sold lobsters and frogs, which Gentiles ate. Huge electric lights lit the market through the night. I led Shosha into a niche and clasped her shoulders. "Shoshele, do you want me?"

"Oh, Arele, do you still have to ask?"

"You'll sleep with me?"

"With you—yes."

"Did anyone ever kiss you?"

"Never. Some lout tried to once, but I ran away. He threw a chunk of wood at me."

Suddenly I had the urge to show off in front of Shosha, to spend money on her. "Shosha, you said just now that you would do whatever I told you."

"Yes, I will."

"I want to take you to the Saxony Gardens. I want to ride with you in a droshky."

"The Saxony Gardens? They don't allow Jews there."

I knew what she meant—under the Russians, Jews in long gaberdines and women in wigs or bonnets had been banned from the park by policemen guarding the gates. But the Poles had since rescinded that order. Besides, I was wearing modern dress. I assured Shosha that we were allowed to go wherever we chose.

Shosha said, "Why take a droshky? We can take 'streetcar No. 11.' Do you know what that means?"

"Yes, go on foot."

"It's a shame to waste money. Mama says, 'Every groschen counts.' You spend a zloty for the droshky and how long is the ride? Maybe half an hour. If you have bundles that's another story."

"Have you ever ridden in a droshky?"

"Never."

"Today you shall ride in a droshky with me. I have a pocketful of zlotys. I told you, I'm writing a play—a theater piece—and they've given me three hundred dollars. I've already spent a hundred and twenty of it, but I've got a hundred and eighty left. A dollar is worth nine zlotys."

"Don't talk so loud. You could be robbed. Once they tried to rob a man from the country, and when he fought, they stabbed him."

We walked down Mirowska Street on the way to Iron Gate Square. On one side was the First Market, on the other a long row of flat shacks where Gentile cobblers sold shoes, boots, even footwear with raised heels and soles for the lame. They were closing up shop for the night.

Shosha said, "Mama is right. God Himself sent you to me. I've already told you about Leizer the watchmaker. Mama wanted to arrange a match between us, but I said, 'I'll stay single.' He's the best watchmaker in all Warsaw. You give him a broken watch and he'll fix it so it will run for years. He saw your name in the paper and he came to us and said, 'Shosha, regards from your fiancé.' That's what he called you. When he said this, I knew that you would come to me one day. He says he knew your daddy."

"Is he in love with you?"

"In love with me? I don't know. He's fifty years old, maybe more."

A droshky came up and I hailed it.

Shosha trembled. "Arele, what are you doing? Mama—"

"Step up." I helped her and got in beside her. The driver in the oilcloth cap with the metal number in back turned around suspiciously. "Where to?"

"Ujazdow Boulevard," I said.

"That's a double fare."

We rode out before Iron Gate Square. Each time the droshky made a turn, Shosha fell against me. "Oh, I'm dizzy."

"I'll bring you home again."

"See how the street looks from a droshky! I feel as if I were an empress. When Mama hears about this, she'll say you're a spendthrift. Arele, I'm sitting with you in a droshky and it seems like a dream to me."

"To me, too."

"So many streetcars! And how bright it is here! Like daytime. Are we going to the elegant streets?"

"You could call them that."

"Arele, since that time I went to The True Mercy I've never been out of

Krochmalna Street. Teibele goes everywhere. She goes to Falenica, to Michalin—where doesn't she go? Arele, where are you taking me?''

"To a wild forest where demons cook little children in kettles full of snakes and naked witches with teats on their navels eat them with mustard.''

"You're joking, aren't you?''

"Yes, my darling.''

"Oh, one never knows what can happen. Mama always teased me, 'Nobody will take *you* except the Angel of Death.' I thought, They'll put me next to Yppe. And then I came home with a cone of sugar and there you were. Arele, what's that?''

"A restaurant.''

"Look how many lamps!''

"It's a fancy restaurant.''

"Oh, see the dolls in that store window! Like alive! What street is this?''

"The New World.''

"So many trees grow here—like a park. And the ladies with the hats, how tall they are! You smell sweetness? What is it?''   •

"Lilac.''

"Arele, I want to ask you something, but don't get mad.''

"What do you want to ask?''

"Do you really love me?''

"Yes, Shosha. Very much.''

"Why?''

"No whys about it. Just because.''

"So long as you weren't there, you weren't there. But if you went away now and didn't come back, I'd die a thousand deaths.''

"I'll never leave you again.''

"Is that the truth? Leizer the watchmaker once said that all writers are like bums, they walk near the soles of their shoes. Leizer doesn't believe there is a God. He says everything came from itself. How can that be?''

"There is a God.''

"Look, the sky is red, just like from a fire. Who lives in these beautiful buildings?''

"Rich people.''

"Jews or Gentiles?''

"Mostly Gentiles.''

"Arele, take me home. I'm afraid.''

"There's no reason to be afraid. If it comes to it that we must die, we'll die together,'' I said, startled at my own words.

"Is it permitted to put a boy and a girl in the same grave?''

I didn't answer her, and Shosha leaned her head on my shoulder.

4

I rode back in the droshky to the gate of No. 7, having decided to walk from there to Leszno Street, but Shosha clung to my arm. She was afraid to go through the dark gate, the dark courtyard, and to climb the half flight of stairs alone. The gate was locked and we had to wait some minutes for the janitor to come and open it. In the courtyard, we bumped into a short little man—Leizer the watchmaker. Shosha asked him what he was doing out so late and he told us he was taking a walk.

"This is Arele." Shosha introduced me.

"I know. I understand. Good evening. I read what you write—including the translations you have done."

It was hard to see him clearly, but in the dim light coming from a few windows I could make out a pale face with big black eyes. He wore no jacket or hat. He spoke in a soft voice. He said, "Mr. Greidinger—or should I call you Comrade Greidinger? It's not that I'm a socialist, but it says somewhere that all Jews are comrades. I know your Shosha since they moved into this building. I used to visit Bashele at a time when her husband was still a respectable man. I don't want to keep you, but she began talking about you the day we met and she's never stopped. Arele this and Arele that. I knew your father, too, may he rest in peace. I was in your house once. It was during a *din torah*—I came to give testimony. A few years ago when I saw your name in a magazine, I wrote you a letter addressed to the editorial office, but there was no answer. They don't generally answer in editorial offices, I know. It's the same with publishers. Once, Shosha and I went to look for you. In any case, you showed up eventually, and I hear that Romeo and Juliet have found each other again. There are such loves, yes, there are. In this world, there is everything. Nature has a pattern for every piece of goods. If you look for madness, there's no lack of that, either. What do they say in your circles about the world—I mean Hitler and Stalin and that scum?"

"What can they say? Man doesn't want peace."

"Why do you say 'man'? I want peace and Shosha wants peace and so do millions of others. I still maintain that most people in the world don't want wars, even revolutions. They would choose to live out their lives the best way they could. With more, with less, in palaces, in cellar rooms, so long as they had a piece of bread and a pillow to lay their heads on. Isn't that true, Shosha?"

"Yes, true."

"The trouble is that the quiet, patient people are passive and those in power, the malefactors, are aggressive. If a decent majority would decide once and for all to take power in their hands, maybe there would be peace."

"They'll neither decide nor will they ever get power," I said. "Power and passivity don't mix."

"Is that your view?"

"It's the experience of generations."

"Then things are bitter."

"Yes, Reb Leizer, it isn't good."

"What will become of us Jews? Evil winds are blowing. Well, I won't keep you. I sit all day in the house, and before going to bed I take a little stroll. Right here in the courtyard, from the gate to the garbage bin and back again. What can you do? Maybe there are better worlds somewhere else? Good night. For me it was an honor to meet you. I still have respect for the printed word."

"Good night. I hope we meet again," I said.

Only now did I become aware that Bashele was standing at the window watching us. She was obviously worried. I would have to go in for a moment. She opened the door, and as we walked up the stairs she exclaimed, "Where have you been! Why so late? I thought the worst!"

"Mama, we rode in a droshky."

"In a droshky? Why, of all things? Where to? How do you like that!"

Shosha began to tell her mother of our wanderings—we had ridden down the boulevards, gone into a confectionary, eaten cake and drunk lemonade.

Bashele arched her eyebrows and shook her head reproachfully. "For the life of me I can't see the sense of squandering all those zlotys. If I'd known you were going to *those* streets, I would have ironed your white dress. These days you can't be sure of your life. I stopped at the neighbor's and we heard a speech on the radio by that madman Hitler. He screamed so, you could go deaf. Since you haven't eaten supper, I'll make something."

"Bashele, I'm not hungry. I must go home."

"What? Now? Don't you know it's almost midnight? Where will you go so late? You'll spend the night here. I'll fix the bed in the alcove. But you have to eat, too."

Immediately Bashele began to pour water into a pan of flour. She lit the stove. Shosha led me into the alcove to show me the iron bed where Teibele used to sleep. She lit a small gas lamp. There were clothes and laundry piled here, along with baskets and boxes accumulated from the time Zelig was a traveling salesman.

Shosha said, "Arele, I'd like you to spend every night here. I'd like to be with you always—eat with you, drink with you, walk with you. I won't forget this night, not till the day they put shards over my eyelids—the droshky, the confectionary, all of it. I want to kiss your feet!"

"Shosha, what's the matter with you?"

"Let me!" She fell to her knees and began to kiss my shoes. I struggled with her and tried to pick her up, but she kept crying, "Let me! Let me!"

<hr />

5

Although I was no longer accustomed to a straw pallet, I fell into a deep sleep in Bashele's alcove that night. I opened my eyes in fright. A white image stood at my bed, bending over me and touching my face with thin fingers. "Who is this?" I asked.

"It's me—Shosha."

It took me a while to remember where I was. Had Shosha come to my bed as Ruth went to Boaz?

"Shosha, what is it?"

"Arele, I'm afraid." Shosha spoke in a wavering voice, like a child about to burst out crying.

I sat up. "What are you afraid of?"

"Arele, don't be angry. I didn't want to wake you, but I have been lying there for three hours and I cannot fall asleep. May I sit on your bed?"

"Yes, yes."

"I was lying in bed and my brain turned like a mill. I wanted to wake up Mother, but she would have yelled at me. She's busy with the house all day long and at night she collapses."

"What were you thinking about?"

"About you. Crazy thoughts came into my head—that it wasn't you, that you were already dead and had disguised yourself as Arele. A demon screamed in my ear, 'He's dead, dead!' He made such a racket I thought everybody in the courtyard would hear and there would be a riot. I wanted to recite the Shema, but he spat in my ear and spoke queer words."

"What did he say?"

"Oh, I'm ashamed to repeat them."

"Tell me."

"He said that God is a chimney sweep, and that when we marry I will wet the bed. He butted me with his horns. He tore off the cover and whipped me you-know-where."

"Shoshele, it's all your nerves. When we are together, I'll take you to a doctor and he will make you healthy."

"Can I still sit a little?"

"Yes, but if your mother wakes up she will think that—"

"She will not wake up. Dead people come to me the moment I close my eyes. Dead women tear at my hair. I'm old enough to be a mother but I still haven't gotten my period. A few times I began to bleed and my mother gave me cotton and rags, but then it all stopped. Mother talked about it to a woman peddler—she sold shirts, kerchiefs, bloomers—and this woman told everyone that I'm not a virgin any more and that I'm pregnant. Mother began to pull my hair and call me ugly names. Bullies in the courtyard threw stones at me. This was years ago, not now. When my daddy heard what happened, he gave Mother ten zlotys to take me to a women's doctor, who said it was all a big lie. A neighbor came to us and said that I should be taken to a rabbi, to get a paper saying that I am a *mukasetz*. This means a girl who lost her innocence without a man, by accident. Your father had left Warsaw years before and we went to a rabbi on Smocza Street. He ordered me taken to a mikvah and examined there. I didn't want to go, but Mother dragged me. The woman in charge undressed me until I was naked, and I had to show her everything. I almost died from shame. She touched me and fumbled around. Then she said that I was kosher. The rabbi had asked thirty zlotys for the certificate and we could not afford it, so we let it go. Now that you're here, I'm worried that someone may come and tell you bad things about me."

"Shoshele, no one will come, and I will listen to no one. I didn't know there were still such fanatics in Warsaw."

"Arele, strange things come into my head—perhaps this, perhaps that. Until I was three, I used to wet the bed. Even now, sometimes I wake up in the middle of the night. The room is cold, but I'm soaked with sweat. The pillow is wet. I never drink before I go to bed, but when I wake up I need to go so badly that until I reach the chamber pot I make on the floor. In the daytime, I go to the outhouse in the yard and it is as dark as night, and there are rats as big as cats. You can't sit down. Once a rat bit me. The doors don't close—where there's a chain, there's no hook; where there's a hook, there's no chain. I try not to go, and I've gotten so used to it that days and weeks go by and I don't go. Porters come there from Yanash's Bazaar, and hoodlums, too. When they see a girl, they begin to say nasty words. In some apartments there are water closets. You pull a string and the water flushes. There is light also and toilet paper. Here, there is nothing.''

"Shoshele, we are not going to live here forever. I don't earn enough now, but I'm writing a book. And then there's my play for the theater. If I don't succeed this time, I will succeed another time. I will take you away from here.''

"Where will you take me? Other girls can read and write, but I never learned how. Maybe you remember when they sent me home from school. I was sitting in class, and the teacher read something to us, but it didn't go into my head. I always saw funny faces. When they called me to the blackboard, I knew nothing and began to cry.''

"What did you see?'' I asked.

"Oh, I'm afraid to tell you. A woman combing her daughter's hair with a fine comb and putting kerosene on it to get out the lice. Suddenly, lice came from all over—bedbugs, too—and the girl began to scream like mad. I don't remember now if she was a Jewish girl or a shiksa. In a minute the lice ate up the mother and the girl, and only their bones were left. When I walked on the street I thought, What will happen if a balcony falls down on my head? When I passed by a policeman I thought, Perhaps he will say that I stole something and take me to prison. Arele, you will think that I'm out of my mind.''

"No, Shoshele, it's nothing but nerves.''

"What are nerves? Tell me.''

"Fear of all the misfortunes that can happen and do happen to human beings.''

"Leizer reads the paper to us, and awful things happen every day. A man crossed the street and was run over by a droshky. A girl from No. 9 tried to get into the trolley car before it stopped, and she lost her leg. Only last week, a tinsmith fixing a roof fell down and the gutter was red from blood. With such things in my head, I could not pay attention to my lessons. When Mother sent me to buy something, I held the money tight in my fist—then when I got to the store it was lost. How can this be?''

"Every person has an enemy inside who spites him.''

"Then why doesn't Teibele have one? Arele, I want you to know the truth so that you won't think that we are fooling you.''

"Shoshele, no one has fooled me. I will help you.''

"How? If it's so bad now, what will happen when Hitler comes? Oy, Mother is waking up!'' Shosha ran from the alcove. I heard the sound of her shirt tearing as she caught it on a nail in the door.

CHAPTER SIX

1

Each day—no, each hour—brought a new crisis, but I had become accustomed to the dangers attending my lot. I compared myself to a criminal who knows that he will be punished but until he is seized he squanders his loot. Sam Dreiman had given me a new advance and Betty had reconstructed my play to suit her whims. She had introduced new characters, even edited my language. I realized with amazement that the passion to write can strike anyone capable of holding a pen. Betty had introduced more action into the drama and added "lyrics," but the play no longer held together. Though Betty mocked and mimicked the American Yiddish, she anglicized mine. The blind musician now declaimed like the villain in a melodrama. Fritz Bander, who had been cast to play a wealthy Hasid in love with the Ludmir Maiden, demanded that his role be larger, and Betty gave him permission to extend it with lengthy monologues. He still retained some Galician Yiddish mixed with German. Fritz Bander also demanded a part for his German mistress, Gretel, who knew no Yiddish. He pointed out that Jews often employed German maids and this was a part she could handle.

Betty had several copies of her version of the play typed up—one for her, one for Sam Dreiman, one for Fritz Bander, one for David Lipman, one for me, and for others. Each person made changes, and the text was typed again and the revisions commenced all over. Sam Dreiman had rented a theater on Smocza Street and ordered the sets, though basic decisions about the production were still to be settled. The Actors Union demanded that jobs be introduced for additional actors as well as for extras. I was forced to write in parts for a beadle, a madman, and an anti-Hasid who berated the Hasidim. The cast grew so large that dialogue essential to its content had to be deleted.

At first, I resisted. I rewrote Betty's and Bander's revisions, corrected their grammar and spelling, but I soon saw that the contradictions, the different styles, and grotesqueries grew faster than I could repair them. I couldn't believe it, but Sam Dreiman also took a hand in the writing. It reminded me of a story I had heard as a child from my mother about a band of spirits who seized a village and turned everything upside down—the water-carrier became the rabbi, the rabbi a bathhouse attendant, the horse thief a scribe, the scribe a teamster. A hobgoblin posed as head of a yeshiva and in the studyhouse preached a sermon filled with blasphemies. The leech, a demon, prescribed goat droppings and calf feathers for the sick, along with moon juice and turkey semen. A devil with the legs of a rooster and the horns of a buck became a cantor and turned the rejoicing of Simchas Torah into the lamentations of Tisha Bov. Such a mystic comedy could have been created from my play.

The telephone in the corridor outside my room never stopped ringing. Tekla no longer bothered to pick up the receiver—invariably the call was for me. The actors and actresses were bickering with each other, with Betty, and with David Lipman, who was threatening to quit. The secretary of the union raised new demands almost daily. The actors complained that the American millionaire had deceived them regarding their wages. The theater owner decided he had signed an unfair contract and would have to have more money. Sam Dreiman screamed at me until I had to hold the receiver away from my ear. If Jews were capable of such deceit and intrigue, he said, then Hitler was right.

I tried to calm the spirits of the others, but I feared a nervous breakdown myself.

The days passed in turmoil. I stopped talking to Shosha and Bashele. When I went to them for lunch, I sat at the table in silence. I even forgot to eat and had to be reminded that the soup was getting cold. At night after two or three hours' sleep I awoke with my heart pounding, the pillowcase drenched in sweat. In my sleep, my own complications had mingled with the problems of the world. Hitler, Mussolini, and Stalin wrangled about my play, and then went to war. Shosha attempted to defend me. I sat up and listened to the echoes of cries and mayhem that still lingered in my brain. My hair pierced my skull. I itched and scratched. I had wakened with a thirst, a gnawing in my intestines, a stinging in my bladder. My nose was stuffed and a shudder kept running down my spine.

Day would be breaking, and I would still sit and take reckoning. I had accepted more money from Sam Dreiman than I had intended. I gave Bashele more for my meals and helped her with her rent as well. I had given Dora a loan I knew I would never get back.

That night I fell asleep at three. At ten to nine, the ringing of the telephone woke me. Tekla poked the door ajar. "It's for you."

It was Betty. She asked, "Did I wake you?"

"Yes, no."

"I had a terrible night. I wouldn't wish it on my worst enemies."

"What happened?"

"Oh, Sam is torturing me. He makes ugly scenes. He says such wild things I'm beginning to think he's losing his mind. Yesterday, he drank maybe a half bottle of cognac. He shouldn't touch it—he has a bad heart and an enlarged prostate."

"What does he want?"

"To destroy himself and everything. He doesn't want the play any more. Every second he gets a new notion. He made such a fuss you could hear him through the whole hotel. I want to remind you that we are rehearsing today. I have about as much strength to perform after last night as you have to dance on the roof, but I can't leave things hanging in the air any longer. At times I'd like to pick myself up and run off to the ends of the earth."

"You too?"

"Yes, me too. He's become jealous all of a sudden. He seems to know about us!" Betty said, changing her tone.

"What does he know?"

"He's listening right now. I have to stop."

I stood by the telephone with the premonition that presently it would ring again. And so it did. I lifted the receiver and said, "Yes, Celia?"

No one answered and I assumed I had been wrong, but after a while I heard Celia's voice. "Have you become a prophet, or a gypsy?"

"The Gemara says that when the Temple was destroyed God gave the power of prophecy to madmen."

"Is that what the Gemara says? You are crazy, but you are also committing literary suicide. I lay awake half the night worrying about you. Haiml sleeps like a log. The minute his head hits the pillow he begins to whistle through his nose and goes on until morning. But I keep waking up. At times it seems that you wake me. I hear you calling 'Celia!' It's all my nerves. One time it even seemed that I saw you in the doorway. Was it your astral body? There's something not of the ordinary about you. My dear, Morris has read your play. Sam Dreiman gave him a copy. I don't want to repeat what he said. I hear it's no longer your play, everything's distorted. Really, what's the sense of it all?''

"The sense is that I'm losing my senses."

2

When I entered the theater for the rehearsal, coming in from the bright light I bumped against the seats and nearly tripped, but gradually I grew accustomed to the dark. I took a seat in the front row. Sam Dreiman sat two rows behind me. He coughed and grunted and mumbled to himself in English. Celia and Haiml were present, too. Critics aren't usually invited to rehearsals, but I spotted one of them in the audience. In their articles, the critics often decried the state of the Yiddish theater and denounced young writers for allowing kitsch to dominate the stage and for not writing serious plays; yet I knew that they hoped my play would fail. They had launched a campaign against Betty Slonim. In the leftist publications they dubbed Sam Dreiman an American "all-rightnik" and a "Golden Calf." Some theatrical writers pointed out that a mystic play about a girl who presided over Hasidic banquets with a veil over her face, preached the Torah to Hasidim, and was possessed by the dybbuks of a whore and a musician didn't befit the tragic circumstances of Polish Jewry. What was called for were plays that reflected the dangers of Fascism and Hitlerism and the need of resistance by the Jewish masses, not dramas that brought back the superstitions of the Middle Ages.

Two seats away from me sat David Lipman and his wife, Estusia. She peeled oranges and handed sections to him. Because of a heart condition he required constant nourishment. He wore a velour jacket and a flowing tie. The whole play wasn't being performed, merely individual scenes. Fritz Bander, portraying Reb Ezekiel Prager, the Hasid, declared his love for the Ludmir Maiden—Betty. Although I had told Bander time and again not to shout, he thundered away. In those places where he should have lowered his voice, he roared; and he whispered or skipped over those places where he should have been forceful. He swallowed words and improvised. He didn't remember his lines and the prompter had to keep feeding him his speeches. Bander jumbled and fractured the quotations from the Gemara, the Midrash, and the books of the cabala. I had assumed that David Lipman, who was allegedly versed in these matters, would correct him, but he kept silent. He was in awe of Fritz Bander because he had performed in Berlin. Once in a while David Lipman made observations and indicated directions, but he ignored essentials and confined himself to petty details. Betty also had trouble with her lines. She made errors in her Hebrew and even in the Yiddish words. Some of the words she pronounced in a Polish accent, others in a Lithuanian.

Where she was supposed to portray both the whore and the blind musician, she lost her bearings altogether.

I sat slumped over, from time to time closing my eyes to lose sight of my disgrace. Betty might be critical of the trash of the American Yiddish theater, but she had adapted its mannerisms. I recalled my mother's saying "words that walk on stilts." Curiously, when Betty spoke to me in private, her Yiddish was fluent and precise. As I gazed at the stage, I knew I had failed completely. My own mistakes were only too clear to me, but I had no idea how to correct them.

The moment the lights went on, Sam Dreiman came charging at me. "We can't put on this monstrosity!"

"No is no."

"I sat there and didn't understand what on earth they were babbling about, and if I didn't understand it, you can't expect anyone else to. I thought you were going to write in plain Yiddish."

"Dybbuks don't speak a plain Yiddish."

Betty, Fritz Bander, and Gretel came up.

"Betty darling, we'll have to postpone the play!" Sam Dreiman shouted.

"Postpone? Until when?"

"I don't know when. I brought you here to be a success, not to have rotten potatoes heaved at you."

"Sam, don't say that."

"Betty darling, the sooner you act on a mistake, the better. Forty years ago I put up a building in Detroit and in the midst of the construction it turned out that the plumbing and everything else wouldn't work. I'd sunk a fortune into the project, but I ordered everything torn down and the building begun all over again. If I hadn't done this, I would have gone to jail. I had a friend, also a builder, and he put up a factory six flights high. Suddenly, while the building was filled with workers, it collapsed and killed seventeen men. He died in prison."

"Well, I knew it! I knew it all! The evil powers have started their tricks again. I'm through as an actress. My luck—"

"Your luck, sweetheart, is as bright as the sun in the sky!" Sam Dreiman hollered. "You will perform in Warsaw, in Paris, in London, and in New York. The name of Betty Slonim will light up Broadway in huge letters, but in a drama that the world wants to see, not in some crazy farce for insane cabalists. Mr. Greidinger, I don't want to be cruel, but what you've given us is unfit for the public. Betty, we'll get another play. He isn't the only writer in Warsaw."

"You can put on all the plays you want, but without me," Betty said. "This is my final card. With my luck, if you put on a masterpiece it would fail. It's all my fault! Mine! Mine!"

"It's mine, too," Sam Dreiman said. "When he brought us the first two scenes and I read them, I saw at once that this wasn't for us. I thought it might be fixed, but not everything can be fixed. It's like that building—the foundation was poorly laid at the start. I fired the architect and began with another. I'll do the same thing right now."

"You can do it, but without me."

"With you, Betty darling, only with you!"

CHAPTER SEVEN

1

At this time, the logic of my pride was that nothing remained to me but to hide from all those involved with me and my profession. I still had over one hundred dollars from Sam Dreiman's third advance—money that I must pay back if I were not to consider myself a thief. My calculations turned around this sum, which was worth about nine hundred zlotys. According to the agreement with the man from whom I sublet my room on Leszno Street, I had to give a month's notice before I moved out, and I certainly did not intend to break this agreement. I considered suicide, but that would be possible only if I could take with me those who had hung all their hopes on me. Meanwhile, I had to be careful with every penny. I stopped sleeping on Leszno Street, which saved me the expense of paying for a taxi when I went home late in the evening. On the bed in Bashele's alcove I covered whole sheets of paper with figures. The publisher for whom I had translated some German books owed me money, but I was far from sure that he would ever pay it. I was working for the literary magazine, but weeks passed without my getting a penny from them. I reminded myself that about three million Jews lived in Poland and managed to make a living somehow. I did not fool Bashele. She knew my situation. I had promised to marry her daughter but we had never set a date. They would not send out warrants for my arrest if I should disappear. Judging by the way Hitler occupied one territory after another and the Allies sat back and did nothing, there was no hope for the Jews in Poland. But running away and leaving at bay those who were dear to me was not in my nature.

Yiddish newspapers in Warsaw reported that the play Sam Dreiman, the American millionaire, had been planning to produce had been canceled. The Yiddish theater season began on Succoth and there was not time for him to find a new play. They also mentioned that he was negotiating with a playwright in America. Of *The Ludmir Maiden,* a journalist wrote in the humor section that it could not be produced because it was possessed by a dybbuk. Leizer the watchmaker read all these stories of my failure to Shosha and Bashele.

In the month of August, a strong heat spell hit Warsaw. When I was a boy, almost no one on Krochmalna Street took vacations and went to the country in the summer. Only the wealthy and rich did this. But times had changed. Workers were now given vacations and they went to Miedzeszyn, Falenica, and even to Zakopane in the mountains. The workers' unions had summer colonies in Karwia at the Baltic Sea in the "corridor" that divided East Germany from West Germany and that Hitler vowed to take back. I heard that Feitelzohn stayed a few weeks in Jósefow with Celia and Haiml. I had spoken to Tekla on the telephone and she told me that Celia kept calling me. Tekla asked why I hadn't come home for so long. She also asked for my telephone number and the address where I was staying so that she could tell people how to get in touch with me. I said I was busy with work and didn't want to be disturbed. Even Tekla knew that my play had fizzled. She heard it from Wladek, who read about it in the Polish Jewish newspaper *Nasz Przeglad*.

During the day I seldom left the apartment on Krochmalna Street. My old bashfulness had returned to me, with all its complications and neuroses. Some tenants of No. 7 knew me. From Leizer they had heard about me and my love for Shosha. They had also read of my forthcoming play. The girls used to watch from the windows when I passed with Shosha on the way to the gate. I was ashamed before these girls now and imagined that they laughed at me. I even avoided going to the outhouse during the day. The heels of my shoes were worn down, but I could not pay to have them fixed. My hat was faded and stained. I would put on a fresh shirt and a few hours later it would be soaked with sweat, and dirty. The little hair left on my head began to fall out. When I wiped the perspiration from my skull, I found red hair on my handkerchief. I had begun to have all kinds of mishaps around the house. Bashele would give me a glass of tea and it would slip from my hands. Each time I shaved, I cut myself. I kept losing my fountain pen, my notebook. Money dropped from my pockets. In my mouth a molar began to loosen, but I could not afford to go to a dentist. Anyway, what did I need a dentist for, since my weeks or days were numbered?

I had brought with me a few of the books in which I always sought solace whenever there was a crisis in my life—which was often. This time I couldn't find a trace of comfort in them. Spinoza's "substance" had no will, no compassion, no feeling for justice. He was a prisoner of his own laws. Schopenhauer's "blind will" seemed to be more blind than ever. Of course there was no hope for me in Hegel's *Zeitgeist* or in Nietzsche's Zarathustra. Payot's *Education of the Will* was addressed chiefly to students whose wealthy parents paid for their board and tuition. Coué's and Charles Baudouin's patients had homes, professions, well-to-do families, accounts in the banks. I sat on the edge of the bed all day long and let perspiration run over my hot body. Shosha sat near me on her little stool and talked to me or to herself. Occasionally she spoke to Yppe. For some reason Bashele frequently left the house. Shosha would ask her, "Mommy, where are you going?" And Bashele would say, "Where my eyes carry me."

Now that I had failed for everyone to see, I realized that the failure was my own fault. Instead of working on the play, I had spent hours with Shosha every day. Even though Betty kept warning me that the work on the play was of the highest importance, she made me go with her to museums, to cafés, on long walks, and sabotaged all my plans for work. I should have gone with her in the evenings to see serious plays from which I could learn about the construction of a drama. Instead, she took me to see silly Hollywood movies from which there was nothing to be learned. I wasted precious hours discussing Yiddish literature in the Writers' Club, playing chess, and telling jokes. I even squandered time with Tekla, listening to her complaints about her mistress and her stories about the village where she came from, her unloving stepmother, and of Bolek, to whom she was betrothed and who had left her to go to work in the coal mines of France. Our conversations always ended by our falling down on the bed together. I wasn't really awake in those months. My laziness, my passion, and my empty fantasies had kept me in a hypnotic amnesia. Now I could hear my mother saying, "No enemy can do to a man as much evil as he does to himself."

"Arele, what are you thinking about?" Shosha asked me.

"Nothing, Shoshele. As long as I have you, there is still some sense to my life."

"You will not leave me alone?"

"No, Shoshele, I will stay with you as long as I live."

2

At night I lay awake for hours. From the heat I continuously ran to the sink to drink water and then I had to urinate. Bashele had put a chamber pot under my bed and it soon became full. I stood without any clothes before the window of my alcove—a little window with four panes—and let the breeze that came into the courtyard once in a while blow over me. I looked at the few stars that could be seen moving slowly from one roof to the other. Though I had nothing to expect on earth when the Nazis arrived except starvation and concentration camps, perhaps there was some spark of hope in the heavenly bodies? However, from the popular books about astronomy which I had read, I knew that the stars consisted of the same elements as the sun and the earth. If other planets were inhabited by living creatures, their conditions could be like those on earth: struggle for a bite of food, for a secure place to lay one's head. I was overcome by a rage against creation, God, nature—whatever this wretchedness was called. I felt that the only way of protesting cosmic violence was to reject life, even if I had to take Shosha with me. The animals and the insects did not possess such a choice.

But how would I accomplish this, actually? If I were to throw myself out the window of my room on Leszno Street, I would risk remaining alive with possibly a broken spine. If I were to fling myself under a trolley or a train, I might end up without feet or arms. Should I get rat poison and slowly burn out my insides? Should I hang myself and burden those who loved me with arranging my burial? After much brooding I decided that the best way to end it all would be to throw myself into deep water, where I would molest no one and would even help the fish with a meal. The Vistula was too shallow in the summer. Every day the newspapers wrote about ships that got stuck in the sand. The only way of doing it right would be go to Danzig or Gdynia and board a ship that sailed the Baltic. A travel agency was advertising a cruise to Denmark for which no foreign passport or visa was necessary. The price was reasonable. It was enough for the passenger to show a Polish inland passport. The trouble was, I didn't possess even this kind of document. In the process of moving from one furnished room to another with my books and confusion of manuscripts, I had lost my draft card, my birth certificate, and all other proof of my citizenship. I would have to travel to the village where I was born and bring to the City Hall witnesses who could attest to the day of my birth or my circumcision feast. The archives of births and deaths had burned down in the German bombardments in 1915. With all my anxiety I had to laugh. I needed to go through a lot of red tape to be able to commit suicide.

That night I fell asleep at dawn. I opened my eyes. Shosha was shaking my shoulder. I looked at her bewildered. It took me a while to remember where I was and who was waking me. "Arele," she said, "a young lady is waiting for you. The actress from America."

After a while Bashele stuck her head in the room. I asked her and Shosha to please leave and close the door. In a rush I put on my underwear, my pants, my shirt, and my jacket. For a minute I thought I had lost the hundred dollars that I carried in the left pocket of my pants. I needed money to buy a train ticket and ship card to go ahead with my plan. Had someone stolen my money? I touched all my pockets with the turmoil of one who wants to live, not to die. Thank God, the banknotes were in a pocket of my vest. My shirt was crumpled, my collar had a spot, I had lost the cuff link of my right sleeve. I screamed through the closed door, "Betty, wait! I will soon be out." The sun was already scorching me through the open window. From the courtyard I heard the voices: "Bagels, hot bagels! Plums, fresh plums!" A beggar was already scratching out a plaintive melody on a fiddle and his female companion was beating on a little drum with bells, calling for alms. I touched my cheeks. Although I kept on losing the hair on my head, my beard grew with wild impetus. The stubble felt stiff and prickly. Disordered and frowzy, I opened the door and saw Betty freshly made up in a straw hat with a green ribbon, a suit that I had not seen, and white shoes with open toes—a novelty to me. I began to apologize for my appearance.

Betty said, "Everything is all right. You don't have to compete in a beauty contest."

"When I fell asleep day was breaking, and—"

"Stop it. I didn't come to look you over."

"Why don't you sit down?" Bashele said to Betty. "I keep asking the young lady to sit down, but she has been standing all this time. We don't live in luxury but our chairs are clean. I dust them every morning. I wanted to make tea, but the young lady refuses everything."

"I'm sorry. I just had breakfast. Thank you very much. Tsutsik, forgive me for coming so early in the morning. Actually, my watch shows ten minutes to ten. I came, as they say in America, on business. If you like, we can go out somewhere and talk it over."

"Arele, don't go for long," Shosha said. "We have prepared breakfast and later we will have dinner. Mommy bought sorrel and potatoes and sour cream. The lady can eat with us."

"We have enough for both of you," Bashele agreed.

"How can I eat if I've had breakfast already?"

"Shoshele, we will only go out for half an hour," I said. "It's not convenient for us to talk here. Let me find my cuff link and change my collar. One minute, Betty."

I rushed into the alcove and Shosha followed me. She closed the door. "Arele, don't go with her," she said. "She wants to take you away from me. She looks like a witch."

"A witch? Don't talk nonsense."

"She has such sharp eyes. You told me yourself that you lay with her in bed."

"I told you? Well, never mind. Between her and me everything is finished."

"If you want to begin with her again, better kill me first."

"The way things are going, I will kill you anyhow. I will take you on a ship and we will both jump into the sea."

"Is there a sea in Warsaw?"

"Not in Warsaw. We will go to Gdynia or Danzig."

"Yes, Arele, you can do with me whatever you want. Throw me in first or take me to Yppe's grave and bury me there. As long as you do it, it is good. But don't leave me alone. Here is your cuff link."

Shosha bent down and gave it to me. I put my arms around her and kissed her. I said "Shoshele, I have sworn by God and by the soul of my father that I will never abandon you. It's about time that you trust me."

"Yes, I trust you. But when I saw her, my heart began to pound. She is dressed as if she were going to a wedding. All new to please you. She thinks I don't understand, but I understand everything. When will you be back?"

"As quickly as possible."

"Remember that no one loves you as I do."

"Sweet child, I love you, too."

"Wait, I have a fresh handkerchief for you."

3

Betty and I passed the courtyard; it looked like a marketplace. Peddlers were hawking smoked herring, blueberries, watermelons. A peasant had ridden in with his horse and buggy, and he was selling chickens, eggs, mushrooms, onions, carrots, parsley. In other streets, this kind of business was not allowed, but Krochmalna had its own laws. An old woman carrying a sack on her back stood near the garbage bin and with a stick poked through for rags to make paper and for bones used in sugar factories. Betty tried to take my arm, but I gave her a sign not to do it, since I was sure that Bashele and Shosha were watching us from the window. We were watched from other windows, too. Girls wearing loose dresses over their bouncing breasts were shaking threadbare carpets as well as featherbeds, pillows, and mangy fur coats that would be worn when winter began. One could hear the noise of sewing machines, cobbler's hammers, the planing and sawing of carpenters. From the Hasidic studyhouse came the voices of young men chanting the Talmud. In the cheder, little boys recited the Pentateuch. On the other side of the gate Betty took my arm and said, "I didn't know the number of the house, but after I called and called you on Leszno Street and the maid always replied that you were not there, I decided you must be here on your beloved Krochmalna Street. What kind of a swamp have you fallen into? It absolutely stinks here! Please forgive me, but this Shosha of yours is a perfect imbecile. She asked me to sit down at least ten times. I told her I preferred to stand, but she asked over and over again. I really think you are mad."

"You are right. You are right."

"Don't tell me how right I am. You are one of those men who like to sink. In Russia they call them *brodyagi*. Gorky wrote about them. In New York there is a street called the Bowery, and you see them lying on the sidewalk drunk and half naked. Some of them are intelligent, with higher education. Come, let's get out of this sewage. An urchin has already tried to grab my purse. You haven't had breakfast, and I am hungry myself from walking so long around here trying to find the house. All I remembered from my first visit was that there was a ditch in the courtyard. But it seems that they filled it up. Where can we get a cup of coffee?''

"There is a coffee shop at No. 6, but the underworld goes there."

"I don't want to stay on this street another minute. Hurry, here's a droshky. Hey! Stop!''

Betty jumped in and I after her. She said, "Would you like to have breakfast in the Writers' Club?''

"Absolutely not.''

"Did you have a quarrel with someone? They say you've stopped coming there. How about Gertner's Restaurant, where we met the first time. My God, it seems so long ago.''

"Madame, where to?'' The coachman turned his head.

Betty gave him the address. "Tsutsik, why are you hiding from people? I met your best friend, Dr. Feitelzohn, and he told me you've severed connections with him and everybody else. I can understand in a way that you wouldn't want to have anything to do with me, because I'm responsible for what happened, although I had only good intentions. But what's the sense of a young writer burying himself in such squalor? Why don't you at least stay in your room on Leszno Street—you pay the rent, after all. Sam is deeply upset about the way you run away from us.''

"I hear he's negotiating a play with some trashy writer from New York.''

"Nothing will come of it. I'm definitely not going to play in that kind of junk. I've told you already it's entirely my bad luck. Everyone who's involved with me shares my miserable fate. But I told you I came on business and I'm not lying. The story is this. Sam's not well and I'm afraid he's sicker than I realized. He's planning to go back to America. We've done a lot of talking in the past few days, much of it about you. Now that there's no longer a deadline I've had time and the peace of mind to read your play again. It's not nearly as bad as that short little critic with the tin-framed glasses made it out to be. The insolence of a writer tearing down a piece before it's been performed! That can happen only among the Yiddishists. Such a malicious worm. Someone introduced me to him and I gave him a piece of my mind. He began to excuse himself and flatter me and twist his tongue like a snake. Actually, I think it's a good literary play. The trouble is, you don't know the stage. In America we have men who are called play doctors. They can't write a line themselves, but somehow they know how to rearrange a piece and make it right for the stage. I'll make it short—we want to buy your play and try it out in America.''

"*Buy* it? Mr. Dreiman already gave me seven or eight hundred dollars. It's his if he wants it. I'm terribly sorry that I'm not able to give him back the money, but he certainly can do what he likes with the play.''

"Well, I can see you're not much of a businessman. I'll tell you something. He's loaded with money. America is beginning to go through a new period of prosperity, and without lifting a finger, he is making a fortune. If he wants to pay you, take the money. He promised to leave me a large inheritace, but according to the law he has to leave a part of his fortune to his Xanthippe, and perhaps also to his children, though they hate him and defy him. With my luck, I'll probably get nothing. If he's willing to give some to you, there's no reason you should refuse. You won't be able to write if you remain where you are now.

I looked into that alcove of yours. It's a hole, not a room. You could suffocate in there. What's the point of it? Even if you want to commit suicide, such a death is too ugly. Here is Gertner's.''

Betty tried to open her purse, but I had the fare ready in my hand and I gave it to the coachman.

Betty threw me an angry look. "What's the matter with you? Do you want to finance Sam Dreiman?''

"I don't want to take any more from him.''

"Well, everyone is crazy in his own way. Bevies of schnorrers run after him and you are trying to support him. Come, madman. I haven't been here in God knows how long. I even thought they might not be open so early. In New York there are restaurants where the day begins at lunchtime. Now you may kiss me. We can never really be complete strangers.''

4

The Headwaiter rushed toward us and gave us the table in the niche that Sam and Betty always got when they ate here. He said he was sorry he hadn't seen her and Sam lately. Even though it was still early, there were people already at the tables, eating fish and meat and drinking beer. Betty ordered coffee with cake for herself and made me take rolls with eggs and coffee. The waiter gave us a look of reproach for ordering a late breakfast instead of an early lunch. Those at the other tables gazed at us questioningly. Betty looked too elegant to be my companion. She was saying, "How long is it since we've seen one another? It seems to me an eternity. Sam wants me to return to America, but in spite of all my disappointments I fell in love with Warsaw. What would I do in America? In New York they know everything that is happening everywhere. In the Actors Union they have surely heard of my defeat, and my stock there will have dropped lower than ever. They sit in the Café Royal and make mountains out of molehills. What's left to them except to gossip? Some of them saved when times were good. Those who have nothing get relief from the government. In the summer they play a few weeks in the hotels in the Catskill Mountains. America has become a country where one is not compelled to work if he doesn't want to. They drink coffee and chatter. They play cards. Without cards and gossip they would expire from boredom. My trouble is that I don't play cards. Sam tried to teach me, but I couldn't learn even the names of the suits. A stubborn instinct in me refuses to learn. Tsutsik, I'm as good as finished. This was my last game. I've nothing left except to commit suicide.''

"You too?''

"Who else? Is this why you are going to marry Shosha—to make her a widow?''

"I'll take her with me.''

"Well, you are, as they say, healthy, fresh, and meshugga. In my case I tried to play year after year after year, and I always failed. Besides, I'm older than you. But why should you fall into such despair? You are a writer of stories, not a playwright. So far as the theater goes, you're still a greenhorn—I think with talent. Oh, here is my cake and your eggs. I used to wonder why those condemned to the electric chair bother to pick out a special last meal. They ask for a rare steak and a tasty dessert. Why should a person care what he eats if he's going to be dead an hour later? It seems that life and death have nothing in common. You may decide to die tomorrow but today you still want to eat for pleasure and sleep in a warm bed. What are your real plans?''

"Really, to get through with the whole botched-up mess.''

"My God, when I was on the ship to Europe I never thought I would drive someone into such a state because of my foolish ambitions.''

"Betty, it's not your fault.''

"Whose fault is it?''

"Oh, it's everything together. The Jews in Poland are trapped. When I said this in the Writers' Club, they attacked me. They had let themselves fall into a stupid kind of optimism, but I know for sure that we will all be destroyed. The Poles want to get rid of us. They consider us a nation within a nation, a strange and malignant body. They lack the courage to finish us off themselves, but they wouldn't shed tears if Hitler did it for them. Stalin will certainly not defend us. Since the Trotskyite opposition began, the Communists have become our worst enemies. Trotsky is called Judas in Russia. The fact is that the Trotskyites are almost all Jews. If you give a Jew one revolution, he demands another revolution— a permanent one. If you give him one Messiah, he asks for another Messiah. As to Palestine, the world doesn't want us to have a state. The bitter truth is that many Jews today don't want to be Jews any more. But it's too late for total assimilation. Whoever is going to win this coming war will liquidate us.''

"Maybe the democracies will win.''

"The democracies are committing suicide.''

"Well, don't let your coffee get cold. If you hadn't decided to carry that silly Shosha on your shoulders, you could easily get yourself to America. There the Jew can still muddle through. I can go back, but the very thought of it makes me shudder. Sam can't stay at home even one night. He always has to go somewhere—usually to that Café Royal. There he meets the writers he supports and the actresses he used to have affairs with. This is the only place where he is somebody. It's funny, but there is only one little place in the whole world— a third-rate restaurant—where he feels at home. He eats the blintzes the doctors have forbidden him. He fills up his belly with twenty cups of coffee each day. He smokes the cigars he knows are poison for him. He demands that I go with him, but for me this café is a nest of snakes. They always hated me, but now that I am with Sam they would like to swallow me alive. The Yiddish theater where he takes me at least twice a week has reached its lowest point. To sit there with him and listen to their stale jokes and see sixty-year-old yentas play eighteen-year-old girls is a physical pain. The sad truth is that for me there isn't *one* place in the whole world where I feel at home.''

"Well, we're a well-matched pair.''

"We could have been, but you didn't want it. What do you say to this Shosha all day long?''

"I don't say much.''

"What is this with you, an act of masochism?''

"No, Betty, I really love her.''

"There are things you must see to believe. You can never foresee them in your imagination: you and Shosha, me and Sam Dreiman. At least he finds some comfort among his cronies. Tsutsik, look who's here!''

I raised my eyes and saw Feitelzohn. He stood a few steps from our table with a cigar in his mouth, his Panama hat pushed back, and a cane hooked over his shoulder. I had not seen him with a cane before. He looked older and changed. He smiled with familiar shrewdness, but I imagined that his cheeks had fallen in, as if he had lost his teeth. He approached our table with small steps. "Is this how things are?" he said with a muffled voice, and then took out the cigar. "Well, really, Tsutsik, I begin to believe in your hidden powers." He leaned the cigar in the ashtray on our table. "I passed by and it occurred to me, 'Perhaps Tsutsik is there.' Good morning, Miss Slonim. I've become so mixed up that I forgot to greet you. How do you do? It's nice to see you again. What was it I wanted to say? Yes, Tsutsik. I said to myself, 'What would he do here so early? He only comes here with Sam Dreiman and not this early in the day.' I was about to continue my walk but somehow my feet brought me in by their own choice. You should be ashamed of yourself, Tsutsik. Why are you keeping away from your friends? We have all been looking for you—Haiml, Celia, I. I called you perhaps twenty times, but the maid had one answer: 'Not home.' What's wrong? You have better friends in Warsaw?''

"Dr. Feitelzohn, sit down with us," Betty said. "Why are you standing?"

"Since you two are huddling in a corner, no doubt you have your secrets. But one can say hello in any case.''

"We have no secrets. We were talking business and we have finished. Sit down.''

"I really don't know what to say," I began to stammer.

"If you don't know, don't say. I will say it for you. You have been a little boy and you will remain one for the rest of your life. Look at you," Feitelzohn said.

"Where did you get a cane all of a sudden?" I asked, just to change the conversation.

"Oh, I stole it. One of my Americans left it to me. Lately my feet have been making monkey business. I walk on a flat road and suddenly my feet begin to run by themselves as if I were ice skating or going downhill. What kind of a malady is this? I will have to ask our literary physician Dr. Lipkin, who understands as much about medicine as he understands about literature. Meanwhile, I have decided that a cane cannot do any damage. Tsutsik, you look pale. What's the matter? Are you sick?''

"He's perfectly well and crazy," Betty said. "A first-class maniac.''

5

Feitelzohn assured us that he had eaten breakfast, and when Betty ordered rolls, an omelette, and coffee for him, he smiled and said, "If one lives in America a few years, one becomes an American. What would the world do without America? When I lived there I complained of Uncle Sam steadily—talked only about his shortcomings. But now that I'm here, I miss America. I could go back if I chose, on a tourist visa. It might even be that I could get a visa as a professor. But in New York and Boston no university would give me a permanent job. And to teach in those small colleges somewhere in the Midwest means dying of boredom. I cannot sit all day long and read like a bookworm. The students there are more childlike than our cheder boys. All they talk about is football, and the professors are not much cleverer. America is a country of children. The New Yorkers are a little more grown up, but not much. Once some friend of mine put me on a ferry to Coney Island. This, Tsutsik, I wish you could see. It is a city in which everything is for play—shooting at tin ducklings, visiting a museum where they show a girl with two heads, letting an astrologer plot your horoscope and a medium call up the soul of your grandfather in the beyond. No place lacks vulgarity, but the vulgarity of Coney Island is of a special kind, friendly, with a tolerance that says, 'I play my game and you play your game.' As I walked around there and ate a hot dog—this is what they call a sausage— it occurred to me that I was seeing the future of mankind. You can even call it the time of the Messiah. One day all people will realize there is not a single idea that can really be called true—that everything is a game—nationalism, internationalism, religion, atheism, spiritualism, materialism, even suicide. You know, Tsutsik, that I am a great admirer of David Hume. In my eyes he is the only philosopher who has not become obsolete—he is as fresh and clear today as he was in his own time. Coney Island fits David Hume's philosophy. Since we are sure of nothing and there is even no evidence that the sun will rise tomorrow, play is the very essence of human endeavor, perhaps even the thing-in-itself. God is a player, the cosmos a playground. For years I have searched for a basis of ethics and gave up hope. Suddenly it became clear to me. The basis of ethics is man's right to play the games of his choice. I will not trample on your toys and you will not trample on mine; I won't spit on your idol and you will not spit on mine. There is no reason why hedonism, the cabala, polygamy, asceticism, even our friend Haiml's blend of eroticism and Hasidism could not exist in a play-city or play-world, a sort of a universal Coney Island where everyone would play according to his or her desire. I'm sure, Miss Slonim, that you have visited Coney Island more than once.''

"Yes, but I never came to your philosophical conclusions. By the way, who is David Hume? I've never heard of him.''

"David Hume was an English philosopher and a friend of Jean Jacques Rousseau before he became a disgusting schnorrer.''

"Here is your omelette, Dr. Feitelzohn,'' Betty said. "I have heard of Jean Jacques Rousseau. I've even read his *Confessions*.''

"It is easy to read David Hume, too. A child can understand him. I'm sure, Tsutsik, you know that $7 + 5 = 12$ has been judged an analytic sentence, not a synthetic a priori one. Hume was right, not Kant. But you still haven't explained what happened to you. You vanished like a wishing ring. I began to think you had gone to Jerusalem and were sitting in a cave trying to bring the Redemption.''

"Dr. Feitelzohn, his cave is on Krochmalna Street.'' Betty turned to me. "May I tell him the truth?''

"If you like. I don't care any more.''

"Dr. Feitelzohn, your Tsutsik has found himself a bride-to-be on Krochmalna Street.''

Feitelzohn put down his fork. "Is that so? According to the way you used to praise that madman Otto Weininger, I thought you would turn into an old bachelor.''

I wanted to answer him, but Betty prevented me. "He could have remained a bachelor, but he found such a treasure—her name is Shosha—that he had to break all his principles and convictions.''

"She's making fun of me,'' I managed to say.

"What? You cannot run away from the female species. Sooner or later you fall into their net. Celia was looking for you desperately. Shosha? A modern girl with such an old-fashioned name? What is she, a fighting Yiddishist?''

Again I tried to answer and again Betty interrupted me: "It would be hard to say just what she is, but if such a connoisseur of women as your Tsutsik decides to marry, you know she has to be something extraordinary. If your David Hume had met her, he would have divorced his wife and run away with Shosha to Coney Island.''

"I don't think David Hume had a wife,'' Feitelzohn said after some hesitation. "Well, mazel tov, Tsutsik, mazel tov.''

Only now did Betty let me speak. "She makes fun of me,'' I said. "Shosha is a girl from my childhood. We used to play together before I went to cheder. We were neighbors at No. 10 Krochmalna. Later I went away and for many years . . .''

Feitelzohn picked up his fork. "Whatever the case, you don't run away from your friends. If you get married, you cannot keep it a secret. If you love her, we want to know her and accept her as one of us. May I call up Celia and tell her the good tidings?''

I saw that Betty was about to come out with some new joke and I said to her, "Do me a favor, Betty, and don't speak in my name. And please don't be so sarcastic. Dr. Feitelzohn, it's not such good tidings and I don't want Celia to know about it. Not yet. Shosha is a poor girl without any education. I loved her as a child and I was never able to forget her. I was sure that she was dead but I found her—thanks to Betty, as a matter of fact.''

"I wasn't being sarcastic. I meant it all seriously''—Betty tried to defend herself.

"Why isn't Celia allowed to know the truth?'' Feitelzohn asked. "Whenever I expect life to remain status quo, something unexpected pops up. World history is made of the same dough as bagels. It must be fresh. This is why democracy and capitalism are going down the drain. They have become stale. This is the reason idolatry was so exciting. You could buy a new god every year. We Jews burdened the nations with an eternal God, and therefore they hate us. Gibbon tried so hard to find the reason for the fall of the Roman Empire. It fell only because it had become old. I hear that there is a passion for newness in the sky also. A star gets tired of being a star and it explodes and becomes a nova. The Milky Way got weary of its sour milk and began to run to the devil knows where. Does she have a job? I mean your fiancée, not the Milky Way.''

"She has no job and she cannot have one,'' I said.

"Is she sick?''

"Yes, sick.''

"When the body gets tired of being healthy, it becomes sick. When it gets tired of living, it dies. When it has enough of being dead, it reincarnates into a frog or a windmill. The coffee here is the best in the whole of Warsaw. May I order another glass, Miss Slonim?''

"Ten glasses, but please don't call me Miss Slonim—my name is Betty.''

"I drink too much coffee and I smoke too many cigars. How is it possible that one never gets tired of tobacco and coffee? This is really a riddle.''

PART TWO

CHAPTER EIGHT

1

Two days before Yom Kippur eve, Bashele bought two hens with which to perform the sacrificial ceremony, one for herself and the other for Shosha. She wanted to buy a rooster for me, but I refused to let a rooster die for my sins. Certain writers in the Yiddish newspapers had come out against this rite, calling it idolatrous. The Zionist supporters proposed sacrificing money instead, which would go to the Jewish National Fund for Palestine. Still, from all the apartments on Krochmalna Street one could hear the clucking of hens and the crowing of roosters. When Bashele went to Yanash's Court to have the hens slaughtered, she didn't return for two hours. The crowd was so large she couldn't get to the slaughterers. Toward evening, the street emptied even of pickpockets. The den at No. 6 was closed down. Candles were lit in the brothels and no visitors were permitted. Even the Communists were hiding somewhere. Bashele had bought a seat in a synagogue. Toward the evening meal, she lit a large candle stuck in a pot of sand—a "soul candle"—and put on a silk holiday dress that went back to the time we had lived at No. 10. She took out of a chest two prayer books she had received as a wedding present, and went off to services. Before leaving, she blessed Shosha and me. She placed her hands on my head and mumbled the benediction as if I were her son: "God make thee as Ephraim and as Manasseh."

I stayed with Shosha for some time. I tried to kiss her and she admonished me that it was forbidden. She had been busy all day long helping her mother prepare for the after-holiday meal, and she kept yawning and falling asleep. She looked pale. She asked me again and again to read some prayers from her grandmother's prayer book, with its faded pages and spots made by tallow candles and tears, but I refused. After a while I wished her a good holiday and left. Dr. Feitelzohn had invited me to spend the evening with him.

A silence had descended over all the Jewish streets. The trolleys made their way empty, and shops were closed. Overhead, the stars flickered like the flames of memorial candles. Even the prison on Dluga Street, the "Arsenal," appeared veiled in reverent melancholy with its dim glow behind the barred windows. I imagined that the night itself took score of its mission. Feitelzohn's apartment was in a house near Freta Street. He had told me no other Jewish tenants lived there besides him. At times I felt that no Gentiles lived there, either. The front windows were never lit in the evenings, nor were there lights at the gate entrance. I climbed the four flights of stone stairs to his place and not a rustle could be heard from behind a single door. I often played with the idea that this was a house of ghosts.

I knocked, and Feitelzohn opened. The apartment consisted of a huge, almost empty room, with gray walls and a high ceiling with a solitary lamp. A door led to a tiny kitchen. How strange, this erudite man owned hardly a book except for an old German encyclopedia. Nor did he have a desk. He slept not in a bed but on a couch, which was covered with a black blanket. Mark Elbinger sat on the couch now—erect, tense.

I had apparently interrupted a dispute between them, for after a long pause Feitelzohn said, "Mark, of all the errors Jews have made, our greatest was to delude ourselves—and later other peoples—that God is merciful, loves His creatures, hates malefactors, and all the rest of it our saints and prophets preached, from Moses down to Chafetz Chaim. The ancient Greeks never nursed this delusion and that was their greatness. While the Jews accused other nations of idolatry, they themselves served an idol of justice. Christianity is an outcome of this wishful thinking. Hitler, savage that he is, is now trying to dehypnotize the world from these fallacies, but—oh, the telephone again! On Yom Kippur!''

I was not in a mood to take part in any discussions and I went over to the window. On the right side I could see the Vistula. A three-quarter moon cast silver nets upon the dark water. Elbinger materialized at my side. He murmured, "A strange person, our Feitelzohn."

"What is he?"

"I've known him over thirty years and I don't begin to fathom what he is. All his words have one aim—to cover up what he's really thinking."

"What is he really thinking?"

"Gloomy thoughts. He is disappointed in everything, but mostly in himself. His father was an ascetic. He may still be alive somewhere. Morris has a daughter whom he last saw in her diapers. I myself have known two women who committed suicide over him. One a German in Berlin, and the other a missionary's daughter in London . . ."

Feitelzohn grunted and put down the receiver. "It's my opinion that woman's number-one passion isn't sex but talking," he said.

"What does she want?" Elbinger asked.

"You ought to know, you're the mind reader."

The conversation turned to occultism, and Feitelzohn said, "There are unknown forces here, yes, there are, but they're all part of the mystery called nature. What nature is no one knows, and I suspect that she doesn't know herself. I can easily visualize the Almighty sitting on the Throne of Glory in the Seventh Heaven, Metatron on His right, Sandalphon on His left, and God asking them, 'Who am I? How did I come about? Did I create Myself? Who gave Me these powers? After all, it couldn't be that I've existed forever. I remember only the past hundred trillion years. Everything before that is hazy. Well, how long will it go on?' Wait, Mark, I'll get you your cognac. Something to nibble on? I have cookies as old as Methuselah."

Feitelzohn went into the kitchen. He came back after a long time with a plate holding two glasses of cognac and a few biscuits. I had told him I was fasting, not because I believed that this was God's will, but to remain in some way a part of my family and all the other Jews. Feitelzohn clinked his glass with Elbinger's. *"L'chaim!* We Jews keep on wishing ourselves eternal life, or at least immortality of the soul. In fact, eternal life would be a calamity. Imagine some little storekeeper dying and his soul flying around for millions of years still remembering that once it sold chicory, yeast, and beans, and that a customer owes it eighteen groschen. Or the soul of an author ten million years later resenting a bad review he got.''

"Souls don't stay the same. They grow," Elbinger said.

"If they forget the past, they are no longer the same. And if they remember all of the pettiness of life, then they cannot grow. I have no doubt that soul and body are two sides of the same coin. In this respect Spinoza had more courage than Kant. Kant's soul is nothing but a false figure in a false system of bookkeeping. *L'chaim!* Let's sit down.''

The conversation turned again and again to the secret powers, and Elbinger said, ''Yes, they exist, but what they represent I do not know. My own experience with them started when I was still a child. We were living in a village so small I could never find it on any map—Sencymin. Actually, it was a hamlet into which two to three dozen Jewish families had moved. My father, a *melamed,* was a pauper. We occupied two rooms—one used for the cheder; the other for the kitchen, the bedroom, and everything else. I had an older sister, Tzipa, and an older brother, Yonkel. I was named Moshe Mottel after a great-grandfather, but I was called Mottele, which later evolved into Mark. I recall a number of episodes in my life as far back as the age of two. My bed was set up in the cheder room, where the children studied by day. The two windows there had shutters and they must have faced east, because the sun shone through them in the mornings. What I'm speaking of now has no connection with the so-called occult but with a feeling that everything is full of mysteries. I recall that once I woke quite early—my parents, brother, and sister were still asleep. The rising sun shone through the cracks in the shutters, and columns of dust rose from sunbeams. I remember that morning with remarkable clarity. Obviously, I was too young to think in the context of words, but I wondered, 'What is all this? Where does it all come from?' Other children no doubt go through the same thing, but on that morning my feeling was unusually strong, and I knew instinctively that I shouldn't ask about this and that my parents couldn't supply any answers. Our ceiling had beams, and a web of sun and shadow played across it. I realized that I myself and what I was seeing—the walls, the floor, the pillow on which I rested my head—were all one. In later years I read about cosmic consciousness, monism, pantheism, but I never experienced it with such impact. More, it provided me with a rare pleasure. I had merged with eternity and I relished it. At times I think it was like the state of passing over from life to what we call death. We may experience it in the final moments or perhaps immediately after. I say this because no matter how many dead people I have seen in my life, they have had the same expression on their faces: *Aha, so that's what it is! If I had only known! What a shame I can't tell the others about it!* Even a dead bird or mouse presents this expression, although not as distinctly as man.

"My first psychic experiences—if you can call them that—were of a kind that might have come in a dream or while I was awake, although I'm as convinced that they weren't dreams as I am that my sitting here with you now is no dream. I remember one time leaving our house at night. Our house—actually, all the Jewish houses were built around a sandy area called the Market. The shops were there, the prayer house and a ritual bath, as well as the tavern. I couldn't say how late it was, but the Market was deserted, all the stores were shut, and the shutters closed. I managed to slip out of bed and open the door. The night was bright—if not from the moon, perhaps from the stars.

"Across the way from us stood another house. The peasant shacks had roofs of straw, while the Jewish houses had crooked shingle roofs. Needless to say, the houses were low. The moment I stepped outside I saw something sitting on the roof across the way. I imagined it was a man, yet different. For one thing, he had no arms or legs. For another, he didn't stand on the roof, he didn't sit—he hovered there. He didn't speak to me, but I understood that he wanted me to come up to him, and I knew that to go up would be the same as going to where my dead brother and sister had gone. Just the same, I felt a strong urge to go to him. I stood gaping in indecision, frightened and disbelieving my own eyes.

"Suddenly I was aware that the man or monster had begun berating me—still in silence—and he lowered a spade toward me. The spade was not a spade at all but something that emerged from his body. It was a kind of tongue, so long and wide that it couldn't have come from any mouth. It stretched out so close to me that I knew it would catch me at any moment. I was overcome by a dreadful fear and ran back into the house screaming. The household wakened. They blew on me and, it seems, uttered incantations over me. My mother, father, Tzipa, and Yonkel—all of them barefoot and in their nightclothes—asked why I was crying so desperately, but I neither could nor wanted to answer them, knowing that I wouldn't be able to find the right words for it, that they would not believe me, and above all, that it would be better for me if I said nothing. Actually, I'm telling this for the very first time tonight. From then on, I became a kind of secret visionary. I saw things that some sense told me not to reveal. In the daytime I often saw shadows on the walls of our house, shadows not connected to the phenomena of light and shade. These were beings that crawled over the walls and into the walls. At times, two came together from opposite directions and one swallowed the other. Some were tall; their heads touched the ceiling—if you could call them heads. Others were small. At times I saw them on the floor, too, and outside on other houses, and in the air. They were always busy—coming, going, rushing. Rarely did one stop for a moment. I tell myself today that I saw ghosts, but this is merely an appellation. One thing does come to mind—I separated them into males and females. I wasn't afraid of them. It would be more accurate to say that I was curious.

"One night after I had gone to sleep and my mother had put out the light and the moon shone in through the cracks in the shutters, I heard a rustling. How shall I describe it? It was like a dried palm leaf shaking, like beating osier branches, like spraying water, and like something else to which there is no comparison. The walls began to hum and buzz, particularly in the corners, and the shapes that till then I had seen only by day now raced in thick whirls. Today, I would express it as a kind of panic among them. They hurried here and there, merged in the corners from which the noise came, raced over the beams and across the floor. My bed began to vibrate. Everything beneath me shook and tossed, and the straw in my mattress seemed animated. For once I was terrified, but I didn't dare cry out, fearing a blow or some other punishment. When I grew older, I speculated that this vibration might have been the result of an earthquake, but when I casually asked my parents and other townspeople if they had ever been through an earthquake, they all replied in the negative. I don't know if Poland has ever suffered an earthquake. The noise and dashing about lasted a long time. You can tell me my venture outside the house and the experiences that night were dreams or nightmares, but I know this isn't so.

"In later years I almost ceased having these visions, or whatever they may have been, but others evolved. I got an urge for girls—for Gentile girls, too— and I gradually realized that if I thought about a girl long enough or intensely enough, she grew magnetized and came to me. I'm not one to ascribe unusual powers to myself. Essentially, I'm a rationalist. I know coincidences occur that, in terms of probability, couldn't happen. When I play the game of dreidel with myself and the dreidel falls on the same letter five or six times because I will it to do so, I can assume that it happened by chance. However, when I spin the dreidel ten times and it comes out the same, I know that chance has nothing to do with it. I'm sure you'd rather hear about girls than dreidels. It came to the point where I would mentally order a woman to come to this and that street, and this and that number—we were then living in Warsaw—and she would come. I can't prove this to you. I can't even demonstrate with a dreidel each and every time. These powers are strangely inclined to be spiteful. They are mischievous, and they hate to be put to the test with pencils and watches. I would say that they hate science and scientists. Believe me, even to my own ears this sounds like nonsense. Who are these powers? Are they living beings? And why should they hate science and statistics? It sounds like a pretext for lying, and I've been called a liar more than once. I myself considered mediums liars if they couldn't demonstrate their powers when they were being controlled, so to say, scientifically. Well, but aren't they, in a sense, antiscience? Morris, if you were told to sleep with a woman in the presence of ten professors with cameras and meters and all kinds of measuring instruments, you wouldn't be such a Don Juan. Well, and what would have happened to poets like Goethe or Heine, if they had been placed at a table surrounded by professors and instruments and ordered to write a great poem? You can play a violin in a bright hall before hundreds of people, but it's a moot point whether Beethoven or Mozart could have written their symphonies under such circumstances. I tell you that although I've managed many things under strict controls and before huge crowds, I've experienced my most significant events only when I've been alone. No one watched for results, and I didn't have to worry that I would be jeered or whistled at. Shyness is a tremendous force— occasionally a negative one. There are many men who would go to brothels, but they don't because with a prostitute they would become impotent. Why should the occult powers be any less capricious than the genitals? I can hypnotize in front of an audience today. I had to learn to do this. I've conquered my fear of failure, but not altogether. If I bang my fist on the table, the table bangs the fist back in return. This is true in spiritual matters as well. Every hypnosis has its counterhypnosis. If I'm afraid that I won't be able to sleep, I lie awake all night, and if professors from another planet sat around me on a single visit, they might conclude that I never slept at all. Why is it so hard to be a good actor and to speak and behave naturally on-stage? At home, every woman is a Sarah Bernhardt. I've seen great scholars face an audience unable to utter a lucid sentence on a subject in which they were world experts.

"Yes, I did things that amazed me and convinced me I could dominate other souls, often those whom I barely knew—perhaps they had glanced at me just once. My success with women was so great that it frightened me. What is hypnotism, anyway? My theory is that it's a language with which one soul communicates directly with another.

"Our conscious hypnotic powers have limits. I don't believe that I hypnotized the dreidel. Perhaps I hypnotized my hand to spin the dreidel in such a way that it fell where I wanted it to. But who says that hypnotism is merely a biological force? Maybe it's physical, too? Maybe gravity is a kind of hypnotism? Maybe magnetism is hypnotism? Maybe God is a hypnotist with such strong hypnotic powers that He can say, 'Let there be light,' and there is light? I heard of a woman who ordered a chair to walk, and the chair walked from wall to wall and even danced. A poltergeist lifts plates and breaks them, throws stones, and opens locked doors. A woman came to me once and swore on all that was holy to her that one time when she entered her kitchen a pot rose, soared toward her, and slowly came to rest at her feet. This was an elderly woman, a lawyer's widow, a mother of grown sons and daughters, a person of education and dignity. She had no possible reason to make up such a story. She came to me hoping I could explain the mystery. It had plagued her for years. She told me that the pot didn't *fall* at her feet but laid itself down carefully. From that day on, she was afraid of the pot. She waited for it to pull another stunt, but no, it remained a pot like all pots. The woman cried as she spoke to me. Could this have been a greeting from her late husband? She spent two hours with me, hoping I could provide her with an explanation, but the only thing I could tell her was that the pot hadn't acted on its own, but that some force—an unseen hand—had lifted it and laid it down at her feet. I recall her saying, 'Maybe the pot wanted to play a joke?'"

"If this story is true, we must reexamine all our values, our concept of the world," Feitelzohn said. "Still, why doesn't it happen that a pot or some other object rises in the presence of a physicist or a chemist or at least a photographer with a camera? How is it that these wonders always occur in quiet widows' kitchens? Why don't they happen in a kitchen where there are several cooks present? Can it be that pots are bashful, too?"

At ten-thirty, Elbinger announced that he must leave. He had an appointment. I wanted to leave with him, but Feitelzohn insisted I stay.

He lit a cigar and said, "That big hero is a hypochondriac. He has hypnotized himself into believing that he suffers from a dozen ailments. He is convinced that he hasn't slept in years. He has ulcers. He is supposedly impotent, too. Women are crazy for him, but he practices celibacy. The history of mankind is the history of hypnotism. It's my firm conviction that all epidemics are mass hypnosis. When the papers announce an outbreak of influenza, people start to die from influenza. I myself talked all kinds of insanities into myself. I can't even read a book any more. At the end of the first sentence, I start to yawn. I'm sick of women. Their talking puts me off. Take our Celia. She would come here for an hour or two, and for an hour or two she would chatter. That Haiml is a homosexual. At times it seems to me I'm another. Don't be afraid, I wouldn't lay a hand on you."

Again the telephone rang. Feitelzohn let it ring. He stood there and looked at me in a new way—there was something fatherly and older-brotherly in his look.

He said, "It's Celia. I see you're tired. Go home if you want. Tsutsik, don't stay in Poland. A holocaust is coming here that will be worse than in Chmielnitsky's time. If you can get a visa—even a tourist visa—escape! A good holiday."

Then he walked over to the telephone, which had kept on ringing.

2

Warsaw was so quiet I could hear the echo of my own footsteps. Candles still burned in the windows. The gate in the house on Leszno Street was closed, and the janitor was slow in coming to open it. He grumbled, as if he knew that I intended to move out soon. Although I had my key to the elevator with me, I walked up the dark stairs.

I knocked at the apartment door and Tekla opened it. She said, "The phone rang for you today maybe a hundred times. Miss Betty."

"Thank you, Tekla."

"You don't go to the synagogue on such a holy day?" she asked with reproof.

I didn't know how to answer her. I went to my room. Without putting on the lights, I took off my clothes and lay down, but even though I was tired I couldn't sleep. What would I do after the few zlotys I had left were gone? I saw no possibility of earning money. I lay there, frightened by my situation. Feitelzohn had at least a semblance of a living from his lectures. He took money from Celia and from other women, too. He had a rent-controlled apartment, for which he paid no more than thirty zlotys a month. I had accepted the responsibility for a sick girl.

I fell asleep and wakened with a start. The phone in the corridor was ringing. On my watch the luminous hands showed a quarter past two. I heard the sound of bare feet—Tekla was running to answer. I heard her whispering. The door to my room opened. "It's for you!" Her voice expressed the indignation of a Jew forced to desecrate the holiest day of the year.

I got out of bed and bumped into her. She was wearing only her nightgown. In the hall I picked up the receiver and heard Betty's voice. It was hoarse and grating, like that of someone in the midst of a quarrel. She said, "You must come over to the hotel at once! If I call you in the middle of Yom Kippur night, it's not because of some trifle."

"What's happened?"

"I've been calling you all day. Where do you wander off to on Yom Kippur eve? I didn't sleep a wink last night and I haven't closed my eyes tonight. Sam is very sick. He has to have an operation. I told him all about us."

"What's the matter with him? Why did you need to tell him?"

"Last night he got up to go to the toilet, but he couldn't pass water. He was in such pain I had to call the First Aid. They relieved him with a catheter, but he requires an operation. He refuses to go to the hospital here and insists on returning to America to his own doctor. The doctor who saw him today told me that he has a weak heart and is not likely to recover from surgery. My dear, I have a feeling he won't make it. He called me to his side and said, 'Betty, I'm cashing in my chips, but I want to provide for you.' He talked in such a way that I couldn't withhold anything from him. I told him the whole truth. He wants to talk to you. Catch a cab and come right over. He's acting like a father to me—closer than a father. I know it's Yom Kippur, but this can't wait. Will you come?"

"Yes, of course, but you shouldn't have told him!"

"I shouldn't have been born! Be quick!" She hung up the receiver.

I tried to put on my clothes in a hurry, and they slipped from my fumbling fingers. The button fell out of my collar and rolled under the bed. I stooped to pick it up and knocked my forehead against the rail. The room was warm, but I felt a chill. I closed the door behind me and began to race down the unlit stairs. For the second time that night I rang the bell and waited for the janitor to open the gate. The pavement outside was wet—it must have been raining. The street lay deserted. I stood at the curb hoping for a taxi to come by but soon realized I could stand all night without one coming. I went in the direction of Bielanska Street and the Cracow suburb. The only streetcar that passed was headed in the opposite direction. I didn't walk but ran. I came to the hotel. The clerk dozed before the honeycomb of key boxes. I knocked on Betty's door. No one answered. I knocked again, this time on Sam Dreiman's door, and Betty let me in. She was wearing pajamas and slippers. Inside, the lights glared with a middle-of-the-night tension. Sam lay with his eyes closed, his head resting on two pillows, seemingly asleep. From under the bedding a little hose ran into a container. Betty's face was sallow and drawn, her hair disordered. "What took you so long?" she asked in a choked voice that hid a scream.

"I couldn't get a cab. I ran all the way."

"Oh. He just now fell asleep. He took a pill."

"Why do you have the room so bright here?"

"I don't know. I'll turn the lights down. I don't know what's happening to me any more. One calamity after another—look at my eyes. Come closer!"

She took me by the arm and pulled me to the other end of the room near the window. She gestured to me to be quiet. She began to talk in a whisper, but from time to time she emitted a shriek as if so many words had collected in her they could no longer be contained.

"I started calling you at ten this morning and on into the night. Where were you—still with that Shosha? Tsutsik, I have no one here but you. I tell you, Sam is a saint. I never knew he had such a noble soul. Oh, if I had known, I would have been nicer to him. I would have been faithful. But I'm afraid it's too late now. He had a hemorrhage in his nose. Tomorrow they're holding a consultation here. I called the American consulate and they arranged everything. They wanted to check him into a private clinic, where he can have the best doctors, but he insisted he would only be operated on in America. In the midst of the commotion he called me to him and said, 'Betty, I know that you love Tsutsik and there's no point in your denying it.' This was such a blow to me that I confessed everything. I began to cry and he kissed me and called me 'daughter.' He has children, but their mother filled them with hate against him. They dragged him to court and tried to grab their inheritance while he was still alive. Wait, he's waking up."

I heard a tossing about and a groan.

"Betty, where are you? Why is the room so dark?"

She ran to the bed. "Sam darling! I thought you would sleep longer. Tsutsik is here!''

"Tsutsik, come over. Betty, turn up the lights. So long as I can draw breath I don't want to be in the dark. Tsutsik, you can see for yourself I'm a sick man. I want to talk to you like a father. I have two sons, both lawyers, but all my life they treated me not like a father but worse than a stranger. I have a son-in-law, and he's no better. Living with him has turned my daughter into a bitch. I haven't felt good for a long time. Old age has suddenly caught me—the head, the stomach, the legs. Twenty times a day I run—if you'll excuse me—to the toilet, but my bladder is blocked up. In New York I have a doctor who watches over me. He gives me a checkup every three months, treats me with massages. He didn't want me to have an operation because my heart is making monkey business. In Warsaw I have no doctor. Besides, we were so busy with the theater I put off everything. My doctor ordered me not to drink—whiskey irritates the prostate and isn't good for the bladder, either—but you don't want to admit you're washed up. Take a chair, sit down. That's it. You, too, Betty darling. What was I saying, eh? Well, I'm afraid God wants me up there with Him. He's probably in the real-estate business and wants Sam Dreiman to advise Him. When the time comes, you got to go. Even if I survive the operation, it won't be for long. I was supposed to lose weight while I was here. Instead, I gained twenty pounds. How can you diet when you're away from home? I love your Warsaw dishes—they have that homey taste. Well . . .''

Sam Dreiman closed his eyes, then shook himself and opened them again. "Tsutsik, today is Yom Kippur. I thought I'd be able to go to the synagogue. I wanted to go to the one on Tlomacka Street as well as to the Hasidim on Nalewki. I bought the tickets. But man proposes and God disposes. I'll be frank with you—if I should pass away, I don't want to leave Betty to the fates. I know about your affair—she confessed everything to me. I knew about it even before. After all, she's a young woman and I'm an old man. I used to be a great lover, I could raise hell with the best of them, but once you pass into your seventies and have high blood pressure you're no longer the big hero you were. She kept on praising you. She accused herself of having brought you bad luck. I hoped the play would be a success, but it wasn't fated. We did a lot of talking. Hear me out, don't interrupt, I beg you, and think over what I'm going to say, because I look at things in a clear-headed way. You're a poor young man. You have talent, but talent is like a diamond—it has to be polished. I've been told you're involved with some sick, undeveloped girl. She is poor, too, and what is the saying? Two corpses go dancing. Things will not end well in Poland. That beast Hitler will soon come with his Nazis. There'll be a great war. Americans will lend a hand and they'll do what they did in the last war, but before that the Nazis will attack the Jews and there'll be nothing but grief for you here. The Yiddish papers are in trouble already, there are no book publishers, and what goes on on the stage is disgusting. How will you make a living? A writer has to eat, too. Even Moses had to eat. That's what e holy books say.

"Tsutsik, Betty loves you and I gather you don't hate her, either. I'm going to leave her a lot of money—exactly how much I'll tell you another time. I want to make a deal with you—a regular business transaction. I don't know yet what's going to happen to me. It's possible I'll leave this world soon, though if God is willing, I may be around for another few years yet. If they remove my prostate

I may not be left a whole man in the true sense of the word. Here is my plan: I want you two to marry. I'll establish a trust fund. A lawyer will explain it all to you. You won't be a parasite supported by his wife but just the opposite— you'll support her. I only ask one promise from you—that as long as I live she can remain my friend. I'll be your publisher, your manager, anything you like. If you write a good play, I'll produce it. When you have a book ready, I'll publish it or give it to another publisher. In America, writers have agents to represent them, and I'll be your agent. You'll be my son and I'll be a father to you. I'll hire people who'll see to it that everything is in order."

"Mr. Dreiman—"

"I know, I know what you want to say. You want to know what will happen to the girl—what's her name? Shosha. Don't think I would leave her to God's mercy in Warsaw so she should starve. Sam Dreiman doesn't do such things. We'll bring her over to America. She is sick and should have help—a psychiatrist maybe. The consul is my friend, but he can't issue a permanent visa. There is a quota and not even the President can get around it. But I've figured how we can manage. We'll take her along as our maid. She won't be anyone's maid, but saying she is can get her a visa. If she's cured there, this would be a hundred times better for her than if she becomes your wife and starves to death here. You have only to agree that Betty can remain my friend and not leave me alone when I'm old and sick, and she won't take you to court if you should want to give your Shosha a kiss or whatever. Isn't that so, Betty?"

"Yes, Sam darling, anything you say is all right with me."

"Do you hear? So that's my plan. It's her plan, too. We talked frankly. Just one thing more—I must leave for America soon, so everything has to be done fast. If you say yes, you'll have to marry at once. If not, we'll say goodbye, and may God help you."

Sam Dreiman closed his eyes. After a while, he opened them and said, "Betty, take him to your room. I have to . . ." He mumbled a few words in English that I didn't understand.

3

In the hallway between her room and Sam's, Betty began to kiss me. Her face was wet from crying, and within a moment my face was drenched. She whispered, "My husband, that's the way God intended it!"

She opened the door to her room for me and immediately went back to Sam's side. She hadn't put on the lights and I stood in the dark. After a while, I lay down on the sofa, my mind blank. I assumed that Betty would come right back, but she was away a long time. The shade was drawn over the window, but it seemed to me that day had started to break. Gradually, I began to take account of the situation. After I had given up on everything, a perspective had opened such as I never dared dream of—a visa to America and the chance to write without worrying about money! I could take Shosha along, too. Something inside me both laughed and marveled. From the time I reached manhood, I had told myself I would marry a girl just like my mother—a decent, chaste Jewish daughter. I always felt pity for men with dissolute wives. They lived with harlots and could never be sure that their children were their own. These women sullied their homes. Now I was considering taking one of this ilk for my own. What Betty had told me about her adventures in Russia and in America stayed in my mind. During the Revolution she had carried on with a Red Army man, with some sailor, with the director of a traveling actors' troupe. She had sold herself to Sam Dreiman for money. Not only did she have an ugly past, but Sam Dreiman had now stipulated that as long as he lived she would remain his friend—which was to say his lover. "Run!" a voice cried within me. "You'll sink into a slime from which you'll never be able to get out. They'll drag you into the abyss!" It was my father's voice. In the light of dawn I saw his high brow and piercing eyes. "Don't shame me, your mother, and your holy ancestors! All your deeds are noted in heaven." Then the voice began to abuse me. "Heathen! Betrayer of Israel! See what happens when you deny the Almighty! 'You shall utterly detest it and you shall utterly abhor it, for it is a cursed thing!'"

I lay there shaken. Since my father had died, I had been unable to conjure up his face. He never appeared in my dreams. His death had brought with it a kind of amnesia. Often, before going to sleep, I implored him to reveal himself to me wherever he might be and to give me a sign, but my pleas had not been answered. Suddenly here he was beside Betty's sofa, and on the Day of Atonement. Glowing and awesome, he shed his own light. I recalled what the Midrash said of Joseph: as he was about to sin with Potiphar's wife, his father, Jacob, appeared before him. These apparitions come only in the height of distress.

I sat up, my eyes wide open. "Father, save me!" As I pleaded, Father's image dissolved.

The door opened. "Are you asleep?" Betty asked.

It took a while before I could answer. "No."

"Shall I turn on the light?"

"No, no!"

"What's the matter with you? Today is more than Yom Kippur for me. Before you came, I took a nap on the sofa and my father came to me in a dream. He looked just as I knew him in life, only handsomer. His eyes glistened. The murderers shot him in the face and crushed his skull, but he stood before me unmarked. Well, what's your answer?"

I could only say, "Not now."

"If you don't want me, I won't throw myself at you. I've still retained some pride. One has to be a saint to treat us the way Sam Dreiman is offering to do. But if it's a disgrace for you to become my husband, say so and don't leave me dangling. I've done some ugly things in my time, but I didn't have anyone then and I owed nothing to anyone. My blood burned like fire. Those men weren't even real to me. I swear to you that I've forgotten them all. I wouldn't recognize them if I saw them on the street. Why was I fool enough to tell you about them? I've always been my own worst enemy."

"Betty, Shosha would die if I did this to her," I said.

"Eh? The truth is, she'd be cured in America, but here she'll starve to death. Already their house reeks of decay. She looks ready for the grave. How long can she go on like that? I don't have to get married—not to you or to anybody. That was purely Sam's idea. A real father wouldn't be as good to me as he has been. I'd sooner cut off my hand than just leave him. I've already told you he is barely a man now. All he needs is a kiss, a pat, a kind word. If you can't even let him have that, then be on your way. If I am ready to take Shosha into my house—that ninny—then you needn't act so superior toward Sam. He has more insight in his little finger than you have in your whole body, you goddamn idiot!''

She went out and slammed the door behind her. A moment later she was back. "So what shall I tell Sam? Give me a straight answer.''

"Well, all right, we'll marry,'' I said.

Betty paused a moment. "Is this your decision or are you just trying to make a fool out of me? If you're going to go around burning with jealousy and thinking of me as a whore, we'll call the whole thing off right now.''

"Betty, if I can look after Shosha, you can be with Sam.''

"What do you think—that I'd post a guard by your bed like that sultan in the *Thousand and One Nights?* I realize you feel close to her. I'm prepared to accept it. But I demand the same from you. The times when a man could indulge all his swinish urges while the woman remained a slave are over. So long as Sam lives—and may God grant him the years he deserves—we must all live together. Try to think of him as my father. That's what he has become. I haven't given up on the theater—I still plan to make another try at it. In America we can revise this play. There no one will harass us or rush us. The fact that you'll be diddling around with your Shosha bothers me as much as last year's frost. I doubt if she's even capable of *being* a woman. Have you got her started yet?''

"No, no.''

"Well, a lion can't be jealous of a fly. All I can tell you is that in a hundred and twenty years, when Sam is no more, I won't be looking for anyone else. This, I could swear to you before black candles.''

"You don't need to swear.''

"We must get married at once. Whatever happens, I want Sam to be there.''
"Yes.''

"I know that you have a mother and a brother, but this can't be put off. If things go well, we'll bring your family over to America, too.''

"Thank you, Betty, thank you.''

"Tsutsik, I'll be better to you than you can imagine. I've already had enough filth in my life. I want to wipe the slate clean and start fresh. What it is I see in you I'm not sure myself. You have a thousand faults. But there is something about you that draws me. What is it? You tell me.''

"I wouldn't know, Betty.''

"When I'm with you, things are interesting. Without you, I'm miserable and bored. Come here, wish me mazel tov!''

———————

4

I had fallen into a deep sleep on Betty's sofa. When I opened my eyes, I saw her standing beside me. It was day. She looked bedraggled and upset. She said, "Tsutsik, get up!''

I had wakened with a headache. It was a few seconds before I could remember what I was doing here.

Betty bent over me with maternal concern. "They're taking Sam to the hospital. I'm going with him."

"What happened?"

"He has to be operated on immediately! Where shall I look for you? You'd better stay in this room so I can call you."

"I will, Betty."

"You remember our agreement?"

"Yes."

"Pray to God for him! I don't want to lose him. If, God forbid, something should happen, I'd be left in the cold." She leaned down and kissed me on the mouth. She said, "The ambulance is downstairs. If you need to go out, leave the key with the desk clerk. If you want to go to Shosha's, you can, but you have to break off with that Celia once and for all. I won't stand for a fifth wheel on the wagon. I would have liked you to say goodbye to Sam, but I don't want him to know you spent the night here. I told him you went home. Pray to God for us!"

She left and I stayed on the sofa. I glanced at my wristwatch. It had stopped at the hour of four. I closed my eyes again. From what Betty said, I couldn't understand whether Sam had already made a new will or was planning to. Even if he had, his family would destroy it. I was dismayed at the trend my thoughts were taking. Money matters had always been alien to me. In none of my fantasies had it ever occurred to me to marry for money or for any practical reason. *It's the visa, not the money,* I justified myself—*the fear of falling into the hands of the Nazis.*

Suddenly I felt as if something had bitten me. Break off with Celia? Betty had no right to make such a demand on me while she remained Sam's mistress. I'd go straight to Celia's! I rubbed my jowls—a heavy stubble had sprouted. I stood up, but my legs had grown wobbly from sleeping on the sofa. A mirror hung over the washstand. I raised the window shade and gazed at my reflection: withered face, bloodshot eyes, a wrinkled collar. I went to the window and looked out. There was no vehicle of any kind at the hotel entrance. The ambulance had already carried them to the hospital. Betty hadn't even given me its name. From the slant of the sun's rays, I estimated that it was not early.

"What shall I tell Shosha?" I asked myself. "All she would understand was that I married someone else. She wouldn't live through it." I stood looking out at the street, the empty streetcars and droshkies. Even the Gentile neighborhoods seemed deserted in honor of Yom Kippur. I took off my jacket and washed my face, even though it was forbidden on this sacred holiday. I went out. I walked downstairs step by step. There was no reason to hurry. For the first time I felt close to Sam. He wanted the same as I—the impossible.

I passed a barbershop and went in. I was the only patron and the barber treated me with particular politeness. He wrapped me in a white sheet, like a corpse in a shroud. He stroked my beard before he began to lather. He said, "What kind of city is this Warsaw? It's Yom Kippur by the sheenies and the whole city acts dead. And this is supposed to be the capital, the crown of our Polish nation. It's really funny!"

He had mistaken me for a Gentile. I wanted to answer him, but realized that the moment I spoke more than a word or two my accent would give me away. I nodded, grunting a single word that wouldn't compromise me: *"Tak."*

"They've taken over all Poland," he went on. "The cities are lousy with them. Once, they only stank up Nalewki, Grzybowska, and Krochmalna Streets, but lately they swarm like vermin everywhere. They've even crawled as far as Wilanów. There's one consolation—Hitler will smoke them out like bedbugs."

I barely kept from trembling. The man held the edge of the razor at my throat. I looked up, and his greenish eyes briefly held mine. Did he suspect that I was a Jew?

"I'll tell you something, dear sir. The modern Jews, those who shave, who speak a proper Polish, and who try to ape real Poles, are even worse than the old-fashioned Hebes with their long gaberdines, wild beards, and earlocks. They, at least, don't go where they aren't wanted. They sit in their stores in their long capotes and shake over their Talmud like bedouins. They babble away in their jargon, and when a Christian falls into their clutches, they swindle a few groschen out of him. But at least they don't go to the theater, the cafés, the opera. Those that shave and dress modern are the real danger. They sit in our Sejm and make treaties with our worst enemies, the Ruthenians, the White Russians, the Lithuanians. Every one of them is a secret Communist and a Soviet spy. They have one aim— to root out us Christians and hand over the power to the Bolsheviks, the Masons, and the radicals. You might find it hard to believe this, dear sir, but their millionaires have a secret pact with Hitler. The Rothschilds finance him and Roosevelt is the middleman. His real name isn't Roosevelt but Rosenfeld, a converted Jew. They supposedly assume the Christian faith, but with one goal in mind—to bore from within and infect everything and everybody. Funny, don't you think?"

I emitted a half grunt, half sigh.

"They come here for a shave and a haircut all year, but not today. Yom Kippur is a holy day even for those that are rich and modern. More than half the stores are closed here and on Marshalkowska Street. They don't go to the Hasidic prayer houses in fur-edged hats and prayer shawls like the old-fashioned sheenies—oh no, they put on top hats and drive to the synagogue on Tlomacka Street in private cars. But Hitler will clean them out! He promises their millionaires that he'll protect their capital, but once the Nazis are armed he'll fix them all— ha, ha, ha! It's too bad that he'll attack our country, but since we haven't had the guts to sweep away this filth ourselves, we have to let the enemy do it for us. What will happen later, no one can know. The fault for it all lies with those traitors, the Protestants, who sold their souls to the devil. They're the Pope's deadliest enemies. Did you know, dear sir, that Luther was a secret Jew?"

"No."

"It's an established fact."

The barber had gone over my face twice with the razor. He now splashed me with eau-de-cologne and dusted me with powder. He brushed off my suit and with two fingers removed some stray hairs from my shoulders. I paid him and left. By the time I closed the shop door my shirt was soaked. I began to race, not knowing in what direction I was going. *No, I wouldn't stay in Poland! I'd leave at any price!* I crossed the street and a car nearly ran me down. This was the most tragic day of my life. I, too, had sold my soul to the devil. Maybe go to a synagogue? No, I would desecrate the holy place. My stomach churned and I felt an urge to urinate. Sweat ran from me, and pain stabbed my bladder. I knew that if I didn't void immediately I would wet myself. I came to a restaurant and tried to enter, but the glass door wouldn't give. Was it locked? It couldn't be—I could see diners inside and waiters carrying trays.

A man with a dog on a leash came up and said, "Don't pull, push!"

"Oh, many thanks!"

I asked the waiter for the way to the restroom and he pointed to a door. But when I walked in that direction the door vanished as if by magic. People looked up from their breakfasts and stared at me. A woman laughed aloud.

The waiter came up. "Here!" And he opened a door for me.

I ran to the urinal, but just as with Sam Dreiman, the urine had become blocked inside me.

CHAPTER NINE

1

I didn't go to Celia. I spent Yom Kippur with Shosha. Bashele had gone to the synagogue. The big commemorative candle she had lit the day before still burned, casting almost no light. I lay on the bed next to Shosha in my clothes, dulled by the sleepless night. I dropped off, began dreaming, and awoke. Shosha spoke to me, but even though I heard her voice I didn't follow what she was saying. It had to do with the war, the typhus epidemics, the hunger, Yppe's death. Shosha placed her childlike hand on my loins. We both had fasted.

From time to time I opened an eye and noticed how the sunlight moved up across the opposite wall. A Yom Kippur quiet lay over the courtyard, and I could hear the twittering of a bird. I had made a decision and knew that I would keep it, but why I had made it was something I couldn't explain to myself or to anyone else. Did it have to do with the vision—or hallucination—of my father? Had the barber influenced me with his poisonous words? I was rejecting a woman of passion, of talent, with the capability of taking me to wealthy America, and condemning myself to poverty and death from a Nazi bullet. Had it been jealousy of Sam Dreiman? Such great love for Shosha? Did I lack the courage to disappoint Bashele? I posed a question to my subconscious or unconscious, but no answer came back. This is precisely the case with those who commit suicide, I said to myself. They find a hook in the ceiling, fashion a noose, place a chair underneath, and until the final second they don't know why they are doing it. Who says that everything nature or human nature does can be expressed in motives and words? I had been aware for a long time that literature could only describe facts or let the characters invent excuses for their acts. All motivations in fiction are either obvious or false.

I fell asleep. It was dusk when I awoke. A final sliver of sunset blazed in the pane of a garret window. Shosha said, "Arele, you slept nicely."

"And you, Shoshele?"

"Oh, I slept."

The room filled with shadows. On the table the memorial candle began to flicker. The flame flared up once and soon grew so small it barely touched the wick. Shosha said, "Last year I went with Mommy to the synagogue on Yom Kippur night. A man with a white beard blew the ram's horn."

"Yes, I know."

"When three stars appear in the sky, we'll be able to eat."

"Are you hungry?"

"When you are with me, it's better than eating."

I said, "Shoshele, we'll soon be husband and wife. After the holidays."

As I spoke, I wanted to caution Shosha to say nothing of this to her mother for now, but just then the door opened, Bashele came in, and Shosha ran to meet her. "Mommy, Arele is going to marry me after Succoth!" She shouted this in a louder voice than I had ever heard from her. She hugged her mother and began to kiss her. Bashele quickly put down her two prayer books and cast a questioning look at me that was full of joyful astonishment.

"Yes, it's true," I said.

Bashele clapped her hands. "God the merciful has heard my prayers. I stood on my feet all day and prayed only for you, daughter, and for you, Arele, my son. Only God in heaven knows how many tears I shed for you two today. Daughter, apple of my eye, mazel tov!"

They kissed, hugged, and swayed, as if unable to break apart. Then Bashele held out her arms to me. There came from her the aroma of the fast, of the naphthalene in which her dress had been lying a whole year, and of something womanly and festive—an aroma familiar from my childhood, when our living room was turned into a women's synagogue during the Days of Awe. Bashele's voice, too, had grown louder and stronger. She began to speak in the style of the Yiddish supplication book: "It's all from heaven, from heaven. God has seen my grief, my broken spirit. Father in heaven, this is the happiest day of my wretched life. Help us, God, for we have suffered enough. Sweet Father, let me live to enjoy the satisfaction of leading my first-born child to the wedding canopy!" She raised her hands high. A motherly bliss shone in her eyes. Shosha burst into tears. Then Bashele exclaimed, "What's wrong with me? He fasted all day, this treasure of mine, my precious heir. You'll soon have food!"

She raced to the credenza and came back with a beaker of cherry brandy. The liqueur must have been standing there from long ago, awaiting some joyous occasion. Shosha received the same offering. We drank a toast and kissed. Shosha's lips did not feel like those of a child but like those of a ripe woman. The door opened and Teibele came in, pretty, in a dress that looked new to me. I had met her for the last time on Rosh Hashanah, when she came to share the holiday feast with her mother and sister. Teibele was tall, erect, and resembled her father with her dark hair and brown eyes. Although she had been only three when the family moved from No. 10 to No. 7, she remembered me and called me Arele. On Rosh Hashanah she had brought a slice of pineapple with which to make the New Year benedictions. As soon as she heard the news, something like a mixture of happiness and laughter appeared in her eyes. "Arele, is this true?"

Before I could answer, she embraced me, held me close, and began kissing me. "Mazel tov! Mazel tov! It's a fated thing! And on Yom Kippur! Somehow my heart told me—Arele, I never had a brother, and from now on you'll be my brother, even closer than a brother. When Daddy hears this, he will . . ." Teibele trotted to the door on her high heels.

Bashele asked, "Where are you running in such a hurry?"

"To telephone Daddy," Teibele called back from the hallway.

"Why him? What does this happy event have to do with him?" Bashele shouted after her. "He abandoned us, sick and lonely, and went off to live with a slut—may all the fires of hell consume her. That's no father but a murderer. If it had been left to him, you'd have all starved to death. I was the one who fed you and gave my last bit of strength so that you should live. God in heaven, You know the truth. It was because of that rascal and his filthy ways that we lost Yppe—may she rest in paradise with the sainted souls."

Bashele said all this to herself, to Shosha, and to me, since Teibele had slammed the door behind her.

Shosha asked, "Where will she call from? Is the delicatessen open?"

"Let her call. Let her suck around him, that old whoremonger. To me he's as *trayf* as pork. I never want to see his face again. He was no father when we starved and ailed and spat out our lungs, and I don't want him as a father now when luck has come to us, may it only stay with us. Shoshele, why are you standing there like a ninny? Kiss him, hold him! He is already as good as your husband and to me he's as dear as my own child. We never forgot him, never. A day didn't go by that we didn't think of him. We didn't know where he was or if he lived, so many young people perished in all the fires. When Leizer brought us the good news that he was alive and writing for the newspaper, it was like a holiday in the house. How long ago was this? My head is so muddled I don't know what or when. *I* will lead you to the wedding canopy, my darling daughter—not your cruel father. Arele, my child, God should only grant you as much happiness as you have granted us this night." Bashele began to cry, and Shosha cried with her.

After a while, Bashele put on an apron and started fussing with pots, pans, plates. The two chickens that had been offered in sacrifice on Yom Kippur eve lay already cooked, and Bashele quickly sliced them and served them with challah and horseradish. Later, she scolded herself that she had forgotten to serve the gefilte fish first.

She hovered over me. "Eat, child of mine. You're probably weak from fasting. For myself, my soul was so burdened I didn't even realize I was fasting. To me fasting is no novelty. More than one night I went to bed without a bite in my stomach so that my little swallows should have bigger portions. Eat, Shoshele, eat, my bride! God hearkened to your longing. Worthy ancestors interceded in your behalf. For you, today is not the end of Yom Kippur but Simchas Torah. What happened to Teibele? Why is she staying away so long? He blotted her out as a daughter and still she keeps herself close to him just because he has a nice apartment and throws her a trinket from time to time. A shame and a disgrace! A sin before God."

Bashele sat down to eat, but every few seconds she turned to face the door. Finally, Teibele came back. "Mommy, I have good news for you, but first swallow your food, because when you get excited, you start to choke."

"What news? I don't want news from him."

"Mommy, listen to me! When Daddy heard of Shosha and Arele he became another person. He fell in love with that redhead, and love makes people mad. Daddy told me two things, and I want you to hear carefully, because he's waiting for an answer. First, he said that he would provide Shosha with a trousseau for the wedding and he would give her one thousand zlotys for a dowry. This isn't much, but it's better to begin with a little money than with none. Second, he said that if you, Mother, will agree to a divorce, he'll give you a thousand zlotys, too. Hush! I know how little this is for all your years of suffering, but since you two can't ever be together again, what's the point of spiting each other? You're not that old, and if you dressed yourself up you could still find a suitor. Those were *his* words, not mine. My advice is, forget the past wrongs and come to a settlement once and for all.''

The whole time Teibele was talking, Bashele's face twisted with revulsion and impatience. *''Now* he's going to divorce me—when my blood is congealed and the marrow is dried in my bones? I no longer need a husband and have no desire to please anyone. All my life I lived only for you children, only for you. Now that Shosha has found her destined one, I have but one wish—that you should do the same, Teibele. He doesn't have to be a writer or a scholar. What does a writer earn, anyway? Nothing with nothing. I would be satisfied with a merchant, a clerk, even a tradesman. Does it make any difference what a husband does? The main thing is, he should be decent and have one God and one wife, not—''

"Mommy, decency is *not* everything. You have to feel something for a husband, to love him, to be able to talk to him. To tie up with some tailor or clerk and begin cooking and washing diapers is not for me. But why waste time talking about that? Better think over what I told you. I promised Daddy an answer.''

"An answer already? I waited for him longer. Hoo-hah, the great squire! The only reason he's got so much gall is that he has money and we're paupers. He'll get no answer today. Sit down and eat with us. In this house, today is a double holiday. We're poor but we don't come from dirt. We had a preacher in our family—Reb Zekele Preacher, they called him. Your father, that skirt-chaser, will have to wait.''

"Mommy, there's an expression—strike while the iron is hot. You know Daddy—all moods. Tomorrow he may change his mind. What will you do then?''

"I'll do what I've done all these years—suffer and place my hope in the Almighty. Arele loves Shosha, not her clothes. You can put a dress on a mannequin, too. An educated person considers the soul. Isn't that true, Arele?''

"Yes, Bashele.''

"Oh, please call me Mother. May your mother live to a hundred and twenty, but you haven't a better friend than me in the whole world. If someone told me to lay down my life for your tiniest fingernail, as God is my witness, I wouldn't hesitate.'' Bashele began to cough.

"Arele, there are no words for how much we all love you,'' Shosha said.

"Well, you two love, but don't try to sell me to some clerk,'' Teibele said. "I want to love, too. If only I could meet the right person, my soul would open to him fast enough.''

That night, Bashele set the date for the wedding—the week of Hanukkah. She suggested that I write a letter to my mother at once in Old Stykov, where my brother Moishe was now rabbi in my father's place.

Teibele, ever practical, asked, "Where will the newlyweds live? An apartment is like gold these days."

"They'll live here with me," Bashele replied. "And when I cook for two, there'll be enough for three."

2

I had committed the worst folly of my life, but I had no regrets. Neither was I elated, as those in love usually are. The day after Yom Kippur I gave notice at Leszno Street that I would be moving out at the end of the month. I might have condemned myself to penury but not yet to death. I still had my room for four weeks. I could pay Bashele for my food until some time after the holidays. I was amazed by my light-mindedness, but not shocked. I had heard that Sam Dreiman had been operated on at the Jewish hospital on Czysta Street and would go off with Betty to recuperate. When Tekla heard that I would be moving out after the Jewish holiday, she came to ask the reason. Was I dissatisfied with the service? Did she, Tekla, neglect to convey an important message to me? Did she insult me in some way? For the first time I saw tears in her pale-blue eyes. I put my arms around her, kissed her, and said, "Tekla dear, it's not your fault. You were good to me. I'll remember you to my last breath."

"Where will you live? Are you going with Miss Betty to America?"

"No, I'm staying right here in Warsaw."

"Bad times are coming for Jews here," she said, after some hesitation.

"Yes, I know."

"If a war should break out, it won't be good for Christians, either."

"Also true. But the history of all peoples is one long chain of wars."

"Why is it so? What do the educated people say—those who write the books?"

"The best thing they find to say is that if there were no wars, no epidemics, and no famines, people would multiply like rabbits and there soon wouldn't be enough for everybody to eat."

"Doesn't enough rye grow in the fields for bread?"

"Not enough for thousands of millions of people."

"Why didn't God make it so there'd be enough for all?"

"I can't answer that."

"Do you know where you will be staying? I'll miss you. I'm off Sundays, but somehow I can't seem to get close to anybody," Tekla said. "The other maids go out with soldiers, with fellows they meet in the street or in Karcelak Place. But I can't make friends with a lout who kisses you one day and doesn't want to know you the next. They drink and fight. They get a girl pregnant and later they don't want to know her. Is that just?"

"No, Tekla."

"Sometimes I think I'd like to become a Jewess. The Jewish boys read newspapers and books. They know what's going on in the world. They treat a girl better than our fellows do."

"Don't do it, Tekla. When the Nazis come, the Jews will be the first victims."

"Where will you move to?"

"No. 7 Krochmalna Street."

"Can I come visit on Sunday?"

"Yes. Wait for me by the gate at noon."

"Will you definitely be there?"

"Yes."

"Is that a holy promise?"

"Yes, my dear."

"You'll be living there with someone, eh?"

"Whoever I live with, I'll miss you."

"I will come!" Tekla dashed from my room. A slipper fell off her foot. She picked it up with one hand and clapped the other over her mouth so that her employer wouldn't hear her crying.

That afternoon I sat down to work on a sketch, and later on a novel based on the life of the false Messiah, Jacob Frank. I had already gathered a substantial amount of material about him. In two days I completed three sketches and took them to the newspaper that had published things from me earlier. All hope was gone, but so was all tension. To my surprise, the editor accepted all three. He even asked me to write other short pieces for him. The power that guides man's lot had postponed my death sentence.

My success with the sketches gave me the courage to phone Celia. I told her everything. Celia heard me out, sighed; from time to time she laughed a short laugh. When I finished she said, "Bring her and let me look her over. Whatever may be, your room still stands ready for you here. You can move in with anyone you like."

"Celia, she's infantile—physically and mentally backward."

"Well, and what are you? What are all writers? Lunatics."

Things began to happen quietly and as if mechanically, I had given up free choice, and causality took over. I let Tekla and her mistress know that I would be staying on another month, and both of them congratulated me and expressed the hope that I would stay even longer. On the last day of Succoth, Teibele called to invite me to her apartment. Zelig wanted to meet me. I put on my good suit, bought candy for Teibele, and took a droshky, so that I wouldn't arrive in a sweat. The girl who shared Teibele's apartment had gone to the opera. Zelig sat at a table in the living room, which was set with liquor and food. With his dyed hair and beard, he looked not much older than he had twenty years ago. He was broad-shouldered, stocky, with a short neck, a pointed belly. His nose was red and had the broken veins of a drinker. He spoke to me with the crudeness of burial-society members. He smelled of alcohol and smoked one cigarette after another. If he were my age, he said, he wouldn't marry a sluggard like Shosha. He complained that Bashele had refused to divorce him and for so many years had kept him from marrying the woman he loved. He compared Bashele to a dog sitting on a pile of hay he couldn't eat himself but wouldn't let another creature have. He told me what I already knew: that he was prepared to come to Shosha's wedding and give her a thousand zlotys' dowry. Like a proper father-in-law to be, he questioned me about my prospects of earning a living at writing. He poured himself half a glass of the vodka Teibele had put out and asked brusquely, "Be honest, what do you see in my Shosha? No front and no behind—a board and a hole is what we'd call her."

"Papa, you shame me!" Teibele cried.

"What's there to be ashamed of? In the burial society we know the truth. A woman can fix herself up for the outside world, cover everything with rouge and powder and corsets, but when we strip her for the shrouds . . ."

"If you don't stop, I'll leave!" Teibele warned.

"Well, daughter, don't be angry. That's how we are. That's why we drink. Without booze, none of us would last. You don't drink, eh?" he said, turning to me.

"Seldom."

"Tell my wife she's waited long enough. It's now or never if she wants to marry again. If she puts it off for a few more years, she can become a virgin again, ha, ha, ha!"

"I'm going, Papa."

"All right, I won't say another word. Wait, Arele, I've got a present for you."

Zelig took a watch and chain from his breast pocket. I blushed and he said, "Whatever I may be and whatever they say about me, I'm still Shosha's father. If she ever has a child—and I can't imagine how, unless they perform a Caesarean— I'll be a grandfather. I knew your father, may he rest in peace. We were neighbors for years. At times when there was a wedding at your house, they called me in to make a quorum. He always sat over his Gemaras. I also remember your mother. Not a bad-looking woman, though too skinny for my taste. You look like her. What will be with this Hitler? People are all terrified, but not me. If things get bad enough, I'll dig myself a grave, take a shot of brandy, and go to sleep. When you see death every day, you stop being afraid of it. What's life, anyway? You give the throat a squeeze and it's all over. Here, take this watch. That's my wedding present to you. It's silver and it has seventeen jewels. Bashele's father gave it to me to sleep with *his* daughter, and now I give it to you to sleep with *my* daughter. If you take care of it, one day you may give it to the fellow who'll do the favor for *your* daughter."

"Oh, Papa, what's to be done with you?"

"Teibele, give up—you can't do anything with me. I have a present ready for you too, when you find the right man. There is no God. I went to synagogue on Rosh Hashanah and Yom Kippur, but I didn't do much praying."

"So where does the world come from?" Teibele asked.

Zelig pinched his beard. "Where does everything come from? It's there and that's all. In Praga, there were two friends and one got sick. Before dying, he made a deal with his friend that if there was another world he'd come back to give him greetings. He told his friend to light the candles in the Hanukkah lamp on the last day of the mourning period and he would come put them out. The friend did as he was told. On the last day of mourning he lit the Hanukkah lamp. But he was tired from working and he dropped off. Suddenly he woke up. A candle had fallen from the lamp and started a fire. His gaberdine was burning. He ran outside and rolled in the gutter. He had to spend two months in the hospital."

"And what's to be made from this?"

"Nothing. There is no such thing as a soul. I've buried more rabbis and holy Jews than you've got hairs on your head. You stick them in the grave and that's where they rot."

No one spoke for a while; then Zelig asked, "Shosha doesn't sleep so much any more? That time when she got the sleeping sickness she slept nearly a whole year. They woke her, fed her, and she went right back to sleep. How long ago was it—fifteen years already, eh?"

"Papa, what's wrong with you?" Teibele exclaimed.

"I'm drunk. I didn't say anything. She's recovered now."

CHAPTER 10

1

Dora was supposed to have gone to Russia months earlier, but she was still in Warsaw. Her sister Liza called me at the Writers' Club to tell me Dora had attempted suicide by drinking iodine. It seemed that Wolf Felhendler, a fellow Communist who had gone to Russia a year and a half before, had broken out of Soviet exile and smuggled his way back into Poland. The news he brought was dismaying: Dora's best friend, Irka, had been shot there. A whole group of comrades who had gone to the Soviet Union were either in prison or had been sent to the north to dig for gold. As word of his report spread, the Stalinists in Warsaw accused Wolf Felhendler of being a Fascist traitor and a spy for the Polish Secret Service. However, within Poland trust in Stalin's justice suffered a mighty blow. Even before this, whole cells had become disillusioned and gone over to the Trotskyites, and many Communists had switched to the Jewish Bund or the Polish Socialist Party. Others had become Zionists or turned to religion.

After Dora's stomach had been pumped out, Liza arranged for her to spend a few days in Otwock. Back in her apartment, Dora telephoned me, and I went to visit her in the evening. Behind the door I heard a man's voice—Felhendler's. I hadn't the slightest urge to meet with him. He used to warn the anti-Communists at the Writers' Club that when the revolution came he would see them hanged from the nearest lamp post. Still, I knocked. In a few minutes, Dora opened the door. Even though it was half dark in the corridor, I could see that she looked pale and wasted. She clasped my hand and said, "I thought you would never want to see my face again."

"I hear you have company."

"It's Felhendler. He'll be leaving soon."

"Don't keep him here. I don't have the patience for him."

"He's not the same person. He's gone through hell."

Dora spoke softly and didn't let go of my hand. She led me into the living room, where Felhendler sat at the head of the table. If I hadn't known who he was, I wouldn't have recognized him. He was thinner, aged; his hair had fallen out. His attitude toward me had always been arrogant—he addressed me as if the revolution already had come and he had been appointed a commissar. But now he jumped to his feet. He smiled and I saw that his front teeth were missing.

He held out a clammy hand to me and said, "I called you at your room, but you weren't home."

Even his voice had grown meek. I couldn't bring myself to take revenge upon a person so beaten, although I knew that, if it had been within his power, he would have subjected me to the very treatment he himself had received. He said, "I've thought of you more than you know. Did your ears ever burn?"

"Ears burn when you talk about someone, not when you think of him," Dora observed.

"You're right, of course. Lately, I've begun to forget things. For a time I even forgot the names of my own family. You've probably heard what happened to me. Well, I've paid my dues, as they say. But I didn't only think about you, I actually spoke of you. I shared a cell with a man by the name of Mendel Leiterman, who had once been a reader of *The Literary Magazine*. Forty of us were jammed in a cell made for eight. We sat on the floor and talked. The greatest privilege was to be next to the wall where you could lean your head."

I assumed Felhendler would say goodbye and leave; instead, he settled down again. His suit hung so loosely that it seemed not to be his size. In the past, he had always worn a stiff collar and tie, but now his collar was open, revealing a scrawny neck. He said, "Yes, I recalled your words. You predicted everything in detail—you might have been some kind of prophet who had put a curse on me. I don't mean this in a bad sense—I haven't yet reached such a stage of superstitious nonsense. But words aren't lost. At night when I lay on the bare floor, sick and grimy, my head reeling from the stink of the slop bucket—that is, if they let me lie and didn't drag me off for an interrogation—and I heard the doors being opened to take someone else to be tortured, I thought, what would Aaron Greidinger say if he could see all this? It didn't occur to me for a second that I would live to meet and talk with you again. We were all condemned to death or to work in the gold mines, which is worse than death. No, they don't let you die so fast and easy. One time they questioned me for twenty-six hours straight. This kind of physical torture—I'm not speaking of the spiritual pain—I wouldn't wish on my worst enemies, not even on Stalin's minions. I don't believe they were as cruel during the Inquisition or that it's being done in Mussolini's prisons. A man can take torture from an enemy, but when your friend turns out to be the enemy, then the anguish is beyond endurance. They wanted one thing from me—to confess that I was a spy sent by the Polish Secret Service. They literally begged me to do them the favor and confess, but I swore to myself, anything but this."

"Wolf, stop talking about it. It's making you sick," Dora said.

"Eh? I couldn't be sicker than I am. I said to them, 'How can I be a Polish spy when I did time in every Polish jail for our ideal? How can I be a Fascist when for years I was an editor of a magazine that attacked the Zionists, the Bund, the P.P.S., and that openly preached the dictatorship of the proletariat? My family was from the poorest of the poor, and all my life I've suffered hunger and want. Socialism was my only comfort. Why would I become a spy for the reactionary and anti-Semitic Polish regime? What military institutions was I being allowed to get near? Where has your sense of reason gone? Even in madness there has to be a trace of logic,' I said. But the fellow who sat facing me toyed with his revolver the whole time, smoked cigarettes, and drank tea while I was standing on swollen feet and everything inside me was shriveling from lack of food, water, and sleep. He glared at me. His eyes were murderous. 'I've heard all your lousy excuses,' he said. 'You are a Fascist dog, a counterrevolutionary traitor, and a Hitler spy. Sign the confession before I tear the tongue out of your pig's snout.' He called me 'thou,' that Russky. He lit a candle, took out a needle, held it to the flame, and said, 'If you don't sign, I'll jam this under your filthy fingernails.' I knew what pain that meant, for the Polish Fascists had done it to me, but still I couldn't label myself a spy. I looked at him—someone who should have been the defender of the working class and of the Revolution—and for all my anguish I started to laugh. This was bad theater, the worst kind of trash. Even Nowaczynski in the wildest stretches of his sick imagination couldn't have dreamed up such an idiotic plot.

"I stuck out my hand and told him, 'Go ahead. If this is what the Revolution needs, do with me as you will.' He was called out and a new executioner took his place—a new executioner who was rested and full. That's how they questioned me for twenty-six hours by the clock. I pleaded with them, 'Shoot me and put an end to it.' "

"Wolf, I can't listen to any more!" Dora cried.

"You can't, can't you? You have to! We are responsible for this. We spread the propaganda to bring it about. In 1926, when the news began to come out against Trotsky, we called him an agent for the Pilsudskis, the Mussolinis, the Rockefellers, the MacDonalds. We stuffed our ears and refused to hear the truth."

"Felhendler, I don't want to rub salt in your wounds," I said, "but if Trotsky was in power, he wouldn't act any differently from Stalin."

A mixture of irony and anger showed in Felhendler's eyes. "How do you know how Trotsky would act? How dare you make assumptions about things that never happened?"

"They've happened in all the revolutions. Whenever blood is spilled in the name of humanity, of religion, or of any other cause, it leads inevitably to this kind of terror."

"So according to you the working class should keep silent over what is happening in Russia, allow Hitler and Mussolini to seize the world and let itself be trampled like ants. Is this what you preach?"

"I don't preach."

"Yes, you do. If you can say that Trotsky would be no better than Stalin, it means that the whole human race is corrupt and there is no hope—that we must surrender to all the murderers, the Fascists, those who instigate pogroms and turn the clock back to the Dark Ages, to the Inquisitions, to the Crusades."

"Felhendler, England, France, and America haven't resorted to inquisitions and crusades."

"Oh, haven't they? America has locked its gates and is letting no one in. England, France, Canada, Australia—all the capitalist countries—are doing the same. In India, thousands of people die of hunger each day. English travelers admit this themselves. When Gandhi, submissive as he is, uttered a word, they threw him in jail. Is this true or not? Gandhi babbles about passive resistance. What a swindle! How can resistance be passive? It's exactly as if you would say hot snow, cold fire."

"Then you're still for revolution?"

"Yes, Aaron Greidinger, yes! If you went to a dentist and instead of pulling a rotten tooth he purposely pulled three healthy teeth, this would surely be a tragedy and a crime. But the rotten tooth would still have to be pulled. Otherwise it could infect the whole mouth—even lead to gangrene.''

"Right! One hundred percent correct!" Dora exclaimed.

"I hate to dash your hopes," I said, "but I will make another prediction for you: Trotsky's permanent revolution, or whatever revolution it may be, will duplicate precisely what the Stalinists are doing now. I do not want you to have to say again that I was right. You've suffered enough."

"No," Felhendler said. "If I were to think in your terms, I'd have to hang myself this very night."

"Enough," Dora said. "I'll put up tea."

2

We drank tea, ate bread with herring, and Felhendler recounted his experiences from the time he crossed the border into Russia and was met by a delegate of the Comintern. He was taken to Moscow and assigned a room with another delegate from Poland, a Comrade Wysocki from Upper Silesia. Every other evening, they attended free performances of the theater or the opera or some new Soviet film. Suddenly in the middle of a night there was a knock on his door and he was placed under arrest. Five weeks he sat behind bars without knowing the charges against him. He comforted himself with the idea that his imprisonment was an error—he had obviously been mistaken for some other Felhendler and everything would be cleared up at the interrogation. He shared a cell with both political and criminal prisoners. The thieves, murderers, and rapists beat the politicals and took away their food rations. They played cards among themselves, using slips of paper, and gambled for each other's rations, clothing, and the right to sleep on the hard bench instead of the floor. When one of the players lost all he possessed, he played for blows—the winner could slug the loser. Many of the criminals practiced homosexuality. A new prisoner who didn't want to participate was raped. The Red authorities made no effort to protect the victims.

Felhendler said, "In the Polish prisons, even in such a tough jail as Wronki, where I spent three years, they gave us books. I went through a whole library there. But in the land of socialism, we—the fighters for justice!—sat for weeks on end going mad. We kneaded chess pieces out of the claylike bread that they gave us, but there wasn't enough room on the floor to set up a board to play on. None of the political prisoners had the slightest notion of what crimes they had been picked up for. Yet nearly every one of them remained dedicated to the cause. They put the blame on the lower officials of the G.P.U. without once accusing Stalin or anyone in the Central Committee or the Politburo. But I slowly became aware of the quicksand in which we were caught. Some of the prisoners confided to me that they had been forced to make false accusations against their closest comrades.''

It was midnight when Felhendler left. The moment he closed the door, Dora burst into tears. "What can one do? How is one to live?"

She clasped me by my wrists and drew me to her. She leaned her forehead on my shoulder and sobbed. I stood there gawking at the opposite wall. From the day I had left my father's house I had existed in a state of perpetual despair. Occasionally, I considered the notion of repentance, of returning to real Jewishness. But to live like my father, my grandfathers, and great-grandfathers, without their faith—was this possible? Each time I went into a library, I felt a spark of hope that perhaps in one of the books there might be some indication of how a person of my disposition and world outlook could make peace with himself. I didn't find it—not in Tolstoy or in Kropotkin, not in Spinoza or in William James, not in Schopenhauer, not in the Scriptures. Certainly the Prophets preached a high morality, but their promises of plentiful harvests, of fruitful olive trees and vineyards, protection against one's enemies, made no appeal to me. I knew that the world had always been and would always remain as it was now. What the moralists called evil was actually the order of life.

Dora wiped her tears. "Arele, I must move from here at once. The apartment isn't mine, and even if it was, I couldn't pay for it. Also, I'm afraid that my ex-comrades will turn me in to the Secret Service."

"The Secret Service knows about you, anyway."

"They could provide the necessary proof. You know how it is with the Stalinists—whoever isn't for them must be liquidated."

"You yourself used to preach this."

"To my shame, yes."

"The Trotskyites follow the same principles."

"What shall I do? You tell me!"

"I can't tell you anything."

"I could be arrested any day. The last time you slept here I was still full of expectation. I even dreamed you might sooner or later come to me in Russia. Now I don't look forward to anything."

"A half hour ago, you agreed with Felhendler's Trotskyism."

"I'm no longer sure. I should have thrown myself out the window instead of drinking iodine."

That night I lay next to Dora, but that was all. I couldn't sleep. Each time I heard the bell at the house gate I assumed it was the police coming to take us in. I rose at dawn and before I went I gave Dora some of the money I had with me.

Dora said, "I thank you, but if you should hear that I've done away with myself, don't feel too bad. I've been left with nothing."

"Dora, for the time being, don't get involved with the Trotskyites. A permanent revolution is about as possible as permanent surgery."

"What will *you* do?"

"Oh, live from day to day—or from hour to hour."

We said goodbye. I was afraid that a secret agent might be waiting by the gate to arrest me, but no one was there. I headed back to my room and my manuscript.

On the way, I glanced at the high tower of the church on Nowolipki Street. In buildings around the enormous courtyard encircled by an iron picket fence lived nuns—Jesus's brides. I often saw them pass in their starched cowls, long black robes, and mannish shoes, their bosoms hung with crucifixes. On Karmelicka Street I passed the "Workers' Home," the club of the left-wing Poale Zion. In there, they espoused both Communism and Zionism, believing that only when the proletariat seized power would the Jews be able to have their own homeland in Palestine and become a socialist nation. In No. 36 Leszno Street was the Groser Library of the Jewish Bund, as well as a cooperative store for workers and their families. The Bund totally rejected Zionism. Their program was cultural autonomy and common socialist struggle against capitalism. The Bundists themselves had split into two factions, one in favor of democracy and one in favor of immediate dictatorship by the proletariat. In another courtyard was the club of the Revisionists, the followers of Jabotinsky, extreme Zionists. They encouraged Jews to learn to use firearms and contended that only acts of terror against the English, who held the mandate, could restore Palestine to the Jews. The Revisionists in Warsaw had a semi-military unit that from time to time paraded through the streets carrying wooden swords and shouting slogans against those Zionists who, like Weizmann, believed in mediation and compromise with England. Nearly all the Jewish parties had their clubs in this area. Each year added some new splinter group and another office.

I had won a moral victory over Dora, Felhendler, and their comrades, but everything had grown so wildly tangled that I could no longer sneer at anyone else's wrongheadedness.

I went to my room, which I now decided to keep until the wedding, but I was too tired to work. I stretched out on the bed, dozed off, and in my mind heard over and over Felhendler's words and Dora's lament: *What can one do? How is one to live?*

CHAPTER ELEVEN

1

A few days before the wedding, my mother and Moishe arrived, and I met them at the Danzig depot. The train pulled in at 8 a.m. I barely recognized them. Mother seemed smaller, stooped, and as old as a crone. Her nose had lengthened; it curved down like a bird's beak. Creases cut deep into her forehead and cheeks. Only the gray eyes still showed a youthful sharpness. She no longer wore a wig; a kerchief covered her head. Her skirt reached the floor, and she had on a blouse that I remembered from the time I lived at home. Moishe had grown tall. He had a ragged blond beard and earlocks hanging to his shoulders. His rabbinical hat was flecked and mangy, and his fur coat was ratty. The unbuttoned shirt collar exposed a soft, childish throat.

He gazed at me with amazement in his blue eyes and said, "A real German."

After I had kissed my mother, she asked, "Arele, are you sick, God forbid? You're as pale and drawn as if you just got out of a sickbed, may it never happen."

"I didn't sleep the whole night."

"We've been on the road two days and nights. The wagon that took us to the train in Rawa Ruska turned over in the mud. It's a miracle we weren't hurt. One woman broke her arm. That's why we missed the train we intended to take and had to wait twenty hours for another. The Gentiles became unruly. They wanted to cut off Moishele's earlocks. The Jew is helpless. If it's this bad now, how will it be when the murderers come? People shake in their skins.''

"Mama, the Almighty will help," Moishe said. "There have been many Hamans and they all came to a bad end."

"Before they came to their bad end, they killed off plenty of Jews," Mother replied.

I had rented a room for Mother and Moishe in a kosher boardinghouse on Gnoyna Street. The proprietor was a Hasid. I called a droshky to take them there, but Moishe said, "I don't ride in droshkies."

"Why not?"

"The seat may be linsey-woolsey."

After lengthy discussion it was decided that Mother would spread her shawl over the seat. Moishe had brought along a basket that closed with a wire and a little lock—the kind once used by yeshiva students. Mother carried her things wrapped in a sheet. Passersby stopped to stare at us. The driver went slowly, since the road was blocked by trolleys, taxis, freight wagons, and buses. The nag looked skeletal; it limped. Moishe began to sway and murmur. He was either commencing his morning prayers or reciting Psalms.

Mother said, "Arele, child, for the fact that I've lived to see you again, and about to be a bridegroom at that, I must thank the Almighty, but why didn't your father, too, live to see it? He studied the Torah almost to the last minute. I didn't realize myself what a saint he was. Alas, I plagued him for dragging us off to such a faraway hole, but he accepted it all in good spirits. I eat my heart out now and don't sleep nights on account of this. Whatever punishment is visited upon me I deserve. Arele, I can't stay in Old Stykov any more. I don't want to speak against Moishele's wife, my daughter-in-law—may she stay healthy and strong—but I can't live with her. She's a country girl, her father is a farmer. In Galicia, Jews were always allowed to own land. She does and says things that displease me. I hear well, thank God, but she screams into my ears as if I were deaf. Her mind is always on petty things. It's true that I've sinned, but how much can a person take?"

"Well, ah, well!" Moishe put two fingers to his lips—a sign that Mother's words were slander and that he wasn't permitted to speak now during prayer.

"*Well, ah well* here, and *well, ah well* there! Certainly my words are sinful, but what flesh and blood can suffer has a limit. She hates me because I read books and she barely knows how to pray. But what do I have now besides my books? When I open *The Duty of the Hearts* I forget where I am and what's become of me in my old age. Arele, I don't want to die in Old Stykov. True, your father is buried there, but the few years or months allotted me to creep around in this world I don't want to spend among boors. It's bitter for Moishele, too. They pay him no wages. On Thursdays the beadle goes around with a sack collecting handfuls of wheat, corn, and groats—the way the Russians pay their priests, beg the comparison. The Gentiles there are Ruthenians and some of them boast that Hitler is on their side. They fight among themselves, too. One of them chopped off a girl's head right outside our window, just because she'd been going around with another fellow. Our lives are in danger every minute.

I pray for death. Each day I beg the Almighty to take me from here, but just because you want to die, you live.''

"Well, ah well!"

"Stop with those *well, ah's*. You won't go to my Gehenna. Arele, I want to say something to you, but I don't want you to get angry at me. I will not go back to Old Stykov. Even if I have to sleep in the streets, I'll stay here in Warsaw.''

"Mama, you won't sleep in the streets," I said.

"Have pity on me. I hear there's no longer a rabbi on Krochmalna Street. Maybe Moishele could get some job here? I myself am ready to go into an old-age home or wherever I can find a place to lay my head. What kind of girl is this Shosha? How did you happen to choose her? Well, it all comes from heaven.''

The droshky pulled up before a gate on Gnoyna Street. Some of the courtyards here were over a hundred years old. There were alleys where farmers came at dawn with their produce from the nearby villages. Eggs were stored in lime in the cellars. In No. 3 was Krel's studyhouse, where I went to read a page of the Gemara on my own after I had left cheder. In No. 5 was a synagogue and another studyhouse. The ritual bath where my mother went when she was a young woman was still in operation nearby. Even the oil cakes, the chick-peas with beans, and the potato cakes sold here smelled as I remembered them.

Mother said, "Nothing has changed."

Several wagons were parked in front of the building where we had stopped. The horses were eating a mixture of oats and chopped straw from feedbags. Pigeons and sparrows pecked at the seeds dropped from them. Men in short sheepskin coats and caps carried sacks, crates, baskets. Through the partially frosted-over windows could be seen bottles, pots, diapers hanging to dry. From one window came the sound of children reciting a chant from the Pentateuch— a cheder. Muddy stairs led up to the boardinghouse on the third floor.

After each half flight, Mother paused. "I'm not used to climbing stairs any more.''

On the third floor I opened a door leading off the dark hallway. The boardinghouse consisted of a sitting room and a few small rooms. In the sitting room one man prayed in his prayer shawl and phylacteries, another packed paper boxes into a sack, and a third ate his breakfast. Two women, one in a wig and the other in a bonnet, sat on a bench mending a fur coat with a huge needle and string. The proprietor, with a pitch-black beard and wearing a skullcap, showed us to a room with two beds, where Mother and Moishe would spend the night.

Moishe said, "It's getting late and I want to pray. Is there a house of worship here?''

"There are two prayer houses in the courtyard—one of the Kozienica Hasidim, the other of the Blendew Hasidim. There is a synagogue, too, but those who pray there are all Litvaks.''

"I'll go to the Kozienica prayer house.''

"Would you want some breakfast?" the proprietor asked Mother.

"Is it strictly kosher?''

"What a question! Rabbis eat here.''

"Maybe a glass of tea for now.''

"Something to nibble with it?''

"I've lost my teeth. Would you have some soft bread?"

"There isn't a thing I don't have." He went to fetch the bread and tea.

A washstand stood in one corner of the room, with a basin of water, a dipper, and a dirty towel hanging on a hook. Mother said, "Compared to Old Stykov, this is a mansion. We live in a shack with a straw roof. It leaks. There is a stove, but the flue is broken and the smoke won't go up through the chimney. When will I get to see the bride?"

"I'll bring her here."

2

It was the first night of Hanukkah. The owner of the boardinghouse lighted and blessed the first of the eight Hanukkah candles for his guests, but my mother and Moishe refused to accept another person performing so holy a ceremony for them. Besides, he had lighted a candle, not a wick in oil. I went down to the street and bought a tin Hanukkah lamp for them, as well as a bottle of oil, wicks, and a special candle called "the beadle," which is used for lighting the wicks. In their room, Moishe poured the oil into the first little bowl, put a wick in place, lit the beadle, touched the wick with it, and recited the benedictions. Then he began to chant the liturgy: "O Fortress, Rock of my Salvation . . ." These were my father's tunes, even his gestures. At first the wick refused to catch fire, and Moishe had to try to light it again and again. When it did burn finally, it smoked and sputtered. Moishe had placed the little lamp on the window according to the law, so that the miracle of Hanukkah should be shown to the world, even though the courtyard below had three blind walls and no one was there. The window was not tight; wind blew in. Every few seconds the little light fluttered, but it did not go out. Moishe said, "Just like the Jewish people. In each generation our enemies rise up to destroy us, and the Holy One, blessed be He, is saving us from their hands."

"It's high time our enemies should be praying for miracles," I said.

Moishe clutched his beard. "Who are we to tell Him what to do and when to do it? Only yesterday you told Mother that the more the astronomers ponder and measure the stars, the larger they become. You said that many of them are larger than the sun. So how can insignificant creatures like us, with our tiny brains, understand what He is doing?"

Moishe spoke with my father's voice. Only a few years ago my father was arguing with me: "You can spill ink but it won't write a letter by itself. The unbelievers are not only vicious but also fools."

Moishe left for the studyhouse after watching the Hanukkah light for half an hour. He found books there that he could never get in Old Stykov. With the little money he had, he bought *The Roar of a Lion, The Responsa of Rabbi Akiva Eiger,* and *The Face of Joshua.* He promised Mother he would not be late. She sat on her bed, propped up by a pillow, and her large gray eyes stared at the flickering light with curiosity, as if she were seeing such a light for the first time. I remembered her being medium in height, even somewhat taller than Father, but now she appeared shriveled. Her head kept nodding in a constant "yes, yes, yes." Then she said to me, "Arele, God forbid, I don't intend to nag you, you are already an adult, I hope you outlive my bones, but what was the sense of it?"

"What do you mean?"

"You know very well what I mean."

"Mother, not everything one does has to make sense."

My mother's eyes showed the beginning of a smile. "What is it? Love?"

"You can call it that."

"There is a saying that love is blind, but even love isn't completely without reason. A shoemaker's apprentice would not fall in love with a princess, and he certainly would not marry her."

"Even this can happen."

"What? In novels, not in real life. When we lived in Warsaw, I used to read the novels serialized in the newspaper. Your father—peace be with him—disliked newspapers and their writers. He said that they defiled the holy Jewish letters. Only when the war broke out and he wanted to know the news did he glance into a paper. Even in those trashy novels there was some logic. Now you come and marry Shosha. True, she's a gentle child, unfortunately sick, perhaps a victim of her father, but couldn't you find something better in the whole of Warsaw? I'm sinning, I know I'm sinning. I shouldn't say these things. I'm losing the world to come. Look, the light is out!"

We sat in silence. The air smelled of burned oil and of something sweet and long forgotten. Then Mother went on, "My child, it's all so destined. My father, your grandfather—he should rest in peace—had the name of a genius. He could have become a rabbi in a big city, but he was content to stay in his little corner in a forsaken village, and there he remained until his end. Your paternal grandfather, the one from Tomaszów, hid from people altogether. All his years he wrote commentaries on the cabala. Before his demise, he called one of his grandchildren and told him to burn his manuscripts. Only one page was left accidentally, and those who read it maintained it was full of the mysteries of the Torah. He was so unworldly he did not know the difference between one coin and another. If your grandmother Temerl hadn't skimped and saved, there wouldn't have been a piece of bread in the house. She was a saint in her own right. When she went to visit the rabbi of Belz, he invited her to sit down on a chair even though she was a woman. What am I in comparison to them? I'm steeped in sin. Of course I love you, and I would like you to get a good wife, but if heaven ordains differently, I should have the power to curb my tongue. I say all this to remind you that you should remember your origin. We didn't come to this world to indulge in our passions. Look at me and see what happens to blood and flesh. I was a beautiful girl. When I passed Lublin Street, people stopped to stare. I had the smallest feet in town and I shined my shoes every day with polish, even when it rained. I used to polish them a hundred times with the brush. I had a pleated skirt, and every second day I ironed the pleats. People denounced me to your grandfather for being vain. How old was I altogether? Fifteen years. At fifteen and a half I became engaged to your father. A year later I was led to the wedding canopy. A girl is not allowed to study Torah, but I stood behind the door and listened as your grandfather lectured to the yeshiva boys. If one of them made a mistake, I knew it. I also began to look into morality books in Hebrew. By that time, I realized that I'm hot-blooded and that I had to control my impulses. How did this come to me? I hope to God that the children will take after you, not after Shosha.''

"Mother, we won't have any children.''

"Why not? Heaven wants there to be a world and Jews.''

"No one knows what heaven wants. If God had wanted the Jews to live, He wouldn't have created Hitlers.''

"Woe to me that you speak such things!''

"No one has ascended to heaven and spoken to God.''

"One doesn't need to ascend to heaven, one can see the truth right here on earth. Three days before Meitel's Esther won the lottery, I saw in a dream the letter carrier handing me a paper full of numbers. I wanted to take it, but suddenly Meitel materialized—she was already dead then. Her face was yellow and she wore a white cowl. She said to me, 'It's not for you, my daughter Esther is going to win a lot of money on this.' And she handed the letter carrier a bunch of straw stalks. I was only a ten-year-old child at the time, I didn't even know that there was such a thing as a lottery. I told the dream to everybody in our house. They shrugged their shoulders. After three days a telegram came saying Esther had won the grand prize. When I had this dream they had not yet drawn the numbers. Two years later, I witnessed a case of a haunted house. For weeks an evil spirit kept on knocking on the window frame in the house of Abraham the ritual slaughterer. Soldiers were sent to search the rooms, the cellar, the attic, but nothing could be found to account for this racket. My child, the world is full of so many mysteries that if the scholars continued to study for a million years, they could not solve even a millionth part of them.''

"Mother, all this cannot give comfort to the tortured Jews in Dachau, and in other such hells.''

"The comfort is that there is no death. Your own Shosha told me her dead sister was visiting her. She's not shrewd enough to invent such a lie.''

<hr>

3

Bashele intended to invite my mother and Moishe for either lunch or supper but Mother told me plainly she wouldn't eat in Bashele's house. Neither she nor Moishe had confidence that the food in her kitchen was strictly kosher. However, in order not to shame her, Mother and Moishe agreed to come for tea and fruit. I don't know how they learned that the late rabbi's wife and her two sons would be visiting Bashele's. Around three o'clock in the afternoon when I brought them from the boardinghouse and opened Bashele's door, I saw to my amazement a room full of people: old women in bonnets of beads and ribbons, men with white beards and sidelocks, also a few young men and girls, who, it seemed, read the literary journal. There were tea glasses, Sabbath cookies, and saucers with gooseberry jam on the table, which was covered with a holiday tablecloth. The old women had brought little gifts wrapped in handkerchiefs—gingerbread, cake, and cookies, raisins, prunes, almonds. My God, we were not completely forgotten on Krochmalna Street! The war, the epidemics, and hunger had worked with the Angel of Death, but a few of those who knew our family remained alive. Bonnets shook, shrunken mouths mumbled blessings and greetings, reminisced about former times. Tears rolled down faded cheeks. The men had all been followers of the late rabbi of Radzymin. He had passed away without an heir, and his court had disintegrated. The Hasidim said that if the rabbi had consented to go through an operation, he might still be living, but to the last day he was true to his conviction that a knife is for cutting bread, not human flesh. He gave up his sacred soul after long suffering. Rabbis from the whole of Poland came to his funeral. He was buried near the grave of his grandfather Rabbi Yankele, who waged war with the demons all his life and performed countless miracles. It was known that corpses came to him at night to confess their misdeeds while alive, and that his garret teemed with spirits.

While the Hasidim greeted Moishe and asked him about the Hasidic courts in Galicia—the courts of Belz, Sieniawa, Ropczyca—the young men and girls introduced themselves to me. They praised the sketches and articles I wrote. They spoke to me in a literary Yiddish with illiterate errors. They had heard about my play that had failed and complained about the state of the Yiddish theater. Civilization was on the verge of collapse, but they were still producing the kitsch plays of fifty years ago. Teibele had come to the reception and she had brought with her her lover the bookkeeper, a little man with a pointed belly and gold teeth in the front of his mouth. Some of the girls gathered around Shosha. I heard one of them ask her, "How does it feel to be engaged to a writer?"

Shosha answered, "Nothing, just like a human being."

"How did you two come together?" another girl asked.

"We both lived in No. 10," Shosha said. "Arele lived in the apartment with the balcony. Our windows faced the courtyard just across the horse stable."

The girls looked at one another and smiled. They exchanged side glances that asked, "What does he see in her?"

Bashele had placed Moishe at the head of the table, with the old men on either side of him. Moishe hinted that it was not in the Hasidic tradition for men and women to sit at the same table, and Bashele put chairs for the old women in the middle of the room. The boys and the girls remained standing. The Hasidim continued to discuss Hasidic topics: What is the difference between the court of Belz and the court of Bobow? Why are the Hungarian rabbis against the world organization of Orthodox Jews? What kind of a saint is the rabbi of Rydnik? Is it true that the rabbi of Rozwadow has inherited the sense of humor of his great-grandfather, the rabbi of Ropczyca? They said it was a pity so little was known about the rabbis of Galicia in this part of the country.

"Why is it important to know?",Moishe asked. "Everyone serves God in his own manner."

"What do they say in Galicia about the tribulations of our time?" one of them asked.

Moishe answered the question with a question: "What is there to say? These are the birth pains of the Messiah. The prophet has already foreseen that at the End of Days the Lord will come with fire and with His chariots like a whirlwind to render His anger with fury and His rebuke with flames of fire. The evil ones don't surrender so easily. When Satan realizes that his kingdom is shaky, he creates a furor throughout the universe. There are dark powers even in the higher spheres. What is Nogah? Good and evil mixed together. The roots of evil reach as far as the legs of the Throne of Glory. Since God had to create a vacuum and dim His light in order to create the world, His face has to be hidden. Without diminishing the power of His radiance there would be no free choice. Redemption will not come at once but gradually. God's war with Amalek is going to last long and will bring great distress and many temptations. One of our sages said about the Messiah, 'Let Him come, but I don't wish to live to see Him.' The Mishnah has foreseen that before the Messiah comes human arrogance will reach its height and . . .''

"Woe to us, the water is up to our necks," said an old Hasid, Mendele Wyszkower, with a sigh.

"What? Evil possesses enormous powers," Moishe said. "In quiet times the vicious try to cover up their intentions and disguise themselves as innocent lambs. But in times of decision they reveal their true faces. Ecclesiastes has said, 'I saw under the sun the place of judgment, that wickedness was there.' The men of iniquity aspire to a world of murder, lechery, theft, and robbery. They want the iniquities to be considered virtues. Their aim is to erase the 'Thou shalt not' from the Ten Commandments. They scheme to put honest men in prison and thieves to be their judges. Whole communities degenerate. What was Sodom, with its judges Chillek and Billek? What was the Generation of the Flood? Who were the rebels who built the Tower of Babel? One sheep can make the whole herd leprous. One spark of fire can burn a mansion. Hitler—his name should be blotted out—is not the only villain. There are Hitlers in every city, in every community. If we forget the Lord for a second, we are immediately on the side of defilement.''

"Oy, it's difficult, very difficult," said another old man, and he goaned.

"Where is it written that things have to be easy?" Moishe asked.

"Our strength is waning," a third old man moaned.

" 'They that wait upon the Lord shall renew strength,' " Moishe replied.

The old women kept still and cupped their ears to hear better. Even the young men and girls who had come to debate culture, literature, Yiddishism, and progress with me became silent.

Suddenly Shosha asked, "Mommy, is this really Moishe?"

There was laughter. Even the old women laughed with their toothless mouths.

Bashele became embarrassed. "Daughter, what's the matter with you?"

"Oy, Mommy, Moishele is a real rabbi, just like his daddy." Shosha covered her eyes with a handkerchief and cried.

4

Two days before my wedding it started to snow and went on without letup. When it finally stopped, frost set in. The streets were buried under drifts of snow as dry as salt. Not even sleighs could make their way through them. Huge icicles hung from the eaves and balconies. The wires running above the rooftops had gown thick and were glittering with sparks of frost. Here and there a bird's beak or a cat's head peeped from the snow. On Krochmalna Street the Place was deserted. Little snow eddies swirled—imps trying to catch their own tails.

The thieves, whores, and pimps were hiding in their cellar rooms or garrets. The vendors who usually sat before Yanash's Court vanished.

The wedding was to take place at eight that evening at a rabbi's on Panska Street. With Zelig's contribution, Bashele had been able to prepare a modest trousseau for Shosha—a few dresses, shoes, and underwear—but I had made no preparations of any kind. From the short pieces I sold and a little money I got from my publisher for translating, I had scratched together enough for my mother's and Moishe's expenses at the boardinghouse, but I had very little left.

On my wedding morning, I rose later than usual. I had stayed awake and could hear the chiming of the grandfather clock and the wailing of the wind until daybreak. It was ten by the time I got out of bed and began to wash and shave.

Tekla pushed open the door. "Shall I bring your breakfast?"

"Yes, Tekla—if you feel like it."

She left and soon came back. "A lady has come with flowers for you."

I had planned to keep everything secret. I started to tell Tekla to let no one in, but at that moment the door opened and I saw Dora. She wore a faded coat, boots, and a hat that looked like an upside-down pot. She held a bouquet wrapped in heavy paper. Tekla grimaced and turned her head.

Dora said, "My dear, there are no secrets. Congratulations!"

My cheeks were covered with soap. I put down the razor and asked, "What kind of nonsense is this?"

"Don't you know you can't keep anything from me? It's true you didn't ask me to the ceremony, but there will always be a kinship between us. No one can erase the years we spent together. Here—may it be with happiness and prosperity."

"Who told you about it, eh?"

"Oh, I have connections. Someone who works with the Secret Service would know everything that goes on in Warsaw."

Dora was referring to the Stalinists who, ever since she had left the Party, had accused her of being an agent for the Polish Secret Police.

I took the flowers from her reluctantly and stuck them into the jug that held my wash water.

Dora said, "Yes, I know everything. I've even had the honor of meeting your bride."

"How did you accomplish that?"

"Oh, I knocked on her door and pretended I was collecting for some charitable cause. I spoke Yiddish to her but she didn't understand what I was talking about, and I thought, She speaks only Polish, but I soon saw that she doesn't know Polish too well either. I don't want to needle you. Since you love her, what difference does it make, anyway? People fall in love with the blind, the deaf, the hunchbacked. May I sit down?"

"Yes, Dora, do sit down. You shouldn't have spent money for flowers."

"I wanted to bring something. I have my reasons. I'm getting married too, and if I give you a wedding present, you'll have to give me one. I have an ulterior motive for everything I do." Dora blinked and sat on the edge of the bed. Rivulets of melted snow ran from her boots onto the floor. She took out a cigarette and lit it.

"Felhendler?" I asked.

"Yes, my dearest. We're both renegades, Fascists, traitors, and provocateurs.

Could there be a more perfect match? We'll stand together on the barricades and shoot the workers and peasants. That is, if we don't happen to be in prison at the time. Do the reactionaries know that we're their friends? By the way, what happened to that play you were supposed to have written? You drifted away from me, but I remember each hour we spent together. When something of yours is published, I read it not once but three times. I hear that Dr. Feitelzohn is planning to put out a magazine."

"He's been planning this magazine for years."

Tekla opened the door with her toe and brought in my breakfast tray.

I asked, "Would you join me, Dora?"

"I've had breakfast already, thank you, but I would have a glass of coffee." While Tekla went to bring the coffee, Dora looked around. "Will your wife come to live here with you or will you move in with her?" she asked. "I'm nosy as always."

"I don't know anything yet."

"I don't understand you—but what's the point of upsetting you with questions? You don't know the answer, anyway. As for me, I don't love Wolf. We're too much alike. Lately, he's become exceedingly sarcastic. He keeps making those awful jokes. Our being together is futile, anyway. Either he'll be arrested or I'll be arrested. The police play with us like cats with mice. But so long as we remain on this side of the bars, we don't feel like being alone. As soon as he leaves the house, I start looking up at the ceiling for a hook. When I go downstairs I have to cross the street to avoid my former comrades. If they see me, they spit and shake their fists. You once told me things that I didn't grasp at the time, but since all this has happened, they're starting to come back to me."

"What things?"

"Oh, that you can't help mankind and that those who worry too much about the fate of man must sooner or later become cruel. How did you know this? I hardly dare say it, but I lie in bed next to him and I think of you. He's both ironic and grim. He smiles as if he knows the final truth and I can't stand that smirk, because he smiled the exact same smile when he was a Stalinist. Just the same, I can't be alone any more."

"He moved in?" I asked.

"I can't pay the rent by myself. He got some kind of part-time job in a union."

The door opened again and Tekla came in with a glass of coffee. Her eyes sparkled with laughter. "Miss Betty is here with flowers," she announced.

Before I could answer, Betty appeared on the threshold in a blond fur coat, a fur hat to match, and fur-trimmed boots. She carried a huge bouquet. When she saw Dora she took a step backward. An urge to laugh came over me. "You, too?"

"May I come in?"

"Of course, come in, Betty."

"It's some blizzard outside! Seven witches must have hanged themselves."

"Betty, this is Dora. I've told you about her. Dora, this is Betty Slonim."

"Yes, I know—the actress from America. I recognize you from your picture in the newspaper," Dora said.

"What shall I do with the flowers?"

"Tekla, could you bring a vase?"

"All the vases are full. The mistress keeps kasha in them."

"Bring whatever there is. Take the flowers."

Tekla held out her hand. She seemed to be doing everything in a mocking fashion.

Betty began to hop up and down in her boots. "A terrible frost. You can't cross the street. It's the way it used to be in Moscow. It's like this in Canada, too. In New York they clear away the snow—at least on the main streets. Help me off with my coat. Now that you're about to marry, be a gentleman."

I helped Betty off with her coat. She was wearing a red dress that clashed with her red hair. She looked pale and thin. She said, "You're probably wondering why I came. It's because you bring flowers for a bridegroom and you bring flowers for a corpse, and when the bridegroom is also a corpse, he deserves a double bouquet." She spoke the words as if she had prepared them in advance.

Dora smiled. "Not badly said. I'll be running along. I don't want to disturb you."

"You're not disturbing anybody," Betty said. "What I have to say everyone can hear."

"Shall I bring more coffee?" Tekla asked.

"Not for me," Betty said. "I've had maybe ten glasses today already. May I smoke?"

Betty took out a cigarette, lit it, and after a while offered one to Dora. Both women seemed to fence momentarily with the tips of their cigarettes. It was like the remnant of some heathen rite.

5

Dora still sat on the bed. I had given Betty my chair and I sat on a bench by the washstand. Betty spoke of Eugene O'Neill, one of whose plays had been translated into Yiddish. She would be appearing in it in Warsaw. She said, "I know it's going to be a flop. They don't understand O'Neill even in America, so how will the Warsaw Jews understand him? The translation isn't any good, either. But Sam insisted that I appear in Poland before we go back to America. Oh, how I envy a writer! He doesn't have to deal with people all the time. He sits at his desk with paper and pen and says whatever he wants. But actors are always dependent on others. At times the urge to write comes over me. I've tried to write a play—a novel, too—but I read what I've written and I don't like it, and I tear it up on the spot. Tsutsik—may I still call you Tsutsik?—here in Poland the situation is deteriorating fast. Sometimes I worry about getting stuck here."

"With an American passport, you've got nothing to worry about," Dora said. "Even Hitler wouldn't start up with America."

"What's a passport? A piece of paper. And what's a play? Paper, too. And what are reviews? Again, paper. And traveler's checks and banknotes are also only paper. One time when I couldn't sleep I started thinking—there was once a Stone Age; now we're in the Paper Age. Some tools have remained from the Stone Age, but from the Paper Age nothing will remain. At night the most bizarre thoughts come to mind. Once, I woke up and began musing about my genealogy. I know only a little bit about my grandfathers and nothing at all about my great-grandfathers and great-grandmothers. Well, and what about the great-great-grandfathers? I figured that when you go back enough generations, everyone stems from thousands of forebears, and from each of them he has inherited some trait. By day, this is nothing more than a passing thought, but at night it becomes terribly relevant and even scary. Tsutsik, you write about dybbuks. The past generations are our dybbuks. They sit within us and usually remain silent. But suddenly one of them cries out. The grandmothers aren't so dreadful, but the grandfathers terrify me. A person is literally a cemetery where multitudes of living corpses are buried. Tsutsik, has this ever occurred to you?''

''All kinds of crazy things occur to me.''

''Among the generations there have probably been madmen, and their voices must be heard,'' Betty went on. ''I'm not only a cemetery—in my brain there's an insane asylum, too. I hear the lunatics shriek their wild laughter. They pull at the bars and try to escape. Heredity cells aren't lost. If man is descended from an ape, he carries the genes of an ape in him, and if from a fish, there is something of the fish in him, too. Isn't that funny and frightening at the same time?''

Dora crushed the butt of her cigarette. ''Excuse me, Miss Slonim, but did you ever consider that such thoughts have a social undertone? If you have the right pieces of paper, as you've described them—the passport, the checks, the ticket to America—you can indulge in the luxury of probing into all kinds of vagaries. But if you must pay the rent the next day and don't have a groschen and you're apt to be forced out into the cold and they're about to put you in jail for some crime you haven't committed and you're hungry besides—that's when you concentrate on reality. Ninety percent of mankind—ninety-nine percent— is uncertain of its tomorrow, and often of its today. What they have to concern themselves with is the most basic needs. When writers like H. G. Wells or Hans Heinz Evers, or maybe even our own Aaron Greidinger, come out with fantasies about wars between planets or about a girl with two dybbuks who want to get married—excuse me for being so blunt—they're talking to each other. I never read the writer O'Neill, but I have a feeling he's one of those who spin dreams. Miss Slonim, you should appear in something that touches everybody. Then you will be understood and you will have an audience. Forgive my frankness.''

Betty bristled. ''What should I play in? A propaganda piece preaching Communism? First, I'd be arrested and they'd close down the theater. Second, I come from Russia and I've seen what Communism really is. Third . . .''

''I'm not proposing you should do a Communist play,'' Dora interrupted her. ''How could you? No one knows any more where Stalinism ends and Fascism—or whatever you choose to call it—begins. Still, it remains a fact that the masses suffer and their suffering grows steadily worse. If the Nazis attack Poland, it's the poor who will be the victims. The rich will all flee abroad. If you can show a bank book with a hundred thousand dollars and if you travel strictly for pleasure, then the whole world is open to you. They'll even let you into Palestine if you can show one thousand pounds sterling. Is that true or not, Aaron?''

''A novel or a play that said all this wouldn't change anything,'' I said.

"The masses already know that's how things are. Besides, you said before the very opposite of what you're saying now."

"I didn't say the opposite. I have my doubts, but the masses remain dear to me. They should be taught how to resist this exploitation."

"Dora, you speak of the masses as if they were innocent lambs and only a few villains are responsible for the human tragedy. Actually, a large part of the masses themselves want to kill, plunder, rape, and do what Hitler, Stalin, and tyrants like them have always done. Chmielnitsky's Cossacks weren't capitalists, neither were Petlura's murderers. Petlura himself was a pauper right up to the time Schwartzbard did him in. He starved in Paris."

"Who sent a hundred thousand soldiers to die at Verdun? Wilhelm and Foch."

"Wilhelm and Foch couldn't have sent them unless a big enough percentage had been willing to go. The ugly truth is that a great number of men—young men in particular—have a passion to kill. They only need a pretext or a cause. One time, it's for religion; another, it may be for Fascism or to defend democracy. Their urge to kill is so great it surpasses their fear of being killed. This is a truth forbidden to utter, but true nonetheless. Those Nazis ready to kill and die for Hitler would under other circumstances be as ready to do the same for Stalin. There hasn't been a foolish ambition or an insanity for which people weren't ready to die. If the Jews were to become independent, you could start a war between the Litvaks and the Galicianers."

"If that is true, then there is no hope."

"Who says there is?"

"A hypocrite!" Betty said after Dora had gone. "I've seen her ilk in Russia. They put on leather jackets, hung revolvers at their hips, and became Chekaists. Now they're being liquidated. They richly deserve it. Tsutsik, come kiss me. For the last time."

CHAPTER TWELVE

1

In the afternoon more snow began to fall. A dusky murkiness showed through the windowpanes. The sky loomed low, gray, neither cloudy nor clear but looking as if, through some change in creation, the world had acquired another climate. Where was it written that the Ice Age couldn't suddenly come back? What was to prevent the earth's tearing loose from the gravitational force of the sun and straying from the Milky Way in the direction of some other galaxy? After Dora and Betty left, it grew quiet in the apartment. The telephone didn't ring, nor did Tekla come to straighten up and take away the tray. I lay down in my clothes on the unmade bed and closed my eyes.

Around seven-thirty I'd have to take a droshky, a sleigh, or a cab and go to the boardinghouse on Gnoyna Street where my mother and Moishe were waiting for me. Mother was undoubtedly sitting on a chair or on the bed, waiting absorbed in *The Duty of the Hearts,* which she had brought with her. My marriage to Shosha had robbed her of the last hope of returning to Warsaw. Moishe was probably in the studyhouse browsing through books there. He hadn't uttered a word against Shosha, but his eyes laughed momentarily when he first heard her name. The boys in the cheder where he went used to mimic Shosha. I was sure he was thinking that those who strayed from the path of righteousness also strayed when it came to worldly matters. Well, and what about Feitelzohn, Celia, and Haiml? Even Teibele had reacted with a hint of contempt when she heard I would be marrying her sister. I had already determined never to take Shosha to the Writers' Club. They would ridicule her—and me.

Evening fell abruptly. My room grew dark. The sky had acquired a violet tinge. I got up from my bed and stood at the window. The passersby were not walking but struggling against the blizzard; occasionally they danced with the whirlwind. Vast piles of snow transformed the street into valleys and hills. What are the sparrows doing now? I wondered. According to Spinoza, the frost, the birds, and I were all modes of the same substance. But one mode whistled, whined, and drove a cold wave from the North Pole; a second hid in a hole in a wall, shivering and starving; a third was getting ready to marry Shosha.

It wasn't yet seven when I went outside to find a droshky. I had put on my good suit and a fresh shirt. Haiml and Celia had reserved a room in a hotel for us in Otwock, where we would spend a week. This was to be their wedding gift and our honeymoon, and I had packed a satchel with manuscripts, some clothing, and a toothbrush. I did it all with the feeling that it was never my decision but that some unknown power had decided for me. The illusion of free choice had vanished from within me. Perhaps this is the way all people marry? Perhaps this is how men steal, murder, go to war, commit suicide? Something in me laughed. The fatalists are right after all. I'll never blame anyone for anything. I waited in front of the gate for fifteen minutes, but all the sleighs and taxis that passed were taken. Nor were any of the trolleys with their frosted-over windows heading in the direction of Gnoyna. I started off on foot, carrying the satchel, and the snow sprayed my face at an angle. My eyelids became swollen. The snow-covered street lights cast trails of fog. I stumbled along in the wintry chaos with the uncertainty of a blind man. Even though I wore rubbers, my feet were soon wet. I passed Solna and Electoralna Streets, and from Zimna came out on Gnoyna. How would I take Mother and Moishe through such a storm to Panska? She could barely take a step in normal weather. I glanced at my wristwatch, but I couldn't read the numbers on the dial.

I climbed the three flights of wet and slippery stairs that led up to the boardinghouse. Mother sat in the living room in a velvet dress, a silk kerchief over her head, her face pointed and white. I could see in her eyes both a pious acquiescence in God's verdicts and a tinge of worldly irony. Moishe had already put on his rabbinical fur-lined coat with the mangy collar and his broad-brimmed hat. There were other men and women in the place, guests who had spent the night there, possibly stranded in Warsaw by the snowstorm. They apparently knew who was expected and guessed the circumstances, for when I came in a tumult broke out and a clapping of hands.

Someone exclaimed, "Mazel tov, the groom is here!"

A whirl of steam covered my face and for a moment I saw nothing and heard only a mixture of male and female laughter.

A youth—he may have been an employee of the house—volunteered to go downstairs and help us get a sleigh or droshky. Mother wasn't able to climb in, and I had to lift her and place her in her seat. Moishe didn't forget to be suspicious that the seat cover was of forbidden cloth, and he spread his handkerchief over it for a partition. The droshky had already started off when I realized I didn't have my satchel. I began to shout to the driver to stop. At that moment the youth—Mother designated him an angel from heaven—raced up and threw it in beside me. I wanted to reward him, but I had no change. I yelled my thanks and the wind blew my words away. The droshky's canopy was up; it was dark inside. I heard Moishe say, "Well, thank the Almighty you came. It was getting late and we were afraid something had happened. You know how Mother worries."

"I couldn't get a droshky. I had to walk the whole way."

"God forbid you didn't catch a cold," Mother said. "Ask Bashele to give you an aspirin."

"It all comes from heaven, it's all from heaven," Moishe said. "In everything man does there are obstacles so that he can discern the hand of Providence. If everything were to go smoothly, man would say, 'My power and the might of mine hands hath gotten me this wealth.' When evildoers achieve success, they believe it to be due to their own ability, but not always is the path of evil successful. That Hitler—may his name be blotted out—will be dealt his punishment, nor will Stalin, that wicked monster, have his way either."

"Until they receive their deserved punishment, who knows how many innocent people will perish," Mother said.

"Eh? Accounts are kept in heaven. Rabbi Sholom Belzer once said, 'Not a pinch of snuff is ignored in the Celestial Council of Justice!' He who knows the truth relies completely on God."

The droshky dragged along, rocking. From time to time the horse stopped, turned his head, and glanced back, seemingly wondering why people should drive in weather like this. The driver said in Yiddish, "On a night like this, a droshky is no good and a sleigh is worthless, too. On a night like this, it's good to sit by the stove and eat broth with noodles."

"You'll have to give him a few groschen more," Mother whispered.

"Yes, Mama, I will."

When we got to the rabbi's, everyone was waiting: Shosha, Bashele, Zelig, Teibele, Feitelzohn, Haiml, Celia. They greeted me with smiles, winks. Celia's eyes seemed to ask, Are you really so blind? Or do you see something the others can never see? Maybe they had suspected I would change my mind at the last minute. Mother's old-fashioned clothes brought a condescending expression from the rebbitzen, a stout woman in a black curled wig; she had a broad face and a huge bosom. There was not a trace of feminine well-wishing in her stern gaze. Counting the rabbi and his son—a swarthy youth with hardly any earlocks and the stiff collar of a half Hasid, half dandy—there were seven males present, and the rabbi sent his son out to collar three men from the courtyard or the street to complete the quorum.

Shosha had on a new dress. Her hair done in a pompadour and her high-heeled shoes made her look taller. When we came in, she stretched out her arms and made a gesture as if to run up to us, but Bashele indicated to her that she should stand still. Bashele had brought a bottle of wine, a bottle of whiskey, and a bag of cookies. The rabbi, a tall, erect man with a pointed black beard, didn't appear pious like my father or Moishe, but a worldly person, all business. There was a telephone in his apartment. Mother and Moishe looked at each other, surprised. It never occurred to Father to install a gadget like this in his house.

Since Zelig had already deposited a thousand zlotys with a lawyer to be paid to Bashele after the divorce, the former husband and wife avoided each other. Zelig paced to and fro in a black suit, a stiff collar, and a tie with a pearl stickpin. His shoes squeaked. He was smoking a cigar. He was already properly drunk, as befitted a member of the burial society. He called Mother *"mechutayneste"* (in-law), and reminded her of the time when we had been neighbors. Feitelzohn was having a conversation with Moishe, displaying his knowledge of the Gemara and the Midrash. I heard Moishe say to him, "You are a scholar, but erudition demands practice."

"For that you need what I lack—faith," Feitelzohn replied.

"Sometimes the faith comes later."

Feitelzohn had already met Shosha at Celia's. He had praised her childish beauty to me, said that she reminded him of an English girl friend of his of olden times, even spoke of having Shosha take part in some future soul expedition of his, together with me. He added, "Tsutsik, in my eyes she has a million times more charm than that American actress—what is her name? If you would have married her, I would have considered it a degradation."

The rabbi sat down to fill out the marriage contract. He wiped the point of his pen on his skullcap. When he asked if the bride was a virgin, Zelig replied, "Certified."

The rabbi's son came back with three men dressed in padded jackets, heavy boots, fur caps. One wore a rope tied across his loins. They didn't want to wait for refreshments until after the ceremony and immediately poured themselves glasses of whiskey. Their faces, raw from the cold outside, blackened and wrinkled from age and hard work, expressed disdain for all the hopes of the young. Their moist eyes behind bushy brows were saying, Just wait a few years and you will know what we know. From behind the stove the rabbi's son brought a canopy and four poles. The rabbi quickly read the ketubbah, the marriage contract written in Aramaic. He swallowed words. I promised Shosha two hundred gulden in the event I divorced her, and the same sum of money from my heirs should she be widowed.

I hadn't bought a wedding ring. Bashele told me that no jeweler would be able to supply a ring to fit Shosha's index finger, which was as slender as a child's. Bashele now gave me the ring that Zelig had given her over thirty years ago. I would use it just for that occasion. She burst into tears when the rabbi began to chant the holy words. Teibele wiped a tear from her left eye with a corner of her handkerchief. Shosha moved her lips several times, as if about to ask or to say something, but each time Bashele shook her head in warning.

I noticed that my mother was barely able to stand. From time to time she wavered and took hold of Moishe's shoulder. Moishe swayed as if he were mumbling a prayer.

Haiml and Celia had planned a reception for us at a restaurant, but it had to be canceled. Mother and Moishe let it be known that they didn't trust the big-city restaurants to be strictly kosher. Besides, the last train to Otwock, where a room stood ready for Shosha and me, departed too early to leave enough time for a reception. Bashele had packed a supper for us to eat on the train. Mother and Moishe intended to go back to Old Stykov the first thing the next morning. Haiml and Celia would take them to the station. When Shosha and I returned from Otwock, we would move in with the Chentshiners.

I knew that all who were present at the ceremony—perhaps even Bashele and Shosha herself deep down where a vestige of sane judgment always remains—felt that I was committing a terrible folly, but the general mood was a kind of jubilant solemnity. Feitelzohn, who was wont to make jokes even at funerals to show how consistent he was in his cynicism, conducted himself almost paternally. He squeezed my hand and wished me good luck. He bent down and gallantly kissed Shosha on her little hand. Haiml and Celia both cried.

Zelig said, "Getting married and dying are two things you can't avoid." And he handed me a stack of banknotes wrapped in tissue paper.

Mother wasn't crying. I hugged and kissed her, but she didn't kiss me back. She said, "Since you went ahead and did it, it was obviously ordained."

2

The train was scheduled to leave at twenty to twelve, but at midnight it still hadn't moved. The car in which we were seated was empty. The tiny gas lamp blinded more than it illuminated. Bashele and Teibele, who escorted us to the train, had gone home. It was nearly as cold in the car as outside, and I put on the two sweaters I had packed in my satchel. Shosha had brought along a fur collar and a muff that may have come from before the war and had undoubtedly belonged to her mother. The collar had a fox head with two glass eyes. Shosha pressed against me and her body vibrated, like that of some small animal.

Had we made a mistake and boarded an empty train that was scheduled to stand all night in the station? I wanted to take a look in the other cars, but Shosha clung to me and said she wouldn't be left alone. Eventually we heard a whistle and the train began to glide hesitantly over the slippery rails.

Shosha opened the bag Bashele had given us and we ate a cold meal. Everything she did took a long time: untying the bag, deciding which portion was meant for her and which for me. She seemed to waver at every bite. I had promised Haiml and Celia, those generous benefactors of ours, that when we lived with them Shosha would help out with the housekeeping chores, since Celia's Marianna had gone off to be married, but Shosha's indecision each time she had to make the pettiest choice convinced me that she would be of little use. She picked up a slice of sour pickle and it fell from her fingers. She took a crumb of a roll, then put it down again. Her slim fingers had almost no nails and I could not make out whether she had bitten them off or whether they had stopped growing. She began to chew and somehow forgot that she had food in her mouth.

We rode past the Praga cemetery, a city of headstones enveloped in snowy shrouds, and Shosha said, "Here lies Yppe."

"Yes, I know."

"Oh, Arele, I'm afraid!"

"Afraid of what?" I asked.

Shosha didn't answer and I assumed she had forgotten what I had asked. Then she said, "The train may get lost."

"How? A train runs on tracks."

Shosha thought this over.

"Arele, I won't be able to have children. The doctor once said I'm too narrow. You know where."

"I don't want children. You are my child."

"Arele, are you my husband already?"

"Yes, Shoshele."

"And I'm really your wife?"

"According to the law."

"Arele, I'm afraid."

"What are you afraid of now?"

"Oh, I don't know. Of God. Of Hitler."

"So far, Hitler is in Germany, not here. As to God . . ."

"Arele, I forgot to bring along my little pillow."

"We'll be back in a week and you'll have your pillow again."

"Without my pillow I won't be able to fall asleep."

"You'll sleep. We'll lie in one bed."

"Oh, Arele, I'm going to cry." She burst out in a clamor, like a little girl. I put my arms around her. She trembled and I felt the beating of her heart. I counted her ribs through her dress.

The conductor came in to punch the tickets. He asked, "Why is she crying?"

"Oh, she forgot to bring along her pillow."

"Your daughter, eh?"

"No. Yes."

"Don't cry, little girl. You'll get another pillow." He threw her a kiss and left.

In the midst of crying, Shosha began to laugh. "He thought you're my daddy?"

"That's what I am."

"How is that possible? You're fooling!"

She became still and I put my cheek against hers. She shivered from the cold, but her cheek felt hot. I was cold, too, yet at the same time I was overcome by a desire different from any I had felt before—passion without association, without thought, as if the body, the corporeal stuff, were acting on its own. I listened to my desire and it struck me that if metal could feel, my feeling was that of a needle drawn to a magnet.

Shosha must have read my mind, because she said, "Oh, your beard pricks like needles!"

I started to answer her, but the wheels made a scraping sound, then came to a halt. We were somewhere between Wawer and Miedzeszyn. A white wasteland stretched beyond the other side of the pane. It had stopped snowing and the sky reflected the snow. For all the frost, it seemed to glow of an other-worldly summer.

The conductor came by and announced hastily that the rails were iced over.

"Arele, I'm afraid!"

"Afraid of what?"

"Your mother has grown so old. She looks near death."

"She's not that old."

"Arele, I want to go home."

"Don't you want to be with me?"

"Yes, with you and with my mommy."

"In a week, not before."

"I want it now!"

I didn't answer. She laid her head on my shoulder. A feeling of despair settled over me, together with the comfort brought about by the awareness that I was not responsible for this entanglement. In the half darkness I winked to my other self, my mad dictator, and congratulated him on his droll victory. I closed my eyes and felt the warmth flowing from Shosha's head to my face. What did I have to lose? Nothing more than what everyone loses anyway.

3

We were the only passengers to get off in Otwock. There was no one from whom to ask the way to the hotel, and we wandered into a wooded area. I must have been half asleep. I started to address someone—it turned out to be a tree. Shosha had become strangely silent. All of a sudden a man materialized as if from the ground and conducted us to the hotel. A servant had been sent to meet us at the station but had missed us. He mumbled who he was and remained mute all the way. He walked so quickly that Shosha could barely follow him. Every few minutes he became lost among the trees and then emerged again in a midnight game of hide-and-seek.

The room they gave us was in the attic and was large and cold. It had one big brass bed and a narrow cot, each with huge pillows and heavy blankets. It smelled of pine and lavender. Through a pane that was not frosted over one could see pines laden with snow-covered cones and draped with icicles like the Christmas trees of the Gentiles. Shosha was ashamed to undress before me, and I had to stand facing the window while she got ready for bed. I had assumed that wandering astray through the cold woods would put Shosha in a panic, but the real danger seemed to have left her indifferent. I saw her reflection in the clean part of the windowpane as she took off her camisole and put on her nightgown. After fussing a long time with buttons and hooks, she got into bed. "Arele, it's cold as ice!" she exclaimed.

Shosha demanded that I lie on the cot, but I lay down beside her. Her body was warm, while mine was half frozen. In my cold arms she fluttered like a sacrificial chicken. Except for her little breasts, which were those of a girl just starting to mature, she was skin and bones. We lay together quietly and waited for the bedding to warm up. Cold came in through the window frame, and the panes rattled. From time to time the wind whistled and dropped to a drawn-out moan like that of a woman giving birth. Sometimes a wailing of different voices could be heard, as if packs of wolves were roaming the Otwock forests.

"Arele, it aches."

"What is it?"

"You're sticking me with your knees."

I pulled my knees away.

"My stomach is rumbling."

"It's my stomach, not yours."

"No, it's mine. Do you hear? Like the crying of a baby."

I felt her abdomen. She shook. "Cold fingers!"

"I'll warm myself on you."

"Oh, Arele, you're not allowed to do this to a female."

"Shoshele, you're my wife."

"Arele, I'm ashamed. Oh, you're tickling me!" Shosha began to laugh, but abruptly the laughter turned into a sob.

"Why are you crying, Shoshele?"

"It's all so strange. When Leizer the watchmaker came to read what you wrote in the newspaper, I thought, How can this be? Is he actually there? I took out the papers you had painted with the colors and they had dried out. We went to look for you at the newspaper and an old man, the one who serves the tea, yelled, 'Not here!' We didn't go back. One evening I played with a shadow on the wall and suddenly it jumped down and slapped me. Oh, you have hair on your chest! I lay sick all year and Dr. Kniasler said I would die."

"When was this?"

She didn't answer. Even as she was talking, she fell asleep. Her breath came quick and soft. I pulled her closer, and in her sleep she cuddled up to me with such force it was as if she were trying to bore inside my guts. How can such a weak creature give off so much heat? I wondered. Is there a physiological reason for it? Or does it have to do with the mind?

I closed my eyes. The tremendous urge for Shosha that had seized me in the train had dissipated. Was I suddenly impotent? I fell asleep and dreamed. Someone shrieked wildly. Animals with long teats dragged me, tore chunks from me with fang and claw. I was wandering through a cellar that was also a slaughterhouse and a cemetery strewn with unburied corpses. I awoke excited. I grabbed Shosha, and before she could even wake up, I mounted her. She choked and resisted. A stream of hot blood burned my thigh. I tried to pacify her, but she broke out in a wail. I was sure she had awakened everyone in the hotel. Had I injured her? I got out of bed and searched for the light switch, but I couldn't find it. I tapped around and bumped into the stove. In my distress I prayed to God to protect her.

"Shoshele, don't cry! People will come running! It was all out of love."

"Where are you?"

I found the switch and turned on the light. For a moment I couldn't see. There was a washstand here with a pitcher of water and two towels hanging at the side. Shosha was sitting up in the bed, no longer crying.

"Arele, am I a wife now?"

4

On our third day in Otwock, while I was sitting with Shosha in the hotel dining room eating lunch, I was summoned to the telephone. The call was from Warsaw. I was sure it would be Celia, but it turned out to be Feitelzohn.

"Tsutsik, I have good news for you."

"Good news for me? That's something I hear for the first time."

"Yes, good news. But first tell me how things are going with the honeymoon."

"Fine, thanks."

"No crises?"

"Yes, but—"

"Your Shosha didn't die of fright?"

"Nearly. But now she is happy again."

"I like her. With her at your side, your talent will grow."

"From your mouth to God's ears."

"Tsutsik, I told Shapiro, the editor of the evening paper—what's it called?— that you're writing a novel about Jacob Frank, and he wants you to write Frank's biography for him. He wants to print it in six installments a week and pay you three hundred zlotys a month. I told him that was too little and he may up it a few zlotys."

"Three hundred zlotys is too little? That's a fortune!"

"Some fortune! Tsutsik, you're made! He told me you'll be able to drag the thing through a year, or as long as your imagination holds out."

"That really is a stroke of fortune!"

"Are you still moving in with the Chentshiners?"

"Now I won't do it. Shosha will pine away without her mother."

"Don't do it, Tsutsik. You know I'm not jealous of you. Just the opposite. But to live there wouldn't be a good idea. Tsutsik, I'll go bankrupt from this call. We'll celebrate when you come back. Regards to Shosha. Adieu."

I wanted to tell Feitelzohn how grateful I was and that I would pay for the call, but he had already hung up. I went back to the table. "Shoshele, you've brought me luck. I have a job on a newspaper. We won't be moving in with Celia!"

"Oh, Arele, God has answered me. I didn't want to be there. I prayed. She tries to take you away from me. What will you do on the paper?"

"Write the life of a false Messiah who preached that God wants people to sin. The false Messiah himself slept with his own daughter and with the wives of his disciples."

"He had such a wide bed?"

"Not all at the same time—or maybe all together, too. He was rich enough to afford a bed as wide as all Otwock."

"You knew him?"

"He died some hundred and fifty years ago."

"Arele, I pray to God, and everything I ask for He does. When you went to the post office, a blind man came up and I gave him ten groschen, and that's the reason God did all this. Arele, I love you so terribly! I'd like to be with you every minute, every second. When you go to the toilet I start to worry that you may have gotten lost or fallen. I miss Mommy, too. I haven't seen her for so long. I would like to be with you and with her day and night for a myriad of years.''

"Shoshele, your mother will be divorced soon and she may remarry. And it will be impossible for me to be with you every minute. In Warsaw I'll have to go to the editorial office, to the library. Sometimes I'll have to meet Feitelzohn. It was he who got me the job.''

"He has no wife?''

"He has many women, but not one wife.''

"Is he the false Messiah?''

"In a way Shoshele—that's not a bad comparison.''

"Arele, I want to tell you something, but I'm ashamed.''

"You have nothing to be ashamed of before me. I've already seen you naked.''

"I want more,''

"More what?''

"I want to lie in bed. You know what.''

"When? Now?''

"Yes.''

"Wait, the waitress hasn't brought us our tea yet.''

"I'm not thirsty.''

The waitress came with two glasses of tea and two slices of sugar cake on a tray. We were the only guests in the hotel. Another couple was expected but not until the next day.

It had stopped snowing and the sun shone. I had been planning to take a walk with Shosha, maybe as far as Świder. I wanted to see if the river was frozen over and how the waterfall looked with its huge icicles gleaming in the sun, but Shosha's words changed everything. The waitress, a short woman with a broad face, high cheekbones, and liquid black eyes, didn't turn back to the kitchen right away. She said, "Mr. Greidinger, you eat everything up, but your wife leaves everything. That's why she's so thin. She barely touched the appetizer, the soup, the meat, the vegetables. It's not good to eat so little. People come here to gain weight, not to lose.''

Shosha made a face. "I can't eat so much. I have a small stomach.''

"It's not the stomach, Mrs. Greidinger. My grandmother used to say, 'The intestine has no bottom.' It's the appetite. My boss here lost her appetite and she went to a Dr. Schmaltzbaum. He gave her a prescription for iron and she gained back ten pounds.''

"Iron?'' Shosha asked. "Can you eat iron?''

The waitress laughed, exposing a mouthful of gold teeth. Her eyes contracted to the size of two berries. "Iron is a medicine. No one is told to eat nails.'' She walked away, scraping her large shoes across the floor. When she reached the kitchen door, she cast an amused glance back toward us.

Shosha said, "I don't like her. I like only you and Mommy. I like Teibele too, but not as much as you two. I would like to be with you a thousand years.''

5

The night was long. We went to sleep before nine and at twelve we both awoke. Shosha asked, "Arele, you don't sleep any more?"

"No, Shoshele."

"Neither do I. Every time I wake up I think it was all a fairy tale—you, the wedding, everything. But I touch you and I see you are here."

"Once there was a philosopher and he believed that everything was a dream. God is dreaming and the world is His dream."

"Is this written in the books?" Shosha asked.

"Yes, in the books."

"Yesterday—no, the day before yesterday—I dreamed that I was home and you came in. After you closed the door you came in again. There was not one Arele, but two, three, four, five, ten—a whole row of Areles. What is a dream?"

"No one knows."

"What do the books say?"

"The books don't know, either."

"How can this be? Arele, Leizer the watchmaker said that you are an unbeliever—is this true?"

"No, Shoshele, I believe in God, but I don't believe that He revealed Himself and told the rabbis all the little laws that they added through generations."

"Where is God? In heaven?"

"He must be somewhere."

"Why doesn't He punish Hitler?"

"Oh, He doesn't punish anybody. He created the cat and the mouse. The cat cannot eat grass, she must eat flesh. It's not her fault that she kills mice. The mice are certainly not guilty. He created the wolves and the sheep, the slaughterers and the chickens, the feet and the worms on which they step."

"God is no good?"

"Not as we see it."

"He has no pity?"

"Not as we understand it."

"Arele, I'm afraid."

"I'm afraid too, but Hitler won't come tonight. Move over to me. So."

"Arele, I want to have a child with you, a little baby with blue eyes and red hair. The doctor said that if they cut up my belly a living child would come out."

"And you would want that?"

"Yes, Arele. Your child. If it should be a boy, he would read the same books as you."

"It isn't worth cutting up a belly to read books."

"It's worth it. I would suckle him and my breasts would grow bigger."

"They are big enough for me."

"What else is written in the books?"

"Oh, all kinds of things. They found out that the stars run away with us. Myriads of miles every day."

"Where do they run?"

"Into empty space far away."

"They will never come back?"

"They will be extinguished and get cold first, and then they will fall back with such might they will grow hot, and the whole swinish business will begin all over again."

"Where do the books say Yppe is?"

"If there is a soul, she is somewhere. And if there isn't any, then—"

"Arele, she was here. She knows about us. She came to wish me mazel tov."

"When? Where?"

"Here. Yesterday. No, the day before yesterday. How does she know that we are in Otwock? She stood at the door, near the mezuzah, and she smiled. She wore a white dress, not a shroud. When she was alive, two of her front teeth were missing. Now she has a full mouth of teeth."

"There must be good dentists in the hereafter."

"Arele, are you making fun of me?"

"No, I'm not."

"She came to me in Warsaw, too. It was before you visited us for the first time—I sat on my stool and she came in. The door was bolted. Mother was out, and she told me to bolt the door because of the hoodlums. Suddenly Yppe was there. How could she do it? She spoke to me, like one sister to another. I had undone my hair, and she braided it. She played cat's cradle with me, but without string. And then that day before Yom Kippur I saw her in the chicken soup. She had a wreath of flowers on her head, like a Gentile bride, and I knew that something was going to happen. You were there, but I didn't want to say anything. When I mention Yppe, Mother screams. She says that I'm crazy."

"You are not crazy."

"What am I?"

"A sweet soul."

"What do you make of it?"

"You might have dreamed it."

"In the middle of the day?"

"Sometimes one dreams in the daytime."

"Arele, I am afraid."

"What are you afraid of this time?"

"The sky, the stars, the books. Tell me the story about the giant. I forget his name."

"Og, the king of Bashan."

"Yes, about him. Is it true that he could not get a wife because he was so big?"

"That is the story. When the flood came and Noah and his sons and all the animals and fowl went into the Ark, Og could not enter because he was so big, and he sat on the roof. Forty days and forty nights it rained on him, but he didn't drown."

"Was he naked?"

"What tailor could sew a pair of pants big enough for him?"

"Oy, Arele, it is good to be with you. What will we do when the Nazis come?"

"We will die."

"Together?"

"Yes, Shoshele."

"The Messiah isn't coming?"

"Not so quickly."

"Arele, I just remembered a song."

"What song?"

Shosha began to sing in a thin voice.

> *"He was called Beans,*
> *Noodles was her name,*
> *They married on Friday*
> *And nobody came."*

She cuddled up to me and said, "Oy, Arele, it's good to lie with you even if we die."

CHAPTER THIRTEEN

1

In the afternoon paper where the biography of Jacob Frank—it was actually a blend of biography and fantasy—had already been dragging on for months, the news worsened. Hitler and Mussolini had met at the Brenner Pass and no doubt reached decisions regarding the destruction of Poland and the Jews, but a large part of the Polish press kept attacking the Jewish minority as if it were the nation's greatest danger. Representatives of the Hitler government came to Poland and were received by the dictator, General Rydz-Śmigly, and his ministers. In the Soviet Union the purges, mass arrests, and trials of Trotskyites, old Bolsheviks, right- and left-wing dissidents, Zionists, and Hebrewists became a permanent terror. In Polish cities, unemployment grew. In the villages, particularly where Ukrainians and White Russians lived, the peasants starved. Many *Volksdeutschen*, as the Germans in Poland called themselves, proclaimed themselves Nazis. The Comintern had dissolved the Polish Communist Party. The charging of Bukharin, Kamenev, Zinoviev, and Rykov with sabotage and espionage and the designation of them as Fascist lackeys and agents of Hitler evoked protests even from sworn Stalinists. But circulation did not drop in the Yiddish newspapers in Warsaw, including the afternoon daily for which I worked. On the contrary, more newspapers were read now than before. The story of the false Messiah Jacob Frank and his disciples had to end, but I was ready with a list of other false Messiahs—Reuveyni, Shlomo Mulkho, Sabbatai Zevi.

There was a time when I had to make up some pretext whenever I came home late or didn't come home at all, but gradually Bashele and Shosha became accustomed to asking no questions. What did they know about the writing profession? I had told Leizer the watchmaker that I served as night editor a couple of times a week, and Leizer had explained the facts to Bashele and Shosha. Leizer came by each day and read to them the latest installment of my biography of Jacob Frank. Everyone on Krochmalna Street was reading it—the thieves, the streetwalkers, the old-line Stalinists, and the new-fledged Trotskyites. Sometimes when I walked down the street I heard the market vendors talking about Jacob Frank—his miracles, orgies, and lunacies. The leftists still complained that this kind of writing was an opiate for the masses, but after they finished reading the political news on the front page and the local news on page 5 the masses needed an opiate.

Before I moved into the alcove at Bashele's she had had the walls painted and installed an iron stove, and thrown out the sacks and rags that had been accumulating for twenty-odd years. Shosha couldn't be by herself even an hour. The moment she was left alone she was overcome by melancholy. On the other hand, I couldn't be with her all the time. I had never given up my room on Leszno Street or told my landlords that I was married. True, I seldom spent nights there, but even Tekla had learned that writers are impulsive and confused creatures. She had stopped asking what I did, whom I spent time with, where I dragged around in the nights. I paid my rent and each week I gave her a zloty. On Christmas and Easter I brought her a gift. Every time I gave her something, she flushed, protested that she didn't need it, that it wasn't necessary. She would seize my hand and kiss it, as peasants had done for generations.

Because I couldn't be with Shosha all the time, coming home to her was always a wonder to me. She and Bashele had food ready for me to eat before I lay down—rice with milk, tea with a Sabbath cookie, a baked apple. Each night before coming to bed Shosha washed herself and often washed her hair as well. She discussed with me the latest installment of the Jacob Frank story. How could a man have so many women? Was it black magic? Had he sold his soul to the devil? How could a father have doings with his own daughter? Sometimes Shosha provided the answer: those were different times. Didn't King Solomon have a thousand wives? She remembered what I had told her when we lived at No. 10.

Basically, Shosha had stayed the same—the same childish face, the same childish figure. Still, changes had become apparent. In former times, Bashele had been the only one to prepare our meals. She hadn't let Shosha go near the kitchen or entrusted her with the marketing. She only sent her occasionally to the nearby store for a half pound of sugar, a few ounces of butter, a piece of cheese, or a loaf of bread—all bought on credit. I doubted whether Shosha knew the value of coins. Suddenly I observed her bustling about in the kitchen. She accompanied her mother to market in Yanash's Court. I heard her discussing with Bashele the vegetarian dishes that wouldn't upset my digestion. This concern for my diet always baffled me. I wasn't accustomed to anyone's paying attention to my needs. But to Shosha I was a husband, and to Bashele a son-in-law. It had never occurred to me that Shosha could sew or darn, but one day I saw her darning my socks over a tea glass. She began to look after my shirts, handkerchiefs, and collars, and to take my shoes to be heeled at the shoemaker's. I couldn't, or didn't want to be a husband in the accepted sense of the word, but Shosha gradually assumed the duties of a wife.

When I came home in the evenings I still found her seated on her stool, but no longer surrounded by playthings. Nor did she read her schoolbook any more. Surprises constantly awaited me. Shosha would be wearing shoes with high heels and flesh-colored stockings not only when she went visiting but also at home. Her mother had bought her dresses and nightgowns with lace. Occasionally she changed the way she wore her hair.

Shosha's interest in my writing increased. The novel about Jacob Frank had come to an end. The new novel, about Sabbatai Zevi, described with much detail the Jewish longing for redemption in an epoch that displayed similarities to our own. What Hitler threatened to do to the Jews Bogdan Chmielnitsky had done some three hundred years earlier. From the day they were exiled from their land, Jews had lived in anticipation of death or the coming of the Messiah. In Poland, in the Ukraine, in the lands ruled by the Turks, and most of all in the Holy Land, cabalists sought to bring the End of Days through prayers, fasts, the utterance of holy names. They probed the mysteries of the Book of Daniel. They never forgot the passage in the Gemara which stated that the Messiah would come when the generation was either totally innocent or totally guilty. Every day, Leizer had to read to Shosha the latest installment and explain to her the references to Jewish law and Jewish history. I heard her say to her mother, "Oh, Mommy, it's exactly like today!"

Teibele still hadn't found a husband. She had been choosy so long, Bashele complained, that she had become an old maid. Instead of a husband, she had taken a lover, a married bookkeeper with five children. Any day, he was allegedly going to divorce his wife, who was a common piece, but two years had gone by with no divorce in sight. Instead of satisfaction, Teibele provided her mother only with shame.

Teibele would often visit her mother and sister. She, too, liked to discuss Jacob Frank, Sabbatai Zevi, and their disciples with me. She brought small gifts for Bashele and Shosha, and occasionally for me as well—a book, a magazine, a notebook. Her lover was spending more and more nights at home with his wife. He had turned out to be a hypochondriac, Teibele said. He had convinced himself that he suffered from heart trouble. When Bashele reminded Teibele that it was getting late and she shouldn't be starting for home at such an hour, Teibele said in jest, "I'll lie down with them," pointing at Shosha and me. Or she would say, "What difference does it make? We're all doomed anyhow."

At night in bed, Shosha no longer talked about dolls, toys, children of neighbors she had known twenty years ago, but quite often she spoke of things I cared about. Was there truly a God up in heaven? Did He know every person's thoughts? Was it true that He loved Jews above all other people? Did He create the Gentiles, too, or only the Jews? Sometimes she questioned me about my novel. How could I be sure of what had occurred several hundred years ago? Had I read it in a book or did I make it up in my head? She asked me to tell her what would occur in the installment tomorrow and in the days after. I began to tell her things I hadn't yet written. I conducted a literary experiment with her—let my tongue wag freely and say whatever came to my lips. I had read and heard from Mark Elbinger about automatic writing. I had also read in a literary magazine about the kind of literature called the "stream of consciousness."

I could test all this on Shosha. She listened to everything with the same sense of curiosity—children's stories I had heard from my mother when I was five or six; sexual fantasies no Yiddish writer would have allowed himself to publish; my own hypotheses or dreams about God, world creation, immortality of the soul, the future of mankind, as well as reveries of triumph over Hitler and Stalin. I had constructed an airplane of a material whose atoms were so densely compressed, one square centimeter weighed thousands of tons. It flew at a speed of a million miles a minute. It could pierce mountains, bore through the earth, reach to the farthest planets. It contained a clairvoyant telephone that tuned me in to the thoughts and plans of every human being on earth. I became so mighty I rendered all wars obsolete. When the Bolsheviks, Nazis, anti-Semites, swindlers, thieves, and rapists heard of my powers, they promptly surrendered. I instituted a world order based on Dr. Feitelzohn's philosophy of play. In my airplane I kept a harem of eighteen wives, but the queen and sovereign would be no one other than Shosha herself.

"And where would Mommy be?"

"I would give Mommy twenty million zlotys and she would live in a palace."

"And Teibele?"

"Teibele would become a princess."

"I would miss Mommy."

"We'd come to see her every Sabbath."

For a long time Shosha didn't speak. Then she said, "Arele, I miss Yppe."

"I would bring Yppe back to life."

"How is this possible?"

I elaborated to Shosha the theory that world history was a book man could read only forward. He could never turn the pages of this world book backward. But everything that had ever been still existed. Yppe lived somewhere. The hens, geese, and ducks the butchers in Yanash's Court slaughtered each day still lived, clucked, quacked, and crowed on the other pages of the world book—the right-hand pages, since the world book was written in Yiddish, which reads from right to left.

Shosha caught her breath. "Will we live in No. 10?"

"Yes, Shoshele, on the other pages of the book we still live in No. 10."

"But different people have moved in."

"They live there on the open pages, not the closed ones."

"Mommy once said that before we moved in, a tailor used to live there."

"The tailor lives there, too."

"Everyone together?"

"Each in another time."

I had gradually ceased being ashamed of Shosha. She dressed better, she appeared taller, I took her to Celia's, and both Celia and Haiml were enchanted by her simplicity, her honesty, her naïveté. I had taught her how to handle a knife and fork. She spoke in a childish fashion, but not stupidly.

On one visit Celia had detected a similarity between Shosha and her own deceased daughter. She showed me a yellowed photograph of the child and it struck me, too, that there was a certain resemblance. Haiml, who was growing ever more inclined toward mysticism and occultism, played with the idea that the soul of their little girl might have transmigrated into Shosha and that I was actually his and Celia's son-in-law. Souls weren't lost. They came back and sought bodies through which to reveal themselves to their loved ones. There was no such thing as chance. The forces that guided man and his fate always united those who were destined to meet.

Elbinger happened to be visiting the Chentshiners that evening and he repeated what he had said about Shosha on an earlier occasion—that he thought she possessed the qualities of a medium. All true mediums that he had met displayed the same primitivism, directness, sincerity. Once, he made an attempt to hypnotize Shosha, and as soon as he told her to, she fell into a deep sleep. Elbinger had trouble waking her. Before leaving, he kissed Shosha's forehead.

After Elbinger had gone, Shosha said, "He is not a person."

"What is he?" Haiml and Celia asked in unison.

"I don't know."

"An angel? A demon?" Celia asked.

"Perhaps from the sky," Shosha replied.

Haiml clapped his brow. "Tsutsik, this is a memorable evening for me. I won't forget this evening as long as I live!"

2

This Friday night, as always, I came home to Shosha. I did not keep the Jewish laws, Shosha did not go to the ritual bath, but I yielded to Bashele and pronounced the benediction over the wine on Friday night and on Saturday morning. Bashele prepared vegetarian Sabbath meals for me. She even baked a vegetarian Sabbath stew with kasha and beans and a kugel made of rice and cinnamon. Shosha blessed the candles every Friday before dusk. She put them in silver candlesticks that Haiml and Celia had given us. Two challahs were covered with a cloth that Bashele had embroidered thirty years ago for Zelig. The family also owned a knife with a handle made of mother-of-pearl on which the words "Holy Sabbath" were engraved. That Friday evening Bashele and Shosha ate gefilte fish with chicken, and for me they made noodles with cottage cheese and carrot stew. They put on their Sabbath clothes and dressy shoes. Through the open window I saw the Sabbath candles in other apartments and heard table chants. The simple Jews sang, "Peace and light to the Jews on the day of rest and the day of joy." The Hasidim sang a cabalist poem by the Holy Isaac Luria, written in Aramaic, about a heavenly apple orchard, a heavenly bridegroom and bride, heavenly bridesmaids and best men—all in highly erotic verses that would shock readers and critics even today. Bashele and Shosha conversed about the facts that food was getting more expensive and that it was increasingly difficult to find a place to hang the wash in the attic. Bashele mentioned with nostalgia the custom of past years to spread yellow sand on the floors before the Sabbath. Peasants from nearby villages used to bring carts of the sand in wooden kegs. They called out their merchandise in the streets. Now this was out of fashion. Today women liked to shellac their floors. Another thing, pious matrons used to go from house to house on Friday and collect challah, fish, and tripe—even cubes of sugar— for the poor. The new generation did not believe in this kind of charity. The Communists came in and asked for money for the Jews in Birobidjan, a region deep in Russia, somewhere at the edge of the world. They said that there was a Jewish land there. Only God knows if they were telling the truth.

"Mommy, what comes after the edge of the world? Is it dark there?"

Bashele shook her head. "You tell her, Arele."

"There is no edge of the world. The earth is round like an apple."

"Where do the black people live?" Shosha asked.

"In Africa."

"And where is Hitler?"

"In Germany."

"Oh, they used to teach us all this in school but I could never remember," Shosha said. "Is it true that in America there is a big Jewish man who must sign every dollar or the money isn't worth anything? Leizer the watchmaker said so."

"Yes, Shoshele. But he doesn't sign by hand. They print his signature."

"On the Sabbath one shouldn't talk about money," Bashele said. "There was a pious little rabbi, Reb Fivke, and on the Sabbath he spoke only in the Holy Tongue. He lived on Smocza Street, but on Friday he used to go around with a sack in Yanash's Court and collect food for the poor. After twelve o'clock on Friday he stopped talking, because Friday afternoon is almost as sacred as the Sabbath. When they gave him alms he just nodded or he mumbled some words in the Holy Tongue. One Friday he didn't come with his sack and someone said that he was sick in the poorhouse. After a few weeks he came again with his sack, but he had stopped talking altogether. He just went from store to store like a mute man. Someone said that he had had an operation on his throat and they cut out his windpipe. One Friday he entered a butcher shop and the butcher gave him some chicken feet or a gizzard. A man from the burial society—a gravedigger—happened to be in the store, and when he saw Reb Fivke, he let out a terrible scream and fainted. Reb Fivke immediately disappeared. They revived the gravedigger with cold water and by rubbing his temples with vinegar, and when he came to himself he swore a holy oath that Reb Fivke had died, that he had buried him himself. People couldn't believe it and said that the man was mistaken, but Reb Fivke never came again. Some curious men investigated the matter and they found his widow. He had been dead for months when this happened. I know, because Zelig still used to come home once in a while and the gravedigger was his best chum."

"As far as I know, your former husband does not believe in such things," I said.

"Now he believes in nothing. Then he was still a decent person," Bashele said.

"Oh, I will be afraid to go to sleep," Shosha said.

"Nothing to be afraid of," Bashele said. "Good people don't become spiteful after death. Just the opposite. Sometimes a corpse doesn't realize that he is dead and he leaves his grave and walks among the living. I heard of a man who came home when his family was sitting shiva for him. He opened the door and when he saw his wife and daughters sitting on low stools in their stocking feet, the mirror covered with a black sheet, and his sons with rended lapels, he asked, 'What's going on here? Who died?' And his wife, who was a mean shrew, answered, 'You!' At that moment he vanished."

"Oh, I'm going to have bad dreams."

"Just say, 'In Thy hands I commend my soul,' and you will sleep peacefully," Bashele advised.

After the dessert, Bashele served tea with Sabbath cookies she baked herself. Then I went out with Shosha on a walk from No. 7 to No. 25; one could walk that far safely even at night. Farther there was danger of being attacked by some hooligan or drunk. On some streets there were Jewish stores that were kept open on the Sabbath, but not on Krochmalna Street. Only one tea shop had its door half open on the Sabbath, and the customers drank tea on credit. Even the Communists were not allowed to pay in cash. Bashele remembered times when gangsters used to attack young couples or newlywed pairs and make them pay a few groschen a week in order not to be molested. But this took place in past years, she told me. At the time of the revolution in 1905 the socialists waged war with the toughs of the underworld, and many thieves, pimps, and racketeers were beaten up. A number of brothels were destroyed and the whores dispersed. The brothels and the thieves came back, but the racketeers disappeared forever.

Shosha and I walked. We passed the almost empty Place. When we reached No. 13, across the street from No. 10, Shosha stopped. "Here we lived once."

"Yes, you say it every time we pass."

"You stood on the balcony and caught flies."

"Don't remind me of that," I said.

"Why not?"

"Because we do to God's creatures what the Nazis do to us."

"Flies bite."

"They must bite. This is the way God created them."

"Why did God create them this way?" Shosha asked.

"Shoshele, there is no answer to this."

"Arele, I want to look inside the gate of No. 10."

"You've done it a thousand times already."

"Let me."

We crossed the street and looked into the dark courtyard. Everything remained as it had been twenty years before, except that most of the tenants had died. Shosha said, "Is there still a horse in the stable? When we lived here the horse was brown and it had a white patch on its nose. How long can a horse live?"

"About twenty years."

"Why not longer? A horse is so strong."

"Sometimes a horse lives until thirty."

"Why not until a hundred?"

"I don't know."

"When we lived there a demon entered the stable at night and plaited little braids in the horse's tail, and in its mane," Shosha said. "The demon mounted the horse and rode it from wall to wall all night long. In the morning the horse was wet from perspiration. It had foam on its mouth. It almost died. Why do demons do such things?"

"I'm not sure it's true."

"I saw the horse that morning. It was all wet. Arele, I want to look into the stable. I want to see if the horse is still the same."

"It's dark in the stable."

"I see a light there."

"You see nothing. Let's go."

We continued to wallk until we reached No. 16. Then Shosha stopped. This was always a sign that she wanted to say something. Shosha could not walk and talk.

"What is it, Shoshele?"

"Arele, I want to have a child with you."

"Why suddenly?"

"I want to be a mother. Let's go home. I want you to do to me you know what."

"Shoshele, I told you, I don't want any children."

"I want to be a mother."

We turned back and Shosha said, "You go away to the newspaper and I am lonesome. I sit there and queer thoughts come to my mind. I see funny faces."

"What faces?"

"I don't know. They grimace and say things I don't understand. They are not people. Sometimes they laugh. Then they all begin to wail like at a funeral. Who are they?"

"I don't know. You tell me."

"They are many. Some of them look like soldiers. They ride horses, too. They sing a sad song, a silent song. I am frightened."

"Shoshele, you're imagining things. Perhaps you're dreaming."

"No, Arele. I want a child to say kaddish for me when I die."

"You'll live."

"No, they call me to go with them."

We passed No. 10 again, and Shosha said, "Let's look inside the gate."

"Again?"

"Let me!"

CHAPTER FOURTEEN

1

Haiml's father died and left Haiml buildings and real estate worth several million zlotys. Friends and relatives advised Haiml to move to Lodz, where he could keep a closer eye on his main properties, but Haiml said to me, "Tsutsik, a person is like a tree. You can't chop it from its roots and plant it in other ground. Here, I have Morris, you, my friends from the Poale Zion. Somewhere in the cemetery here lie the bones of my little daughter. In Lodz I'd have to look at my stepmother's face each day. The main thing is, Celia would feel unhappy there. Who would she have to talk to? Let there only be peace in the world and we'll get through the years somehow where we are."

At one time Feitelzohn planned to go back to America, but he had long since given up this plan. From Palestine a number of his friends wrote that if he were to come there, there was a good possibility of a position at the Hebrew University in Jerusalem, but Feitelzohn refused. "The German Jews run things there," he told me. "Many of them are more Prussian than the Prussians. I would fit in about as well as you would fit in among Eskimos. I'll have to sneak through my years somehow without universities."

We all lived for the present—the whole Jewish community. Feitelzohn compared this epoch to the year 1000, when the Christians in all Europe awaited the Second Coming and the destruction of the world. So long as Hitler didn't attack, so long as no revolution or pogrom erupted, each day was a gift from God. Feitelzohn often recalled his beloved philosopher, Veihinger, and his philosophy of "as if." The day will come when all truth will be recognized as arbitrary definitions, all values as rules of a game. Feitelzohn toyed with the plan of building a play-temple for ideas, for samples of cultural diversions, for systems of behavior, for religions without revelations—a kind of theater where people would come to act out their thoughts and emotions. The audience would be the performers. Those who hadn't yet decided what kind of games they preferred would participate in soul expeditions with him or with someone of his caliber to discover what would amuse or inspire them most.

I heard Feitelzohn say, "Tsutsik, I know very well that it's all sheer nonsense. Hitler wouldn't accept any other game but his own. Neither would Stalin, nor even some of our own fanatics. But I lie in bed at night and imagine a world of all play—play-gods, play-nations, play-marriages, play-sciences. What happened to mathematics after Lobachevsky and Riemann? What is Kantor's A or the "set of all sets" or Einstein's theory of relativity? Nothing but wordplay. And what are all these parts of the atom that grow like mushrooms after a rain? And what is the receding universe? Tsutsik, the world goes in your direction—everything is becoming fiction. Why are you grimacing, Haiml? You're more of a hedonist than I am."

"Hedonist shmedonist," Haiml answered. "If we're fated to die, let us die together. I have an idea! In the Sochaczów studyhouse the greatest joy came on the second evening of a holiday. Let us establish in our house that *every day* should be the second evening of a holiday. Who can forbid us to create our own calendar, our own holidays? If all life is nothing but make-believe, let us make believe that every night is the second night of a holiday. Celia will prepare a festive meal for us, and we'll make kiddush sing table chants, and talk about Hasidism. To me, Morris, you are my rebbe. Your every word is filled with wisdom and love of God as well. There is such a thing as heretical fear of God. You can sin and still be God-fearing. Sabbatai Zevi wasn't the liar he was made out to be. The true Hasid isn't so afraid of sin. You can frighten a non-Hasid with Gehenna and the bed of nails, but not us. Since everything is supposed to be a part of the godhead, why is Gehenna inferior to paradise? I'm looking for pleasure, but to be joyous today people need noisy music, vulgar chansonettes, women in chinchilla furs, and who knows what else, and even then gloom prevails. I go to Lurse's, to the Ziemianska. They sit there gazing into magazines with pictures of whores and dictators. There's not even a trace of the bliss we used to have in the Sochaczów studyhouse, with its torn books, a kerosene ceiling lamp, and a bunch of bearded Jews with untidy earlocks and ragged satin gaberdines. Morris, you know it, and Tsutsik, you know it, too. If God needs a Hitler and a Stalin and icy winds and mad dogs, let Him have them. I need you, Morris, and you, Tsutsik, and if there is no merciful truth, I take the lie that gives me warmth and moments of joy."

"One day we will move in with you," Feitelzohn said.

"When? When Hitler stands at the gates of Warsaw?"

Haiml proposed to Feitelzohn that he publish the magazine he had been planning for years and write a book about the revival and modernization of the play called *Hasidis*. Haiml would finance both and have them translated into a number of languages. All great and revolutionary experiments had originated and been conducted in precarious circumstances, Haiml contended. He suggested that the first temple of play be built in Jerusalem, or at least in Tel Aviv. The Jews, Haiml said, unlike the Gentiles, hadn't spilled blood in two thousand years. Jews were perhaps the only group that played with words and ideas instead of with swords and guns. According to Jewish legend, when the Messiah came, Jews would go to the Land of Israel not on a metal bridge but on one made of paper. Well, and could it be mere chance that the Jews dominated Hollywood, the world press, the publishing houses? The Jew would bring the world deliverance of play and Morris Feitelzohn would be the Messiah.

"Before I become the Messiah," Feitelzohn said to me, "maybe you could lend me five zlotys?"

<hr />

2

I stayed the night with Haiml and Celia. For some time, my relations with Celia had become platonic. There were times when I ridiculed this word and what it meant, but neither Celia nor I had had much interest lately in sexual experiments. Both she and Haiml still tried to persuade Feitelzohn and me, with Shosha, to move into their apartment and live like one family. Lately, Celia had turned gray. Haiml had mentioned that she was under a doctor's care and that in normal circumstances she would have gone to Carlsbad or Franzenbad or some other spa, but he never said what was wrong with her.

That night, as so often before, the conversation ended with the question why were we not leaving Warsaw, and each of us gave more or less the same answer. I couldn't leave Shosha. Haiml wouldn't go without Celia. Besides, what was the sense of running away when three million Jews remained? Some rich industrialists in Lodz had run away to Russia in 1914 and three years later were murdered by the Bolsheviks. I could see that Haiml feared more the bother of travel than the persecution of the Nazis. I heard Celia say, "If I felt that I still had the strength to begin over, I wouldn't remain here another day. My mother and grandmother as well as my father all died at my age—in fact, younger. I keep myself going only with the force of inertia, or call it what you will. I don't want to go to a foreign land and lie sick in some hotel room or hospital. I want to die in my own home. I don't want to rest in a strange cemetery. What more can Hitler do to me? I don't recall who said it, that a corpse is all-powerful, afraid of no one. All the living want and ever hope to achieve the dead already have—complete peace, total independence. There were times when I was terrified of death. You couldn't mention the word in my presence. When I bought a newspaper, I quickly skipped over the obituaries. The notion that I would one day stop eating, breathing, thinking, reading, seemed so horrible that nothing in life agreed with me any more. Then gradually I began to make peace with the concept of death, and more than that—death became the solution to all problems, actually my ideal. Today when I'm brought the newspapers I quickly turn to the obituaries. When I read that someone has died, I envy him. The reasons I don't commit suicide are first, Haiml—I want to go together with him—and second, death is too important to absorb all at once. It is like a precious wine to be savored slowly. Those who commit suicide want to escape death once and for all. But those who aren't such cowards learn to enjoy its taste.''

We went to sleep late. Haiml began to snore immediately and I could hear Celia turning in her bed, sighing, murmuring. She put on the night lamp and put it out. She went to the kitchen to make herself tea, perhaps to take a pill. If everything was nothing but a game as Feitelzohn maintained, our love game was over, or at least postponed indefinitely. It was actually more his game than ours. I always felt his presence when I was with her. Often when Celia talked to me she repeated almost literally things he told me. She had acquired his sex jargon, caprices, mannerisms. She called me Morris and by some of his pet names. Whenever our love play failed, Feitelzohn was lying between us. I even imagined that I could smell the aroma of his cigar. It was dawn when I fell asleep. The morning came up cloudy and a bit damp—it had rained in the middle of the night—but there were signs that it would be clearing later. After breakfast I went to Shosha's and stayed there for lunch. Then I left for my room on Leszno Street. Although it would have been quicker to go down Iron Street, I walked on Gnoyna, Zimna, and Orla. On Iron Street you were vulnerable to a blow from a Polish Fascist. I had laid out my own ghetto. Certain streets were always dangerous. Other streets you could walk boldly by day but not at night. Still others had remained more or less safe for the present. The corner of Leszno and Iron Streets always posed a measure of danger. Although I had turned away from the Jewish path, I carried the diaspora upon me.

As I came closer to the gate, I started to run. Safe inside, I caught my breath. I climbed the three flights of stairs slowly. I had lots of work to do this day and in the days to come. I was behind with my novel for the newspaper. I had promised a story for a literary anthology. I had started another novel about the Sabbatai Zevi movement in Poland. This was intended to be a serious work, not for serialization in an afternoon daily. I rang the bell and Tekla opened the door. She was polishing the corridor floor and had her dress tucked up over her bare legs.

She smiled and said, "Guess who called three times last evening?"

"Who?"

"Guess!"

I mentioned several names, but she shook her head. "You give up?"

"I give up."

"Miss Betty."

"Betty from America?"

"She is here in Warsaw."

I was silent a moment. Feitelzohn had learned from one of the American tourists that Sam Dreiman had died and left Betty a large share of his inheritance, and that Sam's widow and children had contested the will. Now Betty had come to Warsaw. And when? At a time when every Jew in Poland was dreaming of escape. Even as I stood there marveling, the telephone rang and Tekla said, "It's her. She said she'd call in the morning."

3

Although it didn't seem to me so long ago since Betty had returned with Sam Dreiman to America, I barely recognized the woman I faced that day at the Hotel Bristol. She looked years older, middle-aged. Her hair had become thin and was no longer naturally red but an ugly mixture of yellow and red. Her face beneath the rouge and powder appeared somehow broader and flatter; there were wrinkles, and traces of hair on her upper lip and chin. Had she been ailing all this time? Had she grieved so over Sam's death? Something had happened to her teeth, and I noticed a spot on her neck she had not had before. She wore a kimono and slippers. She measured me from head to toe and back again, then said, "Already completely bald? Who wore you out so? I thought you were taller. Is it possible at your age to start shrinking? Well, don't take it seriously, I live entirely by my impressions. I lack all sense for what they call objective truth. I hardly recognized Warsaw. Even the hotel didn't seem the same. Before we left Poland I collected a whole stack of photographs of you and the others, but they got lost along with many of my papers. Sit down, we must talk. What can I offer you? Tea? Coffee? . . . Nothing? What's the sense of nothing? I'll order coffee."

Betty ordered coffee by phone. She spoke in a mixture of Polish and English.

She sat down in an easy chair facing me and said, "You're probably wondering why I came, particularly at such a time. I wonder myself or, to put it more accurately, I've stopped wondering not only about what others do but about my own actions as well. You probably know that Sam is dead. He went back to America and I believed he was well. He threw himself into his business as energetically as ever. Suddenly he dropped dead. One second he was alive, the next he was dead. For all my grief, I envied him. To people like me, death is a long process. We begin dying just as we're starting to mature."

Her voice had also changed—it was hoarser, somewhat shrill. The waiter rang and rolled in a silver service on a cart. It had coffee, cream, and hot milk. Betty handed him a dollar.

We drank our coffee and Betty said, "Everyone aboard ship kept asking the same thing: 'Why are you going to Poland?' They were all going to Paris. I told them the truth, that I have an old aunt in Slonim—the very city whose name I bear—and I wanted to see her before she died. They all believe that today or tomorrow Hitler will start the war, but I'm not so sure. What good would a war do him, since whatever he wants they bring him on a silver platter? The Americans and the whole democratic world have lost the most valuable possession—character. There's a form of tolerance that's worse than syphilis, worse than murder, worse than madness. Don't look at me that way. I'm the same person. It's just that in the time we were apart I lived whole ages. I suffered a complete nervous breakdown. I often heard the term used but didn't know what it meant. In my case, it showed itself in total apathy. One night I went to bed ostensibly normal, and when I woke up I was alive physically but I was neither hungry nor thirsty, nor did I have the slightest urge to get up. You should forgive me, but I didn't even want to go to the bathroom. I lay all day and my mind was blank. After Sam's death I had started smoking heavily. I drank too much, too, although alcohol had never been a passion with me. Sam's Xanthippe and his greedy children took me to court over his will and their lawyer was something it would take the devil himself to invent. Just looking at his face made me sick. I gave up everything and fled for my life. When the actors found out that Sam had left me part of his fortune, they became as tender with me as they would be with a boil. They even offered me membership in the Hebrew Actors Union. I was promised leading roles and whatnot. But my ambition for the stage was gone. What is theater, anyway? False mimicry. Literature is the same. Sam—may he rest in peace—never read anything, and we often argued about this, since I was a voracious reader from childhood. Now I'm beginning to understand him. Why didn't you answer my letters?"

"What letters? I got just one letter from you and you didn't even include a return address."

"How is that possible? I wrote several times. I cabled you, too."

"When? I swear on everything that's holy to me that I received nothing but one letter."

"What's holy to you? First I wrote to the address on Leszno, and when you didn't answer I wrote you in care of the Writers' Club."

"I no longer go to the Writers' Club."

"But that was your second home."

"I decided to stop going."

"And you're capable of sticking to a decision? Maybe my letters are still lying there?"

"What was the cable about?"

"Oh, it's no longer important. Life is full of surprises. If a person thinks no more surprises await him, it's only because he has shut his eyes and doesn't want to know. What about you? Did you break up with that freak Shosha?"

"Break up? Where do you get such notions?"

"How is it you've kept your old room? I didn't call there believing I'd find you—I only hoped they might know your new address."

"I work there. It's my study."

"You have an apartment with her?"

"We live with her mother."

A trace of laughter showed in Betty's eyes. "On that foul street among the thieves and brothels?"

"Yes, there."

"What kind of life do you lead with her, if I may ask?"

"A kind of life."

"Do the two of you ever go anywhere?"

"Rarely."

"You never go out of the house?"

"Sometimes. We take a turn around the garbage bin at night. To get a little air."

"Well, you've remained the same. At least you're crazy in your own fashion.

In New York I was stopped in the street by an actor who made guest appearances here and he told me that you've become a big success and have published a novel everyone is reading. Is this true?"

"I'm having a novel printed in a newspaper and I barely earn enough to feed us."

"You're probably running around with ten others."

"That's not true, either."

"What is true?"

"How about you?" I asked. "Surely, you've had affairs."

"Are you jealous? I could have had. Men still chase after me. But when you're deathly ill and each day isn't one crisis but a thousand, you don't want affairs. Is that hocus-pocus Elbinger still in Warsaw?"

"Yes. He fell in love with a Gentile woman who was the mistress of the famous medium Kluski."

"I think I heard of him once. What did he do?"

"The dead came to him and left impressions of their hands in a pail of paraffin."

"You're scoffing, eh? I really believe that the dead are all around us somewhere. What has happened to that short, rich fellow—I've already forgotten his name. His wife was your sweetheart."

"Haiml and Celia. They are here."

"Yes, them. How is it they've stayed in Warsaw? I hear many rich Jews have escaped abroad."

"They want to die."

"Well, you're in one of *those* moods today. I've missed you. That's the truth."

4

I couldn't believe my ears, but after all those angry words about theater in general and Yiddish theater in particular, Betty Slonim had come to Warsaw with a play and was seeking a producer. I shouldn't have been surprised. Many of my colleagues, the writers, behaved precisely this way. They announced that they were laying aside (or breaking) their pens, and soon afterward they launched a novel or a long poem—even announced plans for a trilogy. They heaped invective upon a critic, maintained that he had no conception of literature, and the next day they begged him to write a few kind words about them. The play Betty brought was her own. I stayed the night, and we read it. It was the drama of a young woman, an artist (Betty had made her a painter) unable to fit into any environment. She couldn't find the right husband or lover, or even any interesting girlfriend. The play featured a psychoanalyst who tried to convince the heroine that she hated her father and was jealous of her mother, while in fact the woman worshipped her parents. There was a scene in which the heroine searches for an end to her loneliness by trying to become a lesbian and fails. The play contained possibilities for humor, but Betty handled everything in tragic fashion. The long monologues were packed with clichés. It ran some three hundred pages and was full of observations about painting by someone who knew nothing about it.

Dawn had begun to break by the time I got through with the fourth act. I said to Betty, "The play is good in essence, but it's not for Warsaw, just as mine wasn't for any place."

"What is for Warsaw?" she asked.

"I'm afraid nothing is for Warsaw any more."

"It seems to me this play is just right for the Polish Jews. They are like my heroine—they cannot fit in anywhere, neither among the Communists nor among the capitalists. Certainly not among the Fascists. At times I think nothing is left them except suicide."

"Whether that's true or not, the Warsaw Jews don't want to hear it. Certainly not in the theater."

I was so tired from reading that I lay down on the bed and fell asleep in my clothes. I wanted to tell Betty that she herself was proof that no person or collective has the strength fully to resign, but I was too exhausted to bring out the words. In my sleep I reread the play, gave Betty advice, even wrote new scenes. Betty had left the lights on and from time to time I opened an eye. She was busy in the bathroom. She had put on a magnificent nightgown. She came over to the bed and took off my shoes and pulled off my shirt. In my sleep I laughed at her and her urge to seize all the pleasures at once. That's what suicides are, I thought—hedonists who attempt to enjoy more excitement than they are capable of. This possibly was the answer to my own riddle.

I opened my eyes and saw that it was day. Betty sat at the desk in her nightgown and slippers, cigarette in mouth, writing something on a sheet of paper. My wristwatch showed a few minutes before eight. I sat up. "What are you doing? Rewriting the play?"

She turned her head toward me. Her face was ashen, her eyes had become strangely stern and determined. "You slept but I couldn't shut an eye. No, not the play. For me the play is dead. But I could save you."

"What do you mean?"

"The Jews here are all going to perish. You'll sit with that Shosha until Hitler marches in. I've been reading the paper half the night. What sense does it make, eh? Does it pay to die on account of such a moron?"

"What do you suggest I do?"

"Tsutsik, after I see my aunt I have no reason to stay here, but I want to help you nevertheless. Aboard ship I met an official of the American consulate and we spoke of various things. He even began flirting with me, but he wasn't my type. A military man, a drinker. They drown everything with whiskey—it's their answer to all problems. I asked him about bringing someone to America and he told me that outside the quota this is impossible. But it's easy to obtain a tourist visa if you apply with some goal in mind and can prove that you won't become a public charge. In America, when a tourist marries a citizen, he immediately gets a visa outside the quota and is allowed to remain. I want to tell you something. I see in advance that all my plans and hopes will come to nothing. But if I can help someone who is close to me before I die, I want to do it, and even though you told me coldbloodedly last night that I have nothing to hope for from you, I consider you somebody close. As a matter of fact, you are the closest person I have outside Sam—may he rest in peace—and my sisters and brothers lost somewhere in the Red hell—I don't even know if any of them are still alive. Tsutsik, since you assure me the play is worth a kick in the ground, as the Litvaks say, I have nothing more to do here, and I can't go back to America all by myself. Between a yes and a no I could arrange a tourist visa for you and you could go with me. Do you have official papers with Shosha? Were you married in court?"

"Only by a rabbi."

"Is it written on your passport that you're married?"

"Nothing is written on the passport."

"You can get a tourist visa immediately if I give you an affidavit. I'll say you've written a play and we want to put it on in America. I'll say I will be appearing in it. There is even a chance that this might really happen. I can show them a bank book and whatever they require. I don't consider death a tragedy. It's actually a release from all trouble. But to live day in, day out with death is too much even for a masochist like you."

"But what could I do with Shosha?"

"They wouldn't give Shosha a tourist visa. If they took one look at her, they wouldn't give one to you."

"Betty, I can't leave her here."

"You can't, eh? That means you're ready to give up your life for her."

"If I have to die, I'll die."

"I didn't know you were so madly in love with her."

"It's not only love."

"What is it?"

"I can't kill a child. I cannot break my promise either."

"If you go to America, there might be a chance you could send for her. You'd at least be able to send her money. As it is, you will both perish."

"Betty, I can't do it."

"If you can't, you can't. According to what you've told me, you never had such consideration for women. When you got tired of one, you found another."

"Those were adults. They had families, friends. Shosha—"

"Well, you don't have to justify yourself. When a person stands ready to offer his life for another, he obviously knows what he's doing. I wouldn't have believed you capable of such a sacrifice, but you never know what a human being is capable of. Not that those who make the sacrifices are always saints. People sacrificed themselves for Stalin, for Petlura, for Machno, for every pogromist. Millions of fools will give their empty heads for Hitler. At times I think men go around with a candle looking for an opportunity to sacrifice themselves."

Neither of us spoke for a while. Then Betty said, "I'm leaving now to visit my aunt and we may never meet again. Tell me, why did you do it? Even if you lie to me, I want to hear what you'll say."

"You mean marrying Shosha?"

"Yes."

"I really don't know, but I'll tell you, anyway. She is the only woman I can trust," I said, shocked at my own words.

Betty's eyes lit up with laughter. For an instant she became young again. "My God, this is the truth. As simple as that!"

"Perhaps."

"You're both a godless lecher and a fanatical Jew—as bigoted as my great-grandfather! How is it possible?"

"We are running away and Mount Sinai runs after us. This chase has made us sick and mad."

"Don't include me. I am sick and mad, but Mount Sinai has nothing to do with it. As a matter of fact, you're lying. You are no more afraid of Mount Sinai than I am. It's your miserable pride, your silly fear of losing your filthy male honor. You once told me what one of your cronies said about the impossibility of always betraying and never being betrayed. Who was it—Feitelzohn?"

"I don't remember. Either Feitelzohn or Haiml."

"Haiml couldn't have said it. Well, it doesn't matter. You're crazy, but a good many other idiots of your kind went to their deaths to save the reputation of some whore. No, Shosha won't betray you—unless she is raped by a Nazi."

"Goodbye, Betty."

"Goodbye forever."

5

I had left the hotel without breakfast—I couldn't have stayed because the room-service waitress would have seen me. For the second time I had given up the chance to save myself. I walked without a definite direction. My legs led me by themselves from Trebacka Street to Theater Place. I didn't have the slightest doubt that to remain in Warsaw this time meant falling into the hands of the Nazis, but somehow I didn't feel any fear. I was tired from so little sleep, from reading Betty's play, and from her talk. I had given her the opportunity to scold me and so made our parting less solemn. Only now did it occur to me that she had never before mentioned her aunt in Poland and that she never had gone to see her. She certainly would not have come to Poland especially to see her now. Like me, Betty was ready to perish. A passage of the Pentateuch came to my mind: "I am at the point of dying and what profit shall this birthright be to me?"

I had thrown away four thousand years of Jewishness and exchanged it for meaningless literature, Yiddishism, Feitelzohnism. All I was left with was a membership booklet from the Writers' Club and some worthless manuscripts. I stopped at store windows and stared. Any day the destruction might begin, but in the meantime, here they displayed pianos, cars, jewelry, fancy nightgowns, new books in Polish, as well as translations from German, English, Russian, French. One book had the title *The Twilight of Israel*. Well, but the sky was summery blue, the trees on both sides of the street were lusciously green, the ladies wore the latest styles of dresses, hats, shoes, purses. The men looked them over with expert appraisal. Their legs in nylon stockings still promised the never-realized delights. Although I was doomed, I too glanced at hips, calves, breasts, throats. The generations that will come after us, I said to myself, will think that we all went to our death in repentance. They will consider all of us holy martyrs. They will recite kaddish after us and "God Full of Mercy." Actually, every one of us will die with the same passions he lived with.

They still played the familiar operas in the opera house: *Carmen, Aida, Faust, The Barber of Seville*. They were just unloading from a truck the faded sets that in the evening would create the deception of mountains, rivers, gardens, palaces. I went to a café. The smell of coffee and fresh rolls whetted my appetite. With my coffee a waiter brought me two newspapers. Marshal Rydz-Śmigly again assured the nation that the Polish armed forces had the means to repulse all attacks from the right and the left. Foreign Minister Beck had received new guarantees from England and France. The old anti-Semite Nawaczynski attacked the Jews, who, together with the Masons, the Communists, the Nazis, and the American bankers conspired to destroy the Catholic faith and to replace it with pagan materialism. He still quoted the Protocols of the Elders of Zion. Somewhere I had had a trace of faith in free will, but this morning I felt sure that man possessed as much choice as the clockwork of my wristwatch or the fly that stopped on the edge of my saucer. The same powers were driving Hitler, Stalin, the Pope, the Rabbi of Gur, a molecule in the center of the earth, and a galaxy billions of light-years distant from the Milky Way. Blind powers? Seeing powers? It did not matter any more. We were fated to play our little games and to be crushed.

<hr />

6

Usually when I didn't spend the night at Shosha's I came home the day after for lunch, but this morning I decided to go back to her early. I was too tired to try to work at my desk on Leszno Street. I paid for my breakfast and went by way of Senator Street to Bank Place and from there to Gnoyna and Krochmalna. In the Jewish streets they bustled and rushed as every day. In the brokerage houses on Przechodnia they figured the value of the zloty against the dollar. Those on the black market paid a few pennies more for the dollar. In the yeshivas they studied the Talmud. In the Hasidic studyhouses they conversed on Hasidic topics. That morning I had the feeling I was seeing all this for the last time. I tried to engrave in my memory each alley, each building, each store, each face. I thought that this was how a condemned man would be looking at the world on his way to the gallows. I was taking leave of every peddler, porter, market woman—even of the horses of the droshkies. I saw in each of them expressions I had never noticed before. Even the horses seemed to know that this was their last journey. There was knowledge and consent in their large eyes, dark with pupil.

On Gnoyna Street I stopped for a moment at the large studyhouse in No. 5. The walls were blackened, the books stained and torn, but young men with long sidelocks still swayed over these ancient volumes and chanted the sacred words with the same mournful chant. At the lectern by the Ark the cantor was praising God for his promise to resurrect the dead. A little man with a yellow face and a yellow beard sold boiled chick-peas and beans that he doled out in a wooden cup. Is he the eternal Jew? One of the thirty-six saints that are the pillars of the world? A disguised Elder of Zion in secret pact with Roosevelt, Goebbels, and Léon Blum to bring about the kingdom of Satan?

I entered Krochmalna and the gate of No. 7. The baker's daughter stood there with large baskets of warm bagels. She must have been one of my readers, because she smiled and winked at me. I imagined that she was saying to me: "Like you I must play my game to the last minute." I passed through the yard, opened the door to Bashele's apartment, and what I saw was so bewildering that I stood in the doorway staring. Tekla was sitting at the table drinking tea or coffee with chicory from a large cup. Shosha sat beside her. Something has happened to my mother, I thought. A telegram must have come announcing that she died! Tekla saw me now and jumped to her feet. Shosha rose, too. She clapped her hands. "Arele, God Himself sent you!"

"What's going on here? Am I already in the World of Delusion?"

"What? Come in. Arele, this Gentile girl came and said she was looking for you. She called you by name. She brought a basket with her belongings. There it is. She said something about a fiancé—I don't know what she's talking about. It's a good thing Mommy went shopping or she might have thought who knows what. I told her you wouldn't be home till lunchtime, but she said she'd wait."

Tekla stood there obviously eager to speak, but she waited respectfully until Shosha had finished. Tekla looked pale and disheveled, as if she hadn't slept. She said, "Forgive me, sir, but something bad has happened to me. Last evening someone knocked on the kitchen door. I thought it might be a neighbor returning a glass of salt she had borrowed, or one of the maids from the courtyard. I opened the door and in came a lout—one of our kind, a Christian. He was dressed in city style. He said, 'Tekla, don't you recognize me?' It was Bolek, my ex-fiancé. He's come back from France from the coal mines and he says he wants to marry me. I was scared to death. I said, 'Why didn't you write all these years? You went away and it was as if the earth swallowed you.' And he said, 'I can't write, and neither could any of the other miners.' Well, between this and that, he sat down on my bed and started talking as if nothing had passed since we last saw each other. He brought me a present, too—some trinket. It's God's miracle I didn't die on the spot. I said, 'Bolek, since you didn't write so long, we are no longer engaged and everything between us is finished.' But he started yelling, 'What's the matter? Got somebody else? Or are you in love with that Jew who wrote those letters to me for you?' He was drunk and grabbed a knife. My mistress heard the commotion and she came running, and he started cursing the Jews and threatened to kill us all. The mistress said, 'So far, Hitler isn't here yet. So get out of my house.' Wladek called the police, but a policeman didn't show up till three hours later, after Bolek had gone. He swore he would come back again today, and he warned me that if I didn't go with him to a priest straight off and marry him, he'd kill me. After he left, the mistress came in and said, 'Tekla, you've served me faithfully, but I'm old and weak and I don't have the strength for such goings-on. Take your luggage and leave.' I persuaded her to let me spend the night. This morning she paid me what was coming to me, added five zlotys, and sent me on my way. You once gave me your address on Krochmalna Street, so I came here. The young lady said she's your wife and that you'd be back for lunch, but where could I go? I know no one in Warsaw. I was sure you wouldn't throw me out."

"Throw you out? Tekla, I'm your friend for life!"

"Oh, thank you. What shall I do? I can't go home to our village, because

Bolek said if I did he'd come after me. He has a whole gang of thugs who served in the army and came back with revolvers and bayonets. He said he'd saved up a thousand zlotys and some French money besides, but my heart is no longer his. He can get plenty of other girls. He stank of vodka and he talked like a roughneck. I've grown unused to that kind of coarseness."

"Arele, when Mommy comes back and hears this, she'll get nervous," Shosha said. "If the man is threatening with a knife, you mustn't go to that place. But what will she do here? We hardly have space to lay our own heads. Mommy says each time she goes out to let no one in. She used to say the same when we lived at No. 10—remember?"

"Yes, Shoshele, I remember. Tekla is a decent girl and she won't give anyone any trouble. I'll take her away in a minute." In Yiddish I said, "Shoshele, I'm going with her for a while. When your mother comes back, tell her nothing."

"Oh, she'll know it, anyway. Everyone in the courtyard looks out the window, and when someone who doesn't belong here goes in or out they know it and start to gossip: 'What's she doing here? What does she want?' The younger women are busy with their children, but the old ones want to know everything."

"Well, I'll be back around lunchtime. Tekla, come with me."

"Shall I bring my basket?"

"Yes, bring it."

"Arele, don't be late. When you're late, Mommy starts to worry that maybe you no longer want us, and things like that. I start thinking all kinds of things myself. Last night I could barely sleep a wink. If she's hungry, I can give her bread and herring to take along."

"She'll eat. Come, Tekla."

We walked out under the watchful gaze of eyes that seemed to ask, "Where is he off to so early with this peasant girl? And what is she carrying in the basket?" I answered them in my mind, "You may try to solve the puzzles in the newspaper, but never the mysteries of life. For seven days and seven nights you could rub your brows like the Sages of Chelm and you'd still never figure out the answer."

In front of the gate, I stood for a long time thinking what to do next. Should I try to find a room for her? Should I go with her to some cofee shop and look up advertisements for maids' agencies? I would have let her stay with Shosha for a while, but I had never told either her or Bashele of my room on Leszno Street. They believed that I slept at the newspaper, and Bashele would begin a long interrogation. Suddenly I knew what to do. The solution was so simple I wondered that it hadn't occurred to me immediately. I walked with Tekla to the delicatessen in No. 12, told her to wait for me by the door, and went inside to phone Celia. Only a few days earlier, she had bewailed the fact that ever since Marianna had left her, she hadn't been able to find a decent maid. I heard Celia's dull voice—one that seemed to say without putting it in words, Whoever it may be, I can expect nothing.

I said, "Celia, this is Tsutsik."

"Tsutsik? What's happened? Has the Messiah come?"

"The Messiah hasn't come, but I have a maid for you."

"A maid? You? For me?"

"Yes, Celia, and a part-time boarder in the bargain."

"Bless me if I know what you mean. What boarder?"

"I am the boarder."

"Are you making fun of me?"

I told Celia what had happened. "I can't stay in my room on Leszno Street any longer. A rowdy peasant is threatening Tekla and me." Celia did not interrupt me, apparently stunned by the turn of events. I could hear her breathing on the other side of the line. From time to time I glanced through the glass door to where Tekla waited. She stood with humble patience. She did not put down the heavy basket but held it in both her hands, pressed to her belly. At home on Leszno Street she showed big-city shrewdness, but overnight she seemed to have lost it all and become a peasant again.

"Will you bring Shosha with you?"

"Whenever she is able to stay apart from her mother."

Celia seemed to ponder the implication of my words. Then she said, "Bring her as often as you want to. This is going to be your second home. Where you go she should go."

"Celia, you are saving my life!" I exclaimed.

Again Celia paused. "Tsutsik, take a taxi and come at once. If I live a little longer, something good may happen even to me. If only it isn't too late."

EPILOGUE

██████

────────

1

Thirteen years had gone by. In New York, I had saved two thousand dollars out of my salary from the Yiddish newspaper. I had also received a five-hundred-dollar advance for a novel that would be translated into English, and I took a trip to London, Paris, and Israel. London still had craters and ruins left over from the German bombs. In Paris, I ate in a restaurant that obtained its food from the black market. In Marseilles I boarded a ship bound for Haifa with a stopover in Genoa. The singing of the young passengers rang through the nights— the old familiar songs, as well as new songs that had come out of the war with the Arabs between 1948 and 1951. After six days, we arrived in Haifa. It was an experience to see Hebrew signs over the stores and streets bearing the names of writers, rabbis, and leaders, to hear Hebrew spoken in the Sephardic style, to see Jewish soldiers of both sexes. In Tel Aviv I stopped at a hotel on Yarkon Street. Although Tel Aviv was a new city, the houses looked old and dingy. The telephone didn't work properly, the bathtub seldom had hot water, and the electricity often went off at night. The food was bad.

There was a notice in a newspaper announcing my arrival, and I began to receive visits from writers, journalists, old friends from Warsaw, distant relatives. Some of them had numbers tattooed on their arms from Auschwitz, others had already lost sons in the battles for Jerusalem or Safad. I heard the same horror stories about Nazi brutalities and the savagery of the N.K.V.D. that I had heard in New York, in London, in Paris, and aboard ship.

One morning as I ate breakfast in the hotel dining room, a tiny person with a milk-white beard that extended like a fan came into the room. He wore an unbuttoned shirt with an open collar, a straw hat, shabby trousers, and sandals on his bare feet. I was sure that I had known him once, but I couldn't identify him. How can such a little man have such a large beard? I wondered. He approached my table with hasty steps. He had young black eyes that resembled the olives on my plate. He pointed a finger and said in a familiar Warsaw Yiddish, "There he is! Peace to you, Tsutsik!"

It was Haiml Chentshiner. I got up and we kissed and held each other for a moment. My face filled with beard. I asked him to have breakfast with me but he told me that he had eaten, and I ordered coffee for him. I had heard that he and Celia perished in the Warsaw Ghetto, but encounters with those supposedly dead had ceased to surprise me. Feitelzohn I knew was no longer alive, for I had read of his death in the paper years ago.

We drank the coffee and Haiml said, "Forgive me for calling you Tsutsik— it remains a term of affection for me."

"Yes, but I'm an old dog now."

"To me you will always remain Tsutsik. If Celia were alive, she'd call you the same thing. How old are you?"

"Forty-three."

"Not so very old. I'm in my late fifties. It seems to me I'm as old as Methuselah. The things we went through during those years! Not one life but a hundred."

"Where were you, Haiml?"

"Where *was* I? Where wasn't I! In Vilna, in Kovno, in Kiev, in Moscow, in Kazakhstan, among the Kalmucks, the Chunchuz, or whatever they're called. A hundred times I virtually looked the Angel of Death in the eye, but when you're fated to stay alive miracles occur. So long as a breath of life remains in the body, it crawls like a worm, and I crawled and avoided the feet that squash worms till I came to the Jewish land. Here again, we suffered war, hunger, steady danger. Bullets flew over my head. Bombs exploded a few steps away. But here no one went like a sheep to the slaughter. Our lads from Warsaw, Lodz, Rawa Ruska, and Minsk suddenly turned into heroes like the fighters in the time of Masada. Piff-poff! The greatest optimist wouldn't have believed it possible. You probably know what happened to Celia."

"Not a thing."

"How could you, after all? How about going out on the terrace? I like to look at the sea."

We went to the terrace and took a table in the shade. A waiter came over and I ordered more coffee and cookies. For a long time we both stared out to sea, which changed color from green to blue. On the horizon a sailboat rocked. The beach swarmed with men and women. Some exercised, others played ball, sunbathed, or lay under umbrellas. Some splashed at the edge of the water, others swam far out. A man urged a dog to go into the water, but the animal was unwilling to bathe.

Haiml said, "Well, a Jewish land, a Jewish sea. Who would have believed this ten years ago? Such a thought was beyond daring. All our dreams centered around a crust of bread, a plate of groats, a clean shirt. Feitelzohn once said something I often repeat: "A man has no imagination either in his pessimism or his optimism." Who could have figured that the Gentiles would vote for a Jewish nation? Nu, but the birth throes are far from over. The Arabs haven't made peace with the situation. It's hard here. Thousands of refugees live in tin shacks. I lived in one of them myself. The sun roasts you all day like fire, and at night you freeze. The women are at each other's throats. Refugees have come from Africa who've never seen a handkerchief—literally people from Abraham's time. Who knows what they are—maybe descendants of Keturah. I hear you've become famous in America."

"Far from it."

"Well, you're known. They used to read your books in the camps in Germany. Things were reprinted in the papers there. Each time I saw your name, I cried, 'Tsutsik!' They thought I was crazy. Today when I saw the notice in *Hayom* that you were here, I began to jump in the air. My wife asked, 'What happened— have you gone mad?' I got married again."

"Here?"

"No, in Landsberg. She had lost her husband and the children were taken away from her to the gas chamber. I was wandering around alone. I didn't have anyone to so much as make me a glass of tea. I remember your words: 'The world is a slaughterhouse and a brothel.' At the time it seemed to me an exaggeration, but it's the bitter truth. They consider you a mystic, while the fact is, you're an out-and-out realist. Still, everything is forced upon us, even hope. The dictator on high, the celestial Stalin, says, 'You must hope!' And if he says you must, you hope. But what can I hope for any more? Only for death. Where is the sugar?''

"Right here."

"This coffee tastes like dishwater. How long is it since I've seen you— thirteen years? Yes, in September it will be exactly thirteen years. Shosha is no longer alive, eh?''

"Shosha died on the second day we left Warsaw."

"Died? On the way?"

"Yes, like Mother Rachel."

"We knew nothing, nothing. News came from others. There were Jews in Bialystok and Vilna who became mail carriers, messengers. They brought letters to wives across the borders. But you vanished like a stone in water. What happened to you? I first found out you were alive in 1946. I came to Munich with a large group of refugees and someone gave me a newspaper published there. I opened it and saw your name. It said that you were in New York. How did you manage to get to New York?''

"Through Shanghai."

"Who sent you the affidavit?"

"Remember Betty?"

"What a question! I remember everybody."

"Betty married a Gentile, a colonel in the American Army, and he sent me the affidavit.''

"You knew her address?"

"I learned it by chance."

"Well, I'm not religious, I don't pray, I don't observe the Sabbath, I don't believe in God, but I acknowledge that some hand guides our world—this, no one can deny. A vicious hand, a bloody hand, occasionally merciful. Where does Betty live—in New York?''

"Betty committed suicide a year ago."

"Why?"

"No one knows."

"What happened to Shosha? If it's painful for you to talk about it, you don't have to tell me.''

"I'll tell you anyway. She died exactly as I saw it in a dream a few years before. We were walking along a road that led to Bialystok. It was toward evening. The others walked fast and Shosha couldn't keep up. She began to stop every few minutes. Suddenly she sat down, and a minute later she was dead. I had told this dream to Celia. Maybe to you, too.''

"Not to me. I would remember it. What a sweet child she was. In her own fashion, a saint. What was it, a heart attack?''

"I don't know. I think she simply didn't want to live any more."

"What happened to her sister—what was her name, Teibele?" Haiml asked. "And how about her mother?"

"Bashele perished for sure. About Teibele, I don't know what happened. She might have run away to Russia. She had a friend—a bookkeeper. Perhaps

she's here, although it doesn't seem probable, since I have heard nothing from
her in all these years."

"I'm afraid to ask, but what happened to your mother and your brother?"

"After 1941, the Russians saved them by taking them in a cattle train to
Kazakhstan. The trip took two weeks. I met a man who was with them in the
same train, and he told me the details. They are both dead. How my mother
could last several months after the experience of this trip, I still don't grasp.
They were taken to a forest in the middle of the Russian winter and told to build
themselves log cabins. My brother died almost immediately after he arrived."

"What happened to your Communist girl friend, what was her name?"

"Dora? I don't know. Got crushed somewhere, either by the do-gooders or
by the do-badders."

"Tsutsik, I'll be right back—don't go away."

"What a thing to say!"

"Anything can happen."

Haiml left and I turned toward the sea again. Two women splashed each
other and lost their balance from the force of their laughter. A father and son
played with a balloon. A Sephardic Jew in a white cloak, barefoot, and with a
scraggly white beard and earlocks dangling to his shoulders, went around begging
from the people on the beach. No one gave him anything. Who would go begging
on a beach? I wondered. He was probably not in his right mind. At that moment
I heard my name called on the public-address system. I was wanted on the
telephone.

2

I came back from the phone. Haiml sat at the table, facing the door with a
childish eagerness. When I came out, he made a move as if to stand, but kept
his seat. I sat down and he asked, "Where did you go?"

"I was called to the phone."

"When you come here, they don't leave you alone for a minute. Well, there
were notices about you in the newspapers, but how did they know it when I
came? People called whom I thought were long buried. Every such meeting was
like the resurrection of the dead. Who knows? If we could live to see the miracle
that the Jews have a country again, maybe we shall see the Messiah come, after
all? Maybe the dead *will* be resurrected? Tsutsik, you know I'm a freethinker.
But somewhere inside me I have the feeling that Celia is here, that Morris is
here, that my father—may he rest in peace—is here. Your Shosha is here, too.
How is it possible, after all, that someone should simply vanish? How can
someone who lived, loved, hoped, and wrangled with God and with himself just
disappear? I don't know how and in what sense but they're here. Since time is
an illusion, why shouldn't everything remain? I once heard you say—or quote
someone—that time is a book whose pages you can turn forward, not back,
Maybe *we* can't, but some forces can. How is it possible that Celia should stop
being Celia? For Morris to stop being Morris? I live with them, speak with them.
At times I hear Celia talking to me. You won't believe this, but Celia told me

to marry my present wife. I lay in that camp near Landsberg, sick, hungry, lonely, dejected. Suddenly I heard Celia's voice: 'Haiml, marry Genia!' That's my wife's name, Genia. Sure, you can explain this psychologically. I know, I know. Nevertheless, I heard her voice. What do you say to that, eh?''

"I don't know.''

"You still don't know? How long can you go on not knowing? Tsutsik, I seem to be able to make peace with everything but death. How can it be that all the generations are dead and only we shlemiels are allegedly living? You turn the page and can't turn it back again, but on page so-and-so they're all right there in an archive of spirits.''

"What do they do there?'' I asked.

"That answer I don't have. Perhaps we are there already, dreaming the same dream. Either everything is dead or everything is alive. I want you to know that it was only after you left that Morris became great—he never had been as great as he was in those months. He lived with us on Zlota Street until the Jews were herded into the ghetto in October of 1940, which was more than a year after the Germans came in. As you know, before the war he could have gone to England as well as to America. The American consul urged him to leave. The war with America didn't start until 1941. He could have traveled through Rumania, through Hungary, even through Germany. With an American visa they let you pass. But he stayed with us. One time I said to Celia, 'I'm ready to die but I want one favor from you and the Almighty if He exists—that I never see a Nazi.' Celia said to me, 'Haiml, I promise you that you won't see their faces.' How could she have promised such a thing? She herself had grown in stature. She wasn't the same Celia any more. Our situation and Morris's moving in with us uplifted her to a degree that can't be put into words. She became beautiful!''

"Were you jealous of him?''

"Don't talk nonsense. I too grew a bit. The Angel of Death waved his sword but I stuck out my tongue at him. Outside, it was the destruction of the Temple, but inside our house it was Simchas Torah and Yom Kippur rolled into one. Next to them I, too, became cheerful. I'm not telling these things in proper order—how can you speak of such things in order? My only uncle died in the month of October. It wasn't possible to go to Lodz—a Jew couldn't show his face anywhere. Still, I dared the dangers. I walked the whole distance on foot. The trip there and back was a real odyssey.

"As you know, Celia had prepared a room we called the Cave of Machpelah. She started to prepare it while you were still in Warsaw, but the day they announced on the radio that all men were to cross the Praga Bridge and you decided to leave together with Shosha, that day the room became Feitelzohn's and my only place. We ate there, we slept there. Morris did his writing there. I had brought money from Lodz—not paper money, but golden ducats my father left with my uncle for me. They were saved from the time of the Russians. Just the fact that I had returned with such a treasure to Warsaw and wasn't searched or killed on the way is beyond belief. But I did come back. Then Celia had her jewelry. At that time you could get everything for money. A black market developed almost at once.

"After my odyssey, I was so depleted that my last drop of courage drained away. Like Morris, I wouldn't go into the street, and Celia became our contact with the outside world. Each time she went, we weren't sure we'd see her again.

Your Tekla, too, ran errands for us. She risked her life. She had to go back to her village because her father died.

"The days were days of sorrow. Our life started at night. There wasn't much to eat, but we drank hot tea and Morris talked. He talked those nights as I never heard him talk before. The heritage of generations had wakened within him, and he hurled sulphur and brimstone against the Almighty; at the same time the words themselves blazed with a religious fire. He castigated Him for all His sins since the Creation. He still maintained that the whole universe was a game, but he elevated this game until it became divine. That was probably how the Seer of Lublin, Rabbi Bunim, and the Kotzker spoke. The essence of his words was that since God is eternally silent, we owe Him nothing. It seems I once heard similar words from you—or maybe you were quoting Morris. True religion, Morris argued, was not to serve God but to spite Him. If He wanted evil, we had to aspire to the opposite. If He wanted wars, inquisitions, crucifixions, Hitlers, we must want righteousness, Hasidism, our own version of grace. The Ten Commandments weren't His but ours. God wanted Jews to seize the Land of Israel from the Canaanites and to wage wars against the Philistines, but the real Jew, who began to be what he is in exile, wanted the Gemara with its commentaries, the Zohar, *The Tree of Life, The Beginning of Wisdom*. The Gentiles didn't drive us into the ghetto, Morris said, the Jew went on his own, because he grew weary of waging war and bringing up warriors and heroes of the battlefield. Each night Morris erected a new structure.

"We could have escaped up to the time they locked the Jews in the ghetto; people went back and forth to Russia. In Bialystok there was a Jew from Warsaw, a half writer, half madman, and a whole martyr. His name was Yonkel Pentzak. He kept going from Bialystok to Warsaw and back again—a kind of holy messenger or a divine smuggler. He smuggled letters from wives to husbands and from husbands to wives. You can imagine the risk connected with such journeys! The Nazis finally got him, but until they did, he served as a sacred mail carrier. He brought me a few letters. Some friends of mine had gone there and they begged us to join them, but Celia didn't want to and Morris didn't want to, and after all, I couldn't leave them behind. What was there for me in that alien world? The whole crew of writers and leaders that sent us greetings had overnight turned about and become ardent Communists. Denouncing one's fellow was now the order of the day. Their writing consisted of praising Stalin, and the reward for this was at first a plate of groats and a bed, and later jail and exile and liquidation. I came to the conclusion that what people call life is death and what people call death is life. Don't ask any questions. Where is it written that a bedbug lives and the sun is dead? Maybe it's the other way around? Love? It wasn't simply love. Tsutsik, do you have a match, maybe? I've gotten into the habit of smoking, actually right here in the Jewish land."

I went to get Haiml matches, and at the same time I bought him two packs of American cigarettes.

He shook his head. "Are those for me? So help me, you're a spendthrift."

"I took more from you than two packs of cigarettes."

"Eh? We didn't forget you. Celia kept asking about you—maybe someone had heard something, maybe something of yours had been printed. After you left Warsaw, where did you go—not to Bialystok?"

"To Druskenik."

"You were able to get there?"

"I smuggled myself over."

"What did you do in Druskenik?"

"Worked in a hotel."

"Well, you did the right thing to stay away from the writers. You couldn't become a Communist, and the anti-Communists were soon sent to Siberia. Later they did the same to most zealous Stalinists. What did you do in 1941?"

"Kept on going."

"Where to?"

"I dragged along till I came to Kovno, and from there I went to Shanghai."

"Got a visa, eh? And what did you do in Shanghai?"

"Became a typesetter."

"What did you set?

"The *Shitah Mekubbetzet.*"

"Well, a crazy race, the Jews. I heard there was a yeshiva there that published books. You didn't write?"

"I did that, too."

"When did you go to America?"

"At the beginning of 1948."

"I left Warsaw in May of 1941. Morris died in March."

"Why didn't you take Celia along?"

"There was no one to take along."

"Was she sick?"

"She died exactly a month after Morris, in what they call a natural death."

3

Haiml and I squeezed our way into a bus going to Hadar Joseph, a suburb of Tel Aviv with housing for new immigrants. The passengers cursed each other in Yiddish, Polish, German, and in broken Hebrew. The women fought over seats and the men took sides. One woman had brought along a live chicken. The bird tore loose from the basket and began to fly over the heads of the passengers. The driver shouted that he would throw out anyone who caused a disturbance. After a while things quieted down and I heard Haiml say, "Well, a Jewish nation. The newcomers are all out of their minds—victims of Hitler, bundles of nerves. They always suspect they're being persecuted. First they cursed Hitler, now they curse Ben-Gurion. Their children or perhaps their grand-children will be normal if the Almighty doesn't send a new catastrophe down upon us. What can you know of what we went through! You haven't said anything, but you're probably wondering why I had to marry again after Celia. Before, Genia and I were two worms crawling separately; then we began to crawl together. Until recently we lived in a tin shack. Later, we got the apartment we have now. How much can a body tolerate? She isn't Celia, but she's a good person. Her husband was a teacher in a Yiddish school in Pietrkow. A Bundist. Genia believed in Stalin for a while, until she got a taste of him. Funny, she knew Feitelzohn. She once went to a lecture of his about Spengler and he autographed a book for her. She's an orderly in a hospital where they bring the wounded in ambulances. The Red Mogen David. It just so happens she's off today. She knows all about you. I gave her your books to read.''

We came to Hadar Joseph. Lines of wash stretched from one flat roof to the other. Half-naked children played in the sand. Cement steps led directly into Haiml's kitchen. Outside, it stank of garbage, asphalt, and something else sticky and sweetish that was hard to identify. The kitchen smelled of sorrel and garlic. Next to the gas range stood a short woman with short-trimmed hair—black, mixed with gray. She wore a calico dress and over her bare feet cracked slippers. She had apparently undergone surgery, since the left side of her face was compressed, full of scars under the chin, and her mouth was crooked. When we came in she was watering a flower in a pot.

Haiml called out, "Genia, guess who this is!"

"Tsutsik."

Haiml seemed embarrassed. "He has a name."

"It doesn't matter. Just the opposite," I said.

"Excuse me, that's how we refer to you," Genia said. "Four years I've been hearing it day and night—'Tsutsik,' 'Tsutsik.' When my husband thinks well of someone, he speaks of him without stopping. I had the honor of meeting Dr. Feitelzohn, but I only know you from a picture that appeared in the Yiddish paper. Finally I see you in person. Why didn't you tell me you were bringing someone to the house?" she said, turning to Haiml. "I would have put the place in order. We battle here constantly with flies, beetles, even mice. Years ago I didn't consider that insects or mice were God's creatures, too; but since I've been treated as if I were a beetle myself, I've come to accept things one doesn't want to accept. Please, go into the other room. Such an unexpected guest. What an honor!"

"You see her cheek?" Haiml pointed. "That's where a Nazi hit her with a piece of pipe."

"Well, why talk about it?" Genia said. "Go in the other room. Excuse me for the state it's in."

We went into the other room. A big sofa stood there, one of those that serve as a sofa by day and a bed at night. The apartment had no bathtub, only a toilet and a sink. This room seemed to serve both as a bedroom and a dining room. There was a bookcase, where I spotted Feitelzohn's *Spiritual Hormones* and several of my books.

Haiml said, "This is our land, this is our home. Here, maybe we'll have the privilege of dying if we're not driven into the sea."

After a while, Genia came in and began to straighten up. Even as we sat there, she swept the floor and spread a cloth over the table. She excused herself again and again for the mess. Evening was beginning to fall by the time she served dinner—some meat for herself and Haiml, vegetables for me. It struck me that the couple mixed meat dishes with dairy. I had assumed that despite the fact Haiml talked like a heretic he would be observing Jewishness in the Land of Israel.

I asked, "Since you aren't religious, why did you grow a beard?"

Genia put down her spoon. "That's what I want to know."

"Oh, a Jew should have a beard," Haiml replied. "You have to be different from Gentiles in some way."

"The way you have lived, you're a Gentile, too," Genia said.

"As long as I have never beaten or killed anybody, I can call myself a Jew."

"It's written somewhere that whoever breaks one of the Ten Commandments must break them all," Genia said.

"Genia, the Ten Commandments were written by a man, not by God," Haiml said. "As long as you don't harm anyone, you can live any way you want. I loved Feitelzohn. If they told me to give up my life so that he could live again, I wouldn't hesitate. If there is a God, let Him be witness to what I say. I love Tsutsik, too. The time of property will soon pass and there will evolve a man with new instincts—those of sharing: Morris's very words."

"Then why were you such an anti-Communist in Russia?" Genia asked.

"They don't want to share—they want to grab."

It grew silent and I heard a cricket—the same sound that came from the cricket that chirped in our kitchen when I was a boy. The room filled with shadows.

Haiml said, "I am religious—in my own fashion. I am religious! I believe in the immortality of the soul. If a rock can exist for millions of years, why should the human soul, or whatever you choose to call it, be extinguished? I'm with those who died. I live with them. The moment I close my eyes they are all with me. If a ray of light can travel and radiate for billions of years, why can't a spirit? A new science founded on this premise will emerge."

"When does the bus go back to Tel Aviv?" I asked.

"Tsutsik, you can sleep here," Haiml said.

"Thanks, Haiml, but someone is coming to see me early in the morning."

Genia cleared the dishes and went to the kitchen. I heard her close the front door, but Haiml didn't switch on the lights. A pale glow shone in through the windows.

Haiml began speaking to me, to himself, and to no one in particular: "Where did all the years go to? Who will remember them after we're gone? The writers will write, but they'll get everything topsy-turvy. There must be a place somewhere where everything is preserved, inscribed down to the smallest detail. Let us say that a fly has fallen into a spiderweb and the spider has sucked her dry. This is a fact of the universe and such a fact cannot be forgotten. If such a fact should be forgotten, it would create a blemish in the universe. Do you understand me or not?"

"Yes, Haiml."

"Tsutsik, those are your words!"

"I don't remember saying them."

"You don't remember, but I do. I remember everything that Morris said, that you said, and that Celia said. At times you uttered ridiculous foolishness, and I remember that, too. If God is wisdom, how can there be foolishness? And if God is life, how can there be death? I lie at night, a little man, a half-squashed fly, and I talk with the dead, with the living, with God—if He exists—and with Satan, who certainly does exist. I ask them, 'What need was there for all this?' and I wait for an answer. What do you think, Tsutsik, is there an answer somewhere or not?"

"No, no answer."

"Why not?"

"There can't be any answer for suffering—not for the sufferer."

"In that case, what am I waiting for?"

Genia opened the door. "Why are you two sitting in the dark, eh?"

Haiml laughed. "We're waiting for an answer."